Crink

Crink

Norman Lowson

Published by Cestria Publishing

A CIP catalogue record for this book is available from the British Library.

ISBN 978-1-9996916-0-8

Book layout and cover design by Clare Brayshaw

Prepared and printed by:

York Publishing Services Ltd
64 Hallfield Road
Layerthorpe
York YO31 7ZQ

Tel: 01904 431213

Website: www.yps-publishing.co.uk

Prologue

The storm that hit New Orleans in 2007 brought huge quantities of household debris swilling into the streets. During the subsequent clearing up operation a small wooden box was found beneath a layer of mud. It was unrecognisable as anything of value, something to be disposed of as junk or burnt as polluted flotsam. Luckily the finder broke the lock on the lid with his spade and found, yellow with age, thick wedges of handwritten sheets of paper.

These papers were, as a Virginian prospector with the colourful name of 'Mulehead' Joe said of a mud encrusted nugget in the '49 gold rush, "gold disguised as sludge." Except the papers were 'historical gold'. Page one was titled: 'Crink's Endeavours: Alabama's saviour of the United States of America during the late Civil War.' An amending line changed this to: 'Lincoln's Spy: How I almost won the war for the South and nearly lost it for the North.'

The papers are an autobiographical account of the adventures of a Civil War veteran during those momentous years 1861–1865. By all accounts, and this is being kind to Crink, research has shown that prior to the Civil War he was a 'born again criminal' who robbed and stole as a career choice. A former President of the United States has suggested that our perception and understanding of the war will never be the same again.

I suspect Crink would reply: "Amen to that."

Notes have been added for those readers living east and west of the Greenwich Meridian unfamiliar with American slang and military terms common in the United States during the Civil War period.

Chapter One

Boston. 1st April, 1895

I have adopted the name Cornelius Crink. Using my real name would run the risk of unwelcome visitors at my door. Those years of civil war between the States festered resentments and feuds that have long survived the ending of hostilities. Former comrades in arms south of the Mason Dixie, once they read my account of what went on, will realise that in truth I was an enemy; a spy for the North.

Although my memory is at times vague as to exact times and dates I saw a lot of the war that began in 1861. From the opening shots at the bombardment of Fort Sumter to the awful slaughter at Gettysburg and Antietam, and the exploding mine at Petersburg to name but a few. There were fights and skirmishes at a dozen other places I would rather forget. As Sergeant Smith, my company sergeant succinctly put it: "Apart from the South's 'Stonewall Jackson' and the North's Ulysses Grant, the Generals on both sides were TISS." (Tactically Inept Strategically Stupid.) If you want a truthful and fresh account of terror, horror, comedy, bravery, ignorance and dumbass stupidity, the last two descriptions being attributed to those battlefield leaders on both sides who, in my opinion, continually got it wrong then read on.

Chapter Two

As I recollect it my meeting with President Abraham Lincoln began on the evening of the 4th April 1861, in a room at the Willard Hotel in Washington.

"Sir, you are a scoundrel."

Not the most memorable speech that Lincoln ever uttered. But when handcuffed to a chair with the dangerous end of an army colt model 1860 revolver pointing at your head, as I was, then you tend to contemplate such words with a thick slice of trepidation and without admiration as to the identity of the speaker. Especially as Lincoln had the ability, when the need took him, to growl like a grizzly in heat. An effect he cranked to maximum level on this occasion.

It wasn't Lincoln brandishing that revolver. No, that was in the hands of a broken-nosed thug wearing Clan Cameron Scottish tartan trousers.[1] Along with the revolver it gave the game away that he was military. It got worse. Positioned in front of the windows, blotting out the light, stood a group of well-dressed toughs. Avidly watched the proceedings they were, to a man, detectives. One I immediately recognised; Allan Pinkerton.[2]

Abe Lincoln contemplating murder?

Whatever history says about the great man, and you will recollect that on this date he was President of the United States, I thought him capable of it. Lincoln's outer shell of decency masked a deep kernel of iron resolve. In army terms his attitude was, 'complete the mission whatever the cost in lives or finance'. It is my considered opinion that a man needs the fires of hell in his head and an everyday willingness to cheat, steal, and lie through his back teeth, to run for the office of President of the United States. The ability to murder to get what you want isn't far away when you possess those nefarious traits. I should know. I have them in abundance; although I am unlikely to run for president. Of course Abe Lincoln could also project opposite characteristics; honesty, honour, wisdom, vision and kindness, everything I'm not. But it ain't possible to get to the top of that greasy political pole that leads to the White House without a thick streak of ruthlessness; and for me Abe Lincoln had that in bucketfuls. You disagree? Look at how he hired and fired generals and members of his presidential cabinet. When you've finished that exercise count the butchers-bill at Gettysburg and Shiloh, Antietam and Chickamauga. Ruthless as a fox with a cornered chicken; that's how I see Abe Lincoln.

Lincoln continued, "No doubt you would answer this assertion of 'scoundrel' as a disagreeable rumour with no truth in it whatsoever. You may even say it is a joke in bad taste."

Pausing for a second to check his pocket-watch Lincoln frowned, before going on, "Adultery and theft Mister Crink are reprehensible. You have those vices in canyon filling capacity. People of consequence have lost money to your dishonest schemes and sensible wives have squirmed and blushed at your redwood thick flattery. Then regretted walking to the rear of a building, or clambering hotel stairs, to discuss empty promises of employment."

"Mister President, those are accusations from jealous men. A vice that breeds insecurity. And 'jealous' stands in the dictionary between 'jazz' and 'jeer'. The first being 'a screeching sound'. The second 'to shout rudely'. Both describe the behaviour of my accusers over the years," I replied hotly.

After a moment's pause I went on. "And what woman would find me attractive? Five feet eight inches in my calloused feet, mud coloured eyes, bow legged, half an ear missing, and a top to bottom scar from eyebrow to jaw."

Lincoln ignored my protestations. Rubbing his nose he reflected for a moment then, narrowing his eyes, continued, "Pinkerton informs me that in the previous five years you've stolen from banks in every state south of the Mason Dixie[3] without getting caught.Marching like some one man invading army. Wandering the south without stirring a whiff of suspicion. Sir, we ask, how did you do it?"

He had me there. That was not something I wished to elaborate on, or even admit to. Truthfully I exhibit a vacant look which, when combined with facial scars, most people misinterpret as an outward display of inner integrity and honesty. Allowing me on occasions in towns and cities from Richmond to New Orleans to wander past my own wanted notices, displaying excellent sketches of myself, without challenge from lawmen or civilians.

All I could manage in reply was a sullen, "Robbing banks. Not me, sir. That was my twin."

An obvious lie that brought a disdainful look that would have made a vulture hop backwards from a slab of festering meat. In the ensuing silence my words hung uneasy, like a trespassing ripe fart at a wedding service. Lincoln sucked on a tooth and looked forlornly at the ceiling, producing the appearance of someone struggling manfully with some hidden vice, before shaking his head and saying. "Yes Mister Crink. A one man march of crime through Dixie to the sea."

With hindsight Lincoln's description of marching to the sea was a prophetic remark if ever there was one.[4] But Sherman's famous journey was three and more years away, an unknown future historical event, yet a small part of me sensed these words were a hidden finger reaching from a million tears in the future. Or, as someone else said, "Forthcoming events cast their shadow before them."

You will appreciate, having been arrested in the street by a pair of Pinkerton's detectives and dragged into this room, that I was shocked and taken aback when President Lincoln marched through the door. So far I had been ten minutes in the great man's presence and there was no explanation as to why he was so virulently clacking his teeth about my damnable past. What had I done to upset him? I had no recollection of cheating him at cards. Nor meeting Mrs Lincoln and laying a meandering hand on her ample posterior. Not unless she had taken to disguising herself with a face mask and singing for a few extra dollars towards the President's campaign funds in one of the seedy bars that I frequent. I watched and waited as Lincoln stared at the ceiling until, taking a deep breath, he said mournfully. "Mister Crink, you are full of can't." He paused, then cut to the chase, "However, even you have it in you to help the North." "Not with a gun at my head," I managed to bleat. "Keeps you interested," growled the soldier holding the revolver.

A grim interruption came from Pinkerton, "Lose interest in our little talk and yours will be the first coffin in the coming war."

"And I have a measuring tape. Just so you'll fit nicely inside it," said the revolver wielding oaf.

Suddenly Pinkerton's comment hit like a vulture pecking my eyes. From the man in charge of the President's intelligence gathering. Hostilities were on the way. I was bug-eyed. A miner gazing at a thousand dollar nugget. While trying to think of some way to extricate myself from this situation I had to keep talking. "You want my help. Why kidnap me?" I said nervously.

Head down, arms behind his back, President Lincoln slow marched to the other side of the room and Pinkerton took over. "May I remind you of your most recent escapade, Mister Crink? Today you betrayed the trust of an army officer by consorting adulterously with his wife." He paused, rather dramatically I thought, but then he is a detective. He rumbled on in his hideous Scots accent, "Worse, her jewellery is missing. During a visit to her hotel room you stole it. Help the North's cause and you will hear no more about this crime."

Mentally, I gagged. Lincoln and Pinkerton and his gang of toughs were stooping to blackmail. Imagine the newspaper headlines if that ever got out. After a few seconds of silence Pinkerton placed his mouth close to my ear and whispered. "Putting it another way. Join us and you get to stay alive."

"By doing what?" I croaked.

I could smell the tobacco on his breath when he whispered, "Work for the agency."

Become a Pinkerton man? How had I ended up in this situation?

Perhaps it was inhaling Pinkerton's body odour that stimulated my thoughts but a flash of insight lifted a blanket of fog from inside my head. I had fallen for one of the oldest tricks since Eve scammed Adam with a piece of fruit. Earlier today, whilst dawdling past the White House, I met Tom Smith, a major I had served with in the Texas Rangers during the Mexican war. After the usual slaps on the back and queries about each other's health, marital status, and current occupations, the Major introduced his wife and explained that although now serving in the artillery, he was detached on special duties here in Washington.

Whilst chatting I watched Smith's wife out of the corner of my eye. Carmen was her name. Twirling her parasol and giving me the occasional appraising glance she was a buxom, sharp-eyed New Yorker, with a foxy smile simmering along a wide mouth and swaying hips that would make a preacher groan. Major Smith explained that he had to present himself at the White House on urgent 'army business' and asked would I be so good as to chaperone his wife for the rest of the day.

"A pleasure," I answered with a flick of a finger to the brim of my hat.

My dalliance with Carmen started a chain of events that would lead me into the horrors and bloodshed of a war that touched all Americans in the four years that followed. The chaperoning began well. Left alone on the street we flirted outrageously and this progressed, as things sometimes do, to an 'unspoken' invitation to move somewhere private. Once in her room in the Willard Hotel it went thus. Carmen points her breasts at the 'mark'; i.e. me; eyes expand as does another part of my anatomy, followed by a fluttering of her eyelashes and mischievous glances at the nearby bed. Hand gropes thigh, clothes heave off, we slink under the sheets followed by bouts of mattress bouncing.

In between action scenes Carmen produced a few bitter, angry rants revolving around her current unhappiness with her adultery practising husband. Along the lines of, "Just takes off and disappears for days. And when little old me asks what he's been up to, there is no denial of being unfaithful. He even boasts who with."

Carmen followed this with by a seductive description of an enormous legacy she would inherit from her father when he 'passed on'; an event expected to occur in the not too distant future; the man suffered from a painful incurable wasting disease that not even the most skilled snake oil trader could cure. After plying me with whiskey, Carmen moved to mooting an arrangement whereby we could use her soon to arrive money and my 'enormous intelligence' and shackle ourselves together in a business deal. By opening a high class brothel for rich businessmen, politicians and foreign diplomats in Washington. And, even with a two-way split of the profits, we would be millionaires before two years were out.

Next she queried as to whether I was in possession of a 'stash' of money, only wanting to know this to be sure that I would be a genuine business partner and not someone who would "take advantage of a dumb helpless girl by vanishing with her inheritance." When I confirmed that indeed I had a cache of hard-earned dollars Carmen skilfully interrogated me as to where they were hidden. (Hey, when I say 'hard-earned', take into account there was usually armed opposition when liberating banks and trains of their money, then paying off sheriffs and a posse or two, not to mention the odd judge; robbing is damned hard work.)

Besotted and drunk, I told all.

Stage two of her con was just as good. Sparkling in plain sight on a nearby table Carmen had placed rings, a necklace, arm bangles and an enormous brooch. Studded with diamonds they were begging to be borrowed. Casually changing the conversation to her 'sparkling baubles' as she described them, Carmen gushed they were worth thousands of dollars and were presents from a besotted banker. And surprise, surprise, she had to hide them from her husband. Soldier boy being a regular visitor to the local church he would 'tan Carmen's ass' with the flat of his sword if he ever found out.

"Not that anything happens between us when I meet mah sweet little banker," she whispered. Which of course was true. The banker was a figment of her imagination.

After a nibble at my ear Carmen wanted to know what I thought of her jewels. Although my gaze had wandered to admiring her cleavage I confirmed that I can occasionally tell the truth by replying, "Most impressive."

Carmen's eyes lit up at this compliment and she went on at length how they were a rare size, the diamonds that is. She then pretended to fall asleep and drunken greed clicked in, which naturally took priority over this 'leaky mouth'[5] festooning herself with diamonds. Scooping the jewellery into my hat I quickly dressed and began tiptoeing towards the bedroom door when it suddenly opened and Major Smith walked into the room.

Chapter Three

Quickly taking in the scene the Major, feigning outrage, started tugging at his holster and, you can guess the next bit, throwing my hat and its contents at him I turned and scuttled out of a window. A few seconds later I arrived in the outside alleyway where another surprise awaited; a posse of Pinkerton's detectives lounging nearby against the hotel wall. Within seconds they grabbed me and marched me back to the room I had so recently vacated. (A dribbling spittoon to the President's pocket watch Carmen and Major Smith were not even man and wife.) And, what a shock, the Major and Carmen had disappeared. In their place stood Pinkerton and his detectives and the President of the United States; Abraham Lincoln. What were the odds, huh?

Lincoln brought me back to my current situation. Glancing balefully at the revolver pointing at my head he said, "Does working as a Pinkerton agent appeal Mister Crink? Speak up you are among friends."

Out of the corner of my eye I could see that Pinkerton's watching baboons were growing restless. Examining their revolvers two of them were throwing irritated looks in my direction. A third made a showy display of removing a gleaming knife from his waist belt and began excavating dirt from underneath his fingernails. Followed by the shrill sarcastic voice from another detective who said, "Mister President, according to Major Smith, apparently Crink was holding his trousers when he turned and ran. The Major swears that he caught sight of a yellow rat tattooed on his ass as he screeched and squawked out the window."

"Yellow and rat. Don't easily forget that combination," said Pinkerton. Comments accompanied by loud laughter from the rest of his agents.

Lincoln and the revolver holding soldier remained scowling.

I wanted to shout that Pinkerton had it wrong because my ass tattoo was in fact a pair of hands, the wrists disappearing south, palms on the cheeks; underneath were the words 'No jail can hold Crink.'

Hell, I was proud of that tattoo, always a talking point with those ladies lucky enough to view it. I did wonder whether I should correct my audience but decided to keep quiet. (Lincoln would be unimpressed and might walk away and find someone else to be an agent. Leaving me to be taken to the nearest jail by Pinkerton's goons.) At this point my nerve went. Everybody has a breaking point and mine had arrived, earlier than most no doubt, and I babbled, "Mister President. It would be an honour to be a Pinkerton agent."

"The prodigal son returns," muttered one of Pinkerton's men.

Lincoln quietened the room with. "Enough banter, gentlemen. Welcome to our cause, Mister Crink." After a short pause the President put a hand on my shoulder and continued, "You were born in Alabama where folk believe in honour, virtue and hand-shaking hospitality. We have assessed the defects in your unique character and whatever your shortcomings our conclusion is that you are a resilient, determined, tough and disciplined individual. Properly guided and controlled you could be an asset to the North and I want to harness your services to our cause. I suspect that deep down, given the opportunity, you would want to atone for the many and varied wrongs you have committed over the years."

When Lincoln uttered those words no mongoose stared as intently at a meandering snake as I did at him. The President remained silent. All to ratchet up the tension, until I chased the moment with a worried, "What do you have in mind, Mister President?" "Enlist in the Confederate army. Be part of our eyes and ears in the Confederacy. At their headquarters if you can," came Lincoln's considered answer.

Mesmerised with foreboding I stared at Abraham Lincoln like a bare-assed cowboy unable to stop walking backwards towards a cholla cactus.[6] Sickening rumblings erupted in my stomach at the thought of putting my life on the line as a spy, I mean where do you go for the training, if any is provided that is. I had to change tack and replied, "Mister President I have never considered being a spy. No sir, ah see myself as a soldier. If you kindly ask this soldier to holster his revolver ah will slip out and join the Union army instead."

Lincoln shot back, "We don't need you as a soldier, Mister Crink. The Union will recruit plenty soldiers in the days ahead. We need you for the long haul. For the war's duration."

For a couple of seconds I stared at my hands then it hit me; Lincoln had said 'war'. My mind hummed. First Pinkerton and now the President of the United States had admitted that soldiers would march and swords would be drawn, rifles aimed and bullets fired. And he wanted me for the duration! My impression during speeches on the secession problem was that Lincoln wanted to avoid war; if he could. Yet here it was, from the man at the top of the political dunghill, war it would be. And, horrifying thought, he wanted me to spy for the Union surrounded by thousands of enemy troops in the south. I had volunteered for the worst job in the army. I nearly passed out at the thought of it. Caught with Confederate secrets and it would end in only one way. Shot.

Probably without a trial. Lashed to the nearest tree and sent to the promised land. To the face twisting displeasure of the rest of the room I let rip an enormous trouser ruffling fart. (Anxiety does that to me.)

"Whoa there Mister President. Shooting, bayonet fighting, attacking artillery, ah will do them all. But sneaking around Confederate camps, writing down troop movements and the like. No sir. That's not for me. Need to be a good actor. Which ah ain't."

My reluctance to accept Lincoln's ridiculous suggestion brought forth another disparaging comment from one of the watching heavyweights, a sour-faced individual with a large beard who muttered, "Can't trust the man. Slimy as a greased anchor chain."

"Grease your damned ass," I shot back. Considering my situation it was a stupid comment which produced a tightening of jaws and drumming of thick tobacco stained fingers against half a dozen thighs. For a few seconds there was a tense silence during which Lincoln put his hands behind his back and began pacing the room. Hopefully my non-cooperation was making him reconsider how to use my talents. In the ensuing quiet, like a drowning man, visions of my past squirreled into my head. After twenty-five years out west trapping and scouting for the army my father settled in Montgomery, Alabama. My mother was Irish who avidly read and believed explicitly what she read in the Bible. She spoke little but drank a lot. Born in the spring of 1826 my upbringing being mainly down to my father, that being heavy in the use of rifles, revolvers, horses, trapping and skinning game, building log cabins and cheating at cards; but light on reading and writing. Or, as he put it: 'If a man can shoot a pine cone at fifty yards, calm a horse, catch his supper in the woods, understand the spots on a pack of cards and hold his own at arm wrestling, what else is there to worry about?' I also followed my father's other inclinations. He being infused with the notion that robbing banks is a virtue and cattle rustling and stealing horses splendid ways to spend a working day.

Mother taught me the basics of reading and writing. Once a week she put her Bible on the table and sat me close and commanded that I read. When I struggled she would help. Until imbibing too much drink when I would feel the back of her hand for not understanding the words in the good book. Not wanting to be hit around the head with a hand the size of a pineapple I did as told, learning quickly how to read and absorbing stories of strange miracle performing folk who trundled in and out of Egypt, Babylon, and every hick town and city in that sand-blasted part of the world. Seems they spent most of the time having their asses kicked by God, invading other countries, fighting amongst themselves, pillaging, treachery, murder, and suffering all manner of diseases. Neighbours persecuting neighbours on an industrial scale. Conduct that reinforced my opinion; if such behaviour was good enough for folk in the Holy Bible, then it was good enough for me.

Pinkerton returned to my side and in a low voice said, "Mister Crink. You don't have much choice."

Stating the obvious I replied, "Forcing me south won't mean much once ah get there. What's to stop me disappearing? Go west? Or take a ship from New Orleans to Europe?" Lincoln gave the cheroot smoking Pinkerton a narrowed eyed glance then said, "Tell him Pinkerton."

"Your hidden, ill-gotten gains. We have them. Want them back? Work for us," said Pinkerton smugly.

I thought for a few seconds then said, in what I hoped was a calm and considered tone, "What ill-gotten gains?"

Knees knocking I watched Lincoln's craggy face. Had he become a judge his courthouse portrait would be titled, 'Noose lover'. Or some such. Throughout our 'discussion' Lincoln had been uneasy; fidgeting constantly with those stubby fingers of his, tapping them on his coat lapels then cocking his head from side to side as if struggling with some inner, inappropriate thought. If he was debating causing harm to me, then his thinking was damned inappropriate. After an agitated glance towards Pinkerton, Lincoln began tapping his toecap on the carpet. He reminded me of a bull getting ready for a charge. After a lifetime spent dealing and conniving with every kind of crook and confidence trickster in creation, I can spot those signs that tell you what a man is thinking, as opposed to the story he's telling you; 'body language' is the current phrase. (Or 'mind walking' as I once heard it described by an educated Comanche.)

The recently installed President was in a hurry to be elsewhere.

"The money from your bank robberies in Dixie. One hundred thousand dollars. Found under the floorboards in that place you rent. Now in protective custody," cut in Pinkerton.

Carmen had a lot to answer for. That money was my retirement funds. Without it I would have to return to stealing or cheating at cards. And, once the North and South had concluded their argument, there might not be any banks or trains left to plunder. It was decision time; time to accept my role as a spy. Rolling my eyes I said, "You win. Ah agree to whatever you want."

Nerves seemingly pacified Lincoln nodded and, putting his hands inside his pockets, resumed that grave tone of his,

"I am pleased that you agree to a commission representing us in the Confederacy."

With this 'commission to represent us', Lincoln was using politician speak, as if packing me off to be a military attaché in a foreign country. My guts were really in motion now and it took a real effort to keep my tightly clasped buttocks from declaring their own independence. In years of ambling around the States Lincoln's 'commission' ranks as one of the most stupid offers I ever received. Up there with an offer of a commission as a colonel in the Mexican Army just before their war with Texas. Tempting though it was with the likelihood of being chest deep in sultry, enormous breasted, eye flashing Mexican women and an unlimited supply of tequila. Plus lashings of gold braid hanging on multicoloured uniforms and a hefty cut of captured plunder. The thought of leading Mexico's finest did not appeal, not when the opposition included a collection of granite hard, lunatic Texas Rangers who rushed to the war, "fer the pleasure of fighting," as one of them smilingly put it.

Lincoln rumbled on, "You will be inserted into the confederacy with an adequate disguise. What Pinkerton and his boys call a cover story. We'll have it circulated how you were disgraced by this scandal with Major Smith's wife and chased out of Washington with a hue and cry about seduction and stolen jewellery. Pinkerton will ensure that the stench of shame, and your resentment at such treatment, wafts deep into the South. Lord knows you've had plenty similar events in your past. So this scandal won't be a surprise to anyone."

Ambling across the room Pinkerton stood close and said, "Don't fret. Your ungentlemanly behaviour will be acceptable to these Confederate boys. When imbibing moonshine they like a bit of scandal to banter with fellow plantation owners around the dinner table." With a cynical grin he added, "Whatever their Southern pedigree."

"If ah am found out. Can you rescue me?" I squawked.

"No. You will be shot. War generates a ruthless mentality," replied Pinkerton breezily. "Should be fun," said the Cameron Highlander and winked.

It went quiet. The collective pleasure of Pinkerton's men at my consent to their ludicrous spying plan was obvious. Flaring nostrils, indrawn breaths, and tight smiles gave that away. Pinkerton broke the heavy silence. After studiously blowing on the glowing end of his cheroot he said, "A gentle reminder Mister Crink. The Major is crushingly offended by your behaviour with his wife. Rumour has it the continuation of your mortality is at the forefront of his mind. Considered opinion is, if you risk it, and run out on us then you won't have time to wash your feet in the Potomac before I repay a favour to an old lawman friend in Atlanta. He will be informed that you were responsible for those unsolved bank robberies in Dixie during the 1850s."

It was getting worse. They had me 'hog down.'[7]

"Without money ah ain't got a life. Step out of line with you guys and ah lose both," I retorted.

A contented smile appeared for a second across Lincoln's face before he took up talking again. "Your task should be given to someone more committed to our cause. But these are difficult times. I say something on Monday and on Tuesday my words stare at me from newspaper headlines. Worse, within hours of presidential meetings in the White House, Confederate sympathisers are telling the south what we have discussed."[8] Lincoln paused, glanced at his shoes, then went swiftly on. "We want, how shall I put this, to return the favour with private sources reporting from the South. Most of our information is gossip; tittle-tattle and hearsay. You are cunning, devious and intelligent. Born and bred in Alabama you know your way around the Southern States. Ingratiate yourself at their army headquarters. Appointment as a General's aide would suit our requirements admirably. Perhaps with General Lee. I hear you two were acquainted in the Mexican war."

I did not like what I was hearing. Stress was gathering another gigantic wind bubble in my guts. I held it for as long as I could but eventually it had to break cover. I delivered it how I hoped my presence in the Confederacy would go; slow and quiet, unheard and unsuspected.

Lincoln cleared his throat and said, "Time to attend to matters with Mister Baldwin.[9] Pinkerton, please take over." He sounded like Saint Peter reading the last chapter from 'Revelation'. As Lincoln walked out of the room I heard him mutter, "We must keep Virginia in the Union."

The North could keep Virginia, lose it, or tow it into the Atlantic and sink it for all I cared. But it crossed my mind that Lincoln and myself had similar missions; he wanted to penetrate and guide the thoughts of folk in the North. And I needed to penetrate and steal the thoughts of the South.

Pinkerton began his briefing. "When you establish yourself in the Confederacy you will need assistance from my agency to pass on information. Don't worry if it takes a while before you hear anything. We intend waiting until you are in a position to communicate intelligence that will help with our military plans. Wherever you end up one of my men will contact you. Eventually," he said in a low voice.

The thug with the revolver chimed in with, "Don't forget to mention your years as a slave trader. Makes your story of leaving the North and siding with the South more believable."

Good grief was there nothing Pinkerton and his goons didn't know about me? Whipping up an index finger Pinkerton pointed it at my head and said, "McCallister is right. Slaving credentials always go down well in the south. Make sure you mention it when you arrive."

Wincing I replied, "That was my father's New Orleans import and export company. We sailed to Africa to trade with the natives. We gave them cotton clothes in exchange for ground nuts, African fruits, and wood," I said. Not much of a defence but better than dumb insolence.

"This wood. Was it black ebony?" growled McAllister. The sarcasm in his voice was thicker than a lumberjack's bicep.

After blowing his nose on a bright red handkerchief Pinkerton went on, "We will ship you to Fort Sumter[10] for infiltration into South Carolina. When the Rebs capture the fort step forward and volunteer your services to the Confederate cause."

How on earth did Pinkerton know what was going to happen at Fort Sumter? "Assuming ah survive any fighting at the fort," I replied sarcastically.

"Born survivor Mister Crink, that's you" retorted Pinkerton with a grin.

Sauntering across the room to stare out of a window Pinkerton started rubbing his eyes and, in the ensuing silence I asked quietly, "When will ah get my money back?"

Pinkerton came back to where I was sitting and said in that doom laden tone only the Scots are capable of and answered, "Do what we ask and one day you will get your money back. That's a promise." Good grief, now that was an evasive answer if ever there was one. I managed not to laugh. Mind you I had asked a stupid question. It was well known that you couldn't trust a Pinkerton man to stand by a promise. Their days were spent dealing with criminals. Meaning, not only did they think like them, they acted like them as well. My thoughts were interrupted when the Scots horror McCallister shook his head and said, "One other thing. Don't leave the South without permission. We shoot deserters as well."

I riposted with the obvious. "Let's see if ah have got this straight. Vacate my post in the south then the Confederates will mark me as a deserter. And if they find me, will shoot me. But, if ah can avoid the clutches of the boys in gray, the north will chase me down, tie me to a range post and blow my brains out instead."

"Looks that way," agreed Pinkerton with a contented smile.

Rubbing my chin I said in a low voice, "Angry Apache in front. Hissing rattlesnake behind."

"Happy days, huh?" agreed the Cameron Highlander.

"How will you make contact with me?" I asked after a further bout of rubbing my chin.

"Wait until the Rebs accept your story. When they do, your contact will be moved south and will get in touch. Whatever happens don't try to contact us. There's more Confederate spies and sympathisers in the North than ticks on a bison's hide."

Pinkerton's sales pitch made it sound as easy as doffing your cap to a lady in the street. Mind you, Pinkerton's confidence that he would know if I had fooled the Confederacy was food for thought. If that was so then there must be other Pinkerton agents in the South. It was comforting to know that I wasn't the only idiot grabbing the wrong end of a branding iron. As I was digesting these thoughts Pinkerton produced a wintry smile, examined his pocket watch, pursed his lips and said to a trio of lounging toughs, "Boys. Look after Mister Crink until he leaves for Sumter."

Then to me he intoned, "When the time comes these detectives will escort you to the ship. Then cut you loose on the South."

"Amen to that," I replied and swallowed heavily.

Pinkerton fixed me with a stare that would have frozen the fire in a blacksmith's forge and said, "Good luck. I've a feeling you're going to need it." After a short pause he pulled an envelope from a jacket pocket and handing it to me added, "Nearly forgot. A letter of introduction from President Lincoln to Major Anderson, the commanding officer at Fort Sumter. The President has explained that you are on a secret mission and he is to provide all assistance you may require to carry it out. Keep your wits and our next meeting will be in a better place some time hence."

Now that comment had to be one for the grandkids. Just what did he mean? Was the better place Washington after the North's victory? Or the great hereafter? Any spiritual meeting would present difficulties for I doubt when departing this earth the two of us would frequent the same environment. That said, it would be interesting if President Lincoln, Detective Pinkerton, and myself did meet in the hereafter; Saint Peter would surely be intrigued at our recollections.

"Thank you for those comforting words, Detective Pinkerton," I replied nodding my head vigorously.

Pinkerton flicked his cheroot out of a window, sniffed, wiped his brow with his red handkerchief then hurried out of the door. Looking sad with eyes full of distrust, probably at not being allowed to use me for target practice, McCallister shuffled off after him. That left the three Pinkerton men who were to look after me until my departure into the maelstrom of anger and hate that would become the Confederacy.

Glancing around I realised why they were looking so miserable. Being detectives they had expected a free bar in the room.

Chapter Four

My custodians having removed my timepiece, remembrance of how long I remained in that hotel room is dim. Neither would they inform me of the time of day, or even what day it was. However, I estimate being there for eight or nine days. Otherwise Pinkerton's boys looked after me. A 'lady of the line',[11] tent-pole slim figure, lithesome, blonde and with adventurous eyes and a delightful finger-twisting way of plucking the lace knots from her blouse flounced through the door every evening and stayed until the early hours of the morning.

"We've extracted payment for her dancing lessons from your detained stash," so an unsmiling detective informed me. Guess he was shy at talking about what we were up to. Or he had a dry sense of humour. The first time she arrived Pinkerton's guards took up post outside in the corridor before I was treated to fast no-nonsense talking from my visitor. "Pinkerton's finest said to keep our conversation short and ask no damn fool questions about who you are and why you are here or where you are going. You can call me 'Stretch'. Trained to be a dancer." After a moment's pause she lowered her voice and said, "And mister scar face ah reckon we have met before. In San Francisco late last year, when the money men were talking about building a railroad."[12]

"Yep. Ah was in San Francisco in November. Playing poker. Took some big men for some big dollars," I boasted then instantly regretted my words. This could be another Carmen scam type situation developing.

'Stretch' went on. "Lots of business for us line girls there. Mainly we worked out of tents. Weren't many well-mannered visitors. Apart from a short, bow-legged, scar-faced man. Had a bad time when I laughed at a drunk unable to make himself available. Got mighty angry. Scar face stopped him slashing my face open. Wore a beard back then but pretty sure it was your face hiding beneath that dribble dam."

The incident flooded back. "You were parading outside your tent, dropping bits of clothing. Nice act. Good way to attract customers. Certainly put heat into mah steam. Naked man tried to force himself on you. Couldn't allow that bad behaviour."

At that she pulled a wad of dollars from underneath her dress and, handing them over said, "Scar face, Pinkerton's gang paid me a week in advance. But you can have it for free." After a short pause she added philosophically, "One good turn deserves another."

In the history of whoring a 'lady of the line' paying a customer has got to be worldwide unique. A story fit for a sermon if I ever attended a church service in the future. Pinkerton's detectives also provided plenty of food and drink, a pack of cards, and a box of cigars during those hours when 'Stretch' was 'working' Washington's high society.

It didn't last. Such contentment rarely does. It was late in the evening, pickled deep in whiskey and dozing in a chair, when a fresh posse of Pinkerton men arrived and announced that it was time for my shipping to Charleston, South Carolina. Elbows gripped between two huge detectives I was hurried out of the rear door of the Willard and unceremoniously heaved into a coach. After a long, fast, bouncing drive the cry of seabirds announced our arrival at a quayside at which point a hood was pulled over my head. Lifted out of the coach I was supported under the armpits and taken on tiptoe, accompanied by the sounds of shouting, singing stevedores and rushed up a ship's gangplank. Taken below decks I was bundled into a tiny cabin where, much to my surprise, Pinkerton's guards shook my hand and wished me the best of luck before hurrying out of the door.

Collapsing on a bunk bed I fell asleep and knew no more until a shifty-eyed, thickset hunchback, shook me awake. Before I could gather my wits and ask how long we had been at sea he grunted something that sounded like 'goat stew' and thrust a plate of meat and coffee into my hands. Then turned and padded quietly out of the door. This became a daily pattern with the same sailor bringing food and drink but ignoring any attempt to engage in conversation. Eventually I gave up trying to obtain information and spent time practising cheating routines with a pack of cards and reading old newspapers I found in a cupboard. After what seemed weeks of this routine the hunchback arrived and spoke; announcing: "Charleston Bay to starboard," then hurried away again. Here the jitters hit. Pacing up and down a thousand scenarios, mainly about diving overboard and swimming for Charleston, went through my head. A pounding on the door followed by the hunchback shouting for me to join him outside pulled me back to reality. Arriving on deck it was night and the air was cool. The ship's captain a peppery individual with a strong handshake introduced himself. To this day his name is vague. Maybe Gowgum or Growtum.[13] Names, especially those with whom I have debts, alas time and drink have addled my memory somewhat.

"What day is this? What time is it?" were my confused questions.

"Tempus fugit[14] Mister Crink," replied the Captain enigmatically. He followed this by handing me a stick of chewing tobacco, wished me a curt 'goodnight', then scurried away to the ship's stern where he stood, muttering and staring alternatively at the sky, the sea, then Charleston. "Lights in Charleston sure look pretty," said a voice behind me.

I turned around to find a large individual wearing the greasiest pullover this side of the Potomac. A unique odour caught my nostrils. A mixture of rotting fish and sweat. In a high pitched voice the sailor said, "Time to go," and escorted me to the ship's rail. He followed this with, "Take hold of this rope and lower yourself into the row boat below. I'll send down your pack when you git on board. The crew are down there."

It was a thousand dollar winning hand to a fleabite that none of this rowing crew would accompany me into Sumter. They would dump me at the gates then scull at speed back to the ship and watch from the safety of the guardrail as the Fort receded into the distance. Returning to port they would brag how brave they'd been sailing within range of the guns in Charleston and how much they really wanted to join 'Old Crink' and the rest of Fort Sumter's heroic garrison but 'orders are orders' and they had to return to port. Yeah, right. And it was my ass that first sang 'Dixie' in the Mechanics Hall, on Broadway, in April of '59.[15]

Feet either side of the rope I gripped tight and slithered down until, friction stinging my palms, I clattered into the boat sending it rocking from side to side. Bringing an angry response from one of the four man crew, a morose looking individual with a sloping forehead who said, "Mister, you just made my face hit the bottom of this boat. You ever tasted a mixture of salt water, tar, grease and tobacco spitting? Plus the keel side droppings of hundreds of boots? Vilest taste imaginable."

"Don't forget the remains of that bird, Sam. Sure did hum," put in another rower; a smiling thick armed man with a bright red bandana tied around his head.

"Yep. Plenty putrid," added a third. Thin as a flagpole with a beard flecked with chewing tobacco.

"His silence says it all," said 'Sloping Forehead'.

"Sorry about that," I muttered and clung desperately to the side of the boat as a rolling swell sent me backwards. I lay staring up at the ship to see a huge figure on the guardrail suddenly grab at the dangling boarding rope and hurl himself outwards. With a lightness that belied his size he rappelled effortlessly into our boat and, offering an enormous hand, jerked me to my feet and said in a slow southern drawl, "Mister Crink. Ah am to accompany you into the Confederacy."

Around six foot six inches tall and half that again in shoulder width, he looked big enough to blot out the moon. Dressed in army uniform he wore a forage cap, sack coat, enlisted man's shoulder scales, trousers, and a beige union army shirt; he looked smart. Which was more than you could say for my crumpled exterior. The newcomer stared at me until, with an idiotic grin usually seen on circus clowns, he said. "How am ah doin' Mister Crink? Do ah look the part of a tough corporal in the Union Army?"

Struggling to keep my balance in the swell I replied with a shake of my head, "Not with that accent. Sounds Alabama." There was a second's quiet then he went on, "Yep, Alabama is right Mister Crink. Same as you. Call me Jack. Not mah real name yah unnerstan'. I'm really called Jim. But yah need to get used to calling me Jack. Just won't do to call me by mah real name in Confederate territory. Us bein' spies, an all."

What kind of an stupid oaf do we have here, I thought. Which came out as, "You really coming with me?"

"Ah just told yah," Corporal Jack replied good naturedly.

"Ah got that," I retorted, "What I meant was, why?"

"Sho' am a surprise for you, ah reckon. Sorry about that. But mah orders are to look after you. See that them Confederate boys don' mistreat you none," he replied with a huge grin.

"Could you spies shut up and sit down," said 'thin man' in a patient voice from behind his oars.

Myself and Jack the jolly giant duly sat on a board in the middle of the boat. Almost immediately it began to move. Slowly at first, then picking up speed until we were skimming at a fair lick across the water. Cynic that I am it crossed my mind that this Alabama loon, apart from his professed protection role, which would be a difficult job for one man, was also here to keep an eye on me; make sure that I stayed loyal to President Lincoln. Jack could be a Pinkerton man. I gave him a corner of the eye once over. Strapped to his waist were a polished black belt with belt cap box, bayonet and scabbard, and a battered cartridge box. Draped across his body were a '58 tin drum canteen and a gleaming '42 musket. Everything was Union blue apart from an infantry overcoat which was strapped to his back; it was gray. He also carried a large knapsack with a red blanket tied to the top. On his feet were what must have been the biggest pair of Brogan boots that ever walked the Atlantic seaboard. If we suffered a biblical flood both of us could take one each and sail to safety. Jack's clothing was worn and discoloured but his fighting equipment was clean and well maintained. In short, as he put it, he was a mean looking professional soldier.

"Jack. Do you want to explain yourself a bit more?"

In an instant Jack transformed from a hillbilly to an alert and articulate man. "Mister Crink, ah have heard good and bad reports from Mister Pinkerton. Everything from when you fought with the Texans in Mexico. Which was the good. To when you was robbing trains down south and lassoing slaves on the African Coast. Which was the bad. Ah also hear in the gold digging forty-niner days you were ejecting trouble making drunks from yor California bordello. Fists jabbing so fast even 'Old Smoke' Morrissey would not see them coming.[16] You are a tough son of a bitch but Mister Pinkerton reckoned you could do with some help. Spread the load. Watch yor back. In drink us southern boys can be mean. But talk too much. So here ah am."

Talk about first impressions being deceptive. Jack was an actor. And a good one. Gone was the slow speaking idiot he initially portrayed. Plus that comparison with 'Old Smoke' Morrissey was a heavy compliment. And everyone takes pleasure at flattery, laid on thin and quietly it can sway even the most cynical; except me of course.

"Pinkerton said that once settled in the Confederacy someone would arrive and help move information north. Would that be you Jack?"

"No. Signal expert's job. Could be a while afore he joins us."

"Nice to know I'm not alone."

"Ah think we will get along fine Mister Crink."

There was a pause during which we stared at each other. Me wondering if Jack had ever strode into the ring with 'Smoke' Morrisey. He had a boxer's cold ruthless look in his eyes. I reckoned he would cut a throat with about as much thought as flinging the lining of his nose into a spittoon.

It didn't take long for my thoughts to return to their usual selfish level. In a low voice I said, "Jack, we're two bad asses together and as some sailor type once said, 'All is set fair for the south'. But ah do have one problem that needs spilling some bile. Before leaving Washington there was mention of mah money stash being moved to a safe place. Would you know anything about that?" I paused before adding, "Like where it is hidden. Tell me and ah will cut you in for a percentage."

"Nope. Can't help," he answered with a shake of his huge head.

"Come on Jack where the hell has Pinkerton hidden it? Make me concentrate more on the job in hand if ah knew," I blurted out. I'm not one to be diplomatic with important questions; at least not until trying bluster.

"Maybe under President Lincoln's bed. Reckon it would be real safe there," he replied with a wide grin. Jack's delivery had returned to hillbilly mode.

"Doubtful its under Lincoln's bed. The President would not want to risk his toes colliding with Mrs Lincoln's chamber pot and sloshing the contents over mah dollar bills."

"Jesting, right. Ah do not believe that lovely woman has a pot under her bed."

I grinned and warming to my story went on, "Talk in town is that inside the presidential bedroom there is a souvenir piss pot from when George Washington scuttled into town looking for an all over massage. President and Mrs Lincoln need their sleep and won't want to stumble out of bed, knees clamped against hairy legs, scuttling down corridor for all to see. Ain't elegant."

"Whoa there Mister Crink. Ah reckon you are a mite upset about this. Don't worry none. If President Lincoln or Mister Pinkerton has your money it will be well taken care of," he said adding an elaborate wink that would have put a horse off its feed.

"As long as Pinkerton doesn't work it so that my money looks after him," I growled with a resigned sniff.

In the ensuing silence I looked around at our rowers. To a man they were rowing and also staring at us; fascinated at our conversation. (Can't be every day you overhear a discussion about the presidential chamber pot.) The fourth member of our crew, an authoritarian type with only half an ear, spoke up, "Whereabouts of that money won't get us to Sumter. Grab an oar. Dig water. Help git the job done quicker."

"Sure can," answered Jack grabbing an oar from the bottom of the boat.

That was the only spare oar, so after drumming my fingers together for a few seconds, I started rotating my head from left to right; keeping lookout. Although not having a clue what I was looking for, I hoped it made it out to the crew that I was earning my keep.

Eventually the dark outline of Sumter appeared ahead. Like a wedding vow, 'for better or worse', my future beckoned from inside the fort.

Chapter Five

Although I am an optimist at the back of my mind was the thought that if the boys in Fort Sumter noticed our approach they might think that we were an attacking Confederate force and start shooting. Then something else pulled my eyelids apart in sheer fright. Looming out of the night on our right hand side, 'starboard' to our tetchy rowers, came another row boat. Skimming along from the direction of Fort Sumter towards us, its sudden appearance made my guts freeze.

"Damnation, its heading our way," I said out aloud.

It was travelling fast and on a parallel course with about fifty feet between us but our crew's exertions and the sound of splashing oars drowned out my shout. In addition, concentrating on the work in hand and not admiring the view, our crew did not notice the new arrival. Pointing a finger at the fast approaching interloper I opened my mouth to yell a warning but, before I could speak, our combined speeds saw us move past one another. Luckily without any excitement from the other boat. Inside it I counted four men. In the dark it was difficult to be precise but three of them looked to be in Confederate army uniform. They were doing the rowing. The fourth was in civilian clothes and he was staring towards the lights of Charleston. All had their backs to us. Meaning no one was looking in our direction.

Unable to take my eyes off the boat and expecting one of the crew to suddenly turn and spot us I muttered, "Any second now. One of those 'Tar Heels'[17] will notice there's a second row boat roaming the waves in Charleston Harbour and then the fun will begin."

Our luck held as the other boat swished by and on into the darkness without any yelling or signalling towards us. Before it disappeared I heard one of the crew shout, "Colonel Chesnut, when we get back to Charleston have ah got time to weed the garden afore the war starts?"

Out of the night the Colonel's faint reply floated back.

"Captain Lee. Ah don't rightly know. But sometime shortly Sumter's garrison will be available as compost. So get your request in early."

I heard faint laughter then silence closed in again.

North and South were about to start tearing themselves apart and one of those Confederate soldiers was joking about the state of his garden. Or was it a nonsense comment? Southern sense of humour that no one north of the Mason Dixie line has ever really understood. Open-mouthed, stomach tight, I turned and looked at my rowing companions. All heads were down concentrating on propelling our boat forward, seemingly no one but me had noticed the one hundred percent increase in sea traffic. A few minutes later my lookout duties ceased when we pulled alongside a lichen and moss encrusted jetty beneath the dark outline of Fort Sumter.

"Here we go," I said to 'One Ear'.

"Keep your anchor clean," he replied in a low voice. A nautical witticism that sailed way over my head.

As the boat rode the waves 'Thick Arm' whispered, "Git moving. Can't hang around. Not with the Nina patrolling hereabouts."

"Nina? Who's she?" In my nerve-raddled state I imagined Nina to be a patrolling mermaid protecting the watery approaches to the fort.

"Reb picket boat," answered Thin Man nonchalantly leaning across his oars as if on a sightseeing trip.

"Forget about the Nina. Ah saw it skip past us a few minutes ago," I hissed.

"Why didn't you say something?" asked One Ear testily.

"Ah did. But you damned pirates were too busy heaving away to hear me shouting and pointing as it went past." Pausing, I finished lamely, "Ain't up to much. Just a row boat. Same as this."

"The Nina ain't a row boat. Its bigger than that," put in Sloping Forehead.

"Who cares. It's gone. Let's get out of here," said One Ear through gritted teeth.

"Yep, time you two went spying," said Thick Arm staring intently at Charleston.

Nerves getting the better of me I was about to remonstrate that our boat was moving up and down faster than a New Orleans whore with a queue of impatient sailors and perhaps we should trundle around the harbour for another hour so that I could get the hang of disembarking when Jack, grabbing our packs, solved the impasse by leaping nimbly onto the jetty.

Once the boat stopped rocking it was time for me to go. Steadying myself and praying for a soft landing I jumped. Unfortunately, as one foot went into space I pushed the other foot down hard on the rail, sending it lurching upwards on the other side. From the crew came an outburst of angry shouts, accompanied by some words I had not heard in a long while; including some clearly nautical terms I had never heard before. The noise diminished when Thick Arm and Sloping Forehead were tipped into the water. With their combined shrieking and splashing I was surprised that no one in Fort Sumter, or in Charleston, thought that the war had started and opened fire. In the meantime I crashed stomach first against the jetty. As I lay, winded, more cussing and hollering came from the swimmers. A suggestion from Thick Arm that I share a bed with an excited 'long eared chuck wagon',[18] an eyebrow lifting idea was the most interesting. Especially considering the smell. The animal. Not me. Ignoring the insults I clambered to my feet and looked at the sally port gate. It was shut. For a few seconds we stared hoping a patrolling sentry would show himself but the Fort was wreathed in a silent, brooding darkness. Then the fun began. Grabbing my pack I started rummaging inside. "Where is it?" I grumbled.

"What yah looking for?" asked Jack.

"Union flag,"

"Here. beneath mah shirt," he replied and with a wide grin pointed at his chest. His booming voice sounded like a cannon going off. Jack went on, "Ah saw it peeping out of the bag. So ah decided to keep it safe and wrapped it round mah chest. Keeps me warm."

"Not so loud. Ah want Anderson's men to see the flag, then us. If they spot us first in the dark they might think we're Confederates and blow us into the harbour. Thing to do is spread the flag on the ground then attract someone's attention," I whispered.

As Jack produced the flag I heard the splashing of oars as our boat pulled away from the jetty. Although the insults had stopped nobody shouted good luck. Guess they were glad to be rid of us.

"Unfurl the flag," I whispered.

What a toil that was. Twisted in large knots it took Jack's strength to disentangle it. On reflection it was a situation mirroring the political standing between North and South. Both sides enmeshed in knots of snarling claims and counter claims, each accusing the other of bad faith. Eventually we prised the flag loose.

Still whispering Jack said, "Can't see anyone above the gate. No movement on the western scarp wall. Ah suggest we hold the flag between us and start shouting. Should make a sentry come running."

"And hopefully keeps his finger away from the trigger," I replied and then yelled, "Hello. Can anyone hear me? Cornelius Crink. Envoy from President Lincoln here." Then added as an afterthought, "Outside your gate, that is."

Still nothing. All that my straining ears could hear was the slap of waves hitting the causeway rocks. What had happened to the garrison?

"Maybe they've left. Surrendered," said Jack in a low voice.

"Or maybe the Confederates have attacked and slaughtered them," I said with a worried scratch at my chin.

Suddenly a voice came from the parapet above. Sounding like a squealing hog someone yelled, "Ah kin hear someone shouting. Is that the Reb colonel again?"

After a furtive glance at Jack I whispered, "The Colonel is probably one of those soldiers on that row boat I saw. Must have paid a visit here." Then I shouted, "We've been sent by President Lincoln to speak with Major Anderson."

More yelling came from above. "Think I'm stupid? Nearest Union troops are scratching their armpits in Washington. Nobody hereabouts but you Rebs. Reckon it's time to shoot a couple of yah and start the war." This was followed by the noise of metal scraping over stone.

"Just slid his rifle across the top of the wall," I said.

"Sentry must be suffering from war fever," said Jack pointing at a dim shadow on the parapet.

Frustration boiled as I yelled, "You dumb 'castanet catch colt'. Union infantry here. Look at our flag."

"What in the hell is a 'castanet catch colt'?" whispered Jack with a frown.

"Castanets. Tried them in Mexico. Kept hitting mah fingers. Dumb of me huh? And 'catch colt' is cowboy talk for an illegitimate child."

"Used a lot of air to call the sentry a dumb bastard mister Crink. Good job he don't know what you mean," whispered jack.

"What did you say?" yelled the sentry.

Ignoring the sentry I said, "Jack, spend time at card tables and you pick up cowboy money and cowboy talk."

"Ain't answered mah question. Don't trust yah. Stay there," shouted the sentry.

"Can't walk on water like that guy in the good book. Guess we'll have to stay?" said Jack with a grin.

I broke the ensuing silence with, "Jack, we could make history. How does this sound? Two Alabama men fighting for the North standing outside a Union fort in the secessionist state of South Carolina get shot at and start this interstate brawl."

Before Jack could reply a voice yelled, "Sergeant Chester, night guard sergeant.[19] What's going on? You Confederates back again? What's your intentions this time?" His accent was Scottish. (Hopefully no relation to Pinkerton's Cameron Highlander.)

Even in those early naïve days in the confrontation between North and South one thing stood out in that sergeant's questions. Did he believe that a potential enemy would tell him what they intended doing? I considered replying, in my best sarcastic Alabama voice along the lines of: "We're trying to sneak inside the fort. If yah object, then we intend attacking. Yah have a problem with that?"

Instead common sense won out and I said to Jack, "You can yell the loudest. Tell him we're on special duty from the army in Washington and would he kindly open the gate. Tell him that ah have cigars to give away. Might tempt him."

"Hell Mister Crink, we ain't trading with Indians. Whiskey might be a better offer."

Before I could reply Jack put his own interpretation on what I had said and yelled, "Yah great idiot. We're here with supplies from President Lincoln. Tobacco. Licker. Swing these damned gates open."

Jack's Alabama bred throat stirred the Sergeant. "That's a real Dixie twang soldier. You sound like a Reb serpent.[20] Don't move while I turn out my officer," was the Sergeant's surly reply.

"Sergeant as dumb as the sentry. Surrounded by water and thousands of Confederate troops and he tells us to stay put. Ain't many places we can disappear to," I said sarcastically.

The voice of the Sergeant came again, "You hear me down there?"

"Yeah, we hear," shouted Jack.

From above came the sharp crack of a rifle shot.

Jack was the nearest piece of cover but before I could manoeuvre behind his broad back he dropped to a kneeling position and aimed his rifle at the Sergeant. If Jack returned fire that would surely jerk the garrison into action; in short it would start a gunfight. The noise of which would undoubtedly stir Charleston's politicians into violent action. Itching to remove Major Anderson and his garrison from Fort Sumter it would be the excuse they needed to order an attack. Confederate newspaper headlines would be easy: 'War. Treacherous Unionists in Fort Sumter open fire on our brave boys in Charleston.'

President Lincoln's political tricks and shenanigans would count for nothing.

Courtesy of two Northern uniformed Alabama men, war was a rifle shot away.

Chapter Six

To my relief Jack held his nerve and stayed his trigger finger until the Sergeant yelled, "Yoh, down there. That was an accident. Dumb assed sentry tangled his finger against the trigger. No harm meant." He followed this with, "Captain Davis is here."

"Stupid as a woodpecker pecking tin. Hope the rest of Lincoln's army is more sensible than that sentry," muttered Jack.

A new voice came from the gorge wall parapet, "This is Captain Jefferson Davis. Who's down there?"

"Mister Cornelius Crink. Pinkerton agent." I paused then whispered, "Jack what in the hell is your family name."

Jack finished our introductions by shouting, "Corporal Jack Claybutt. 7th New York Militia."[21]

Vaguely I heard the sentry say, "Sound like a pair of Rebs, Captain." Obviously unimpressed with the sentry's comment Davis shouted, "Can't open the gate. I'll throw down a rope ladder."

Which he duly did.

"Appears Davis is a trustworthy type. Or history appreciations need revising at West Point," I commented out of the corner of my mouth as I grasped the ladder.

"How come?" whispered Jack.

"Ancient war somewhere in Europe. England ah guess. Army of bushwhackers couldn't batter their way into a city. So they built a large wooden horse and left it outside the walls. Sort of parting gift, showing respect for how well the city folk had fought. Bushwhackers rode off in a supposed sulk. But those guys were real sneaky. Wooden horse was hollow and inside they hid a whole bunch of their men. Dumbass city people opened the gates and dragged the horse inside. Night came and out jumped the bushwhackers. They rushed the guards, opened the gates and back came their army and the city went the way of the Alamo."

"We ain't exactly an army."

"Anderson don't know that," I replied and started climbing the ladder.

"Welcome to Fort Sumter, Mister Crink. I'm Davis," said a smiling lieutenant who saluted and extended a gauntleted hand to myself and Jack.

After shaking hands I said, "Pleasure to meet you Davis. We are on special duties from President Lincoln in Washington. Please escort me to Major Anderson."

Looking suitably impressed at my description of ourselves Davis replied, "Certainly. Major Anderson is inspecting our magazine. Follow me."

Entrance to Sumter Fort, part one of our mission, was accomplished. I doubted that part two, enlistment in the Confederate army, would be as easy. Lieutenant Davis escorted us across the yard where in front of a pair of bomb proof traverses stood the flagpole. In the breeze, making cracking noises, fluttered the United States flag which myself and Jack saluted. Looking at the flag it crossed my mind that not many of us can resist a feeling of pride in a piece of coloured cloth that represents all Americans whatever religion, or profession, or whichever side of the legal fence their boots straddle. Or at this date in our history whether your uniform was blue or gray. Even after secession most of the Confederate soldiers I met, out of respect to their prior allegiance to the Union, would flick a salute to the stars and stripes. Or, if that stuck in the crop, give it a respectful nod.

All was quiet at the magazine. Nobody was sure but it was suggested Anderson had departed to his quarters. Our group about turned and once again marched off to find the Major. Inside the fort buildings lack of adequate light meant it was a struggle to keep Davis's bobbing hat in sight. Aids to vision inside buildings were candles brought in by soldiers wives. Plus, an idea from Fort Sumter's light keeper, homemade candles built from tin tubes fitted into cork discs floating on whale oil placed inside coffee cups. Flickering flames produced eerily dancing shadows, adding an atmosphere of mystery and foreboding. Meandering owls would have flitted around without difficulty but for us it was walk a pace then trip two more. "Kinda spooky around here," shouted Davis over his shoulder.

"Just thinking the same thing, Lieutenant," I replied then went head first over a box on the floor. Dusting me off the Davis said soothingly, "Not far to go Mister Crink. Turn right into the corridor at the top of this stairwell."

As we progressed I noticed a group of men huddled in a group at the top of the stairs energetically huffing and puffing at something cupped in their hands. Noticing my narrowed eyes watching the men Davis explained, "Ain't no tobacco left. Those guys are sucking their lungs out on yarn. Don't suppose you've got any to spare?"

As if on cue one of the yarn suckers began coughing.

"No yarn. Only cigars." Delving into a pocket I nonchalantly handed Davis a couple of large cigars.

"Hey, thanks Mister Crink. I will make sure they get these," he said warmly.

I could feel his smile in the dark. Mind you, as always, there was an ulterior motive with my charity. If I needed assistance whilst resident in 'Fort-Doom-Sumter' then Lieutenant Davis would be my first port of call to wheedle any favours. During the Mexican War I quickly realised certain priorities should be put in practice when Soldiering, priorities that sometimes needed assistance or advice from fellow soldiers:-

(i) In case you have to retreat at speed memorise the location of the nearest road or dirt track that leads to safety. And my definition of safety is the furthest point that a sharpshooter's bullet will travel before it loses the force needed to cause damage to your posterior; this area being one of the larger parts of my body. Back then, if we had to retreat, we would run five hundred yards before hunkering down again. (Sniper's optimum distance.)

(ii) Your first friend should be a cook. (Preferably a competent one.)

(iii) Locate the nearest thunder box. Or, as was so often the case, if there ain't one then build your own. (Maintain sufficient distance so that sleep is not disturbed by the smell. Or noise; big man equals big ass; equals impressive sound.)

(iv) Find a safe spot to lay out your bedroll. As in out of sight from soldiers senior to yourself, marching troops, meandering wagons, and horses. A respectable distance should be maintained from the latter even when stationary. Horseshit ain't that bad a smell but uncomfortable if it lands on you. Especially if you don't wake up until it's all over. (Yep, stating the obvious there, but you'd be surprised at how many guys had to learn the hard way. Mind you some farm boys just laughed, brushed it off, and whistled their way through the rest of the day.)

(v) Once bedded down for the night put on your cap and wrap your arms around your rifle and keep close to hand ammunition, a full water bottle, a day's bag of food, and your boots. Putting it another way. If you have to move fast in the night the bare necessities to survive should be near to hand.

(vi) Carry as many spare dry pair of socks as possible. Although in war personal hygiene tends to be optional; i.e. it often takes a back seat when you're feeling tired or how busy you are. Sweat and wet conditions can cause trench foot so socks should be washed as often as possible.

(vii) Be on the best possible terms with your sergeant. Usually they've forgotten more about soldiering than you will ever know. Plus you don't want to be ordered to the front row during a bayonet charge. Last but not least. Stay cheerful. If you're marching you're not fighting. So smile. You're still alive and nobody's shooting at you.

Ushered inside the Major's quarters we found Anderson sat at a table, fingers intertwined, twiddling his thumbs; which I took as a sign of frustration at his situation rather than boredom. Behind him, and to one side, stood a bareheaded Captain; he looked alert but uneasy.

Major Anderson began with a stinging greeting. "Two of you. Is that it?"

Throwing a pair of fingers against my hat, old habits die hard, I fished out Lincoln's letter from a pocket and handing it to Anderson replied through gritted teeth, "Don't need many men to carry this letter, Major." After a pause I added, "The name is Crink. Mister Cornelius Crink. Pinkerton agent. And this is Corporal Jack Claybutt, 7th New York Militia."

Accepting the letter Anderson said with a frown, "That so. Don't care for your tone mister. Nor do I see any point in a Pinkerton agent appearing on my doorstep." The Major paused, cocked his head to one side then said, "Speaking of tones, yours is distinctly from south of the Mason Dixie. Is this another request from South Carolina's Commanding General, Brigadier Beauregard inviting me to surrender the fort?"

"Doubt that a Pinkerton agent would be given such an assignment, Major. And if you read that letter you will see it is from your commander-in-chief," I answered sourly.

"Sounds like you have a touch of the 'lampers', Mister Crink."[22]

"Difficult, Major. Ah ain't a horse."

A thin smile of approval at my comment appeared on the bareheaded captain's face. Which is reassuring when you are with strangers and trying to orientate yourself in a place your boots have never tramped before.

Slitting open the envelope and extracting the letter Major Anderson squinted at it then, throwing me an inquiring look, pointed at the letter and said in a perplexed tone, "Originating address is the White House. This some kind of a joke Mister Crink?"

Still in my sour mode I replied, "Read it. Might want to give us some respect when you do."

Holding the letter in the air Anderson said to the bareheaded captain in a voice coated with sarcasm, "Mah eyes are stinging from poking about in the magazine. Abner, what does our commander-in-chief want?" The Captain took the letter but before he could say anything Anderson went on, "Captain Abner Doubleday. Mah second in command."

I nodded at the Captain and received a nod in return.

Doubleday began reading. Within seconds his eyes opened wider than I thought possible and, after an astonished glance at me and Jack said, "Best if you read this, Major," and returned the letter to Anderson.

The gingerly way that Doubleday handed over the letter you would have thought he was handling his mother-in-law's underwear. Major Anderson swiftly read the one page letter and, placing it face down on his desk said in a respectful voice, "Never seen anything like this before. Have to offer you every assistance in your endeavours to infiltrate Confederate lines. All requests for help are to be treated as if coming directly from the President of the United States himself. And signed by President Lincoln."

There was curiosity and wariness in Anderson's eyes when he said,"One hell of a recommendation Mister Crink. Can't think of anything higher. Not in this world anyway. But your names are not mentioned in this document?"

"As Pinkerton agents, the President didn't want to put our names in there in case it fell into Confederate hands."

For a few seconds there was silence as Anderson studied me and then Jack. I decided to change tack with a verbal handshake,"Perhaps we got off on the wrong foot Major. At this moment in time you have the worst job in the United States military. And ah consider it an honour to meet you."

"Ah reciprocate the compliment, Mister Crink."

In Anderson's eyes there was now a chunk of pity mixed with curiosity. The Major's tone was all concern when he said, "Intelligence work. Ain't none of our business. But sticking your tails inside confederate territory in their present rebellious mood is dangerous. How can we help?"

"Major, as you've guessed myself and Corporal Claybutt are to operate behind enemy lines and intend infiltrating the South from Fort Sumter. Ah would respectfully ask that everyone in the fort is sworn to secrecy about us. On a

Bible if possible. When the garrison march out they should not divulge to anyone how and when we arrived. If our coming to Sumter in the middle of the night is discovered the Confederates might suspect that we are not genuine Reb sympathisers. It's human nature for soldiers to be curious. But loose talk could jeopardise our mission."

"Sounds melodramatic. But I think that can be done. Chaplain Harris can be made available."[23]

"Assuming the garrison walks out of here and is not carried out," said Doubleday in a low voice.

"Could go either way Captain. But ah am confident that an honest appraisal of the military situation will determine Fort Sumter's future status," I said.

"You've got a way with words, Mister Crink," said Anderson thoughtfully.

"Major Anderson ah think you are the kind of person who appreciates an honest opinion. Any objections to mah appreciation of your situation?" I said quietly.

"Go ahead."

"War is about to break out and Fort Sumter is where it will start. Sumter is deep inside secessionist South Carolina and the artillery boys across the bay in Charleston are pawing the ground with frustration. They want to fire their cannons. For political reasons President Lincoln also wants the South to fire the first shots. The question is, do you wait until the Rebs start shooting and put on a show of defending the fort by returning fire? Then after a face-saving interlude surrender. Which ah suspect is President Lincoln's expectation. Or do you prevent unnecessary loss of life by running up the white flag now. And seeing it out of mah eyes that latter decision is preferable. Meaning, if a slugging match starts between Charleston's cannons and Fort Sumter's artillery and myself and Corporal Jack become casualties then our mission has failed before it has even started."

"Accurate appreciation, Crink." Turning his head Anderson said quietly, "What do you think, Abner?"

Pursing his lips for a second Captain Doubleday replied, "President Lincoln is our commander-in-chief and his view should be our priority consideration. Unless, Mister Crink, your mission is of such importance to the Union that under no circumstances should we put you at risk. Can you tell us anything about your mission?"

"No. Ah cannot." (Which was true. I didn't have any specific instructions myself! That wouldn't come until I met my contact who was to ferry intelligence north.)

"Playing Devil's advocate, Abner. Do the President's instructions for us to assist Mister Crink override his wishes that the Confederates start hostilities with us?" said Anderson.

Doubleday frowned and after scratching his head and smiling wryly said, "Don't recollect such a scenario ever presented for discussion at West Point. Seems a 'stalemate'. My impression is perhaps the President has put Mister Crink's plan together at short notice and has not considered what takes priority. Is it Mister Crink and Corporal Claybutt's mission, or his desire for the South to be seen to start hostilities? On the little that we know I would have to say that we should follow the President's design for the South to be seen as the aggressor and hunker down until they attack. Putting it another way. The history of the United States will have to show that the South started the war. Pulling down the flag and surrendering without a fight will raise Confederate morale and cause resentment and anger with our soldiers against our leaders. In short it will send the wrong message to both sides."

"Back to you, Mister Crink," said Anderson grimly.

"Ah have to agree with Captain Doubleday. Except to say the North has very little intelligence coming out of the South, but plenty of it going the other way. Truth is, President Lincoln did not mention how important our mission is. But to measure our mission against the President's wishes that the South has to begin hostilities, it would be foolish to think that we should take priority."

"Well spoken," said Anderson with an agreeing nod of his head.

Considering Lincoln and the rest of the North was mighty interested in what was happening at Fort Sumter it was a good bet that today's discussion would eventually reach the President's ears. Assuming Anderson survived any Confederate attack and escaped Sumter and made his way to Washington, then his 'after action report' would undoubtedly include my comments. And it would not be difficult to predict how a man with Lincoln's Presidential powers would react if I had said the opposite of my speech. Probably jail. Certainly my money would disappear. But hopefully my ill-gotten gains would now be kept safe for my return. Maybe even a medal. (Yeah, I know, the Medal of Honour would be pushing it a bit. It's for bravery in front of the enemy, not making bootlicking speeches.)

"You planning on joining the Confederacy when they take over the Fort?" said Doubleday quietly. The Captain had worked out what myself and Jack were, hopefully, about to do. There was no way I could confirm his question.

"Whatever happens to the garrison myself and Corporal Claybutt are to remain in the South. That is all ah can say, Captain." Which I thought a reasonably ambiguous answer. When in a fix always try to give an answer that satisfies the question but doesn't explain what scheming you're up to. A politician's reply; i.e. respond but don't answer in depth.

Raising an eyebrow Major Anderson said, "Abner, ah think that we have taken our conversation about Mister Crink and Corporal Claybutt's mission as far as we can. Mind you, ah would have thought President Lincoln would have sent some troops with you two. Couple hundred infantrymen wouldn't go amiss. Help keep the fight going a bit longer."

"Sounds as if you've decided to put up a fight, Major," said Jack.

"Sounds that way, don't it?" answered Anderson nodding his head.

You had to doff your cap to the man. He was standing his ground against the whole of the South with his eighty-odd garrison soldiers which included eight musicians, who could maybe perforate a few Confederate eardrums if they played loud enough when they came over the walls; plus forty or so civilian workers and myself and Jack. Anderson's reaction was that of a loyal West Pointer; meaning when the President and the rest of the United States is watching stick out your chest, feel your collar with the back of your neck, and stand your ground come what may. After my experiences in the Mexican War it's an attitude that still annoys me. Major Anderson was a graduate of West Point, class of 1825, and at fifty-five years of age he was at the rear end of his career rather than the front. Although serving bravely in the Blackhawk, Seminole, and Mexican Wars, for me the Major should have been 'salvage cut'[24] and retired to a rocking chair, drinking and scratching himself stupid, rather than in charge of one the most sensitive military situations in the history of the United States. Yet here he was, in charge at Fort Sumter, flashpoint and potential genesis of America's civil war. But there was nothing to be done but wait for the God of war to roll the dice and get on with whatever evil 'norther' blew our way.[25]

An uneasy silence descended which I broke with, "How did talks with Brigadier Beauregard's emissaries go, Major?"

His voice ringing with contempt Major Anderson spoke slowly and deliberately, "Brigadier General Beauregard wants me to surrender Sumter immediately. Those aides of his first arrived yesterday afternoon. Uninvited, same as you. Ah refused to abandon the fort. Told them in a few days we'll run out of food, so leave us alone until then. Meaning, we walk out of Sumter in our own time."

Anderson stared at his fingers for a moment then continued, "They returned just before you arrived. Came with a second message from Beauregard. To the effect that, to avoid an 'effusion of blood', ah was to state when ah intended evacuating the fort. If ah refused then Sumter would be reduced."

Extracting a sheet of paper from his jacket Anderson thrust it into my hands saying, "They sure are impatient. This is the ultimatum delivered by Chesnut and Lee. Have a read."

I took the paper. From memory, and a powerful memory is one of my few virtues, the note went: 'Sir: By authority of Brigadier-General Beauregard, commanding Provisional Forces of the Confederate States, we have the honour to notify you that we will open fire with our batteries on Fort Sumter in one hour from this time.'

It was signed by James Chesnut and Stephen Lee. Aide-de-camps.

As I pondered Beauregard's ultimatum Anderson said, "Dammit Crink, what kind of a comment is 'effusion of blood'? Why not come right out and say they'll blow us to Kingdom Come?"

When you're tired and bleary eyed and surrounded by water and thousands of enemy troops and there's no route to slip away, that is not the comment you want to hear.

After a moment's silence Anderson said, "Anyway, I told them provided that I did not receive contradictory instructions from President Lincoln, or further supplies, I would evacuate Sumter on the 15th April."

Hallelujah.

Chapter Seven

Glancing at Anderson, Captain Doubleday enlightened us about Beauregard's use of language in his note. "Brigadier General Beauregard's comment 'effusion of blood' was first spoken during a war between the English and the Irish over two hundred years ago. English General called Oliver Cromwell used the expression outside the besieged Irish town of Drogheda. Beauregard is saying that we should note the similarity between Drogheda and Sumter. Both places under siege and Cromwell won the English civil war. The Brigadier is hinting that the South, like Cromwell, will win the coming war."

"So that's who they were," I said out aloud.

"Who?" queried a frowning Anderson.

"Beauregard's visiting 'aide-de-camps.' It was their boat I noticed rowing past us on our way across the harbour." Turning to Jack I continued, "Counting the ship that transported us to Charleston, plus the boat that brought us to Sumter. Add that 'Reb' picket boat, the *Nina*, plus the row boat with Sumter's Confederate visitors. Charleston Harbour was a wagon train of wandering boats."

"And apart from you Mister Crink, none of those meandering sailors, soldiers, or civilians appear to have noticed each other." said Jack with a surprised grin.

"Got to hope nobody in Chesnut's boat saw you headed this way. Dumbest dish washer in Charleston would wonder what you were up to. Might even stir South Carolina's finest into thinking you were spies." said Anderson. (Bit of sarcasm there I thought.)

"Nobody in that Reb boat noticed us," I said confidently.

"Sure of that?" asked Doubleday warily.

"Too busy looking at the fort and discussing what mischief they would commit against its inhabitants."

"Major, what time did your visitors leave?" asked Jack.

"Around 3.30 am. Not a bunch of time left before they start their bombardment," replied Anderson raising his eyebrows.

Flicking open the cover on his pocket watch Captain Doubleday said, "Fifteen minutes."

It was going to be long fifteen minutes. At the back of my mind I was considering scouting out a safe place to skulk. If there was any fighting inside the fort I didn't see the point of any heroics on my part. Besides, as I kept telling myself, the object of the mission was to stay alive and infiltrate the South; to obtain information not to fight. And just in case South Carolina's militia cutthroats couldn't contain themselves when they swarmed over the parapets I was carrying a white flag in my sack.

"Major, got much in the way of provisions?" I asked.

"Abner estimates five days food left."

Doubleday piped up with, "Two days ago we ran out of bread and some of the boys were grubbing around on the floor picking up spilled rice. Which ain't much fun. Not when there could be glass mixed in with it."

Jack broke the silence that followed with a loud, "Glass?"

"Had us some firing practise with our artillery earlier and bust a few windows. Bits and pieces of glass fell to the floor," answered Doubleday gloomily.

I shivered at the thought of glass shards slicing through my innards.

"An hour firing canons then haul down the flag?" I queried.

With a glance at Doubleday, Anderson replied, "Whoa there Crink. Reckon we can take a day of discomfort before dropping the flag."

Captain Doubleday nodded his head in agreement.

"Any idea of the Confederate war menu Major. Bombardment only? Or cannon fire and infantry assault?" I asked and gripped the sides of my trousers. (Tension brought on by thoughts of bayonets dripping blood. My blood.)

"Suppose for starters they'll serve mortar shells. Followed by a main course of artillery for a day. Then a rest period while they digest how much damage they've caused. It's a well built fort so a dessert of more artillery is likely. Further courses will depend on how much brickwork is still standing. If we resist for a couple of days ah can see them sending in the infantry." Anderson wearily rubbed his eyes before continuing in a low monotone, "Might be prudent to write a Will."

My immediate thoughts, in respect of a Will, would not impress a benefactor. It would go along the lines of:- 'Dear relative or concubine. I leave all my worldly goods to you:-

(i) That being the sum of one hundred thousand dollars. Whereabouts unknown.

Don't get too excited about this money. You will have to trek to Washington and persuade either President Lincoln, or his detective Mr Allan Pinkerton, to reveal its whereabouts.

(ii) A saddle. Stolen from the sheriff's office in Tombstone Arizona.

(iii) Two revolvers. Likewise, stolen. Forget where.

(iv) A pair of boots. One with a 'plains' spur; the other California style. Present from 'Shifty Eyes' Amy; bartender in Tombstone. Good luck. p.s. If you approach either Lincoln or Pinkerton and they are elegantly attired, living in a new house apiece and wearing expensive watches, then I suggest you

> leave them be. p.p.s. Persist in requesting that these gentlemen hand over the money then you run the risk of being arrested for Conspiracy to Possess stolen money. Claiming ignorance as to its pedigree has about as much chance of being believed as I have of becoming President of the United States. So, dear relative or concubine, you will end up with a pair of boots plus a pair of spurs. Ain't I generous?

"Nothing to leave anyone, Major," was the only answer that I could come up with.

"All ah own is mah boots," put in Jack cheerfully.

"Actually, Mister Crink, you have something very valuable that you could give to the Union cause," said Doubleday. He paused, rather theatrically, then went on in a low voice, "Your life."

"Horrifying thought Captain. But true," I grumbled.

After a wry smile Captain Doubleday whispered in Major Anderson's ear. Followed by Anderson replying, "Agreed. Go warn the men to expect Beauregard to start the war anytime soon."

As Doubleday disappeared out of the door at a brisk trot Anderson said, "Mister Crink, for the record you will appreciate us Kentucky folk don't give in easily. And without direct orders from Washington ah have struggled for hours wondering what to do."

"Major ah suggest you partake of a Kentucky breakfast. Then think again," said Jack with a smile.

Displaying deep red gums Anderson laughed out aloud. "Kentucky breakfast?" I queried. Anderson provided the answer. "A three pound steak. A bottle of whiskey. And a dog nearby."

Leaning forward Jack said to me in a low voice, "The dog gits to eat the steak."

For the second time in five minutes, still smiling at Jack's suggestion, Major Anderson stuck a hand into his tunic and yanked out his pocket watch. Carefully scrutinising it he gave me a resigned look and said, "Four thirty. Reckon its noise and smoke time. Beauregard's one hour grace has expired."

"Brigadier Beauregard could be having second thoughts," I said hopefully.

"Could be. Maybe leaving his final decision until later in the morning," said Jack.

As Jack finished uttering those twelve words South Carolina's artillery intervened in our deliberations and fired a shell into Fort Sumter. As the resulting explosion reverberated throughout the fort the Major said dryly. "Bang on time. Mind you mah watch is a few seconds slow. Bit like its owner."

On time or not, that lump of metal changed the history of the United States forever.

Out of the mouth of a cannon rather than any misty-eyed presidential address from Abraham Lincoln or Jefferson Davis, war had been declared. I have heard it argued that the first shots of the civil war were in fact fired three months before on the 9th January 1861, at the *Star of the West*, a ship attempting to reinforce Sumter with troops and supplies. When fired upon by the Confederate harbour batteries from Fort Morris the ship turned and retreated. (Suppose January to April could be described as 'stroking the chin time'.) But that shell fired at Fort Sumter meant that President Lincoln could point the finger of blame for the commencement of hostilities at the Confederacy. Quite simply Lincoln had kept his cool and out-thought the South. President Lincoln's future, and that of his generals, depended now on finding a strategy to out-fight the South.

My thoughts went to another conflict. When young and stupid I went to fight in the war against Mexico. As I stood at our door ready to leave my father placed a hand on my shoulder and said: "Cornelius, it's easy to start a war. Words from a politician is all it takes. But damned difficult to stop. Pride and stubbornness prevent politicians admitting they called it wrong. They believe their views and ideas are right and the rest of us too stupid to understand what they've set in motion. Reckon our leaders hear voices in their heads telling them to keep the war going. Probably believe its God speaking; confirming their own self-righteous convictions that they made the correct call. So the soldiers keep pulling the trigger and its damnation to the blood and expense." Snapping out of my memory trip I grimaced and said, "Permission to leave and take shelter, Major."

"Granted Mister Crink. I will inform the chaplain to administer your requested oath of secrecy to the garrison."

At that Anderson thrust Lincoln's despatch into my hands and, with Jack hard on my heels, I hurried out of the door. The sound of another arriving shell made us take cover behind a bombproof traverse next to the parade ground, close to the sally port door leading to Charleston Harbour. No sooner had we done so than I heard a loud voice. Looking around a corner of the traverse I saw a bearded officer, who I later learned was Captain John Gray Foster the fort's engineer, standing on the parade ground shouting, "Come on. Outside. Roll call. Get on parade."

Impatiently tapping a foot on the ground, Foster stood, one hand on his waist belt, the other waving encouragement at passing soldiers to join him. Amongst the throng another three of Anderson's subordinate officers arrived; Captain Jefferson Davis, Assistant Surgeon Samuel Crawford, and First Lieutenant Truman Seymour hurried to come to attention in front of Gray. The order to muster had come from Anderson who left his quarters to join the parade. The screech of another shell landing on a wall encouraged the Major to direct his collection of grim-faced officers and soldiers to take shelter alongside myself and Jack. Once everyone was in orderly lines roll call was taken. While this was going on the men kept glancing anxiously at the sky and whispered profanities reached us from within their ranks. Suddenly things became worse. It rained shells. As I remember it most of those early artillery shots either hit the water or the outside walls.

Major Anderson took charge of the parade and said, "Men, the South has begun its bombardment of Fort Sumter. (Oh really, is that what the noise is all about!). Move around in the open with care. Don't take any unnecessary risks. Take cover and may God protect you. In due course we shall return fire. You can now go and have breakfast."

Time has dimmed my memory of his exact words but that recollection is close to it. Soldiers had been made to leave shelter and listen to Anderson's eve of battle speech. Gettysburg address it wasn't. Rank stupidity more like. I mean was there ever an officer who needlessly exposed his troops to enemy fire more than Anderson did at Fort Sumter; just to tell them the obvious. Setting an example and showing coolness under fire is one thing but a single shell could have taken out most of the garrison. The shelling went on and on. Nearby Confederate occupied forts joined in, with barrages arriving from Fort Johnson and Fort Moultrie. Floating batteries close to Sullivan's Island and Cummings Point also let rip. Firing without respite. Bright flashes followed by long curving arcs of hot steel rained down. The Confederates weren't very accurate until a misty daylight arrived and then their aim improved somewhat. As the day went on it was more of the same;

with succeeding crashes, bangs, cracks and explosions playing havoc with everyone's nerves. I heard a sergeant say that Captain Doubleday fired the first counter battery shot, which was around 7.30 a.m. Aiming his salvo at Cummings Point. This was followed by Lieutenant Davies banging away at Fort Johnson. Next, Crawford started lobbing shells at Sullivan's Island. We were later told that a Crawford shot knocked out a gun on the floating battery, but these efforts were a token reply against a vastly superior force who had us surrounded and who battered away at Sumter to their hearts content.

Myself and Jack stayed away from the inside of buildings. Remaining behind the bombproof traverse. Mind you the secure feeling at being surrounded by solid brick was tempered by what would happen if a building suddenly collapsed on top of us. (The word terrifying comes to mind.) As for the soldiers the longer it went on the less upset they became. "You bastards are enjoying this," I shouted at a nonchalantly whistling soldier. This was after a trouser filling moment when a shell hit the parade ground and showered myself and Jack in dirt and grit. The soldier grinned, waved a hand, then sauntered away. Although I did notice his shoulders were slightly hunched and his left eye twitched somewhat.

With most of our artillery situated on top of the fort walls it was an obvious place to attract attention and, with increasing frequency, it was there that Confederate shells hit. Eventually Major Anderson ordered everyone off the walls and under cover. An order that stuck in the throats of two sergeants. For they went, bent double, scurrying to the top of a wall where a 10-inch columbiad cannon stood. A loud boom and a cheer signalled the sergeants had struck back. A courageous action brought on by frustration at not being able to trade equal amounts of shells. That said, the sergeants' second shot was their undoing. A lanyard was tugged to fire the gun and it fired alright, but flew from its carriage and came to rest at the head of a nearby stairwell. Luckily neither sergeant was injured.

Honour satisfied the two sergeants hurried back under cover.

On and on it went. Shell after shell gouged holes in Sumter's walls and large cracks appeared in buildings. Thick pillars of brick dust, clouds of smoke, and wood soot wafted skywards. The shells came throughout the morning and early afternoon of the twelfth. Never before had I felt so impotent and frustrated, including when pinned to a church organ and nearly smothered by Tombstone's 'Suction Thighs' Snibbings, as I did during that bombardment of Fort Sumter. We sat, swore, smoked, and took it.

Months later I wrote to father about our ordeal at Sumter: "What a pounding we received," was one of the expressions I used; I didn't need to exaggerate, the truth was bad enough. Waxing about such horrors failed to impress father. The current doe-eyed 'horizontal worker' told me his reaction was along the lines of "Hey, sugar. Cornelius got himself 'rim rocked'[26] in that Fort Sumter fight. Wonder what dollar making confidence trick he was pulling in South Carolina. Can't have been taking sides in the war. Ain't his style. Whatever he's up to must be worth a lot of whiskey money. Holed up in a fort and getting shot at is dangerous. Should stick to cards, dancing with rich wimmen, selling fake drink and robbin' banks to earn his keep. Don't understand what he's complaining about. Seems those Reb shells missed him. Lot of fuss about nothing." Followed by heaving my letter into the fire.

Then it happened. About 3 p.m. on the 12th April, the barracks were smoking and crumbling nicely while myself and Jack skulked in a shelter in the south-east scarp. After a meagre lunch of dubious pork and mouldy bread we'd found in a discarded knapsack, Major Anderson came prowling along on a morale boosting foray. "Mister Crink. How are you and Corporal Claybutt making out?" he queried.

"Thinking about swimming to Charleston," I grumbled.

Anderson thought I was joking. After a thin smile and a wagging finger he walked away. Suddenly, in a shower of glass, wood and dust, a shell screamed through a window and landed with an explosion that sent me and Jack flying backwards to land on the floor in a dust covered heap. Dazed, I lay wondering whether it was the end of my world and if I was about to meet someone with horns and a pointed tail who, giving the thumbs down, would thrust a large shovel into my hands. Staggering to my feet I did a quick check. Everything between the legs was still capable of swinging back and forth. Head locked to shoulders. Arms and legs had reported for duty. Nothing was missing. Apart from some cuts and bruises and a sharp ringing in my ears, I was sound in wind and limb; especially the wind department. They say the devil looks after his own. He certainly did that day. God bless him. Mind you, I must have been in shock. I remember shrieking a pathetic 'help' then stumbling around in circles shouting arrant nonsense about the ridiculous rise in the price of slaves and damning the North for causing me problems in the South. Which, after returning at speed to re-join us, is how Major Anderson found me.

"Mister Crink, hope you've only lost your mind and nothing else," boomed Anderson lumbering out of the darkness.

According to the Major I shook a fist at him, grinned inanely, then sat on a jagged bit of wood, which sent me hurtling upright again. With tears streaming down my cheeks Anderson started pummelling my head with the palms of his hands. This cleared my mind and restored my ability to think somewhat but did not quite return me fully to the land of the sane and sound of wit. Roaring profanities I ran towards a hole where a window had once been. Until an artillery shell destroyed it the window looked out at Charleston. Scrambling up a ramp of brick rubble and broken planks of wood I imagined it somehow offered an escape to the outside world.

"Come back yah idiot," bleated Jack.

But there was no reasoning with me. Scrabbling on bloodied hands and knees, screeching about having to 'escape this hell hole', I made for the opening intent on performing a diving header into oblivion. About to hurl myself through the hole I tripped on a lump of brick and landed face down in a pile of brick dust. Gasping for breath I stared uncomprehendingly at Charleston harbour. Effortlessly lifting me to my feet Jack rasped, "Let's have yah away from this window."

Tut-tutting with concern Jack produced a piece of cloth the size of a barmaid's dress and, spitting on it, began wiping dust and grit from my face. (A cloth saturated with spittle is not much different from water. It's wet. Assuming there were no infectious diseases lodged in Jack's mouth, that is. Which is a distinct possibility with an Alabama man. Still, it's the thought that counts.)

"We need to get under cover," Jack shouted as another shell landed nearby.

I answered with, "Pinkerton, where the hell are my dollars?"

Which goes to show although disorientated and confused as I was, greed for money was still my priority.

No change there then. Then everything went black. I either fainted or Jack forgot the size of his feet and stood on my head. Whatever the cause I was out cold for about ten minutes. When I re-opened my eyes I was flat on my back on somebody's bed. A black face, with red rimmed eyes, stared at me. It reminded of a bank robber who had rode with me down south.

"Not very hot," I said to the face.

"What?" retorted the face.

"Are you the devil?" I stammered.

"It's me. Jack."

"What happened to your face?"

"Piece of cloth. Lot of stinging dust hereabouts." So saying Jack removed the cloth and grinned. Then leaning to one side he grabbed a pair of Union blue trousers from a chair and said, "Going to need these Mister Crink."

"Why?"

"Exploding shell shredded yor trousers. For a moment your bare ass was in the window, facing towards Charleston. Reb sharpshooters must have thought the moon was rising. So held their fire."

My sense of humour was still absent and all I could come out with was, "Why am I shivering?"

"Concussion and shock. You'll be alright," said a voice out of sight. Turning my head I saw surgeon Crawford sitting in a chair. On the wall behind him hung all manner of surgical instruments, bowls and piles of dark stained towels. Crawford went on, "Hit your head. No great harm done. Suppose that would be difficult anyway. You being an Alabama man."

Jack laughed. But I couldn't find my sense of humour, not yet anyway.

"Been lucky Mister Crink. Apart from a weakness in yor head and torn and singed clothing is all," said Jack.

"Where's the luck. We're in hell. Trapped in a fort being bombarded into bits of grit." A thunderous crash provided a timely reminder of my statement of the obvious.

"Why don't we just surrender?" I said through chattering teeth.

"We will. All in good time," crooned Crawford.

"Need to stick it for a while longer. Give the wrong impression if we run soon as the shootin' starts," said Jack with a wink.

Befuddled or not I was still looking for answers. "Crawford. What's your take on our situation?" I asked.

Putting his hands behind his head Crawford answered, "Lincoln has acted smart. In simple terms the President needs to be seen as the good guy. If the Confederates want out of the Union then they have to shoot first. President Lincoln can open his hands, look the Union and the Confederate States in the eye, and say war was forced upon him. He's looking to the future. When the war is over he wants reconciliation. That will be difficult if the North attacks the South first. It will leave a festering mental boil of an accusation that we started the war. Stabbed the South in the back. So they took up arms to defend themselves. In that scenario only the good lord could know when the fighting would stop."

Here Crawford paused, cocked his head to one side and went on, "Lincoln's other dilemma is the honour of the Northern States. Can't surrender Sumter immediately. We have to resist. Put on a show. Like the Alamo. Except don't go the same way they did. Fort Sumter's garrison needs to walk away. The cry has to remain: 'Remember the Alamo.' Not 'Remember the Alamo and Sumter'. That's what I think."

"Sounds good, Lootenant," said Jack appreciatively.

The bombardment went on. A whirling blur of noise, flames, flying dirt and eye-irritating dust. With hindsight this was tame compared to most battles that lay in the future and, amazingly, we lost only one soldier at Sumter. And that was an accident when a cannon exploded during the garrison's salute to the Union flag before the fort was evacuated. I failed to witness the accident. Fatigue and stress sent me to sleep and it was Sunday the 14th April when I awoke. Standing next to me was a Confederate captain. My first thought was; 'Hallelujah, our nightmare bombardment is over.'

With hindsight a new nightmare was about to begin.

Chapter Eight

After the garrison left Fort Sumter they were taken on board a Confederate ship, the *Isabel* until the next day when they were transferred to the *Baltic*; a Union ship waiting for them outside Charleston Harbour Bar. Myself and Jack had already presented ourselves to a posse of Confederates who had swarmed into the fort when Major Anderson ran up a white handkerchief on the flagstaff. It was difficult to tell if the group that approached us were soldiers or civilians pretending to be military. They were wearing a variety of civilian clothes, red sashes, carrying swords and described themselves as aides to officials of the State of South Carolina. Although they ignored queries as to who these officials were. Stony-faced they stared and exclaimed how puzzled they were as to why we had not left with Major Anderson and the others. However, once I requested to be escorted into the presence of Brigadier-General Beauregard so that we could offer our services to the South, their demeanour changed to smiling, hand shaking friends.

On arriving in Charleston, a Confederate Major from the Charleston Ancient Battalion of Artillery, who was dealing with recruitment in the city, informed us that Beauregard was very busy and had more pressing matters to deal with than conversing with a pair of lowly recruits such as ourselves. (He spoke as arrogantly as it sounds.) When I informed the Major that I was acquainted with the South's President Jefferson Davis, having served together during the Mexican War, his attitude of indifference noticeably changed to one of polite interest and he promised to get a message to Davis that I was looking to enlist with the

Confederacy. Before departing the Major placed us in an unoccupied house in Tradd Street, overlooking the Ashley River, home of a cotton plantation owner currently in residence at his second home in Flatrock, North Carolina, who had graciously allowed his Charleston house to be used by 'any Southern military gentlemen in need of accommodation during the current crisis between the States'.

Free to wander Charleston while we waited for instructions as to our disposal from the artillery major, myself and Jack split up and strolled the streets watching and listening to local civilians and men in uniform, visiting shops, saloons, and in particular sidling into business premises such as the *Charleston Mercury* and the *Charleston Daily Courier* newspaper offices to chat with staff about the political situation in the country and preparations for hostilities. (For me journalists and bank robbers are much better at finding out what is going on than police detectives. But then I'm biased.) Although useful practice in information gathering tactics it was early days in the war and unlikely that we would pick up anything of consequence that would interest Pinkerton or the military.

One April evening, while Jack was drinking and listening to bar talk in the Mills House Hotel, I strolled past the city market and on a whim decided to eat in the nearby Charleston Hotel. The restaurant was full and I was about to walk back into the street when a woman, sat by herself in the middle of the room, came to my rescue. Poking me in the ribs with her parasol she announced that I could draw up a chair and share her table.

In her thirties, Mrs Sarah Riley made it obvious she had taken a shine to me. After a short period of introductory banter about our backgrounds she complimented me with,

"It is such a delight to meet a well-mannered Southern gentleman such as yourself Mister Crink. Even though you are from that backward, rough and tumble, tobacco chewing spitting State of Alabama," and accompanied this with a coy smile that would have made a chicken squawk with fright.

A woman with enormous protruding buttocks she reminded me of the rear of a trail wagon. Nevertheless she was cheerful and talkative. The widow of an itinerant engineer who had travelled the South servicing and repairing 'cotton gins'[27] within minutes she was talking about the history of these 'amazing machines', especially McCarthy Gins that her husband had so enjoyed fixing in Florida, Georgia and South Carolina. Mrs Riley also exclaimed how much work her husband had done for the famous Colonel Wade Hampton[28] on his plantations in South Carolina and Mississippi.

Moving mind and mouth to politics Mrs Riley described how she 'dearly wished' to give that rascal Abraham Lincoln a piece of her mind for causing this 'uncalled for ruckus' between the States. After an hour of being an entertaining and pleasant companion, too much whiskey moved the evening on to Mrs Riley talking nonstop on many things; from how annoying cowboys are when slurping coffee to the untimely death of her husband, who was bitten by a whore's pet snake in Atlanta, Georgia.

Mrs Riley explained: "Mah husband Jonathan, God rest his soul, was sorely maligned by a woman of ill repute. She claimed that Jonathan was having a dalliance with her when he was attacked by her pet snake; which went by the name of Thomas. Apparently she kept it for protection. Truth is mah Jonathan was a highly principled man and was passing by when he heard her shouting for help. On investigating what the problem was, sweet Jonathan found the snake about to attack this woman. He tried beating it with a whip he found under the bed, but that annoyed it even more and it turned and bit him on his bare ass."

Mrs Riley stopped talking to sink a glass of whiskey in one swallow then leaning forward she whispered, "That woman did not own a horse, so why did she keep a whip in the house?"

Another pause and Mrs Riley returned to her normal voice with, "To this day ah do not understand why mah sweet Jonathan had no clothes on. According to a lawyer, who just happened to be passing in the street, that snake was the biggest ever seen in Atlanta. Apparently the woman brought it all the way from Tombstone, Arizona. Only thing ah can think of is that the clothes were ripped from his back while fighting that snake. His demise caused such a loss of income that ah was reduced to eating 'grass fat' beef for months."[29]

Eventually my eyes glazed over and I developed an ache in my neck from nodding and shaking my head as she constantly wagged her mouth. Had the widow Riley not slipped a foot from her shoe and started rubbing it up and down my shin I would have left the table to attend to nature and then strolled out into the street; leaving her to pay the bill. As the evening wore on I slipped a hand under the table and tickled her foot, which produced a bright blush and an embarrassed giggle in the by now intoxicated lady. Having moved into a whiskey generated mood of generosity I paid the food bill and arm in arm escorted Mrs Riley, at her insistence, out of the hotel.

As we rolled and barged our way along the street and I explained where myself and Jack were billeted Mrs Riley trilled, "Ah have always wished to inspect the home of a rich plantation owner."

"And it will be my pleasure to escort you around the building," I said and promptly tripped over a dead dog and landed face first in a puddle.

Arriving in Tradd Street at around midnight Mrs Riley blundered through the doorway of my temporary home, came to a standstill, placed both hands on her hips and after scanning the interior announced her satisfaction with the furniture and her delight at the interior decoration. Then, eyes bulging and attempting to stifle the noise with a hand over her mouth, she enlivened the evening by producing an enormous belch for which she apologised profusely. Then her mood changed. Turning around she puckered her octopus sucker sized lips, closed her eyes and advanced in my direction. For once in my life I was unsure what to do. Did I pull this swaying, whiskey-sozzled bison-sized woman into my bedroom thereby risking suffocation. Or should I run? A decision she made for me. Lurching forward she grabbed me around the legs and, effortlessly hoisting me across those steer-sized shoulders, carried me into the bedroom. Mrs Riley's behaviour became stranger. Throwing me across the bed she barrelled out of the room and began rummaging in the large evening bag she hauled around, to return wearing a black blindfold and brandishing a huge Bible in the air. Reminding me of those Mormons who went to Utah in the 1850s and 60s. Waving Bibles during their journey, presumably to attract divine assistance, those folk pulled and pushed handcarts containing their belongings all the way. (Why? Perhaps they thought horse drawn wagons were creations of Lucifer? One ancient disillusioned Mormon told me: "Stupidest thing ah ever did. Lost lots of shoe leather. Gained nothing but blisters.") Mrs Riley presumably transported around her Bible to pray and ask for divine forgiveness after lapsing into bouts of carnal bouncing. Which when considering her appetite for bedroom contortions must have been a daily occurrence.

Hurrying to re-join me the widow stumbled against a chair then a table, scattering and knocking them to one side, before crashing on the bed and dragging me under the blankets. As dawn broke, exhausted and bug-eyed and unable to sleep because of her voracious demands I lay staring at the ceiling. Suddenly, with a speed that belied her enormous size she heaved herself into a vertical position, grabbed my neck in a one of her paw-like hands, and began whacking me about the head with the bible. Muttering incessantly "Fornication is the devil's work" she leapt out of bed, replaced the blindfold, dressed herself and repeating the earlier furniture moving display staggered out of the room. And so it went on. Unable to summon the courage to say no to Mrs Riley's visits, night after night like a moth to a flame, via a door left open by yours truly I invited her into the house. As always it was the same performance. She would blunder her blindfolded way to my room where, quivering with fear and lust, I lay staring up at the ceiling. By morning, much to Jack's headshaking laughter, I would shamble around zombielike with fatigue and massaging Bible-thumped lumps on my head and shoulders. Why none of the half a dozen servants who looked after the place came to investigate the bangs and shouts of pain as Mrs Riley crashed in and out of the building and into my bedroom, I never did find out. Maybe this was normal Charleston behaviour.

Occasionally she would stand in the bedroom doorway waving a handkerchief in farewell. Another time Mrs Riley turned around, burst into tears and after curtsying in my direction, hurried away. On one famous occasion Jack queried why she was stood, waving a tablecloth-sized handkerchief at me and hitting the side of her head with a Bible and yelling: 'Damn you, Satan.'(Feelings of guilt?)

Curiosity also provided a visit from the famous diarist Mrs Mary Boykin Chesnut; wife of Colonel Chesnut one of the occupants of the row boat that sculled close to our boat in Charleston Harbour. Damned woman arrived unannounced and nearly caught Mrs Riley and myself on the carpet communicating horizontal grunts and groans Luckily Mrs Chesnut tripped on the front porch and pitched herself face forward into the door. The noise of the collision and her accompanying angry words, blaming the position of the porch rather than her carelessness, gave ample warning for us to make ourselves decent. Mrs Chesnut was great at talking about herself and gibbered a nonstop monologue of virulence against the world in general. But mainly she railed at her inability to produce children. Her constant song was a burning ambition to produce a child saying: 'why, oh why, had the good Lord made her barren'. On one memorable occasion she came right out and laid the problem at her husband's door saying, "Maybe the problem is elsewhere." If memory serves me right she then added: "Perhaps Colonel Chesnut's long working hours have caused mah dear husband an injury and he can no longer function as a man should." A sad observation delivered with an intense stare in my direction.

In the absence of Mrs Riley I would have offered a second opinion as to where the fault lay; alas the opportunity did not arise.

Yet all good things, eventually, have to end.

Having requested a staff officer post at army headquarters I guessed someone would be checking my credentials and asking questions about my past before I was considered for a commission in the Confederate army. Meaning my induction would be delayed. The South badly needed infantry soldiers so Jack would have no problem enlisting. His problem would be an allocation to the same unit as myself. At the beginning of the Civil War, the South, same as the North, was kept busy organising armies and planning war strategies and whatever else senior officers in every war since Hannibal's elephants stumbled across the alps and the British army kicked Napoleon's ass at Waterloo, occupy their time with. So in early May I decided to try and move my recruitment along and contact Confederate headquarters direct. (Meaning. After announcing myself. Look up, blow the clouds a kiss, and hope for the best.)

On the 30th May, I sent a telegraph message addressed to Confederate President Jefferson Davis at the Confederate Capital in Richmond explaining my situation and how keen I was to serve the South. As President of the Confederate States, only God held higher rank than him. Leastways that was the view of the South. As luck would have it Davis also served in the Mexican War and our paths briefly crossed at Buena Vista, when he led the famous 1st Mississippi Regiment. We'd met after attending to nature one evening and expended a lot of wind arguing over who owned a pair of socks I had found on the ground. Eventually, accepting that Davis had a stronger claim to ownership, I handed them over dangling from the end of a long stick. He must have been short of socks for, notwithstanding the smell of stale sweat and fresh horse shit, he grasped them between an extended thumb and finger and eagerly stuffed them into a trouser pocket. Later I discovered neither of us owned them. They belonged to a dead Mexican. Hell, I didn't think Mexicans wore socks.

In my telegram I reminded the President of my generous capitulation as to the ownership of those socks, followed by praising my prowess as apolitical aide-de-camp who would best serve the South pouring military advice into his ears; rather than my expert talents being wasted on the battlefield. (Needless to say the word 'wasted' hung heavy on my mind.) It would be a quite a coup if I could work with Davis. Potentially it was a post where I could obtain invaluable intelligence for that other President, Abraham Lincoln, and it would also place me a long way from the sharp end of the war. I doubted that a man as busy as President Davis would read my letter. Plus he had only arrived on the 29th May from Montgomery, Alabama, after the Confederate Congress voted to move the South's capital to Richmond. So it was unlikely that he had unpacked or splashed around in the bath with his wife, never mind finding time to read correspondence from the likes of me. Hopefully, one of his staff would read the telegram and decide that I could be the South's answer to those wily, perfidious, Northern politicians and its military buffoons who provided advice to Lincoln on what strategy would win the war. (That was the South's views, not mine.) Luckily my message impacted with someone on Davis's staff for within two days I received a telegram from Captain Walter Herron Taylor, of the 3rd Virginia Infantry, aide-de-camp to Major General Lee, summoning me to attend the General's headquarters in Richmond. Perhaps that 'someone' remembered times from their own upbringing when they walked without socks.

Leaving Charleston myself and Jack made a slow ride to Richmond arriving on a blustery morning which, if my memory serves me right, was the 6th of June. A date remembered because on the 8th June, Virginia's Governor John Letcher, at the insistence of President Davis, issued a proclamation transferring Virginia's army and navy to the national army of the Confederate States. And as Lee was the commander of Virginia's forces it meant that he would in effect be redundant; no army to boss around; no job to perform. Not that that situation would last for long. Lee was too competent to be kept out of the South's line of battle. Immediately we arrived in Richmond, while Jack took the horses to be fed and watered, I went to the Mechanics Institute at Ninth and Franklin Streets where I was met outside General Lee's office by Captain Taylor who, warmly shaking my hand said, "Good to meet you Crink. Welcome to the hub of the Confederacy."

It crossed my mind that although hubs are an important part of a wheel too much pressure can cause them to collapse. On this occasion, unusual for me, I kept that smart ass thought to myself and instead replied with a lopsided grin, "Pleasure to meet you in the hub, Captain."

Taylor explained that he had been tasked to interview me about my desire to serve the Confederacy. So it was to the Captain that I pleaded my case and my intuition told me that Taylor knew more about me than he would ever admit. So wariness was uppermost in my mind. I kept it short. In essence I employed a two track approach, saying, "Firstly, ah want to plead allegiance to the ideals and way of life of the South. As a former Texas Ranger, born and bred in Alabama, I would rather stand alongside the Confederate flag. Ah do not consider black hugging northerners worthy of coexisting in the same nation as our abused and misunderstood Southern States."

Pausing to dramatically shake my head I went on, "Secondly, I am a man wronged by the wicked behaviour of others in the North and keen to repay them."

"Well said Crink," replied Taylor solemnly. Nodding his head he went on, "Would this have anything to do with an incident at the Willard Hotel in April?"

Although ready for any revelations as to my nefarious past, I was still stung with a spasm of surprise at Taylor's knowledge of the 'Carmen' incident. Mentally crossing my fingers that he knew nothing about Pinkerton's involvement I recovered swiftly to indignantly reply, "Certainly has, Captain. So-called former comrade of mine shamed me by making a false allegation that ah seduced his wife. It was slander but once you start that kind of prairie fire it grows a life of its own. People want to believe it and it becomes difficult to stop and ah was chased out of Washington. Truth is, it was a lie put out by this former comrade who could not face the embarrassment of knowing it was his wife who seduced me."

Pinkerton had obviously set in motion the story about this incident, so my version should confirm what was already in circulation and show that I was not afraid to face such allegations head on. (Mind you, the speed that it had travelled south was rather surprising.) Hopefully the Captain would be broadminded enough to smile and put such an allegation to one side as nothing but Northern propaganda. For good measure I added that the Major was also angry at losing a bucketful of dollars to me in a poker game.

At this point Taylor fell silent and, sure in my own mind that Robert E. Lee would support me, saving the best till last, I jumped in with, "Ah also met General Lee in the Mexican war when we served at Cerro Gordo. It was an honour to have served with him."

Captain Taylor smiled, nodded his head then said, "Crink, we need men such as yourself to safeguard the sacred lifeblood of the Confederacy." Pausing to gauge my reaction to this comment, he tilted his head to one side then went on, "General Lee speaks highly of your service in Mexico. In particular he remembers your welcome presence at Cerro Gordo during a dangerous reconnaissance mission of the enemy's positions."

I thought Taylor's 'sacred lifeblood' delivery a bit pompous but my opinion of him, even on such a short acquaintance was that the man was nobody's fool, so I needed to be careful with what I said. Before replying a flashback of my meeting with Lee at Cerro Gordo crowded into my mind. Although well known that Lee found himself in a difficult position during a reconnaissance mission prior to the Battle of Cerro Gordo, what is not known is that I played a vital part in assisting him to escape what ultimately turned into a dangerous situation. The date, impossible to forget, was the 15th April 1847, during my service with the Texas Rangers. Having fought in the Battle of Vera Cruz in March I had my immature eyes opened to the reality of war when on the receiving end of some accurate artillery fire which, quite frankly I found terrifying. The army's next destination was the strategically located mountain pass at Cerro Gordo on the route to Mexico City. Still shaky from the Vera Cruz battle I figured that I was too young to go to the 'sand hills'[30] and leave my bones in that bleak excuse for a country. Time to leave; yep, desert.

As part of my escape plan I intended volunteering for a reconnaissance mission against the Mexican lines. However, instead of noting troop dispositions and looking for the most advantageous line of attack amongst the surrounding geography at Cerro Gordo, I would sneak into the Mexican camp and steal a horse. For me the Mexican army were an unprofessional bunch. Although brave in battle, in the main, they were peasant conscripts who preferred to sleep rather than soldier. Meaning their camp guards would not be paying much attention to what was going on around them. Once I had a horse I would skirt the Sierra Madres then move north. After laying low in a frontier town for a couple of weeks I would move to Arizona or California where I would start a new life; perhaps open a brothel or a saloon. And for once luck was on my side when an escape opportunity came my way from none other than the army commander, General Winfield 'Fuss and Feathers' Scott.

While Scott was visiting my Texas Ranger unit, on a 'show his face to the Rangers' mission, I dropped into a conversation I had with him and his staff 'hangers on' that I had some experience as a scout having helped in that well known hunt of '53 when a band of cowboys retrieved four hundred of Samuel Maverick's missing cattle.[31] 'Fuss and Feathers' took the bait. "Got just the job for you Crink. There's a pass near Cerro Gordo which needs reconnoitring. Needs a man with a cool head and an ability to read the geography on the ground. Think you can handle it?"

"Be a pleasure General. And I would insist on carrying out the mission alone. Two men usually argue and I prefer my judgment every time," I replied breezily.

After a short scrutinising stare General Scott nodded his head and said, "Good man Crink. You've got the job. Report to my headquarters in half an hour for a briefing."

What I didn't know was that half an hour earlier Captain, as he then was, Robert Edward Lee and a guide called John Fitzwalter had been detailed to scout the same area. I suppose Scott sent two patrols in case one of us didn't make it back. Although I found out later that Fitzwalter had already supposedly scouted this area but filed a report that was vague and missing details that Scott required. A colonel from Scott's staff briefed me on what route to take and what was expected from the mission which was, basically, to scout the Mexican lines and discover flaws in their defences and the general layout of the pass. As the General wanted answers fairly swiftly I left during the hours of daylight.

Keeping low and moving slowly and carefully on foot I set out on the two mile journey towards the pass until, around two hours later, I suddenly heard Spanish voices close by. Without realising it I had stumbled on a group of Mexican soldiers. Specifically I was in a ravine thick with trees and vegetation with a track approaching from the south, also the direction from which the Mexican chatter was coming from. Stopping to ponder my next move I noticed a large spring off to one side. Bending down to top up my water bottle I heard someone, on my right, running at speed. Dropping to the ground I drew my knife just as a man ran past me. He disappeared before I could make out if he was a Mexican soldier or a civilian. If the runner was a Mexican soldier then he was in for a shock, he was heading towards the American camp. Within seconds the sound of running feet dimmed and apart from the chatter of Spanish voices it went quiet again. I lay for a few minutes wondering whether to press on or get out of there and re-join my fellow Americans but my next move was decided for me when, about twenty yards away, I noticed a pair of legs sticking out from under a fallen tree. Must be a Mexican guard taking a siesta, I thought, but if he woke and glanced my way then the game was up. To be taken prisoner was not an option so, sliding my knife out of its sheaf, I crawled towards the owner of the legs.

Chapter Nine

Cutting a man's throat would be a first for me but there was no way I could get around him, not without the risk of being noticed or heard. Either by him or his companions further down the track. Therefore needs must. I arrived a few feet from the man's position and raised myself to one knee. Holding the knife high above my head I readied myself to plunge it into his neck; then froze. The man was wearing American army trousers, jacket, and shirt. Either hearing me or sensing my presence, his face displaying fear and astonishment, his head whipped up and he said fiercely, "Who the hell are you?"

Still with my knife in the air I replied, "Crink. Captain, Texas Rangers. And you?"

"Lee. Captain, Corps of Engineers."

Lowering my knife I said, "Reconnaissance Lee?"

"The same."

"Why are you here?"

"Scouting for General Scott. What's your business?"

"The same. Looks like one of us has strayed from their objective area," I replied with a good dollop of sarcasm.

"I'm where I should be," Lee retorted indignantly.

Peering around as if checking my position I said, "Reckon you are Lee. I should be further over to the left."

"General Scott never mentioned anyone else would be prowling around here. Must have been worried one of us might not make it back, " grumbled Lee.

"Sounds about right."

"Anyway, welcome to my tree Crink. The Lord works in mysterious ways."

"Why? What's he done now?"

"Couple of minutes ago my guide, Fitzwalter,[32] ran off when a Mexican wandered past. Seconds later you appear. Good to have your company. Together we can finish the mission."

Not if I can help it, I thought. But answered with, "Reckon I just saw Fitzwalter disappearing at speed towards our lines. Must have lost his nerve."

"He'll lose something else when I report back to General Scott," said Lee peevishly.

My thoughts went in a different direction. Along the lines of: 'Now isn't this just fine and dandy. Can't move because of Lee on one side and the Mexican army on the other. If I stick to my plan and slink away on a stolen horse then Lee will report my performance to Scott and I would be labelled a deserter, with all the problems that entailed; so for now I was stuck with Lee.' Seconds later it got worse. The sound of tramping feet and loud voices came from our left. Wending their way towards the spring ambled a line of Mexican soldiers. Chattering and gesticulating at each other their lack of noise discipline and relaxed appearance displayed a collective opinion they believed that their enemy was far away.

A frame of mind that has cost the lives of many soldiers.

"Crink. Mexicans coming for water. Get under the tree," hissed Lee.

Ducking down I joined him. Luckily the surrounding vegetation was thick enough to cover us completely. We lay there for around an hour as a parade of Mexico's finest came and went; filling canteens and on a dozen uncomfortable occasions standing uncomfortably close and pissing to all points of the compass. On one breath-holding occasion a Mexican oaf splashed Lee's trousers and my boots. (Hey, it's only smelly water. Could have been worse.) Most of the time they chattered in a dull, dispirited tone, speaking too fast or indistinctly for me to understand. On a few occasions my Spanish was good enough to make out, amid bursts of laughter, that they intended shooting lots of Americans; especially Texans. Which made me wonder what they would do if they caught an Alabama man? One gravelly voiced braggart described in detail how he would eat a Texan tongue between slices of bread. Another intended to use a prisoner to hoe weeds and tend vegetables in his garden. Another wanted a Yankee to wash and clean babies and scrub floors.

Disaster beckoned when a soldier sat astride our tree trunk and, with one foot dangling a couple of inches in front of Lee's nose, jabbered nonstop about missing his wife's cooking and how he wanted to increase the number of his children when the war was over. Thankfully he was looking in the direction of his comrades when he spoke. After an absent-minded scratch at his chest the soldier sighed loudly before meandering back down the trail. A couple of hundred yards away half a dozen stragglers were arguing with each other about what to eat for their evening meal.

"Can't take much more of this." Lee's words hinted that he had a problem. Either he was buckling under the strain of our close proximity to the Mexicans or a hissing snake was about to grab his nose.

"What's up?" I growled.

"I have to go."

"Go? Where?"

Without answering Lee lurched to his knees. Everybody has a breaking this was Robert Edward Lee's. In a second, pulling him to the ground, I had my bowie knife at his throat and whispered, "Calm down Bob. Stay under the tree. Or those hungry Mexicans will be slicing human beef. Ours."

I needed to distract Lee from his current predicament. Bit of pain should do the trick. Gently pressing knife point against one of his ears I waited until a pinprick of blood appeared. Although the pain was minimal it was sufficient to jerk Lee out of his panic moment.

"Stay on the ground," I ordered before withdrawing the blade and returning it to its sheath.

Breathing deeply he relaxed. Taking a few more deep breaths he said, "Thanks, Crink. Lapse of concentration. Won't happen again." After a pause he continued, "Can we keep this between ourselves?"

I reassured him with, "At some point in a campaign everybody reaches a point where they consider running. Shrug it off. No need for anyone to know when your time came. In fact, ah don't see any reason to mention our meeting here at all."

"Agreed. Thanks for that," he said with a shudder of relief.

We shook hands.

Captain Lee's ability to conduct himself in the manner befitting an officer in the United States Army would remain intact. And just as important for a gentleman of the south so would his reputation as a man of honour and integrity. However, we both knew that my silence was necessary for the continuation of his military career. And, it has to be said, the fact that Lee was beholden to me might be useful someday. A cynical view but that was the way of the world. My world, that is. Yet there was also frustration at my current situation. My cynical view was that once we'd finished this mission any attempt at moving in a direction other than toward our lines would provide an opportunity for Lee to inform Scott that he was of the opinion that I had deserted. Thus removing the future threat of my talking about what had happened.

What to do?

One obvious solution, murdering Bob Lee, did not appeal. Desertion is one thing. It is possible to weave a tale of being captured by the enemy, or claim a blow on the head caused a loss of your thinking process, which made you stagger away from the army without permission. But murder coupled with disappearing would see you shot on the spot. We had each other by the throat, the only difference being that Lee didn't realise it. The only sensible conclusion was to remain with the Rangers and I rated Lee as just another face to watch amongst a posse of people who preferred me out of the way. Permanently, if possible. In jail, otherwise.

My memory of Cerro Gordo receded as Taylor's voice swung across my ears again. "Did you hear me, Crink? What happened in Mexico?"

If I wanted to strengthen my chance of any favours from Lee, it being a certainty Taylor would repeat to the General anything said between us, I had to add more shine to General Lee's reputation. I grinned and replied, "Sorry Captain, ah was remembering my time with General Lee. He was the best reconnaissance man ah ever served with. Together we scouted Mexican lines at Cerro Gordo and had to hide under a tree for hours while a whole bunch of Mexicans wandered around nearby. One nearly stood on my leg, which made me panic. But the General kept his nerve; calmed me down. Saved our lives."

With an energetic nod of his head Taylor said, "That's also General Lee's recollection. Although he didn't go into details."

At this disclosure my mouth dropped open but I recovered quickly and said, "Modesty. The mark of a great man." The great man was also a liar. (Which we all do. Just some more than others.)

Pursed lips and a cool appraisal told me Taylor had noticed my reaction about Lee saving my life. Possibly he was wondering what exactly had gone on at Cerro Gordo but, being a Southern gentleman and sensibly not wanting to discover anything potentially embarrassing about the General, he refrained from questioning me any further. It came as no surprise that Taylor hastily put an end to the interview when he shook my hand and wished me good luck for the future.

As I went to leave the Captain casually said, "Ah will recommend that you be granted an officer's commission in the Confederate army. However, I am unable to clarify which arm of service it will be. General Lee has stated that he must be consulted first."

I left the Mechanics Institute with a slight feeling of foreboding. Perhaps General Lee wanted to make the final decision as to where I would serve to ensure I went into an infantry regiment. Which tends to be the most dangerous occupation in any army. But as it turned out my future took another unforeseen twist. The next morning a message arrived from Taylor requesting that I immediately attend the Mechanics Institute for 'consultations' with President Jefferson Davis's military advisor; who of course was Major-General Robert E. Lee. Life had turned a full circle since Mexico. Except this time I wouldn't be wielding my bowie knife.

Although it had been only one day since talking to Captain Taylor he warmly shook my hand as if I was a returning prodigal son and said, "Good to see you again, Crink."

In seconds I was ushered into Major General Lee's presence and subjected to a strong and prolonged handshake from the General. It was fourteen years since I had seen Lee in Mexico when he was forty years of age. Back then he had determination and pride in his eyes, a bushy black moustache and dark hair; now there was a weary, wary look in his eyes and the moustache had turned into a gray beard and overall he looked older than he was. I suppose, considering he had hitched his reins to the Confederacy, the colour of his beard was appropriate.

Our handshaking was accompanied by, "Good to see you again, Crink. Been a long time." Followed by, "Too long. Far too long. How have you been? You look well." Plus a few more effusive comments you would expect from someone who owed the rank on his shoulders and his ass warming a General's chair to my silence.

Like for like I boomed, "Good to see you as well, General Lee. Plenty years slid by since Mexico."

Pulling a face Lee replied, "More than I care to think about."

After a cup of coffee and more chit chat and a short, final appraising stare, Lee got down to business. "Crink, combat is an experience not shared by many of our army recruits. Most are keen to fight but need preparing for the rigours of war. No matter what advice or description of combat is given, a recruit cannot be fully aware of the real thing. They need training. And crucial to this is excellent leadership. Then we can send them into battle knowing we have done our best for them. Of course only the real thing provides experience. So, we need people like yourself. Someone who has fought on the battlefield. He paused then went on, "Recruits have an unrealistic expectation of what warfare entails. They see themselves charging heroically across the battlefield and it will be the enemy who loses his life. Or is injured. Or the man standing next to him who goes down. Never himself."

Lee looked at the ceiling and sorrowfully shook his head. It was early days in the war and I guessed he was worried at the thought of how the South's army of new recruits would perform when they went into combat. It was that age-old military problem common to all armies; how to put an experienced head on a pair of young shoulders. I decided to make my pitch and solemnly replied, "Mexico was fourteen years ago General. Ah am a bit old, as you put it, to go charging across a battlefield. Giving advice to senior officers at Headquarters is more my expertise."

The vacant look on Lee's face suggested that my request had caught him by surprise. Opening his mouth to reply General Lee was interrupted by a knock on the door followed by Captain Taylor poking his head inside the room and whispering in a wary voice, "General Lee. The President is here."

Abraham Lincoln's glowering face flashed into my mind sending my buttocks into cramp mode. Of course Taylor meant President Jefferson Davis. In unison myself and Lee jumped to our feet, ran hands through what remained of our hair, straightened our jackets, and stood at relaxed attention.

"Show him in Captain Taylor," said Lee quietly.

Before Taylor could move, hands clasped behind his back, in stalked the President of the Confederate States of America; the timing of his entrance meant he had to have been listening at the door. (Disgraceful behaviour, huh?) "Good morning General Lee," said Davis. Then, pointing a forefinger at me, he thundered. "Crink, you scar-faced wart. Still grieving over losing those sweaty, mud infested Mexican socks are you?"

Lee gave me a wondering look.

Taylor raised an eyebrow then left the room.

Grinning hugely the President advanced forward and energetically shook my hand. The handshakes from Davis, Lee, and Taylor had all but mangled my right hand and as I use that hand to cheat at cards this was a bit worrying. While Davis clasped and pumped my hand he gave me a shrewd, scrutinising once over then said, "Sit down, Mister Crink. You as well General Lee."

There was a moment's silence as the three of us settled into chairs before President Davis said, "General Lee, ah heard about Crink's telegraph message and the invitation for him to visit Richmond. So decided to drop by and get reacquainted."

Surprise lifting his eyebrows Lee said, "You know each other?"

Davis nodded his head and replied, "Met Mister Crink in the Mexican war when we argued over a discarded pair of socks."

Interlocking his fingers Lee placed his hands in his lap and staring at me said thoughtfully, "Crink. You get around."

"As you know General Lee, ah am always willing to help."

Accompanied by a wondering smile, my reply produced an expression on President Davis's face that suggested he was wondering what lay behind my not so subtle quip.

Pulling a trouser leg up Davis pointed at a sock and said, "Recognise this?"

"Ain't you changed them since Mexico, Mister President?" I answered with a deadpan expression.

Throwing back his head Davis roared with laughter. "Same old cheek. Ah recollect you handing me those socks with a disgruntled grimace. Rumour went around you intended retrieving them at the point of that bowie knife of yours."

Mentioning the knife caused Lee's right foot to jump an inch or two and his eyelids to flutter, followed by a worried glance in my direction; it wasn't hard to work out what the General was remembering. I kept the subject going, "Talk about retrieving those socks at knifepoint was exactly that, Mister President. Talk from folk with nothing better to do than sit around a fire, chew tobacco, spit, whittle wood, drink whiskey and make up stories."

Nodding his head Davis said solemnly, "Just as I thought." After drumming his fingers together and narrowing his eyes Davis stunned me with, "Crink. Do you think the Northern President is an abolitionist?"

Hell, I didn't give a bucket of buffalo shit to Davis's Mexican socks what Lincoln thought. As an Alabama man slaves were a fact of life, at least a fact in my life. What Lincoln wanted to do with them was not something that ever crossed my mind. My father summed it up when he said: "Slaves are just passing shadows. They have no substance."

This was tricky. Why was Davis asking such a damn fool question? Was this a loyalty test? Walking with politicians you need skin as thick as an alligator and the ability to crawl lower than a snake's belly. After a bout of coughing to gain thinking time I concluded Lincoln must be an abolitionist. Else why this war? But what answer was Davis fishing for? Time to imitate a politician and give a meaningless answer; in other words answer the question but leave listeners wondering and unsure of what you said. Mentally crossing my fingers I replied. "Ain't sure about that Mister President. Northern politicians sit alongside angry rattlers and demented coyotes howling at the moon. Don't want to shake hands with any of them. Why do you ask?"

Jumping to his feet Davis grabbed the lapels of his jacket and, after an agitated bout of pacing along the carpet, came to a standstill opposite me and with an intensity that set my teeth on edge said. "I need ideas. Thoughts from such as yourself. People who have seen life both North and South. I want sympathy and support for the Confederacy to refute propaganda daily billowing from Washington. We need to find fault with that other President. Is Abraham Lincoln an abolitionist? Or are his words a cynical ploy to gain support during this war? What do you say to that?"

Feeling backed into a verbal corner I thought furiously then answered, "When he took office Lincoln swore to uphold the Constitution. Yet there is nothing in that document, or its amendments, about the abolition of slavery." Not much of an answer but the best that I could come up with.

A wintry smile crossed Davis's face before he replied, "Well said. A politician's answer. Perhaps you should become one."

As someone who would rather kiss a rattlesnake than enter politics I kept quiet. In any case Davis was riding point on the conversation, so it was polite to leave the floor to him. The President selected a document from his pocket and gravely intoned, "In his inauguration speech in March the Northern President said: 'I have no purpose, directly or indirectly, to interfere with the institution of slavery in the states where it exists. I believe I have no lawful right to do so.' Is the Northern President a hypocrite? He has publicly stated that he has no lawful right to interfere with the institutions of slavery. Yet because of slavery we are at war with the North. Therefore once again I ask is Lincoln a hypocrite?"

That had me foxed. I had been called a hypocrite before but wasn't sure what it meant. It sounded like a wandering tribe in the Bible. But I couldn't recollect mother mentioning anyone in the 'Good Book' spending an afternoon smiting hypocrites. Nor had I heard of any Indian tribes of that name. Unsure of an appropriate reply I examined my fingernails before saying, "Maybe it was an attempt to send a signal to us Southern boys. Reach out. Make us think again. Ah think the expression is to 'offer an olive branch'. Last ditch effort to stop Southern States from seceding." Pausing for enlightenment I went on, "But was he really trying to reach us afore war broke out? Or was he just leading us on? In mah family we have a saying: 'Trust the Devil before a Yankee.' Let's just say mister President, hypocrite or not, Lincoln does not get mah vote."

Davis swung a fist into the palm of a hand and said excitedly, "Mister Crink. You are perceptive and intelligent. I think the South can use you." There was silence while Davis did another turn or two on the carpet. Then staring at me went on,. "Ah am persuaded you shall best serve the Confederacy in the infantry. Such men as yourself are needed to guide our inexperienced men on the front line. Yet we cannot fight a war with soldiers alone. The South needs money. Lots of it. So, before allocation to a regiment, I have an important mission for you mister Crink. I want you and Corporal Claybutt to carry out an important mission in Lynchburg, Virginia."

Thank goodness the verbal jousting with President Davis was over. I could feel the sweat dripping inside my clothes. As my mother would say: "Cornelius the smell from your armpits would make a coyote howl." At Davis's mention of infantry my bowels curdled, then settled when the mission to Lynchburg was mentioned. "What do you have in mind?" I asked guardedly.

"Ever heard of the Thomas Beale papers?"[33]

"Virginia is thick with whispers about those papers mister President. On mah travels around this great country of ours ah have heard rumours about Beale in every dust ridden, tumbleweed infested town from Oregon in the west to northern Nebraska. Plus Alabama and Louisiana in the south. Fishing folk have laughed at such talk in the Great Lakes."

"Same for me. Beale's papers have figured in table gossip at dozens of plantations ah have visited. Never really believed in the story," said Davis crossing his legs and flicking a piece of lint from his trousers.

Deciding it was time he said something General Lee sniffed and took up the topic with, "Ah have also heard Beale mentioned in houses in New York and Washington. A mysterious story of gold, buried somewhere in Virginia."

Running with the two of them I said, "It's hogwash. Another damn fool story made up by drunken miners grasping at any excuse to sneak away from their wives. They return to Virginia year after wasted year searching for the big one. The retirement ticket that will keep them in women, drink and song until the undertaker lays them out."

"Be plenty drinking and womanising but not much singing if gold is found," said Lee with an absent-minded tug at his earlobe.

Pulling his chair close to mine Davis said in a low voice, "Crink, things have changed. Documents have recently come to our attention indicating there might be some substance to these rumours. Gentleman by the name of Robert Morriss, resident of Lynchburg, recently visited Richmond and spoke to Captain Taylor. Morriss asked to speak to General Lee in private. Said he had information that would help the Confederate cause."

Here Lee took up the story. "When ah met Morriss he looked just like another locoweed[34] eating eccentric wanting to give advice on how to fight the North. We get plenty of these characters presenting themselves. Usually after a drinking session in one of the local saloons." Lee paused to clear his throat then went on, "Yet Morriss was different. For a start he was sober. After introducing himself he produced an iron box and claimed it contained documents about a matter of importance that would assist us. Ah decided to ask president Captain Taylor to join us. Always have a witness. Apart from security there needs to be someone who can corroborate what is said. Strange man, Morriss. Stared at me with piercing blue eyes the whole time he talked. Touch of the fanatic about him. Also an air of toughness."

Lee nodded at Davis then walked to a nearby table and poured himself a glass of water.

Davis continued. "Morriss's box contained sheets of papers full of random numbers and scrawled writing. He explained that his box and its contents were given to him by a Thomas Beale, in 1822. The writing in the papers told a story that Beale took a hunting party to Santa Fe in 1817. Two or three hundred miles north of Santa Fe, the party were following a herd of buffalo when they stumbled across a vein of gold in some rocks. Lots of gold."

Then it was Davis's turn to take a drink of water.

Sitting down again Lee took up the tale. "According to Beale, after eighteen months digging they found and extracted around two thousand nine hundred pounds of gold. Apparently Beale eventually hid it in Virginia. In the Lynchburg area. Morriss wants us to have the gold to help finance the war and is willing to sell the box and its contents for two thousand dollars. Unfortunately the pages that tell where the gold is buried are in code."

Like all good entertainers Lee stopped speaking. He was saving the best till last. With an excited grin he went on, "Morriss states that he has deciphered one of these coded pages. It says that Beale deposited the gold in a vault about four miles from Buford's Inn, in Bedford County, Virginia. Unfortunately the page does not give us the exact location. That is on another of the coded pages which has not yet been deciphered. Of course Morriss could be a fraudster out for money, so ah probed the truthfulness of his story which unfortunately upset him somewhat. Morriss jumped to his feet and left. Returned to Lynchburg, taking the box with him. On reflection President Davis and myself think it worth investigating this story further. If there is any truth in these papers then we should pay for them. We think five hundred dollars would be sufficient payment. Our signals people can then try and make sense of those coded numbers."

The talking went back to Davis. "Mister Crink, ah want yourself and Corporal Claybutt to travel to Lynchburg and contact Morriss and make him an offer of five hundred dollars for these papers. An offer ah hope he will be pleased to accept."

As he finished speaking Davis pulled a sheet of paper from his pocket and scrutinising it said, "Excuse me gentlemen. I must be elsewhere." After shaking hands with myself and Lee, the President wished me good luck then strode out of the room.

Dropping his voice to a whisper Lee said, "Crink, if this Morriss is adamant about wanting two thousand dollars then I suggest you confiscate the box. Use any means necessary. If we find Morriss's gold, you will be well rewarded."

At the age of twelve when I first realised that I could hold a revolver in one hand, and stroke a woman's thigh with the other, wealth in all forms has seen me sniffing the wind of opportunity. No surprise then when I replied, "Mighty generous General. Me and Claybutt accept the task."

Scratching around Lynchburg looking for gold sounded a better deal than showing raw recruits how to use a rifle and bayonet. I was sure Jack would accept the challenge. Being a solider don't suppose he had much choice.

I then realised why Davis had left the room. Should anything go wrong in this hidden treasure adventure he needed what politicians call 'plausible denial'; meaning he wasn't present when illegal methods were authorised by General Lee and would deny any knowledge if anyone tried to associate him with what had been said.

"Excellent," replied Lee beaming.

Trying not to sound too excited I asked, "General, how much would that reward be?"

"A pair of socks," answered Lee roaring with laughter. Once he stopped laughing Lee went on, "Only kidding. We think fifty pounds weight in gold. To be divided equally between you and Corporal Claybutt."

(Hallelujah. Never doubted that my mother's screeching from the 'Good Book' would, eventually, reach the good Lord's ears.) Needless to say I saw no reason to inform Pinkerton of this potential windfall. The tone in Lee's voice became serious when he said, "One other thing Crink. For the duration of this mission you will hold the rank of Captain in the army of the Confederate States of America seconded to my headquarters." Picking up a book from a nearby table Lee heaved it in my direction and said, "Mah Bible. Raise your right hand."

Catching and holding the Bible against my chest and right arm aloft General Lee duly swore me in as Captain

Cornelius Crink, seconded to Confederate States Army Headquarters Richmond, Virginia. After a backslapping cheerio from Lee I left the building reflecting that I was now in the unique situation of being on two missions. The first for President Abraham Lincoln in the North, who temporarily owned my money. The second for President Jefferson Davis in the South, who temporarily owned my body. Flesh and money, my two hallowed possessions

Both could be so easily lost if I bluffed my hand the wrong way.

After a morning recalling those Mexican memories from the two most powerful men in Dixie I re-joined Jack in our hotel. "How did the meeting go?" he boomed.

"Ah am now Captain Crink. You're going to have to get used to calling me 'sir' and saluting me, Jack. Reckon you should also bring me coffee in the morning and clean mah boots," I said and laughed.

Jack responded with a solemn salute and a loud belch.

"Tomorrow we're off to Lynchburg, Jack. You heard of it?"

"Better than that Captain. Been there."

"Doin' what?"

"Lookin' for gold," he replied in a low voice.

Chapter Ten

No surprise to say that I was stunned at Jack's gold hunting revelation.

Nodding his head Jack went on, "Happened six years ago. Me and mah uncle Jerome were wandering Virginia selling 'Hercules Powder'.[35] Came out of the Blue Ridge Mountains in the summer of '55 and stayed couple of weeks in Sulphur Springs. Small town. Nobody has secrets in small towns. Never have. Never will. In a bar one night met a bunch of prospectors passing through after years of searching Virginia for gold. Dozens of them. Doublejackers, dynos, hard-rock miners, sluicers, of foreign 'cousin jack miners' and lots of 'shovel stiffs'.[36] Couple of them got really drunk and bragged a story of gold secretly buried thirty years or so ago in Bedford County, near Lynchburg. Said they'd bought a map in Lynchburg marked with information 'bout this buried gold. Said they found nothing because there were mistakes on the map. Think they were drinking 'moonshine' and talking 'moonshit'. Mistake they made was buying that so-called map. Reckon it showed nothing but 'moose pasture'[37] and the gold story was set away and kept alive by town folk keen to maintain interest in a quiet place like Lynchburg. Brings money to flour makers and keeps shelves stocked with beans. Ain't no poor bar owners neither. But those miners fired Jerome with prospecting fever and ah followed him. We made rapid tracks to Lynchburg, see if we could pick up a trail. Plenty of hints and whispered advice and opinions by Lynchburg folk about this hidden gold but nobody really knew where it might be. And we couldn't find anyone with maps to sell. After six or seven months our pockets were empty, so that was it; unhitch the horses and return to Alabama."

"Grab a shovel Jack. We're going to Lynchburg. Search for that gold again."

"You're kiddin' me?"

"Nope."

"Who's idea is this?"

"President Jefferson Davis, and General Robert E. Lee no less. If there's gold near Lynchburg, they want it. Help fund the war."

"Only gold in Virginia is fools' gold. And we'll be fools goin' looking for it," Jack grumbled.

"Maybe so. Got to be better than getting shot at when North and South saddle up and start the war for real."

"Ah notice you only want one shovel. That for you, or me?"

"Ah am a captain. Reckon you can figure that one out, Corporal."

"Hey, you are learning fast Captain Crink."

"Only kidding Jack. Bring two shovels."

We left Richmond in the early hours of a Monday but, other than the journey passing in a mind numbing blur, ain't no point in describing the ride through Virginia. We took our time arriving in Lynchburg in the afternoon of another Monday. Tired, irritable, needing a feed followed by a gallon of beer we dismounted outside a small, rundown, grimy hotel in the 'Buzzard's Roost' area.[38] Infamous for prostitutes and drunkenness and most other debauched vices mentioned in the Bible and including some that ain't. It was to be our home for however long it took to finish the task.

Staring up and down the street Jack said, "Ah feel uncomfortable."

"What's up?"

"Remembering Uncle Jerome. Couldn't shake that gold out of his head. Saved money, borrowed money, and stole money just so he could return. In '56 he came back to plan another prospecting expedition. Bought a general store and took up with a Swedish woman called Magda. A missionary. That woman entered every saloon and whorehouse in Lynchburg; praying, reading from the Bible, singing psalms, and yelling future damnation at everybody in the building. Nobody listened, only laughed. Made her angry. So Magda burned a whorehouse to the ground and shot a couple of clients in the ass as they ran out. She was shooting them at the front of the building. Uncle Jerome was lucky, he ran out the back. Judge gave Magda sensible Virginian justice."

"Which was?"

"Gave her a choice. She could hang. Or work in a whorehouse and use her earnings to pay the cost of rebuilding the one she burned down."

"Reasonable judge."

Jack laughed and said, "Sure was. He owned the whorehouse."

"Magda work off her debt?"

"Certainly did. Not before she stole Jerome's horse and tried to escape out of town though. Posse of the judge's men dragged Magda kicking and screaming into another whorehouse. Also owned by the judge. Worked of the debt. Got so Magda enjoyed herself. Lynchburg men enjoy cracking whips. So does Magda. She spent a couple of months whacking ass then took up with the judge. Last count they employed couple of hundred horizontal workers."

"Magda still here?"

"First she retired to a ranch couple of miles out of town.

Kept cattle and hogs for the judge to occupy his time. Judge's mind went. Read law to the cows and sneaked up on the hogs and tried to shoot them. Never hit one yet. Got so the hogs just ignored him. Then the judge accidently shot himself in the head. Ricochet. Fine funeral. Every whore in Virginia turned out. Much to Magda's surprise seems he was running most every brothel in the State. Became a rich widow. Hear she took over a hotel here in Lynchburg."

Nodding my head wisely I replied, "Hogs got a better deal than the cows from the judge."

When Jack stopped laughing he said, "Magda could be useful. Whores know about everything going on in their town. And in her case the State of Virginia."

"Maybe we should look her up," I said raising an eyebrow.

"Sounds good, Captain."

"What happened to Uncle Jerome?"

"Stayed a year. Ran down every rumour and story about buried gold. Never found anything. Chased out of Lynchburg at the wrong end of a rifle for jumping the queue in the judge's whorehouse. Judge's daughter was working there that night and seems the judge's nephew was next in line for her services. Seems like the nephew read poetry to her while she entertained him. She liked that. Upset her somewhat when Uncle Jerome staggered in drunk and pushed the nephew down the stairs. Then Jerome blew cigar smoke in her face and started flicking lice out of his shirt at her. Eventually judge's daughter drew the line at him wanting to stay all night and offering her a pan of beef, a boiled potato and a cup whiskey in payment. So she yelled rape."

"Sounds like a contradiction in terms."

"A what?" replied Jack pulling a face.

"It was the daughter's occupation. Should not bother a whore none who is queue jumping and stoking their boilers. Just carry on knitting and ask for couple of dollars more. Or in her case a couple of potatoes, more beef, and another cup of whiskey."

"That wasn't all," said Jack sheepishly.

"Ah can guess what's coming," I said with a shake of my head.

"She was only sixteen."

"Thought so. Sixteen. Not too bad. Old for an Alabama man," I said raising an eyebrow.

Jack grinned, shrugged his shoulders and said quietly, "Virginia folk have long memories. Hope the townsfolk don't turn on me because of mah Uncle Jerome."

"Only one way to find out. But let's find a bed for the night first."

Both the hotel bar and its eating room were making a lot of noise. About to hit the reception bell I was saved the bother when the upper torso of a woman suddenly shot up from behind the counter. Six feet six inches tall with horse sized shoulders, breasts a full uddered Hereford cow would be proud of, protruding facial cheeks that looked to be hiding apples, carrot sized fingers and forearms as big as melons; add a scarlet dress a company of soldiers could disappear into and you have a picture of the biggest, most formidable, woman I ever met. (And that includes Dodge City's 'Fetlock Fingers' Amy.)

"You the clerk?" I asked.

"Hotel ramrod.[39] Owner. Clerk. Barmaid. Do everything around here. You want a good time or a bad one?" answered the woman patting her hair. Her accent was deep, foreign, sexy.

"What's the difference?" I asked.

"Good times are at mah card tables with one of mah girls running their fingers through your hair, licking your ears, and taking your orders at the bar. Bad times are next door with the town preacher. Only thing his fingers connect with are coins. Your coins. Both situations cost money. Difference is, mah heaven is here and now. His is somewhat delayed."

There was a sudden shout as Jack took over the conversation shouting, "Magda. Slim as ever, ah see. You on the menu tonight?"

Through suspicion narrowed eyes Magda stared at Jack until, arching her eyebrows in recognition, she yelled back. "Hey, 'Iron Jaw' Claybutt. Long time, no see. Still boxing for an extra dollar?"

"Nope. Nose hair hangs in the air like mah horse's tail these days. Itches a lot. Can't scratch it wearing boxing gloves."

Jerking a thumb at me Magda said, "Is scarface with you?"

"Sure is. This is Captain Cornelius Crink. Waiting for allocation into a Confederate army regiment. As am I."

"Army. What brings you to Lynchburg?"

"Giving the town a look over for General Robert E. Lee. The General is thinking about setting up Confederate headquarters here. He needs a report on how good the facilities are," I lied.

"Sounds good. Could do with more business," said Magda with a wink that would have made a horse blush.

"You got two rooms?" I asked.

Magda grabbed two keys from a drawer and said, "Sure have. Come on boys got a good Rincon[40] just for you." Then looking at the floor she said, "Wait there Puke.[41] Don't go into the bar. Ah need you sober."

"Puke?" said Jack.

With a wry grin Magda replied, "Tobacco worker. Originally from Missouri. Just got paid. Lot of dishonest poker players in this hotel. Prefer it if Puke loses at my table, not theirs."

Magda gave us two adjoining rooms and, before returning to whatever adventure she and Puke were undertaking, pointed to a notice pinned to the reception desk and said, 'House Rules'.

There weren't many:-

(1) Don't add to the washing in this hotel. Piss in the pot under the bed. Or out the window. Don't water the flowers. Reckon they don't like it. And my cactus plants bite. Painfully.

(2) This is civilisation. Ain't the Sonora Desert. Throw coffee dregs into the rain tub outside. Not on the carpet.

(3) Feeling sick. Use the bucket next to your bed.

(4) Treat my girls with respect. In Texas they use a girl's underwear to rub down revolvers and boots. Not in Virginia. Use your neck rags.

(5) The girls are paid to take their clothes off for the purpose of sending you cross-eyed. Time is money. Play poker downstairs.

(6) Bullet holes in the walls have been counted. Don't add to them.

(7) Shoot anyone then leave enough to pay for his funeral. (Which means no one will chase you.)

(8) Ain't happy? Don't start a fight. Leave.

Before Magda could say anything further the beginnings of a bar fight hastened her down the stairs. According to Jack fighting had always been a nightly event, not that anyone took much notice, drinking and gambling took priority over reeling, dribbling drunks, trying to punch each other and usually hitting a wall; or the piano.

We took a couple of days to settle in, drinking and playing poker alongside hotel regulars occupied most evenings. Occasionally we entertained Magda for an hour or two at the bar; meaning we bought her drinks while she made eyes at whoever took her fancy. Sometimes we played poker with Magda and occasionally she brought tears to my eyes when her bear paw hand squeezed my thigh under the table. Other than that, she was good company. Magda's size put me off wanting to get to know her better. No fun in wallowing in a passionate clinch with a woman who can literally surround you. Being smothered ain't my idea of departing this life. Such a sized woman is possessed of sufficient suction in her lips to empty your lungs, another unattractive method of passing on. But deep down I knew it was only a matter of time before she dragged me upstairs for a bout of horizontal exercise. Yep. Most places I visit there are envious voices whispering that I have a certain effect on women. When I find out what causes that 'certain effect' I intend bottling it. Reckon it would make plenty of money in Georgia. Men in those parts need assistance. Not an opinion of mine I hasten to add. Just something I heard in Texas.

Magda could also match most men drink for drink and, when playing poker, she could spot and outplay 'tinhorns'[42] at their own game. According to Jack she knew everything there was to know about Lynchburg and its inhabitants, especially folk who had previously lived here or passed through. So it looked as if Magda was going to be the one to ask about Beale's gold. Particularly the whereabouts of the mysterious Robert Morriss.

One cool afternoon, about a week after we arrived, myself and Jack caught Magda in a more sober moment sitting in her rocking chair shooting a revolver at empty whiskey bottles at the back of hotel. We indulged in half an hour's general chit chat before I asked, "Magda, you know anyone in Lynchburg by the name of Robert Morriss?"

"What's he mean to you?" she asked suspiciously.

Jack moved into the conversation going in with both feet and hands. "Hear he knows about gold secretly buried somewhere in Virginia around forty years ago."

"Sounds like you're looking for Beale's gold," she replied pinching one of Jack's cheeks between a vice that was a thumb and forefinger. Pausing for a moment to knock back a glass of whiskey Magda thought for a moment then continued, "Reckon it's time to talk. Time to get a second opinion on what went on all them years ago. Town gossip has it that old man Morriss moved to Loudoun County, Virginia, from Maryland at the beginning of the century. Not sure when. Married Sarah Mitchell and came to Lynchburg and took up buying and selling tobacco. Became bankrupt. Then ran the Washington Hotel in Lynchburg. In 1820 Morriss first met Beale when he arrived in town and the two became friends. Apparently Beale left Lynchburg in that same year of 1820. Returned in 1822 and met up with Morrriss again. No idea what they talked about. Rumours drifted around town that Beale buried gold somewhere in Virginia and gave Morriss documents showing its location. Then Beale left in the Spring of 1822 and as far as I know he never came back to Lynchburg."

"Old man Morriss still in town?" asked Jack.

"Nobody seen or heard of him or his wife for a while. Seems he turned into a recluse and rarely ventured out into the street. Neither would he receive visitors. Talk has it he up and left town couple of years ago. Left in a hurry. Morriss and his wife supposed to be hiding in an old miners' shack in West Virginia. Blue Ridge mountains somewhere. Could be hiding under straw in the livery stable. Nobody really knows," declared Magda with a shrug of her massive shoulders.

"Hiding from what?" I asked.

"Debtors, mainly."

When fishing for information it can pay to remain silent and wait for the other person to pick up the conversation. With a glance at Jack I refilled our glasses and waited. It worked. Checking no one was in earshot Magda said in a low voice, "There's someone else supposedly with a copy of these Beale papers. Wandering prospector. Old timer called Mulehead Joe. He's so old he saw the Whitehouse burned by the British in 1814. Nobody knows West Virginia better than Joe. Roamed for thirty years or more searching for Beale's gold. Trustworthy. Votes Democrat. Drinks whiskey. Hates Mexicans. Last heard of in the Blue Ridge for the past six months."

"From that description he must be Texan," said Jack.

"Doubtful. Don't swagger when he walks. Don't boast. Ain't tall. Don't wear shiny spurs and don't wear a big hat. And Joe plays good poker." Magda paused, sniffed under her armpits, wrinkled her nose then went on, "Ain't met a Texan yet who can play poker. Not like Joe. Don't cheat neither. So honest he'd make God blush."

"Know where we can meet Joe?" asked Jack.

"Due to hit town any day soon. If I can coax him to talk and you find Beale's El Dorado,[43] what's in it for me?" Magda replied quietly. She was suggestively fingering a bow at the top of her dress. Undo the knot and I visualised Magda's enormous breasts tumbling and swinging down to her waist; an ear warming thought.

I had to be truthful. "Ain't my option Magda. We're working for President Davis and General Lee. Got to be their decision. They're in charge of the Confederacy. We find anything though and ah will mention your assistance. Without you helping us along guess me and Jack would be sitting playing cards in your bar until sagebrush grew over the roof. Got to take notice of that."

Magda thought about it then with glazed eyes said, "Jack, no offence meant, but it seems that Captain 'Scarface' Crink here is the main man. Me and him need to go someplace quiet to discuss this further. You hurt any at that?"

"Nope. Ah will move indoors and play a hand of poker," said Jack breezily and lumbered away.

"Where to Magda?"

"Boneyard. Nobody goes there. Unless they have to. Then they git carried, for free," she replied with a roar of laughter that sent her breasts bouncing frantically up and down. Expecting her dress to tear under the heaving weight my eyes followed their juddering progress until she gave me a playful dig in the ribs with her elbow. Playful to her but it left me gasping for breath.

We walked to the graveyard where we snuggled down behind a lopsided wooden cross with the inscription: 'Here lies squint-eyed Joe Dull. Died in a gunfight. Left eye looked right. Right eye looked left. Fooled himself. Shot his horse. Dull in name. Dull in wits. Amen to him.'

"Cornelius before talking about Mulehead can I tell you a bit about mahself. Need to work my jaw muscles. Mah way of thinking. Talk and think at the same time. Help figure out what to tell you."

"Sounds good." (It didn't. But hey, sway with the music.)

"Always wanted to be a singer. Even when ah was a missionary. One day ah want to entertain folk in those fancy theatres in Washington and New York. Listen to this song and tell me what you think. Is my voice good enough? Tell the truth. Don't try to impress me with your Alabama bullshit. Ain't going to let you talk me into lodging between your spurs. Leastways, not yet."

Magda promptly lurched to her feet and started screeching some nonsense about a cowboy and a sheriff's daughter strolling through this same graveyard in the summer of 1800 and how they tripped and stumbled into a freshly dug grave. After falling asleep in each other's arms their romantic interlude came to an end when a recently shot bank robber was thrown at them by a posse of grinning gravediggers.

Finishing her song of love, red-faced and happy, Magda grabbed a handful of my shirt and growled, "Well, you ugly runt. Impressed? Good enough to head north and sing in a theatre full of Yankees?"

Sing? Hell's teeth, Magda would make coyotes slink away in fright. She was awful. In full voice she could strip quills from a cactus and on this performance the nearest she would get to a stage would be sweeping it. Instead of the truth I went into 'trying to impress attitude' and said, "Sure am. Hairs on my chest are standing at attention in admiration."

"Attention, Cornelius. That's what I like to hear."

At that we kissed. Which brought a new meaning to that underwater experience described as 'coming up for air'; hallelujah Magda had lungs like a blacksmith's bellows. I realised then that our relationship was destined to be short-lived. Collapsing onto her back she pulled me with her and, with some disinclination on my part, we kissed again until the suction in her lips had my eyes bulging like a raccoon in heat. I pushed her away and bleated, "Whoa there Magda. You were thinking what to tell me about Mulehead Joe and Beale's gold."

"Ah sure was," said Magda reluctantly.

Staring at the surrounding headstones she sighed then said. "Cornelius, truth is folk have scratched acres of Virginia searching for Beale's gold. Apart from Mulehead nobody bothers much now. Got 'gold colic' real bad.[44] Prospects in Bedford County day in, day out. More soil under his fingernails than coffee in 'Cheyenne' Bill's store."

"You mentioned Mulehead has some papers about this gold."

"Yep. Joe mentioned that. Drunk as a judge at the time. Told me he won a wedge of papers in a poker game in the old Washington Hotel. Had them for years. Discussed them with me. Trusted me. Doubt he discussed them with anybody else. Joe is like that. Very secretive." Magda paused then said in a quiet voice, "Don't forget. Find any gold do you promise to put in a word for a reward. Ah don't want a large slice. Say half a percent."

"Sounds fair. Can but try." I paused then continued, "South's leaders seem to be reasonable men living in unreasonable times. But ah cannot promise they'll pay up."

Truth was I didn't trust Jefferson or Lee as far as I could carry Magda. And as I wouldn't be able to lift her three hundred pounds of blubber without the assistance of another dozen men, I wasn't holding out much hope of a reward coming Magda's way. (Should such a situation arise, that is.)

"Just have to wait and see. Ah suppose," said Magda with a sniff.

"Did Mulehead mention who he won those papers from?"

"Yep." Magda followed this single word explanation with a whiskey smelling belch and continued, "Won them from a cousin of Bob Morriss. Believe the cousin copied the original Beale papers without Morriss's permission."

"So you're saying there's two sets of identical papers about Beale's gold?"

"That's right. Original papers are with Morriss. Mulehead Joe has a copy. There's a problem though. Joe confided in me that the papers are in code. Reckon you need to tell him how good you are at figuring out puzzles with numbers. Maybe that way he'll let you have a look." Magda paused then whispered, "Don't tell Joe that ah mentioned these codes. Might upset him that ah have betrayed his confidence. But ah will help wheedle him into talking when he hits town."

In code. That did not sound good.

"When will Mulehead hit town?"

"Anytime now. Comes in every three months or so for supplies. Plus a belly full of drink. Day and night poker and a fondle in the livery stable with one of mah girls."

"Why the livery stable?"

"Old fashioned ah suppose. Grew up working in stables. Likes the smell of hay and saddle leather."

After a moment's silence an incentive to leave presented itself when a stone, pressing into my side started to hurt. "Reckon it's time to make away," I said with a grimace.

Magda ignored me and said, "Cornelius, I kinda like you. You planning to stay?"

"Lynchburg? Or snuggled here with you and squint-eyed Joe Dull?"

"Lynchburg, you clown."

"Me and Jack will stay a while longer. At least until we sort out this Beale business. But there's a war on. General Lee sends for us then we gotta go."

"How about taking me?" she replied breathlessly.

"Can't take a woman to war, Magda. Ain't easy to cook and clean when someone's shooting at you."

"Stop teasing. Take me, here and now."

Clearly Magda had moved on from thoughts of gold. With a loud sigh I laughed and said, "Magda, amount of drink ah have had it will be difficult raising an eyelid. Never mind perform carnally."

That got her going. Eyes wider than a constipated cow she frowned then yelled, "You been sniffing rattlesnake spittle Cornelius? What does 'carnally' mean?"

"Another time Magda and ah will give a demonstration. But mah leg is hurting. Time to go."

Staring a Joe Dull's wooden cross Magda said, "Finding gold could be my road north. Else one day ah could end up here. Next to Joe."

Lurching to my feet I said, "Magda, don't get your hopes up. Half a percent of nothing, is nothing."

At that we staggered back to her hotel and to the nightly routine.

As in most saloons during the civil war inebriation and stupidity went together. Magda's hotel was classic in this respect. Drunken customers, especially on pay night, were met with caressing hands, encouraging kisses, enormous winks and suggestive leers from her 'Calico Queens'[45] followed by an invitation to get better acquainted upstairs. Then they were hurried to a bedroom for an in-depth search for their dollars. Rather than a hotel it was more a 'crib'[46] criminal enterprise. The noise in the bar never dropped below loud and gambling was the main business occupied by everyone who frequented the place. Success at the tables never escaped the attention of the 'Calicos' neither. They watched for dollar waving winners like owls scouring a field for mice. Once spotted Magda's painted girls would sidle up and sweet talk their 'marks' into buying drinks or pull them to a dark corner for more intimate attention. Or, like the payday drunks, they were marched upstairs.

Picking pockets was another expertise Magda's girls excelled at. Allegedly hired to entertain with singing and dancing the 'Calicos' began their evenings clumping around card tables squawking something vaguely resembling a song. On payday nights the crowds at the bar and card tables were huge. A multitude of gibbering, feeding baboons thrusting a mass of prodding fingers, caressing hands and puckered lips towards the strolling 'Calicos' whose cold, experienced eyes flicked from side to side like human chameleons; their mission to find 'protruding wallets' and empty them. Then move on.

The day after our discussion in the boneyard myself and Magda were talking in the hotel bar with a regular called Pinkham, a so-called mining engineer who passed his days panning for gold in rivers and streams throughout Virginia. Pinkham talked nonstop about equipment and gold mining expressions with mysterious names, such as gold canoe,[47] gold borer and a strangely named gold monkey; gold blossom, gold brick and gold dirt. I reckoned he was also looking for Beale's gold. (Although, sober or drunk, he never mentioned Beale's name.) Pinkham's mouth dispensed a barrage of prospecting technical terms that I guessed were an attempt to impress people, such as myself, who were ignorant of the world he and many others inhabit. Pinkham was a bore. He could make a spittoon yawn, grow legs and run. But the day was saved when the saloon clamour was drowned out as the place erupted into a roaring din of "Mulehead Joe."

Chapter Eleven

In he came. An entrance that would have had them standing and cheering in the North's finest theatres. Ignoring the hotel sign that said: 'No animals, lawmen, snake-oil salesmen, or Yankee preachers', Mulehead Joe entered the room dragging behind him two hee-hawing mules. The mules were festooned with boxes, picks, shovels, blankets, tin pans, a rifle, a huge frying pan, a large mug, bulging boxes and sacks and bits of equipment that resembled nothing that I had ever seen before. He could have been any age from eighty to one hundred. Around six feet tall, his face was tanned almost black with deep creases around the eyes, and sunken cheeks radiating more lines than a railway junction, no teeth and a gray beard reaching from a sickle moon shaped head down to a thin chest. He wore a battered weather stained army kepi hat and a shirt black with ingrained grease, grime and sand. His many patched trousers were likewise black with age, encrusted dirt, and dried mud. As he trudged into the saloon a thin covering of trail dust fell to the floor.

"Skunks must hide upwind when he rolls by," said Jack shaking his head.

"Joe smells like a bison in heat but he's a real gentleman. Don't dribble down a girl's cleavage or spit chewing tobacco on mirrors or mah walls."

Glancing at Magda I asked wonderingly, "This really the man with documents about the Beale gold?"

"He's the one," replied Magda grinning from ear to ear.

"That why you allow him to drag those stinking mules into the bar?" queried Jack.

"It is," Magda replied with a weary sigh. Pointing at one of the mules said, "That one is 'Bad Ass' Susannah. Named after a woman who figured somewhere in his life. The other is 'Nat Trapper'. Named after his father. An army spy in the Blackhawk war. Brave man."

"Nobody object to their disturbing the peace with their hee-hawing?" I asked.

Magda bristled and said, "Don't dare. Have me to argue with if they did. Joe spends a lot of money in here. For which I am most grateful. Ten years ago he struck gold out west. Sonora, I think. Came home to Lynchburg to spend it. Have to keep him happy. When Joe hits town he marches straight in here. Invites everyone to join him and buys drinks all night. Do more business at the bar and card tables than a barking preacher on apocalypse day. Make him tether the mules outside and they'd quickly disappear. Most folk think there's gold dust in Joe's travel bags. Mules go missing, he would go looking. Might never come back. Meaning profits drop. Simple as that."

As an afterthought Magda added, "Most of the customers stink same as Joe's mules. Mules don't complain. So ah don't neither."

"Some smell worse," I muttered.

"Where does he sleep?" asked Jack.

"Upstairs. In the bridal suite."

"And the mules?" I queried.

"Tethered to his bed."

"Do you clean his room with a shovel?" I asked grinning.

"Joe takes care of the mule dung. After a night's drinking he's kinda lazy and just shovels it out of a window." Glancing at Mulehead who was upending his third beer since entering the bar Magda added, "Gave Joe strict instructions when heaving mule dung to use the same window every time. When he's in town folks give that side of the hotel a miss. Or pass underneath holding an umbrella. Ain't pretty when they forget."

A 'Calico Queen' sidled up to Magda and in a low voice said, "Time for the game, Magda?"

Pinching the woman's pale cheeks between a thick forefinger and thumb Magda replied, "Sure is Jenny. Go get the buckets." A grinning Jenny blew Jack a kiss then flounced away.

From behind the bar Jenny picked up two large wooden buckets and walked to the mules. A signal for everyone in the room to push back chairs, surround Joe, wave money and begin shouting bets. Joe moved fast, taking money like a well-oiled 'tinhorn', from a bunch of gamblers as eager and noisy as any you would see on the Mississippi boats.

Raising my voice above the din I asked, "What is Joe taking bets about?"

Magda replied, "Only game in the bar is poker and a house rule is that my girls always hold the bank. Makes for a lot of 'honking' from mah regular boys but they can go elsewhere, if they want. Exception is Joe and his mule game. He holds the bank. That's why this bunch of 'galoots'[48] get excited and wave beer stained dollars at him. They think betting on his game will change their luck."

"So what's the mule game?" asked Jack.

"Watch Jenny," said Magda.

"Already was," said Jack his eyes firmly fixed on Jenny's rear as she arrived alongside Joe's mules.

Jenny placed one bucket on the floor in front of 'Bad Ass' Susannah and the second underneath its tail.

"Fill it," yelled Magda. Three barmen hurried forward and tipped a pitcher of beer each into the front bucket. Closely followed by the mule dipping its head to drink.

The watching crowd went wild. Shouts, whistles, pushing and pulling, arguments and fists flew in the crowd as money was waved and thrust into Mulehead Joe's face.

Betting finished when Joe raised his hands and bellowed, "Back off you stinking steers. 'Bad Ass' is nearly finished imbibing. No more bets."

A voice from the crowd shouted, "What's imbibing mean."

"Somthin' wrapped around a baby's neck," another voice replied.

"Sounds about right. Plenty baby stink in the air," muttered Jack. Dragging a chair next to 'Bad Ass' Susannah's rear Jenny sat down and, producing a pocket watch, alternatively stared at it and then at the empty bucket. As the mule noisily slurped its beer an expectant quiet fell in the room. Silence broken by an occasional cough, a fart, or a striking match.

Mystified I whispered, "Magda, ah still don't get it. What's the bet?"

"Yeah. How does this game pan out?" put in Jack.

"Simple. Just pick the time that the beer reappears into that bucket under the mule's tail."

Shaking my head I said, "Joe makes. You make. And this crowd get to lose their money in a different way."

Shrugging her enormous shoulders Magda said, "Not even Joe. Only winner is me. Joe's mule dollars end up spread across my poker tables. Rarely beats the bank. His age, Joe don't care. Long as he gets to gamble. Drink. Fondle the girls and sleep in the bridal suite. Joe's happy. I'm happy. Everybody's happy." After a short pause she added, "Mah girls would appreciate Joe occasionally washing his hands. But they get paid plenty to grin, roll their eyes, brush the sand off their clothes and take him for another fifty dollars."

The unnatural silence continued to cloak the room until a sudden hissing sound announced the arrival of a deluge of splashing urine from the mule. A cascade that broke the tension with a clamour of waving hats, head slapping, foot stamping, swearing and angry drunken shouts. There was one winner. The local undertaker. A top hat wearing drunk who was flat on his back, asleep in a corner of the room; a spreading puddle beneath his legs betraying his un-witting entry into the spirit of Mulehead Joe's game.

Wandering across to Mulehead, Magda whispered into his ear and then indicated for us to follow. Magda's room was well stocked with furniture, plants, carpets, heavy curtains and a dozen paintings of scantily clad women. Once myself and Jack were settled into a sofa, Magda sat Joe on the floor; that being his preferred chair. 'Bad Ass' Susannah and 'Nat Trapper' were tied to a nearby table. Momentarily forgetting about the bits of Virginia festooning Joe's clothes Magda removed his kepi and affectionately ruffled a frying pan sized hand through his sparse tufts of hair. An action that transferred ownership of a sheen of soil, dirt and sand to her hand.

Grimacing Magda energetically wiped the hand on her dress and said, "Have a glass of whiskey, Joe. On the house."

Drinking it in one gulp Joe held the empty glass towards Magda and said, "Mighty kind. Refill?"

"Not yet. Me, you, and these Confederate army gentlemen need to talk first." Smoothing her dress Magda paused then did the introductions, "Little Scarface over there is Captain Crink. And man mountain next to him is Corporal 'Ironjaw' Claybutt. They want information about Beale's gold."

Nothing like cutting the crap and getting down to it I suppose.

Joe's face changed from looking like a rusty apparition of the moon to a wary smile and shaking our hands said, "Pleasure to meet two of Lee's men." Joe then turned to Magda and said, "Afore we talk reckon you should put another bucket under 'Bad Ass' Susannah. There's a lake of piss left in her."

Once she had dealt with Joe's suggestion Magda joined him on the floor and said in a low voice, "Joe, time to discuss business."

With a suspicious glance in our direction Joe said, "You said information. Now its business. Which is it?"

"Both. Couple of years ago you talked about a box full of gold hidden somewhere in Virginia. Remember?"

"Sure do. Man's got to talk to somebody 'bout his secrets. Bottling up information is bad for your health. Pressure can blow your head inside out. Seen men talking to the sky to dampen down problems. Remember lawyer Graham. Ran around Lynchburg wearing only boots and a cowboy hat, firing a rifle at the sky and screaming he didn't want to go into court no more." Joe replied then said, "Only told you about the gold though."

"Much appreciated Joe. Seems you never did find it. If you had then you and most of Lynchburg would be emptying my bar of drink and shouldering my 'Calicos' upstairs. You think it time to get help to find this gold?"

Joe took a while to answer but after slowly nodding his head he glanced at myself and Jack then said, "Yep. Time ah talked Magda. Held it inside too long. Ah lied about winning them papers about buried gold in a poker game. Truth is they were sold to me by a no good, son-of-a-bitch Scottish confidence man calling himself Thomas Jefferson Beale. Ah was twenty when he rode into Lynchburg with two of his men in January 1822. Stayed three months.

Should have realised he was no good. Fooled us all. Ah mean, what foreigner would baptise a child 'Thomas Jefferson'? Only one man carried that name and he was President of the United States."

Joe paused, scratched his chest, then went on, "Beale was a man you never forgot. Spent most of his time in the Washington hotel. Same as me. Unlike me, when he spoke, people listened. Good talker. Folk bought him drinks just to listen to the words drumming along his tongue. Sort of barked. Like an army officer. Strange voice. Tried to sound Virginian but his words hit the air with the background noise of a Scotsman. Faint Spanish burr there as well. Met some Scotsmen out west; in Tombstone. Hard workers. Liked whiskey; hated the English. Scared horses with strange music they squeezed and blew out of a leather contraption. Some days they would wear fancy coloured skirts. Never understood that. Maybe they liked wind blowing up their legs. Caused plenty problems when the boys drifted into town from outlying ranches on paydays."

"Strange man," said Jack.

Pausing to drink, Mulehead thought for a moment then went on, "Beale was impressive. Tall, strong looking. Everything about him was dark. Skin almost black. Long black hair. But those eyes of his. Big, shining fever mad, and black as mah feet after six months in the mountains. Had a bad stare. Like a lot of miners during the gold rush in '49. In drink a mean streak oozed through those eyes. Kind of man that shoots a preacher in the morning and sings hymns in his church in the afternoon. Smooth as owls' feathers with women. Ladies would surround him and make a fuss, trying to impress. Got so they left the room to fart. Reckon he used perfume. Gave a head start over us mountain men. Smelling of horseshit, camp fire smoke, sweat and wet hay, as we do. No saloon girl charged for a night bouncing around in his bed. Did it for free. Caused bad feelings with Lynchburg men, but nobody dared go again him. Split an apple at twenty paces with a knife; or revolver."

While Mulehead rolled himself a cigarette, I said, "Sounds like he could have been Mexican."

"Maybe a 'cabron'.[49] Drifted east looking to rob a bank," said Jack. A comment that made me shift uneasily.

Mulehead stayed silent. No doubt remembering the Scotsman. Then with a sigh he continued, "Sometime in February of 1822, happened me and Beale played poker for two days nonstop. No surprise to say he cleaned me out. When the game was over we went outside to pull some air. Sun came up and he talked about its golden beauty. Sneaky way to introduce gold into our conversation. Then Beale said: 'Speaking of which, reckon a prospecting man like you would appreciate hearing a success story' and started talking about how he and thirty men had tumbled across a lot of gold in the ground near Santa Fe. They dug out a heap of it and Beale and three of his party came and buried the gold somewhere in Bedford County. Never explained why they went to Bedford County. Although Beale hinted that he was born and raised there. Gave a tale that these four wrote the location of where this gold was buried in coded numbers on pieces of paper then returned to Santa Fe to re-join the rest of the miners to dig for some more. Said they had to go back because there was lots of gold near to the surface waiting to be dug out. Only those four who buried the gold knew how to unravel the combination of the codes. That way everybody stayed together. At least until the mine worked out."

"Heavy temptation there Joe. Those who buried the gold could have rode away with it," I put in.

"Ah said the same thing. Beale explained that his men at the mine figured the lure of lots more gold would make sure they would return. According to Beale they did go back," replied Joe with a tight grin.

Eyes glinting Magda asked, "Then what?"

"Beale offered to sell me his coded papers. Said a doctor told him that he had some disease or other and didn't have much time left on this earth. Claimed he caught something in one of those fancy whorehouses in Santa Fe. Leastways ah hope he did. Hope his pronging pole turned green and dropped off. Anyway, Beale said he wanted to go east and enjoy himself before his time was up and a thick fog of greed closed across mah mind. Ah was hooked. Especially when he explained he'd managed to translate one sheet confirming that gold had been buried in a vault in Bedford County, close to Buford's tavern. So, being young and stupid ah bought them. Sure enough those papers contained lots of numbers which ah have never understood. Can just about count on mah fingers and toes, never mind figuring out codes. Beale said if ah studied them long enough or got help, ah would eventually translate them. Being greedy ah didn't want anybody's help. Nothing but bad luck since ah owned them papers. Mah shack burned down and mah woman left me for another woman."

"Another woman!" exclaimed Jack.

Joe shook his head and said, "Goes on more than you think. Knew a banker in Texas who stood in a shack doorway at the edge of town taking payment for us to watch his wife and sister provide entertainment. Didn't do a lot. Chased each other around the room. Flicking dresses in the air to show a bare ass, then ten minutes mud wrestling. Something different. Sent lots of guys rushing to the whorehouse."

"Banker own the whorehouse?" I asked.

"Sure did."

"Joe, stop giving me ideas," said Magda wincing.

Joe stuck out his glass and Magda refilled it and he went on, "The two other sheets of numbers still ain't translated. Supposed to give the exact location of the hidden gold and the names and addresses of the thirty miners and their families. Far as ah am concerned they are rubbish. Made up numbers that don't mean anything. Ah was plain stupid to believe those papers were genuine. Anyway, ah went to Bedford County and followed mah instinct, as us old timers sometimes do. Been prospecting that long ah kin spot abandoned diggings and old filled in holes. Some dug by me. Spent thirty years or more watching the ground, searching for this Beale gold; waste of time. Ah have dug so many holes in Bedford County people got to be careful where they walk."

With a shifty eyed inspection of her fingernails, Magda said, "Joe, just because you can't translate those numbers don't mean they ain't genuine. You just haven't figured them out yet. Been too long searching by yourself. Time to loosen up. Get help for the problem."

"Could be right. Could be time to share them," replied Joe quietly.

"Anybody else in town have these numbers?" asked Jack.

After a quick glance at 'Bad Ass' Susannah Joe answered, "Rumour has it old man Robert Morriss has copies. That Scotsman maybe told him the same story he told me. Don't rightly know. No matter who asked, Bob Morriss always denied having them."

"Joe, lot of painful brooding about finding nothing," said Magda who paused and with a shrewd glance at myself and Jack continued, "Reckon Captain Crink and Ironjaw might help. Could be they understand things like codes and numbers. Might open up that gibberish and make some sense of it afore you get thrown in a sack and dumped in the ground."

With an energetic scratch at his beard Joe replied, "Yep. Could be right Magda."

"Captain Crink, do you understand this line of work?" purred Magda.

Figuring it best to show Joe some confidence I replied confidently, "Always had me a head for figuring puzzles. Especially numbers on cards."

If we got hold of Muleheads papers we would return to Richmond and hand them over to Lee's Signal Corps. Meaning we would leave town in the middle of the night with strips of Magda's dress wrapped around the horses hooves. Thoughts that were interrupted when a sudden hissing and splashing reminded us that 'Bad Ass' Susannah and her bladder were still functioning properly. As was the bucket. It was three quarters full and no leakage. If nothing else good buckets are made in Lynchburg.

Joe stared at his mud encrusted boots for a short while then, after a loud sigh, he looked at me and Jack and said, "Dammit. Judgement day can't be that far away. Been a slave to those numbers too long."

Once again it was head swivelling time when we were interrupted by another release of the mule's bladder. "Lord almighty, the bucket is overflowing," shouted Magda. Jumping to her feet she rushed to a cupboard, grabbed another bucket, and swapped it for the full one.

"Happen a lot?" asked Jack grinning.

"Once the mules start they keep going. Same for anyone who drinks beer. Although excessive amounts have other consequences for men," said Magda with a sad shake of her head. She continued, "Ah always keep a spare bucket ready. But the mules catch me out every time." Flicking one of 'Bad Ass' Susannah's ears she added, "Time the bucket was cleaned. Newest 'Calico' girl gets the disagreeable jobs. So ah will give little Mary a shout."

As Magda wandered into the corridor Mulehead Joe, still in reflective mood, said in a low voice, "Ah can still hear Beale's insistent voice when ah hesitated about buying them pieces of paper: 'Joe, time is running out. You won't regret it.' Beale was a good talker alright. How ah wish that Scottish thief would return to Lynchburg. Would be worth jail time kicking his ass."

"Joe, it happens. You were young. Anyway, it was forty years ago. Time to forget," I said sympathetically. I should know. Having strung a few cowboys along with similar tales.

Having re-joined us Magda snorted, "Dammit Joe, he 'four flushed' you."[50]

Joe blew a deep breath of tobacco smoke into the air and said, "Reckon so. After Beale disappeared rumour went around someone conned the bank for five thousand dollars. Reckon that was Beale. Bank manager never spoke about being hustled; too embarrassed ah suppose."

Mulehead went silent again. Brooding on that bad time forty years ago.

It was time to dig deeper. "Joe you still have Beale's papers?" I asked.

"Yep. Don't know why ah kept them. Better off burning them."

"Can we have a look?" asked Jack.

"Sure. Translate them if you can. Make about as much sense to me as eating wood shavings sprinkled on beaver fur."

Leaning forward Magda said, "Joe. You never can tell. If Captain Crink and Ironjaw can make sense of it all and find that gold then you can have a free double portion of pork and beans and drink as much beer as you want for a month."

"Generous as always, Magda. Got the papers here." Taking off his battered cavalry kepi Joe extracted a sweat and dirt encrusted linen pouch, handed it to me and said, "Here be Beale's gold."

Chapter Twelve

"Now I know why you never take your hat off," exclaimed Magda.

At that moment the door flew open. Framed in the doorway, a cigar in one hand and a wooden club hanging from his belt, a barman shouted, "Magda, fight in the bar."

"Tobacco men?"

"Ain't it always. Pay-day," replied the barman with a tired grin.

"Dammit, more broken furniture," muttered Magda. She hesitated, torn between seeing Muleheads papers and protecting her livelihood. Finally she yelled, "Don't want them setting fire to the bar again. Be back after waving mah revolver around and blasting more holes in the ceiling."

Followed by Magda and the barman rushing down the stairs.

Opening Joe's pouch I found six sheets of paper. Covered in scrawled handwriting faded and yellow with age. They were legible; just.

"See anything interesting?" asked Jack.

"Headaches and sleepless nights," put in Joe with a roar of laughter.

Holding the sheets of paper in the air I said, "Jack we've got two letters. One dated 4th January 1822, and the second dated the 5th January 1822. There's also some papers covered in numbers."

After reading the letters I said aloud. "The first letter must be a scam. Keeping it short. It explains that in May 1817, Beale and his thirty-strong gang were north of Santa Fe. Seems they took off to hunt buffalo, bear, and game.

During their travels they claim to have discovered a gold lode in some rocks. Took eighteen months but they dug out a whole heap of it. In 1819 they decided to transfer the gold elsewhere for safekeeping. Eventually they moved it to Bedford County where four of them put it into a vault in the ground near Buford's tavern. Then they went back to the mine and dug out more gold and put that into the vault as well. Seems at some time Beale and his gang decided to confide in someone they could trust as to the location of this gold in case anything happened to them. So Beale and three of his men came to Lynchburg to find someone to leave a coded location for the gold."

With a snort of derision Joe said, "Numbers ain't disguising anything. They're gibberish."

Turning to me Jack pointed at Joe's papers and said, "Old man Morriss must have got hold of a similar set of papers."

"Same tale to Morriss. Same lies," said Joe and flung his empty whiskey glass at a sketch of Magda on the wall. It depicted her playing cards, revolver by her side, with a mixed group of top hat wearing men and a pair of serious-faced Chinamen.

"As for the second letter," I said squinting at the opening couple of lines. "It's almost illegible. Ain't much written here. Says that one of the sheets with those coded numbers contains the names and residences of relatives of those other thirty men with Beale. Seems Beale and his men wanted their kin to receive a share of the gold."

Picking up the next three sheets of paper I looked at them, tipped my hat on the back of my head and said in a low voice, "And here are the three sheets with coded numbers."

As I finished speaking Magda, eyes narrow slits and carrying a revolver and a shovel, re-entered the room.

There was a loud clang as she dropped the shovel onto the floor. Sitting heavily in a rocking chair Magda growled, "Had to shoot a couple of more holes in the ceiling to quieten those damn tobacco men. Dozen of them fighting over 'Stumpy Leg' Margaret. She has one leg shorter than the other. Lurches rather than walks and it kinda interests some of the tobacco men. They pride themselves in trying out a new girl first." Pausing to swig from her whiskey bottle Magda went on, "Anything interesting in Joe's papers Cornelius?"

After explaining to her what I had read so far I said, "Coded numbers look mighty strange to me Magda."

Magda pointed her whiskey bottle at me and said, "You saying Beale's papers need to be taken to Richmond for the army to look at?"

"Seems that way," I replied with a shrug of my shoulders.

"No offence Cornelius. But that could be the last we see of them," said Magda with a tired grimace.

"Could be right," I agreed.

For a while nobody said anything until the quiet was broken when Jack asked, "Why the shovel, Magda?"

"It's for Joe. Mules could release their meals anytime soon."

Holding a pack of cards a senior member of Magda's 'Calico' pack burst into the room. "Looking mighty nervous, Jenny. Worried you didn't knock before joining us?" said Magda sourly.

Staring at Magda, then at Joe, Jenny said, "Don't have time for politeness Magda. Could not help overhearing about them Beale papers you was talking about. Ah might be able to help."

"Listening at keyholes," said Joe scornfully.

"Ah am a lady. And ladies do not listen at keyholes. Ah was in the room above collecting a new deck of cards when ah noticed a hole in the floor. Your voices were loud and so ah overheard your conversation," replied Jenny indignantly.

"How can you help Jenny," I asked. Now it was me cutting the crap and moving things along.

After a loud sniff she said, "Joe's description of Beale reminded me of a painting in the loft. Shown to me by an old bartender, Jim 'Wooden Leg' Hall. Remember him Magda. Died last year. Dozen spooked horses ran over him in the street. Jim said it came from the Washington Hotel a long time ago. Arrived with a wagon load of glasses, furniture, and paintings they was throwing out."

Frowning Magda asked, "Ain't noticed any paintings in there?"

"I'll show you," Jenny replied and made for the door.

"Jenny, take this revolver. Those tobacco boys ah just threw into the street might come looking for trouble again. Your turn to throw them out if they do," said Magda with an angry glance out of a window.

Jenny took us up some rickety stairs to a loft in the roof. The entrance door was locked and we used the usual key; Jack's boot. With no windows the room was dark, dusty, and damp. It was full from floor to ceiling with furniture most of which was broken or full of bullet holes, damaged paintings, oil lamps, cracked crockery, the remains of a roulette wheel, bits and pieces of beds, neatly stacked torn and ripped bartenders' uniforms, and an enormous mirror cracked from top to bottom. It looked to be a storeroom for junk from the war of independence to this week. Pushing and wading through the debris, with the rest of us following, Jenny made it to the far end of the room where she tugged open the door of a lopsided wardrobe. Inside

I saw a pile of old rags, bits of wood, and almost hidden beneath a pair of threadbare carpets a large painting of a man in military uniform. Dragging the portrait from the wardrobe I gazed at it. The man depicted looked middle-aged, dark-featured, black hair, thick muttonchop sideburns, barrel-chested, neck pushed back into his collar. Overall he simmered with hostile arrogance. A man of power; or a man possessed by madness; perhaps both.

Even more distinctive the painter had caught the eyes. They told of the real man. Glowing with insidious cunning and ruthlessness they shouted here parades evil. Someone who would smile and whistle a happy tune as he hacked off a foot to steal a shoe. His uniform reeked of pompous flamboyance favoured by European and South American senior military officers. Draped in a high-collared blue uniform jacket on which large gold coloured buttons marched from throat to waist, his chest festooned with medals, huge gold shoulder tassels. In his left hand he held a large hat; a hat that sprouted a mini copse of white ostrich feathers embossed with a huge foreign army badge. The index finger of his right hand pointed angrily at something not caught by the painter. Perhaps a dog cocking a leg against his boots; or commanding a slave to kneel to be used as a footstool. If asked to name the painting I would call it: 'Disdain for Humanity'. As father would say: "When generals represent unimportant countries. The more importantly they represent themselves."

Pointing at the picture Mulehead yelled, "Hey. That's him. Thomas Jefferson Beale."

Before anybody could react there was an almighty bang; swiftly followed by a second loud bang. Dropping the painting I fell to my knees and hid behind Magda; being well used to a daily dose of gunfire she stood her ground.

Even Jack threw himself sideways. A loud crash followed by the splintering of wood told that he had collided with the wardrobe. Joe shuddered and closed his eyes and hunkered down on the spot. Having heard a few bangs and explosions over the years I knew shots had been fired. Yet instinctively I roared, "What the hell was that?"

"Hate rats. Two less in Lynchburg. But they'll do for tonight's soup," said Jenny smugly.

Picking up the painting Joe said, "This was probably painted by the preacher's wife back in '22. Strange woman. Always drawing and painting folk. Should leave that nonsense to onion eating Frenchies and cheese making Dutchmen. In Virginia women should bake bread, darn socks, patch holes in shirts, wash their man in the bathtub and carry him home from the saloon at night."

Taking the painting from Joe, Jack turned it over, squinted at it then exclaimed, "Some sheets of paper jammed between the frame and the painting."

Leaning forward I extracted the papers and stared. They were pages of a letter dated March 1822 and addressed to 'The townsfolk of Lynchburg.' With the other three at my elbows I read half a dozen lines then said, "Joe, same handwriting as in Beale's letters of January 1822."

"Coded numbers?" queried Magda frowning.

"Nope. In English."

"Readable?" asked Jack.

Staring hard at the writing I replied, "Ink is faded and the writing jumps all over the place but ah can read it."

"Bad writing could have been caused by someone Thomas Jefferson Beale annoyed. Hopefully by sticking a steer's horn where the light don't shine," said Joe grimly. As an afterthought he added, "That would have been most of Lynchburg's male population back then."

"Wishful thinking, Joe," said Magda rubbing his jacket sleeve. An act she instantly regretted. Pulling a face she wiped the offending hand on her dress then said, "Read it to us Cornelius."

I began: "Spring. 1822. Washington Hotel, Church Street, Lynchburg. To the citizens of Lynchburg, Virginia. Subject: My departure from Lynchburg: One: First, I mention your preacher. A man whose mentality where the conduct of his wife and myself were concerned expanded with suspicion as did her girth during my stay in this strange town. His wife's situation was caused by her preacher husband. Yet this so-called man of God blames me for her condition and loiters under my hotel window, wringing his tiny hands and bellowing nefarious insults concerning false assertions that I meet his wife five times a week in the livery stable. Not since I assisted in the liberation of parts of South America have I suffered such a dreadful libel. Two: This preacher's outrageous activities and atrocious lies have encouraged other disreputable folk in this woe-begotten town of tobacco farmers, corn grinders, and flour millers, to fling similar false claims of my consorting irresponsibly with their women. Such a flagrant miasma of untruths have caused me hurtful mental turmoil. Because the inhabitants of this little enclave of Virginia, having proved they are an evil abomination, I have decided to depart Lynchburg and never to return. Such a consequence has not been visited on earth since Moses left Egypt for the promised land. My intention is to travel to where my expertise in promoting efficient and honest government will be better appreciated. Perhaps Florida. Or return to South America."

I paused to moisten my lips with a drink of beer then carried on: "Three: You will have realised by now that Thomas Jefferson Beale is not my true identity. Thomas Jefferson being an esteemed presidential name that would, and indeed did, impress those simple souls I met in Virginia. (Especially Lynchburg.) Had I not taken the name Beale then certain servants of the Spanish empire in South America, who have good cause to hate me, could have discovered my presence in Lynchburg and would try to extract revenge for my military successes in Bolivar's service. Four: Those citizens of Lynchburg who hold expectations of receiving thousands of dollars in return for investing small amounts of money with myself reveal their true selves. Displaying depraved greed. My story of a group of thirty compatriot miners discovering gold north of Santa Fe saw their eyes light with the avarice of Judas and his thirty pieces of silver. In truth this makes them brothers and sisters to Judas. They will receive nothing. Five: Those fools wishing a refund of the money they have donated should note that I consider these loans to be outright gifts, for my use as and when I think fit. Six: The name that I have used in Lynchburg has been taken from the initials of those persons and places that have impressed me most during my travels: Bolivar – General. Eyre – Colonel.

Arismendi – General. London – England. Edinburgh – Scotland. London and Edinburgh being cities in which I have lived and which have nurtured my genius. Signed: Gregor MacGregor.[51] Cazique of Poyais and General in the army of Venezuela."

"Who, or what, is a Cazique of Poyais?" asked Magda with a puzzled frown.

Scratching my head I answered, "Judging by the tone of this letter a lunatic political status for a lunatic."

Stamping a foot on the floor Mulehead exclaimed, "Forgot to mention. When Beale was taking mah money he claimed that his brother was involved in a business venture in a South American country called Poyais. Claimed the natives were not very friendly and he might have to sail there to assist his brother. Meaning there could be a delay before he returned. Been thirty-nine years. Some delay huh?"

Pausing to rub his forehead Mulehead went on, "Beale also said if his brother was making a success of his business then he might stay a couple of years to help expand it. But the gold would be put into a Poyais bank and promised that he would authorise the bank to send mah money to me in return for trusting him with the loan. What a fool ah was, huh?"

"Cazique must be a false status in a make-believe country," said Jack quietly.

"Poyais. Can't say that ah have 'chewed the dog'[52] with anyone claiming to have been there," said Magda.

"Quite a tale coming out of those bits of paper. McGregor was a fraud from beginning to end. Only came here for one purpose. To cheat Lynchburg folk. Took their money and ran," put in Jenny with a sad shake of her head.

Admiring how McGregor worked I kept quiet.

"Let's see what else we can find," said Magda who began rummaging inside a mound of wooden planks, chair legs and window frames.

Jack, searching inside the wardrobe, shouted. "Old copy of the Declaration of Independence here," and began waving a battered, grubby pamphlet in the air.

Taking it from Jack's outstretched hand Joe gazed at it then said, "Ah remember this. Old man Morriss nailed it against a wall at the Washington Hotel. Good reading material for a hotel with that name."

"Declaration of Independence should be prominently displayed in all hotels. Show foreigners how to run their countries," said Jenny over her shoulder.

"Hunting rats Jenny?" asked Joe. "Sure am. Skin them and they can join the other two for tonight's soup. Ladle that soup between your teeth and it'll make your hair grow Joe. Make you handsome again. Women will fight to run their hands through your sticky locks. That appeal?"

"That it does. Reminds me of John Augustus Sutter[53] one of the first forty-niners. Met him April of '49 told me to rub a bottle of coyote brains on mah head. Said it makes hair grow. You can see that didn't work real well. Cost me plenty too. Means ah need something extra to entice women into mah bedroom. Reckon a large bag of pipe tobacco, bottle of whiskey, a pan of pork and beans and insect free bread will give me plenty stamina. Heaven will have arrived for Mulehead Joe. Hallelujah Lord. When that day arrives I shall sing your praises," chanted Joe wistfully.

"Virginia man's paradise. Breath smelling of whiskey and tobacco, belching, farting pork and beans and a naked woman tickling his chest," said Magda dryly.

"Joe's menu more'n likely curl a man's eyeballs backward. Help spot Bluecoats sneaking up," said a grinning Jack.

Looking over Muleheads shoulders Jenny said, "Declaration of Independence impressed someone. Words circled. Scribbles, notes, and numbers in the margins. Looks like that lunatic General McGregor's handwriting."

Glancing at where Muleheads dirt encrusted fingernail was moving across a page Magda said, "Looks like his handwriting. Maybe McGregor really did bury gold and used the 'Declaration' as a key to unravel the code in his papers."

"Getting complicated," I put in.

"Like playing poker with Joe," said Magda. Followed by her pointing at the remains of a chair next to Jack and yelling, "Jenny. Rat. Shoot."

Jenny duly responded. Swinging the revolver out of her pocket, without aiming, she fired from the hip and blew the rat's head off.

Standing next to Jenny my ears were ringing from the blast.

"Another one for this evening's soup," said Magda happily.

"Impressive shooting Jenny. Must teach me how you do it," said Jack with a slow moving wink.

"Let's get out of here before Jenny forgets where we're all standing and somebody follows that rat," I grumbled.

As we left the room I heard a giggling Jenny mutter, "Magda you reckon kissing Jack would taste better than rat soup?"

Magda looked thoughtful. But said nothing.

Chapter Thirteen

At the end of June I sent a telegraph message to General Lee. Unfortunately, it was good news and bad news. In paragraph one I outlined our discovery of Mulehead Joe's copy of the Beale's papers. Followed by a second paragraph in which I described McGregor's written confession of fraud. Captain Taylor later told me that on reading the first paragraph the General jumped to his feet and shouted, "Holy Hannah, he did it. Crink found a copy of Morriss's documents."

Followed, after reading the second paragraph, by Lee sitting down on a chair with such force that both he and it flew backwards onto the floor. After recovering himself the General put a hand to his forehead and said, "Holy Hannah. Beale was a swindler. There is no gold."

Within hours a telegraph arrived from Taylor ordering me and Jack back to Richmond and to expect the arrival of two soldiers to escort us. The few days it took for the soldiers to arrive we spent trying to understand why anyone rarely won at Magda's poker table. I suspected she was cheating. Such behaviour is an art that requires a lot of practice. It is also a dangerous occupation. Anyone caught can expect a very rough ride; sometimes inside a coffin. And Magda being a woman would not guarantee her safety. Although I can usually spot a marked deck or a player using a hidden mechanical device such as a spring loaded frame, or a sleeve holder, I could not see anything obviously amiss at her table. Magda's cards were clean and she played with her arms bare; forearms thick with hair that would hide a nest of mice but insufficient to conceal a mechanical device. When Jack grumbled at his run of bad luck Magda said, "Jack, poker is like a shootout in the street. It's the luck of the draw. Sometimes you win. Sometimes you don't. Only difference is you walk away from mah table."

"Magda, outcome of a gun fight is fatal to the body. Cards at your table is fatal to the wallet," replied Jack with a wry grin.

One quiet afternoon when tobacco smoke was not so thick and the noise not so loud, I began to suspect Magda was using a large glittering glass ring on her index finger to cheat. She would turn the ring around so it was facing the cards as she dealt them As she started dealing, by holding the cards at a certain position, they reflected into the ring. Once Magda was dealing, always slowly, she would continuously flick glances at the ring; she was memorising her opponents cards. Sitting next to her I bent down and pretended to scratch my ankle and, glancing up, sure enough as Magda dealt I could see the cards reflected into her ring. When you are a stranger in town there is no point in making a fuss. Just quit playing and store the ploy behind your eyes for the future. Maybe use the same trick with a female partner elsewhere.

That same afternoon our army escort rode into Lynchburg.

Magda and Jenny provided the farewell entertainment. As we mounted up ready to leave, leaning out of an upstairs hotel window, Jenny waved a Confederate flag and shouted, "Jack. If ah have a son ah will name him after you. See yah back here at the end of the war."

Before Jack could reply Magda arrived alongside Jenny and shouted, "Cornelius, if ah have a girl, ah will call her Cordelius. Sorta rhymes with Cornelius."

"Sorta does," I yelled back.

Accompanied by our escort, with a wave of our hats, we rode out of town. After a few minutes riding I gave Jack a sidelong glance and said, "Jack. You reckon Jenny took up with you because of those coded numbers?"

"Yep. Figured that. Told her we might decipher those numbers someday. Which kept Jenny mighty interested. Jenny talks a lot. Reckon she will drop hints and spread rumours that the Confederate army is wandering around the area looking for Beale's gold. Get the prospectors fired up to come back to Lynchburg and go hunting. If there is any gold buried in Virginia maybe they'll find it 'afore Lee's Signals soldiers figure it out. Prospectors boots wandering through Lynchburg will be good for the town's prosperity as well. And Magda's," he whispered.

"Funny. Ah said the same thing to Jenny."

"You sneaked into her room as well?" exclaimed Jack and laughed.

"Sure did. And ah reckon you paid a visit to Magda."

"Happen you're right, Captain."

"Happen ah am. Alabama men, Jack. Difficult to trust," I riposted with a sad shake of my head.

"Ain't they just."

"Thing is Captain. Any children arrive then we ain't going to know which of us owns what," said Jack with a similar sad shake of his head.

"Well, if they have a boy apiece maybe one will be called George Washington Claybutt."

"The other would have to be Thomas Jefferson Crink. Problem of ownership kin be sorted by applying Crink's Alabama observance."

"Sounds good." A few frowning seconds later Jack asked, "That observance. Anything to do with giving up drink?"

"Nope. To do with flipping a coin."

During our journey back to Richmond myself and Jack spent hours trying to make sense of MacGregor's code in the untranslated Beale papers. We also discussed the Cazique of Poyais's explanation of what he had done and why he did that gargantuan confidence trick. Thumping the saddlebag containing McGregor's confession letter and the coded papers I said, "Reckon he wrote the letter admitting what he'd done because the son-of-a-bitch wanted to gloat. Taunt his victims. Make them feel real miserable. But ah do wonder, Jack."

"About what, Captain?"

"Why didn't McGregor distribute that bragging letter so that the rest of Lynchburg could read it. A person in his frame of mind ah would have thought he would drop it into a newspaper office. Or slide it under a judge's door as he rode away. Ensures that knowledge of what he's done circulates faster than a 'chaparral'[54] chasing a lizard. Which would have warmed McGregor's son-of-a-bitch evil mind for months. At least until he pulled that trick in another town."

"Perhaps McGregor just didn't think of it."

"Or he left Lynchburg in a hurry," I said slowly.

Pausing to take a swig from his water bottle Jack thought for a while then said, "Maybe McGregor did bury gold in Bedford County. Stands to reason that everybody he conned was given a copy of the Beale papers. That letter admitting everything was a confidence trick might have been another attempt to mislead folk. Make them lose interest in trying to decipher these codes and find the gold. According to McGregor he needed dollars to take back and rescue his miners. Which was a problem. He couldn't sell the gold to get dollars without agreement from his gang of prospectors. So he came up with the idea to borrow money.

Initially he was not going to repay the loans. Hence the letter. But maybe changed his mind. Couldn't go through with stealing the money and threw the letter into the back of the wardrobe. He really did intend coming back to pay the good folk of Lynchburg but something happened to prevent his return. Maybe Indians did for him. Or disease."

"My experience Jack that kind of reasoning is wishful thinking. McGregor's story is just one of life's strange tales that appear every so often; you live and learn. Face facts. The man was a confidence trickster. In terms of finding gold or anything of monetary value that will assist the Confederacy our mission has been a failure. Nope. My opinion. These Beale papers are a fraud."

After a sad sigh Jack said, "Yeah, happen you're right Captain."

"Happen I am, Jack."

On arriving in Richmond myself and Jack were taken immediately into the presence of Major General Lee at the Spotswood Hotel. Lee shook our hands and thanked us for our efforts in Lynchburg. We didn't stay long. The General was disappointed that nothing had been discovered about Beale's gold and that was it, we were dismissed with the parting words, "Speak to Captain Taylor. He will sort out rooms here in the Spotswood." Then he shook our hands again and wished us, "Good luck." As we left the room I turned my head for one last glance at Lee. In return he gave me the Plains Indian hand signals for: 'Keep your knife close', and grinned.[55]

Our remaining stay in Richmond was a blur of watching the arrival and departure of men and supplies as the Confederate army began to expand and get organised under Major-General Lee's leadership. Occasionally I paid a visit to Camp Lee, near Richmond, where volunteers for the army were drilled and taught the basics of military life. Mentally I noted the type of men the Confederacy were recruiting and their reaction to being moulded into soldiers. Information for forwarding to Pinkerton as and when my contact with the north announced himself. Most of the recruits were country boys. In the main they displayed good and bad points. As soldiers must they were used to tough living and looking after themselves but could be infuriatingly stupid when it came to understanding discipline. An attitude summed up by one sallow-faced, sour-voiced volunteer, who demanded: "Ah need to return in the mornings to mah parents farm to milk the cows."

As the recruits saw it they wanted to fight Yankees, not march around holding rifles in different positions and be told what position to take up prior to firing at the enemy.

Then it happened. Early in July Captain Taylor informed myself and Jack that a decision had been made about our future. We were to be allocated to the 33rd Virginia Infantry. Their nickname was 'lousy', because of an infestation of lice rather than a description of their prowess as soldiers. The 33rd Virginia were in the 1st Brigade under the command of Brigadier General Thomas Jackson; which was one of four Brigades in General Johnston's II Corps. To say I was unhappy with a posting to an infantry regiment was an understatement, yet there was nothing I could do about it: "The good lord provides and the good lord takes away" would have been mother's take on it. (At this point I would have happily returned to living with mother and her screeching extracts from the Bible.) I wondered if Lee, acutely embarrassed at my arriving back in his life, was despatching me towards danger in the hope that I would not return. I could have read it wrong but it would be understandable that Lee wanted to prevent what went on during our reconnaissance mission in Mexico leaking out. He obviously didn't trust me. (Quite right too!) Any blemish on his military reputation similar to what nearly happened at Cerro Gordo, leaving his post in the face of the enemy then his position in the Confederate army could be in jeopardy.

Whatever the truth of my posting, once again I was off to war.

On 15th July myself and Jack joined Jackson's Brigade in the Shenandoah, at Winchester, and I was given command of a composite infantry company made up of spare men who had not yet been processed into the regiment. Usually for reasons such as sickness or recently arrived and had received very little training. The 33rd Virginia were composed of ten companies and my soldiers were billeted in tents close to 'K' company, the Shenandoah Sharpshooters. Jack went to another company so I was on my own. In fact I was not to see Jack until we went into battle at 'First Manassas'.

After Fort Sumter's surrender the first major battlefield clash of arms came in July 1861 at 'First Manassas';[56] or 'First Bull Run', depending on which flag you saluted. A battle that came about after a Confederate army found itself in danger of attack at Manassas in Northern Virginia by a superior force of federal troops led by Brigadier General Irwin McDowell. With Union forces trundling towards Manassas who did the South have in command at Manassas? None other than the victor of Fort Sumter; Brigadier General Pierre Gustave Toutant Beauregard. Our paths first crossed at Vera Cruz during the Mexican War. My company sergeant, an enormous Texas Ranger, with a money winning line in arm wrestling, pointed at a nearby swarthy army engineer and said. "Sir, never trust a man who doesn't need to remove his shirt for a suntan."

The object of the Texan Sergeant's disdain was Beauregard; at that time a lowly lieutenant. Although I didn't know it back then, even though Pierre Beauregard made a name for himself as an excellent engineer in the Mexican war, the Sergeant had made an excellent observation. I queried his reasoning and, after squirting a large brown ball of chewing tobacco in Beauregard's direction, he answered: "That man is ambitious. And ruthless. Both necessary assets to be a successful army officer. But also arrogant and stupid. A conflict of character that has lost battles in every war there has ever been."

Quite an observation for a sergeant who only learned to read and write when he joined the army. Beauregard's swarthy appearance came from French and Welsh blood irrigating his veins; he also inherited the more dramatic extrovert aspects of this mixed lineage in bucketfuls. Even his name makes you cringe. I mean, who names a child Pierre Gustave Toutant Beauregard? Perhaps his parents were hoping he'd become a male dancer. Or perhaps they imbibed too much 'moonshine' on that historic day he entered the world. In Mexico, Lieutenant Beauregard never struck me as incompetent. But at 'First Manassas' he was never going to follow in his hero's footsteps; Napoleon Bonaparte. Whatever his misguided and self-important opinion of himself, Beauregard never achieved military greatness. Nearest I heard of him being praised as such happened when I overheard a wheat stalk chewing private soldier mutter: "General Beauregard must be a great General. Because he has a French name. Same as that famous General Bony Part." That private soldier was from Alabama. No surprise there.

Leading the other side was General Irwin McDowell. A strange man among a herd of senior Union soldier eccentrics. Had McDowell taken on the south in a pie-eating competition, then the civil war would have finished that same day. Which gave rise to the insulting rumour that

McDowell took hours to give orders to his subordinates because his mouth was always full. (Captain James Fry, McDowell's adjutant, told how the General when eating a meal would: "Gobble the larger part of every dish within reach.") General McDowell also had a problem with remembering the names and faces of his soldiers and found the easiest way to deal with this was by ignoring them. Not surprisingly there were a lot of riled junior officers. Not that that bothered McDowell. Often he would be found silent, absorbed in his thoughts, and indifferent to those around him.

After experiencing the Mexican War I should have known better, yet I told myself that the forthcoming clash of arms at Manassas would end in a swift victory for the North. Followed by a cavalry charge to Richmond and that would be it. The war would be over. Couple of months at the most. Then a return to Washington and claim my money back from Pinkerton.

Christmas at the latest. Amen to that.

Unfortunately that's not how 'First Manassas' panned out.

In my opinion the South's secret weapon in the days before the battle was a heap of petticoats; yep, for me Rose O'Neal Greenhow won the day at 'First Manassas'. Confederate soldiers still had to fight and defeat the Union army but it was she who paved the way for the South's first victory. Miss Greenhow was a Confederate spy in Washington. In her own words she summed herself up as: "A southern woman born with revolutionary blood in my veins."

Rose O'Neal Greenhow was recruited by Captain Thomas Jordan, former quartermaster in the federal army, who resigned his commission and joined the Confederate army. Jordan became Beauregard's adjutant and information flowed to him and then to Beauregard and the rest of the South's Generals. According to Confederate Navy Secretary Mallory, Miss Greenhow was 'the clever one', meaning that like most people involved in treachery and double dealing she mixed easily and comfortably with all manner and members of Northern society. Including politicians such as former President of the United States James Buchanan and Senator Stephen Douglas who were taken in by her soft talk and flattery. Rose Greenhow was also at home with those who doffed their caps and touched the forelock to others. Especially servants who wandered the corridors of power, cleaning furniture and floors, serving drinks and spooning food onto plates. Servants. People who were inside a room but socially invisible and ignored, deemed stupid and incapable of understanding what they were overhearing; of no consequence to those important people chattering about the conduct of the war and how it should be fought. In short, servants were a readymade spy network in the North and a security weakness to their masters. Moving quietly from room to room listening to the chattering leaders, or those aspiring to be leaders, then whispered all to Miss Greenhow.

As for Thomas Jonathan Jackson, our brigadier. One thing that I am good at is appraising the character of my fellow man. A lifetime of skulduggery has honed that particular trait real sharp. Had I met Jackson before the muskets started firing at 'First Manassas' then I would ran out of the camp as fast as my stumpy legs would rotate. Brigadier Jackson was as mad as a brain-frazzled buffalo licking piss off a cactus plant. Stemming from his religious beliefs Jackson had a messianic outlook on soldiering. As someone once said: "He lives by the New Testament and fights by the Old." People with those rabid beliefs can never be wrong and are rarely shifted from an opinion. Every army since Alexander the Great has laboured with a General holding those traits. Some win the battle. Others destroy themselves and their army. Poke your nose into Jackson's saddlebags and you would find, alongside his spare ammunition, a Bible.

Jackson wasn't the only fanatic though. In my opinion, at 'First Manassas' Early and Hampton matched him for aggressive energy and commitment on the battlefield. Colonel Jubal Anderson Early, known to his troops as 'Old Jube', was cantankerous and exasperating. It was said his peppery disposition came about because by training and occupation he was a member of 'Satan's brigade'; yep, a lawyer. For me I think Early was full of 'hell' because of his rheumatism. Pain can make a man want to take his ire out on everything and everybody and never mind the consequences. Colonel Wade Hampton was a perfectionist and an organiser but he was born in the wrong era. Had Hampton been around at the time of Joshua his aggression would have seen him hack a way through the walls of Jericho with his teeth. With more senior officers like those three fighting for the South, then the war would have lasted longer than it did.

Speaking of the war, by July 1861, how was it doing? Forget Fort Sumter and early skirmishes between North and South. The real war began when word reached Beauregard from Miss Greenhow that the Union army was on the march and heading towards Manassas. Eventually twenty thousand Confederates and thirty thousand Federal soldiers manoeuvred themselves into positions in and around the Bull Run River.

Over fifty thousand men about to start fighting.

All excited at the prospect.

Apart from me, that is.

Chapter Fourteen

My opinion is that 'First Manassas' should be known as the confused battle. Simply because nobody really knew, especially senior officers, what was going on. Put it down to the inexperience of those early days in the war but mistakes and incompetence by both sides were common. And me? Yep, I took part in 'First Manassas'. But like salmon in a bear's paw I did not want to be there. My buttock clenching recollection of Manassas is the name Henry, a name that has been pinned, by doting parents on many men over the years. Most accept Henry without thinking too deeply about it. Hell, there's worse. You won't be surprised when I say Pierre Gustave Toutant Beauregard comes to mind. However, for me, Henry reminds me of a nightmare on 'Henry House Hill' where I experienced terror not felt since my service with the Rangers in the Mexican War. Even now, two decades after the battle, whenever I hear the name Henry I shift uncomfortably. I fought in worse battles involving more carnage in dead and wounded but this was the first large battle in the war. And like a first in anything it stays long in the memory. Recently, while taking the air, I heard an irate mother shout at her young son: "Henry wipe that mud off your shoes." I froze to the spot until her next bellow of: "Henry stop strangling that duck," sent me scuttling off to hide in the nearest bushes.

I also fidget with embarrassment when recollecting another occasion when playing poker on a Mississippi boat and being introduced to an opponent as 'Bishop Henry'; after turning the colour of puce I let rip an almighty fart. Fear can cause that reaction. Leastways it does in me. An eruption of wind thundering around the table caused by remembered battlefield feelings at 'First Manassas' jumping from a hidden recess in my mind. Although the venerable nose twitching bishop did not appreciate this at the time. On recovering his composure the bishop said, "Lovely day for it." Whether meaning the poker game, or my wind, I didn't have the nerve to ask. But something impressed his wife. A note appeared underneath my cabin door with a scrawled: Every evening 'Bishop Henry' visits Cabin 6 between eight and ten. Call on me during this time in Cabin 9 for Bible study lessons and I will be pleased to receive you.' I figured her interest had something to do with my nickname. On the Mississippi boats I was known as 'donkey', which came about because of my large ears; but she wasn't to know that. Anyway, if she was disappointed, she never said.

As for my company of soldiers. Although full of fighting spice and keen to shoot themselves 'a Yankee or two', I was apprehensive as to how they would react in battle. A few had combat experience in the Mexican War but most were ignorant of disciplined fighting when under fire from canon and rifle. Once the bullets began flying and men were knocked to the ground the reaction of these 'green' troops could only be guessed. Some would run, some would freeze, but hopefully most would stand their ground. As in all battles there would be casualties. The fate of many of Southern boys and their Northern opponents before the war was over.

"Slovenly looking bunch," I muttered to myself. "What did you say sir?" asked Sergeant Smith.

Smith was my company sergeant. Formerly a career soldier in the North he had switched sides and joined the Confederacy. Which he did for the usual reason. Smith was born and bred in the south; South Carolina to be exact. Bovine-faced and much given to spitting it didn't come as much of a surprise that he was regimental champion at moving the watery contents of his mouth, and hitting selected targets, usually insects; with the accuracy of a 'Plains Indian' skewering a rattlesnake through the head with an arrow. Which doesn't sound a lot to brag about until I discovered that spitting competitions could, and did, earn Smith dozens of dollars in bets. On one memorable occasion I witnessed him swivel one hundred and eighty degrees and drown a meandering fly ten or twelve feet away. (Useful asset when eating outside.)

This particular evening Smith was walking alongside me as I wandered around company lines. "Fine looking body of men, Sergeant Smith," I replied.

It doesn't do to fall out with your Sergeant after only a couple of days acquaintance and as I hadn't had time to figure out Smith's views on our Company yet, I reckoned it would be best to praise the men until I got to know Smith better. In reality, to a man, they were scruffy and unkempt and looked as if they had been dragged through a hedge backwards and then rolled in a tub of dust. I changed tack to get the Sergeant's opinion on their fighting prowess. "They keen to get to grips with the enemy?"

"Sure are Captain. They reckon on sending those federal boys back to Washington after a couple of weeks fighting and then march on the White House to loot as many souvenirs as they can find," he boomed. After a swift glance over his shoulder the Sergeant went on in a low voice, "Truthfully Captain. Ah ain't so sure. They ignore us old soldiers. We tell them: 'Time comes to start shooting don't pull the trigger on your rifle, squeeze it. And don't fire until you can see brown-stained Yankee teeth and kin smell the tobacco on their breath.' They just laugh. Always the same. Old lessons are forgotten and have to be learned again."

After a pause to scratch his chin Smith surprised me with his follow up perception of the men when he continued in the same low voice, "Sir. One thing universal at the beginning of any war, anywhere, is the initial enthusiasm of civilian volunteers who rush to the colours declaring they want to see action before the bugles sound an end to proceedings. There is an illogical assumption, both by soldiers and their civilian supporters, that their cause is the correct one and that with God's help allied to their superior fighting abilities they will triumph swiftly on the battlefield and win the war. Along with this wishful thinking is the belief that, because the fighting will only last a short while, the war will be over before they have the opportunity to enjoy themselves and shoot at the enemy. Ah reckon both you and me know that as this war lumbers bloodily on, which it will, and casualties start to mount cynicism sets in and morale suffers with a realisation that it is going to last a lot longer than they thought. Soldiers, both Confederate and Union, are the same in this respect. Main problem for us is that this is just the beginning and recruits are woefully short on training and equipment."

"Very perceptive Sergeant. And ah agree. Gray and Blue recruits have swaggered to the call to the arms believing their cause is 'right and just' and their boasts are full of the usual beginner's brash eagerness to close with the enemy. Yesterday ah overheard a raw recruit brag that the Yankees can no more fight than planting a feather will grow a chicken."

Sergeant Smith sucked a tooth then said, "Thousands of civilians have shouldered packs, pulled on their boots, hugged their loved ones and laughed at old timers' words to take care. Then marched happily away. Both sides straining to close with each other. Each convinced they can hurry the other back to Washington; or Richmond."

Smith paused to glance at our soldiers who were stood around talking, smoking and throwing us the occasional casual look. No doubt wondering who we were talking about. But being crafty, cynical Southern boys, I guessed they probably realised it was them Hitting his stride again the Sergeant took up the verbal slack with a whispered, "Captain when this war is over both sides will shake their heads and wonder how politicians would not listen to reason. Today great dribbles of stupidity splash out of their mouths. Our Generals ain't much better. Look at Lee. He's with the south because he feels more affinity to Virginia than the United States. Somehow things just don't seem right with that stance. Don't get me wrong. Ah have gladly chosen the Confederacy. But as an officer in the Union army since 1829 ah would have thought that General Lee would command Federal forces. Not us rebels. Suppose what ah am trying to say is that you, me, Lee and every other Southern boy has an awful choice. Fight for the home State or stay with the Union. Like General Robert E. Lee, ah will fight for the Confederacy to the best of mah ability."

"Must confess, ah feel uneasy at what is going on Sergeant," I said quietly.

This situation of an unstoppable roll to war was well summed up by a former Confederate colonel I met in a bar in Abilene, Texas, after the war: "In the beginning we were wide-eyed and naïve. It took four years for us to realise that war is a dumb way to settle our differences. But neither side would stop and talk. Even after six hundred thousand graves, we just kept fighting. When Anderson surrendered Fort Sumter, Confederate canons in Richmond fired a victory salute. Hell, we should have fired them at the politicians. Then gone home."

Something clicked inside my head and I asked, "You the only one in your family in this fight?"

Head down kicking at a tuft of grass Smith replied, "Some South Carolina folk have sided with the Union and one of mah brothers is fighting on their side. Last ah heard he went north and enlisted in the 14th New York Militia."

Now that had to be a conversation stopper.

It is well known that individual States provided volunteers for both sides in the Civil War. Although it seemed that most Southern boys enlisted with the Confederacy there were some, uneasy with slavery, and others who preferred the Union to continue as the government. So they followed that little voice in their heads that told them to join the North's army. Others cited the rebellion by the secessionist States as akin to treason and marched north. On occasions, as with Sergeant Smith, family loyalties were split with fathers, sons and brothers taking opposing sides. There were many stories told around campfires in the months to come of angry words in households, both the North and South, about families arguing and shouting at each other as to which side to support; and ultimately which side to fight for. Hot words followed by blows sent some striding angrily out of homes and marching in different directions. For those in this situation, when things had calmed down, went the unspoken fear: "What if my father. Or son. Or brother, appears to my front just as I am about to pull the trigger?"

What came first. Family? Or the ideals of the south and establishment of a new nation? I was glad I didn't have to make that choice. In my case assistance being provided by President Lincoln and Pinkerton who put their muddy boots against my ass and pushed.

"Any idea where the 14th New York are right now?" I asked quietly.

"Heading for Manassas."

"Sorry to hear that Sergeant. Hopefully you'll both come through this coming ordeal without meeting. Or either of you coming to harm." After a suitably polite pause I went on, "How are the men with discipline? That a problem with these newcomers?"

"Sadly lacking. Apart from the former soldiers ah have found them argumentative with those in authority, that mainly being myself and the corporals. They constantly query instructions and orders and still think and behave as civilians. Especially with me, a foreigner from South Carolina."

"Anyone from another State is a foreigner to Virginians," I said with a grin then continued, "From rumours ah hear that there ain't much time before this war really gets going. We've got to stick at teaching the boys the basics of soldiering."

"Absolutely Captain. But you try explaining the concept of orders and the necessity for discipline during the chaos of battle. Ah tell them that discipline is vital and when a command is given it should be obeyed without questioning the whys or wherefores. Ah finish mah talks with telling them that not reacting promptly could cost them their lives."

At this point a group of soldiers from my company wandered away from their tents and stood nearby, staring at myself and Smith. Private Aster, a farm worker small in height but broad-shouldered and strong with bulging forearms that could lift half his body weight straight from the ground and hold it over his head, put a hand towards his cap in some form of a salute and said slowly, "Excuse me Captain. We could not but help overhearing you and Sergeant Smith talking about our lack of discipline. Could you please tell me what's so vital 'bout us doing what you tell us to do. Ah reckon we need time to think about your orders. Make sure what you're telling us is right."

This was immediately followed by a comment from Private James. A raw-boned former trapper missing an ear and two fingers after a fight with a bear in the Blue Ridge mountains who chimed in with, "Captain, what if you get it wrong? Ah mean you could be a real duffer with them orders of yours.[57] Our ideas might be better. Could at least listen. Might save your life."

Needless to say patience was the only way to proceed when dealing with men who could not, as yet, understand why their ideas and opinions were not considered or listened to. I answered with, "In battle there won't be time to sit and discuss plans. You need to carry out orders as quickly as possible. Gets the job done, as well as saving lives."

Another soldier, notable for a beard that would put an Old Testament prophet to shame and spookily called Jerome Jonah Jeremiah, intervened with a surly, "Captain, we don't need anyone to tell us when to shoot. Soon as a blue uniform appears, that's the time to pull the trigger."

Sergeant Smith joined in with, "Soldier, never pull the trigger. The rifle will jerk. You will hit crows in trees or remove your comrades hats. Or worse. You squeeze the trigger. Keeps the barrel steady. Sends the bullet where you're aiming." After a moment staring at his boots Smith sighed and said slowly and loudly, "Another thing. See a blue uniform, wait. Don't immediately open fire."

"Why's that?" asked Aster with a perplexed scratch at the back of his neck.

Here I took over and said, "Because there are other Confederate army units wearing blue uniforms. That's why."

"This is complicated. Some Confederates are wearing Yankee blue.What is going on?" asked Private James loudly.

"Years ago those in charge of militia units in different States decided what colour uniforms their regiments would wear, not the government in Washington. When thConfederacy was seceding State militia units were wearing all kinds of uniforms. Happens some are blue. There ain't been time to issue everyone with Confederate gray. If you doubt me on that then I suggest you take a wander around camp.You'll see plenty of blue," I explained.

There was a moments silence while this information was thought about then Aster stubbornly returned to his dispute about discipline. "Captain, I still ain't persuaded you will give the correct orders when the time comes for us to hunt Yankees."

Before I could have another go at explaining to Aster that it was my 'thinking' that counted a new voice joined in. Corporal O'Halloran gave his contribution to what was fast turning into a company discussion. "Captain, ah am a former soldier. Most of the boys are farm hands who have done a lot of hunting. Ah believe that where shooting is concerned they can fire straight and load fast. And we ain't frightened of anyone who crosses the Virginia State line looking for a fight. Especially Yankees."

With close set eyes and a similar build to Aster and with hair down to his collar O'Halloran, originally from Kentucky, had only left the army four or five months ago. On hearing the news about Fort Sumter's capture he re-enlisted and volunteered to serve the South. A plain speaking man O'Halloran was one of those who candidly admitted to re-joining the army: "Fer the fun of it"; had he been living in the North then it would have been to them he would have offered his services. Money in his pocket, food in his stomach, and tobacco in his pouch were all that mattered to him. The politics of what this war was about were of no concern; his take on this war was simple: "Shoot the enemy afor' he shoots you."

Which made me ask the question, "O'Halloran how do you feel about shooting fellow Americans?"

"Don't know Captain. Ain't shot one yet," was his philosophical reply.

I decided it was time to retreat to my tent and think of a better way to explain how the army operates. Walking away alongside Smith the Sergeant summed up my ragtag array of soldiers when he said, "Sir, the men are dusty, scruffy, and don't know a lot about discipline. But most are from backgrounds where they have to learn how to use a rifle so they can eat. Their rifles are clean and they know how to use them."

Truthfully, they knew the most important part of soldiering. How to use a firearm.

With a farewell touch to his hat Sergeant Smith turned and walked off to his own tent.

Deep in thought I didn't notice, walking towards me, a slave carrying kindling wood. Slaves are not an unusual sight in camp and other than displaying a certain dignity in his bearing, he was not someone I would show an interest in; he was merely part of the Confederate camp scenery. As we drew level the slave stopped and stared at my face, probably wondering about the scar on my right cheek, I thought. Lots of people have shown an interest in this souvenir from the Mexican war and many a tale of 'adventure and bravery' have I conjured from my imagination as to how I obtained this injury. Usually concerning a skirmish with a dozen bloodthirsty Mexicans. Truth is, full of drink, I fell over and collided with a rock. With an indifferent glance at the slave

I walked on. On hearing footsteps following me I stopped. In close attendance the footsteps stopped. I moved again. The footsteps behind me resumed. The slave was following me. Curious as to what he was up to I turned and with a lazy wave of a hand ushered him close. However, before I could speak the slave pointed at my company's tents and said, "Your soldiers look plenty ready for a fight, Captain Crink."

There are times when we hear only what we want to hear and mentally blot out unpalatable truths that don't agree with our thought processes. That happened when this slave mentioned my name. Church bells should have rung in my head. Apart from being a slave he was also a total stranger. How did he know who I was? He could have had me pointed out by someone else in camp. But, whatever the reason, his greeting of familiarity did not register. Although alert and puzzled at his speaking to me almost as an equal did register. Narrowing my eyes I replied, "My company are ready to go to war." After a moment's pause I went on in an irritated tone, "Not that it's any business of yours." "Ready or not Captain, there will be casualties in their ranks before this war is finished. Families will suffer. When the soldier is killed his pain is over. For the folks at home it is the beginning of their anguish," the slave replied with a sad shake of his head.

Silently I stared at him. That was a profound statement, for a slave. Bobbing his head up and down a couple of times he added quietly, "My brother, clouds of tear filled sadness approach. In the coming years a thunderstorm of grief will descend on both sides."

His 'brother'? That was a stunning comment.

What was he on about? The slave obviously didn't mean that we were sired by the same father and being a slave he was not someone who had accompanied me when wandering around any bars; nor did I recollect him in tow holding my clothes when visiting any of the bordellos I frequent. Nor helping me cheat at cards. In a lifetime of being hit with unpleasant surprises I have learned not to show emotion; always present a straight face no matter what. But I failed on this occasion. My cage was well and truly rattled. Trying to understand what was going on top and bottom teeth separated and I gaped at the slave.

Recovering my composure I blurted out, "Brother! What the hell are you on about?"

Stony-faced, he ignored my question.

I stared. My brain slowly revived itself and I waited. Expecting a cheeky smile to suddenly appear and the slave's head to drop in embarrassment at his temerity. Some of them possess an insolent sense of humour and occasionally produce audacious jokes that involve white folk. An attitude that appears now and then when they are feeling sorry for themselves, usually after labouring through a hot day in the fields. It crossed my mind to search out a whip to crack across his back but, before I could stir myself, there was more impudence when he said, "We really are brothers."

I had had enough. "This 'brother' nonsense is crass insolence. Any more of it and ah will kick your ass from here to Washington," I retorted.

Leaning forward he whispered, "Don't you remember me?

"No, ah don't. No reason to? You're a slave. You all look the same."

A few seconds of dumbfounded silence encouraged yet another ludicrous comment, "Don't be afraid, Captain. But be assured, you are my brother. And you are beholden to me."

Eyes narrowed to furious slits I answered, "How the hell can ah be your brother. You're a different colour."

Out of the corner of my eye I noticed a group of my soldiers idly watching our verbal exchanges. They were far enough away so that I doubted they could hear what we were saying but their facial expressions were unhappy, bordering on hostile. My angry scowls must have indicated to the soldiers that I was not amused at what was being said. I had to be careful. A dramatic shout from me could rile these Southern boys and cause them to intervene and push this slave on his way; perhaps even give him a beating; or worse. I had to steer clear of controversy, even with a slave. Yet I needed to find out who he was and what these ludicrous claims of being his 'brother' were about. But not here. Shouting at him for his verbal buffoonery and browbeating an explanation from him would have to be done in private.

Then it got gut wrenchingly worse when the slave whispered, "Look close. I am Yankah. I saved your life on the Cape Coast?"

Those thirteen words brought an explosion of memories! Sixteen years since I had seen Yankah. His hair was gray, but his facial features were the same as when we first met. In the fall of 1845 I was slaving with father on the West African Cape Coast between Accra and the Volta River. A horrible place clogged full of every disease in Africa. In particular, as medics later discovered, malaria. Having slave collecting arrangements with a number of Fanti tribal chiefs my father visited this area on a regular basis. The chiefs would round up suitable 'merchandise' grabbing them from tribes they'd fallen out with; tribal hatreds were endemic in Africa. Or kidnapping trespassers on tribal land. The chiefs would even let us have their own people. Those who had upset them, meaning anything from suspected rebellion, breaking tribal laws, or merely falling asleep in the great man's presence. Prisoners would be traded for goods we had brought. Father wanted good relations so he gave decent, expensive goods. Well-made furniture, large mirrors and especially alcohol.

One thing never traded, for obvious reasons, were firearms. Especially as the *Amistad*[58] incident was always uppermost in slavers minds. As word of father's way of doing things spread, we gained more and more 'business' contacts. Although on some trips the locals would get wind of our arrival and a lot of 'material' slipped into the jungle or hid in remote villages further inland. Because father was very popular his slave providers would go hunting flesh for us. A service that saved us time and effort chasing them down.

On this particular trip, owing to a navigation error, we landed in an area never visited by us before. Rather than search for where the ship should be berthed father decided to have a 'hunt' in this locality. Being strangers we would make a fast 'snatch and grab' of any suitable natives without announcing ourselves. Saving us time by not having to go through bargaining procedures with local tribal chiefs. I went ashore with twenty crew but, not finding any mature male or female natives in the nearest half a dozen villages, concluded our arrival in the nearby bay must have been noticed.

On frustrating occasions such as this, after a long voyage from the States, some of the crew would haul old or unfit female natives from their huts and rape them in nearby patches of jungle. I tried to prevent this but, boss's son or not, half a dozen pistols pointing in my direction quickly made me back off. Yep, I know, hard to believe but Cornelius did feel uncomfortable at this kind of behaviour.

(If they'd been young and nubile I would have joined in.) I did hear that some slaving crews would tie old men to trees and use them as target practice; sheer badness I suppose. Which is murder; but to them it was sport.

Moving further inland we searched a dozen village without finding any natives worth putting in chains. There was nobody but a selection of listless looking old hags, mostly huddled around large cooking pots, or sleeping, so we moved further into the interior. After walking through another dozen smelly villages populated with pot-bellied old men, screeching infants and dozing crones, none of whom would last a journey to the States, I stopped to relieve myself. A call of nature was such a common occurrence there wasn't much point in telling my companions what I was doing. By the time I finished they wouldn't have gone very far and I would quickly catch them up. Except this time I failed to notice they had moved into a patch of thick jungle and were out of sight.

As I lurched away in the direction where I surmised the men had gone I found myself walking along a narrow track. Although navigation has never been my strong point I found myself following a lot of footprints, which made me confident that I was heading on the same compass point as the rest of my posse. Hurrying down the track I emerged into a clearing beside a fast-moving stream where I found, kneeling and leaning the upper part of her body into the stream, a naked Fanti woman. In her early twenties she was noisily splashing and sloshing water under her armpits and across her belly. With delightful curves that made the blood pound behind my eyes she began dipping her head into the stream sending her pert rump bobbing up and down. I knew she would be a delight to practise on and within seconds I was dribbling saliva like a howling coyote. The woman's facial features and bodily curves reminded me of one of my father's slaves. A woman who had kept me amused for many an hour when father was away on business; or in jail; or both. They could have been sisters. Possibly they were. But it wasn't a discussion about her siblings I was interested in.

"At last. Something decent to play with," I crooned under my breath.

On occasions when I least expect it bursts of biblical verse surface from hidden crevices in my mind. Years of mother stuffing religious drivel into my head I suppose. After a minute admiring the Fanti woman I began quoting the Good Book to myself: "Prepare the way of the lord. Make his paths straight. Every valley will be filled."

And how appropriate that quote was on this riverbank. The area was deserted so my way ahead was prepared with a straight path towards that cavorting rear. I knew which valley to fill. In short, I had to have this woman; there and then. There would be no negotiation over a price with her or her village elders and hopefully she would not display any indignation at being the lucky recipient of my attention. Wrong colour of skin for that. It was turning into a fun day. Or so I thought. A couple of weeks roaming the high seas has this effect on most slavers. Now, older and more dignified, I would open my wallet first.

The Fanti was so engrossed in her ablutions that I managed to creep up and grab her from behind before she could react. Pinning her arms to her side, amid a bout of screeching, angry grunting and irate gabbling in her hideous West African dialect, I began dragging her towards a copse of nearby trees. Just in case any of her friends came wandering along I intended jumping her bones out of sight. What happened after I had finished depended on her demeanour. I always carry a pair of shackling irons and if compliant she could trot alongside me to our ship for a free passage to the States and spend a couple of years or, depending on how quickly I became bored, some months entertaining me and my father. Any trouble or noisy tantrums between here and the ship then I would dispose of her. In the African jungle too much noise attracts unwanted attention and any nearby clansmen of hers would come running. As I was on my own her rescuers, especially armed ones, could cause trouble. I would have to dispose of her. Meaning, dumping her in the river. If she could swim, a spot of sport would be in order. Such as my boot pushing on her head for a few minutes.

Hopefully once I began she would mind her manners and keep quiet.

Unfortunately for me the afternoon's amusement was rudely interrupted when a huge native, wearing only a loincloth and with extensive slash scars across his face and shoulders and carrying a long gleaming spear, crashed into the clearing from out of a dense patch of jungle. Face screwed into an expression of hate the newcomer roared what I guessed would be the Fanti equivalent of "Take your filthy bulldogging[59] hands off her, you hairy son-of-a-bitch foreigner."

Chapter Fifteen

At this uncalled-for and frightening interruption during my attempt at getting to know the Fanti girl better I swiftly released her then, putting my hands palm first in the direction of the newcomer, announced in a loud, nervous voice, "It's not what it seems. Just trying to make friends with this lady. You can have her instead. Do what you want, ah don't mind. Ah will help hold her down."

My words were met with vacant-faced incomprehension from the Fanti native.

"Dumb native. Ain't got a clue what ah am on about. Time to retreat," I muttered.

Although furiously back-pedalling away from the spearman, there was no way I was about to turn my back on him, the situation got worse. Levelling the weapon at genital height, my genital height that is, the new arrival set off jogging towards me. Blood draining from my face I must have paled the colour of flour. Panicking I turned around and started to run. Big mistake. The Fanti woman reversed roles by lunging forward and grabbed my waist in a bear hug. Clinging on like a raccoon in heat she let out a hideous growl and swung me around so that once again I faced the advancing spearman. How ridiculous I thought. I haven't done anything vicious or painful to this woman, not yet anyway, and I was now in imminent danger of becoming a eunuch; or much worse a dead eunuch. What a way to end your days. Testicles skewered to the ground in this acre of foetid African swamp land that had not made a mark on any known map, and probably never would. And, apart from people I owed money to, no-one would miss me when I failed to return to the States. Father would merely shrug his shoulders, laugh, fart and say: "Way to go, Cornelius."

Terrified I bellowed at the woman, "Let go you horrible creature. That's an order."

The things you say when under extreme stress.

Clearly this woman did not understand English either for she merely grunted and promptly tightened her grip. What strength. It seemed that I had picked on West Africa's woman wrestling champion. Our tussle turned into an almighty free for all, with me shouting, twisting and turning, trying to throw this Amazon to one side. At the same time revolving my head this way and that to keep the snarling spearman insight. All to no avail. I was bolted to the woman. Frantic shouts for help attracted no one. In seconds the point of the spear arrived within jabbing distance of my stomach and a bloody end beckoned. By now we were teetering close to the edge of the stream and it crossed my mind, ludicrous I know, that there would probably be all manner of unknown reptiles and diseases lurking in that water. Why a matter of such secondary danger should come into my head as I was about to be stabbed into oblivion is one of those mysteries of the inside of my head; but it did.

Hallelujah, salvation temporarily arrived when both myself and the Amazon lost our footing and we fell over. Luckily we hit the ground, rather than the river. The Fanti woman landed on her back with me, still pinioned by her arms around my waist, staring at the sky. There was no let-up in her grip; her strength would have won praise from a champion rodeo rider and I was starting to feel faint. Lack of oxygen I suppose. They say in this situation your past flashes through your head. It's true. Into my mind jumped snatches of my childhood; recollections of me laughing as I beat a flapping fish to death with a pole; pulling the wings off a fly; followed by my hands around the throat of a boyhood friend leaving him half-throttled. I stared, horrified, at the Fanti towering above me. Drawing back his spear to thrust it into my innards I panicked, frantically shouting, "Ah have gold. You can have it."

Ridiculously I went on with, "Is your bank nearby? Ah can pay it in tomorrow."

Then I started screaming.

Desperate times brought desperate strength as, with a gigantic heave, I rolled myself and the Amazon over and in the process somehow managing to turn myself inside her arms so that her back was uppermost and facing the spearman. Meaning we were now face to face. At this range, nose touching nose, her face revealed more pockmarks than those strange looking blotches on the moon; and her breath stank of fish. They say the devil looks after his own, one of whom must be me, or you could say a bucketful of Alabama luck appeared with the entrance of another Fanti native. A male also wearing only a loincloth who, carrying a similar spear to my attacker, darted out of the jungle. Yelling his head off, eyes bulging, he pointed his spear at my would be attacker. Possibly a rival suitor for this woman's affections. Or maybe his tribe was engaged in a vendetta against the spearman's tribe. Equivalent of a 'range war' out west. Whatever the reason for the newcomer's timely intervention he stopped and, in a blur of movement and balance, raised his spear to shoulder height then hurled it.

With a sickening crunch the spear thudded into the would be rescuer's back and pitched him, spread-eagled and screaming, on top of the Fanti woman. To this day his screams occasionally wake me in the night.

Here, not surprisingly, I fainted.

I awoke to find my rescuer slapping me repeatedly across the face and shouting, in English, "Master. Are you alright? Wake up." Followed by my panicking thought that if this was the entrance to the pearly gates then Saint Peter must have a strange sense of humour; he had an African gate guard. Followed by the further ludicrous thought of: 'did this mean St. Peter was against the slave trade?' If that were the case then my slaving history meant that I was in grave danger of being refused admittance and transported elsewhere. But they are minor thoughts. Whenever I think back to that fight five things have vividly remained in my memory. One: The woman's glorious backside hefting itself skywards as she bathed in the river. Two: Her excruciating bad breath as we manhandled each other towards the riverbank. Three: The menacing sight of that Fanti native advancing with his spear pointed at my guts. Four: The screams of the dying Fanti. Five: Never before, or since, have I seen a man so placid after killing another human being.

A few yards away the speared native lay face down with the Fanti woman bending over him. To my stressed mind she was to blame for what had happened. In the sense that by refusing my friendship she had instigated an attack by this deceased native. It took a lot of restraint on my part, suffering from shock, shivering with fright, and wondering why the front of my trousers was wet, not to start kicking the dead man. A pointless exercise, but it would have soothed my frayed nerves somewhat. Instead I unthinkingly babbled at my saviour. "The President of the United States will give you a medal and shake your hand for saving mah life."

After reassuring myself that the Fanti was still horizontal on the ground and not crawling towards me, I stared at my rescuer for a few seconds, before gibbering further rot. "If you find yourself in America, look me up. Mah father could spare a couple of dollars and a shirt or two. Or a job cleaning the house. We pay well. Three meals a day and a bucket of beer at the end of the week. Plus a night with a female slave once a month."

I waited for my rescuer to speak.

When a stranger is standing to my front what you might call Crink's policy has been not to talk too much about myself, nor tell the truth until knowing why he, or she, was there. Especially if they're displaying a friendly smile. They can be trying to put you at ease but in reality their minds are seething with memories of some long forgotten quarrel. Or claiming that you owe them money. Or you cheated at cards. Or in this case the newcomer could be remembering his family being dragged to a slave ship and, rather than watch the dead Fanti skewer me, wanted the pleasure of revenge instead. His blood dripping spear draped across a shoulder my rescuer calmly said in very good English, "My name is Yankah and you are now in my debt."

In shock or not I did not take kindly to this introduction; in his debt?

Friend Yankah then frightened the life out of me by springing forward and tying a small canvas black bag to my waist belt. After whispering some Fanti bilge he said loudly in English, "The fetish inside this pouch is now part of you. Aidoo's spirit resides inside and protects you. Averting the evil eye, calming wild animals, and will repel those who would do you harm. Be they thugs, thieves, or those seeking revenge for adultery."

Amen to that last category. Although it was worrying that Yankah realised that one of my special interests was adultery. (Hey! Why get married? End result is you hitch poker playing money in your wallet to the upkeep of someone else's daughter.)

Naturally curiosity made me ask, "Who is Aidoo?"

"My woman's mother."

A surprising reply that took away the happy edge to the day. Had I thought about it, why was my saviour giving me this ridiculous present in the first place? I put my failure to ask what was going on down to shock from the dramatic interlude with the woman's would be rescuer. If he thought I would keep such a ridiculous present then he didn't realise who he was dealing with. Once Yankah disappeared back to his jungle hovel then that little canvas house and his mother-in-law would fly into the nearest clump of African shrubbery. Truth is though, I have never been able to get rid of that pouch. I could always remove the belt from my waist but my arm locked whenever I tried dispose of belt and pouch. It was the same in reverse. When getting dressed some strange force made me pick up the belt and pouch and strap it around my waist. Thirty years on and it still hangs on my belt. Try explaining what's so special about that damned pouch to a lady friend when you don't know yourself what's going on.

Yankah then brought on another potential trouser-smelling moment when he leapt forward and, placing a hand on my forehead, said in a high-pitched voice, "I am a Fanti priest. Henceforth your life is beholden to me. And to the spirit of Aidoo."

Now I realised. Yankah was a Voodoo practitioner. A 'Bocor'.[60]

I had come across them during my slaving forays in Africa. It was unusual to scoop one up and transport them across the Atlantic; rumour had it Bocors knew when we were we coming. Occasionally though, it happened. Father thought they allowed themselves to be shackled because, for reasons known only to themselves, they wanted to come to the States. Nothing wrong with that; but as a slave? Perhaps they wanted to ensure that Voodoo travelled with the slaves; sort of Voodoo missionary. Certainly I had heard of Voodoo ceremonies on plantations in the South and their Bocors were well known to be highly intelligent, evil, and not to be crossed.

Yankah walked to the dead native and, accompanied by muttered Fanti claptrap, he pulled his spear out of the body and taking a machete from his waist belt began hacking at the corpse. Swiftly removing the eyes, tongue, an ear, four or five fingers and some of the contents of the man's stomach. Presumably Yankah wanted these bits to help prepare concoctions connected to Voodoo rituals. No surprise that I was not about to ask what he had in mind. Bar room talk has it that Bocors change moods faster than a lunging rattlesnake and I didn't want Yankah taking umbrage at my curiosity and begin relieving me of any bodily attachments necessary to keep me trundling happily through life.

Muttering constantly to himself Yankah began stuffing his harvested bits of blood dripping meat into various pouches around his waist belt. As he worked my saviour looked at me once, a cold look out of the corner of his eye that said: "I have your measure. Some day this blood debt will be claimed." The awful thought crossed my mind that staying here any longer and Yankah might insist that we dine on bits of the dead man. A sort of bonding ceremony. Consecrate our brotherly pact, so to speak. But, on finishing his grisly task Yankah merely said, "Never forget what happened this day."

With a shudder I replied, "Forget? Not much chance of that."

The Fanti woman was hunkered down on the riverbank, arms across her knees, staring at me with an expression of pure hate and with an intensity that would curdle fresh bear puke. Pointing at the now partially dismembered native I said to Yankah in a low voice, "Someone may seek out this dead man. This woman is a witness and might tell lies about me. She also saw what you did. His friends might want revenge."

My tone humming with false concern I went on, "Just give the nod and getting rid of the woman will take but a moment. Surely those chunky curves can be turned into much sought after magical assets. If you don't want her bits then others in your tribe surely would. Use your spear. Or machete. Or dump her in the river. Sort of sacrifice to a river God, or some such foolery."

Yankah produced a thin mirthless smile, shook his head and said, "No. Goodbye my blood brother. Perhaps some day we will meet in America."

I knew the effects of shock were wearing off when, ungrateful as always, I thought that if ever Yankah appeared in the States he would be shackled at the wrists and ankles. I mean, what would my Alabama neighbours think if he knocked on my door claiming to be my brother, and wanting access to the house? Selfishly I spat out an irritated, "What are you on about. Ah am not your damned blood brother."

Pointing at the dead native he answered, "I killed for you. His blood begins a debt of honour to me." At this point I did wonder why Yankah had taken my side in this incident. Not liking the way things were going I said, "Your help is much appreciated but ah must leave and return to my ship. It sails shortly," and shook his hand. Which was a first for me. Shaking an African's hand, that is.

"I too must go. Goodbye Mister Crink. Pray every day to Aidoo," Yankah replied solemnly. Silently, without a backward glance, Yankah and the Fanti woman left the clearing at a trot. In seconds they blended into the jungle and disappeared.

Those African memories flashed through my mind in an instant. Aware of an audience of curious soldiers from my company watching us from outside their tents I said in a stern whisper, "Now I remember. You saved my life in Africa. At that stream. Keep your voice down and do not mention any nonsense about me being your brother. Those soldiers standing behind you will not understand. Such talk will anger them."

Yankah said in reply, "It is good that you remember. The woman was my sister and the man I killed was another Fanti priest. A stranger trespassing in our territory. Like you he came across her on the riverbank. Unlike you, his mind was poisoned with thoughts of rape and murder. You gave her protection with your body. Not many white men would do that."

His sister! Now this announcement and blaming that native for ruining her wash day was unexpected. Yankah must have thought the dead native was up to some Voodoo. A rape session followed by turning her into a zombie. Then Crink played the hero and threw himself between her and the attacker. This could be useful. Cynical. But sometimes you just have to shrug your shoulders and run with whatever rubbish floats your way.

"No one should force himself on a woman. Whatever her colour. It was outrageous conduct," I said harshly.

For a few seconds we stared at each other. Then it hit me.

Once we had gone our separate ways Yankah's sister would have explained what had really gone on. She was a blood relative therefore her word would be accepted as the truth. Yankah must know that the native with the spear protruding out of his back had been trying to protect her from me. So why the pretence then that I was her would be rescuer? All I could come up with on the spur of the moment was my suggestion to Yankah, should he ever cross the Atlantic, that I would find him work with my father. Coincidently bumping into me here in camp and thinking quickly on his feet, Yankah was putting down roots in an attempt at building a relationship. Putting it another way, one good turn deserves another. After all he had saved my life. So I owed him one. Looking for an easy life wasn't Bocor thinking. It was common sense.

Or had he thrown the dead man's bones and foreseen he would sail across the Atlantic and become a slave? Which possibly meant that our meeting was not accidental. A worrying thought and mentally I shuddered at being beholden to this Voodoo priest and what he might have in mind. Like a vulture eyeing the innards of a dead cow, Yankah looked at my waist belt and whispered, "Aidoo is still with you. That is good."

"Tried a couple of times to open the pouch but those drawstrings are tied tighter than a nun's underwear," I said grimly.

It was the strangest thing. On those occasions when I tried to open Aidoo's pouch I found it impossible to untie the drawstrings. And when I persevered my arm would freeze. No matter how much I wrestled with that pouch I could not open it or separate it from the belt. Damn thing stayed put, part of my daily baggage: belt with revolver, ammunition, knife, and Aidoo's pouch. In Tombstone, Arizona, a Jesuit missionary performed an exorcism over it. Unfortunately that ritual rebounded when the priest suddenly flew backwards and landed beneath the wheels of a passing stagecoach. For me religious ceremonies are a waste of time. It's the same with so called 'charms', whether rabbits feet, saints toenails, or the Christian cross. They appeal to the gullible and those insecure enough to believe that they can provide protection from life's calamities. My opinion; they are of no more use than a one-legged man in an ass-kicking contest.

It was time to move on. I said, "Don't think me ungratefulYankah. But what happened in Africa was a long time ago. Ah am a busy man and shortly we may have to fight a battle. Best if you leave and go about your duties." A sudden thought made me pause and add in a whisper, "Before you go ah would be mighty obliged if you could remove Aidoo's pouch from my belt. Ain't done me any favours."

Yankah whispered in reply, "My brother. In the name of Aidoo's spirit ah want satisfaction of your obligation to me. Our gods have decided that you must help our cause. We must win this war. Slavery must end. To assist us, Aidoo remains with you."

It's not every day you hear that kind of rubbish talked. Yankah made it sound as if there was some dark and mysterious plan involving me in playing a major part in winning the war. How in the Hell could I do that? I could shoot a few Rebs but that wouldn't make much difference. There were too many. Even marching Confederates past in columns of threes, with me shooting as they went, I could never get rid of them all. They would breed so fast at the end of the queue it would be an unending quest.

Yankah stood, head cocked to one side, silently watching my face. Deep cunning and canyon-wide intelligence flickered in his eyes and, it has to be said, a sliver of aggression. The moment was broken by Private Aster. Ambling forward he stopped a few feet from me and, cradling his rifle across his chest, looked at my 'slave brother' and with a slow shake of his head asked in a puzzled drawl. "Captain Crink. Did ah hear this slave say that he was your brother. Was he being disrespectful to you?"

Aster's intervention moved this situation to a more worrying level.

I answered with what I hoped was an acceptable lie. "This slave recognised me. Couple of years ago he belonged to my father. He's lazy and sleepy, so we sold him to a tobacco boss hereabouts. Wants to know if ah can help find his brother. He's an officer's servant somewhere in our camp."

Staring with a distrustful look in his eyes Aster pointed a stubby finger at Yankah and asked, "Who might you belong to?"

Loud and shrill Aster's voice was thick with menace, bringing an air of tenseness to our little group. An act of unpleasantness loomed. Things could get nasty if Aster and the rest of the company thought a slave had been acting above his station with me. The fact that I was also a Confederate army officer, therefore a man worthy of respect in these soldiers' eyes, could make things worse. Time to move things along. Fast. Speaking in an impatient manner I said, "Private Aster, don't delay the slave. If we keep him any longer his owner will send out a search party. Time to send him on his way."

Aster was not easily put off. "Maybe he's looking for some extra work Captain. Company could do with help, cooking and cleaning."

I had to keep Yankah out of the company's clutches. Voodoo is severely frowned upon and if they found out that he was a Voodoo priest they might string him up. Or worse, they might find Aidoo's pouch and lynch me as well! Further lying was out. Only the truth would do, so I went for it.

Chapter Sixteen

"Ah would not want this man working for the company. Ah did not want to admit it, but ah owe him. Years ago he saved mah life when we were shackling slaves in West Africa. If he wants a new owner, reckon he should work just for me," I said and mentally crossed my fingers that this explanation would stop Aster's questions.

It worked. Aster's expression relaxed and, grinning from one earlobe to the other, he about faced and yelled, "Boys. This here slave saved the Captain's life. In a place called Africa."

"Where's Africa?" muttered a voice from a gaggle of avidly watching soldiers.

Another soldier, barefoot and scratching at a straggly beard, said. "Way east of Richmond. Somewhere near Florida. Ah guess."

A tall gangly youth with trousers a size too big and tied in the middle with twine put in, "Ah have never spoken to a slave. None worked on our farm. Ah am real curious to know where they come from. Heard campfire talk in Texas that this Africa place is south of here, past New Orleans. Sail in any direction for a couple of months and you'll find it. Full of plantations. Natives singing as they pick cotton. Dancing and playing drums, getting drunk, eating raw meat and sleeping on rocks and wood. Am ah right, Captain?"

Before I could answer another soldier, sitting outside a tent washing his feet in a bowl of gray scummy water, shouted. "Naw, you fool. Ain't no place called Africa. Met an old sailor called 'Blind Doc' White in Nevada City during the '49gold rush. Did lots of slave runs. According to him Africa is a made up name. He said sail south of

Dixie for a year and you come to England. That's where you find slaves. You must know that, Captain Crink. Hey, you ever meet 'Doc White' in this Africa place?"

At this point, not wanting to get into a discussion about geography of which I knew little, I tried to lighten the moment by butting in with, "Of course there's a place called Africa. Lose this war and old daddy Lincoln will send us there. Swap us for more blacks. Better behaved than us Southern boys."

Here I crossed my fingers that nobody would ask how Yankah had saved my life. It worked. To a man they were laughing and nodding their heads in agreement. After a moment Sergeant Smith stepped out of the shadows of a tent opening and settled the debate with, "Let's just say Africa is way east of here. And you get to go across a sea to go there. Ain't no sailors in this company, so none of you will ever visit there. Let's get back to cleaning rifles."

Out of the corner of my eye I noticed Yankah ambling away, which was a relief. Likewise in ones and twos, some deep in conversation, others vacant faced and probably wondering what the discussion had been about, my soldiers returned to their tents. When only Smith and myself were left the Sergeant stared down the track where Yankah had disappeared and said, "Sir, it would have been better to have threatened to kick that slave's ass to a city in the South. Rather than Washington. Guys might wonder. You being an Alabama man an' all."

"Don't miss much Sergeant."

"Goes with the job, Captain." He thought for a moment then went on in a low voice, "Sir, ah really don't give a monkey's tail which way a man's sympathies lean. Just so long as he does his job when the bullets start flying and men start dropping."

"Ah am with you on that," I answered in a similar low voice.

Smith said goodnight with a finger to the brim of his hat and a loud, "Good hunting sir."

I did not reply. It is a recognised rule that sergeants have the last word whatever army they serve in. As I wandered back to my tent I wondered what quirk of fate had brought Yankah to this part of Virginia then, with a start, I found my hand touching Aidoo's pouch. Glancing sheepishly around I muttered under my breath, "Should maybe find me another Jesuit. Could be the first one made a mistake and said the wrong words during that eviction ritual against Yankah's mother-in-law."

Pausing for a moment I glanced again at the pouch then continued, "Maybe thousands of slaves in Africa and America carrying pouches inhabited by relatives they want rid of. Priest succeeds in throwing Aidoo onto the street, word will spread. Crink's mother-in-law eviction ritual. Could be a dollar earner."

As I finished speaking something stirred inside Yankah's pouch and a stab of pain hit my forehead. What followed made me skip backwards as, into my mind, came the image of a ceremonial African tribal mask. I recognised it from my 'business' visits to West Africa. Its eyes were a pair of red hot points burning with an intensity that grew in size until all I could see was a vision of churning fire. Terrified I covered my face, which was pointless, the damned thing was inside my head.

The apparition ended with five words crashing from side to side inside my skull. "Obey the gods. Obey Aidoo."

Such pain in my head. Now I knew how cattle feel when hit with a branding iron. Yet, as quickly as it arrived the interference inside my skull disappeared. Anxious, head down, I marched back to my tent. As I moved I could feel something chipping at the back of my mind, something I couldn't quite focus on, a black cloud of memory that hovered and wanted to reveal itself; to be understood. It concerned something Yankah had said during our meeting all those years ago in Africa. But I was damned if I could remember what. At the tent entrance I was distracted by the sound of energetic scrubbing. Inside I found Yankah holding one of my boots in one hand and a small cleaning brush in the other. My second boot stood nearby. Both were covered in the usual mix of mud and horseshit. Yankah's presence filled me to the brim with anger but, remembering my recent head pain, I controlled myself and quietly said, "Yankah, why are you cleaning mah boots?"

"Need cleaning, Captain."

"Ah thought you agreed to return to performing your duties?"

"Sure did. And here I am. Tending to your equipment. Boots need cleaning, which you ain't been doing. Next I will wash your shirts and clean the tent.

"Whoa, now just hold on a moment. Ah do not want your owner charging around here, raising the roof of mah leaky tent with harsh words because he thinks that ah have stolen you."

"Won't happen."

"Why's that?"

"Ain't on any owner's list in the South. Escaped. Find my name on a reward poster dated March 1855. Forty dollars offered for an escaped slave called Cronkiss Brink."

"Stupid as that name sounds, it's a bit close to my own," I snarled.

"Captain, when I arrived in America I decided to adopt a western name. So gave myself something similar to your own. Shows affinity between us. After all we are blood brothers." After wagging an admonishing finger he went on, "And you did say that if I ever came to America, to look you up."

Yankah had me there. My big mouth was in danger of having me disinherited and disowned by an unbelieving and unforgiving, father. The rest of the Crink clan would then pat father on the back and hold out a hand for my inheritance to be diverted into their sweaty palms.

"You must have been brought to the States on a slaver?"

"Certainly was. But salvation came when me and six others were taken north to Philadelphia by Miss Minty in '55."

"Who?"

"Miss Araminta Ross. Underground railroad's famous 'conductor'. Now married and called Mrs Harriet Tubman."[61]

My initial irritation had cooled and I said in an admiring tone, "Yep, heard of Mrs Tubman. Mighty brave lady. Made fools of plenty plantation owners and vigilante gangs. Caught conducting slaves north she would probably have been killed out of hand. You work the same plantation as her?"

"No. Miss Minty slaved in Dorchester County, Maryland. I worked a plantation in South Carolina. She went north six years before me, in '49. Couple of years ago she recruited me to work in her 'railroad'; mighty dangerous occupation. But each slave we move north is one worker less in Hell." Sticking his head out of the tent he checked no one had wandered within earshot then went on, "Couple of days ago I hid in the false bottom of a wagon and moved south. Dropped off a few miles away. Moved at night to Winchester before strolling into your camp. Thousands of people, black and white, milling around so one more black man don't excite attention. Easy searching you out as well."

"Let me guess. Aidoo helped locate me," I said sarcastically.

"Learning fast, Captain."

Should I believe him? Or was he being mischievous?

Stroking my chin I asked, "You a spy, Yankah?"

Yankah proudly replied in a low voice, "Captain Crink, I serve the Northern lawyer."

Now that was a conversation stopper. There was only one lawyer that expression could refer to; Abraham Lincoln. But Yankah needed to be told that speaking in such a voice about the northern lawyer was, to Southern ears, almost an admission of being a spy. "Not so loud Yankah. Careful what you say. Lincoln ain't exactly popular around here." After a pause to think I went on, "What do you want from me?"

"Captain Crink, I am Mister Pinkerton's go-between. You discover Confederate plans, write them down, and I send a message North."

Surprised at this unexpected revelation I hollered back, "So you're Pinkerton's contact man?"

It was Yankah's turn to remonstrate. "Easy there." He paused before saying with a thin smile, "Let's just say I work for a man who speaks with an accent stranger than my own. And like me he comes from across the sea.

"Pinkerton is from a place called Scotland. Don't ask me where it is. Ah have heard it's a province of England. And they own half the world. Could be anywhere between here and China. Wherever that is." Glancing nervously around went on, "How will you contact Pinkerton?"

Waving my boot in the air he replied, "If you wanted to transmit a message today you write it down on a sheet of paper and drop it inside one of your boots. I retrieve it when I clean them. Translate it into disguised words and walk out of camp and pass it to one of my men hunkered down nearby."

"Then what? He jumps on a horse and gallops to Washington?"

"No. Have to be careful of Confederate patrols. A rider or someone on foot can be caught. Could be a message need passing quickly. We use drums. Hollowed out logs. Hit them with wooden hammers. Long and short sounds. High tones and low tones. Log drumming is an old African skill and can be heard up to twenty miles away. A skill I have taught other slaves. African trackers find Confederate army camps and a pair of drummers hide nearby and wait for spies in the camp to smuggle out messages. This information is sent down a line of drummers stationed every ten miles or so until it reaches the nearest Union army camp. Mister Pinkerton has a drummer and one of his detectives attached to army units in Union territory. From here the message travels to Washington by horse and rider. When a Confederate unit moves camp my trackers will follow. Logs yoked across shoulders my drummers go with them." Smiling wryly Yankah carried on, "African slaves have lots of experience carrying lumps of wood across their necks."

Returning his wry grin I asked in a surprised tone, "How long has this been going on?"

"Just getting started, Captain. At this moment there are drummers and trackers north of here on a training exercise watching this camp. First to be deployed."

"Sounds dangerous work. How do your men move around? On foot or horse?"

"Open countryside they travel by horse and at night. Rough country and forests, on foot. It's unlikely that they will be noticed. Moving unseen is easy for anyone with experience of tracking in the African bush."

After glancing towards some nearby trees I frowned and asked, "A disguised message? How's that done?"

"It's called a code. We use a book written by a clever Englishman."

"An English codebook?"

Once again he surprised me with, "No, a book of stories and theatre plays by Mister William Shakespeare. Any book can be used. The code is formed from words taken out of his book. These are written down in number form and sent as a message."

"Sounds complicated. But ah have heard of William Shakespeare. Famous writer. Ain't read any of his stories though. How come you use him?"

"My master at the plantation that I worked in South Carolina was a good man. As far as slave owners go. But he had a difficult daughter, Miss Annie. Wasn't much interested in education. Only wanted to chase boys, throw rocks at us slaves, and beat us with sticks. On Miss Annie's birthday my master gave her Mister Shakespeare's book. Hoped she would learn something from it. Short while later a local white boy made Miss Annie pregnant. She was mighty angry. Nearest thing to her throwing hand was Mister Shakespeare's book. She grabbed it, screamed she hated it, and couldn't understand anything in it. Then threw it through a window. Part of my routine was following Miss Annie around. Carrying shopping, collecting things she dropped, tidying up after her. Reckon Miss Annie didn't want the book no more, so I picked it up and took it to Mister Roberts, her father. He didn't read very well, so gave the book to me."

"How does this code and Mister Shakespeare's book pan out?"

Yankah thought for a moment then continued, "To put a message into code I pick a page at random from his book. That page number is the first thing sent. For instance we might send page 49. If the first word of the message is 'Confederate', I find a word in page 49 that begins with the letter 'C'. I note what line that word is in. If the word is in the third line down, I then put down the number 3. Then count along line three and note what position the word beginning with 'C' is in. For instance the word could be the fifth word along line 3. Ah then put the number 5. To send the letter 'C' we drum 49-3-5."

Yankah then pulled a pencil and a piece of paper out of his pocket and wrote down:- 49 = Page number; 3 = Third line; 5 = Position of the word in line 3.

Holding up the piece of paper Yankah pointed at the numbers and said, "Like this. The rest of the words in the message will be sent in the same way. Easy code to understand. Easy code to send for the drummers."

"Seems long-winded. Could be drumming a long time."

"It is. But we drum fast. Secret is, keep the message short."

"What happens when the numbers are received in Washington?"

"Using another copy of Mister Shakespeare's book a Pinkerton detective changes the numbers back into letters of the alphabet. Only way Confederates can read the code is if they know we are using that particular book."

For a moment I stared at him then said, "Using those drums is mighty impressive. But noisy. Only needs a slave working for the South, who understands your drums, to mention it to an officer. Once the Confederates are told the drumming consists of only numbers they will realise it's a secret communication system. Search parties will be sent out. They find the drummers, torture will discover the code. Let's hope there ain't any traitors in your team."

"The drummers are unaware the code is based on a book. Only person that knows is me. And only important or urgent messages will be sent. Anyway noise is difficult to pinpoint, especially at night and we only drum for short periods. Maximum fifteen minutes. If the full message is not finished in this time the drummer moves to a new location. Hopefully messages will be few. Besides not many Africans are sympathetic to the Confederate cause, Captain."

"Who decides if a message is important or urgent?"

Staring intently at me Yankah replied, "You do."

"You get caught with that Shakespeare book and Confederate signals officers will be mighty suspicious. Must be unique for a slave to carry that around. Find out what's going on, they'll shoot you," I said quietly.

"Captain, that's the price of freedom."

Thinking deeply, impressed with Yankah's brave statement, I dug my top teeth into my bottom lip and started to nod my head in agreement. An unusual mood for me. Perhaps I wasn't all bad back then? Then again maybe Yankah had caught me in a weak moment? Thoughts that swiftly left me as, from somewhere deep inside my head a bad feeling began to scratch at my memory lockers, making the fingers of both hands beat against my thighs. That earlier feeling had returned; Yankah had said something disquieting when saving my life in Africa. Suddenly it hit me with a force that snapped my head back. When Yankah and his sister had disappeared into the jungle, he had called me 'Mister Crink'.

How the hell did he know my name? We'd never met before that day of horror.

"Maybe it was Yankah's mother-in-law. Interfering cow," I whispered.

Immediately followed by the thought of how ridiculous I was getting hooked on this Voodoo business. I had probably misheard or imagined Yankah mentioning my name. Of course try as I might those imps of doubt that afflict us all sometime during our lives would not go away. But it was a mind churning thought that Yankah knew who I was all those years ago. And certainly it seemed that Yankah and his mother-in-law were firmly anchored in my head. This was confirmed when, realising that I had just called Aidoo an 'interfering cow', I glanced warily at her pouch. Nothing stirred. She had to be a good age. Maybe it was afternoon nap time? Could Aidoo have a sense of humour. Or was she in a good mood. (Thus does madness arrive.)

My ruminations were interrupted by Yankah who asked, "What was that Captain?"

"Talking to mahself. Wondering if it ain't time to bed down. Been a long day."

"Me too Captain. Before I go, Mister Shakespeare has descriptions for plenty of situations we meet in life. Got one here for war. Maybe cheer your soldiers on. Want to hear it?"

"Go ahead. Words don't hurt the pocket none."

"Comes from a play called Henry the Fifth. Goes like this: 'But when the blast of war blows in our ears, then imitate the tiger. Stiffen the sinews. Conjure up the blood. Disguise fair nature with hard favoured rage.' That sound a good way to prepare for what's coming Captain Crink?"

"Sure does."

With a wintry smile he nodded, turned, and walked away.

I looked at the lines of tents belonging to our 33rd Virginia Regiment. Hundreds of Southern soldiers preparing themselves for the coming fight. Most going about their business with a grin or whistling happily to themselves. Ready to stand alongside the Conderate flag and declare they wanted to see action before the bugle calls time on the proceedings. It wouldn't be long before their initial bubble of cheerful eagerness was burst.

I was no different. It was wishful thinking but into my mind came the thought that surely there would be quick charge from the north sending the Confederates reeling back to Richmond and it would all be over. Six or seven months should see it finished and I could return to Washington and collect my money.

Christmas at the latest.

Amen to that.

Chapter Seventeen

At dawn on the 18th July I heard a heart stopping shout: "Git ready 33rd Virginee. We are leaving Winchester."

Wearing only a towel I hurried outside the tent and, guessing that a nearby jogging corporal was doing the shouting, I stopped him and asked, "What's going on soldier?"

Spitting out a stream of liquid chewing tobacco, which landed across my bare feet, the soldier inhaled deeply and replied, "We're marching."

"Where to?"

Looking me up and down and obviously not impressed with the fact that I was wearing only a towel he asked with narrowed eyes, "Who are you? Ah been told to be careful who ah speak to. Could be federal spies hereabouts."

Little did he know.

"Captain Cornelius Crink, 33rd Virginia Regiment. With Jackson's Brigade," I replied in a low, conspiratorial voice.

Seemingly satisfied he answered, "Orders from Brigadier Jackson, sir." After spitting out another lump of liquid tobacco across my feet he added with Blue Ridge mountain man logic, "We're leaving camp. Marching backwards."

With a vision in my head of thousands of soldiers facing the wrong way and walking heel first out of camp I said, "What the hell are you on about? You saying we're about to retreat?"

Rolling his eyes the soldier said loudly, "That's right. Ain't moving forwards. So we're going backwards." With a sniff he added, "Be better if you washed your ears out on a morning, Captain."

Having clarified what the soldier meant, I smiled. Good news at last. What was not so good was the tobacco dribbling between my toes. Glancing down I grumbled, "Soldier, any thoughts about this mixture of tobacco and mouth moisture on my feet?"

Following my glance he replied, "Good stuff sir. When mah sergeant spit out his chew ah collected the tobacco and cleaned away the mud and horseshit. Then took a chew of it. Still some strength in it though. If you're short of tobacco, here's mah spoon. Scoop a mouthful." After patting me on a shoulder he added further mountain man logic, of the legal variety this time, "Ah don't mind none. Sorta lost ownership when it hit your feet."

"No thanks. Never been partial to chewing tobacco mixed with mud and horseshit. Anyway, how do you shout and chew tobacco at the same time?"

"Wedge it agin mah cheek. Then holler. Practice a while. It's easy."

With a sigh and clap on the soldier's back and a resigned, "Course it is. Miracle you don't choke," I sent him, shouting his message, on his way.

The day got worse. Yankah appeared as I was hauling on my boots and whispered, "Captain, important information from a slave who helps groom Brigadier Jackson's horse. We're not retreating. Moving out to fight. At a place called Manassas."

So much for the notion of moving 'backwards' to a safer location.

Yankah's message had to be one of the most dispiriting messages I ever received. Up there with being told that Abilene's 'Bouncing Jenny' had died from a strange disease and anyone who had been entertained by her over the previous year needed to see a doctor for treatment with the latest remarkable disease curing snake oil. (She was one of those 'savvy' business orientated people who provided a mobile brothel in her 'Prairie Schooner'[62] covered wagon on the Oregon Trail.)

Yankah went on, "Sounds important, Captain. Time for our first message? Maybe a few words such as: 'Confederate force marching eighteen July to Manassas.' Might help the North prepare a battle plan."

Yankah's suggestion made sense.

"Yep. Got to start sometime. Risky though. Its daylight. But if your drummers are well hidden then go ahead. Send a message. Use the words you just mentioned. Be careful. Once you start every ear around here will be listening and these Confederate boys will not begin dancing to the tune your drummers bang out. Curiosity will send them searching. Looking for the owners of the hands making the noise."

I must admit at the back of my mind I was half hoping that Yankah and the rest of his African drumming band would get caught. It would remove one almighty burr on my ass; my 'blood brother' Yankah. Which would leave his mother-in-law to be sent packing from my waist belt.

"Yankah ah do not know from where the Confederate force will march on Manassas. Nor how many troops will comprise the force. Which could mean Union headquarters, hoping for further information, will dither and delay taking action and end up not doing anything until it is too late."

"Could be right, Captain."

What a situation. If Captain Cornelius Crink sent a message the advantage in this coming battle could shift to the South and it was too late to do anything about it. Best if the Union leaders made their own decisions. Mentally crossing my fingers I reasoned that our messaging service would improve over time. (Hopefully before the Confederate flag flew over the White House.)

"Reckon we'll leave things as they are. You agree."

There was no reply. Yankah had gone. Silently vanishing into the surrounding countryside.

Within thirty minutes of Yankah's disappearance came the sound of drums. A strange noise that quickly grew on me. It almost made me want to grab Jack and start dancing. The effect on passing soldiers and slaves was even stranger. Trying to locate the source of the drumming I watched heads being scratched and eyes gazing around and about, then upwards, until with indifferent shrugging of shoulders and puzzled head shaking they returned to what they were doing. Turned out, so I later learned, that this was the effect throughout the camp.

After the drumming stopped I wondered if Yankah had ignored me and sent a warning North. Or had he merely given his drummers a bit of a practice run and sent a line or two of gibberish from Mister Shakespeare's book? Yankah later told me that did indeed drum a practice run, sending a fictional account of General Jackson rising at dawn to sacrifice a slave to Voodoo gods. Which would have had them scratching their heads in Union army headquarters. A sense of humour was absent from most generals in those early days of the war.

On that day, the 18th of July 1861, we marched out of Winchester.

Jackson's Virginian Brigade moved first. And, typical Jackson, we moved at speed. So fast that we left our tents for the troops who followed behind to gather and carry to Manassas on our behalf. Being under the impression we were retreating meant my company were an unhappy looking bunch as, in company with the rest of the

Confederate army in Winchester, they wanted to fight Yankees. Not producing painful blisters trundling aimlessly around Virginia.

Although a battlefield scenario was about to happen I later learned that for security reasons only senior officers knew our march was not a retreat but, in reality, we were moving to support Beauregard at Manassas. Plus of course myself, Yankah, and the slave who brushed Jackson's horse. Turned out that Jackson's horse brusher also whispered our real destination to every slave he came across. Meaning word swiftly spread to hundreds of slaves who worked in the brigade. You have to shake your head. The camp slaves knew more about was going on than us soldiers. Mind you, I can't say that I was happy with this knowledge. As I found out too much brooding on what was about to come can cause eye watering headaches.

During a rest period, after putting a fair number of miles under our boots and coating our lungs with dust, Brigadier Jackson announced that in fact we weren't retreating but marching to confront and fight Union troops advancing on Manassas. As word spread tired faces smiled and dust covered hands slapped backs. A situation best put by Jackson himself who commented that when the Virginians heard this news: "The soldiers rent the air with shouts of joy." (Hey, I know one who didn't.) Brigadier Jackson also read aloud General Johnston's orders;[63] "Our gallant army under Brigadier General Beauregard is now attacked by overwhelming numbers. The commanding general hopes that his troops will step out like men and make a forced march to save the South."

Jackson saw himself setting forth on a messianic mission hurrying us on our way to 'smite' Lincoln's invading heathen northern hordes. And those words certainly roused 33rd Virginian Regiment, sending it marching with renewed vigour eastward. Statistically we marched seventeen miles to the railhead at Paris. Followed by a rest then a six mile march to Piedmont where we would take a freight train and ride the final thirty-four miles on the Manassas Gap railroad. It was a tiring journey and, not surprisingly, the troops enthusiasm waned when wading across the Shenandoah. Even in July that water was cold. It was dark when we crossed the river which worried some of the more military experienced men, who complained an ambush would see us shot before we even saw the opposition. But we kept going until the early hours of the next day until our Brigadier rewarded us with a rest period. We collapsed into an exhausted sleep. One story has it that while we slept Jackson kept watch. I doubt that this story came from anyone who was on that march. Nobody would have been awake to notice what our commander was up to.

War plans and the current strategic situation along the Bull Run river did not greatly concern soldiers of the 33rd Virginia Regiment. But the weather did. Marching in that July heat to the railroad at Piedmont our only interests were water and food and we grumbled long and loud that our tired legs and aching feet needed rest. But Jackson drove us on until further hard marching saw us arrive, at dawn, at Piedmont. Here we thankfully boarded railway wagons for the remainder of our journey.

Looking at a map of Virginia, any gumboil can see Manassas is an important rail junction. The Orange and Alexandria railroad chugs its way from Manassas to the Confederate capital at Richmond and meets the Manassas Gap railroad as it wanders west to the Shenandoah. Manassas was, in both Union and Confederate army terms, a junction of strategic importance. In those early days before the shooting started in earnest, as the two opposing armies converged on Manassas, similar thoughts on strategy must have stirred in the minds of Presidents Lincoln and Davis. Such as Manassas was twenty-six miles south-west of Washington and any delay in organising and dispatching Union forces to confront the Confederacy would allow Beauregard time to spy the land between his positions on the Bull Run and be ready for an attack. Raising fears that Lincoln's army could be ambushed and potentially leaving the route to Washington open and unguarded. Followed by the nightmare of Confederate forces spitting on their hands, hitching up their trousers, shouldering arms, and marching on the White House. With the possibility of it being burnt to the ground for a second time.[64]

Switching directions. Gazing north and seeing the situation out of Confederate eyes those twenty-six miles between the opposing flags had to set President Davis's innards rumbling. If the Confederacy lost this first battlefield encounter Union forces could dash a path through Virginia straight to Richmond and strangle the Confederacy at birth. In reality the two presidents were in similar political situations. Both had only been in post for a short time and, depending on who was displaying an inane grin on top of the body pile when this war finished, ultimately one of them would become a former President. It was a hand wringing, nervous thought. Davis had the most to worry about. The North could, in theory, sling him into the slammer and put him on trial for treason. Davis could spend a long time in jail; highly unlikely but possible. One day strutting around as President of the Confederacy; the next in a cell yelling at rats instead of generals. Cynics might say there's little difference between the two. If Davis won the war and marched his army into Washington then, unless he was wise enough to build bridges by offering

Lincoln a heavyweight political job, then Lincoln would probably retire. An undignified scuttle back to Illinois to dig vegetables and read law books. Almost as boring as sitting in a rocking chair on the porch watching the sun go down. (Hey, it drops over the horizon every day. See it once is enough.)

Although most of us didn't realise it at the time, win or lose at Manassas, Davis never envisaged invading an economically stronger north. Rather he wanted to keep the federal army at bay and gradually wear Lincoln's forces down and wait, hopefully, for foreign intervention on the South's behalf. England in particular. A lot of cotton was exported to English mills and, not wanting their supply of fluffy white gold cut off, the Confederacy reasoned that England would come to the South's assistance. If asked I would have told Davis that after fighting two wars against the United States, England would not want a third. For me it would stand on the side-lines and declare a non-interventionist line in respect of both North and South, then secretly sell goods to both. A policy to be adopted until it was known which side won the war then support the victorious side.

Interestingly, in February 1863, the Charleston Mercury owner Robert Barnwell Rhett allowed me read a note given to him by Robert Bunch,[65] England's recently departed Consul in Charleston. It was a copy of what Viscount Palmerston, England's Prime Minister, had written to his Foreign Office on 20th October 1861. It succinctly summed up England's fence sitting policy: "It is in the highest degree likely that the North will not be able to subdue the South, and it is no doubt certain that if the Southern Union is established as an independent State it would afford a valuable and extensive market for British Manufacturers, but the operations of the war have as yet been too indecisive to warrant an acknowledgment of the Southern Union."

In Dixie-speak Palmerston said: "Reckon those Southern boys won't be licked. But just in case they are, we'll smile and wink at both sides until we know for sure who's spurs are jingling in the winner's corral." British policy was the cynical way of the world: 'a foot in both camps until one side pulls up the tent pegs, cuts the guy ropes, then scuttles over the horizon'; duplicitous or what? In the cynical nineteenth century I reckon that was a magnificent policy. In a three words: 'Double deal everybody.' In fact they've been doing that to the world for over a thousand years. Which I agree wholeheartedly with. Why fold a winning hand?

We arrived clattering into the rail junction at Manassas, if memory serves me right, early afternoon on Saturday the 20th July 1861, behind rail engines belching black smoke, hissing steam, clanking wheels and transporting our brigade of two thousand six hundred bloodthirsty Virginians, four artillery cannon, and noisy wind emitting me. We were sent to the right of the Confederate forces close to Blackburn and Mitchell's Ford on the Bull Run river. A few days earlier there had been skirmishes in this area and I felt the atmosphere change as my soldiers, looking thoughtful, stared at the loose earth covering former comrades. For a short while the winds of war ceased blowing in their sails. I had seen plenty of soldiers graves in Mexico, theirs and ours, but you never get used to them, especially when they contain people you know. One minute talking of home, wives and children, or lady friends they want to get to know better; occasionally singing quietly, some playing a musical instrument that can fit into a pocket, or just sitting staring into space. All soldiers are the same and whenever I see a grave it makes me reflect on the fleeting nature of time and the unwanted thought arrives: 'that could shortly be me.'

Sergeant Smith caught the mood when he ambled up and, pointing at a grave, said in a sombre voice, "I have seen enough of one war never to wish to see another."

"Very thoughtful Sergeant Smith," I replied in a similar tone.

"Not a quote from my head, Captain. That was President Thomas Jefferson."

With a wry smile I replied, "Sergeant Smith, we were both in the Mexican fight. And here we are, about to partake in another."

"Hopefully it will end soon, Captain."

"Amen to that."

I couldn't have summed it up better than those six words from my sergeant.

For our brigade the Battle of First Manassas began on Sunday the 21st July. Sunday being a day that Brigadier Jackson did not, in the manner of a rabid Christian that he was, want to make war. For him the day should be spent on your knees in church. It was also his wife's thirtieth birthday. But he was a faithful soldier who knew that his duty lay, not only to God, but to the Confederacy as well; and a battle beckoned. For those who have never experience war the following is a description of what all men, and women, have felt wherever they fought and in whatever war they took part in.

When involved in a battle your experiences and recollections are limited to your immediate vicinity. What is happening to your left and right, the good Lord not having given us eyes like a lizard, is usually a mystery. In particular you see what is to the front of your position, invariably meaning you are staring at a section of the enemy's defensive line or, God forbid, a mass of bayonet fixed charging troops. Occasionally, assuming gunpowder from cannons and rifle smoke is not too dense, anxious turns of the head will provide a sight of what your nearest neighbours are doing. But what is happening to the rest of your army or the enemy's formations, rarely can anything be seen. Many soldiers, including myself, have read later accounts of where they fought and scratched their heads wondering if they were in another battle, in another place, on another day. The bigger the battle you're in, the less you see of it. Only birds can see the whole of what is going on.

And from start to finish that state of ignorance was First Manassas.

Jackson had already foreseen the problems of different coloured uniforms in the chaos of our forthcoming battle. Even Jackson was wearing the blue uniform of his previous position at the Virginia Military Institute. To help recognise soldiers from our brigade he ordered white strips of cloth to be tied around our hats. While readying our company for what was to come, as usual, Sergeant Smith neatly summed it up with: "In battle thousands of men do their own thing. Surrounded by the bangs and crash of cannons and rifle fire, yelled commands, shouts of pain, and soldiers rushing by going to somewhere you can't see and you will wonder should I be running with them. Don't agonise about it. Just stand fast and watch and listen for your officer's commands. In the overall battle who is doing what, where they are doing it, and which side is winning the fight will be difficult, if not impossible, to know. All you can do is shoot the first son of a bitch who points a rifle at you."

My recollection of that hot Sunday when Jackson took the Virginians into battle is 'noise and confusion.' Such as

Beauregard riding around sending orders and messages telling his brigade commanders what he wanted them to do. Unfortunately this added to the ongoing bedlam on the battlefield caused by inexperienced officers and men who were struggling to understand what was going on. A lot of Beauregard's information either did not arrive where it should have or went to the wrong place. Worse, on occasions, Beauregard even forgot to communicate information to troops in the front line.

Once again Sergeant Smith dryly summed up First Manassas with the later sarcastic comment, "It would have helped if Brigadier Beauregard knew the location of his troops and what they were doing."

Turned out our brigade's major clash with the North would be at Henry Hill when we went to the assistance of three other Confederate Brigades. Henry Hill is named after the Henry family who lived in a farmhouse on the hill and were represented in the property that morning by Judith Henry, a bedridden eighty-five-year-old widow; along with her son John and daughter Ellen. The family were in an unfortunate position. Their farmhouse stood in the way of the advancing Union army's outflanking right hook. Although initially unnoticed McDowell's forces raised so much dust that eventually Confederate forces realised what was going on and the rush was on to confront the Union advance. Prior to descending on the Henry family farmhouse McDowell's troops first moved across another obstacle called Mathews Hill. Strategically located a mile to the north of Henry Hill it was here, at around nine forty five, that Union forces were challenged by South Carolinians and Louisianans from Colonel Nathan 'Shanks' Evans' 7th Brigade (I Corps). And the battle was on. Evans's men confronted the advancing Union troops and although outnumbered they plugged the gap until reinforcements arrived. In effect, for me, Evans gained the South crucial time for the major event of First Manassas. The Battle for Henry Hill.

Evans's men fought hard but were heavily outnumbered and after bitter fighting for an hour were forced to retreat. As a South Carolina man said to me after the battle: "Apart from vicious fighting we struggled with the heat and rifle powder swirling around. Most of that skirmish on Mathews Hill ah could hardly see for smoke. And ah do wonder, when thinking about those of us wearing blue, if in fact ah shot fellow Confederates by mistake. For the final ten minutes on Mathews Hill ah stopped shooting and stumbled around dizzy with thirst, searching for a friend with a canteen of water."

Even in our brigade with our white bands around our hats it was still dangerous to wear the same colour uniform as your enemy. Not that this worried Brigadier Jackson. For him prayer was the answer. Pray hard and God would watch over us; maybe even change uniforms from blue to gray. I reckon Jackson was thinking if Jesus could change water into wine then the colour of a piece of Confederate cloth should be no problem. All you had to do was pray; long and energetically. Of course nothing like that happened. Possibly the good lord was distracted by other things that day. Captain Cornelius Crink certainly was. Next into the fray were Brigadier Bee's Alabama troops along with Mississippians of 3rd Brigade (II Corps). Then Georgians of Colonel Bartow's 2nd Brigade (II Corps) joined in, but there were insufficient Confederate forces to halt the Union advance. An hour and a half later Confederate units began to pull back from Mathews Hill. A retreat that quickly turned into a rout with hundreds of troops stampeding away. Stumbling and falling, yelling and running, they fled across the Warrenton Turnpike and made their way toward a ravine east of Henry House.

As for our brigade. We began our day at First Manassas trudging around looking for someone to shoot at. Initially ordered to support Brigadier Longstreet's Brigade, close to the Bull Run river at Blackburn's Ford, Brigadier Jackson was disappointed to find nothing happening there. We then hurried away to support Brigadier Bonham and Colonel Cocke's brigades who were on our left near Mitchells Ford but, much to Jackson‘s frustration, there was nothing doing there either. So far, so good.

Then things changed; dramatically. And became not so good.

Standing, sweating, breathing hard, wondering what was going on we heard the sound of battle further over to our left. To Jackson's ears it must have sounded like a heavenly choir of avenging angels summoning him to a holy crusade. As you would expect our Brigadier did not wait for orders but moved at the double towards the clamour of war. Eventually, at around half past eleven, we arrived on the eastern side of Henry Hill and Jackson positioned us about a hundred yards from the Henry farmhouse. As soldiers from Evans, Bee, and Bartow's brigades rushed south I could see four of our six pounder artillery smoothbores in action. This battery, commanded by Captain John Imboden, was positioned close to the farmhouse and his guns were trading shots with units of Union artillery firing from Mathews Hill. Under continuous fire, Imboden later commented that the ground around his artillery unit: "Looked as though it had been rooted up by hogs." But he kept firing until the guns were down to three shells then pulled back to our lines.

For a while Imboden's artillery was the only unit pointing anything lethal towards Union troops. Our retreating infantry could only display their various sized rear ends at the enemy and according to Sergeant Smith: "During that encounter our infantry held the civil war record for the most wounds in the ass." Which with hindsight was unfair. Outnumbered and outgunned those soldiers had stood and fought as long as they could. Everybody has a breaking point. On Mathews Hill when one man turned and ran it caused a ripple effect, an infection of resolve, at first sending a trickle of men running that quickly grew into a deluge of panicking, desperate to get away soldiers.

Then our turn came.

Chapter Eighteen

For me, heroic though John Imboden's actions were in standing his ground, it was McDowell's slow moving units who lost Union forces the initiative. Maybe it was the sun's heat, or supreme confidence as they cheered and laughed at Confederate troops running from Mathews Hill, but instead of pushing forward they dithered. Instead of seizing the moment and moving forward they stood still. Maybe they thought the battle was over, or maybe they were drawing breath, composing themselves for the final push. Whatever the reason it was calamity time for the North. Their delay allowed swarms of Confederate reinforcements to come to the rescue and plug the gaps in Confederate lines. Guess who became involved in that exercise? Yep, it was our turn. Jackson's had us Virginians lined up, waiting to charge into the fray.

As we stood and waited for our brigadier to tell us what our next move would be Confederate soldiers were still escaping from the fight on Mathews Hill. A ragtag collection of panicking soldiery from the earlier brigades that had entered the fight before us scurried past in droves. Streaming through our lines; around our sides; and had it been possible would have jumped over the top of us. Some hollered that the battle was lost and lamented the dire fate of Dixie. An exhausted, hatless, hunched over soldier clasping a hand to a bloodied arm stopped opposite me and yelled, "How in the name of Hades did we get into this damnable fight. Run. Get away afore the Yankees arrive."

A situation not encouraging to us newcomers to the battlefield. (Especially me.)

Yet here Jackson showed his military skill. Instead of charging up Henry Hill to block a Union advance, ploughing through our retreating infantry in the process, he placed us out of sight among a line of pine trees a couple of hundred yards behind the forward crest leading to Henry Hill. A position of relative safety from high flying shot and shell. To do this Jackson had to swing one half of our brigade to the right and the other half to the left. Which would be a complicated manoeuvre with experienced soldiers in peace time, never mind in the middle of a battle. This positioned 33rd Virginia on the right of the brigade. We came to a watchful standstill and, thankfully, Jackson made us lie down. As is sometimes is the way of things when you don't want to be close to your commanding officer, for fear of being noticed and given a dumb order such as: "Fix bayonets and attack that fortified position over there"; somehow I unwittingly found myself and my company within reaching distance of 'Little Sorrel's stirrups. As I watched Jackson, sitting calmly on his horse, he nudged it to the ridge crest and stared intently at the Union lines about a mile away. They were too far away to shoot at accurately, and instinctively I wondered if our brigadier was contemplating a damn fool bayonet charge. That course of action was not on. I mean closing with McDowell's men would put us within spitting distance of hostile Union rifle barrels and sharpened chunks of pointed metal. Literally that could be a fatal move.

Although the situation did not look good it improved somewhat when a group of senior officers rode around in our vicinity in an effort to rally the men fleeing from Mathews Hill. Yelling at them to return to the line and fight. And to a certain extent they succeeded in whipping a lot of runaways into skirmish lines behind our Brigade. Not that many of us noticed. We were too busy staring at what was developing to our front. And nobody ever stared at anybody as anxiously as I did at Jackson that hot July day. My concentration was eventually broken when a distressed looking Brigadier Bee rode up, nodded at Jackson, and said, "General they have beaten us. Drive them back." Or something similar. That hit home. I mean what on earth was I doing here, staring at a couple of thousand Union troops, waiting for our fighting mad brigadier to give an order to set away and attack them?

A sudden increase in the distant noise of canon fire and bullets flying overhead meant that I only heard three words of Jackson's reply: "Perhaps the Bayonet."

Obviously Jackson was thinking of a charge.

I was horrified. The expression 'over my dead body' flashed inside my head. Which I instantly regretted. A frightful thought at any time but especially so when the possibility of a painful demise loomed nearby. I had to do something or else my mortal days could shortly be over. It was now or never. Striding forward I waved at Brigadier Jackson with one hand and reached out with the other towards 'Little Sorrel's bridle. My sudden movement scared the horse, causing it to lurch to one side. Turning towards me and controlling his horse at the same time, Jackson gave me a cold stare and calmly asked, "What do you want, Captain?"

Concentrating hard on what words to plead with Jackson that he should stand his ground and not charge Union lines, full of intense stress, I mixed up what I wanted to say. Unable to control my tongue I was horrified to hear myself shout, "Brigadier, use the bayonet."

Said the wrong thing there alright.

A small twitch at the corner of Jackson's mouth, indicating his equivalent of a normal person's delight at hearing something pleasant was followed by, "Captain, you are perceptive. I was wondering if that was the best tactic to use. Your suggestion has persuaded me."

That moment had to be one of the most awful in my life. My mind went numb at my abject stupidity. Then some other cowboy spoke to Jackson. My recollection is that it was Brigadier Bee who repeated what he had said earlier. "They are driving us." Followed by, "What is to be done?" That was easy. Retreat.

There was no reaction from Jackson. He ignored Bee and remained staring towards Union lines. Wild-eyed, tired and confused Bee rode away to re-join his brigade; or what was left of it. Horrified at what was about to happen because of my foolish suggestion I shouted, "Brigadier Jackson, I made a mistake. I meant to say, don't use the bayonet."

My words must have been distorted by the movement of Jackson's horse, artillery firing, rifles shots, yells and clattering wheels. Jackson raised a finger above his head and said, "I heard your excellent suggestion the first time Captain. I wait for the good lord to announce the moment."

Events overtook us. Opposing Union artillery moved first.

Jackson leaned forward. Gazing with the look of a religious fanatic, which of course he was, our brigadier had noticed something happening in Union lines. My presence and everyone else in his brigade was now irrelevant. Two artillery batteries were being moved in front of their infantry. An unusual operation. Artillery usually support infantry, here it was the other way round. These batteries were deployed into a field close to Mrs Henry's farmhouse. One was placed north of the house and the other positioned to its south. Unlimbering the guns and setting themselves up to commence firing the artillery men received a shock when rifle fire started hitting them. It looked as if Confederate infantry, decamping from Mathews Hill, had stopped running and taken refuge in Henry House and started firing at the Union guns. At first neither us, nor the Federals, knew where those shots were coming from. Eventually the Federals figured out that it must be coming from Henry House.

With practiced speed an artillery piece was manhandled into position to return the favour to the farmhouse occupants. Which they duly did. Unfortunately, bedridden Mrs Henry and her son, daughter and a servant girl were also inside the house. Even had the Union artillerymen realised those civilians were there it would not have stopped them opening fire. Once battlefield hostilities begin any civilians caught in the line of fire have to look after themselves and decisions as to leaving, or staying put, become their own responsibility. I call it 'sideshow consequences'. For Union artillerymen not to defend themselves against Confederate riflemen would demonstrate lack of military effectiveness; you have to defend your soldiers first even if it puts non-combatant civilians in danger.

And there was my unique situation. Facing two ways. Stuck bang in the middle of the Confederate 'real enemy' and about to fight on their behalf, but owing secret allegiance to the North. Unfortunately to those Union artillerymen, similar to the Henry family dilemma, anyone in a gray uniform was a target and once they had sorted out the Henry farmhouse they would turn and start shooting in my direction. Even knowing that I was on their side would not have made a 'rat's ass' difference. Surrounded by thousands of Confederate soldiers. No artillery weapon then, or now, can tell the difference between friend or foe. Be damned good if they could. (A recurring thought of mine at First Manassas.)

Such is war.

While Union artillery were banging shells at Henry House, Jackson's horse edged further away and a gap of about thirty yards opened up between myself and the Brigadier. The battlefield situation was also deteriorating. Although if you thought like Jackson, it was getting better. Someone in the Union camp had taken the initiative and decided it was time to move the battle along. Lines of their infantry began advancing past Henry House and heading towards us Virginians. Unfazed at their approach Jackson was in his element. He yelled, "All's well. Wait until the enemy get within fifty yards." Then adding after a short pause, "Then charge with the bayonet."

Which had me muttering, "Not me, Brigadier. Show me a line of retreat and your brigade will be short of at least one officer when the bugle blows tonight."

Sometimes stupidity heavily effects battles. (My mistaken advice to Jackson for one.) But the other side showed that they were not far behind in that department. At around fifty yards from the 33rd Regiment's front line, with me having difficulty in controlling my legs and bowels, the Union advance came to a standstill. Followed by shouts from Union soldiers wanting to know who we were. Their confusion caused by blue uniforms in our ranks and ignorance as to the precise location of their own units. Camp talk later described a Colonel Gorman of the Union 1st Minnesota yelling to his men not to open fire because the 33rd Virginia were 'friends'. He should have been called 'Gormless' because our retort at his misidentification came back at him in musket volleys. Needless to say, for me, this was preferable to jabbing and sparring at each other with those mini-swords stuck on the end of our rifles. Within ten minutes both sides stopped shooting and those Union forces began retreating back to their start lines. I was relieved that we did not lunge forward and set away chasing after them. That job was done by Colonel Jeb Stuart's cavalry who suddenly appeared, whooping and yelling, and rode into the fleeing Union troops.

It was here that Brigadier Bee made Civil War history. While still hunting for troops from his brigade, Bee queried the identity of a mob of soldiers milling around behind our Brigade and was told they were, one of his regiments; the 4th Alabama. Bee didn't appear too embarrassed at this 'sweat obscuring his eyes moment' because, waving and pointing his sword towards the Federals, he rallied his disorganised throng of Alabama soldiers by shouting, "Will you follow me back to the fight."

Their composure recovered, 4th Alabama, which included Jack, waved their fists and yelled that they would follow and obey Brigadier Bee's orders. But Bee wasn't finished with his confidence building. Pointing his sword towards Brigadier Jackson he hollered arguably the most famous words in the whole of the Civil War. According to the Charleston Mercury it went: "There is Jackson standing like a stone wall. Let us determine to die here, and we will conquer. Follow me."

For me, if that quotation is correct, I fail to understand how 'determining to die' would assist the Confederacy. For me, dead men rarely 'conquer.' Either Bee was tired and emotional when he said those words or the journalist who wrote that piece made it up. No doubt mother would disagree and say Jesus was murdered, but his Christian tribe prevailed and 'conquered' the minds of the ancient world.

According to Brigadier Beauregard, Bee yelled: "Look! There stands Jackson like a stone wall. Rally behind the Virginians."

Like most soldiers that day I didn't hear Bee's words. No surprise there.At the time Bee was creating Jackson's famous 'Stonewall' nickname he was charging around out of my sight. Probably somewhere behind our regiment. (A 'real' wall to take cover behind would have been more useful.) Since the war there's been talk that Bee was actually angry and being sarcastic. Bawling out that our brigadier instead of getting a move on and closing with the enemy and assisting Confederate regiments already in the battle, was doing nothing; sitting immobile on his horse; like a 'stone wall'. But for me knowing Jackson's determination to close with the enemy, preferably at the point of a bayonet, he was watching; biding his time; readying himself; judging the correct moment to enter the fight. Whatever Bee said and whatever he meant, it worked. His soldiers rallied and at the head of his 4th Alabama remnants, away went Bee, charging two Union artillery batteries on Henry Hill. Twelve guns that tore great holes in their ranks. Including Brigadier Bee who was hit and later and died of his wounds. Once again 4th Alabama made no progress and their decimated ranks about turned and retired back to Confederate lines. So without an explanation from Bee the mystery of what he meant with that famous cry of 'Stonewall' can never be known.

It must have been around this time, so I later discovered, that Brigadier Beauregard and Brigadier Johnston arrived on Henry Hill with a posse of reinforcements they had corralled on their way to join us from the Bull Run. I didn't see them. Ain't saying those two weren't there, just didn't notice them. Anyway, who would challenge our two most senior officers as to where they were during the battle? End up on a court martial for insubordination.

Then, as is often the way of things on battlefields, the situation changed again.

Arthur Cummings the 33rd Virginia's Colonel was a thorough man and had, because of the problem of the two sides wearing a variety of different coloured uniforms, devised an extra identification sign. In addition to Jackson's order to wear white strips around our hats, Cummings ordered that on confronting another soldier and were unsure as to which flag he followed, a hand was to be raised to the head and we had to shout: "Sumter." Can't remember what the reply was, logic would suggest "Fort"; but when did logic ever ring loud in the barnacle encrusted minds of the military at the beginning of Civil War hostilities? Even today, fifteen years after the war finished, I still wonder if any soldiers in our regiment shot a comrade because he was unable, in the heat and stress of battle, to remember the reply to that password. Not the kind of thing you own up to is it? After First Manassas a story circulated in Richmond that two 33rd Virginia men, who were chasing the same girl, came face to face while attending to nature behind adjoining trees. One wearing a blue uniform and the other gray. When challenged with Colonel Cumming's password by the soldier in gray, soldier blue replied sarcastically: 'Billy you know who ah am. Ah suggest you get used to the fact that 'Hognose' Kate will marry me when this war is finished. So stick that bayonet on the end of your rifle up your ass.'

His would-be rival in love allegedly replied: "That's kinda insulting Joe. And ah am looking at the wrong coloured uniform and hearing the wrong words. And as you insist on putting your arm around mah sweet Kate's waist the wrong behaviour," and then shot soldier Joe. (Pity I didn't meet anyone dressed in the wrong coloured uniform at First Manassas who I owed money to.)

And here, much to my disquiet and from lord knows where, Colonel Cummings suddenly appeared.

Unfortunately, being my commanding officer and yet another military man who had served in Mexico, Cummings was aware of my reputation as a good soldier and leader of men with the Rangers. (Anyone who served with that outfit is good for at least one free drink in most bars in the Mexican border area of the South West United States. Rumour also has it that on the anniversary of the Mexican War's end, Ranger old timers in the Alamo area are plied with drink and carried to their beds by good looking, doe-eyed women. It's a long way to go to find out if that story is true, so I cannot vouch for its veracity.) Positioning himself alongside me Cummings stared towards the Union lines until, seemingly struggling to make up his mind about something, he gave me an intense sidelong glance. I ignored him. After stroking his chin for a second or two he gave me that intense look again. Which I found worrying. What was he setting me up for? Whatever was exercising his mind I reckoned it would be something dangerous. I was about to step away and mingle amongst a gaggle of my quietly watching soldiers when Cummings decided it was time to try and move the battle along. Finger shaking with nerves or fatigue, or both, Colonel Cummings pointed at two artillery pieces moving along Union lines and said, "Crink. What are they up to? Should I move against them?"

Possibly he was caught in two minds and wanted reassurance as to what action he should take? That scenario happens a lot in life. Suppose that's why generals have chiefs of staff to turn to for advice. A reply to turn 33rd Virginia around and march them in the opposite direction would not find favour with the Colonel, but I did ponder whether to yell those words at him and damn the consequences. But before I could say anything those meandering Federal cannons started firing at nearby Confederate artillery, which in turn was followed by the sudden noisy appearance of Colonel Bill 'Extra Billy' Smith's 49th Virginia battalion. They lined up behind us and guess what happened? Yep, Smith's arriving troops caught the eye of a Union commander who ordered two artillery pieces manhandled to point in their direction. Meaning towards us. Cannons taking on infantry usually means canister shot which, even to experienced troops, can be devastating.

Turned out the 49th Virginia didn't think too much about those artillery pieces because they either moved around us, or through us, I forget which and then advanced towards them. For some reason that I've never understood those Federal cannons were suddenly turned away and began firing at our artillery again. A mistake they paid for when Colonel Smith's arriving Virginians levelled their rifles and fired a volley that blasted the attendant artillerymen and their horses. Colonel Cummings then ruined everything by yelling the command to charge. Dumbfounded at this crass order I stood my ground until sheer weight of numbers, plus choice language by some of my men to get my legs into motion, propelled me forward. I have an impossible to forget memory of 33rd Virginia, howling and screaming, running towards those artillery pieces. Later I realised that this was probably the first 'rebel yell' of the war.

Still trying to recover from the 49th's rifle fire it didn't take long for the 33rd Virginians to scatter the Union artillery survivors. Not that I took much part in this bloody bayonet brawl. After slipping on a severed forearm I pitched forward and hit my head on the barrel of a discarded rifle. Stunned, in shock, wondering what was happening a passing wild-eyed Virginian hauled me to my feet. One hand grasping my rifle and the other swatting at clouds of smoke I staggered a few yards before tripping and falling across a dead horse. This time I was pulled to my feet by Sergeant Smith who, arriving from a cloud of billowing smoke, was a familiar welcome sight. Not that he remained for long; with a yelled, "Keep going Captain," he ran towards a Union cannon abandoned a few yards away. What he intended to do with the artillery piece I was not about to hang around and find out. Mind-numbing fear was shuttling around inside my head and it was time to depart this hell hole. Which of course didn't happen. Not yet anyway.

Within seconds of my decision to quit the field with hundreds of Virginian soldiers milling around in huddled, confused pockets, and amid shouts of "Where the Hell is Colonel Cummings?"; a surging counter charge from the unmistakeable red-trousered 14th New York Regiment (the 'Brooklynites'), crashed into us; producing a savage bloody melee. Both sides were locked so close it was all hand to hand fighting. Bayonet work, stabbing, thrusting, parrying; clubbing each other with gun butts and rifle barrels. It was here that the 33rd displayed their inexperience. Fighting in such close proximity to the enemy they were disorientated and confused. Amid all the noise and rolling smoke they were oblivious to shouted orders from officers and sergeants trying to organise a defensive line to deal with this federal push. Deadly confusion that was too much for me. Gritting my teeth and narrowing my eyes I backed a few paces away from the fight when a Union infantryman suddenly appeared out of the smoke. (Any soldier will tell you not to turn your back, if at all possible, when enemy troops are close. Running away or not.) Marching forward holding his rifle and bayonet extended to his front the soldier was in the classic lunging position, ready to attack the first Confederate soldier he came across. Which was me. The Union soldier reacted fast, pulling his rifle back ready to make a stabbing movement. In slow motion the bayonet moved forward and, grimacing, I tensed my muscles for the jolt and pain that was about to hit. There was pain, but it was in my head. Once again I heard the sound of drums and in my mind's eye appeared a West African tribal mask. Frightening. Then suddenly, to my intense relief, a small red hole appeared in the soldier's forehead and he collapsed in a heap at my feet. "How you doing Captain Crink?" yelled a familiar voice.

Turning around I was confronted by a grinning Jack. God love us, the man was in his element.

"Enjoying yourself, Jack?"

Grinning, reloading his rifle, Jack replied, "Between the eyes. Not bad shootin' Captain. Reckon you owe me one."

With an effort I controlled my clacking teeth and shouted, "Reckon ah do."

"Got to find 4th Alabama," shouted Jack and with the wave of a large hand he dashed away.

By now it was total chaos. Unable to stem the momentum of the 14th New Yorkers our regiment was pushed aside. I was lucky. As the Union troops passed through us towards the rest of our Virginia Brigade I was nicely hidden in a cloud of swirling cannon smoke; which stung my throat but I could put up with that. Then another drama appeared. Stumbling and cursing, wrestling with a red-trousered Union soldier, Sergeant Smith arrived out of the fog. Walking backwards with his forearm around the soldier's neck Smith was shouting, "Stay still. Stop fighting me yah ungrateful son of a bitch. You are mah prisoner."

"No. You are mah prisoner," shouted Smith's prisoner.

"Seems to be a dispute as to who is in charge of who," I shouted.

"Sure is Captain. This is mah younger brother. Arthur. The war is over for him. But he won't see it that way."

Now that has to be one for a dinner table conversation. There were fifty thousand men, give or take a thousand, stumping around the Manassas battlefield. I mean, what were the chances? By now, grunting and gasping, Smith and his brother were rolling around on the ground. Their fight didn't last long. Drawing back a large fist Sergeant Smith hit his brother full in the face. Dazed, eyes rolling from side to side, Private Smith junior allowed Sergeant Smith senior to hoist him across his shoulders. With a wave and a grin Sergeant Smith trotted away with his human burden in the direction of the Bull Run river.

As Sergeant Smith disappeared to the rear we arrived, so armchair strategists said after the battle, at a critical point in the struggle. An appraisal gleaned from the testimony of dozens of watching Confederate soldiers who described Brigadier Jackson as sitting calmly on 'Little Sorrel' watching the oncoming New Yorkers. With a nod of his head, and a raised forefinger,[66] Jackson sent a spasm of excitement through the massed ranks of his impatiently waiting 4th and 27th Virginia Regiments; he had sensed the time for action had arrived. Raising his ass out of the saddle Jackson drew in a deep breath and yelled, "Wait until they are fifty yards away. Then fire. Then charge and yell like Furies." Which is what those two sister regiments of ours did. Holding their nerve and waiting for the order to commence firing.

It seemed Union troops were more than fifty yards away when the Virginians opened fired but hey, I wasn't complaining; just get rid of those New Yorkers; fast. Further volleys from the 4th and 27th crashed out and that was it, the Federals had had enough and started to run. Prompting Jackson to turn in his saddle and yell, "Charge them now and drive them to Washington."

Rifles levelled. Bayonets glinting. Away sprinted the 4th and 27th Virginians.

At this point with New Yorkers running towards me and being followed by the 4th and 27th Virginians, I was in danger of being trampled to death by hundreds of boots. I stared, searching for gaps in the rushing throngs of multicoloured soldiers, through which I could run to safety. Possibly I could get away by jogging alongside the fleeing New Yorkers. It was quite a scene. Yelling at the top of their voices as they came forward the Virginians were an awesome sight and in this headlong rush they suffered heavily from cannon and rifle fire, but kept going until they hit against Captain James Ricketts 1st United States artillery. At this point I changed my mind and thought it might be a better idea if I ran through the gaps in the 4th and 27th and joined Brigadier Jackson in the rear. Staggering a few paces in Jackson's direction I again blundered against a dead horse and fell flat on my face.

Crawling around the horse I stopped to get my breathing back to normal. Staring at the surrounding, heaving, moving mass of men and horses brought tears of frustration and anger running down my cheeks and I thumped the ground with a clenched fist; which was stupid; I hit a stone. In pain, dropping my rifle, grimacing, holding my hand and wondering if I'd broken a bone, I pretended to be a casualty and curled into a sobbing ball. Eventually I calmed down and opened my eyes to check what was happening around and about. And what was the first thing I saw? The distant figure of Brigadier Jackson. Still in the same spot. Sitting motionless and unperturbed, towering above his soldiers on 'Little Sorrel'. It would have taken the good lord's second coming to cause that man to blink, never mind display anxiety. As if trying to catch a low flying bird I watched Jackson repeat that strange oddity of his when this time, palm facing outwards, he launched his left arm into the air. I needed someone to blame for my situation and Brigadier Jackson was my ideal target. (According to an article by some fancy European 'mind doctor' I read in a New York magazine, apparently I was directing blame and anger away from myself and 'transferring' it to Jackson.) Whatever was happening inside my head, in an instant my temper boiled over. Pushing myself to my knees I pulled my rifle against my side, clasped it tight, and fired a shot in Jackson's direction. It wasn't an aimed shot or even a shot that I hoped would hit the Brigadier, more an unthinking release of anger towards the senior officer I felt responsible for my presence on this battlefield. Which was ridiculous. Jackson had played no part in my allocation to his Brigade. It was my nefarious past and the skulduggery of Abraham Lincoln and Allan Pinkerton that had landed me at Manassas.

Within a second or two of pulling the trigger Jackson's left arm flapped to one side. I had hit him. Grasping the arm with his right hand he laid it across his horse's neck. Would you believe it? My angry snap shot had hit Jackson's middle finger. Horrified, I looked around to see if anyone had noticed what I'd done. Nobody was looking in my direction so, jumping to my feet, I was in time to see another Confederate unit on our left, 6th North Carolina, mount an attack. Seems they were fired up by the sight of the 4th and 27th Virginians stampeding towards Union lines. Wearing their blue militia uniforms 6th North Carolina added further confusion and noise to First Manassas.

The sight of soldiers from both North and South rushing past seemed never-ending as thousands of combatants swilled around Henry Hill. Yet many lives were spared as soldiers wiped sweat from their eyes, peered at each other and, unsure which flag the man opposite supported, shook their heads and took up running again. Later, when the battle was over, some soldiers admitted to shrugging their shoulders and smiling at the man standing in front of them before running off. One Confederate soldier told me he recognised a friend from his home town who he knew was fighting on the Union side but neither could summon the courage to shoot the other. Apparently they asked how each other's family were 'doing', shook hands, then hurried away. Scenarios impossible to foresee at West Point. Or when giving pep talks in camp before a battle. Elsewhere panic caused others to shoot or stab men in dusty coloured uniforms. Friend of foe? Some would have been enemy. Equally, some would have been friends.

The fight on Henry Hill dragged in more and more troops from both sides and bloody clashes and skirmishes seemed to go on forever. The hill resembled the scene of a brutal hack and thrust struggle familiar to the likes of that Frenchie, Napoleon Bonaparte, and his British opposite number the Duke of Wellington, fifty years ago. Few troops knew where their commanders wanted them to be and in the excitement of a bayonet charge most didn't care. Especially me. And I didn't want to stand around and wonder how bad an injury I had caused our brigadier. Surrounded by a multicoloured carpet of dead and dying soldiers, both Confederate and Federals, it was time to move away before I joined them on the ground. But where was a safe refuge amongst this carnage? Something that became obvious when I noticed, a couple of hundred yards away, the Henrys' farmhouse. I ran and bundled through a door hanging to one side and, panting and wheezing, arrived inside the building. Close to the doorway lay the body of a soldier. Searching for somewhere to hide I took in the damage from artillery shells. The main room was a shambles of building debris and broken furniture. It was also eerily quiet. If Confederate sharpshooters had distracted Rickett's cannons from inside this house then they had departed to carry on the fight elsewhere. Boots crunching on glass, bits of wood, and broken crockery, I walked warily into the middle of the room. Then suddenly my movements were interrupted by a sudden outburst of sobbing from a nearby fireplace.

Swinging around I saw a woman in a bright red dress, hands pressed against her ears, tears streaming down her cheeks, kneeling inside the chimney recess. She stared with the wide-eyed intensity my mother displayed when ranting about the radiance that will shine from the Lord when he decides to put in an appearance in Alabama on Judgement Day.

Nerves taut I levelled my rifle at her and demanded, "Who are you?"

"Ellen Henry. I live here," she stammered and pointing at a nearby doorway went on, "My mother is in there. I think she's dead."

I found Ellen Henry's mother lying on her back on the splintered remains of a bed. She was elderly, ashen-faced, with blood seeping from wounds to her neck, side, and with a pool of blood surrounding a mangled foot.[67] Mrs Henry was in a bad way. Sitting on the edge of the bed I could see she was breathing with difficulty. I had seen men in this condition in the Mexican War and the end could not be far away. In an attempt to provide some comfort I took hold of one of her hands and leaning forward whispered, "Hang on Mrs Henry. We'll get you out of here and take you to a doctor."

Mrs Henry groaned opened her eyes, jerked her hand out of mine and uttered what turned out to be her last words, "Yankee. Go to hell." After another loud groan she closed her eyes and resumed her laboured breathing. Peeved at this ingratitude to what, for me, was an unusually sympathetic demeanour to someone else's suffering I said loudly, "Ah ain't no Yankee." Then muttered, "Could go to hell though. Me being an Alabama man."

After a few seconds of silence a further surprise arrived when from underneath the bed a woman's singsong voice interrupted my thoughts. "Mister soldier, you have upset Mrs Henry because you is wearing a blue hat. Even ah know that is the wrong colour for a Southern gentleman."

Looking under the bed I saw the chubby, pockmarked face of a black girl. "You Mrs Henry's house slave?" I asked.

Vigorously nodding her large head she replied, "That ah am. Name is slave Lucy Griffith. Ah am trying to help Mrs Henry, who is very ill. But those Yankees outside keep shooting at us."

Grunting and groaning slave Griffith crawled forward and, rolling on to her back, poked her head out from under the bed.

"Well slave Griffith ah would also like to assist Mrs Henry if ah can. Even with her unfriendly attitude." Pausing I sniffed and went on, "Do not be fooled by mah hat. It is indeed blue. Mah shirt and trousers are covered in dust making it difficult to see their true colour; gray. Ah am Captain Crink. 33rd Virginia Infantry Regiment."

With a frown she cheekily replied, "And ah am the Queen of Sheba."

Ignoring an urge to swipe my hand across her head for that sarcastic comment, I said pompously, "Ah will put your ignorant and insulting comment down to stress, fear and a lack of familiarity with the uniforms and deportment of the Union and Confederate armies. A lack of knowledge of such important matters shows the non-appliance of any military education by your master. How can you perform your duties correctly without knowing such military information?" (Yep, those utterly ridiculous words had to be down to my own reaction to stress and fear.)

Rolling her eyes and shaking her head slave Griffith replied, "Mister Blue-hatted, Confederate soldier, how will an education in military information help me. Mornings ah clean the house, cook meals and wash clothes. Afternoons ah sweep the porch, clean windows, and shovel buckets of horseshit from out front. You would not believe the amount that those horses drop in a day."

Not used to such talk from a slave I just stood and stared at her. Before I could think of a suitable reply a stray artillery shell crashed into the side of the house. With a yelp of fear I dropped to my hands and knees and rolled under the bed alongside the slave girl.

"Captain Crink. Would you be so kind as to remove your arm from around mah waist?" said slave Griffith calmly.

Withdrawing the offending arm I replied, "Ah did not realise what ah had taken hold of."

"Now you are gripping mah ass," she said in an slightly irritated tone.

Clamping a hand on her ample-sized posterior was another natural, unthinking movement. However, it was thought provoking that when my hand clamped itself against her buttocks they clenched tighter than the leather on a cowboy's saddle. A situation where I was tempted to forget the war and apply Crink's all over massage which, biased though I am, would surely have changed her surly attitude. It would also be helpful if the artillery boys left us in peace and those marauding soldiers outside went elsewhere to continue the fight. There was also Miss Ellen Henry to consider, but she seemed happy enough in her fireplace, and I doubted that she would stray far for an hour or two. Time enough for myself and the slave girl to get better acquainted.

Alas it was not to be. Suddenly a hand the size of a blacksmith's anvil grabbed the front of my tunic and, hauling me from under the bed, hoisted me into the air.

Chapter Nineteen

"Who the hell are you?" I stammered at a red-faced, bull-necked soldier wearing a gray uniform. He looked to be from the same mould as another Corporal; Jack Claybutt.

Meaning he stood around six and a half feet tall, barrel chested, square jawed and a sun tanned face from which protruded a flattened nose and a large chin. Add shoulders that would support a chuck wagon when it had problems with its wheels on a trail drive and he was a twin to Samson of the Good Book. Holding a rifle in his other hand, sweat dripping off the end of his chin, he held me as easily as a child flying a kite.

The soldier snapped in a broad Irish accent, "Name is O'Sullivan.[68] Rank, corporal. Serving in Emerald Company. 33rd Virginia Regiment."

Instead of telling him that I was a captain in the same regiment and threatening a firing squad if he didn't let go of my shirt I stupidly gasped, "What are you doing in this house?" Nerves and stress again.

"I was bringing water from the well for Mrs Henry when I thought I saw a Union soldier run into the house. And here you are, pawing my slave."

"Careful Corporal O'Sullivan. The Captains is choking," said slave Griffith.

Keeping his hand propped under my chin O'Sullivan loosened the grip on my shirt and then lowered me until the tips of my boots were touching the floor. Ignoring a growing pain in my throat I said, "How can slave Griffith belong to you?"

"Mrs Henry is done for and the house is destroyed. So the slave is now in need of a new master. Under 'Irish Derelict and Abandoned Farm' rules the first person who enters a derelict house, and is verbally told he can have property situated inside the house by the owner, then that person becomes the new absolute owner of the property. Even where the property has been left to another under a valid Will." After a cough to clear his throat and a narrow-eyed stare to see how I was taking this oral rubbish, O'Sullivan pointed at Mrs Henry and continued,"When I first arrived here and spoke with Mrs Henry she explained, because of her injuries, she expected herself to shortly die. Therefore, I could have slave Griffith. Job done."

As he finished speaking O'Sullivan broke into a broad grin. Obviously he found speaking gibberish good fun. Needing to extract myself from the grip of this lunatic Irishman I gabbled out my own hokum, "Don't forget Virginia bare knuckle boxing rights. When a slave is staked in a verbal bet, between bare knuckle fighters, the slave passes immediately to the victor of the fight. And can be claimed as a legal right as if passed as an inheritance under a Will."

Frowning O'Sullivan said,"What are you on about?"

"Like you ah am a bare knuckle fighter. If ah were to challenge you to a fight and you staked slave Griffith as forfeit if you lost. If that happened then ah could claim her. You win. You get to keep her."

Wagging a finger O'Sullivan said,"How did you know that I was bare knuckle fighter?"

"Your flat nose. Disfigured ears and heavily scarred knuckles," I said crossing my fingers that I had got it right.

O'Sullivan produced a large grin, released my throat from his grip, and dropped me in a heap across his boots. Staring at him I said, "Corporal O'Sullivan ah challenge you to a bare knuckle fight. But with this battle going on, ah declare you the winner. You are now the proud owner of slave Griffith."

Smiling, staring intently at me, head tilted to one side O'Sullivan said, "Mister, I've forgotten when someone last stood up to me in the blarney game."

Now that O'Sullivan was in a good mood, and I outranked him, it was time to stick up for myself. "And ah have not forgotten that ah am a Captain in the 33rd Virginia, Corporal. Reckon it is time we went our ways."

O'Sullivan didn't look too impressed with my revelation that he had been ill-treating an army captain. Although my feeling was that this corporal wouldn't be embarrassed if I was Brigadier Jackson. I continued, "What about Mrs Henry's daughter? Best check she doesn't have anything to say about ownership of slave Griffith."

Placing his nose within an inch of my face the Irishman whispered, "Listen little man, Confederate captain or not, I am getting on in age. Couple of months this war will be over. Then I can take it easy. Owning this slave will please both me mother and the parish priest back in Ireland. She wants grandchildren and he thinks it's time I acquired a woman to cook me meals and fill a glass with beer. Slave Lucy Griffith is mine. Leave her alone or I will bury you." There was another short silence until, with an attempt at humour, he went on. "The good news would be me wielding a shovel when I buried you. The bad news would be trying to find a Catholic priest who wouldn't blackmail me after I confessed to murdering a high and mighty Confederate officer."

Staring up at a pair of eyes that bubbled with battle madness, I believed his threat.

O'Sullivan produced a mischievous grin and putting his hands under the slave's armpits dragged her from under the bed and said, "Lucy Griffith soon as I've punched the lights out of these Yankees we're off to California. Start packing."

Things brightened with the distraction of a woman's suntanned legs arriving next to my face. The feet were bare and covered in dust and numerous scratches. The hem of a red dress suggested that the owner was Miss Ellen Henry. This was confirmed when a loud, sad wail, was followed by the owner of the feet shouting, "Mother has gone." Then Miss Henry fainted and collapsed on top of me. Putting out a hand to push her to one side I caught hold of one of her melon-sized breasts; unfortunately this brought Corporal O'Sullivan back into action.

Shouting, "She's mine as well," O'Sullivan grabbed Miss Henry and heaved her to one side. I winced sympathetically as, with a crunching crash, she collided with a rocking chair. I shuddered to think how O'Sullivan thought Miss Henry was 'his'. Then it was my turn. Taking hold of my tunic in the chest area O'Sullivan again hoisted me into the air and, holding me at arms' length above his head, said in a menace-laden voice, "Don't care who you molest, do you?"

Squirming in his iron grip I managed to pant, "That was an accident. And ah order you to put me down."

"Don't think so. Reckon you're one of those strange Yankees who sneak around jumping out of bushes to caress a woman's chest. Or rub their legs. Mother warned me about the likes of you." To emphasis his next point the Irishman pointed a banana-sized finger at my face and went on, "No matter how much tobacco or hay you offer for my horse. When I get a horse, that is. Miss Henry and slave Lucy Griffith ain't for borrowing. Or selling. You want to argue about that?"

I struggled to comprehend his accusation that I hid in bushes and attacked passing women; that was not something I would do; not when sober anyway. Nor was I happy with his accusation that I was a 'strange Yankee'; O'Sullivan seemed incapable of realising the difference between Yankee and Dixie twang. It was time to mollify this madman and I gabbled, "Corporal. Ah will not molest these ladies. Nor will ah hide in bushes, or behind trees, and jump out and grab any part of their bodies. That I swear and promise as a gentleman from Alabama."

Eyes wide and shaking her large head slave Griffith said, "First time anyone called me a lady. But hey, ah like it."

Corporal O'Sullivan just stared, wild-eyed and dripping sweat, but said nothing.

Then the pain in my neck muscles stirred me to heave frantically at O'Sullivan's arm until, with an enormous heave, I pulled it to one side. Swinging my knee against his knee I made him yelp with pain. In an instant the big Irishman stood, fist raised, and was about to punch me into oblivion when I gasped out the verbal oil that calms most arguments, "Don't hit me. Ah have money."

O'Sullivan grinned, patted the top of my head, and whispered, "How much?"

I guessed that not only was this Irishman illiterate but his travels in the States would have been as far as his house to the pens where his family kept their animals and the nearest bar on a Saturday night. Followed by a hungover trudge to church the next morning. So his knowledge of gold would be minimal. With a flourish I pulled a pair of bone craps dice from my coat pocket and whispered in return, "Two solid gold squares. Must be worth eighty dollars at least. Minted last week by the Virginia money board. Lots of thieves around, so ah disguised them with red paint and white spots. Fools people that they're 'craps' dice. Scrape away the red paint and you will find gold."

Taking the dice he held them up to the light and said, "There real gold beneath this paint?"

"Sure is."

After a pause O'Sullivan flashed me a suspicious look and went on, "What does minted mean?"

"Made officially and legally in a Confederate gold factory in Virginia."

Eyes bulging with excitement Corporal O'Sullivan said, "Is that right? In that case you can buy one of these women. Me trying to keep two of them happy will be mighty time consuming. Cost you both gold stones though. Which one do you want?" After a furtive glance at Mrs Judith Henry he continued in a low voice, "If it was me I'd take the slave. She'll do as told. Miss Henry is a Virginia girl. They have a mind of their own. Always arguing and telling men what to do. Some don't even drink. But I prefer a girl with spirit. Good excuse to crack them with a backhander. Or wallop them with a belt."

Before I could answer those ever turning wheels of fortune, that have ran with me ever since leaving Alabama, once again changed direction. During this interlude of verbal sparring with O'Sullivan I had been aware of the constant background noise of cannon and rifle fire. Although the noise level from when our brigade first arrived in the vicinity of the farmhouse had diminished, my thoughts that the battle could be sliding to a location elsewhere changed drastically when artillery shells began hitting the house again. The sound of splintering wood and clouds of flying dust were a brutal reminder of what the two armies were doing to each other on the other side of the farmhouse walls. (What was left of them, that is.) This noisy interruption sent O'Sullivan hurrying to a hole where a window had once stood and, after stuffing my dice into a shirt pocket and glancing at what was happening outside, the Irishman shouted over his shoulder, "Got to re-join the war. Thanks for the gold. Miss Henry. I'll come back for you when this fighting is finished."

With a wave of his kepi and surprising agility for such a big man, the mad Irish corporal leapt over the remains of a farmhouse wall and ran into the smoke and noise. Needless to say his claimed ownership of Miss Henry and slave Griffith was a load of rubbish. But I had no intention of chewing on the claimed legality or otherwise of that bone with these two ladies and, staring at the point where Corporal O'Sullivan had disappeared from view, the three of us maintained a dignified silence. A silence during which I could feel and hear my teeth clacking together. I started shivering and talking under my breath about the unfairness of life. On reflection I could have been suffering from what a Confederate army doctor explained, after dealing with the wounded at Gettysburg, with what he called 'mind disturbance'; a strange 'gazing trance' brought on by mental suffering. His recommended cure was a drunken haze for four or five days, accompanied by nights 'foraging' in a tent or hotel room with an understanding woman who would not be upset by your tears and screams; although the doctor drew the line at howling at the moon as advised by some Swedish immigrants. Apparently this ridiculous behaviour is done from inside a hot steamy wooden box. (Don't reckon there's anything in that tale. Sounds like something mountain men would do. Or Texans.)

Judging by the silence of Miss Ellen Henry, who was sitting on a large travelling chest hugging her knees and moaning quietly, she looked to be suffering from 'mind disturbance' as well.

Slave Griffith brought me back to reality when she asked, "What happens now, Captain?"

“He leaves,” That yell came from a man who had suddenly appeared in what remained of the main doorway. Broad-faced, muscular armed and broad-chested as most farmers are, he was dressed in a torn civilian shirt, working trousers, heavily scuffed boots, a broad panama style hat and covered in dust. Dressed as he was I guessed he would not be involved in what was happening outside the farmhouse.

“Hell and damnation, now what!” I exclaimed. Quickly retrieving my rifle I held it at the ready and added, “Who are you?”

“John Henry. Son of the lady who owns this property,” said the new arrival.

With a shout Ellen Henry ran and grabbed her brother around the neck, pushed her face into his shoulder, and between loud tearful sobs I heard Miss Henry say, “John, Mamma is dead. Those murdering Yankees have done for her. Wounded her all over. Then blew part of her leg off.”

Occasionally glancing in my direction, cooing words of comfort to his sister, John Henry held her tight against his shoulder. Slave Griffith broke the silence saying in a hushed voice, “Master John is visiting us from Loudon County. Afore you arrived the three of us tried to carry Mrs Henry to safety. Could not find the buggy. Yankees must have stole it. Soldiers shooting and cavalry waving swords charging around everywhere so we had to stop looking. Mrs Henry was too badly injured and too heavy to carry in this heat. So we brought her back here. Then Master John went outside to get assistance from some of you soldiers. Nothing doing there either. Too busy shooting each other.”

Pursing my lips to collect my thoughts, and about to ask the slave if she knew where John Henry’s horse was tethered, the noisy arrival of an artillery shell against the roof sent the four of us diving to the floor. In the following silence slave Griffith let out a sudden cry of pain. She was holding her ankle. Seemed she had been hit by a sliver of wood from the roof. Covered in dust Miss Ellen looked unconscious. (Turned out she'd fainted.) John Henry was clutching his sister tight against his chest and staring at his hat which had flown off and wafted inside his mother's bedroom.

Otherwise we four were alive and breathing.

Outside the noise of the fighting grew louder and seemed to be moving closer to the farmhouse. It crossed my mind that after considering the length of time both sides had been attacking each other surely one of them must be ready to say they'd had enough and retreat; or surrender. Unfortunately not yet. I could see swarms of men from both sides rushing around, some stopping to aim and fire their rifles, some suddenly throwing their hands in the air and pitching head first to the ground where they lay curled in silent heaps. Others twisted violently and fell down. Some screamed, most dropped silently.

"Got to get away from this madness," I said in a low voice.

"Good luck, Captain. Come visit us after the war," shouted slave Griffith. (Nothing wrong with her hearing then.)

It was about four o'clock in the afternoon and I vaguely remember clambering over a collapsed farmhouse wall and crouching alongside a dozen dead soldiers. Rifle pointing to my front watching the too-ing and fro-ing of soldiers and riderless horses, wondering in which direction to run, I remained there for what seemed like hours but would have been about ten minutes. Before I could summon the courage to move fresh waves of Union soldiers, coming from God knows where, which from their flags were 5th

and 11th Massachusetts Regiments, stormed across Henry Hill. Clashing with 4th and 27th Virginia Regiments, the Federals succeeded in pushing the Confederates away from what remained of Rickett's battered cannons. With their intervention I decided it would be best to sit tight and wait until Henry Hill was clear of anyone wanting to cause me harm. Then I would disappear.

It was not to be.

Bright lights flashed in front of my eyes and a growling noise rushed through my head and, without a conscious decision on my part, my legs jerked into movement and to my horror I stood up and went charging towards the newly arrived Massachusetts Regiments. Within seconds of setting away I heard yells and the pounding of boots behind me, a torrent of noise that grew louder as I ran. Glancing over my shoulder I saw a sea of charging, yelling, Confederate infantry. Flapping in the middle of this rushing mass was the flag of 5th Virginia Regiment. Someone in that outfit must have seen me start running and decided to join in. Which had a ripple effect. The whole damn 5th Virginia followed. Glory be, I was exactly where I did not want to be; out in front, point man, leading an infantry regiment in a headlong charge. Worse, the trailing Virginians were fifty yards behind and if I kept this pace up I would arrive in the Massachusetts lines first.

Try as I might I could not slow down. If anything, I was picking up speed.

Assuming I didn't get my head blown off, I would be swallowed up, disappearing into the midst of this fast approaching mob of blue uniforms. Meaning, for about ten seconds, there would be a single target for them to shoot at; Cornelius Crink! Then I ran into a bank of swirling smoke. Stumbling along I could see, vague and indistinct, clumps of soldiers moving soundlessly around me. Massachusetts men , no doubt, as lost as I was. Coughing and spluttering I emerged from the smoke and came to an astonished standstill. I had ran through the Union lines and emerged in their rear. To my left and right there was no one. Only sun-twisted grass and clusters of trees. Then to my astonishment, immediately to my front, were lines and lines of empty horse-drawn carriages and tethered horses. Sitting and standing on the grass, surrounded by hampers of food and drink, were hordes of chattering civilian men and women. Visitors from the North come to watch 'these upstart Confederates' get trounced on the battlefield.[69] At present all had one thing in common. They were staring, some through opera glasses, and pointing at me.

Comments from the crowd drifted my way. Such as: "Is he one of ours?"

And: "Hey, this is exciting. Is he going to start shooting at us?"

And: "Mean looking son-of-a-bitch. Must be from New York."

One man got it right when he shouted indignantly, "He's facing the wrong way. Must be deserting."

As the only soldier visible this side of the smoke engulfing the Union infantry, and with my gray uniform covered in dust, these were understandable reactions. It was my hat they were noticing. Strangely it was still showing blue. In a deep part of my mind I heard father's voice say: "Whoa there Cornelius. Slow down. Stumble, fall over, slip up. Get out of the way. This is mighty dangerous territory."

During my terror filled moments on Henry Hill I had forgotten about Yankah's pouch and its non-paying tenant. But father's voice was a background whisper drowned out by another insistent voice that ran across my mind. I heard,

"Keep going. All is well"; so involuntarily my legs kept going. Fanti interest had clearly not ceased. It had to be Yankah or his mother-in-law in control as I hurtled, rifle levelled in a fighting stance, straight towards hundreds of bug-eyed, avidly watching civilians.

The voice rattled into my head again, "Your bravery will assist the Union cause and you will gain fame for your actions today."

"How the hell does that work out. Looks like the Confederacy is wining this battle," I yelled at the sky.

Which I suppose was a new take on talking to yourself.

There couldn't have been many soldiers yelling that kind of rubbish blundering around Manassas battlefield and I was now within hearing distance of a group of watching civilians. Seems my words had quite an effect. Not impressed at my ranting and thinking I was the first man in the South's advance guard, a puffy-faced bulbous-nosed woman sitting by herself on a buggy a few yards away enthusiastically chewing on an apple, stared with horror filled eyes at my bayonet. Putting cannonball-sized hands against the sides of her head she screamed, "He's a Rebel. The Confederates have won. Run."

Having done her civic duty in shouting a warning 'bulbous nose' panicked and, forgetting she was sat on a buggy, hitched up her skirt, clambered to the ground and waddled away in the general direction of Washington. Hearing 'bulbous nose's fearful shrieks and watching her lumber away, folks on either side of her began mounting horses, or heaving themselves into carriages, and moving north at speed. It was the ripple effect again. Close to me dozens of men and women were chasing carriages whose panicking drivers were cracking whips against horses flanks and leaving passengers standing, shaking fists, swearing and cursing. Years later I met a sour faced civilian woman who, stranded at First Manassas complained: "Mah husband betrayed me. Stranded me at Manassas. Ah was quietly nibbling a biscuit and enjoying watching those soldiers running around; shouting; moaning; groaning; blowin' bugles; horses gallopin' past without riders. Cheering when cannons fired. Hey, don't you men have all the fun. Then a short, ugly Confederate officer appeared, leading thousands of soldiers our way. That man was fierce and brave. Looked a bit like you Cornelius. Weren't as good looking as you though. Put the fear of God into us civilians, so we left. Would have departed in a dignified manner as befits Godfearing, church-going Washington folk. But ah had to hoist mah skirts and run because that no good son-of-a-bitch husband of mine pushed me off our buggy and drove back to Washington without stopping. Ten years gone and ah have still not seen mah husband. Only escaped when ah caught a stray cavalry horse and rode it home. Don't know what happened to its owner but the saddle was covered in blood. Ruined mah dress. You would think somebody would have cleaned it. Men are so inconsiderate."

Me 'fierce and brave'? Another undeserved Crink legend.

From where I was standing with hundreds of panicking civilians milling around, it was a jaw-dropping sight. Drivers yelling and impatiently cracking whips. Men and women angrily jostling each other out of the way; folk who had been pleased to call each other 'dear friend' were punched and pushed over. Hems of dresses caused women to trip, sprawling to the ground, to be trampled on by family and stranger alike. A well-dressed twenty-something blonde beauty rushed past and, not watching the ground her tiny feet were traversing, tripped and spread-eagled herself across a mound of steaming horse manure. With a look of consternation creeping across her face the Northern beauty stood up and began frantically brushing manure from her dress until, staring disgustedly at her hands, she burst into tears, stamped a foot and yelled, "Father, mah church dress is ruined. Come back and clean me up. Then shoot the horse that left its insides on the ground for me to trip over."

Noticing me standing nearby the northern beauty held up her hands for me to inspect and shouted, "Ah thought they trained horses to do this sort of thing in their stables."

My reply was an amused smile and a shrug of the shoulders.

Then an angry voice shouted, "Hey you. Soldier boy."

Turning to one side I saw a purple-faced man in his forties wearing a white straw hat, brilliant white shirt and expensive looking red trousers standing, feet splayed wide apart, rocking up and down on the heels of well-polished boots, thumbs hooked into eye catching blue braces. Purple face carried on in the same loud voice, "Never thought ah would see the day Northern boys ran from Southern militia rats."

Purple face had, obviously, mistaken me for a Union soldier.

"Me neither," I replied with a tired shake of my head.

Uncurling a hand from his braces, purple face shook a meaty fist in the air and in a quieter voice said, "Our boys are a disgrace. Nobody in mah regiment behaved like this in Mexico. It should not happen. Stand your ground. Go. Rally your comrades."

The man's stupid outburst made me angry. Cupping a hand against my mouth I shouted. "Listen up purple head. Ah was also in Mexico. Texas Rangers. Couple of thousand Confederate are on their way here. Reckon they'll enjoy sticking a bayonet or two in your pompous ass. Stick around. Brave former soldier like you can help send these rebels back to Richmond."

The man's purple face changed to a deeper purple and he angrily yelled, "How dare you insult me, sir. Ah will have you whipped. What is your regiment? Who is your commanding officer?"

"33rd Virginia. Jackson's Brigade."

A large streak of fear appeared in purple face's eyes as he digested my information.

"You a Confederate?" he stammered.

"Certainly am. Noise behind me is the rest of mah brigade. Any second now they will charge out of this smoke and make straight for you."

Just as I thought, at the mention of the imminent arrival of Confederate troops, purple face's bravado disappeared. Nervously scanning the ever-increasing number of Union civilians and troops heading north purple face decided he'd said his piece and, after giving me an angry glare, put life before wanting to be the saviour of Northern honour. Mounting his horse he galloped away.

As purple face disappeared from sight another horse and rider appeared. However, this was different; he was coming from the north. Slowly and skilfully threading his horse through a morass of fleeing soldiers and civilians the rider was heading in my direction. Meaning he was heading in the opposite direction to everyone else. As the horse came closer I realised that the rider was a woman. Sitting bolt upright, a large unlit cigar clamped in her mouth, holding the reins in one hand and a large black book in the other, she looked familiar. In a lifetime of surprises both good and bad, but mainly bad, meeting the widow Riley again took some beating. Memories of our bedroom and Bible bashing days in Charleston came tumbling back.

Once over my initial surprise at seeing Mrs Riley, waving frantically, I ran towards her. The widow would be my ticket away from this bloody carnage. Pinkerton was welcome to my money. I had had enough. The urge to live a little longer was a stronger incentive than Lincoln and Pinkerton's blackmailing threats. As to why this strange southern belle was amongst a throng of retreating Northern troops and civilian sightseers, I had no idea. Nor did I much care. Whatever her reason it moved into second place against removing Cornelius Crink to safety. Mrs Riley's lumberjack-sized forearms would easily hoist me and dump me onto the back of her horse. If she refused assistance then it would take but a moment to grab the horse's reins and pull her to the ground. A swift blow to the face with my rifle butt would shut her up. And in all the confusion and clamour around and about us I doubted that anyone would notice what I was up to.

Having experience of quickly forming a swift exit in desperate situations, usually criminal induced ones, stood me in good stead. In seconds I formed a rough escape plan. A fast ride to the Shenandoah valley. Lay low in a small town for a couple of weeks before heading west. Maybe pan for gold in a some old worked out mines in California. I always thought there was still gold in some of those abandoned workings. A few months should satisfy my curiosity. Maybe even make a small profit. After things quietened down and everybody north and south of the Mason Dixie, especially Mrs Riley, had forgotten about me I would reappear in some sleepy Alabama town and return to cheating folk at the card tables. Even better, if the war finished while I was in hiding, both sides would be busy making friends again and I could reappear in my old haunts in New York and Washington. Lincoln would not need my services any longer. So, even if that hairy horror

Pinkerton found out that I had returned north which, with his contacts he probably would do, then those grim-faced, knuckle-dragging in the dust detectives Pinkerton employed to chase the likes of me around would, hopefully, leave me alone. At most, just to tidy up and close their file, Pinkerton might ask a few questions as to where I had disappeared to at the conclusion of First Manassas. But that could be taken care of with some well-crafted lies; a particular expertise of mine.

Standing next to Mrs Riley's saddle I could see that the book she was holding was her Bible. (She and my mother would have got on fine. Quoting the Bible. Drinking whiskey and Indian arm-wrestling.) I waved a hand to get her attention but, staring straight ahead, she ignored my presence. Just as I was about to shout for assistance Mrs Riley shifted her gaze to the sky and said in a loud voice, "Hallelujah. Captain Crink. The Lord's work is not finished. There is nothing for you in California. Return to Richmond. Fight on."

In a lifetime of vicious shocks and nasty surprises that had to be the conversation stopper to beat them all. I stared open-mouthed. I mean how on earth did Mrs Riley know that I was thinking of running to California? It crossed my mind that Yankah might be using her as his assistant. Compelled by Voodoo to do his will, sort of thing. With this kind of thinking my situation seemed to be moving from strange to dangerous. But I refused to accept such gibberish. Hey, supernatural powers and magic are just old wives and rabid spouting preachers tales.

Aren't they?

Finally, Mrs Riley glanced at me then started rummaging in her saddlebag until with a flourish, she produced a large Union flag. Leaning forward she dropped the flag at my feet and said, "Captain Crink. Pin this flag to the ground with your bayonet."

"What the hell for?" I demanded.

Leaning forward she replied in a low voice, "Confederate newspaper will love it: 'Hero of Manassas. Captain Cornelius Crink, 33rd Virginia Infantry Regiment. Found on the battlefield lying across a Union flag. Before falling unconscious the brave captain showed his disdain for Lincoln's Northern butchers when he stabbed their flag and pinned it to the ground with his bayonet. Around Captain Crink lay a dozen dead Union soldiers, evidence of Captain Crink's ferocious fight with the enemy. On opening his eyes Captain Crink indicated towards the Federal dead and said: "This is how to treat the north. This is the only language they understand. Long live the Confederacy."' Make for a lot of backslapping and shaking of your hand and maybe a post at General Lee's Headquarters."

"Whoa there lady. Ah ain't falling to the ground for nobody. Too many panicking soldiers and frightened horses running around hereabouts."

Before I realised what was happening, grinning maniacally, Mrs Riley leaned towards me, grabbed my rifle in a large hand then proceeded to swing it around her head. Using it as a spear she threw it at the Union flag. The bayonet hit dead centre sticking the flag firmly to the ground. I wanted to turn and run but couldn't, my legs were stuck fast. Which wasn't Yankah's or his mother-in-law's Voodoo; just plain old fashioned terror. Jerking my eyes away from the skewered flag I looked up at Mrs Riley, just in time to see her Bible swinging towards me. The last thing I remember was the picture of a gold cross and the sorrowful eyes of two biblical figures on their knees with arms extended towards the cross. For a split second I was confused. I thought I was back in Alabama and my mother was administering her usual punishment at my inability to recite the requested biblical text. Then a sharp pain in my head.

Followed by darkness.

Chapter Twenty

Call it delayed shock or just plain relief at being alive but my memory of moving from Manassas battlefield, on my back, in an old wheel squeaking wagon is vague. Until I arrived in Manassas town that is. Because of the large numbers of wounded, Confederate army medics commandeered wagons from Manassas and the surrounding countryside to move casualties to the rear. Pulled by two ancient horses my transport moved slowly. The wagon had been borrowed from a farmer passing through the town and the smell of its previous cargo of freshly cut firewood mingled with the stink of bloody bandages wrapped around my two traveling companions; both from the 5th Virginia Regiment. Competing smells that lingered in my nostrils for days after the battle. A squint through half-opened eyes told me those two soldiers were beyond hope of recovery; whereas I lay there with only a headache. Found unconscious on top of that Yankee flag I had decided, on opening my eyes, to feign an injury caused by a supposed blow to the head. So I groaned long, loud, and complained of being surprised by a ferocious rampaging Yankee who had struck across the temple with his rifle butt. (It certainly felt like it.)

No doubt I had to rethink my strategy. My dash to escape the battlefield, and that unexpected encounter with Mrs Riley, made me realise that escaping from here would have to be put on hold until I could assess my new situation. Also, in the long run, if I was stuck in the South for the foreseeable future did I try to get appointed to a staff post in a Confederate headquarters behind the front lines, preferably Richmond; or attempt to desert again? Staying in the South did not appeal. Yet, if the war was as short as most people thought it was going to be, then Richmond was about as far as you could get from the sharp end of the conflict that was about to unfold. Mind you, I never thought that the South's victory at First Manassas was any indication of the eventual outcome of this war. Even to a dumbass crook like myself the North was superior both economically and politically. Meaning the North could grind out a military campaign for a longer period than the Confederacy without its economic infrastructure collapsing. I also thought the North could absorb more human casualties than the South. Putting it another way; without a swift victory by the Confederate States there was only one winner; the North.

The Union also had Abraham Lincoln.

And as things stood after First Manassas, Richmond was an excellent place to carry out my spying duties. A few months seeing out hostilities alongside the Confederacy's commanding generals would suit me fine. Desertion? Both North and South would have an interest in catching me if I took off. The North desperately needed intelligence on what was going on South of the Mason Dixie and Yankah and his drummer boys, and me, were a good intelligence investment. Caught by the North I reckoned Pinkerton, with Lincoln's ruthless agreement, might make an example of me to the rest of their spies and shoot me, then send someone else in. Then again, depending how much I was in Pinkertons's good books, he might ship me back to the South. If the Confederacy caught me first then it would be a ten minute hearing and despatched to the promised land. All in all the sensible thing was to spend a couple of days resting in a medical tent and then as per Mrs Riley's request somehow get myself transferred to the headquarters of the Confederacy at Richmond.

As we clattered into Manassas one of my wounded companions, a thin, ginger-haired youth with the wispy beginnings of a ginger beard opened his eyes, stared at me and said, "Captain ah recognise you. When we charged those Yankees at the end of the battle you were way out in front of mah regiment. Shouting and hollerin' like an angry hog. You are a mighty brave man sir. Ah reckon that charge won us the day. Ah am real proud to meet you, sir. What is your name?"

"Captain Cornelius Crink, 33rd Virginia Infantry," I replied modestly. After a pause to think I went on, "Those invading Yankees made me mad. The South deserves freedom from those prevaricating liars. All ah want is to send them back North and independence for the Southern States."

The second soldier, gray-faced and clasping at a wound in his chest, coughed and in painful gasps joined in the conversation with, "Sir, ah like what you are saying. But ah was raised never to swear. What does prevaricate mean?"

"Truth is ah don't rightly know what it means son. Mother often claimed mah father prevaricated. Ah figure the North are worse than him. So they must prevaricate as well," I said with clever Crink logic.

After a pause to cough again the second soldier said, "When ah get home do you reckon ah can use that word in front of the folks?"

"Ain't a good word. Reckon its mild swearing. Let's say that Lincoln's men are not the kind of people your folks should be inviting to tea," was the best I could come up with on the spur of the moment.

"Best not greet the good lord with that word then," said the ginger-haired youth with a faint smile.

Even old cynics like me can show compassion now and again and I replied, "Hey, hang on there, soldier. You ain't going anywhere but to meet a doctor. And he'll patch you up and have you on your feet in a couple of days."

'Ginger' replied, "Thanks for that sir. But ah guess it's the end. Will you say a prayer for me."

"That ah will," I replied. And I meant it. And I did. Four years later when passing through Manassas on my way north. Late but keeping myself alive took priority. Also, on every anniversary day of First Manassas I remember that conversation with those young soldiers. Two early casualties at the beginning of awful slaughter that was to come. I have to admit tears were welling in my eyes and my throat was hurting after 'Ginger' made his request for me to intercede on his behalf with the Lord.

It got worse when 'Gray Face' stuck out a hand, which I shamelessly shook, and said, "You are a brave man Captain Crink. Keep fighting for what you believe in. You will get your reward someday."

"That I will soldier," I said in a loud voice then whispered to myself, "Return of my money would be nice."

In the ensuing silence that followed our conversation and, probably for the first time in my life, I felt shame. I mean the deep down, hand-wringing variety, that keeps you awake at night. These two soldiers had misunderstood me and my motives during that final charge at First Manassas. In their eyes I was a hero. Thankfully this feeling only lasted a short while and I quickly returned to wondering about my situation again. As I did so 'Ginger' closed his eyes. He was still breathing but died a few hours later in a medical tent on the outskirts of Manassas.

Out of the corner of my eye I noticed the wagon driver, a barefooted slave wearing a wide-brimmed hat, blue pants two or three sizes too big for him and a frayed grubby white shirt, tilting his head to one side and avidly listening to our conversation. Quickly realising that the driver would be useful in spreading the story of what brave Captain Crink had supposedly been up to at First Manassas. I thought it might be a good idea to tell the driver to repeat what he had heard from these two wounded soldiers to as many Southern army officers as he could. Also few lies about saving the life of Mrs Henry's slave girl to the wagon driver wouldn't go amiss. So I flapped a hand and shouted to gain his attention, but gave up when he appeared unable to hear me; he was also singing some damned awful church hymn.

Which was damned inconsiderate of him, so I returned to thinking and staring at the sky. A few seconds later I sensed that the driver had turned and was staring at me. Glancing in his direction I noticed his hat was now perched on the back of his head. What I saw stunned me and I felt my eyes opening wider than the Grand Canyon. It couldn't be, but it was; our driver wasn't a man, he was a she. I had never been able to forget that pockmarked face and hate-filled eyes of the Fanti woman I had tried to rape all those years ago on the West African Coast.

The wagon driver was Yankah's sister.

Staring at me with a look of loathing that would have given a bison the squirts she hissed, "Praise the Lord, Captain Crink. We are going to Richmond," then hit me on the chin with the thick end of her whip.

Once again I flopped down, horizontal; unconscious.

(Note: At this point, with my 'Chinese concubine' tugging at my elbow and calling me to the dinner table I will end this first manuscript of my recollections. Hopefully, should I survive the night, then I will continue writing in the morning.)

Notes

1. Crink's observations refer to a soldier in the 79th New York Highlanders. A distinctive regiment in the Union army. It was formed in 1859, mainly from Scottish immigrants, and modelled on the British army's 79th of Foot (Cameron Highlanders.) Part of their full dress uniform consisted of kilts, garters, and silver-buckled shoes.
2. Allan Pinkerton: A Scotsman who emigrated to the United States in 1842. Founder of the famous Pinkerton Private Detective Agency. In his autobiographical book: *The Spy of the Rebellion*, Pinkerton describes his time during the war between the States as 'Chief of the Secret Service.' He mentions: "Scarcely had the reverberating tones of the guns upon the batteries in Charleston Harbour died away upon the air, than I was called into the service of the military branch of the government." (Pinkerton is alluding to the bombardment by Confederate guns of Fort Sumter on the 12th April 1861 which began the war.) However, Crink describes his 'meeting' with President Lincoln and Allan Pinkerton in the Willard hotel as occurring on the 4th April. Interestingly therefore, from what Crink says, Pinkerton's Union service may have started at least eight days before Pinkerton claims that it did. A scenario bolstered by Lincoln's journey to Washington as president-elect, in February 1861. During this journey, because of a plot that Lincoln was to be assassinated en-route in Baltimore, Allan Pinkerton accompanied Lincoln in the train as

his bodyguard. (On arrival in Washington, until Lincoln's inauguration on the 4th March 1861, the Lincolns' stayed in the Willard Hotel.)

3. Mason Dixie line: In the eighteenth century a line drawn to settle a border dispute between Pennsylvania and Maryland. Eventually it came to symbolise the cultural and geographical dividing line between the North and South.
4. March to the Sea: Major General William Tecumseh Sherman's famous overland campaign, November and December 1864, through Georgia from Atlanta to Savannah and the Atlantic Ocean. Living of the land and deep within enemy territory Sherman demonstrated that an army could fight, and win, without guaranteed lines of supply or communications.
5. Leaky mouth: Cowboy expression for someone who talks too much.
6. Cholla. Pronounced Choy-yuh. A high growing spiny cactus that grows in the American South West. Described in Win Blevins 'Dictionary of the American West' as "having soft, clingy spines that are meaner than your mother-in-law's tongue."
7. Hog-down: To tie a cow to prevent it escaping. As when 'branding.'
8. Crink's recollection of Lincoln's comments accord with the facts. On the outbreak of war the Confederacy had a widespread espionage system operating in the North. Well-placed sympathisers in Washington and elsewhere kept the South informed of what was being planned. There being no Confederate government in existence until the start of the Civil War, the reverse was not true.

9. Baldwin: John Baldwin was a Virginian Unionist. He met with President Lincoln on 4th April 1861 during Virginia's State convention. Much speculation has centred around whether Lincoln offered to vacate Fort Sumter in return for the adjournment of the convention without Virginia seceding from the Union. Unfortunately President Lincoln did not elaborate in Crink's presence as to how he would approach the discussion with Baldwin.
10. Fort Sumter: Flashpoint for commencement of hostilities between North and South. A coastal fort garrisoned by Union troops and situated in the middle of Charleston harbour, South Carolina, Fort Sumter was deep in Confederate territory.
11. Lady of the line: Western expression for a prostitute.
12. In November of 1860 there was a meeting in San Francisco to discuss financial backing for the proposed extension of Central Pacific Railroad from Sacramento to the California coast.
13. *The Star of the West* was involved in trying to resupply Fort Sumter before the Civil War broke out. It was captained at this time by a John McGowan. A name that resembles Crink's recollection. Crink could have heard McGowan's name mentioned during his travels. Not knowing the exact date that Crink boarded it is not possible to categorically state that he travelled on this ship.
14. Tempis fugit: 'Time flies.'
15. 'Dixie' (1859). A favourite and famous song of the war. Although thought of as a song of the South, both sides sang it. Composed in New York by Daniel Emmett. Its actual title was 'Dixie's Land'.

16. 'Smoke' Morrissey: In September 1853 John 'Old Smoke' Morrissey beat 'Yankee' Sullivan in a bare knuckle fight near the small town of Boston Corners (about one hundred miles north of New York.) This established Morrissey as a champion prize fighter in the United States. Morrissey gained his nickname from an earlier prize fight during which he fell on top of a bed of red hot coal embers that had been knocked over by his opponent, Tom McCann. Both men carried on fighting until McCann grabbed Morrissey and held him down with his back pressed against the embers. Ignoring the pain Morrissey extricated himself and fought on. Eventually he knocked McCann out.
17. Tar heels: Nickname for citizens of North Carolina. Thickened turpentine or pine tar was the main product of coastal North Carolina.
18. Long eared chuck wagon. A mule carrying food.
19. Sergeant James Chester: A Scot who emigrated to the United States and joined the army in 1854. (See: *The Longest Night* by David Eicher. Published by Simon Schuster in 2001) It appears he was not related to Pinkertons's Cameron Highlander.
20. Reb serpents. An expression used to describe southern secessionists by folk in the north.
21. 7th New York Militia. (Nickname the Old Graybacks.) One of the first units to go to Washington during the Fort Sumter crisis in April 1861.
22. Lampers: Inflammation inside a horse's mouth.
23. Although no records have come to light concerning Crink and Claybutt's time in Fort Sumter it is always a possibility that another soldier, who was there, has mentioned it in a letter or correspondence either

during or after war. If so perhaps it will be found by someone involved in historical research work. As things stand it would appear nobody ever divulged the arrival of Crink and Claybutt in Sumter.

24. Salvage cut: Cutting down trees that are dying or damaged before they lose their worth.
25. Norther: Freezing gale that blows across the American Southwest from the north.
26. Rimrock: Steep rock on the side of a canyon. To be 'rimrocked' is to get penned in. A situation difficult to get out of.
27. Cotton gin: A machine for separating the seeds from the fibre of cotton.
28. Colonel Wade Hampton: Before the war Hampton was well known in his home state of South Carolina. Having graduated in law from South Carolina University he went on to serve in South Carolina's State legislature. A speech he made against reopening the slave trade was not a view popular with those who ran slave Plantations in his home State. When the civil war broke out he fought for the South. Initially enlisting as a private soldier and then he went on to raise his own 'legion' of infantry, cavalry and artillery. By the war's end he was Lieutenant-General. In a few words he was "a brave and chivalrous officer."
29. Grass fat beef. A cow fattened only on grass. Someone eating such meat was once regarded as being poor.
30. Sand hills: Blackfeet Indian expression. On dying they go to the 'sand hills.'
31. Maverick's missing cattle: In 1847 Colonel Samuel A. Maverick took four hundred cattle in payment for a debt. Maverick did not look after his cows very well, in that the Colonel did not brand them

as belonging to him. They were also allowed to wander the countryside untended. As a result they multiplied and many of these unbranded cattle became scattered far and wide. This situation was known to other folk in the area and unbranded livestock became known as a 'maverick'. A situation ripe for unprincipled cattle owners to take and brand them with their own brand. In 1853 Colonel Maverick sent out a band of cowboys to round up his cattle. A lot were rounded up but many were not. This created a new word – 'maverick'; an unbranded stray animal without an owner's brand. (Usually one that has been seized unlawfully.)

32. John Fitzwalter: He was Lee's guide on this reconnaissance mission. Fitzwalter had scouted this area on an earlier occasion but appears not to have made a very good job of it. On the approach of Mexican soldiers Fitzwalter bolted. (See *Robert E. Lee* by Emory M. Thomas.)

33. The Thomas Beale papers: In 1885 James B. Ward published, in Lynchburg Virginia, a twenty-three page pamphlet entitled 'The Beale Papers'. This pamphlet describes three encoded messages containing details of buried treasure. (Gold and silver worth millions of dollars.) The treasure was allegedly buried in 1819 and 1821 near Buford in Bedford County, Virginia. One message describes the location of this treasure. A second describes the contents. The third contains a list of the owners of the treasure and their next of kin. As far as I am aware no one has ever verified if the alleged author of these documents, Thomas Beale, ever existed. But see page 128 of my manuscript for Mulehead Joe's

purported identification of Beale. There are entries and discussions about the veracity, or otherwise, of Beale and his documents on the internet.

34. Locoweed: Toxic plants found in the mountainous west. If eaten by livestock it can make them act crazy. In particular astragalus and oxytopis plants. Loco is also an expression used to describe someone who is thought to be crazy.
35. Hercules powder: nitrate of Soda. An explosive charge used by miners.
36. Shovel stiffs: Miner who works with a shovel.
37. Moose pasture: A term to describe an area that is, in mining terms, of no value.
38. Buzzard's roost: An area in Lynchburg of ill repute.
39. Ramrod: Working boss on a ranch.
40. Rincon: A good location.
41. Puke: Nickname for someone from Missouri.
42. Tinhorn: A gambler. Usually someone who cheats at cards.
43. El Dorado: Term to describe a place where a man thinks he will find his fortune. Usually mythical.
44. Gold colic: In a fever to find gold.
45. Calico queen: Another expression for a prostitute.
46. Crib. A saloon, or gambling area, or whorehouse. Often all three combined into one establishment.
47. Gold canoe: A cradle.

    Gold borer: An auger.

    Gold monkey: Locating rod.

    Gold blossom: Gold bearing rock detached from the vein.

    Gold brick: Gold made into a 'brick' for transportation.

Gold dirt: Earth containing gold in amounts worth mining.

48. Galoot: A man who has the reputation as being a bit of a character.
49. Cabron: An outlaw.
50. Four flusher: Someone who bluffs. Originates from the game of poker.
51. Sir Gregor MacGregor: The most authoritative book I have found on this outlandish confidence trickster who invented the fictitious country of Poyais is *The Land That Never Was* by David Sinclair. Published in the UK in 2003 by Headline Book Publishing. (A division of Hodder Headline, London.) Refer back to note 33.
52. Chew the dog: To talk.
53. John Augustus Sutter: German immigrant who, bankrupt, fled Germany and pitched up in the United States. Described as a pleasant and well-mannered he was also a conman; in that for years he was either heavily in debt or bankrupt. Had a huge reputation for not repaying his debts. Arriving in California in 1839 Sutter built a stockade at the confluence of the Sacramento and American rivers. In 1848 gold was discovered by James Wilson Marshall, a partner of Sutter's, fifty miles north-east of Sutter's stockade. By the year's end the famous Californian gold rush was on.
54. Chaparral: Thick tangled shrubbery. In Crink's context it means a 'Chaparral Cock'; a bird. (The well-known road runner.)
55. Plains Indian hand signals for 'keep your knife close'. as per *Indian Sign Language* by William Tomkins. Published by Dover Publications, San Diego,

California in 1969. KEEP: With right hand grasp left index finger firmly and move hands slightly to right and left. YOUR: Point to the person with the knife. KNIFE: Hold right flat hand close to face, lower edge just over the mouth; move the hand upwards and to the left two or three times, as if trying to cut with lower edge of hand. CLOSE: Slightly curved right hand well out in front of right shoulder, draw hand downwards and in towards body, holding hand flat and upright.

56. First Bull Run/First Manassas: The Union army tended to name their battles after a geographical site where the battle took place; i.e. Bull Run River. The Confederates named them after a topographical site; i.e. the town of Manassas.

57. Duffer: A stupid person. Although a well-known term in the United Kingdom, this word was also used by cowboys in the American West.

58. In 1839 a ship called the *La Amistad* was carrying slaves to Cuba. During the voyage the slaves murdered the captain and a sailor and took control of the ship. They told the crew to take the ship to Africa. However the crew sailed it to Long Island, New York, from where the ship was taken by the United States navy to New Haven, Connecticut. The slaves were put on trial for murder and piracy. Eventually, in 1841, the Supreme Court of the United States ruled that all human beings, even if they have committed dreadful acts, have a right to fight for their freedom and they were released and allowed to return to Sierra Leone.

59. Bulldogging: Steer wrestling.

60. Bocor: A male voodoo 'witch' available for hire.

Practises both good and evil magic. Reputedly has the power to create zombies. Including the capture of zombie astrals; i.e. souls or spirits. Which are put inisde a 'fetish' bag. (Which apparently happened to Crink.) A scenario that enhances the Bocor's powers.

61. Miss Harriet Tubman: Called the 'Moses of the People'. She escaped from her Maryland plantation in 1849 and trekked north to the free state of Pennsylvania. Once there she decided to become a 'conductor' and return south to assist others to escape. Risking her life each time she returned south Miss Tubman is credited with bringing around 300 slaves north to safety. During the Civil War she served in the Union Army as a cook, laundress, and nurse. CONDUCTOR: A guide who led captive slaves to freedom.

    UNDERGROUND RAILROAD: A system of routes and attendant guides to assist slaves travel, by foot, from slave owning southern States to the north; or Canada.

62. Prairie schooner: In the nineteenth century it was the 'covered' wagon of choice that moved thousands of migrants to the western United States.

63. General Johnston: Joseph Eggleston Johnston graduated from West Point in 1829. (As did General Robert E. Lee.) Johnston was another who served in the Mexican war and in the Seminole and Florida wars. A Virginian by birth, on the outbreak of the civil war, Johnston joined the Confederacy. On 4th July 1861 he was Commissioned as a Brigadier General and assumed command of Confederate forces in the Shenandoah Valley. At First Manassas, Crink mentions that Brigadier Beauregard commanded

the Confederate army of the Potomac. When President Davis ordered Brigadier Johnston and his army to move from the Shenandoah to Manassas to reinforce Beauregard, which Johnston duly did, Beauregard found himself the junior of these two Brigadiers. However, when briefed by Beauregard as to how he had proposed fighting the coming battle, Johnston approved the plans and allowed Beauregard to continue exercising general field command of Confederate forces at Manassas.

64. Burning the White House: On the 24th August 1814, during the war with Britain, the White House was burnt to the ground by British soldiers. (But not before eating a meal found abandoned in the main dining area.)

65. Robert Bunch: From November 1853 until February 1863, Bunch was Britain's Consul in Charleston, South Carolina.

66. Jackson's raised finger: Brigadier 'Stonewall' Jackson had a habit of raising a finger, palm forward, in the air. Some officers in his brigade thought he was making an appeal to God to intercede favourably on his behalf. Jackson was wounded in the left hand when he raised it above his head at First Manassas. For years after the war Crink's responsibility for firing the shot that hit Jackson's hand has been discussed and argued about in bars in the south. Such debates usually beginning shortly after someone, heavily in drink and fitting Crink's description, ran out of the building.

67. Mrs Henry: Crink's observations of Mrs Henry's injuries are consistent with those she suffered during the battle.

68. Corporal O'Sullivan: There is a Corporal O'Sullivan listed as a casualty at the battle of First Bull Run.

69. Hundreds of civilians left Washington and descended on the outskirts of the battlefield. Expecting to see a Union victory they were sorely disappointed and, as Crink describes, they fled back north when Union troops retreated. Thereafter this panic stricken retreat by the north's army was known as 'the Great Skedaddle'.

LAZANTIS RISING

World Leaders ✦ Benevolent Aliens

URSULA DYCK

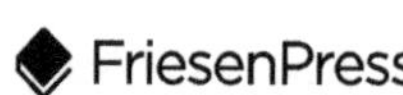

One Printers Way
Altona, MB R0G 0B0
Canada

www.friesenpress.com

First Edition — 2022

Author photo on the cover: Evelyn Tanner

ISBN
978-1-03-913905-3 (Hardcover)
978-1-03-913904-6 (Paperback)
978-1-03-913906-0 (eBook)

1. FICTION, FANTASY, EPIC

Distributed to the trade by The Ingram Book Company

Table of Contents

I dedicate this book to the World Wide Web that provided all the background research for places, names and events. Thank you WWW! Without it, this story would not have been made possible. Also, I dedicate to my lit-up world globe, a companion by my side. Being the armchair globetrotter I was, it provided me with an overall view of where countries were situated in the world, an invaluable tool for this novel. I also dedicate to my roster of music Youtube downloads of eclectic music that inspired me night after night, while writing. A special dedication goes out to English musician Mike Oldfield for his song called 'Surfing', released in 2005 from the album Light + Shade that started me on the journey. Last, but not least, I am grateful for the numerous friends, clients and family members with their words of encouragement, for their laughter and spirit to help me forge on.

Chapter One

The Blue-ray Light

April 2018 . . .

The morning sun streamed through her bedroom curtains as Ushaya rose out of bed, yawning and stretching to shake off the night and greet a new day. With slippers and housecoat on, she wandered to the kitchen to drink her lemon water and take her health supplements, and then began her breakfast. Eggs sizzled in the pan.

Her husband had passed away five years earlier, from a rare lung disease. They had been happily married for forty years. Last year, she retired from Trends & Styles, a magazine company, and purchased a small property in the mountains of central BC, in a little town called Crestfield. Although it was a modest place, she was happy and content. Now sixty-four, she filled her days with pursuing her hobbies and relishing her flower gardens. She picked up the newspaper from the front porch and went back inside.

As she sipped her coffee and gazed out the bay window at the trellises and rosebushes along the fence, she suddenly remembered one glitch in her little paradise and looked at her phone, mumbling, "What time is that city appointment? One o'clock. OK, I have some time." While perusing legal documents on her table, she became increasingly frustrated. Her neighbour Emily Barker argued that the property lines were not accurate on the deed, which would reduce the back of her property by twelve feet and the width by ten feet. Debates ensued back and forth, and now it was up before the Land Titles Office. Today, the adjudicators should decide.

Emily popped up on the other side of the fence to put out the garbage. Their eyes met, and Ushaya quickly turned to her papers. Everything about

Emily annoyed her—her shrill voice and her meticulous attention to her gardens, getting down on hands and knees, cutting grass with scissors. She had made complaints to the city about her staying up at night with dim lights on, which the city had always dismissed. Her yapper dog Mimi always barked the minute she left the house.

One o'clock arrived, and two adjudicators sat at the table. The city determined that the width of the property remained the same, according to the deed, but the length still needed more consideration. This was good news for Ushaya: one battle fought and won.

Days later, her son Brad called up. He was thirty-five years old with a stocky build, receding hairline, and clean-shaven face. Working for GeoFindX as a geologist meant days of travel from his home in Manitoba. He was a likeable chap, meeting friends easily wherever he travelled. "How are you doing, Mom?" he asked.

She replied, "Pretty well. I won in court the other day." She lit up a cigarette and sat down in her living room. Brad was planning a vacation for New Mexico, and they chatted a while, catching up on the latest news, then hung up.

Later that day, a text came in from her daughter, Meg: "When are you coming? I'm working on getting time off work." Meg lived in Wellington, New Zealand, with her husband Devon and their two children, Tyler and Chelsea, whom Ushaya adored. Meg was forty years old, with medium-length brown hair, a curvaceous body, and a pretty face. She owned a spa, named CALM, and Devon was manager of Hakai Tonga Resort, a prominent resort by the ocean.

Ushaya texted Meg, "I booked tickets for October. Will send you details."

"Great, let's chat on the weekend," Meg texted back.

Then she called up her sister, Amelia, who held a PhD in biology specializing in infectious diseases, which meant travelling all over the world. Amelia met her husband Paul at a kayaking club in Sechelt, BC, twenty years ago. He was known for his great sense of humour, and they had been together ever since. They had no children.

No sooner than Ushaya had hung up with Amelia than her brother Kevin called. He had been married to Maria for twenty-five years, and they lived on a small ranch outside of Calgary, and had no children, either. He was a tall, chubby man, clean-shaven, sporting a head full of silver hair, and he recently took up running to lose some weight. He was manager of a large retail store in Calgary called Top Box, while Maria took care of their two horses on the ranch. They chatted a while and hung up.

Ushaya spent the rest of the day organizing boxes in the attic, before retiring to bed. All night long, dreams had kept her in restless slumber, as she tossed and turned. When she woke up, the air was still, and she had pulled the covers to her chin. An electric blue light had beamed through the curtains of her window, and a blue haze had followed, scanning the entire room from left to right and right to left, pausing above her. Frozen, she could not speak or move. Then the blue light disappeared through the curtains. Zip! Gone.

Startled, she sat up in bed. The room was dark and silent. She reached for the iPhone by her bedside to check the time. It was midnight. An uneasy feeling washed over her, and in spite of her fears, she had to investigate, or she would be awake all night. She crawled out of bed and peeked through the curtains, and saw nothing. She crept down the dark hallway and peered out the living room windows, and saw nothing. She tiptoed onto her back deck and stared into the starry night sky, feeling the cool breeze upon her face, and seeing nothing, she turned back inside and locked the door, and crept down the hall, back to her bed.

The following morning sun flickered across the bedroom walls. It was 8:00 a.m., later than her usual wake-up time, as she swung her legs to her bedside, remembering her dream, wondering what it meant. With housecoat and slippers on, she followed the scent of coffee percolating in the kitchen, and went about her usual morning ritual, soon settling down to breakfast, with coffee in hand. While browsing news sites on her laptop and swishing the last piece of bread in her eggs, something had caught her eye. Her hands and arms were glowing a soft blue aura. Gasping, she rushed to the bathroom mirror and saw the same aura glowing around her entire body. Her wavy black hair, with silver streaks running through it, also showed hints of blue. Clumsily slamming into the bathroom door on her way out, she walked down the hall toward the kitchen, continually observing her hands and arms. By the time she had taken her next sip of coffee, the blue aura had faded, and she muttered, “I must see my doctor.”

CHAPTER ONE

After breakfast, she wandered to the bedroom to prepare for her morning walk, which she had enjoyed every day since her retirement a year ago. She dressed in her black jeans, a loose white shirt, and a light-grey cotton jacket, which hung to her thighs. With silver sneakers on, she stepped onto the front porch and smelled the fragrance of morning dewdrops that filled the air and heard the birds chirping in the trees.

As she turned to her right along the ridge pathway, a ripple surged through her body and she began hopping and skipping, feeling giddy with happy childhood memories of hopscotch, roller blades, scooters, rubber balls, and hide-and-seek. Suddenly, she jumped twenty feet down the road and stopped in her tracks, looking behind her. *Well, that was quite the jump*, she said to herself. Without conscious reason, she jumped another forty feet, and looked behind, in astonishment.

Gentle breezes swayed through bushes and small trees on either side of the ridge as she made her way to the path that forged up the mountainside to a row of houses. She passed a large boulder at the base and began her ascent. It was a steep climb, about sixty feet, and she usually took breaks, huffing and puffing, but this time, she walked straight up that mountainside, feeling not tired or strained. The urge came, again, to take the jump. She wondered: *Can I do it?*

With one final push, she leaped high above the ridge and ascended, in one fell swoop, landing on the gravel road, with knees bent and hands on the ground, like a crouching cat. Yes, she could and she did!

Her face was bathed in the morning sun as she gazed at houses that wound along terraced pathways toward the river below. Miss Helen Chu opened her curtains from a nearby house, and waved to her. She had emigrated from South Korea thirty years before, and settled into Crestfield. Like a good neighbour, Ushaya waved back, realizing she had to watch it around here; the mountains had eyes—best be careful.

Well, I've come up this far, guess I must go back down, she said to herself, and took one, and then two steps down. The loose gravel made it slippery, and there were times she descended uncontrollably and had no intent on doing this now. Three steps down, another step, and onward she went. She looked up for a moment, and suddenly her left foot stumbled over a small rock and, just as she feared, she slid uncontrollably on her back with arms flung out wide, among pebbles and sharp gravel. She tumbled in a landslide, desperately trying to move her body upright to avoid that familiar boulder that loomed at the bottom.

Suddenly, she levitated right over the boulder and hovered freeze-frame in mid-air before slowly descending to the ground. "What the hell?" she cried out, looking up and down the road, thankful that no one was in sight. There were scratches on her arms and legs. Feeling nauseous and afraid and wondering if she was going nuts, she jumped, floated, and ran, blazing a trail all the way back, stumbling onto the front porch. With one last leap through the door, she bolted the lock from inside, as if she was afraid of someone or something chasing her. It dawned on her that she may be afraid of herself, and the thought did not comfort her. Dizzied from her morning walk, she trudged to the couch and collapsed.

Superpowers

Birds chirped outside her kitchen window. Flipping her hands back and forth and relieved to see there was no blue aura, she brewed another pot of coffee. Visions of levitating in the air flashed through her mind. Brushing the troubling thought aside, she kept herself busy, for there was laundry to do, emails and text messages to catch up on, plants to pot, and phone calls to make.

Ushaya was taking out garbage to the backyard bins when Emily stepped onto her balcony to shake a rug, and said, "Your hawthorn bushes keep dropping branches onto my side and I have to keep cleaning up the mess. You should cut them back."

"I will do my best to tie them," Ushaya conceded, trying to keep the peace.

Emily kept on. "Your bird feeder attracts such squawking sounds that it upsets my precious Mimi. The other day, she ran crazy around the house, toppling one of my heirloom teacups."

"Well, Mrs. Barker, I find the sound of morning birds very sweet. Too bad your doggy doesn't enjoy one of life's most precious things." Arguments ensued until Ushaya had had enough of this pettiness and walked back to her house, yelling, "Get a life!" She slammed the door with such force it shook the whole house, and even startled her. To take her mind off the upsetting encounter, she went back to the computer to check emails and pay bills.

An hour later, she stood in her living room, silently gazing at the ceiling, when something triggered deep inside her, and she began to rise three feet above the floor. Exhilarated, with arms outstretched, she twirled about. She actually and truly was levitating! A fit of laughter struck her uncontrollably.

Gaining her senses, she continued floating to the kitchen as if nothing had happened, and wrapped her arms around the fridge. Then she lifted it in the air and set it down five feet away. Stepping back in shock, she looked at her hands and remembered why she had wanted to move the fridge in the first place.

With rubber gloves on, she bent down on her knees to scrub the cruddy marks on the floor until the task was finished; then she rinsed the last pail of dirty water into the sink. Once the area was dry, she lifted the fridge and glided it back into position. After, she lifted her couch and placed it back down, and then she lifted her bed, amazed and confused, crying out, "What is happening to me?"

She glanced at her phone. It was noon—plenty of time for a flyby, she thought, and with a burst of excitement, she flew out the back door to discover her newfound strength. It wasn't long before she found things to lift. There was a large grey boulder in a nearby field and a stone statue in a local park and a fifteen-foot white van. She lifted her own car.

Weeks went by and her powers advanced—now she could lift a twenty-foot trailer, an empty city bus, and a rusted-out tractor in a farmer's field. She found some steel rebar at the same site that she bent into a complete circle, to her amazement. It was tricky, at first, balancing her body underneath cars, buses, and tractors with two legs straddling, knees bent, and arms stretched above her, but in time, she became adept at it.

One day, the doorbell rang. Annoyed at unexpected company, she mumbled, "Who would that be?" It was her old friend Mandy. She gave her big hugs and smiled, "Hi my dear! Come in," she said, gesturing her toward the couch.

Mandy sat down and advised, "I am only here for a short while, as I am off to Revelstoke to visit family tonight."

Ushaya offered her a glass of wine and asked, "When did we last see each other?"

Mandy mused, "About six months ago." They chatted for two hours, catching up on their lives while drinking wine and snacking on crackers and cheese. Mandy got up to leave and said, "Let's have a holiday in the Mediterranean, eh?" They exchanged long hugs and promised to keep in touch, and Ushaya watched Mandy drive away along the ridge, happy to have seen her dear friend again.

The evening was still young when she stood on the back deck, wondering what to do. Gazing at tall ash trees, she began her ascent to the highest branches, and startled birds whooshed out from the leaves. Pondering this precious moment in the treetops, she suddenly sprinted up, up the mountainside until she reached a lookout precipice jutting from a rock face, and wondered if hikers had ever reached this place before. It felt much cooler up there along the snow line.

Trees stood silent, tall, and majestic, and while admiring the breathtaking view, she had the urge to jump. Cautiously peering over the ledge to 8,000 feet below, she felt fear grip her and she no longer felt confident, for all her life she'd had a fear of heights. She moved back on the ledge, pacing back and forth and wondering what to do.

Another fear gripped her then: being stuck all night on this ledge with visions of a helicopter rescue. How would she explain being up there with no proper gear or warm clothing? *And the embarrassment of it all, with the event maybe hitting the news*, she thought. *No, no, that can't happen*, she said to herself, still pacing back and forth. The sun was beginning to set and it was getting cold. She must get off this ledge!

Starting back at running position, she made a dart for it. Her sneakers hit the ground . . . Thump, thump, thump, and she reached the edge and froze. It was a long way down. Backing away, she crouched against the rock face, feeling like a cat caught up in a tree that couldn't come down.

But then she convinced herself that it was no different than being in her living room. She got up and said out loud, "If I could do it then, I can do it now." She ran for it . . . Thump, thump, thump, and flung herself over the edge in freefall, her body spiralling downward and her arms in a flurry of erratic movements. Convinced, that she would meet her ultimate demise, she cried out, "Ahhhhhh," her voice trailing behind, "The living room, the living room!" Plummeting to earth, halfway down, she came to a standstill, hovering in the air. Feeling exhilarated yet strangely calm, she experienced a growing personal power that day. No words could describe how she felt as she began to soar, softly whispering, "I am truly flying." Inexplicable joy filled the very core of her being, as she darted in and out of the rock surfaces like a hummingbird, while chuckling to herself, wondering if this is how hummingbirds felt. They must be in constant ecstasy!

While passing over meadows and streams and waterfalls, she became lost, and slowed down to a full stop in midair, and glanced about. Not having the honing instincts of a hummingbird, she pulled out her iPhone from her jean pocket and set her GPS for home. As she flew across the evening sky, the cold began to settle into her bones. She had neither goggles nor gloves to protect her. Her hands, face, and eyes were dry, and the rest of her body was perspiring. She felt thirsty, hungry, tired, itchy, bitchy, sweaty, and cold. And if that was not enough, good old "nature" was calling. It was time for a pit stop in the mountains and a squat in the forest.

With a quick spin in the air, she headed to her little town, flying as fast as she could. Gliding above rugged, pristine forests, she found her house and reeled clumsily onto the front porch with such a loud racket, she feared her neighbours would come out to investigate. "Well, that didn't go as planned," she muttered, dusting herself off. Her body ached from head to toe and her skin tingled from the cold.

She poured herself a glass of wine and sat on the couch, pondering, *I DID fly, didn't I? Was I not in trees, watching birds?* Memories flooded her, of clouds in the air, tiny cars meandering along highways, and rivers and streams and alpine meadows—so many that she could no longer think. The previous hunger had passed, and she headed for bed for some much-needed rest. With her clothes on, so numbed and dazed to undress, she closed her eyes and fell asleep.

Jake Simmons

A receptionist answered: "Dr. Fritz's office. May I help you?"

"Hi, it's Ushaya. I wish to book an appointment."

"The usual fifteen-minute consult?"

"Uh, I might need more time. I have some issues with my . . . my feet." But Ushaya was not having problems with her feet, and so changed her mind.

"I am having problems with my stomach," she blurted. "I mean, I am having issues with vertigo." But she was not having issues with vertigo—quite the opposite. Not making any sense, she backed out of the call. She imagined her doctor listening to her story. With the professional training and knowledge of any doctor, he would prescribe a battery of tests and suggest a very good psychiatrist, who would arrange for a nice padded cell. Fear and paranoia set in, and she stammered, "I have some minor stuff going on, but nothing important right now."

"No problem, just give us a call when you're ready." The receptionist hung up, wondering if Ushaya was OK, and reported the call to Dr. Fritz.

Ushaya stared at her phone. As much as she had a wonderful rapport with her doctor, she was not yet ready to talk to anyone—not her doctor, her kids, her family or her friends. She must think this through. It all started with the Blue-ray light, and she was not any closer to the source of her new-found powers. After her shower, she dressed in fresh clothing and wandered to the kitchen to make breakfast. She spent the rest of the morning tending to emails and sorting out files.

With chores out of the way and a list in hand, she drove down the hill to the local food market. While browsing the aisles, she flung products into the cart, clearly pleased with her feat, chuckling out loud, "Bullseye!" An old man stopped nearby and stared at her. She caught his gaze and looked down, and, to her own shock, she was hovering one foot above the floor. Smoothly descending and without looking back, she continued along the aisles, thinking, no one would believe an old man anyway.

While standing in a long lineup, overcome by rising heat, she became annoyed and impatient. To make matters worse, the urge to levitate was so great that she had to use the utmost willpower not to do so. "Stay grounded, for God's sake!" she whispered to herself. The woman in front of her turned to see what was going on, and Ushaya feigned ignorance. "C'mon, c'mon, get moving," she muttered under her breath. She had to get out of there. All the noise and overhead announcements, the clamour and crowds, the bright lights, and freezers humming and babies crying, took their toll on her. It was time to pay, and out the sliding doors she went, of course mindful to walk and not fly! When she arrived home, she parked her car in the driveway and floated to the front door with grocery bags in both hands, chuckling, "This makes things easier." Mimi the dog was yapping away from her neighbour's front porch.

Days later, her computer guru Joel Dalton came for a visit to teach her GPS tracking on her iPhone for a road trip. He explained, "See these icons? Here is how you save files, and over here is where you check your speed and distance, and over here is where you track your moves. Does that make sense?"

"Oh, yeah, it's clear as mud," she replied.

"Call me anytime and I would be glad to help you," he said, and left.

There was one more thing she needed to do, and that was visit Valhalla Outfitters, the largest outdoor shop in the region. Manager Jake Simmons greeted her. "Can I help you, my dear?" He was a good-looking man in his thirties with blue eyes and long lashes, sporting a boyish haircut swooped to one side of his face. He wore stylish clothes, and judging by his demeanour, appeared to be as gay as they came.

Ushaya smiled. "I'm looking for a hang-gliding suit."

Noticing her age, he motioned with his finger, "Right this way. We have several types to choose from. Do you wish a summer or winter suit? It does make a difference, you know."

"One of each, I suppose," she replied.

He pulled out a cold-weather suit from a rack, which matched her size, "This material is made from the latest infusion of nylon and Gore-Tex, good for weather between minus thirty and ten degrees Celsius. Try it on," he suggested.

In the dressing room, she put on the suit. The fabric felt like brushed cloth over a thin layer of nylon. She raised the attached hood around her face. The sleeves went to her wrists and the leggings down to her ankles, and there was a front zipper down to her waist. The entire suit fit snugly, showing her curves. She stepped out of the dressing room and posed in front of a three-way mirror.

Jake studied her. "Darling, you look fabulous. It suits you well, pardon the pun."

"It's very comfortable," she smiled.

"Try this," he said, handing her another suit, "It's the fair weather one."

She slipped back into the dressing room and tried it on, and then took one final look in the mirror. It was a thinner, sleeker fabric, with a silvery sheen to it. For a moment, she felt like she was in a space suit. She stepped out to a waiting Jake, who stared at her and said, "You look splendid, my dear."

“I will purchase both of them,” she said. While posing in the mirror, she asked, “Is it possible to alter them with zippers sewn along the lower legs and upper arms? It gives the choice to zip up or down while gliding in all weather conditions.”

Jake thought for a moment, and replied, “I do know someone who makes custom orders to fit. When you’re done, meet me at the till and I will give you his card.” He sauntered back to the front desk to search through his drawers.

With both suits over her arm, she began browsing the aisles, and all kinds of gizmos and nifty things caught her attention. She found a rod flame starter. *This may come in handy*, she thought, and placed it in her shopping basket. She passed the kayak section and found a vest, which she also placed in her basket. A rose-tinted set of visors across the aisle caught her eye, and goggles at a nearby kiosk attracted her, too, before she found her way to the till.

“Have you found everything you’ve been looking for?” asked Jake.

She smiled and said, “It must be my lucky day,” and, glancing at a counter display of thin, lightweight gloves, added, “I’ll take these, too. They’re better than the ones I have.”

He handed her a card and said, “His name is Stanislav Kominsky. Have you heard of him? He’s famous around here.”

“I can’t say I have,” she said as she took the card. It had a satin sheen surface. His name was embossed in gold lettering against a soft ochre background, reminiscent of parchment. In the upper right-hand corner was an unfamiliar stylized crescent moon with six blue stars circling it. Under his name, Prof. Stanislav Kominsky, was an email address and phone number, and nothing else. “What is he famous for?” she asked.

He replied, “He is an inventor and master craftsman extraordinaire—cabinetmaker, cloth-maker, remote flying gizmos, you name it and he’s done it. At one time, he was an avid hang glider himself, even entering into competitions. That made him a living in those days.”

“What did he invent?” she asked.

He replied, “He grew up in Poland and became a professor in meteorology. During the Warshank uprising, he immigrated to Canada and went on to graduate with a degree in textile design. He was discovered by our Canadian Space Agency for his space-age cloths, which were used in suits for astronauts. That’s what put him on the map. You can read about him online.

He doesn't have his own website, but others have written articles and done interviews with him."

"Oh, really," she replied.

Jake whispered, "He's eccentric, if you know what I mean."

"No, what do you mean?" she wondered.

He leaned in to her and said, "Wait until you see his mansion, then you will know."

Intrigued, she placed the card in her pocket and asked, "How much for all of this?"

Ringing up the bill, he replied, "That will be $1,573."

She wondered if this was another one of her impulse buying sprees. She perused the gear one last time, and promptly paid the bill.

Lessons in Tenderness

One glorious evening, while wearing her summer suit, vest, visor, and gloves, she soared across the warm skies in a final burst of flight, chasing the last beams of the setting sun. It was time to go home, and while checking her GPS, she realized that she had travelled 500 miles in one hour! In disbelief, she set her coordinates and returned eastbound, following lines of least resistance, hugging mountainsides, with arms thrust forward, feeling the wind whistle around her, as she sped through the air. The g-force mounted against her windswept body, but she didn't care—*just keep going*, she thought. Soon, her little house came into view, and as she slowly descended to the front porch, a bright idea occurred. Landing on her left foot, she brought her right foot forward, behind, and then even with her left foot, stabilizing herself. It worked like magic. She repeated loudly, "Land, forward, back, and stabilize. Yeah, that will work." Aching from head to toe, her body still numb from the cold, her skin weathered and dry, she headed for bed. Totally exhausted, she pulled up the covers and muttered, "For cripes' sake, I'm in my clothes again," and fell asleep.

Days blended into nights, and nights blended into days, as she lost all track of time, forgetting breakfast, lunch, and supper routines, eating sporadically, whenever she could remember. She tried to keep up with emails that continued to pile up. She played back her twenty phone messages: "I haven't heard from you lately, is everything OK?" Next message: "Hi there, just wanted to see how you're doing. Give me a call." Next message: "This is an important message from your credit card company. Please call us to discuss your account at . . ." Next message and next message . . .

Her dual reality became normal life for her and she loved both sides. On the one side, she would make calls to family and friends. She would shop and do her chores and errands, and would study her investment portfolio and pay her bills, all the while remembering to eat and sleep.

In the other world, she was soaring among clouds, clocking speeds of 1,800 miles per hour, as she weaved in and out of earth's great majestic terrain. She would join geese in flight returning for the spring season. She would lift trucks, tractors, buses, boulders, and boats, all the while remembering to write in her daily diary, and to eat and sleep.

Online research led her to esteemed US astronaut Clay C. Anders, who explained about gravity, space, and g-force. He helped her with simple calculations that she could relate to. She began to realize that she was travelling in different speeds, and called them "Fast, Super and HypeMo". Theoretical calculations on propulsion and speed led her to physicist Professor Daniel Smirnoff from Russia, who attempted to answer her questions. She was elated to be in the company of venerated physicists, astronomers, and mathematicians, and explained her reason for contacting them: that she was writing an article on superpowers as part of her creative writing class.

Professor Woody Oldfield, who specialized in ratios and relative weights, advised her to begin a comparison chart. The ratios didn't seem to make sense, but they looked something like this:

OBJECT	**ACTUAL WEIGHT**	**USHAYA FELT**
Fridge	360 pounds	Five
Couch	300 pounds	Five
Large boulder	4,500 pounds	Ten
SUV	5,000 pounds	Fifteen
Tractor	19,000 pounds	Twenty
Greyhound Bus	20,000 pounds	Twenty
Abandoned train caboose	50,000 pounds	Forty

Some of her houseplants had died from neglect, much to her dismay. Sometimes, she got a good night's sleep, and other times, she would return in the wee hours of the morning and sleep until noon. One day, old man Wally, the gardener, dropped by with new topsoil for her terraced garden beds. She'd had to hire a gardener—she was too busy flying to attend to them.

She'd forget her strength at times. One day, about to get out of the car in her driveway, she found the door was stuck, preventing her from opening it. It was an ongoing problem that needed fixing. Frustrated, she kicked at the hinges. An indescribable sound of screeching steel separated from their bolts, and the entire car door fell off, swivelling round and round on the pavement with such a racket, that she feared the neighbours would come out. Stunned, staring at the door, she got out of her vehicle. The tow truck drivers arrived, and Ushaya feigned ignorance, trying to explain, "Somehow it just fell right off. I don't know what happened."

Scratching their heads, the men hoisted the car with chains and levers, and lifted the broken door onto their flatbed, advising her, "We'll get you a loaner while your car gets fixed."

Discovering her strengths made her ultra-sensitive to everyday objects, like holding a flower or working a thread through a needle, or shutting a door. One day, while prying open a stuck lid from a jar of olives, she crushed the glass into pieces, its contents exploding all over the kitchen counter. The glass cut her hand and the blood flowed down her arm. She may have grown stronger, but there were lessons in tenderness and mindfulness.

Day after day, with no one to talk to, weary of hiding her powers, she became distracted, entangling herself in treetops and slamming into buildings. One time, she almost knocked people over on city sidewalks. Fear and paranoia crept in, fear of injury to herself and others.

Jake had recommended that inventor who could make a custom suit, and she asked herself, "What's his name again?" From her den drawer, she pulled out his card. "Ah, yes."

Chapter Two

Stanislav Kominsky, the Inventor

Lucy the Robot

July 2018 . . .

Ushaya drove down a country lane through evergreen forests, passing a babbling brook, until she arrived and turned off the engine. Slowly stepping out of the car, she pulled down her shades. It was like a magical kingdom, far, far away. A four-storey mansion stood in the clearing with steps to a wrap-around deck. Strange glyphs were carved in stone pillars on either side of the landing, overgrown with ivy. Spiral staircases wound around the back, ending nowhere, reminding her of an Escher painting. Steeples and turrets perched on rooftops.

A buzzing sound came from a gizmo stationed at the eaves to her right, beeping, following her with a mechanical eye as she made her way up the steps. *Nothing like a warm welcome*, she thought wryly, lifting the Medusa head knocker on a large cedar door. Knock, knock, the sound clanged alarmingly.

The door opened to a tall, slender man, perhaps in his sixties, who appeared every bit as eccentric as the house. He wore black silk pants that creased elegantly around his ankles, and a pair of well-shined pointy shoes. His white satin shirt hung loosely to his waist with coattails trailing over his hips. His long, white hair fell neatly over his shoulders, and he wore blue-tinted shades and sported a thin moustache and tiny goatee. Stanislav spoke in a soft, dignified voice. "You must be Ushaya. Do come in."

She extended her hand and said, "It's nice to meet you. Jake highly recommended you." He offered to carry her pack, and she followed him to the great space.

"Jake's a good man, and I am sure anyone he recommends is coming to the right place," he said, motioning to her. "Have a seat, and would you like some iced tea? It's freshly made." He placed the pack next to her.

"Thank you, that would be most kind," she replied.

He bowed and left, and, now alone, she glanced around the great space. Books and magazines lined shelves here and there. The place was filled with photographs, art paraphernalia, and odd, eclectic statues. In front of her was a wooden coffee table, and beyond it, rose an imposing stone fireplace. Above the fireplace hung clocks of all sizes and shapes, ticking away, showing time around the world—Houston, London, Delhi, and Beijing. A globe perched on a five-foot wooden tripod to the right of the fireplace, and rod-iron poker sticks and stacks of birch logs sat to its left. At the far left was a table strewn with bits of cloth and papers.

Suddenly, a large black critter pounced on the coffee table. Ushaya screeched and jumped onto the couch. It was a ghastly sort of creature with six legs and rising antennae, looking like a drenched cat with scraggly whiskers and tiny, slanted yellow eyes, clicking and snickering, as it stood on its hind legs. "Aahh!" she cried out.

Stan arrived in time, barking, "Lucy, stand down!" The critter skittered off the table to a corner of the room, curling up in a resting position.

Ushaya could barely breathe. She whispered, "What is that thing?"

While placing cups and a pitcher of tea on the table, he replied, "I apologize. You should not have seen this—my great error." Sitting across from her on his sofa, pouring tea, he explained. "She is an AI robot, often my daily companion. I had forgotten to dock her."

"Fascinating." Ushaya sipped her tea, studying the robot.

He continued: "I am on contract to develop voice-and facial-recognition features, activated by command-control software programs for small devices. It's nothing new; this technology has been around for some time. Consider drones and R2D2." They chuckled.

She asked boldly, "Are you working for national intelligence or something?"

"I am not at liberty to say who my employer is, at this time. I've said too much already," he replied, placing his cup on the table.

"Of course, I didn't mean to pry, my apologies," she said, realizing, they both had their secrets. "The tea is delicious, Stanislav."

He leaned back and said, "Just call me Stan. Now, what brings you here? You mentioned vests and suits for this new club of yours, is that right?"

She reached into her pack to bring out the summer suit, thinking about her kids and son-in-law. Having rehearsed her story many times before, there was no turning back now, and she replied, "We are the Seniors Flying Club, SFC for short, but we are not official yet. There are four members so far, and we want to do an air show next year for Canada Day celebrations."

Stan examined the suit and said, "I can certainly make new suits. What are the alterations you wish?"

She cleared her throat. "Can you put zippers along the outer shins and lower arms? We're seniors and flying is physical work, as you know. It would be nice to have that option to cool down or warm up."

"I would suggest magnetic flaps, instead of zippers, which get stuck. With magnetic studs and flaps along the legs and arms, you can open and close them much easier," he said, adding, "but keep the front zipper. Regarding the vests with pockets and loops, they can easily be made." He placed the suit next to her and examined the paper with sketches and measurements. Silence fell, save for the gentle ticking of clocks. He asked, "So you are requesting four suits and four vests?"

She placed her cup down and replied, "There's one more thing. I know it's the beginning of July and awfully short notice, but could you have these made by end of month? Our members will be gathering next month in Manitoba for a fly-about."

Casually nodding, he placed the sketches on the table and replied, "I can have these suits ready by then, no problem."

"Really? You don't know how much this means to me," she said, breathing a sigh of relief.

He rose from the sofa and said, "Let me show you the sewing room."

"The what?" she asked.

He motioned to Lucy. "Could you come here please?"

The critter jumped on the table, flailing its scrawny arms and legs. It looked like a freaky skinny cat with eyes that appeared fierce one second, and soft the next, baring tiny teeth, nattering and chattering in strange clicking sounds.

"Don't worry, she is quite tame," Stan assured her. "Lucy, meet Ushaya. Ushaya, meet Lucy."

Ushaya bowed politely, "It's nice to meet you." Lucy squawked and clicked and screeched, while prancing about.

She looked at Stan. "What does that mean?"

"She says, it's nice to meet you, too. Now that you two are acquainted, would you mind if she tags along?" He sauntered through the French doors to the grand winding staircase that led to the second floor.

They scampered up the stairs and wandered down corridors lit with flickering torchlights and filled with paintings on either side. Lucy dashed down the hall ahead of Stan, curling into a ball before springing back to a six-legged creature. Then she walked upright, her head and arms swaying back and forth like a human.

Ushaya giggled, "I think she is more than a robot—she's an entertainer."

"Now, settle down, Lucy," he muttered, adding, "I must not feed her so much."

"What do you feed her?"

He stopped and turned to her. "Data," he said, and disappeared to the right.

She followed him up a narrow, winding staircase and down the hall. A door opened wide, and she stepped in and gasped.

The Sewing Room

It was a gigantic room with vaulted ceilings and beautiful stained glass windows. There was a noisy hum, and the place appeared like a small factory, with crisscross rows of cabinets and racks of hanging cloths and textiles. She turned left to the end of the aisle, where nothing could have prepared her for what she saw next. Six metallic tables stood side by side, about five feet apart, each with long, wide drawers and computer consoles. Sewing machines were bolted to each table, but these were no ordinary sewing machines. Strange wiry arms projected out of hoods with separate needles and threads, stitching back and forth in unison along cloths bolted to their surfaces. Each machine appeared to be working on a different design, and it was as if the entire metal surface was their stitching area, not just the normal three-inch metal plate. Bobbins threaded along grooves that joined with vertical spools of coloured thread, were fastened in place at the back of the hoods.

"What is this?" she sputtered.

"These are about to transform the garment industry!" Stan boomed over the din, "A collaborative effort with national and international partners. I have invented the programs and our partners contributed to the design of the machines."

She stopped at the first table and asked, "What is table No. One trying to sew?"

"A man's silk grey jacket, one of a hundred that we are producing in different styles and colours," he replied.

"How can you make so many?" she wondered.

He pointed to the five narrow shelves beneath the table, explaining, "This is where I layer the uncut materials, about twenty to each shelf, and these cubby drawers hold accessories, such as buttons, zippers, clasps, and things." He then turned to her and, with a commanding voice, said, "Now observe!"

To her amazement, an oblong metal plate emerged from the centre of the table, raising the next piece of fabric. Finger-like projections began to align the inside sleeves of the pre-cut cloths around the plate, with needles sewing the right and left armholes, and down the arms, moving the cloth along. Then "fingers" repositioned the front and back inner parts of the suit together, sewing the lapels, the collar, and inner lining. She shook her head, "There are no pins to keep the fabric in place."

"No need to—the fingers do all the walking. Why have pins that perform only one function when the fingers can do many?" he replied.

The machine paused. Fingers sewed upper and lower pockets to the jacket. Needles zoomed back and forth, while vertical spools spun away from behind the hood. Buttonholes were stitched to the left and right edges of the sleeves. Delicate fingers lifted the cloth over the plate and reversed the sleeves, and the plate lowered back down, flush to the surface of the table. The jacket was now complete, with folded collars and lapels, hems sewn, and buttons fastened. A set of brushes emerged to do the final dusting before receding back into the hood. Then fingers hung the jacket onto a coat hanger attached to a line of wire at the back of the table, along with the other jackets.

"Is this for real?" she asked, incredulous.

He proudly replied, "As real as you and me."

"I'm not so sure about that either," she smirked.

He smiled. "Can you imagine a jacket in five minutes without lifting a finger?"

They moved onto table No. Two. It was a woman's blouse with complicated stitchery using coloured threading along the sleeves and under the breast outline. "What nationality is this?" She asked.

He replied, "A Kandyla blouse worn by Greek women, as part of their traditional dance."

Glancing at the rest of the room, she asked, "Who is your market?"

He replied, "We are aiming for lower and middle markets around the world, in Bangladesh, Africa and South America, to reach the everyday people, especially in China and India." While tapping the computer console, he continued, "This is a wonderful start up business that can flourish anywhere. The costs are low with rapid output once the machines are installed and mastered. The machines do not require that much room either. It could even begin in one's home, although it would require a steady supply of electricity and a trained computer programmer on site."

She shook her head and said, "You run these by yourself?"

"Yes, I test the programs. Eventually, we will move operations to a facility, which is being built as we speak, just outside of Whitby, Ontario," he said.

They moved onto No. Three, where he explained about the two large black uncut pieces of cloth lying on top. He paused the machine from the panel keypad and lifted the material to expose rows of teeth in grooves along the surface. He explained how the fingers would turn the cloths in different directions, while scissors cut them into many pieces.

Lucy stood up excitedly on her hind legs, clicking and clacking.

"What is Lucy doing?" she asked.

He chuckled. "She gets excited, for this prototype has a lot of scissors. Mind you, all of these use scissors. This one is special; it produces smaller items in greater quantities at the same time." Stan pressed the keypad to resume and said, "Ushaya, you're about to see the beginning of its next cycle. Observe!"

Several scissors attached to arms and ball joints cut rapidly across the surface, turning the fabrics into shapes of gloves, while fingers simultaneously sewed threads in and out, weaving back and forth. Then the scissors came to a halt. Clamps unleashed and the hood swivelled to the back of the table. Fifteen sets of gloves were sewn in a matter of minutes, perfect with buttons, metal clasps, and fancy stitching. She watched the fingers lift and clip them to a string along the back table.

Stan noticed her gaze and whispered, "That's thirty gloves in a few minutes. Now multiply that by the hour, the week, and the month."

They stopped at table No. Four. Fingers were smoothing the sash of a black silk pair of pants. It was near completion. *The pants go very well with the grey jacket at No. One*, she thought. "What is the name of your company?" she asked.

"Dream Seam Machine is the name," he replied.

No. Five was weaving a beautiful crisscross maze of stitchery on heavier material. Silk threads began to reveal a scene of deep red roses among swirls of patterns. Ushaya watched the needles zoom back forth halfway through the material, and asked, "What is it?"

He smiled and said, "It's a tapestry. This machine is geared for materials like the vests I shall make for you, or shawls, bedding, curtains, projects like that."

She was curious. "How are you going to prevent the big fish scooping up your partners, once they get wind of new emerging markets? How long will it take to make a profit?"

He explained, "The more machines we manufacture and sell, the more profit. The more programs we lease out to entrepreneurs, the more profit. As with all start-ups, confidentiality clauses are built into agreements, and ours include a five-year term. After that, when the markets have flooded, partners can branch out on their own. If they want to sell up to a larger fish, they can do so, for we will have achieved our success by then."

Ushaya wondered if she was in the presence of a madman, but something distracted her at table No. Six. Her eyes widened, dazzled by layers of ivory chiffon and lace overflowing the table. Gazing at needles sewing back and forth over the bodice's multiple leaf motifs, she cried out, "A wedding dress! How beautiful. Who ordered this?"

"My niece Naomi is getting married next year. This gives me thoughts about brides around the world," he said, pondering.

"And you run this all by yourself? I don't see anyone around," said Ushaya, looking about.

Stan reminded her, "Remember, it is mostly automated. Come, I will show you."

They sat in swivel chairs in front of a flat table, and suddenly Lucy sprang up onto the surface. Stan admonished her: "Lucy, you know better than that," and she reluctantly hopped back down.

Ushaya was surprised, and asked, "If you don't want her jumping on the table, then why program that into her?"

He answered, "I didn't. Algorithms allow for spontaneity and discovery. As I track her progress, it is interesting to see the choices she makes." Then he pressed a button under the table and a laptop and two screens rose up. "Now if you don't mind, I need to unlock the computer," he said.

"Yes, of course," she said, moving her head discreetly to her right, gazing down at Lucy, by her side.

Stan punched in a series of numbers and codes. A voice commanded, "Right thumb print." He placed his thumb on the pad.

The voice commanded, "Activating Facial Feature Recognition." A light scanned his face.

"User ID." He punched in his ID.

"Password." He put in his password, muttering about Google Authenticator, which came next. Then came eye scan and voice scan, and then he punched in the name of the model of his first car and the name of a dead relative.

Ushaya crossed her arms and rolled her eyes. Too curious by then, she stared back at him, "All this security?"

Stan cried out, "We're in! It's necessary in my line of business."

"And you don't mind me sitting next to you throughout all this?" she asked.

He leaned toward her and said, "The codes and questions change constantly." Multiple screens opened in the air. He slid them back and forth, and said, "Let's take your measurements, so I can complete your order."

She heard a beep and asked, "What's that sound?"

He looked at his laptop, for it meant something was not right. Examining No. Six, the wedding dress, he realized his stupidity, and replied, "I forgot to feed her."

"Data, right?" she piped up.

"No, pearls," Stan stood up and asked, "Would you mind waiting a bit longer for your order?"

She replied, smiling, "It wouldn't be right to keep a wedding dress waiting, now would it?"

He disappeared down the rows, his voice trailing, "Follow me, we must find the pearls!"

Ushaya swivelled around and glanced at her robotic friend. "I fear that we have fallen down a rabbit hole. Do you know what that means?" Lucy scratched her head, perplexed.

"I didn't think so," she got up from her chair and said, "First, we must find your master." Lucy sprang into action through a maze of rows, until they found Stan searching for No. 645.

"Ah, here they are," he said, as he scooped up pearls with a trowel, and closed the drawer. Ushaya followed him along the walkway, passing rows of cabinets, while admiring the stained glass windows, streaming speckled lights across the floor.

The din and noise filled the air, as they arrived back at the sewing machines. Standing in front of No. Six, he poured the pearls into a cavity and closed the drawer. Cupping his right ear, he said, "It should resume now." The sewing machine began humming; threads on spools began turning. Smiling, he turned to her and said, "Let's get to your order," and guided her to a wall, "See this mat on the floor? I want you to stand on it, with your arms outstretched and your face forward." He began swiping programs in the air, and then called out, "Keep still, with your eyes down. I will pass a beam of diffused light to scan your body. You won't feel a thing."

Bathed in blue light, she felt memories of that fateful night flood her mind. While the beam was scanning down her legs, a growing fear gripped her, and she was no longer enjoying this. Her heart pounded, and sweat poured down her face. She couldn't wait for this to be over. The beam stopped, and Stan called out, "Perfect. You may now step off the mat."

She stepped away, agitated. "What was that blue light?"

Stan shrugged and replied, "The normal light we use for these scans."

"Normal? There is nothing normal about any of this," she cried out, trying to remain composed, "Who are you?"

"Are you all right?" he asked, most concerned.

She sighed and said, "I had a flashback of something. I am OK now."

He softly said, "Come, sit down, and I will show you your scans." A 3D green-coloured graph of her entire body suspended in the air, against a deep blue background. She gazed up in awe, forgetting her fears. He then retrieved a set of gloves from a drawer and said, "Try these on—a popular item among my customers."

She slid on the gloves with magnets attached to the fingertips and thumbs. Flicking her fingers outward, they all opened in one smooth move, much to Stan's surprise. Then she flipped them toward her, and the magnets snapped back into place. She took off the gloves and said, "I will have four sets, please," and asked, "How long will it take for you to complete the order?"

He keyed in specs and stats in the air and replied, "I would say, less than two hours, including the initial programming and prep work."

She couldn't believe her ears. "Four suits, vests, gloves, and programming in less than two hours? How's that possible?"

Unfazed, he pointed to the machines and replied, "No. One is for the suits, and No. Three for the gloves and No. Five for the vests. Once I set them up, the sewing will only take a half an hour." He placed the gloves back in his side drawer, adding, "I can text you when they are ready for pickup, would that be fine?"

Ushaya softly gushed, "Yes, that would be wonderful. It appears that I have all I need, and now the bill, please."

He opened up his accounting program and began clicking, "Give me a moment here. The bill, with taxes, will be $7,850.63," he replied.

She had already spent $1,500 for the gear from Valhalla, and now $10,000 would be sunk into this mission, with no way of knowing if it would work with the kids. Without skipping a beat, she set up the e-transfer payment from his computer, and the deal was done. She smiled and said, "Thank you for this amazing tour. I wish you every success in your endeavours."

Stan turned to Lucy and said, "Kindly escort Ushaya to the main lobby. I will catch up soon."

Following Lucy to the doorway, Ushaya said, "You're quite the robot."

Lucy stopped in her tracks, appearing indignant, chattering and jumping up and down, flailing her arms about.

Ushaya didn't understand a word and called out, "Stan?"

"Yes?" he answered from the far side of the room.

"You must program English into Lucy," she said.

His voice rang out, "It's in the works, and many other languages!" A voice commanded from his computer: "Activating Shutdown Sequence."

Ushaya followed Lucy down the alcove staircase and along the hall of many portraits, one of them a large, framed photo of Canadian Prime Minister Jerome LaBerge, presenting Stanislav with the Golden National Science Award.

Lucy pounced ahead down the hall, chattering back to Ushaya, urging her on.

She gazed one more time at the photo and called out, "I'm coming," and walked briskly down the hall, until she stood at the top of the grand, curved, sweeping staircase, made of ornate golden relief designs. It took her breath away, for she hadn't remembered much on their way up to the sewing room. A large chandelier hung from the domed ceiling. She descended the staircase, gently gliding her right hand along the railing, savouring a moment of wealth and class. All that was missing, she imagined, was her glittery gown and golden slippers. Her grey sneakers touched the floor, and her reality turned no less fantastic, as she strode across the room to Lucy, who was waiting at the door. She turned her gaze through the open French doors, wondering, "I imagine Stan should be here soon, ah, there he is."

His white sleeves flapped in the breeze as he quickly descended the staircase to join them. "Your order is set to go, and I will let you know when they are complete."

Ushaya turned to Lucy and said, "It's been a delight to meet you." Lucy pranced up and down, clicking and clacking.

Stroking his goatee with a glint in his eye, Stan asked, "What do you suppose she just said?"

"Likewise," replied Ushaya.

He frowned and said, "I thought she was wondering how you did that finger flap trick with the gloves, back at the sewing room. Lucy had never seen anyone flick the magnets off all fingertips at the same time."

Swinging her backpack around her shoulders, straightening the straps, Ushaya quipped, "Oh? Then clearly there's more work to do."

He chuckled and opened the door, and said, "Please don't hesitate to call if you need anything," and watched her skip down the steps, carrying a heavy backpack like it had no weight.

She turned at the bottom of the steps to face him and called out, "It's been a pleasure meeting you today."

"Likewise," he answered, watching her pull out a pair of sunglasses and sprint to her car. The engine started and he closed the front door. Pausing a moment, he turned to Lucy and said, "There's something about her. Do you think she is one of us?"

With the engine idling, Ushaya wondered out loud, "What the hell? Lucy? Sewing machines?" She glimpsed through the windshield at the mansion, and then drove through the open gates with her backpack next to her. *As long as he can make these suits, that's what matters. I've got to tell Jake*, she thought.

It was a glorious summer's day with bright blue skies as she steered leisurely along the highway listening to music, passing cars, following transport trucks up steep mountain passes through ever-changing landscapes. A smile crossed her face, for she had forgotten how much she enjoyed the open road.

Chapter Three

First Contact

Gargoyles and Angels

Early August 2018 . . .

Birds chirped outside her window as the morning sun filtered through the curtains. Reaching for her phone, Ushaya blinked in astonishment. It was 8:00, but two days later. From a jumble of disjointed dreams, there was not much she could remember, and she mumbled, "I guess I crashed."

She lit candles day and night, meditating upon the Blue-ray light, asking with the greatest of reverence, for a message from beyond, about these powers. No answer came to her plea. She demanded to know, and then she asked, not so politely, and then she tried bartering. Then she became angry in righteous indignation, and cried out, "How can you abandon me? It's outrageous!" But no answer came.

Sinking further into despair, she felt paranoia begin to set in. Was she going mad? Enough was enough! She thought, *I must find something to watch over me, a talisman, but what?*

One day, while browsing the local Valley Garden Shop, she eyed a pair of gargoyle statues. They stood four feet tall with piercing eyes glaring out intently. Their wings were covered in exquisite swirly designs. Their claws grasped the stone slab foundation with a quiet strength emanating from their sentry stance, which attracted her.

A female clerk approached, asking, "Can I help you?"

Ushaya inquired, "What can you tell me about these gargoyles?"

The clerk scrolled through her iPad and replied, "They replicate originals commissioned by a Spanish count, circa fifteenth century, and are completely made of stone, quite heavy, I would say. It comes with a booklet on the history of gargoyles and the craftsmen involved. Do you like them?"

Before Ushaya could answer, something else caught her eye: two angel statues made of stone of a similar size, standing behind her. Glancing back and forth, she announced, "I'll take the gargoyles, please."

The clerk proceeded to complete the sale, suggesting, "You can always come back for the angels," and asked, "What is your address?"

Ushaya could easily fly the gargoyles home at the laughable ounces they felt like to her, probably in a few minutes. But, alas, unable to reveal her strengths, she was once again reminded that she no longer was like other people, and with a heavy heart, she gave the clerk her address. Days later, their fierce eyes glared over the valley from either side of the front porch, and she gazed at the majestic beasts guarding her world, and saw that all was good.

That evening, thunder roared and lightning flashed through the bathroom window, as she stood naked in front of the mirror, illuminating how toned her body had become. Wrinkles were fading from her face, and she was turning more youthful in appearance. She ran her fingers through her wavy black hair that draped over her shoulders, with wisps of silver running through it. Then she pulled out a mirror to examine her itchy back. All appeared normal and she stepped down from the sink counter.

Lying in bed, she wondered if she was crazy or lonely, or both. It was nice to feel empowered and fly about with birds and all, but with no answer from the source and not a soul to confide in, she felt abandoned and lost. She curled into a ball with her last drifting thought, *the gargoyles are here; the angels will come*, and fell into a deep sleep.

Retirement Bash

One day while soaring across the sky, Ushaya began planning out her strategy on how to fly the kids. They couldn't just lock arms together—it was too risky. Instead, they would be harnessed with ropes through their vests. She researched online for various slipknots and rope techniques, imagining ten feet apart for space between them.

One day, she picked up the phone and called Brad, who answered, "Hello?"

"How are you doing?" she asked.

"Not bad, I left messages, eh?" he replied.

"It's been busy lately. How's your work going?" she asked.

"I just got back from collecting rock samples up north. We're exploring the Churchill region for rare minerals. We may have found something to interest our stakeholders," he said proudly.

"Sounds interesting. Actually, I am wondering if I could visit for a few days," she said.

"Sure, I have some time off next week. Is everything OK?"

She stammered, "I need to see you. I—I can't explain it over the phone."

"What, are you sick?"

"No, I'm not sick."

"Are you in trouble?"

"No, why would I be in trouble?"

"Then what is it?" he pressed on.

She took a deep breath and said, "I have developed special powers, and I want to demonstrate them to you."

He wondered, "What do you mean, special powers?"

She boldly replied, "All I can say is, what you shall witness will blow your mind."

Silence fell between them. He had been concerned about Mom lately, for she would become forgetful, often repeating herself, and now she was playing cryptic games. "Of course, why don't we just book the flight right now," he suggested. They booked her flight, and he offered to pick her up at the airport.

What was the point of driving all the way to the airport, parking his car, and waiting around luggage carousels, she thought, when she could easily fly ten minutes to his place with her GPS and luggage, weighing less than a few ounces. "That's all right, I will take a taxi. Look forward to seeing you. Love you," she said.

"Love you, too," he said, ending the call, wondering what was going on with her.

The contact with her son sent her deep into contemplation. Where would she go after her visit with the kids? Nights filled with candles burning, as she scribbled names of world leaders, starting with Canadian Prime Minister Jerome, followed by US President Ronald. Then, perhaps, Germany, Africa, maybe Mexico, the Middle East, China, and Russia. It was all a jumble in her head. Not one for following politics, other than through tabloid news, she needed to know more. While standing in the checkout lineup at the local library, holding an armful of books and CDs, she bumped into Marcus, a neighbour two roads up. "Nice to see you," she said, smiling.

Marcus glanced at her books, inquiring, "Getting into politics, eh?"

"Uh, just a research project I've got going," she said.

He reminded her of his barbecue retirement bash that weekend. As he was leaving the library, he waved at her and called out, "Be there!"

"I will," she said, waving back, and then she proceeded through the checkout.

The weekend came, and the backyard filled up with guests, about forty milling about. Everyone was enjoying the music, dancing, drinking, and smoking pot. Ushaya helped Marcus at the grill, flipping burgers, chicken, and salmon slabs in one quick succession after the other. He stared at her. She had so much fun all night long, and by 10:00 p.m., it was time to leave. She embraced her friends and exchanged phone numbers with new acquaintances. After congratulating Marcus on his retirement, she found her way down the winding path, looking for her car, slightly inebriated and stoned. "Ah, there it is," she whispered. Swaying in the dark, fumbling with her key fob, she accidentally set off the alarm. Woo, Woo! Quickly she turned it off and pressed another key. The front headlights flashed. She turned it off and pressed another, but nothing happened. "The heck with this," she muttered, placing the fob into her pocket.

Straddled under the car, lifting it with both hands, she began to fly down the pathway, manoeuvring among bushes and parked cars. Her house sat only two roads down. *Not far to go*, she thought, when suddenly, the left headlamp smashed into a tree trunk in front of her, and she backed away. The rear fender hit a boulder with an awful sound of grinding steel, sending her zigzagging over the hill, scraping bushes, and bang! Smash! Crunch! She landed the car onto her driveway. Standing back to examine the damages, she shook her head and went inside, lamenting, "Another insurance claim." She closed the door behind her, vowing to no more drink and fly.

Days later, she got a text from Stan: "Your order is ready for pickup," and, the following day, she sprinted up the steps to his door.

Stan motioned her in. "You have a different car," he remarked.

"Mine is in for repairs," she replied. They chatted a while. Then with suits, vests, and gloves packed into a suitcase, she left.

Closing his door, he turned to Lucy and said, "She must be one of us."

She got into her car. "What if the powers should fail?" she said. The ultimate test to her sanity was about to begin.

Visit with Brad

An announcement crackled over the sound of engines high above the clouds, "This is Captain Conrad speaking. Welcome aboard, ladies and gentlemen. Our weather forecast shows light winds and sunny skies. We'll be cruising at an altitude of 24,000 feet and will arrive at Brandon Airport by 12:30 p.m. Complimentary meals, coffee, and tea will be served shortly, and alcoholic beverages can be purchased with Visa or MasterCard, for your convenience. We hope you have a pleasant flight, and thank you for choosing North Jet."

She retrieved three large metallic trunks from the airport carousel, and, finding an outside hidden corridor, secured them to her belt. With GPS set, she flew up, up in SuperMo toward her son's house. She landed a few minutes later in front of his driveway. The living room curtains ruffled, and the front door opened wide. Brad grinned and gave her a big hug. He stared down the street, and asked, "Where's the taxi?"

"It left already," she replied, entering the house.

He closed the door, and stared at three large metallic trunks and her backpack for a five-day stay. "You're not moving in, are you?" he asked.

She chuckled and replied, "No, just a few things to show you."

He hauled her luggage down the hall to her room and said, "Your room is all set up. By the way, you're looking great."

"Thank you," she said, motioning to him. "You can set the luggage over there."

They soon settled back in the living room, and for an hour, they chatted about their lives, about family, his work and about his new girlfriend,

Cheyenne, who lived in another city. They talked about investments and money, and then it turned to her visit.

While standing in the kitchen, pouring two cups of coffee, he called out, “You mentioned special powers, what’s that all about?”

“I think you should sit down for this,” she hollered out.

“Nah, just go ahead and say it,” he hollered back, stirring in the cream.

There was a long pause, before she spoke. “I can levitate and fly.”

Brad froze. It was worse than he feared. He returned to the living room with their coffees, shaking his head, and said, “Nobody can fly or levitate.”

“Oh, yes,” she argued, taking a sip of coffee. “There are instances in history, and even now, there are people capable of such feats. I know I can.”

“Really? OK, show me,” he said, as he sat on the adjacent couch. It pained him to be so direct, but dementia and delusions were very grave concerns, and he had to assess how far she was into her psychosis, and figure out what to do.

Ushaya got up from the couch. They stared at each other, each in their thoughts. One thing was for sure—both worlds were about to collide and change their lives forever. With arms by her side, she rose five feet and hovered in mid-air. Brad’s mouth dropped and his eyes grew wide. She rose higher, circling the ceiling, twirling around in figure eights, before she sat back down.

“Holy crap. I can’t believe it. It’s no trick?” he cried out, sprinting off the couch.

“It’s no trick,” she replied, secretly joyous that the feat had worked.

“OK, so how did this all start?” he asked.

“Before I begin my story, I wish to demonstrate strength.” She floated to his heavy wooden bookcase, filled with electronic equipment and audio speakers, and various magazines, books, and knick-knacks. After disconnecting the cables, she moved one end of the bookcase from the wall, and, grasping the back panel, tilting the bookcase upon her, she began lifting it in the air, swaying slowly across the room.

“I don’t believe it!” he exclaimed, watching her return the bookcase down in place and wiping the dust from her hands.

She headed for the front door and said, “I can lift boulders, tractors, cars, and beds; you name it. Matter of fact, why don’t I lift your truck right now?”

Warily, he looked back and forth down the street, and replied, “I don’t think that’s a good idea. What will the neighbours think?” She scanned down the street and could see no one around. Against her son's protests, she began lifting the one-ton truck, and rose eight feet in the air. He stumbled back, crashing into garbage cans, exclaiming, "Oh shit, shit, can't believe this." Collecting himself, he straightened out the bins.

Meanwhile, old man Harvey O'Brien sat in his wheelchair in his living room, staring out the window at Brad's house, across the street. An oxygen tank hissed rhythmically, feeding precious life force to his nostrils. His feeble fingers reached for a button, and his long-time aide, Nurse Caroline, entered the room, a plump, middle-aged woman, who spoke: "Is everything all right?" She adjusted his blanket, ensuring to cover his swollen ankles.

He motioned her closer with his fingers. Caroline leaned closer. Faintly coughing, he whispered, "I just saw a woman lift Brad's truck in the air."

She stared out the window. Brad's truck was parked as usual, with no one around, and she replied sympathetically, "If you see anything else, let me know, OK? Your lunch is almost ready." Then she left the room, wondering if his medication needed changing. Harvey nodded in silence, and continued gazing out the window.

All afternoon, Brad chased his mom around the house in childlike playfulness. She lifted his bed, the fridge, his couch, and dining table. She explained about her theory of three speeds, Fast, Super, and HypeMo.

Brad shook his head. "Can you do it again, that's just crazy shit, and you call this HypeMo?"

She shrugged. "I am here by the kitchen, right?" Suddenly, she disappeared. A faint voice called out, "Yoo-hoo, I'm over here."

He walked over to the front window and pulled back the curtains. Waving from the front steps, with an impish twinkle in her eye, she asked, "Can I come back in now?"

Before he could respond, a door shut, and a voice came from behind, "I'm over here." He spun around and saw her floating by the kitchen entrance. Meanwhile, old man Harvey sat quietly eating his lunch, watching strange things going on, across the street.

Brad returned from the kitchen with platters of cheese and crackers, and sat down at the table in the living room, insisting, "OK, you have to tell me how this all started."

She began the tale of her encounter with the Blue-ray light. The stories continued into the evening over a bottle of wine for her, and bottles of beer for Brad, as she recounted her many adventures. Then she checked her invisible watch on her left wrist and announced, "It's almost midnight. I have suitcases to unpack."

"You don't have a watch," he chortled.

"It's a new habit of mine," she replied. As they walked down the hall toward their bedrooms, she stopped. "There's one more thing, and it involves you, but we can talk about it tomorrow. You've been through enough today."

He asked, curiously, "What is it? I won't sleep until you tell me."

She paused for a moment and said, "I want us to fly together."

"Out there?" he exclaimed, gesturing wildly.

"Yes, out there," she replied. "After all, if I can fly buses and cars, surely, I can fly you. How much do you weigh?"

"Uh, 200 pounds, I guess. But I have a fear of heights."

She softly said, "I know you do. Why don't we start from your living room? I've brought suits, vests, gloves, visors, and rope to help you fly." She told the story of her encounter with Stanislav, the inventor.

Feeling overwhelmed by it all, he yawned and said, "Let's call it a night and talk about this in the morning. Love you."

"Love you, too. Good night." She closed her bedroom door.

Land, Forward Back and Stabilize

The sun streamed through his bedroom window while Brad listened to birds chirping their morning songs, enjoying a moment of peace. But there was another sound. He opened his eyes to see a large common fly dive-bomb toward his face, and flung his blankets, and sat up in bed, annoyed by the intrusion. "There it is," he muttered, following its orbital path around the room. He got up and coaxed the fly out the open window. "Out you go, little fella," he said, and slammed the shutters tight. He sauntered down the hall to coffee percolating, and joined his mom in the kitchen. "How was your night?" he asked.

Rummaging through the fridge for cream, she said, "I had a great sleep. How was yours?"

"Out like a light," he replied. They went about their morning routines, taking showers and eating breakfast, checking emails and online news feeds. Eleven o'clock rolled by, and he stood at the dining table, and announced, "I want to fly with you." She glanced up from her laptop.

By noon, all geared up, she asked, "Are you ready?"

"I think I am," he replied, patting his suit and vest. Suddenly, he levitated five feet in the air. "Holy crap!" he cried out, staring down at the floor.

Ten feet of rope hung lax between them, and she gasped, "Why are the ropes just hanging? I should be lugging you like a potato sack against the force of gravity, just like boulders."

"You always rope boulders?" he asked.

"No I just lift them," she replied.

"Then how is this possible?"

"I don't know," she said, staring at the ropes. "Perhaps, it's some kind of thought transference with organic objects like you, instead of inanimate objects."

"So, now I have been reduced to organic matter," quipped Brad.

They gently glided across the living room and into the kitchen, and then down the hallway and back again to their starting point. While hovering five feet in the air, she announced, "Now pay close attention: we are about to land."

He chortled, "Land? It's only five feet down."

"For every takeoff there is a landing, and you must not stumble. We must come down in unison, especially out there," she replied, adding, "Learn my technique, and it will soon be instinct, like driving a car." She then asked, "So which is your strong foot?"

"My right," he answered.

She demonstrated. "On my count, you land with your right foot first. Then you place your left foot forward and back behind you, and then stabilize. See?" Together, they practiced in the air, and he heard her repeat, "Land, forward, back, and stabilize."

"Is that what you usually do?" he asked.

She replied, "No, I land with both feet. But you are a beginner."

He heard the countdown sequence, "Three, two, one," and they landed perfectly, breaking out in jubilation. When the excitement had settled down, she had an idea. Touching baby fingers only, they ascended together in complete awe, and floated about the room, before descending to the floor. From her suitcase, she pulled out visors, gloves, and ear buds, and said, "Here, put these on."

All suited up, they flew out the front door. A neighbour two doors down was parking his car in the driveway. "We need to hide!" she exclaimed, moving them to a nearby bush for camouflage.

He chuckled at the irony and said, "We're supposed to be flying, and here we are in a bush."

"Welcome to my world," she whispered. Soon, the neighbour went inside and the coast was clear.

They blazed a trail eastward over hills and valleys, until his town long faded behind them. Tiny cars meandered along the highway, giving way to scenes of farmers' fields and communities. Hills turned into rivers and small lakes as they flew and flew, marvelling at an osprey soaring alongside them. While descending into the ever-changing landscape, they pointed to a coyote running into a bush below. Bear and moose and elk were roaming across the lands. They glided above marshes, filled with bullfrogs croaking among the bulrushes and reeds, while the call of a loon echoed its song from shore to shore. Winding rivers cut through rolling hills and low-lying fields, toward the distant peaks of a mountain range.

Speechless, exhilarated, and in spite of his fear of heights, Brad was not afraid. Instead, he wondered: *Am I dreaming*?

Wisps of smoke rose above a campsite, with the aroma of burning wood bringing back fond memories from their camping days. Eventually, they found a grassy alpine meadow, and landed on their backs, gazing up at the sky, playing a game of "bursting the clouds."

"I love Canada," he said.

"Me, too," she said.

"Let's come back here to fish."

"We can hire a charter."

"I don't think charters exist in the alpines."

"Then I will fly a boat here," she said, and they giggled.

Suddenly, he sat up and asked, "Where are we?"

She glanced at her phone and replied, "We travelled one hundred miles and have crossed the border into Ontario. We're not in Manitoba anymore." Brad could not believe what he was hearing.

She began adjusting their ropes and vests, and said, "Let's go home." With GPS set, they flew westbound above the ever-changing landscape, feeling the breeze blowing across their faces, until they arrived on the front steps of his house. At that moment, Harvey was peering through binoculars pointed at Brad's place, gaping in awe at what he saw.

Untethered from his ropes and gear, quietly sitting at the kitchen table, Brad asked dreamily, "Did you hear the loon?"

Ushaya replied, "Yes, and did you see the dust storm?"

"No, I didn't, but did you see the motorcycle gang, cruising along the highway?"

"No, but did you smell the fires burning from campsites?"

"Yes, I did," he said. He was silent for a moment and then asked, "Where are you going from here? I mean, what do you want to do with these powers?"

"I want to meet world leaders," she replied, floating to the kitchen.

He followed her, wondering, "Which leaders?"

She opened the fridge and said, "I'm working on it. Firstly, I shall start with our own PM Jerome, and then onto US President Ronald. From there, perhaps, Mexico could be next. After that, it's somewhere in Europe and Africa. From there, I don't know, perhaps China and Russia."

He pressed on, "So how are you going to demonstrate these powers?"

"The same way I demonstrated them to you," she replied, handing him two frozen pizzas from the freezer.

Brad placed the pizzas into the oven, setting the timer for twenty minutes. "What, you're just going to strap them together and fly?" he asked.

"That's the plan. It worked for you, didn't it?" She passed him the lettuce, tomato and avocado for a salad.

He began chopping, pressing on, "How are you going to pay for all those flights to different countries?"

While grating cheese, she answered, "I am hoping leaders will cover the expenses."

"Do you know what you are saying?" he asked, laying out the cutlery on the table.

Ushaya followed him to the dining room, and, placing the salad bowl on the table, said, “There is one more thing.”

“Oh, for cripes’ sake, now what?” he cried out.

She calmly said, “I want Meg and Devon to fly with us together. Four custom suits have been made, thanks to Stan. And they have holidays this week.”

Brad sat down at the table and propped his elbows, holding his head. “What? Meg? I guess that would be cool, but why Devon?” he asked.

Shrugging, she replied, “They are like two peas in a pod. It would be difficult to keep this secret from him. He has been a good man to our family. I can have you back in time for work later this week. What do you say?”

Brad agreed, “OK, when do we leave? We would fly by plane, right?” He wanted to be sure. The sound of a buzzer startled them. Pizzas were ready.

They ate their meals in silence, and soon after, were sitting before his laptop. Meg and Devon appeared on screen. Megan piped up, “Hi, guys. Wow, Mom, are you really in Manitoba?”

“Yup, sure am,” she said, adding, “Hi, Devon.”

“Hi there,” he responded, with his usual cheerful smile.

Meg asked, “You want to visit right away, so what is happening?” Ushaya cleared her throat and replied, “I have developed special powers lately, and we wish to demonstrate them to you. I cannot explain over Zoom. It needs to be seen to believe.”

Meg inquired, “What powers?”

Devon was hoping for a little more and said, “Sure, come anytime, but can you say something about this power?”

“No, I cannot,” replied Ushaya, and she whispered to Brad, “Help me out here.”

Brad piped in, “It’s completely true what Mom says. What you will experience will blow your mind; it has to be seen.”

Devon asked, “So how long do you want to visit for?”

“Just three days, right, Brad?” Ushaya looked at him.

“Yeah, I have a short break,” he replied, barely able to contain his excitement.

Ushaya inquired, “What are the grandkids doing this week?”

Meg answered, “They will be home for only a day or so, before they go on holidays to visit friends.”

Ushaya smiled. “It would be nice to see them before they go. And one more thing: say nothing to them about our reason for coming.”

“It is that powerful,” Brad chimed in, while gazing at his sister Meg and brother-in-law Devon across the screen. Soon after, they ended their call.

Meg frowned at Devon, wondering, “What was that about?”

He shrugged. “We’ll soon find out.”

Flights were booked for the following morning. While sorting through items for the trip, Brad hollered from his bedroom, “With all that seventy feet of rope and gear, why don’t we split the load? My duffel bag has room.”

“Good idea,” she hollered back, gazing at stuff strewn across the living room floor, not knowing where to start.

Chapter Four

The Kids

Touchdown, Wellington, NZ

Brad chose the aisle seat. Ushaya took the middle, and a young lady named Amy sat by the left window. They introduced themselves to each other in pleasant exchanges. The plane accelerated along the tarmac, lifting 300 people into the morning sky, when loudspeakers crackled over the roar, "This is your Captain Riley speaking, and welcome aboard, ladies and gentlemen. Our arrival time will be . . ."

But Ushaya heard, "Welcome aboard, ladies and gentlemen. You are in a straitjacket and have no doubt taken your meds to cope with the gruelling journey ahead. By the end, you will have watched four movies, you will not remember tomorrow. You will have eaten countless meals, and have slept three hours with your eye patch on, curled up in one of our complimentary blankets. And if you were smart enough, you would have chosen the aisle seat. The cabin crew is pleased to serve alcohol, so have your credit card ready . . ." and she jolted back to the captain's last words: "Thank you for joining Can Air International, and have a pleasant flight."

While cruising 500 miles an hour, they watched their movies, and ate their food and drank their drinks. Nighttime fell, and cabin lights dimmed, and Brad asked Mom, "Have you ever flown a 747?"

She leaned over and replied, "I can't imagine lifting a jet, much less fly one."

Amy was browsing sites on her tablet, and the glare from the screen was annoying everyone around them.

Ushaya whispered, "We're going to fix this."

"How?" he whispered.

"HypeMo," she replied. She scoped the area, and, poof! Disappeared.

Amy looked at Brad and said, "Wasn't your mom just here? I just saw her."

"Apparently so," was all he could say, glancing ahead to find her standing at a lavatory door, waving. Poof! She was back in her seat. He looked away, like he didn't know this woman.

Amy shut down her tablet, wondering if she was going crazy. All was dark in their corner, and with headrests and blankets on, they curled up in their seats.

"Thanks Mom," whispered Brad.

"You're welcome," she replied.

The plane touched down on the tarmac, and customs check-in went surprisingly smoothly. Meg greeted them at the gate. "How was the flight?" she asked.

"Interesting," said Brad.

She raised her brows and said, "Oh? Let's get your luggage."

Three big metal trunks came down the carousel, and Ushaya stacked them effortlessly onto a cart. Her backpack soon followed, and she threw it on top.

"All this for three days?" asked Meg, noting how strong her mom had become.

Brad retrieved his duffel bag and replied, "Trust me, she needs them."

An hour later, they arrived in front of ocean views with palm trees swaying along sandy shores. A villa nestled among garden groves and fields. Brad greeted Baxter, a little brown shaggy dog, wagging his tail, and he bent down and whispered, "Hi, little fella." Devon greeted them in the foyer, and knowing it was almost midnight, he guided them to their rooms.

Chelsea's City of Lights

The following morning, Ushaya joined them at the dining table.

"How was your sleep?" asked Meg, sipping her coffee.

She replied, "Out like a light. How about you guys?"

"I slept pretty good," said Brad, as he got up for more coffee, asking, "Mom, do you want one?"

"Yes, please," she replied. Baxter came to her side, wagging his tail. She hugged him, and said, "Hi, my sweetie."

From the kitchen, Devon hollered out, "The kids should be down soon."

Brad had returned with coffee, when Chelsea popped around the corner. She was a tall, beautiful redhead, aged twelve years old, with long wavy hair, wrapped in a ponytail. "Grandma Ushi, Uncle Brad!" she cried out, and ran to them, and they all embraced.

Tyler stood at the entrance with hands in his pockets, acting cool at the age of fourteen. He was slight of build, and his blonde hair parted to his left, and his right side was shaved in a smart slick style, and he had the most wonderful blue eyes.

Brad couldn't believe how handsome he had become. "Come on over and give us a hug," he said. Tyler gave them warm hugs, clearly pleased to see them.

Meg cried out from the kitchen, "I've got the dishes."

"Salt and pepper, Tyler," said Dad, popping bagels into the toaster.

"I'll get the cutlery," said Ushaya.

Chelsea wandered into the melee, "Do we have yogurt, Dad?" she asked.

"In the fridge," he replied, sprinkling fresh-cut chives over the eggs sizzling in the pan.

They sat down to a morning feast of fried eggs and bacon, bagels and cheese, and cantaloupe and yogurt. While buttering his bagel, Devon said, "Tyler has an announcement to make."

"My stunt kite is finally finished, and it's called Black Rider," said Tyler, digging into his meal.

Ushaya asked, "Is that the two-handle one with eight strings and a ten-foot wingspan?"

"Yeah, that's the one," he replied, adding, "And I also made two more kites, a Box kite with streamers and an orange Swordtail fish."

Brad glanced at Meg and said, "We used to go kiting as kids, remember?"

Meg took a sip of juice, reminiscing. "Yeah, it was so much fun," she replied.

While munching on cantaloupe, Brad said, "So Tyler, I hear that you're going on a trip."

Tyler's best friend, Maxwell, had invited him for five days on their family houseboat. The boys grew up together, and were in the same class at school. They were bound for Blue Nelson Lake, to enjoy breathtaking views, and to snorkel and fish in its crystal clear waters.

"And you, Chelsea?" inquired Ushaya.

Chelsea would be staying a week with her friend Rebecca, and her family. They were planning to visit Wapaki City to watch the annual carnival, and afterward, do some sightseeing, and catch a movie and visit museums, and swim in the ocean.

They finished their breakfast, and headed for the car. It was Chelsea's last day at school before the holidays. They were bringing home her City of Lights project from the classroom. Meg explained to them that, for their final mark, students had to build a joint project between father and child. It could be any project they chose, and students came up with some pretty interesting displays.

Devon, who sat behind the wheel, added, "If there was no father, then it could be an uncle or a brother or a male mentor. Many in her class got an A, and the City of Lights was featured in the final school assembly."

"I can't wait to see it," beamed Ushaya. In jumped Baxter for the ride, for on this special occasion, he was allowed to come, and soon the family headed out to celebrate the last day of school.

Mrs. Fisher, the homeroom teacher, greeted them warmly, "Welcome to New Zealand. I'll get extra chairs. Chelsea, can you show your family around?" Many dads were mingling about, for they too, had projects to bring home. The room was filled with maps and brightly coloured drawings, and shelves were layered with students' projects on one side of the room. A blackboard spanned the front of the class, with chalk pieces and brushes resting neatly on a metal shelf. A large computer screen stood on the teacher's table. Desks and chairs were arranged in groups, with iPads in front of students.

When everyone had settled in, Mrs. Fisher pulled down the window shades and commanded Brad to turn off the lights. Chelsea pressed a switch on her remote. Her project lit up like a decked out Christmas tree. Wow! On the table sat a multi-media cardboard display, three feet wide by two feet deep and one foot tall, a three-dimensional cut-out of New York City and its famous landmarks. Twinkling lights emitted through high-rise buildings, along roadways, and over the Brooklyn Bridge.

Brad walked around and said, "Very cool, Chelsea, and look, the Empire State Building, and over here, the Statue of Liberty."

Ushaya wandered around the display. "Fifth Avenue, Guggenheim Museum, and Greenwich Village," she said, surprised to see props, such as trees, park benches, and lampposts in Central Park.

"Times Square and Staten Island," said Brad, pointing.

"Turn on the 9-11 Memorial and the Tribute in Light," said Dad.

Chelsea pressed a button on her remote. Two blue rays shot up intercepting at the ceiling. Ushaya's jaw dropped, "Wow! How did you make this?" she asked.

Chelsea pushed back the curtain and turned on a flashlight, "Here underneath," she replied. They peered in and saw a jumble of tiny wires and electric bars, all leading up through the cardboard floor.

While peering over skyscrapers, Ushaya inquired, "Why did you choose this project?"

"Remember me and my family went to New York City last year?" she began.

The teacher corrected her, piping in, "My family *and* I," and the class chuckled.

With emphasis, Chelsea said, "My family and I flew over the city at night, and the lights were so amazing that I thought it would make a great project." Chelsea wanted to become a city planner when she grew up.

"Hmm, fly over New York City at night? I might just do that one day," said Ushaya. Brad shot her a glance. "May I take some pictures?" she asked.

"Go ahead," said Chelsea, motioning her.

Soon the lights were turned on and the window shades opened. Students buzzed around their projects, while Baxter the dog weaved through the crowd, getting lots of pats. One project was a triptych display on greenhouse effects. A globe stood in the centre, surrounded by charts and recommended books to read.

Another was a homopolar motor demonstrating electromagnetism. A round magnet was placed on the bottom of a triple-A battery. A spiral-shaped copper wire surrounded the battery, with top ends touching, and voilà! The copper wire spun and spun. Another project was a flying gizmo, and everyone enjoyed taking turns with the remote. There was the invisible ink experiment, where they would dip a brush in lemon juice and write down their message on paper. When heated over a candle flame for a few seconds, voila! The secret message would appear. Tyler was admiring a metallic robot, one foot tall, painted in traditional Maori motifs. Sounds bleeped, lights flashed, its head swirled, and arms and legs moved in typical robot style. It belonged to a bright young boy named Kauri, whose father was an aerospace engineer.

Ushaya gazed out the window, in thought. Chelsea was now in Grade 7, sending her down memory lane to when her kids were that age and further in time many moons ago to when she was that age. A lot had changed over the years. But some things hadn't changed—the "feel" of a classroom, the desks and blackboards and hallways filled with lockers.

Students helped lift Chelsea's project into the extended cab of the family car. As they stood around, they all gave their farewells. "Have a great summer, Chelsea," they said. She was popular among her peers. She waved out the window as their car drove away; there was one boy named Travis waving back, who took quite the fancy to her, but he was shy.

Tyler's Kites

The family gathered at the back of their property. Each kite was hand-painted, and materials were carefully chosen. There was the Swordtail Fish, which could "swim" in the air, and his prized Black Rider was mounted on the grass. "Who wants to fly the Box kite?" asked Tyler.

Brad examined the see-through material. It had a black frame with green and red streamers, trailing out from the bottom corners. "I'll take it," he said, and picked up the spool, letting out more and more string. Floating higher, its cubed edges struck a black contrast against the bright blue sky, and he cried out, "Pretty cool kite, Tyler." Chelsea took the Swordtail kite and proceeded to release string into the air. Devon turned on his video and began recording.

Ushaya was shielding her eyes to the sky when Tyler snuck up behind. "Grandma, do you want to try my Black Rider?" he asked.

Flabbergasted, she said, "Well, I don't know. It's been years since I've worked a two-handle. Why don't you demonstrate?" She stood in the field waiting for his command.

He called out, "Bring it up!" She let go, and it lifted in the air, zoom, zoom, back and forth it went. "Keep your wrists apart and move both hands together, like this," he said, demonstrating. After steering for a while, he landed the kite and gave her the handles, and said, "OK, now you try."

Meg grinned and said, "This, I got to see." Devon followed with his camera.

Ushaya grasped the handles, and called out to Tyler in the field, "I'm ready!" Black Rider swooped up and was airborne. She could feel its drag in the brisk wind; a surge of adrenalin raced up her arms, thrilling her. With feet firmly straddled on the ground, she kept a steady eye, as it whizzed back and forth, adeptly making adjustments with her wrists.

Tyler piped up, "You are doing great!" Suddenly, she whipped around in circles, over and over. Voom! Voom! She couldn't stop, so transfixed. He was beginning to worry his kite will crash.

"Mom, slow down!" cried out Meg. But she wasn't listening, twirling, hanging onto the handles with all her might, voom, voom, swish, swish, voom, swish. She was out of control. Chelsea gazed over at the commotion.

"Hold my kite," said Brad, and he ran to them. Chelsea was now steering two kites.

He cupped his mouth and called out, "Mom, you're in HypeMo! Slow down!"

"HiMo?" asked Meg, gawking at Brad.

"I'll explain later," he said.

Regaining her breath, Ushaya slowed to an even stride, and Black Rider soon whizzed gently back and forth. She asked, "Tyler, where do you want me to land this?"

He ran across the field, yelling, "Where you started." She brought down the kite in a perfect upright landing on the grass, and cheers followed.

Meg asked Devon, "Are you recording this?"

"I sure am," he replied.

Ushaya apologized, "Sorry about that, I don't know what happened out there."

"Why don't you take the Box kite," suggested Brad.

Tyler and Brad took turns flying Black Rider, while Ushaya and Chelsea continued guiding their kites. Two hours later, Devon announced, "Time for lunch, reel them in."

They moaned, "So soon?" With lines reeled in and kites stowed away, Ushaya joined Brad, as they walked back to the house. She softly said, "It wasn't HypeMo, more like FastMo, but anyway, it worked out. I'm so embarrassed."

He sputtered, "Watch what you do with those powers, OK?"

"Yeah, right," she replied, and they trudged on.

"I enjoyed kiting today," he said, smiling.

"Me too," she said, smiling back.

Late that afternoon, gathered outside, waiting for Rebecca's car to arrive, Chelsea announced, "Here they come." They shook hands with Mr. and Mrs. Walsh. Their daughter, slightly overweight, with long blonde, wavy hair and a pleasant face that matched her pleasant smile, introduced herself. "I'm Rebecca, nice to meet you. Have a great stay in New Zealand." They helped pack Chelsea's luggage into the car and were soon waving, as they drove away.

While waiting for Tyler's friend to arrive, Ushaya apologized for what happened out there.

He shook his head and replied, "I don't know how you did it, but you can fly Black Rider anytime." Maxwell and his family had arrived, and he excitedly introduced Grandma Ushi and Uncle Brad.

Hugging Tyler, one more time, Meg said, "You'll be out of range sometimes, so stay in touch."

He hugged his dad, and climbing into the car, he said, "Don't worry, I will."

The car pulled away, and everyone waved, crying out, "Bye! Love you! Have a great trip!"

Meg gazed out wistfully, "Well, at least you got to see them," she said.

"You have two beautiful kids," replied Ushaya.

"We sure do," said Devon.

FastMo and SuperMo

The three sat silently on the couch across from Ushaya, who was gazing at the rafters, which were about twenty-feet high, and featured a nice skylight, when she bluntly came to the point and said, "I can levitate and fly."

"Huh?" said Meg, turning to Brad.

"Just listen," he said.

Standing before them with palms upward, Ushaya rose six feet in the air. Meg hushed in disbelief. Devon stared at his mother-in-law floating in his living room. Glancing over at Brad, he asked, "Aren't you amazed?"

"Seen it before," he grinned.

Gliding in loops and swirls, while other times, darting back and forth so fast that the kids could barely follow, she twirled one last time and slowly sat back in her sofa. They exploded in giddy laughter, and conversations bubbled into the early evening. Ushaya told the tale of the mysterious Blue-ray light that one fateful night, of her first levitation on gravel roads, and how she eventually flew great distances at great speeds, reaching 2,300 miles an hour over mountains, valleys and towns in all weather conditions (she preferred to stay out of the rain).

She told her tales of strength, lifting cars, fridges, trucks and tractors. Then she lifted their own couch, buffet and dining table, and they were awestruck. She told the story of the busted car door rattling on her driveway, and they howled with laughter. Transfixed by then, they were eager to hear more.

She told them about Valhalla Outfitters, run by manager Jake, who turned her onto eccentric Stanislav the inventor, about his mansion resting two valleys over, and how he dressed in style, and about his sewing machines. But not a word was spoken about Lucy, for she had sworn secrecy to Stan. Then came stories of physicists, mathematicians and scientists, whom she had met online for advice on speed, weight and mass, and she would write every day in her diary. Then she stopped talking.

So many questions swirled in their minds. What was the blue light? How heavy was a tractor, and how did she lift it? How did she navigate in the sky?

Ushaya broke the silence, "I can travel in different speeds."

Brad cut in, "You have to see this. She calls them FastMo, SuperMo, and HypeMo."

"What do you mean?" asked Devon.

Ushaya recounted the advice given by Astronaut Clay Anders, an expert in aerodynamics propulsion, that she had been travelling in different speeds. "For instance," she began, "I asked him: If an airplane travels at 400 miles per hour through a living room, and is forty feet long, how fast would it be going? He replied, four hundred miles per hour." The kids chuckled.

She straightened up and continued, “So I rephrased the question. How fast does an airplane travel through forty feet of space at 400 miles per hour? While hearing his keyboard clicking, Clay Anders came back with the answer—1.5 seconds in forty feet.”

“Wow,” said the kids.

“That’s FastMo,” said Ushaya, and she gave another example, “Imagine, you’re in the front seat of a racetrack, watching cars go by, zoom, zoom. You barely see them, right? Or imagine a common fly buzzing around, and you can’t catch it. You see the object, but cannot describe what you see. The professor wondered what kind of story I was writing. Of course, I couldn’t tell him, that I actually was really flying.” They all laughed, and Ushaya took another sip of wine.

Brad asked, “Can you catch flies?”

She nodded. “I often do in my kitchen, and release them out the window.”

“So what is SuperMo?” asked Devon.

Ushaya paused and then began, “Imagine something spooked you, like a ghost. You turn around, but nothing is there. I use this mode all the time, say, my parked car at a supermarket, and foop, I’d be gone. People around the area would sense something had happened, but just carry on. That’s SuperMo.”

“Foop?” repeated Devon.

She told the story of her conversation with Professor Oldfield, who was punching in formulas on his computer. He asked, “Ushaya, do you know that a blink of an eye lasts one tenth of a second?”

“No, I didn’t,” she responded.

He continued, “Let’s suppose, a half of a blink of an eye, one-twentieth of a second, is about right to see that ghost of yours, will you agree?”

“OK,” she replied.

With more clicks on his keyboard, muttering about terminal velocity and speed, he looked up and said, “But according to your calculations, you were travelling 2,300 mph, which means 3,373 feet per second. That’s the speed of a supersonic missile, do you understand?”

Ushaya ended the story of the conversation, and folded her hands. They all fell silent.

Meg whispered, almost afraid to ask, "So, what is HypeMo?" Suddenly, she remembered, and said, "Oh, I get it, Brad. That's what you said when she was flying Tyler's kite."

Brad corrected her, "Actually it was FastMo."

The Disappearing Act

They took a break to clear their heads. Meg wandered to the back patio for some fresh air. Brad pulled another beer from the fridge and sat in the den with his laptop. Devon went to the garage to sort out tools, and pulling out a bottle of rum, he took a swig. While sifting through suitcases in her bedroom, Ushaya had found what she was looking for. It was a deck of playing cards, and a smile crossed her face.

Assembled back in the living room, she unwrapped the cellophane packaging, and announced, "I'm going to demonstrate HypeMo."

"You mean a card trick," said Devon.

She fanned the cards face up, and replied, "It's no trick. As you can see, this is a brand new deck. It has all the suits and Jokers too." They looked at the cards.

Ushaya commanded, "Devon, pick up the deck and shuffle well."

He shuffled and shuffled, and after splitting the cards several times, he placed them on the table.

Then she said, "Brad, cut the deck." He leaned over and cut the deck.

She turned to Meg and said, "Pick the top card, and you guys look at it. Say nothing, and place it back down."

Meg picked the first card and showed the others. It was the eight of clubs. Ushaya watched intently as she lay it face down on the pile, for this was her split-second chance. "Meg, turn it over," she said.

With her hand barely off the card, Meg turned over the ace of diamonds, and cried out, "I can't believe it!"

Ushaya smiled and said, "Now go to the front porch." Meg walked over and opened the door.

"Eight of clubs, right?" hollered Brad.

"Yup." She walked back in, and placed it on the table.

With a twinkle in her eye, Ushaya commanded, "Turn the top card. Is it still the ace of diamonds?"

Meg flipped the top card, and it was now the ten of spades.

Ushaya said, "Now check the bottom card."

She flipped the bottom one, exposing the ace of diamonds, and they were amazed.

"This is some trick," said Devon.

"Not a trick, a demo," reminded Ushaya.

Brad was gazing out thoughtfully, combing his hand through his hair, when he said, "You just demonstrated HypeMo, and not only did you disappear, but the cards also disappeared. That's really powerful."

Ushaya replied, "Very good, Brad, you catch on quickly. I've been practicing different objects in HypeMo, but without proper instruments and only my stopwatch to measure this speed, which registers six digits after the dot, I have no clue what this means."

"What the hell are you saying?" asked Meg, frowning, "All we saw was some cards disappear."

"Then, I shall disappear," said Ushaya.

"Go right ahead," said Devon.

"A piece of cake," snorted Brad.

Poof! She was gone. The kids jumped up, looking around, wondering where she went. A faint voice called out, "Over here . . ."

"It's coming from the kitchen," exclaimed Devon.

"I think it's the front door," said Brad, listening.

"She's upstairs," said Meg, and they followed her up the stairs and down the hall, arriving at Ushaya's bedroom. Gently pushing the door open, they saw her in bed with a laptop, smiling impishly, asking, "What took you so long?"

"Now, Mom, you just can't disappear and reappear whenever you feel like . . ." and suddenly, Meg whirled around and said, "She disappeared again."

"I know where she is," said Brad, and they followed him back down the stairs to the living room.

Ushaya sat on her sofa with a book in her hand, and softly said, "So, my dear family, what you have just witnessed is HypeMo."

Stunned, the kids settled back on the couch. Meg wondered, "How fast can you go in HypeMo? Did the math guys tell you?"

She replied, "Professors Smirnoff and Oldfield are working on the formulas."

Brad told the story of their plane flight and Mom's disappearing act, which helped them get some sleep! They all chuckled.

"How far can you go in HypeMo?" wondered Devon.

"About a mile so far," said Ushaya. Then she told the story of flying with Brad to the alpine meadows.

Meg and Devon cried out, "You flew together?"

Brad replied, "Yep, we seriously travelled one hundred miles and ended in Ontario. I couldn't believe it myself. It feels weird to say this, but that's what happened. Even with my fear of heights, it felt safe. I was airborne, and the sights from up there, you guys, you can't imagine."

"How? You didn't hold hands, did you?" asked Meg.

He explained, "We did it with ropes wrapped around both sides of me to hang onto, and the ends were attached to a hook on Mom's belt. My arms and legs were free."

Ushaya dropped the final bombshell: "Let's all fly together."

"What?" Meg straightened up.

"That's why the suitcases, for the rope and gear," said Brad.

"What kind of gear?" asked Devon intrigued.

Ushaya floated back and forth, in an absented-minded way that she often slipped into when excited or deep in thought, and, counting on her fingers, replied, "Well, there's suits, vests, gloves, visors, ropes, hooks, backpacks, water bottles, safety kits, and things like that." Sitting back in her sofa, she continued, "This is a first for me, too, but I am confident it can be done. If a bus weighs twenty tons, then surely I can fly you all. We can practice in the house, like Brad and I did before we headed out."

They had completely missed supper, yet weren't feeling hungry. Devon slowly nodded and said, "I'll give it a go, if Meg wants to, but right now, let's call it a night. It's been a hell of a day and I'm bagged." Ushaya yawned, glancing at the invisible watch on her left wrist. It was eleven o'clock.

"You don't have a watch," said Meg.

They wandered down the hall to their bedrooms. Brad called out, "Good night, guys. Looking forward to this."

In unison, they answered back, "Good night, Brad."

Meg closed the door and turned to Devon, whispering, "Fly together?"

After her shower, Ushaya slipped into her nightgown and under the covers. She turned off the lamp and closed her eyes, softly whispering, "Ah, sleep."

Echo Canyon

The following morning, after they had their breakfast, the kids assembled back in the living room, wearing suits, vests, and gloves. Ushaya weaved one rope through her right vest loops, continuing through Meg and Devon's left and right loops. She did the same with Brad to her left. With plenty of rope to spare, she wrapped the loose ends twice around her waist, before securing them in a triple knot to large hooks attached to separate belts. All suited up, she explained, "Once in mid-air, hang onto your parallel ropes. They keep you stable while you fly." It would help her too, for she could control them, like a pair of wings. Suddenly, they levitated seven feet in the air. Meg gasped, as they glided to the skylights. Keeping them close to her sides, Ushaya gently descended and floated to the kitchen, and then down the hallway and back again to the living room. With one thrust outward, she straightened them in a line, hovering five feet above the floor.

Devon glanced at the ropes and asked, "How come they are slack, and we're floating between them?"

She replied, "We're not sure. Brad and I think it's some kind of thought transference. I haven't roped inanimate objects yet, like a bus or a rock, but when I do, I bet they won't stay lax like this." Pointing to the floor, she added, "We need to land."

"Land? Just take us down," said Meg.

She explained, "That is a different animal. While you were airborne, I had control over your moves, but now, I cannot control how your feet will land, only you can do that. You must learn my technique, and once you know, it will be as automatic as driving a car."

"So, what do we do?" asked Devon, staring at the mere five feet below.

"Which is your strongest foot?" she asked. They were all right-footed. She said, "Then land with your right foot and knees bent. Immediately bring your left foot forward, and then behind you, and then bring it even with your right foot, all steps in one smooth movement, like this." She demonstrated, adding, "No flopping over. The whole idea is that everyone moves in unison, like a dance."

"Can you show us again?" asked Meg. Over and over, they practiced, until they heard, "Land, forward, back, and stabilize." They landed perfectly, and high-fived each other, so happy they had accomplished their mission. Ushaya made her rounds to ensure the ropes were secured, that their vests, packs, visors, gloves, and ear buds were on. With smartphones tethered from their wrists to their vest pockets, they floated out the front door.

"Very cool," said Meg, examining the magnetic flaps at the end of her fingers. The kids pulled down facemasks over their noses, chuckling, feeling like spies on a secret mission.

Ushaya gazed at clouds forming in the north, and, satisfied, secured her GPS for fifty miles, and up, up they flew into the sky, her entourage trailing behind in taut ropes.

Frantically looking about, Meg cried out, "Oh, God, so fast!"

"We're moving twenty miles an hour, do you want me to go slower?" asked Ushaya.

"Hell, no!" cried out Brad, pulling down his visor, flinging his arms in the air.

Devon called out to Meg, "Are you OK?"

A pleasant breeze was caressing her face, when she replied, "I'm OK. How far up are we?"

"About 2,000 feet," said Ushaya, picking up speed, veering northeast over farmlands and valleys and hills and towns shrinking below them, reaching one hundred miles an hour. In breathless glee, they continued their journey, until they came upon a narrow canyon, and, gliding between the sheer-ridged sandstone cliffs, they came to a full stop.

"I know where we are, Echo Canyon, a popular destination for hang gliders," said Devon. He let go the ropes, pulled down his visor, and called out, "All right!" Echoes ricocheted across the canyon, "All right all right, right, right all right, right all, right . . ."

Brad cupped his hands and yelled, "Anybody out there?" Echoes resounded from every direction, "Out there, anybody, anybody out, there out, there out, anybody there, there, out there . . ."

Meg called out, "I can't believe it!" Echoes reverberated: "I can't believe it, believe, I leave it, leave it, leave it . . ."

Suddenly, they heard hissing sounds. Ushaya stopped floating and said, "Shh, quiet. Something strange is going on." Words echoed back, 'Shh, strange, quiet, going, strange, sshh, shh, isssh, hisssss'.

"I'm getting spooked," said Meg. 'Spooked, spook, getting I'm, spooked, ha-ha, spooked, am spooked, sshh quiet, strange, hissssss . . .'

Huddled together, Ushaya whispered, "From now on, text only. Do not speak." Words echoed back, 'Shh, quiet, text, ha-ha spooked, text, strange, speak, speak, hissssssss'.

Brad texted, "What's happening?"

She texted back, "Not sure. Visors on, and hang onto your ropes."

Suddenly, black ghostly shapes appeared all around them with menacing bright yellow eyes, snaking through their ropes, swirling above their heads and below their feet, hissing and whispering. Before Ushaya could react, they disappeared.

"What was that?" cried out Brad. 'Wassss that, wass that, what, wasss, wasss, hissssss . . .'

Something tugged at Meg's right sleeve, and she shrieked. Her piercing cries echoed unbearably.

Ushaya stopped dead in her tracks. The black ghosts had returned in greater numbers, thirty or forty of them, everywhere hissing and whispering. She locked onto one figure. It had a black tail and horrible yellow glowing eyes with sharp-pointed teeth. Their bony fingers yanked at their ropes and pulled at their backpacks. One of them made off with Meg's left glove. Terrified, they began swatting this way and that way, but their hands went right through thin air. They had no defence against them.

Brad sent out a frantic text, "Get the hell out!"

Suddenly, Devon yelled, "Help me!" His voice echoed down the canyon. Two black creatures were lifting his arms, pulling the ropes taut, and the kids cried out in horror.

With fierce eyes and the claws of a tigress defending her cubs, Ushaya lunged toward Devon, screeching, "Aaaaaahhhhhh!" Then something extraordinary happened. Bolts of electric currents shot out from her fingertips, and she zapped the ghosts on either side of him. The creatures disintegrated, releasing Devon from their grip. She looked above him, and zap! Another ghost to his left, zap! Twirling to the front, two more zaps! A strange vision transported her to the Wild West days in a town shoot-out, her posse defending right behind her.

Meg shouted, "Mom, to your right!" Four ghosts were barrelling down upon them, and zap-zap-zap-zap! Proudly razing them all, puffing out imaginary smoke from her fingers, she jumped on her imaginary horse, and called out, "Hang onto your hats!" Her voice boomeranged, "Hang on, hang on, your hats, hats, hats, hissssss . . ."

She continued zapping creatures, left and right, and Brad cried out, "Mom, your left leg!" A creature was about to sink its teeth, and, zap! They began accelerating into SuperMo, barely able to breathe, with cheeks vibrating and teeth rattling, and their gloves hot on their ropes, passing wisps of black shapes, blurring by, when suddenly, they were out!

Ushaya came to a full stop a mile away, exhausted, with hands on her thighs. Slowly, they turned and faced the canyon. Meg was visibly shaken. Devon pulled out his canteen and took a gulp of water, and wiped his mouth. Brad threw off his visor and hood, exclaiming, "What the hell just happened?"

"I don't know," said Ushaya. She turned to Devon and asked, "What is this place again?"

He replied, "Echo Canyon, but more like Shadow Valley."

"They weren't shadows, more like ghosts," said Brad.

"More like creatures," said Meg.

"They were demons," said Devon, adding, "Did you see their yellow teeth and eyes?"

Meanwhile, Ushaya was gazing at her hands.

Meg lit up and said, "Show us the sparks, Mom. I could actually hear crackling in the air. Do you think it's a new power?"

Ushaya moved back to give space, and, concentrating, she flicked out both hands, pffft, pffft! But nothing happened. She flicked her fingers here, there, and everywhere, wondering why it wasn't happening, when Brad interrupted. "It's all right, Mom. We know what we saw."

Meg suggested, "Maybe she needs to be in the right state of mind."

Devon raised his brows and chortled, "Yeah, like sheer terror?"

Ushaya hung her head and said, "I was hoping for a pleasant adventure, and now, this happens." They confirmed amongst each other that Meg had lost her glove, and Devon was almost taken away.

"They were creatures," said Meg.

"Monsters," said Devon.

"Ghosts, right, Mom?" asked Brad, looking at her. She wasn't listening; she was studying her hands.

Danger in the Sky

Meg pointed to the clouds above, and said, "Let's go there."

Devon jibed, "You're getting brave, aren't you?"

"We're here already. They don't seem far away. What do you think, Mom?"

Ushaya scanned the cumulative clouds above them. *It might be a nice distraction*, she thought, *away from the trauma they had just experienced.* She pulled out an extra glove for Meg, and soon they rose.

Devon sniffed the cool air. "It smells like ozone or something, and it's quiet up here."

"It usually is," said Ushaya, "Of course, I have to be on the lookout for birds and planes." Their suits glistened with moist droplets.

"Brad gazed around, and spoke. "The clouds are beautiful."

A swift breeze blew past her face. Ushaya sensed that something was not right. Soon, they were engulfed in thick whitish-grey clouds, obscuring everyone's sight.

"Whoa, this is really neat," said Devon, staring blankly into the greyness, "Meg, are you there?"

"I'm here. What about you, Brad?"

"Roger. Mom, what about you?"

"I'm here. Jesus, we can't see anything. I'm concerned about the down draft."

"What does that mean?" asked Devon.

"It means that more cloud is accumulating underneath. We're right in the thick of it and, shh! Quiet."

"What is it? I'm getting spooked again," said Meg. There was no denying it. They all heard the distant roar of an engine.

Brad looked wildly about, "Where is it coming from?"

"I don't know." Ushaya tried to get a lock on it. The sound was getting louder, and she knew what it was, crying out, "It's a jet!" With two strong yanks, the kids were instantly reined in.

"It's getting louder," said Meg, clearly worried.

Devon hollered, "Where's it coming from?"

Clouds darkened from the plane's shadow above them, and Ushaya cried out, "Hang on! We're going down!"

Meg screamed, "Aaahhhhhhh," her cries deafened by the roar above. With butterflies in their stomachs and hearts leaping out of their chests, there was nothing they could do but endure the breathtaking vertical descent, plummeting to earth in SuperMo. They came to a dead stop, 1,000 feet above the ground. Coughing and spluttering, they steadied themselves in the air before gazing up at the plane in the sky.

"That's no jet, it's a military plane," said Devon.

"How far up were we?" asked Meg suspiciously.

Ushaya replied sheepishly, "About 10,000 feet."

"Are you kidding me?" said Brad.

Devon pointed, "Look! It's turning around and heading our way."

Corporal Terry Smith peered out his right window and said, "Captain, have a look at this."

Captain Magnum Forrest got up and peered out the window.

"What do you make of it, sir?" asked Cpl. Smith.

"Probably a bunch of skydivers," replied Cpt. Forrest.

Smith was worried. "Shouldn't their parachutes be deployed by now?"

"Why didn't they come up on our radar, and where's their aircraft?" asked Forrest.

"My sentiments exactly," said Smith, as he began keying into multiple screens, "I am unable to locate any aircraft." Zooming in on the skydivers, he added, "There appears to be a ringleader, and they have backpacks. But they have ropes between them all, how is that going to work, sir? Wait, they're on the move, but still no parachutes."

Forrest commanded, "Alert the authorities and follow up with a report, ASAP."

"Right away, sir," said Smith.

While descending over ever-changing terrain, their cheeks began to warm in the lower altitude, and the city skyline sparkled in the distance. Sunbeams shimmered through rows of yellow aspen trees among the quivering leaves, as they glided along a country lane, and letting go of the ropes, free from their cares and woes, free of body and mind, they flew into bliss . . .

A familiar sight showed on the horizon, and, closing in, Ushaya called out, "Remember your landing gear." Three, two, one, and they landed on the front porch, home at last! Exploding in giddiness and awe, they removed their gear and suits. Ushaya reminded them that during flight, bodily "needs" suspend, but once back on earth, they become urgent. The kids ran to the loos, while she collapsed in a lawn chair on the back terrace to have a smoke. Devon returned with a daiquiri drink, which she gladly accepted. Soon, the rest arrived with drinks in hand and sat in their chairs, each deep in thought.

Devon gazed at the sky, and said, "There are no words to describe how incredible that was."

Ushaya frowned, exclaiming, "I almost got you killed, not once, but twice!" She stared at their lily pond, and finished with her cigarette, she said, "I'm going for a nap, is that all right?"

"I'm tired myself," admitted Devon.

Brad said, "I'm pretty wired, actually."

"Same here," said Meg.

The card game

Two hours later, Devon stumbled into the kitchen and gave his wife a peck on the cheek, asking, "What's cooking? Smells good."

Meg was stirring noodles in a pot, and replied, "We have a salad and fettuccini Alfredo coming."

"I had a crazy dream," he said, poking his nose in the sauce. "Something about riding a horse in the sky, and there was this fireball coming my way, and the horse threw me off, and I was falling to earth."

"Sounds like normal around here," chortled Brad, setting the table.

The phone rang, and it was Chelsea.

They gathered around, using Face-time. "How are you doing, sweetie?" her dad asked.

"We went to the museum, and now we're at the beach," Chelsea said.

"Don't let the sharks bite," he teased her.

She giggled and said, "There are no sharks here. You know that." Brad's face came into view, and she exclaimed, "Uncle Brad! Are you having a good day today?"

At first, he didn't know what to say. "It's been nice. We're resting and are about to have dinner," he replied.

"Where's Grandma?" she asked.

"She's sleeping," he answered.

Chelsea nodded and said, "She must be tired after all that travelling." They couldn't agree more, and soon afterward, they ended their call.

Meg asked Devon, "Can you check on Mom?"

Devon knocked on her door, and she invited him in. He was surprised to see her up already. "Who's that you are writing to?" he inquired.

Ushaya looked up from her screen and replied, "A physicist I befriended online."

Devon gazed at her screen and said, "Well, supper is ready."

She smiled and said, "I'm famished and will be right down." When he left the room, she continued writing: "If that quantifies at the speed of a quark, then, how fast do electrons . . ."

Suddenly, Meg hollered up the stairs, "Mom, are you coming?"

Ushaya joined them at the table. Meg scooped noodles onto her plate, and said, "You missed Chelsea; she just called."

"Oh, darn," she said, dismayed.

A text came in from Tyler on Meg's phone, "How's your day going?" Meg didn't know what to write.

Brad suggested, "Just say, we're having an interesting visit, learning lots of new things."

Ushaya shook her head and said, "No, he will wonder what kind of new things. Just say it's been a special day and . . ."

"Oh for cripes' sake," interrupted Devon, and he grabbed Meg's phone and began texting: click, click, click, and sent the message.

Tyler glanced at the incoming, "We're having an awesome day and are about to watch TV."

They ate their meals in silence, save for the occasional, 'Pass the salt please, and nice weather we're having'. After their meals, and dishes had been cleared from the table, Brad pulled out a beer from the fridge. Meg chose a cider, and Ushaya poured a glass of red wine. Devon poured a shot of rum, and together, they settled in the den to watch TV. They decided on an old movie called Stopwatch. None of them had seen it before. At the end of the movie, all slouched in their couches, Devon shut off the remote, and said, "That was a great movie."

Megan wondered, "It's nine o'clock. What do you want to do now?"

Brad piped up, "Let's play cards. We all love cards, right?" They looked at each other.

"I'm game for a few rounds," said Ushaya. She was hoping they would open up about what happened that day. Also, she wanted to unveil her future plan.

They moved to the kitchen table, where Devon retrieved a deck of cards from the buffet. "We're not using yours, no offence, Ushaya," he said. They chuckled and took their seats.

Brad asked, "Poker?"

Devon replied, "Five-Card Stud, Seven-Card Draw, wilds or no wilds, Texas Hold'em, Omaha, Blackjack, Lou, whatever you want. Low card deals first."

"What are the stakes?" asked Meg.

Devon returned with sixty poker chips for each, five dollars per chip, and they placed their ante into the pot. Ushaya glanced across at Meg in front of her. Devon sat on her right and Brad sat on her left. They cut the deck, and Devon had the lowest card. Dealing face down, he announced, "Five Card Draw, no wilds."

Proceeding clockwise, Ushaya glanced at her cards. A straight was forming from nine-to-queen in different suits, and she discarded one on the table. Brad held two jacks and discarded three. Meg held two kings and discarded three. Devon held two tens and two eights—a full house was forming, and he discarded one. It was a long shot, he thought. He needed a ten or an eight to win the game, but at least, he had a two-pair.

Brad raised his brow at Mom, and asked wryly, "You could easily cheat, how do we trust you?"

She raised her brow and said, "True, I could go HypeMo and check all your hands, but I cannot anticipate your moves. It would be no fun that way, too much work. So shall we play?" She opened the bet. Brad raised her bet, and Meg raised his bet. Devon raised theirs in a flurry of hands, chipping in the pot.

They soon began to open up about what happened that day, and placed their cards down on the table. They talked about flying in sync through country lanes, and how thrilled they were. They bragged about narrowly escaping a military plane, and then they talked about their fears in Echo Canyon.

Meg said, "Those horrible creatures, what were they?"

"Ghosts," said Brad.

"Ghouls," said Ushaya.

Devon changed the subject, "So, you wish to open a casino one day, is that right, Brad?"

He shrugged and replied, "Well, you know, it will take millions. It's just a pipe dream."

"Very different from geology, but, hey, anything seems possible around here," said Devon wryly.

Meg glanced at Mom, wondering, "Where do you want to go from here? You mentioned world leaders."

Ushaya replied, "It's best to start with our own PM Jerome, then to Ronald of the USA and onto Mexico, maybe. Then Europe, Saudi Arabia, and Russia, I don't know. I just know to start with Jerome."

Devon returned with more rum from the kitchen, and sat down. "How are you going to meet the prince of Saudi Arabia? You don't know a thing about their language or customs. I mean, no offence or anything."

"I'm sure he speaks English," she said. "I shall find a mentor, perhaps, our own Jerome can help."

Brad wondered, "Why not start small and work your way up, like in your own town?"

Ushaya returned from the kitchen with another glass of wine, and began, "Sure, I could demonstrate to neighbours in local town squares and public parks. Word would spread of a great magician, and soon, crowds would gather in every city, in every country, and the act would become an international sensation. But where would that lead me?"

"You could approach power brokers, movers and shakers in science and technology, and find rich entrepreneurs, who could fund your mission," suggested Meg.

Ushaya began floating about the room, and said, "Not a bad idea, but who? Nah, it's best to approach world leaders first. They have the authority to execute plans. Furthermore, I wish to form a secret society. After my visits with each leader, then we should form an assembly meeting to demonstrate the powers, so that we witness them together. And most importantly, we must meet incognito; after all, it would be a secret society."

Brad returned from the kitchen with another beer, and asked, "How are you going to meet Jerome? I'm sure there is heavy security."

"Don't know. I will have to intercept him somehow," she admitted.

"Let's check it out," he said. Being the computer guru, they all followed Brad to the living room, where his laptop lay on the table. He explained, "There is a program called Low Hanging Fruit (LHF), not exactly legal and has underground networks around the world. It used to be called Shake the Apple Tree, but morphed to LHF. Authorities keep trying to shut it down, but have been unsuccessful so far." He brought up the site and logged on, and continued, "You place your keywords in the field here; for example, the time when Jerome sits in Parliament, or his political activities of the last two years. It will pull all events and activities tracked by media reports, newspaper clippings, private citizens using pseudo names, and anything else from the net. You then organize your info, like how often he travelled to the US, or something like that."

"How do you know about this site?" asked Ushaya, intrigued,

He smiled and replied, "I have many interests. So what do you want to know?"

She thought for a moment and asked, "Where does Jerome frequent the most in the area; for instance, where does he go for lunch?"

Brad typed in key words and clicked "submit." Scrolling through headlines, they discovered that Jerome frequented a local café called Bon Matin, and took a break between 12:30 and 1:30 each day, and that his favourite dish was quiche, according to an article published by CNR a year before.

Ushaya got excited, "Meg, come over here! We found something."

Joining them on the couch, Meg chortled, "Oh great, now you two can have quiche for lunch."

Ushaya was sipping wine, gazing at the screen. "Find a map of Parliament Hill and surrounding areas," she commanded.

Brad typed in the algorithms to work their magic, and clicked "submit."

Devon pointed to a link and said, "Open that one." It showed aerial views of the entire Ottawa Parliament compounds. Brad zeroed in to a nail on a lamppost, and then zoomed out.

"Brilliant! Bookmark it," exclaimed Ushaya.

"You have to set up your own account, but I can help you," said Brad.

Meg asked, "Why would you want to meet world leaders who have corrupt governments and human rights abuses, and all that?"

Ushaya glanced at them and replied, "All governments are guilty of corruption and human rights violations, even Canada. Don't forget the good things they do for their countries, too. Besides, I'm approaching them with a higher mission and don't want to get involved in their politics—that's their business."

"And this higher mission of yours?" asked Brad.

While floating back and forth, she said, "Our secret society should form their own expert teams in fields of science, engineering, health and genetics, etc. I would offer myself in a battery of tests, like blood pressure and cell counts, X-rays, CAT scans, ultrasounds, and things like that. There will be tests on cognitive and memory skills, and then endurance, strength, and speed, to push my limits. Perhaps, one day, I shall dodge a flying bullet."

Devon stared at her. "You're talking science fiction."

She bent her head in sadness.

Brad frowned, "What's the matter?"

She whispered, "The source of the Blue-ray light has not revealed anything about these powers since my first encounter. Perhaps world leaders can."

"Aren't we in a card game?" reminded Meg.

With fresh drinks in hand, they returned to the table. Devon dealt out the replacement cards. Ushaya held out for a straight, but the last card failed, and she folded. Brad got a third jack! But Meg got an extra king. Devon held out with his two-pair, tens and eights. Brad opened the final round of betting, each raising the other, and then came showdown. "Ohhh!" Everyone cried out.

Brad whined, "You had to have three kings." Meg chuckled, gathering in her loot.

Devon glanced at his phone in disbelief, and looked up, "It's eleven o'clock. One game in two hours?"

Ushaya got up, weaving toward the front door, and said, "It's been a hell of a day, and I'm going out for smokes."

Meg scolded her, "No, you're not. You're drunk."

She assured her, "I promise not to fly."

Devon stumbled up the stairs in a drunken stupor, heading for a much-needed shower. Brad picked up his laptop from the living room, and winded up the stairs, retreating to his bedroom.

Feeling alone, gazing at the mess on the table, Meg called out, "Mom, I'm coming!" She found her puffing on a cigarette, waiting for her. Their arms locked, and they floated five feet above the garden pathway in the warm midnight air, with porch lights guiding them through the darkness.

Ushaya confided, "My eyesight is improving, and I'm going to have to change my prescriptions." They landed before ocean waters gently lapping the shoreline. A quarter moon hung high in the night sky, filled with twinkling stars. Meg marvelled, pointing to a shooting star, while Ushaya gazed up at the celestial heavens, and smiled.

As they floated back to the house, along the path in the semi-darkness, Meg yelled, "Look out!" They were about to crash into a large bush, and swerved in time. She retorted, "Well, your eyesight may not be as good as you think, or is it the wine talking?"

Ushaya replied, "A simple case of neither of us paying attention, my dear," and in fits of giggles, they glided all the way back to the house.

After they cleared the card table and tidied up the kitchen, they tiptoed up the stairs to Brad's room, and rapped on his door.

He turned from his laptop and said, "Come in."

Meg entered, blurting, "We flew arm-in-arm without the ropes."

He bragged, "We touched baby fingers and floated around the room. But, hey, what you did is pretty neat."

"Why don't we touch baby fingers, right now?" asked Meg.

Ushaya yawned and replied, "It's a pretty tricky move, another time. Let's get some shut-eye, eh?" They all hugged, and Meg left the room. Ushaya sat next to Brad while he showed her a link of an article from an unknown source. Jerome recently held a private meeting with First Nations, and it appeared Canada was on the brink of unveiling a master plan for the Aboriginal people, not yet revealed in daily newsfeeds. "And look here, bribes in the caucus," he said. He then helped her set up her own LHF account (Low Hanging Fruit), and soon after, they called it a night.

Dragon's Pond

The following morning, Brad knocked on the door.

"Come in," she called out.

He placed a hot, steaming mug on her bedside table and said, "Thought you'd like some coffee."

Ushaya rubbed her eyes and sat up in bed, asking, "What's that racket out there?"

"Devon is working on the roof, trying to fix the eaves or something," he replied.

"At this time of morning?" she asked incredulously.

"Well, you know him. He's an early riser. See you later," he said, and closed the door behind him.

While sipping coffee, feeling rested, and listening to birds twittering outside her window, she began flipping through her diary, and realized it was their last day. Their flight would leave that afternoon. She sauntered to the kitchen and made herself breakfast. By 9:00 a.m., she stepped out to see what Devon was doing. He appeared frustrated. "What's the problem?" she asked.

"My ladder just broke, so now I can't finish the job replacing the eaves," he replied, shaking his head.

"I can help, if you teach me how to use the rivet gun," she said, glancing at long metal casings on the ground. Soon, he was hollering directions, as she floated along the roof edges, raising piece by piece.

Meg joined outside, smirking, "Putting her to work, I see."

"Our ladder broke, and she offered," he said, peering up at Ushaya, who was almost finished with the job that would have taken him all day, and he hollered, "Nice work up there!" An hour later, landing in front of the kids, she dusted off her clothes.

Meg asked sheepishly, "Can you do us another favour?"

"What's that?" she asked.

Meg answered, "There is this big boulder we want to move from the ravine to our lily pond."

Devon nodded and said, "A backhoe is scheduled for next month."

They were headed for the ravine when Brad stepped out of the house. Meg said excitedly, "Mom's going to move a boulder."

He grinned and said, "This I got to see."

Ushaya peered down the sloped incline and saw the rock they were talking about. It was very large—over twenty feet high and thirty feet wide—and entrenched among tree roots and small bushes along the steep embankment. Floating halfway down, she pressed her hands against the boulder, feeling its energy, and then commanded, "Everybody, stand back." The kids retreated ten feet. With all her might, she huffed and puffed and pushed and pulled. The earth shook, with roots and branches lifting from the soil in a cloud of dust and stones and debris, cascading into the gulley. The kids retreated twenty feet more, and the boulder gave way. With concerted effort, Ushaya balanced herself underneath and rose in the air, holding it up with both hands, as she floated across the grassy field toward the lily pond.

Devon pointed into the gaping hole and gasped, "There's something shiny down there."

"Yeah, what is it?" wondered Meg.

"We better catch up with her," said Brad, and they all ran across the field.

Ushaya asked, "Where do you want me to lay it?" The kids couldn't decide—maybe here, no, maybe over there. "Make up your mind, it's getting heavy," she said.

"Over there," said Devon.

Ushaya slid the boulder to the ground, and stepped back, thinking it was an interesting rock for their new landscape. The four of them stared across the pond at the monolith.

"We could plant trees," said Devon.

Meg added, "And trailing vines."

"And flowerbeds, our Shangri-La," he said, squeezing her hand.

While gazing across the pond, Brad said, "You know, it looks like a Stegosaurus, don't you think?" Indeed, they saw the profile of a dinosaur. He often found dinosaur bones during his geology expeditions, which turned into a side passion for paleontology. He continued, "Dragon legends came about when early man stumbled upon well-preserved specimens of these great beasts, and they handed down their oral tales, dancing around campfires. Definitely, we have some of that reptilian DNA."

"Sure, I always thought that giant lizards were part of my ancestry," quipped Devon.

"A tail disappears in the embryonic stage of pregnancy," said Meg, jabbing him.

Ushaya agreed, "Maybe we have some of that DNA."

"Now we're talking," said Brad.

Meg gazed across the pond and announced, "Since dinosaurs are our ancestors, let's call it Dragon's Pond."

"I didn't quite say that, but yeah, nice name," said Brad. In silence, they touched baby fingers only, and floated in awe back to the house.

Hours later, while driving to the airport, Devon glanced at Ushaya in the rear-view mirror, and said, "Don't forget to cancel that October trip. We totally understand."

Meg turned to Mom in the backseat and said, "We believe in your mission, you have our full support."

Ushaya gazed out the window and said, "Remember, if you get caught in a flashback, breathe deeply and tell yourself you'll be OK. Write down your questions and I'll answer them. I'm here for you."

Brad, who sat next to Mom, inquired, "What about that manifesto?"

She replied, "It will outline expectations, tenets of conduct, respect, oath of secrecy, and such things, and how to assemble teams to study the powers. I'll send you a draft before I leave for Ottawa."

They soon boarded their plane for Canada. Ushaya sat at the left window, and Brad sat in the middle. A man in his late fifties sat in the aisle seat. Brad whispered to Mom, "No monkey business, all right?"

"Agreed," she replied, strapping in her buckle.

Under the relentless drone, they were well fed and had watched several movies when conversations began with the man in the aisle seat. Arthur

McCormick was of burly size. They learned that he was a farmer, born and raised in Manitoba, who owned large hectares of wheat. He wanted to retire, but couldn't decide which of his three daughters should take over the business. He, in turn, listened to their stories of their family visit, and learnt a thing or two about flying kites, and he was impressed with Chelsea's school project. He, too, had visited Echo Canyon many years ago, and recounted his great adventures hiking up the cliffs. When he heard the story of their backyard pond, he said, "That's mighty impressive. Right now, I have a backhoe digging in my wheat fields to build a new silo for my crops."

Darkness descended and the cabin lights turned off for passengers to get some shut-eye. Arthur began playing a fantasy game on his laptop, which cast an irritating glow among thunderous sounds blaring from his speakers. Ushaya glanced at him, annoyed.

Brad put on his eye mask and lay back in his seat. Suddenly, he felt the familiar whoosh breeze by, and, lifting his right eye patch, he saw Arthur grumble loudly, punching keys on his laptop. It turned off, and Arthur turned it back on, off and on, over and over. Frustrated, he closed his laptop and put it away. All was dark in their corner. Brad pulled down his eye patch and leaned to Mom, whispering, "Is this your doing?"

"Not at all," she replied.

The Manifesto

Back home in her little Crestfield town, safe and sound, Ushaya busily prepared for her visit to Ottawa. Airline tickets confirmed her departure for early November, with a four-day stay at Rideau Chalet, not far from the Parliament Buildings. She had three months to pull this off, and the enormity of the task overwhelmed her. *So much to do*, she thought, *and what if it fails?* What if she didn't find Jerome? What if he summoned guards and she had to retreat in HypeMo?

Weeks later, she called up Stan to commend him on his suits, exclaiming, "We loved them! The members got a kick out of the flip-top finger hoods."

Feeling pleased, Stan inquired, "How was the weather?"

"It was perfect, mostly sunny and warm," she replied, and clearing her throat, she continued, "I have another order for two winter suits, if you could make them by end of October. I am meeting a new member in Ottawa. His name is Jerome, age late forties."

"Do you have his measurements?" he asked.

"I'll email them shortly," she replied, having discovered many things on the LHF site.

While steadily crossing items from her "to do" list, she began to notice her skin had turned blemish free, and her breasts had become firm, no longer sagging. Her body showed defining curves, and she was pleased at how strong and fit she had become. But there was one worry on her mind as she stared in the bathroom mirror. Dark vertical ridges ran down either side of her spine. They were beginning to rise under the skin, and were itchy as hell.

Meanwhile, Devon obsessed day and night, searching the embankment for that shiny object, only to return to the house in fruitless efforts. Meg gazed out the window at Dragon's Pond, worried about his state of mind.

Days flew pleasantly by, and Ushaya had some down time to enjoy a walk among bare-branched trees in a nearby forest. She bought a pumpkin for Halloween and carved out a scary ghoul, and set the pumpkin on a table by the front door, next to burning candles and sprigs of oregano. Children dressed in costumes would walk up past the gargoyles and knock on the door. She would greet them in a scary black ghost costume, while floating in the air, laughing a scary laugh. The children would run away, screaming. They had their trick, but no treat.

A text came in from Stan, and the following day, she arrived at his country mansion. An hour later, she left with two winter suits. Stan closed the door and said to Lucy, "There's something about her."

She had arranged for her gardener Wally to check on the house in her absence. The kids anxiously waited to hear from her. A text arrived on their phones, "I'm about to board the plane."

Meg texted back, "Have a great journey. Good luck. We love you."

Devon had stepped out from his hotel meeting, when he got the message, and texted, "Have a safe trip."

Brad was digging in his backyard to replace mulberry bushes for next springtime planting when he got the text. Opening the link, he read:

Manifesto

> "My name is Ushaya Landau. Welcome to the assembly. Our mission is to research the powers of levitation, flight, strength, and speed, witnessed by all present in this room. The intent is to establish respectful groups to test and explore the above said powers, and in cooperation, to share our collective information toward the betterment of our nations.
>
> "By democratic vote, we shall decide upon a name for our secret society. Members must conduct all activity in utmost secrecy under oath and media blackout. No mention of names, teams, and involved persons shall be made public outside the assembly until dates are agreed upon for doing so."

The document was signed by Ushaya and dated November 3, 2018.

It needs more work, Brad said to himself, and texted back, "You can do this. Love you, Mom."

Chapter Five

Canadian Prime Minister Jerome LaBerge

Operation Intercept

It was early November when Ushaya arrived at the Ottawa airport, which was bustling with foreigners. She placed her luggage onto a cart, like everyone else, and headed into the evening chill, which was hovering around five degrees Fahrenheit. Finding a secluded nook, she hooked the trunks to her belt. While setting her GPS for Rideau Chalet, she heard footsteps coming, and had to act fast. With her left arm raised, she burst into SuperMo, and soared high above the buildings, eventually slowing down to FastMo to enjoy the views. Winds howled and city lights glistened under the falling snow, and flakes landed on her trunks, her goggles, her hood, and gloves. She soon arrived at the hotel nestled on the banks of the St. Lawrence River. When she stepped out of the bushes, she looked like the Abominable Snowman. After dusting herself off, she lugged her trunks through the hotel entrance, where she met the head concierge guiding her to the front desk. "Right this way, ma'am," he said.

Settled in for the night under the bedcovers, she whispered to herself, "Tomorrow is a big day. I can't back out now."

The following morning, she peered through binoculars, while perched in tall evergreens. It was 9:00, and Jerome should have been exiting after a morning caucus meeting. She waited. An entourage piled out at 9:30, and he was among it. She followed him to another building, and put down her binoculars. Too risky, she decided, for he was never alone. Expectations were on target, according to her findings on the LHF site, that he would not be available at this time. She moved to another set of evergreens, and watched and waited. With a couple of hours to kill, her mind drifted idly as she observed people and traffic below.

Suddenly, Jerome was coming down the path. She overhead him request his two bodyguards to return to the building and retrieve a satchel he had left behind, insisting that he would be fine alone. As the bodyguards turned back to the building, she flew off her perch, coasting parallel with Jerome on the other side of the trees, both moving in sync. He had not noticed her. Then there was a break in the trees and it was time to intercept. Swooping in, she landed twenty feet ahead of him.

He stopped, startled, and asked, "Who the hell are you?"

Dressed in grey garb from head to foot, she pulled down her goggles and replied, "Do not be alarmed. My name is Ushaya Landau. There is something I must show you." It sounded rather lame, she realized.

"I am a busy man. Contact my office and follow the usual channels. Now, if you don't mind, I have important business to attend to," he said, slightly annoyed.

"I cannot do that. I must speak with you, and you alone," she pressed on. Then she flew up twenty feet into the trees.

Taken aback, he said, "That's quite some trick."

She flew back down and continued, "One day, I was visited by a Blue-ray light, and the next day, I had the ability to fly." She flew up into trees on his left, adding, "One more thing: I have discovered strength."

"What do you mean?" he asked, gazing up at her.

She descended and replied, "I can lift a truck, a boulder, a bus, and even a tractor."

He had had enough. Clearly, she was some crazy woman, and he began to reach for his right lapel to call in security when suddenly she lunged forward and wrapped her right arm firmly around his waist. Side by side, they rose above the trees against his protests and expletive hollers before chaotically landing fifty feet down the path, where she let go and pulled back ten feet. He dusted off his coat and straightened his tie.

Looking him straight in the eye, she said, "If I say I can lift a truck, then I can lift a truck, sir." They stood in a Mexican standoff.

A smirk crossed his face and, glancing at a nearby parking lot, he said, "All right, see that white van over there? Go ahead and lift it." Off she flew. Confident her scheme would prove to be a fraud and that he could finally remove this crazy, he stopped muttering. The van rose out of its parking spot twenty feet in the air and then descended back down. Excited and confused, he called his secretary, and said, "Rania, I know it's short notice, but can you please reschedule my afternoon appointments? Something has come up. Oh, and one more thing, hold my calls. Thank you."

Something about her disarmed him, but he didn't know what. "OK, you have my attention," said Jerome. "Shall we go back to my office? I want to know more." He looked at her and said, "You'll have to get a visitor's pass, but you can't go in looking like this."

She placed down her pack and pulled out a thin poncho, and then ditched the facemask and put on a fall hat, covering her black, swept-up hairdo. "Is this better?" she asked.

He nodded and said, "Much better." His bodyguards showed up, and Jerome explained to them that all was well, that this woman was a friend of his, and together, they entered the main entrance. With Visitor ID in hand, she followed him down hallways and corridors, greeting many people before entering the elevator. The doors opened to the fifth floor and, discreetly passing his secretary who wasn't looking their way, they disappeared into his private chambers. Jerome closed the door and punched in security codes on the wall console.

It was a large room with three tall bay windows overlooking garden plots and the city below. Gracious alcoves were filled with stained glass windows. Furniture was styled in subdued elegance with a rounded couch in the centre of the room. Stately portraits of important people adorned the walls. One photograph showed Jerome embracing newly arrived immigrants from Syria. Ushaya sauntered over to another portrait. A consortium of Aboriginal and First Nations Chiefs gathered at a large table, signing the Indigenous Reconciliation and Unification Accord.

One of the alcoves had a leaded glass window with an old-fashioned latch. "They don't make these anymore. May I open it, sir?" she asked.

"Sure, go ahead, and just call me Jerome." Standing at the bar, he asked, "Would you like a drink, wine or beer? Coffee or tea?"

Turning the lever and swinging the window wide open, she breathed in the fresh autumn air, and then closed it again. She returned to the rounded couch and replied, “I’d like a small glass of red wine, thank you.”

He brought a glass of wine for her and a beer for himself, and sat down next to her. “Tell me more, how did this all start?” he asked.

While slowly sipping wine, noticing a portrait of Queen Julia II on a wall, she began the tale of the mysterious Blue-ray light, and how she was able to levitate and eventually fly 2,300 miles per hour. Jerome quietly listened to her fantastic story. “Go on,” he said, when she paused.

She continued her story about strength, and how she could lift buses, tractors, and boulders. She told him that loneliness had set in and that she began to lose grip with reality, hiding her powers from others. As she grew stronger with each passing week, she realized that she was living in two worlds. She wondered why she, an ordinary senior woman, recently retired, would suddenly be catapulted into a world of superpowers. She had to admit, though, she enjoyed flying. An hour had passed while she floated a foot above the floor with a wine glass in hand, deep in her tales.

Jerome fired off a series of questions, which she answered.

“When did this start?” he asked.

“Seven months ago,” she replied.

“Where in BC do you live?”

“In a town called Crestfield.”

“Do you have children?”

“I have one son, Brad, aged thirty-five, and one daughter, Meg, aged forty.”

“Do you mind if I ask more personal questions?“

“Go right ahead.”

“How old are you?”

“Sixty-four.”

“What did you do for a living before retiring?”

“I worked for a fashion magazine in Vancouver, as assistant editor.”

“Are you married?”

“My husband Eddie passed away five years ago. We were married for forty years, and I still miss him.”

“I’m sorry to hear that,” said Jerome.

Pausing for a moment, Ushaya then proposed, "Choose any object here that is not bolted, and I will lift it."

Jerome looked around and pointed to his massive desk, suggesting, "How about that?"

She asked, smiling, "May I have a glass of water to wash down the wine? I wouldn't want to accidentally throw it out the window."

He returned with a glass of water, and wryly said, "I would be hard pressed to explain a flying desk out the window."

She walked over to the desk and asked, "Can you lift it?"

"I never tried," he said. Bemused, he stood at one end, and, squatting down, attempted with all his might, but it would not budge.

Slowly, she lifted the massive desk ten feet in the air upon her upstretched hands, with legs slightly spread, and began floating around the room. Then she descended, laying the desk down on the floor. Jerome was speechless. The two sat back on the couch, and she explained, "If a bus weighs twenty tons, then I can lift your desk, which weighs only half a ton, so no problem there." She recounted the strange adventures with her kids, as they flew together, tethered with ropes, wearing vests and suits.

"Your kids know about this and you flew together?" he asked, surprised.

She answered, "So far there are only five in the world that know—you, me, my two kids, and my son-in-law, Devon. No one else." Then she explained how she could fly at different speeds: FastMo, SuperMo, and HypeMo.

"What do you mean by disappearing in HypeMo?" he asked.

Ushaya placed her glass of water down on the coffee table, and said, "Well, I'm here on the couch, right?"

He shrugged his shoulders and replied, "OK."

"Goodbye," she said, and disappeared. Jerome jumped up. *Where did she go?* "I'm over here," a faint voice called out.

He walked down the hall and saw her standing before a portrait. "I had this commissioned," he began, when suddenly she was gone. Flustered, he called out, "Where are you now?" He followed the voice to an alcove, where she stood examining a sculpture bust. "Incredible, just incredible," he sputtered.

She explained, "I can reach a mile in less than a second. The power is increasing, and where it will take me, I have no idea."

Jerome Gets to Fly

"There is something else I wish to show you," she said.

Jerome retrieved his laptop from his desk and sat next to her. "What, you're going to tell me you bend steel?" he asked wryly.

"I can bend steel," she said, matter-of-factly. Then she reached into her pack and pulled out his suit, goggles, gloves, vests, and ropes, and laid them across the table, and said, "I'd like to take you on a fly-about, just like I did with the kids."

"Out there?" he asked, incredulously.

"I flew you this morning without the proper gear, and, with all due respect, I apologize for my transgression. But with vests and ropes, it will be much safer," she assured him.

He picked up the suit and lay it back down, asking, "Where did you get these made?"

"Ah," she lit up and replied, "That is the work of Stanislav Kominsky, the great inventor, who lives two valleys over from me. I learned about him through Jake, who is manager at Valhalla Outfitters and . . ."

Jerome interrupted, "Who did you say?"

"Stanislav Kominsky," she said, then, lowering her voice, added, "You should see his mansion." She told the story of his plans to bring sewing machines to the world through an alliance of interested stakeholders.

Staring at her, he said, "I cannot say much about this, but Stanislav is contracted by our CSIS team on a special mission."

She dared not tell him about Lucy the robot, and, changing the subject, she asked, "How much time do we have?"

He looked at his watch and replied, "We have three hours. My secretary leaves at 5:00."

"I can have you back in an hour, and I am thinking of the Ondanga Bluffs—you know them?"

"I know the Bluffs well, but that's forty miles away, if I recall."

"You'll be there in thirty minutes at 100 miles per hour."

"We'll be going that fast?" he asked.

Shrugging her shoulders, she replied, "The kids managed, no problem."

After a long pause, Jerome asked, "How are we going to leave the building?"

Ushaya guided him to the stained glass window and cranked the shaft open, and said, "We can fly out from here."

Jerome peered over the ledge, assessing his risks. His mind swirled with the events since her arrival, and he wondered if this was his day to die by falling out of a window. He should think not, and announced, "All right, let's do it," and disappeared down the hall to put on his suit and gear.

She called out, "Keep your undergarments on and ditch the tie. It flaps in the wind."

Several moments later, he stood in the great space, wearing boots and a suit, with ropes tethered through his vest. They chuckled at the sight of each other. While walking around, patting his suit, he asked, "What are those things clipped to your goggles?"

She answered, "They're for close-up vision. I'm thinking of outfitting them with windshield wipers."

Tea had finished brewing, and he filled two thermoses, adding cream and no sweetener for both. She found mixed nuts in a canister on the kitchenette counter, and bagged them for their journey. They looked at each other, chuckling at the absurdity of it all. Standing silently, she counted out loud, "One, two, three," and up they levitated, six feet.

Jerome gasped, "Ooh, wow!"

They glided down the hall of portraits and then returned to the great space, hovering five feet above the floor. She then taught him the landing moves, and was surprised at how quickly he learned the steps. Soon, they sidled through the stained-glass window and were out!

This was her territory. With ears pricked and eyes open wide, she felt an enormous responsibility to guide her leader safely, as they glided over rooftops of Parliament Hill, feeling the cold breeze brush past their faces, when suddenly she yanked him into nearby evergreens to hide, and said, "People are coming."

Jerome whispered, pointing down, "That's Bagua, minister of foreign trade."

She smirked and said, "Don't wave to him now," then gazing at grey skies that hinted at snow flurries, she whispered, "Shall we push on?"

With ropes taut, they soared northwest over citadels and steeples and roadways and busy sidewalks and suburban communities, which soon gave way to farmlands and fields and rolling hills and small towns, dotting the landscape, and up, up, up into the open sky, they flew, enthralled, continuing their journey in silence.

Gazing left and right, feeling strangely safe, Jerome said, "The scene is constantly changing."

"I wonder what birds must think," she replied.

"It's quiet up here," he noticed.

The Ondanga Bluffs came into view, and landing in perfect unison upon the mesa, they removed their goggles and sat down, with legs dangling over the edge. It was a 1,000-foot drop of sheer vertical rock face. While sipping tea and eating nuts, admiring the vast, barren landscape lightly dusted in snow, she asked Jerome, "If you had one wish in the whole world, what would that be?"

Reflecting a while, he replied, "I wish less bickering among the provinces and territories, and less government red tape, so that citizens can be served in a timelier manner, especially in health services. The immigration process needs to speed up, and I aim to push through policies to that effect in the next year. The problem is that I have a minority government with a Parliament that slows down my progress considerably. Then, there are ratification agreements with Indigenous nations, a very complex area to navigate. There's the matter of affordable housing and investments into electric cars, and so on."

She gazed across the snow-covered terrain and said, "Government should give citizens a basic amount to survive. No one should have to struggle in this country. When people are empowered, they provide prosperity, and in turn, use fewer government services."

He confided, "We are working on a policy along those lines."

"And what about US relations?" she asked.

"Oh," he replied, "Don't get me started on Ronald, unless you want to be here all day."

Changing the subject, she said, "I'm glad you legalized pot."

"You smoke pot?" he asked.

"Sometimes," she said, adding, "Government has cornered the market on four vices—gambling, booze, cigarettes, and pot, I see."

He gazed out and said, "We should head back."

They scrambled to their feet, and, checking their gear, she asked, "How strong is your heart?"

"I have a strong heart, why?" he asked.

She gave him two options and said, "It took a half an hour to get here, cruising at an altitude of 6,000 feet at 100 miles per hour. Or, we can fly back in five minutes. What do you think?"

Surprised, he asked, "Did your kids fly that fast?"

She said, "It's called FastMo, 400 miles an hour, and, yes, they did, but not as long as five minutes. We can start slowly, and as we pick up speed, I'll check on you. So which do you prefer, a half an hour or five minutes?"

Gazing out at the terrain, feeling chilled, he replied, "I'll take five minutes."

She pushed off the bluffs, heading southeast, as Jerome spread out his arms, gliding gently back and forth. This was his favourite part of flying. Then he heard, "We're picking up speed, 120 miles an hour." A rush of excitement filled his veins as he continued to accelerate. Then he heard her announce, "Two hundred miles." Soaring through the skies exhilarated, almost breathless, he cried out, "Yes! YES!"

Ushaya glanced back and said, "Don't forget to breathe."

He gave a 'thumbs up'. Forging into the bitter cold, surpassing 300 miles an hour, he heard her announce, "Four hundred miles." The landscape whizzed by, as he hung onto ropes for dear life. The g-force pressed against his chest. His body was numb to the bone, and, no longer able to feel his face, wondering if it had fallen off, he descended into the downtown core, landing in tall evergreens.

It had been the craziest day of his life, he thought. Holding onto a branch and to his sanity at the same time, he realized, he had to surrender to the journey, wherever it was taking him. Yet, his biggest challenge lay ahead. They took one giant leap through the air and landed on a green turret above his alcove window. A sheet of thin ice covered the surface, as Jerome desperately clung to the iron steeple rods, staring down at the relaxed ropes between them.

Ushaya gazed up at him. There was only one thing left to do, she thought, and ran down the turret . . . thump, thump, thump, reining him in as he flung over the edge, airborne. His cries rang in her ears, and within seconds, they floated in front of the window. Breathless, he pulled down his goggles, so relieved to see his little alcove. Rubbing his hands to circulate the blood, he sputtered, "Thank God we're alive!"

She apologized for the detour, pointing down to her left, "See that couple walking?"

He glanced down and replied, "They would have seen us, if we had landed sooner, is that your logic?" She nodded.

Jerome suggested, "May I take the lead?" Floating past her, he reached inside and turned the latch wide open, and they entered through the window.

Following him toward the ceiling, she asked, concerned, "Where are you taking us?"

"I'm still practicing," he replied. With ropes taut, gliding them down the hallway and back again around the liquor bar and kitchen, he then called out, 'Three, two, one," and they landed in the open space.

"How magical!" she cried out.

He appeared serious and said, "That's thought transference."

"I see," she whispered, unhooking the ropes between them. They removed their vests and gloves, and sat down in their grey suits on the rounded couch, feeling not hot or cold, just comfortable.

He continued, "You'll be visiting very powerful people. Don't let anyone coerce you into doing something you don't want to do. Remember, they cannot fly. Only you can, and you hold the reins, pardon the pun. Until we learn more about this thought transference mechanism, we have no idea." She nodded, understanding what he meant.

He further advised, "For that matter, the powers that you demonstrated today should be added to your manifesto in more detail. We, as leaders, are accountable for your safety and protection at the highest levels," and lowering his voice, he added, "It is a living document of intent that will take time to grow and manifest."

Brainstorming

Ushaya floated to the kitchenette and opened the fridge, asking, "What's there to eat?"

Jerome was studying her notes on the table, when he replied, "Anything you can find. I'm starved."

She pulled out croissants and a jar of red bell peppers, and smoked salmon cream cheese and a handful of spinach leaves, and laid them on the counter. She then eyed a carton of organic orange juice and some bananas and strawberries, and pulled them out, too.

She chopped, diced, and arranged croissants onto two plates. Next, she found a small blender in his pantry. She added orange juice, banana, strawberry, a spritz of soda, crushed rosemary, drops of vanilla, and half a teaspoon of honey, and blended the ingredients together to produce a smoothie. She put the plates of croissants and two large goblets on the table.

Jerome took a sip and said, "Hmm, it's delicious, you must send me the recipe."

"I'd be glad to," she replied, munching on her croissant.

While leaning over his report, dabbing his mouth with his napkin, he said, "To recap so far, you propose a secret society dedicated to the research of your powers." He pulled out a blank sheet of paper from a drawer under the table, and continued, "I believe in your mission. Now, let's figure out which countries, OK?"

She asked, "Do you have a globe?"

He returned with a globe and set it on the table.

Pointing to Canada, she began, "It starts with you. Then she pointed her finger to President Ronald Thump in the USA, and then onward down to President Carlos Sabrador in Mexico." Resting her finger, she said, "From here, I am not sure. I only know to end my journey in Russia."

"Why Mexico?" he wondered.

She replied, "We share a NAFTA agreement with the US and Mexico."

Jerome turned the globe across the Atlantic Ocean, and, pointing to the UK, said, "You should visit the queen and prince, for sure."

She gasped, "The queen and prince?"

"You do realize Prince Herbert is in a wheelchair. How are you going to fly him?" he asked.

She replied, shaking her head, "Such a dreadful car accident ten years ago, and now he has a spinal cord injury. Thankfully, he still has use of his arms." She thought for a moment and said, "I shall find a way." Then she asked, "How old are they, again?"

Jerome replied, "Julia is seventy and Herbert is seventy-two." He brought his finger down the globe, asking, "Now which country in Europe?"

She suggested, "How about Germany? I was born in Dresden, and it's been over forty years since I've visited my homeland. They have a great female leader right now."

"Yes," he reflected loudly, "Chancellor Irena has a most difficult mandate to pull the EU together. With the refugee crisis, the unstable Eurodollar, and Brexit looming, I think she is doing a fantastic job." He jotted down the names of the queen and prince, and Chancellor Irena of Germany. Then he looked up and asked, "Which country in Africa? I propose Cyrak Hosan of South Africa."

"Nah, too many problems with apartheid," said Ushaya, studying the globe, suggesting, instead, "I prefer President Mimbauwe of Rwanda."

"What do you know about Rwanda?" he asked.

She replied, "Not much, but I do know, it is one of the fastest-growing countries in Africa, both economically and in their social reforms. A lot has changed since the Tutsi genocide by the Hutus in 1994. The country has become super clean. Police bribes are no longer allowed, and no one lives in straw huts anymore. Even the poorest people are receiving social housing. Female genital mutilation is no longer practiced there and they have abolished the death penalty, and many women have been elected into congress." She paused and said, "Botswana is another fast-growing country."

Jerome looked at her and said, "There are many fast-growing countries in Africa, but I will go with your first choice." He jotted down Mimbauwe of Rwanda and then asked, "Which country in the Middle East?"

Ushaya sat back on the couch, sighing, "I suggest Crown Prince Muzaffar of Saudi Arabia. He rules over the largest landmass in the Middle East. With his Vision 2030, he is making huge reforms for his people."

Jerome jotted down Prince Muzaffar, and then suggested, "Prime Minister Yadgiri of India, for sure."

She nodded and said, "Absolutely, a country that holds one-seventh of the world's population, a growing superpower."

He scribbled the names of Chinese President Zhangwei and Japanese Prime Minister Hashimoto, and looked up at her, with inquiring eyes.

"Yes, both are world powers. By the way, have you noticed that Japan's landmass is shaped like a dragon?" she asked wryly.

Nodding in amusement, he turned the globe and said, "President Yaegar of Russia?"

"Most definitely," she replied.

Jerome opened a new folder on his laptop and entered the names of eleven countries: Canada, USA, Mexico, Britain, Germany, Rwanda, Saudi Arabia, India, China, Japan and Russia.

She nodded appreciatively and said, "Another thing. I want to visit leaders in an orderly fashion from west to east, just like what we did here, starting with you in Canada and around the globe ending in Russia."

"What is the timeline between each visit?" he asked.

She pondered for a moment and replied, "I'd say one every month, which means ending in Russia later next year." She bit into her croissant and asked, "I have a question, Jerome. What if a country opts out?"

He answered, "No country will opt out, you just watch."

The conversation was getting serious. She looked at him and said, "The meetings must be in secret, so no entourage, just the leaders alone; otherwise, I will not meet with them."

Jerome stroked his chin, wondering, "How would you meet them?"

"Through an open window would be great," she replied, while floating around the room, "That way, they wouldn't have to leave their compounds. I would need their GPS coordinates, and would just fly to them. Good for me, for I can bypass all that damn ground traffic, you know." She stopped in mid-air.

Gazing up at her, he asked, "What if they want to meet you outside their compounds, instead?"

"Then we must decide the location and come incognito, in disguise," she replied.

"What kind of disguise?" he asked, finishing the last bite of his croissant.

She shrugged and said, "I don't know, perhaps, a beard, moustache, or dark sunglasses. They are smart leaders and can figure something out. Either way, I will work with them if they work with me."

Jerome glossed over the names, dabbing his mouth with his napkin one last time, and said, "According to our list, your next visit is with Ronald. I will personally call him and strongly state my case that he meet with you."

"What if he declines?" she asked, taking the last sip of juice.

"Then we will approach Carlos first, and that ought to put a fire under him," he replied.

She set down her goblet and said, "We'll have to come up with a name for our secret society."

"Yes, for sure, but one step at a time," he advised.

She cleared her throat and asked, "I have a concern about flight expenses and hotel stays, and all that, and I was wondering if . . ."

He interrupted, "Your visit was not on my dime. I will reimburse you for all you have incurred, even the gear and flights to Ottawa. And furthermore, consider your visit with the US president all expenses paid."

"Thank you. I guess our time is near," she said, glancing at her invisible watch.

"Yes, unfortunately," said Jerome, as he got up to put dishes into the dishwasher. He called out from the kitchenette, "I would like to meet your kids. In fact, they should become members."

Ushaya stopped packing, flabbergasted, and called back, "I'm sure they would be most honoured."

He joined her in the great space and said, "There is something else. It has to do with your friend Stanislav. I fondly remember signing off a Prime Ministerial Order two years ago regarding his secret work with us. Do you realize who you are dealing with?"

"What do you mean?" she asked.

"He is not a stupid man, and will become suspicious. What reason did you give him for your suit and vest orders?"

"I told him a lie, and said I was starting a seniors flying club."

Jerome shook his head and said, "He needs to know the truth, for he is responsible for the suits that world leaders will be flying in. He may even improve on their design once he knows the purpose of our mission. No, he must become a member." He paused and continued, "The good thing is it won't breach any privacy contract with Canada, since he is operating as an independent. If there is a man who can keep a secret, it is Stan."

Ushaya thought about Lucy, and, taking a deep breath, she said, "So, now we have the three kids and Stan, and, including myself, it brings a total of seventeen members at the assembly."

He insisted, "We must set this up right from the beginning,"

"OK, when do I tell Stan?" she asked.

He thought for a moment and replied, "I would hold off until after your visit with Ronald." She had finished packing when he asked, "What are your plans for your stay?"

Tightening the straps of her backpack, she replied, "I have another two days and was thinking of some early Christmas shopping, and maybe a fly-about." She added, "So we agree that no one should know about this—not your sister or brother, not your wife or kids, not even your goldfish."

"How do you know I have goldfish?" he asked.

Thinking of LHF, she replied, "I have my ways."

"Don't forget your security pass," he reminded her, as he walked over to the desk to retrieve it.

She replied, "Right, of course, but couldn't I just fly out the window, eh?"

Remembering the ordeal of slipping past his secretary, he waved his hand and said, "OK, out the window you go."

She cranked the lever open and slipped out the window, and, turning mid-air to face him, she asked, "What will you say to security?"

He leaned over the ledge and replied, "That you simply left the building and forgot to hand in your pass." While gazing at the evening sky, he warned her, "You're in with the big boys, Ushaya. It's a totally different world out there."

With a slight smile, she said, "Frankly, there are days I do not know what world I'm in." She put on her goggles, and receding farther away and waving at Jerome, she slowly faded into the distance.

A trance-like state overcame him. What had just happened? He *did* fly, didn't he? Who was this woman? Had he gone mad? In a daze, wandering down the hall, straightening out pictures, his mind was filled with floating desks, ropes and fir branches, and icy rooftops. He changed back into his business attire, and carefully stowed the suit and gear, under lock and key, in one of the cabinets. He fed the paper list of names to the shredder and checked his watch. It was 5:10, time to face his secretary. Glancing one more time across his chambers, he shut off the lights and closed the door on his way out.

Ushaya sat in the hotel café with her laptop, writing her report, and she couldn't stop thinking about their day. Two hours had passed, and the café was filling up with people, so she paid the bill and retired to her room. The night was young. Flipping through TV channels, she watched a sitcom, and ended the evening engrossed in a movie. By eleven o'clock, she had her shower and crawled under the sheets of her comfy bed, and turned out the light.

That same evening, Jerome sat around the family dinner table with his three kids and wife, Kaitlyn, who was an attractive forty-five-year-old with brown eyes and long, brown hair. His fourteen-year-old son, Sebastian, was a well-built, sturdy lad with a head full of black curly hair. He proudly announced, "I got on the soccer team today."

"Congratulations," said Jerome, smiling. "I know you worked hard for this."

Ten-year old Annabelle, who aspired to become a rock star, piped up, "I can't wait to start singing lessons." She was slightly overweight and had stunning blue eyes and brown wavy hair that hung to her shoulders.

"You have a lovely voice, sweetie, I'm sure you will rock the world," said Kaitlyn, forking into her scalloped potatoes.

Little five-year-old Adrian had a head full of blonde hair and cute dimples. He asked, "Daddy, when are we going sailing again?"

Jerome replied, "Maybe next spring." Conversations went back and forth, as they dug into their sumptuous meal.

Later that evening, he retreated to his private den to make a call on his private line. The phone rang three times, and Ronald answered, "Hello?" An hour later, Jerome ended the most intense call of his life. Letting out a sharp breath, he leaned back in his chair with his feet on the desk and his arms folded behind his head, and smiled.

Frogfish and Twelve Spheres

Ushaya was sipping her morning coffee and eating breakfast, pondering the kids and Stan joining as members. Grateful for a good night's rest, she continued writing for another hour in her report, before getting up to stretch. It was time to go shopping, she thought, and turned on the TV.

While browsing through hotel brochures, something distracted her on TV. It was a program about the Great Canadian Shield. A team of outdoor enthusiasts was surveying the northern regions near Hudson Bay, hiking through provincial parks, flying aircraft over rugged, pristine evergreens, and canoeing along winding streams. *Gosh, what a beautiful country*, she thought, longing to see the north, for it had been decades since she had last visited. *That pure, fresh Canadian air*! *Should I do it*? she wondered.

While locking GPS coordinates into her phone, she cried with glee, "Perfect!" She might be able to strike this off her bucket list, after all, and be back in Ottawa to do that shopping.

It was almost noon, and all geared up, she whisked out the hotel and sprang into the air, accelerating in SuperMo until the city was far behind her. Towns and farmlands changed into rolling hills, as she weaved along the Ontario-Quebec border in the land of deer and moose, and forests and lakes, feeling the stinging cold through her mask.

She arrived at her destination and sat on a boulder, sheltered among barren trees hugging the shorelines of a narrow, winding shallow stream. Glorious autumn leaves, in many colours, lay fallen on both shores. The waters had not yet frozen over, and the rippling sounds soothed her mind. It was where she wanted to be. In this vast land of solitude, she felt at one with nature's grandeur, and the spirit of the earth awakened her soul.

She pulled her sandwich from her pack, thinking about Jerome and his wishes, and how noble but difficult to achieve they were. Something caught her eye downstream to her right. Waters were bubbling and swirling, and a large group of fishlike creatures was dipping in and out of the water. There had to be forty, fifty, sixty of them, she thought, thrashing over the rocks, passing her by.

Hastily, she lay down her sandwich, and put on her backpack and followed them, while filming the scene on her iPhone. Carefully, she ducked under overhanging branches, observing creatures rise out of the water and back under, when suddenly they all disappeared into the sediment. She floated back and forth, wondering, *where did they go*? Nothing stirred for several minutes, and she stopped recording.

As she floated downstream, back toward her boulder, an emerald-green ball shimmered among the surrounding grey pebbles. She pulled off her right glove and plunged her hand into the icy water, and brought up a perfectly round sphere, about the size of a billiard ball. Studying it, she realized it had weight, perhaps granite or ore, she wasn't sure. But it was exquisitely beautiful. Deciding to bring it with her, she dropped it in her pack. Another ball glimmered in the streambed to her left, and with her left glove off, she reached in and brought out a cobalt sphere, the same size. Mesmerized by blue and gold striations, she threw it into her pack, hearing it clink against the first ball. Continuing on, there was another and another, and another, and over here! She couldn't believe where these sphere balls were coming from. Her fingers were numb, but she didn't care. There was a black ball close to the shore, under a rock overhang. She retrieved it and let it drop in her pack, hearing it clink against the others.

Settled back on her boulder, she pulled out twelve spheres from her pack, and began studying them. They were totally smooth with contrasting swirls and colourful striations across their surfaces. She wondered how there could be so many perfectly round balls.

While munching on her sandwich, the waters downstream, to her left, began bubbling again. Annoyed, she cried out, "Can't I finish a sandwich around here?"

The creatures returned in greater numbers—hundreds, thrashing, jumping, leaping over each other. The entire stream frothed in frenzy, as her camera clicked away. She caught a glimpse of a head with bulging eyes on a fish body with fins, and front legs like a frog. Click, click, click, the shutter went, and not paying attention, she almost dropped her phone in the water! Then the stream turned silent.

She took a gulp of orange juice from her thermos, grateful for the shot of rum she had spiked it with before leaving the hotel, feeling the warmth spread through her body. She wondered what these creatures were, and how they could survive at this time of year. Where did they come from, and where did they go? While browsing through photos, she was astonished at the clarity of the images, and, zooming in closer, she whispered to herself, "They look like some kind of frogfish, how odd."

Suddenly, she realized, here she was shopping for early Christmas gifts, and right here, was a unique gift for Jerome. While staring at the sphere balls strewn across the rock around her, the phone rang and she answered, "Hello?"

"You sound far away, where are you?" inquired Jerome.

"Up north in the Canadian Shield," she replied.

"Why am I not surprised?" he asked wryly.

"Jerome, I have discovered something very interesting. I'm sending you videos right now," she said, "They appear to be some kind of frogfish, hundreds of them in this stream."

He watched the video downloads, totally intrigued, and said, "I've travelled all through Ontario and Quebec and have never seen anything like this. I don't know what they are."

She said, "Neither do I, and, by the way, I found twelve spheres in the same stream. I'm sending you pictures right now."

Gazing at his phone, he said, "They're beautiful, but what are they?"

"I don't know, but consider them my Christmas gift to you," she replied, holding one sphere in her hand.

He felt honoured and said, "That's very kind of you. But whatever for?"

She insisted, "Would you like me to drop them off before I leave?"

He replied, "No, keep them for now. For that matter, bring them to the assembly meeting. It might be useful information about your powers."

"I assume there is a reason for your call?" she asked.

He began, "Ronald is very interested to meet you. I spoke to him last night for an hour, and another hour this morning. It took some convincing, with him poking at my mental sanity, but he is intrigued enough, and will send the official invite, and is aware of the secret status that you wish."

She softly said, "That is great news."

He asked, "With Christmas around the corner, Ronald wondered if you two could meet in early December. How do you feel about that?"

Barely containing her excitement, she replied, "Yes, I can make it."

He assured her, "Remember, I am here to assist, OK?"

She asked, "I'm heading back home tomorrow. What should I do next?"

"The first thing you must do is send me that smoothie recipe," he said in his most serious tone.

She smiled and said, "Yes, sir."

He continued, "Once you are settled in, we can talk about your upcoming presidential meeting, and also about your kids and Stanislav." He didn't want to hold her up any longer, and concluded, "Have a safe journey home, and we'll be in touch."

She was stunned. Was this her lucky day? Carefully stowing the spheres back into her pack, she hovered above the quiet, rippling stream, one last time, and said to the frogfish, "So long, my friends, may we meet again."

With GPS set, she forged on in SuperMo across the sky, feeling the afternoon sun rays cut through the icy cold, until she arrived in Ottawa's old city core, famous for its quaint shops. While wandering through the streets, she entered a novelty gem shop. Approaching a young female clerk, she asked, "Good afternoon, I was wondering if you have velvet pouches with drawstrings, big enough, say, for a billiard ball?"

The clerk turned down one aisle and replied, pointing, "They come in all colours and patterns."

Sifting through the pile, Ushaya picked out twelve pouches and paid for the order, and was soon standing on the sidewalk. With a quick spin in the air, she soared over the old city toward her hotel. Back in her room, she carefully placed each sphere in a velvet pouch, drawing the strings snug.

Feeling hungry, she went down to the café with her laptop and sat by a window. The waiter took her order of Caesar salad and avocado Tuscan linguine, and a glass of red wine. Her first entry began with the TV documentary that morning, which led her to the Great Canadian Shield. This led her to the mysterious frogfish, and the twelve spheres she gifted to Jerome. She ordered cheesecake and another glass of wine, as she continued writing her report. The kids and Stan were about to join as members, and she was about to meet the president of the USA!

A Curveball

Days later, back in Canada, she drew a simple map of the Canadian Shield, marking the Gagnon Stream with a big X, where she found the frogfish and the twelve spheres. She added the GPS coordinates above and below, and rolled the finished parchment, tying it with a red ribbon. Then she placed it in a faded blue, wooden chest, which she had retrieved from the attic, and turned the key, and locked it.

Ushaya had arranged a group Zoom call with the kids to recount the story of her visit with Jerome. "We invite you to become members, and he wants to meet Stanislav, too," she said.

Excited to hear the news, Meg wondered, "What are we going to say to him?"

She replied, "He wants to hear your stories. Just think about it, you get to meet world leaders. Jerome and I want to know, are you in or out? Take your time to consider this." Questions exploded.

"What do we do? What is the name of the assembly?"

"I don't know," she answered.

"Are there more meetings? What if new leaders want to join? Where is the assembly taking place?"

"I don't know," she answered.

"And what is my role?" Chatter escalated.

Devon's voice boomed out, "I'm in!" Everyone turned silent, and he continued, "It's an experience of a lifetime I would not want to miss."

Meg nodded and said, "I'm in, too." All eyes were on Brad.

"What," he looked back and forth, and said, "Of course I'm in."

"Well then, that settles it," beamed Ushaya. "Welcome to the assembly. I don't know where this is going, quite frankly, but together we'll find some answers. Remember, one step at a time, eh?" And they ended their call.

As she stood on the front porch, gazing past the gargoyles, she began to ponder the events of the last seven months. Now, the kids were coming on board, and Stan would be next.

Days later, Jerome called her up and said, "Thank you for the recipe."

With morning coffee in hand, she smiled and said, "The kids have agreed to become members. They have many questions, which is to be expected, but isn't that wonderful news?"

"I'm pleased to hear that," he said, adding, "Ronald emailed his formal invite, and I have secured airline tickets and hotel arrangements. However, he does not want to meet at the White House. Instead, the tickets are for West Palm Beach, Florida, just north of Miami, at his private resort called Dolce Maria Villa. Personally, I think he is looking forward to the flying part."

"Good to know. I'll contact Stan to order his suit and gear," she said.

"Keep a tab on your running expenses, and, one more thing," he advised. "Do not put Ronald through the speed I went through. I don't think he could take it."

"Agreed. Where shall I meet him?" she asked.

He replied, "By a swimming pool under a red rooftop. I'll send you the flight details shortly."

Ushaya called up Stan the following day, to order a summer suit, vest, and gloves for a large man in his late sixties, and they ended their call. She googled "Frogfish and the Canadian Shield," but her research came up empty, for this kind of fish was nowhere to be found. Next, she removed the spheres from their pouches and lay them on a table in her den. For days, she would pick up a ball, here and there, wondering what they were all about.

Then she noticed two spheres had switched positions. She was sure the black ball had been at the far left, and now it was at the far right, and the red ball at the far left. "Hmm," she wondered. It happened again the next day, and the next day, and the next. Two spheres kept changing positions. That night, she set up a tripod, and let the video run overnight, while she slept.

The following afternoon, she fast-forwarded the recording, and stopped. A blue-marbled sphere rolled over to fourth position, and an orange ball rolled over to tenth position. The recording clearly showed they had moved at 2:00 a.m. *I have to tell Jerome about this*, she said to herself, totally mystified.

Meanwhile, Stuart McCallum, personal aide to the US president, sat at the Oval Office, holding a clipboard in his lap. He was a mild-mannered man in his mid-forties, short in stature, with speckles on his face. His brown hair was neatly groomed, and he wore a two-piece suit and polished black shoes.

With hands clasped on the desk, Ronald barked, "I want my schedule cleared for two days between December 5 and 6. Make it quiet, no fanfare, only between you and me, not even my wife must know about this. I want a total media blackout, that way no chance of fake news. I damn well need a vacation, do you understand?"

McCallum nodded, "Yes sir," he said and asked, "What should I say to your wife, the staff, and media?"

He replied, "Just say I am debriefing notes, and if they press on, say you'll get back to them." Ronald stood up to leave and said, "I'll take it from here.

From now on, we communicate through texts only, no tweets," and he disappeared down the hall.

McCallum was used to his multiple personalities. Sometimes he was brash and swaggering, often leaving his team with vague commands, but other times, he was kind and generous. He always talked straight from the hip, and that he liked about him. Ronald may be controversial in his presidency, but he was much loved by his people.

It was the end of November when Ushaya received a text from Stan, advising her that Ronald's suit and gear were ready for pickup. The following day, she stepped out of her car and pulled down her shades, gazing up at the chimney emitting smoke. A dusting of snow sprinkled the ground, and the air was nippy.

Stan heard her coming up the steps and opened the door, pleased to see her. "Do come in," he said. He took her backpack to the great space, while Lucy clicked and clacked, whizzing about. He showed the suits, vests, and gloves on the table, and remarked, "This is an improved product from what your buddy Jerome wore, a material called Azacron."

Ushaya examined the gear. With orders tucked in her backpack and the sale completed, she stood at the door, promising to be in touch after her southern trip, and then she left. Stan closed the door and looked at Lucy, and said nothing.

Ushaya headed out the door to meet the president of the USA.

The following morning, the gardener Wally entered her house for his first round of check-ups, knowing nothing of the sphere balls, for they were hidden under lock and key. A tattered piece of paper flew off a shelf onto the floor as he walked by. He picked it up and read:

Wish List
Stake out the White House
President's itinerary
He must be alone
Bring suits and gear
How to dodge a flying bullet

He placed the paper on the shelf, wondering what she was up to.

Chapter Six

US President Ronald Thump

Children of the Sky

It was early December when Jerome texted Ronald, "Ushaya is on her way. She will change your life."

Ronald texted, "You owe me one."

Jerome texted back, "No, after this, *you* owe *me* one."

Having circled the Dolca Maria Villa in West Palm Beach, Ushaya landed at the swimming pool under a red roof. The water was drained, and stacks of tile lay around the deck. After pacing for twenty minutes, she phoned up Jerome, lamenting, "There's no sign of him. Does the president usually keep people waiting?"

Jerome dialled up Ronald and asked, "Where are you?"

He moaned out loud and replied, "There are two swimming pools, both under red roofs. I bet she's at the wrong one."

Jerome sighed and said, "This is why I asked for the exact GPS coordinates."

He barked, "My assistants do this work for me," then suggested, "I guess I should get over there."

"No, don't, she'll find you," said Jerome, and they both hung up.

Ronald had barely laid down his phone when an apparition appeared before him. She pulled down her hood and tussled her hair, and then extended a hand, introducing herself. "Hello, I'm Ushaya Landau, so pleased to meet you."

For once in his life, he didn't know what to say, and scrambling out of his chair, he shook her hand and said, "I apologize for the confusion."

"No worries, mistakes happen," she said, while removing her pack and gloves.

Half-grinning that signature smile of his, he moved to the bar and asked, "Would you like a drink? Wine, beer, or juice?"

"A glass of red wine, thank you," she replied.

He popped the cork from a very nice wine and poured a drink, and then poured a glass of orange juice for himself. They sat back in cozy lawn chairs in front of a pool filled with sparkling water. Lush hanging flower baskets and trailing vines adorned the fences around the patio.

Ronald couldn't stop gazing at her. She had to be five foot six, he thought, with a nice figure and long slender legs, and wearing silver running shoes. Her wavy black hair, with a hint of silver, draped around her neck, and she had the loveliest brown eyes, which sparkled. He began, "I understand your superpowers came from a Blue-ray light, is that right?"

Ushaya nodded and replied, "It started eight months ago." She told the tale of her adventures, the story of Stanislav and the kids, and the story of Jerome, and the frogfish and the twelve spheres.

Silent for a moment, he said, "Your plan is to visit eleven countries. I agree, but this assembly thing you're talking about is not possible."

She gazed about the patio and suggested, "Let me demonstrate for you, Ronald. Pick the heaviest object that is not bolted, and I will lift it."

Together, they walked down the path, and, pointing to a cement truck, remembering contractors on his compound, he asked half-jokingly, "Can you lift that?"

With folded arms, she replied, "I've never lifted a cement truck before, but I can do it."

"Be my guest," he motioned her.

After studying her best entry point, she began squatting between the huge drum and connective cables to the front cab. Then clamouring underneath, shifting her balance, with knees bent and hands spread above her, she slowly raised the beast in the air.

He couldn't believe his eyes. "How heavy is that thing?" he asked.

"About ten tons, but feels like a sack of potatoes," she replied, as she slowly landed the cement truck back on the gravel road, then brushed the dirt from her hands.

They returned to the villa, where he pulled out two serving trays from the fridge, filled with pastries and breads and cheeses, and they moved to the main living room. After he had fetched their drinks from the patio, he sat down next to her and said, "I understand your kids are joining as members. What are their names again?"

She answered, "Brad and Meg, and my son-in-law Devon." While gazing around at the lavish gold décor, she wondered, "Did your wife Karina do the decorations?"

She spearheaded the project, yes," he replied.

"She has amazing talent."

"That she has; it's what I love about her."

"Can I ask a personal question?"

"Sure, go ahead."

"Why did you not have children?"

He answered, "It was simply a choice we both agreed on, and don't go believing that fake news about infertility; it isn't true. But we can chat about that another time. I want to hear about your powers."

While snacking on cheese, Ushaya went on about the different speeds and how scientists were working on the formula for HypeMo.

He was about to bite into a French pastry when he said, "Show me this disappearing thing you do." He stopped and began pacing. Where did she go? After three demos, he sat down with that signature smile of his and said, "You could make a killing with this act." Waving his hand, he added, "I know, I know, we have a bigger mission here. You're right to meet world leaders, and I am totally on board with keeping this a secret."

"Glad to hear that, sir," she said.

"Just call me Ronald," he smiled, and after taking a sip of orange juice, he suggested, "Instead of Mexico next, why don't you visit Prince Muzaffar? I have a meeting with him to discuss some business. It may help with our negotiations."

She plopped a green olive into her mouth and replied, "I've had this conversation with Jerome about zigzagging around the world, and how leaders constantly change their schedules. So, what am I going to do, pull a name out of a hat? No, an orderly fashion will give us time to prepare, and Russia completes the circuit."

He was quiet for a moment and said, "All right, I'm not here to mess with your plans, but this two-day assembly meeting you are proposing is too long; it may raise suspicion."

She agreed, "It will be tricky and has to be meticulously planned, and I am confident that you leaders can figure something out—remember, a total media blackout."

He folded his arms and asked, "Assuming this meeting takes place, what about logistics, such as food and computers and all the equipment we need?"

While sipping wine, she replied, "It will be a group effort when the time is right."

Always looking at fresh angles to be the first and most powerful in the world, he offered, "You know, we can host this meeting right here in the US."

"I'm honoured to hear that, but let me complete my mission, and then we can decide," she said.

He asked, puzzled, "Aren't you hot in that suit?"

She put down her wine, and replied, "The material breathes and keeps my temperature regulated, and, speaking of suits, I would like to take you on a fly-about."

His eyes lit up. Feigning modesty, he said, "Me?"

"Of course," she said, smiling. "It's a big part of my mission." From her pack, she pulled out his suit, gear, and ropes and laid them onto the table, and said, "First, you need to remove your suit and tie. Leave your undergarments on, and ditch the brown leather shoes, and put on socks and running shoes. Then slip into your suit and put on your vest." He disappeared down the hall with his gear.

While floating around the kitchen, she pulled out papaya juice from the fridge and filled two thermoses she had found in a cupboard. When she returned to the great space, she filled lunch bags with snacks from the food trays, and then sat down, waiting for him.

Ronald appeared at the entrance, walking stiffly, playfully, pretending to be an astronaut, "Actually, this suit feels very comfortable. How did you get my measurements?" he asked.

She thought of LHF and replied, "I researched online."

"You don't say. It fits me too well, shows all my curves," he said.

She restrained a smile and replied, "I've put together some snacks and juice for our journey."

"Where are we flying to?" he asked.

"Where do you want to go?"

"How about Miami?"

"Too far, how about Fort Lauderdale? It's fifty-five miles from here," she said.

He nodded and said, "I know of a very private spot called Pasadia Beach."

"We can do that," she said, tapping coordinates into her GPS. Then she gave him his lunch and thermos, and said, "Here, put these in your pack."

As he watched her slip the ropes around them, fastening the ends to her belt, he began to have second thoughts, and asked, "You're sure we can do this?"

"Absolutely. If I can fly a cement truck, then you're a walk in the park," she replied.

"Right, I did see you do that," he said.

"You're the weight of a tomato, more like a feather, so are you ready?" she asked.

"Ready for what?" he asked.

She counted out loud. "One, two, three," and up they rose six feet in the air. While floating through the villa, she taught him the landing moves, repeating, "No, Ronald. Land with your right foot first, left foot forward, back, and stabilize." They tried again and he landed perfectly.

With ropes taut, and hanging on for dear life, he flew out the patio doors over the deck and pool, over chalet rooftops and palm trees swaying in the breeze. They headed southbound along the ocean shoreline, and up, up, up until cars were tiny specks weaving along the highway below. Higher and faster, he flew across the grey expanse under thick clouds forming above, feeling the cool, damp air upon his face. Ushaya slowed down and looked behind her.

Ronald broke into a broad smile, and letting go of the ropes, cried out, "Look, no hands!"

She felt happy that he was enjoying the flight, and said, "We're breaking a new record, cruising at 12,000 feet altitude. Even the kids haven't flown this high."

Suddenly like a child, he couldn't stop giggling, "Hee, hee, hah, hah, haw, haw, ah, ah, ah . . ." His voice choked up. She turned her belt around and floated backward, facing him, concerned that the altitude was getting to him.

Sputtering, catching his breath, he cried out, "I didn't believe Jerome, and now here we are! Ha, ha, ha, heh, heh, heh, eh, eh, eh," holding his stomach.

She herself began to giggle, "Huh, huh, huh, huh, huh, huh," and soon they were at a standstill, pointing fingers at each other, unable to finish a sentence, laughing so hard.

Smiling, wiping his tears, he cried out, "I haven't had this much fun in ages." She brought out a tissue to wipe the tears from her visor. While looking about, still in shock, he said, "We are flying, right?" She burst into laughter, and they laughed and laughed, rolling around in fits of hysteria. Soon they began their descent under foreboding clouds, and landed on a secluded beach. Not a soul was in sight, for tourists had stayed away due to the imminent rains.

The Argument

Ronald sat on a log feeling grounded and relaxed as he watched gentle waves lap the shore. He pulled out a sandwich from his pack and said, "Isn't the ocean beautiful? I feel like I've had ten vacations in one day, away from all that damn politics."

Ushaya took a sip of papaya juice and replied, "You must have a lot on your plate."

He confided, "I've tabled a bill in Congress to reduce refugees entering the US."

She took another sip of juice and blurted, "Germany let in a million refugees."

His face turned red, and, raising his voice, he barked, "I don't' care what Germany did. I will not let one illegal refugee cross our borders. We cannot have terrorists from asshole countries enter this great country of ours—not today, not tomorrow, and not yesterday."

Pondering a moment, she replied, "It's sad that these leaders don't care about their people. All they care about is money, politics and power."

Ronald sat on the sand, leaning against the log and said, "You got that right. We're dealing with autocratic rulers who vastly oppose our values and ideologies. In other words, we don't get along with them, and never will."

She replied, "Yet you continue trading with these countries for their commodities and resources."

"Ushaya, it is not up to us to fix their problems," he said, adding, "Trade must continue, but in some cases, embargoes and sanctions are our best options."

She asked, "Do you think sanctions really work? Or don't they just end up hurting the little people?"

"Sanctions have worked," he replied.

"Oh? Tell me when," she said.

Conversations were not going well, and not long afterward, they started on the wall. One of the promises Ronald had made, should he get into power, was to erect a physical barrier along the border between the US and Mexico.

"That's another thorn in my side," he said, "Do you know how many thousands of migrants flood our border each year? It is overwhelming, and we can no longer sustain the impact this is having on our economy."

She countered, "You mean, the impact it is having on your flawed immigration system, which needs reforming. Besides, the costs in maintaining the wall will be astronomical, not to mention, it will affect wildlife migration patterns on both sides, disrupting their natural habitats."

He bit into his sandwich and said, "Do you realize, illegal immigrants that enter our country every year have strained our social programs, along with billions of dollars in lost tax revenue?"

She retorted, "Well, at least don't build detention centres at the border, separating children from their families. How can you let that happen? Build bridges, not walls, Ronald."

"I thought we weren't going to talk politics," he said.

While eating her sandwich, she quietly said, "There are many problems in the US. Do you think a wall will make America great again?"

A full-blown argument broke out, with neither of them listening, each pointing a finger at the other on a variety of issues, from the Second Amendment to bear arms, to international arms trade deals with dubious countries. They argued about abortion rights, about bigotry and racism, about legalizing cannabis, and about climate change denial. They argued about steel trade agreements, about Iran nuclear warheads, about tax levies on China, about Germany owing vast sums of money to NATO. They argued about the US's withdrawal from the Paris Climate Agreement.

They stopped yelling, and turned away in silence, with arms crossed, both stubborn.

Ronald slowly faced the ocean and said, "This is ridiculous. Here we are having the most amazing experience of our lives, and we're bickering."

She turned toward the ocean and said, "Ronald, you are accomplishing great things, too."

"Oh, please, do tell me," he said, taking a swig of papaya juice from his thermos.

She began, "You are expanding your support among non-white voters, which is a good thing. Plus, your Republican party has gained new seats in the House, preventing Democrats from taking over the Senate. I am sure that is a feather in your cap."

He screwed the lid tight on his thermos and replied, "Go on, I'd like to hear more."

She continued, "You are brokering multiple Arab-Israeli peace deals to establish further stability in the Middle East."

"That I am," he said proudly.

She continued, "The US Space Force (USSF) is becoming a separate branch of the Armed Forces, under the Department of the Air Force. It's a historic moment for your country. From what I understand, this will reduce costs and help coordinate their efforts toward space exploration."

He leaned into her, confiding, "If I don't get a second term, that's all right. I will be more powerful from behind the scenes. I will not be finished yet. Besides, I got a few words for the Federal Reserve and their cronies." He slapped his knees and said, "Let's agree, no more politics." Ushaya had started on Obamacare when he stopped her and said, "Remember?"

"Right," she said, and backed down.

Then he started on Russia meddling in their US elections, and about fake news, when she stopped him and said, "Remember?"

"Right," he replied.

If You Had One Wish

While gazing at pebbles along the beach, Ushaya asked, "If you had one wish, what would that be?"

Ronald let out a sigh and replied, "Opportunity for every citizen to realize the American dream—that is, to realize their greatest potential, regardless of what class they were born into. And I wish to levy higher taxes on the rich that do offshore business, and entice them back to US shores with economic incentives." He took a bite into his sandwich and continued, "I want our troops to come back home from overseas. And one more thing, I wish to change the system between Congress and executive committees to give me more presidential powers." He paused, "I wish I had a crystal ball, you know, to be on the cutting edge of business opportunities."

She gazed at the grey skies and replied, "Yeah, sure would be nice, wouldn't it? It's going to rain. Shall we push off?"

He suggested, "Jerome flew 400 miles an hour, and I'd like to beat that. How about 500?"

Tightening the ropes around his vest to ensure they were snug, she looked at him and said, "There's a twenty-year age difference between you and Jerome. How strong is your heart?"

"From what doctors tell me, my heart is in great shape," he replied.

Putting on her gloves and visor, she said, "I cannot go past FastMo, the g-force will be too great—sorry, Ronald. I'll start slowly and check in to make sure you're OK. We'll be back in five minutes, which is a nice bonus."

They glided northbound along the ocean shoreline toward West Palm Beach, and Ronald heard her announce, "One hundred miles per hour." He hung onto the ropes, and the sandy shoreline whizzed by. As they accelerated across the sky, he heard, "Two hundred miles." She looked behind, and he gave the thumbs up. While blazing through the sky, he heard, "Three hundred." A bolt of lightning streaked across the dark clouds, and thunder clapped in shock and awe. The rain was about to burst when he heard, "Four hundred." He hung on for dear life, his suit glistening with moisture and his visor plastered to his numb face. Unable to find his feet, and wondering if he had cracked the sound barrier, he barely escaped the torrential downpour. They entered the calm grey atmosphere, and slowly descended all the way to his villa. He staggered inside, clutching his chest, and collapsed on the couch.

"Are you OK, Ronald? Say something," she said, most concerned.

There was a moment of silence, and then he asked, "Did you see the aircraft below us?"

"That I did, and did you see the tornado?" she asked, as she began removing the ropes and vests.

He answered, "I did not, but did you see Cape Kennedy launch pad from Canaveral?"

"No, I did not," she replied.

While gazing out pensively, he said, "Your visit was not on my dime. Jerome paid for it. Consider your visit to Mexico all expenses paid, and I will personally call Carlos to insist he meet with you. Now, if you will excuse me, I need to head to the restroom," and he ran down the hall.

She called out, "Thank you. That is most kind."

A Game of Golf

When he returned to the great space, still in his grey suit, he piped up, "Let's do a round of golf."

"Golf?" she asked, perplexed.

Heading to the door, he said, "My private grounds are just around the corner. We can walk there."

She followed him and said, "But I don't know a thing about golf."

"Then it's time you learned," he replied.

They soon arrived at a small clubhouse and, retrieving the electric cart loaded with golf clubs and balls, he drove them to the starting point on the greens. She disembarked, gazing at the neatly trimmed grass with little flagsticks stationed around cup holes.

Ronald opened the first round and hit the ball from the tee directly across the fairway into a hole, with one stroke, acing his first play in a record move. "Your turn," he said, motioning Ushaya.

Straddling awkwardly above the tee, she asked, "Where am I supposed to aim?"

He pointed and said, "Anywhere over that stretch of green. Try to pocket the ball in a hole, and avoid sand traps. Give it your best shot. I know you can do it." He stood back with that pride and confidence that only Americans know.

Swaying to and fro, she raised her club and swung. The ball whizzed off the tee high into the air, disappearing over a grove of tall trees, past the edge of the greens.

Resting his hands upon his iron while gazing into the blue yonder and back at her, he said, "That constitutes a penalty for out of bounds."

"What's beyond those trees?" she asked.

"A bog," he replied.

And thus ended their golf game.

The Gemball and alligators

The following morning, Ushaya was on the phone with Jerome. "His heart nearly gave out and we had a big argument, and I couldn't even get the golf game right," she said.

"Stop right there," he said, and lowered his voice, "Ronald was incredibly impressed. In fact, we'll be able to reach leaders must faster now, do you understand?" She nodded.

Changing the subject, he asked, "So, what are your plans for today?"

"I'm thinking of visiting the Everglades, and then doing some shopping in Miami," she replied.

Jerome remarked, "By the way, your frogfish videos and the twelve spheres are very mysterious indeed. I look forward to the assembly meeting. Perhaps, together, we can learn more about them." They ended their call. While poring over emails, he heard his wife, Kaitlyn, call out, "I'm going Christmas shopping. Back in a few hours."

"OK, honey, see you later," he called back.

Ushaya stepped out of her hotel. It was high noon. With coordinates set, she blazed across the sky in SuperMo, ending in the Everglades. She followed barges and boaters meandering down rivers, admiring green foliage and mangrove trees; then the terrain turned into dense swampland. Hovering ten feet above tangled roots and tall barren trees, she glanced at the murky waters and muddy pools swirling around dead and decaying roots, emitting a stench. It felt like Spookville. She swiped through her GPS, thinking there had been some kind of mistake, when something moved in the swamp.

An alligator was coming straight for her, swishing its tail. It suddenly snapped its huge jaws in the air. Alarmed, she backed off and floated farther down the river, manoeuvring through twisted dead branches, looking warily behind, asking, "Why is it following me?"

A second alligator, with snaggleteeth and green eyes, slithered toward her. Sandwiched between the two, she immediately scrambled up a dead tree. The second alligator leaped in the air with something bright lodged in its jaws. It slapped its belly upon the mucky waters, and rose up again. This time, she got a better view; it looked like a shiny ball. They clashed, with tails thrashing and bodies writhing, lunging and twisting each other in an epic battle, and she took pictures, click, click, click . . . Bloodied, and hissing at the other, the second alligator dropped the ball, and the two disappeared into the waters, wounded, and all went silent.

She descended to the muddy bank, and looked both ways, ever watchful. With her left glove removed, she plunged her hand into the muck, and the stench filled her nostrils as she searched around the mess of tangled roots. Then she felt something hard, and raised a shiny ball from the gooey slime. While gazing at it, she thought, "So this is what they were fighting over."

Out of Spookville to greener pastures along the Everglades, she washed the ball thoroughly in a river, and settled back on the grassy banks, holding it in her hands, studying it. It was the size of a human skull, crystalline and opaque in appearance, with soft yellow-white striations gleaming under the sun. It had some weight, she thought, and wondered what it was made of. Then she lightly tapped it. Coloured patterns swirled across the surface, and elephant images appeared. Then the scene changed to a marketplace, perhaps in a foreign country. Then the scene changed again to a silver pond. She placed the ball on the grass, and the images disappeared.

Stunned, she held it up again and tapped it lightly. Swirling mists cleared to a scene of butterflies swarming a dark, foreboding castle, and then the scene changed to Stanislav hunched over formulas on his desk. Startled, she placed it back on the grass, muttering, "Something strange is going on." Then she wrapped it in cloth and placed it her pack, and flew off into the sky. *I shall call it Gemball, a fine Christmas gift for Ronald, something unique from the Everglades*, she said to herself.

She never made it to Miami; instead, she flew straight back to her hotel, exhilarated, light-headed, and giddy. For the entire day, she did nothing but gaze into the Gemball, asking questions, enchanted by the moving images.

When she would put it down, it would turn opaque. She discovered that she didn't need to speak out. She could just think of the question, and images would form. The clearer her question was, the clearer the answer.

She asked out loud, "What are the grandkids doing now?" Swirls of contrasting colours changed to a scene of Tyler playing a video game and Chelsea in bed, with a head cold. She texted Meg, "Hi, I'm still in Florida. Is Tyler playing a video game, and is Chelsea in bed with a cold?"

A text came back, "Yes, how do you know?"

Ushaya texted back, "I found the all-seeing Gemball. Will explain later." She sat back in her chair, stunned. She asked more questions, and each time, images formed, giving an answer. One time, she asked a silly question, "Who will be the first person I talk to when I land back at Crestfield Airport?" Images cleared to a scene of an elderly Indian woman dressed in a sari, asking for help with her luggage.

She then asked, "What are the lottery numbers for the Booster Triple play in Florida's game tonight?" Six numbers floated into view. She quickly wrote them down: six, fifteen, nineteen, twenty-five, thirty-two, and forty-four. Excited at the prospect of getting rich, she bought the ticket online, and now had to wait.

That evening, Ronald joined Ushaya on screen, "How was your day?" he asked.

She replied, "I've been to the Everglades and had this most amazing experience." She told the story of the alligators, and he couldn't believe it. Sliding the ball on a white velvet cloth into view, she announced, "I have found a gift for you. Meet the all-seeing Gemball."

He peered into the screen and said, "It's quite large."

She remarked, "As you can see, it is opaque—yellow-white, almost crystalline—but the surface is totally smooth like a marble." Then she tapped the ball once, and as it lit up, she said, "Now gaze into the ball and ask a question."

"Through the screen?" he asked, incredulous.

"Yeah, let's try it," she suggested.

He cleared his throat, and asked out loud, "What is Karina doing right now?" The Gemball turned soft pink with yellow hues, and an image appeared. They gasped. Karina was standing at a side table in a living room, looking down at papers. Her phone was on a nearby couch.

Ushaya could see the same image through the reflection on her screen, and exclaimed, “My God, she’s wearing a green dress, right?”

“Yes, exactly,” he said, and then he had an idea, “I’m going to call her. Let’s see what happens.” He picked up his phone and dialled a number. They watched Karina sit down on her couch to answer the call.

“It doesn’t record sound, does it?” he whispered to Ushaya.

“Apparently not,” she replied.

“Hello, honey? Yeah, I’m still at the White House,” he said, adding, “I look forward to our dinner date tomorrow. By the way, are you wearing a green dress?” Karina appeared surprised, and nodded, while moving her lips.

“No, honey, I love all your clothes. You wear them like a First Lady should. I’m just calling to say that I will be home tomorrow,” and the two hung up. They watched Karina happily rise from the couch and walk back to her papers, and then the image faded to opaque.

Ushaya spoke gravely, “It’s a powerful weapon. If everybody could spy on each other, there would be mayhem and chaos. Can you imagine? Do you realize the implications here? For instance, wife spying on husband to find him in bed with another woman, or spying on your neighbours, or your family and co-workers.”

Pondering a while, he replied, “This capability cannot get into the hands of ordinary citizens, but it could help round up criminals.”

She shook her head and said, “That poses new problems. If it gets into the wrong hands, it could have serious consequences.”

“I don’t intend to pass the ball around. I assume the members will know about this?” he asked.

“Yes, it’s always meant to be open dialogue,” she replied.

He sat back, totally flummoxed, and then said, “This is all so fantastic. I do ask one favour though. Could we have a few more sessions when you are back in Canada, when you have time?”

“Of course,” she replied.

He lowered his voice and said, “Thank you for our amazing experience.”

“It’s been wonderful, Ronald,” she replied. Then they signed off.

She eagerly waited for the lottery to open online. One by one, the numbers rolled in: three, seventeen, twenty-four, thirty-three, thirty-five, and forty-one. She checked her ticket in shock. Not one number was right. Turning to the ball on the table, she tapped it once, and asked, "Is this some kind of joke?" Numbers floated in and out across the surface. Angry that she had not won the lottery, she muttered, "How do I shut this thing off?" Trying something different, she gave it two taps and, to her astonishment, the ball turned off. She tapped it once and it lit up again. *So, one tap to open and two taps to close*, she said to herself. Obsessed, she gazed another two hours, and finally had to stop.

Late that evening, while reading the report in his chambers, Ronald phoned up Jerome, wondering, "It appears Ushaya found twelve spheres for you and one big Gemball for me. What do you make of this?"

Jerome shook his head and replied, "I don't know, but flying with her was undeniably real."

"That it was," said Ronald, and they hung up.

The plane touched down at Crestfield Airport at eleven o'clock the following morning, her final destination, at last. Ushaya picked up her luggage from the carousel and glanced at her invisible watch, thinking she would be home in a few minutes.

An elderly Indian woman, dressed in a colourful sari, was standing by her, when she asked, "Excuse me, madam, please, can you lift my luggage that is coming down the carousel? My son hasn't arrived yet."

Ushaya lifted the suitcases into the old woman's cart. Shortly after, her son arrived, and the two thanked her before going on their way. *How mysterious. It predicts some things after all*, she thought.

Days lingered as she caught up on household chores and the flurry of emails. Texts were sent to Jerome and Ronald, "I have arrived safely and will be in touch." She called up Stan, requesting a block of time in his schedule, for there was something important she needed to discuss. He was surprised, when she asked him to make another winter suit, vest, and gloves for himself, and they agreed to meet in three days.

She emailed photos of her New Zealand visit to her sister Amelia. A reply popped up, "Photos are lovely, glad you had a good time. I just got back from Zambia, been there for three months, as you know, studying the baka-baka root, which shows promise of a new strain against the Zika virus. Tomorrow, I head out to Vancouver to analyze the data." Before signing off, Amelia added, "Let's chat during the holidays."

An email came in from her brother Kevin: "Nice photos. The grandkids sure have grown. I'm glad you enjoyed the trip. Maria and I are building an extension to the ranch for an extra guest room."

The following morning, Ronald called up Ushaya, and spent an hour gazing into the Gemball across the screen, asking many questions, feeling astonished with the answers. "Thank you for your gift, Ushaya, and I look forward to the assembly. In the meantime, go ahead and experiment with it. I have to go now to attend a rally," he said, and hung up.

Gift of Genius

Ushaya was enjoying the country drive through mountain ranges on her way to Stan's place. The sun had broken through a dump of snowfall, and she watched snowplows clear the highway.

When she had settled in the grand space of his mansion, she asked, "Are you staying for the holidays or going somewhere?"

Stan poured cups of tea and replied, "I'll be home for Christmas, and my brother is arriving with his family. How about you?"

"I'll be home, too. After all this travel, it will be good to relax," she said, taking a sip of tea. Then she looked about and asked, "Where's Lucy?"

"She's downloading files. She'll be around soon," he replied.

"No, don't call her. Let's just talk," she said.

"Sure, what's up?" he asked, intrigued.

Ushaya began her story of the Blue-ray light that fateful night, and how she had developed superpowers, flying in great speeds in a single bound, and lifting heavy objects with the greatest of ease. She told the story of Fast, Super, and HypeMo. She told the story of her visit with the kids, how she'd flown with PM Jerome, and how she found the twelve spheres and the frogfish. She told the story of her visit with President Ronald, and how she discovered the Gemball through the mouths of alligators.

Stan listened, marvelling, "That's quite some tale," he said.

She demonstrated strength, by lifting a heavy bookcase by the granite fireplace. They chased each other in FastMo through one room after another. Then she demonstrated HypeMo, returning to the great space.

Stan sat down and said, "So your mission is to approach world leaders."

Smiling, she replied, "Which brings me to my next mission. I want to fly you, just like the rest of us did. That's why I asked you to make a suit for yourself. I've got the ropes."

While silently pacing the floor, with his hands folded in front of him, he slowly began to speak, "I have a confession to make. One night, I also encountered a mysterious blue light, and ever since, my Dream Seam Machine project was born. You are right, I am the only one operating the machines, but of course, I purchased all the supplies."

"What about your investors and stakeholders, was that a lie?" she asked.

He answered, "No, I have stakeholders, it's not a lie."

"So, you saw the Blue-ray light?" she asked.

He told his story, "Days later, a man came to my door selling material swatches, which I accepted, and then suddenly he was gone, like in thin air, no payment, nothing. I thought it strange at the time. Shortly after, I went into SuperMo, as you call it. It was as if my mind began to accelerate, exploding with creative inventions, and charts and formulas, beyond anything I had ever realized my entire life."

She asked excitedly, "What else do you know about the Blue-ray light and the source of our powers?"

He answered, "I have received no further messages or revelations since that time. I am completely mystified."

She wondered, "We may not be the only ones, and that man you met might be a catalyst from the Source. Look at the frogfish and the alligators. It's as if I was guided to find a gift, on top of it all. She lowered her voice, "Perhaps, we are pawns in a larger scheme."

He rubbed his goatee, also wondering, "Surely, we can't be the only ones; but what kind of scheme?"

They soon forgot their worries, whisking through the mansion in their suits and vests while she taught him the 'forward, back, and stabilize' moves. Then they flew into the crisp blue skies, heading east above evergreens hung low under blankets of snow. They dipped into mountain gorges over icy streams and bridges, and scaled down frozen waterfalls. They flew past people skiing down mountainsides and children skating on a pond, and then up, up, up, they continued soaring over small towns dotting along the highway. Ushaya pointed to her home below. Enthralled, frolicking under the winter sun, they landed on her favourite lookout point in the Selkirk Mountains, and sat down with legs dangling over the ledge of an 8,000-foot drop into the fjord below. While sipping hot tea from her thermos, admiring the cascading mountains, she asked, "If you had one wish, what would that be?"

Stan watched a lone osprey gliding in the sky, and replied, "I would like my sewing machines to succeed around the world, and I also want to know the source of our powers."

"As do I," she said, gazing out. And then turning to him, she asked, "So, will you become a member? You must, we can't do this without you. After all, it's your gear the leaders will be flying in."

He pondered for a moment and said, "I don't know where this is going, but yes, I accept to become a member."

She smiled and said, "Welcome to the assembly. We're in this together, you know."

Feeling the cold through his suit, he put on his goggles and said, "The suit could use a few design modifications. I must admit, though, the ropes you chose are perfect." From the rock, they glided westward, engaged in small talk along the way, clearly enjoying the scenery.

Suddenly to their right, an avalanche thundered down the mountainside into a cloud of debris, taking trees with it. They rose higher, watching in awe at one of nature's most terrifying spectacles. Something was happening to their left: first, crackling sounds, and then, bang! A hydro transmission tower blew a circuit, and electric discharges zipped haywire down the poles, sending a blast of current across the sky. It knocked the two of them out of the air, sending them hurtling toward earth. Sputtering, catching their breath, they slowly steadied themselves over another valley. Ushaya pulled down her goggles, blurting, "Are you all right?"

While patting his vest, Stan's face lit up, "A wonderful, splendid idea is coming to me, it's a new invention!"

She put on her goggles, and they continued gliding westward. For a man of few words, he couldn't stop babbling incoherently about formulas and trajectories and strange things she didn't understand.

He exclaimed, "You have given me the greatest gift, it's genius."

"I didn't find a gift, and you are already a genius," she said.

"This feels different. I've got to write this down. Push on, Ushaya, push on!" he cried out. Then he heard her say, "Two hundred miles per hour." He hung onto ropes for dear life, when he heard, "Three hundred miles."

Back in the great space with vests, gloves, and ropes removed, they sat down, sipping tea from their thermoses, and bubbling with excitement over their adventure in the great outdoors. Stan pulled out a blank piece of paper from a drawer, and sat down, madly scribbling the invention that he had envisioned. Feeling satisfied with his jotted bullets, he placed down his pen, and said, "I will remember this."

Feeling so happy for him, she replied, "Jerome will send you the official invite to join as a member."

He glanced at her paper with names, and said, "I assume you want a suit made for President Carlos; he's next on your list of leaders." She nodded.

One day, while standing on her porch, gazing past the gargoyles, Ushaya got a call from Meg, who seemed worried, "I have to talk to you about Devon. Remember the boulder you lifted from the bank, and we saw something shiny in the dirt?"

"Yeah," she replied.

Megan continued, "Devon has been digging for months. One night, I went out with a flashlight to ask him to stop obsessing, but he wouldn't listen. Frankly, I am worried about his state of mind and the toll it's taking on his body."

Ushaya pondered a moment and said, "Hmm, perhaps, he has moved further down the ravine, and is no longer searching in the right place."

"It's possible," said Meg, shrugging her shoulders.

Ushaya was pacing the porch, when she got an idea and suggested, "Why don't you sit on your couch one day, and say something like, 'Honey, with all that digging you're doing, I asked Mom about it, and she insists that you cease digging, and will personally help you the next time she visits.'"

Meg said doubtfully, "I don't know, but I'll try." And they both signed off.

That evening, Ushaya drew maps for Stanislav and Ronald, carefully marking a big X over where gifts were found, drawing in GPS coordinates above and below. She sat back, sipping her wine and taking a drag from her cigarette. Then she wrapped the maps with red bow ties and placed them in the blue treasure chest, and turned the key to lock it.

Meanwhile, she and Ronald continued gazing into the Gemball, right up to a week before Christmas.

You take Beijing and I'll take Berlin

Ushaya watched her little town turn into a winter wonderland of silence, covered in a blanket of fluffy snow. Finished with her decorations, she stopped to admire the tree, which was lit up with brightly coloured baubles and icy streamers. She whispered to herself, "How beautiful."

One day, Ronald called up Jerome and asked, "Have you sent out the official invite?"

Jerome sat back in his chair in his private den and replied, "Yes, we're about to see how the crow flies."

"Good work, I'll give Carlos a call," said Ronald. He then piped up, "I'll take on Saudi Arabia and Russia, if you take on Rwanda."

"Sure, and I'll reach out to the queen and prince," said Jerome.

"Agreed, and can you take on India?" asked Ronald.

"Sure, if you take China," said Jerome.

"I'll take Beijing, and Hashimoto in Japan. But what about Irena?"

Jerome paused. "I'll take Berlin," he replied.

"Merry Christmas, Jerome," said Ronald.

"A Merry Christmas to you, Ronald," said Jerome.

It was late December and the festivities had subsided. One by one, the leaders opened their official invites and read the reports. Carlos was peering into his screen at Jerome and Ronald, wondering if they were both infected with the same mental illness. He said, "Excuse me, gentlemen, but do you know what you are saying?"

Chapter Seven

Mexican President Carlos Martinez Sabrador

Falling in love with Mexico

January 2019 . . .

Dressed in his finest white shirt and black pants with gold stripes, Carlos straightened his bow tie and adjusted his gold cufflinks in anticipation of her arrival. Avocado trees cascaded over green, rolling hills, and high above the terrain, he opened a stained-glass window from the Angel Villanueva Chapel. Suddenly, he noticed a figure fast approaching. "Dios mio," he whispered.

She slipped through the window and landed on the wooden rustic floor. Then she lifted her visor to her head and extended her hand, and said, "Hello, my name is Ushaya Landau. It is very nice to meet you, your Excellency."

"The pleasure is mine," he said, as he took her hand and kissed it.

She blushed, letting her backpack straps slide off her shoulders, while he motioned her to the front pews. Gesturing around the room, he began, "You may be wondering why I chose this place. You see, I grew up not far from Chiapas, and I know this chapel well. Madam, I'd like the pleasure of showing you around."

She smiled and said, "Please, just call me Ushaya."

"And just call me Carlos," he said, smiling back. Then he began to show her around, explaining the history of each windowpane.

Ushaya was on cloud nine in the presence of this most gracious man, who, though in his senior years, looked very well preserved. Upon a six-foot statuesque build, taller than the average Mexican, his neatly combed black hair showed hints of white, and his face was covered in lines. He was a formidable sight of impeccability, oozing old-world charm, as he continued explaining the different icons on the altar. Then he waved his hand dismissively, and said, "But of course, you are not here to learn about a chapel."

She was falling in love with his accent, and said, "That's all right. By the way, you chose a great place to meet. It's peaceful here."

He wasted no time and began, "I must admit, I was not convinced to meet you today, until my conversation with Ronald."

She replied, "I assure you, every word he said was true." Then she looked around the chapel, and suggested, "Let me demonstrate strength."

Carlos scanned his eyes across ornate velvet-covered chairs and rows of pews, and then gazed down at the floorboards, bemused, "I suppose you shouldn't lift these?"

Ushaya looked at the floor and replied, "No, I mustn't." They chuckled out loud, and then hushed, for they were in a house of worship. She whispered, "How about HypeMo, instead?"

His eyes darted back and forth, and he cried out, "Where are you?"

"Behind you," she replied.

Startled, he turned around, sputtering, "What sorcery is this?" Then she disappeared again, and he spun around to find her standing at a large vase, sniffing fresh-cut flowers.

"Would you like to fly?" she whispered.

He combed his hand through his hair, and replied, "I have a weak heart. A stent was placed in one of my valves years ago."

"I promise to go slow," she assured him.

Letting out a sigh, he said, "All right. I'll do this." From her pack, she spread out the gear across the front pews, and he disappeared down the hall to a private chamber. Moments later, he returned, patting his vest and suit, and said, "My shoes do not quite match the outfit."

"It's not a fashion contest," she said, smiling.

"Are you sure we are not flying to the moon?" he asked.

"We'd need oxygen tanks for that," she replied. They laughed out loud, and quickly hushed, for they were in a house of worship.

With ropes secured to her belt, they whisked out through the stained glass windows, gliding under the Mexican sun, over rolling landscapes and farmlands and coffee plantations. They flew over spectacular Mayan ruins to their left and a mining operation to their right. They flew over small settlements, hidden under jungle canopies. They continued gleefully, with not a word between them, since they left the chapel. Then they descended to an empty field, and, finding two tree stumps under a grove of tall dead trees, they sat down for a rest.

Carlos pulled down his visor, spluttering, “I have no words to express my complete and utter astonishment. I must congratulate Stanislav for his fine craftsmanship. The suit is very comfortable.”

“Where are we?” she asked, gazing about.

“An abandoned farmer’s field, I believe,” he answered, while scanning the parched landscape. There was not a soul in sight. Insects were buzzing in the air, and a large lizard was sunbathing on a nearby rock.

“You have family, from what I have read in the reports,” she said, while sipping water from her canteen.

Carlos took a swig from his canteen and replied, “I am happily married to my wife Rosalina for thirty-eight years. We have one son, Geraldo, who is an archaeologist, and we have no grandchildren.”

She took another sip and asked, “Carlos, if you had one wish in the whole world, what would that be?”

He pondered the question for a while before he spoke. “I wish to rein in the drug cartels, and I wish to end bullfights. I aim to open up micro business incentives between the rich and the poor, whereby both sides can prosper.”

“Those are noble ambitions,” she said, gazing at the clear sky. She turned to him and asked, “What can you do to stem the flow of migrants crossing the US border?”

He replied, “I aim to make our country great again, a country so great, our people will have no need to search elsewhere.”

He concluded with his final wish, “I am troubled by my ancient heritage, which goes back further than the Aztecs, a mysterious chapter with conflicting stories on both sides of my family, lost in history.”

Suddenly, there was a loud crack, and a dead tree began lifting from the parched soil, falling toward him. With quick action, Ushaya caught the tree, barehanded, just inches above his head, and holding it horizontally, she placed it on the ground. The lizard skittered away.

Visibly shaken, he cried out, “Dios mio! You saved my life.”

She shook her head, asking, "Why do these things keep happening to me?"

"Because you have been given a great power, and sometimes it will be tested," he replied.

"Shall we head back to the chapel?" she asked, clearly shaken by the event.

Carlos felt the vest ropes tighten under her soft yet strong hands. Gazing upon the face of an angel, he glided westward, not wanting the journey to end, but, alas, he entered the chapel window.

Clover and the Ancient Relic

The following morning, as she stepped out of the Corazon Ranchero, she began to ponder which way to go. A young Mexican woman approached her and asked, "Estas perdida?"

Ushaya smiled politely, and answered, "No, mi estoy perdida, gracias." (No, I am not lost, thank you.)

Her intent was to avoid big cities like Tuxtla, so she headed south, soaring over valleys and crop fields and small town churches. A massive butterfly migration began to appear in the distance. Tens of thousands were fluttering in the air, in every shape, size, and colour, with blue, orange, yellow, and speckled wings glistening under the sun.

Together, they fluttered side-by-side, when suddenly, the swarm approached and landed on her entire body. Some would land and leave, while others took their places. She was in ecstasy, covered head-to-toe in butterflies. With outstretched arms, she followed their journey, wishing this moment would never end. But, alas, shaking off a thick cluster from her hand, and wiping butterflies from her visor, she reached for her phone, and was shocked to discover that she was only a few miles from the Guatemalan border. She shook the butterflies from her body, and quickly backed out of the swarm, "This is where I leave you, my friends," she said. The butterflies continued southward, disappearing into the distant sky.

There was a clearing in the jungle below, where she decided to land. The air was hot and insects buzzed. A snake slithered around a branch to her right, as she cautiously walked through the underbrush, feeling rather spooked. Something big and black whizzed above her head, which frightened her, and she tripped and fell flat on her face. Annoyed, she got up, dusting leaves and dirt from her suit. Then she turned around, wondering what had tripped her.

It was a large, winding root, half-embedded in the ground, and she followed it into a little forest, overshadowed by the jungle canopy. Something shiny caught her eye at the base of a nearby tree. With curiosity, she brought out a hand trowel from her pack, and began carefully digging around the soil, chipping at the hard surface of tangled roots. Occasionally, she would brush away the dirt, growing more excited at a stone object beginning to emerge, sprinkled in gold dust.

The high noon sun peeked through the canopy, and temperatures were rising. She pulled down her hood, opened her flaps, and zippered down her suit, then took a big drink of guava juice from her canister. Returning to her task, she gently pulled and prodded and cut through the tangled roots, until the object gave way. Raising it from the earth, holding it in her hands, she sat against the tree, in awe and wonder, marvelling at the ancient relic. *How magnificent!* she thought.

It was ten inches tall, eight inches wide, and eight inches deep. As she stared into a half-man-half-beast statue, a grimacing face stared back at her, with bulging eyes, a large nose, a slanted narrow forehead, and drawn-down lips. It wore a five-inch headdress, half the entire height of the statue, with elaborate reliefs surrounded by precious gems. The rest of the body parts convoluted into a jaguar, she thought, with two front paws resting over three stone slabs, etched with indiscernible glyphs. She drank the remaining guava juice, and then carefully packed the relic, happy to find a gift for Carlos. As she looked around one more time, she saw creepy crawlies skittering along the jungle floor; it was clearly time to leave.

She proudly whizzed up through the canopy, but when she reached the top, a razor-edged palm leaf cut her left hand. The blood poured out, soaking her suit. "Oh, no!" she cried out, pulling off her glove. It was a nasty gash, baring deep layers of white fatty flesh and cartilage to the bone, from the wrist to the base of her fingers. She squeezed the wound together with her right hand, but the blood kept flowing.

Quickly, she descended into a patch of clover, adjacent to the forest, and pulled out a safety kit. Then she began pouring rubbing alcohol over the wound; it stung like hell. She frantically wound a piece of gauze around her hand and used her teeth to clench a knot, and then looked at it. The blood kept pouring through the bandages. Rummaging wearily in her pack, she pulled out a second piece of cloth and wrapped another layer. The blood kept seeping through the second layer, and, worse, the knots had loosened into a big gooey mess of wet cloths. The sun was blazing down, and she broke out in a sweat. She pulled out her water bottle, but it was empty. Delirious and rapidly weakening, she dropped to her knees, wondering if she had been poisoned, whispering to herself, *I cannot die alone in a Mexican jungle. Is this my fate?* And she fell forward into unconsciousness.

Sparky the Crystal

The evening rains pounded hard on the skylight above. Meg decided to take her mom's advice and talk with Devon about the ravine. She sat with her laptop on the couch, waiting for him to come home.

The front door opened and closed. "Honey, where are you?" he asked as he came around the corner. He saw her resting on the couch, and placed his briefcase on the coffee table.

She looked up, and asked, "How was your day?"

"It was pretty routine. Hmm, it smells good. What's cooking?" he asked.

He seemed in good spirits, she thought, and began, "I chatted with Mom before she left for Mexico about you digging in the ravine."

Alarmed, staring at her, he asked, "What for?"

"I needed to talk to someone," she replied.

He removed his tie and threw it on the couch, snarling, "It's nobody's business what I do, and certainly not your mother's."

Meg tried to stay calm, and replied, "Mom says to stop searching, and the next time she visits, we can explore the area together." Voices escalated and arguments ensued. She yelled, "Besides, you could be searching in the wrong place. Go back to the beginning!"

Devon stormed out the door, and, grabbing a flashlight and shovel from the veranda, he headed for the ravine. Slamming her laptop shut, Meg got up to remove the chicken from the oven. She placed it on the stove and, slapping her oven mitts on the counter, sat down at the dining table and wept.

Soaked to the bone, slipping and sloshing in his business suit and leather shoes, Devon continued to dig and dig, and then stopped. The rains had washed most of the mud into the gulley, and resting in the dark, he remembered her words, "You're searching in the wrong place, go back to the beginning." As he stumbled back along the embankment, he saw something shiny, and, reaching into the muck and tangled roots, pulled out what he was looking for.

A glow surrounded an octagonal blue gem, emitting rainbow rays, like a sparkler. He closed his fist around the object, and sparkles continued emitting through his fingers. He hurried up the bank and stormed into the house to find Meg wiping her tears. Totally drenched, he sat down at the table, and resting on one elbow, holding it in his hand, he softly gushed, "I found it."

Meg gasped, "What is it?"

He gave her the gem and said, "I don't know. Why don't you hold it?" and began removing his muddy shoes and suit jacket.

The blue gem floated above her palm, emitting sparks in all directions. Its core glowed softly, and shrunk and grew like the base of a candle. Meg tapped the crystal, and it moved two feet in the air. Startled, they scrambled out of their chairs, and backed away.

Devon reached out and tapped the crystal. It moved three feet in the air, radiating beautiful colours. Meg tapped it lightly, and like a balloon, it rose up ten feet and returned to them. They began to chuckle in delight. Devon tapped it ten feet in a different direction. Frolicking like children, they flicked their fingers, and the crystal bounced up the stairs and down the hall. Megan remembered the chicken growing cold on the stove, and blurted, "We've got to hide it from the kids. They'll be home soon."

He took her hand and they lay back on their bed. He looked at her and said, "I'm sorry I made you cry." While the two gazed up at the crystal floating above them, he whispered, "I think we found a gift."

Back in the Jungle

A full moon lit up the midnight sky, shining upon the Mexican jungle. Birds pecked at her suit and snakes and insects crawled over her body. Ushaya slowly opened her eyes, and blinked a few times through a hazy scene of violet light. Her head jerked, and, struggling to sit up, she looked around in disbelief. The clover patch glowed all around her with soft, heart-shaped, violet leaves upon bright green stems. Grateful to be alive, she gazed up at the stars and back down at her left hand. The blood had stopped flowing, and tufts of velvety clover petals stuck to the wound, which was now closing.

The patch, where her hand had laid, was soaked in blood. She pulled out her phone from her vest pocket, and was shocked, realizing, she had been unconscious for ten hours.

Convinced that the clover was healing her hand, she gathered a clump of tender leaves and pressed them upon her wound, and then wrapped her hand with more gauze bandages. Then she dug into their roots, using her trowel, and, lifting a chunk of clover, she wrapped it in cloth, and stowed the leaves in her pack. Unsteadily, she rose to her feet, wondering if she had the strength to carry on. Slowly, she glided northbound under a full moon, with renewed strength and faith, for she had died and been reborn.

The cut, which was crusting over, was ugly looking, but much better, she observed back in her hotel room, and was grateful that she did not need to go to the hospital. *It may still get infected though*, she thought, as she looked around for any salve or ointment. Then the idea struck her. *Heck, just add more fresh clover*, she said to herself, and then wrapped the hand up with more bandages.

The following day, with left fingers barely able to move across the keys, Ushaya finally sent her report to Carlos.

Aghast, he immediately arranged for a Skype meeting that evening. "What happened? How is your hand?" he asked.

She unravelled the bandages and showed him a narrow red scar, replying, "Just yesterday, it was cut to the bone." Then she turned out the lights and closed the curtains, and shoved leaves into the viewing screen, announcing, "Meet Clover, my gift for you."

He stared in wonder at violet leaves glowing upon bright green stems, like lilies in a pond. Their petals turned every which way to capture whatever light source they could find. "They're beautiful," he whispered.

Then she presented him with the second gift, announcing, "Meet the Ancient Relic."

He gazed at the half-man-half-beast statue, wearing a headdress, its fierce face staring back at him. Stony stairways were dusted in gold, etched with glyphs and symbols below. Suddenly, he shrank back in shock.

"What's the matter, Carlos?" she asked.

He answered, "In my youth as a freedom fighter, I once landed in prison, and while there, I met a tattooist. When we were released, I had a vision one night." He ripped his shirt open, baring a tattoo of the identical relic on his chest above the heart. Ushaya was speechless.

"Please keep the gifts, for now, and bring them to the assembly meeting," he said, buttoning up his shirt.

She found it odd that none of the leaders wanted their gifts in advance. Perhaps, it was a kind of political courtesy, she thought. No one wanted to be the first to say, "Yes, please, send it by FedEx." She asked, "May I take some clover with me, on my visit to the queen and prince?"

"Of course, take as much as you need," he said, adding, "And let me arrange a private jet for your return home."

She replied, "Thank you, but the power is growing. I shall make my way home by myself. Please cancel my return flight."

Brad and the Map

While trudging along his snow-covered street, Brad began thinking back on his mom's visit, wondering if someone had seen his truck rise in the driveway. Old man Harvey was sitting in his wheelchair, waving out the window from his house. Brad waved back, and decided it was time for a visit, so he walked across the street and up the salted steps, and knocked on the door.

Nurse Caroline answered, "Come in. Are you here to see Harvey?"

"Yes, how is the old boy doing?" he asked, entering the living room to the sound of a hissing ventilator.

She replied, "He is doing well, but I have to admit, this is usually his nap time."

"I won't be long," he said.

The nurse left the two in privacy, and while holding his fragile hand, Brad asked a question that had been on his mind for some time: "You've lived here your whole life. Do you know anything about the original owner of my house?"

Harvey beckoned him closer and said, "Look for a crack in the concrete floor of your garage."

"Pardon me?" he asked, perplexed.

Harvey raised a bony finger, and, with a raspy voice, he replied, "Old man Byron was a miner in his heyday, and he died with many secrets, leaving no heir." Suddenly, he began choking.

Brad cried out, "Nurse!"

Caroline came running in. She adjusted the ventilator, while asking rapid questions, "Are you all right? Can you breathe? Are you in pain?" After wrapping his blanket snug, she turned to Brad and said, "I think you should go, it's time for his nap."

Harvey's voice boomed with sudden clarity, "I saw your truck rise in the driveway."

Caroline whispered, "Don't mind him, we're going to adjust his medication."

Brad held Harvey's hand and whispered in his ear, "You saw right, my friend. Mom has developed superpowers, and the truck did rise in the air, I swear to God. Will explain later." They let go of their hands. With a satisfied look across Harvey's face, the nurse wheeled him away.

Brad wandered around his garage, looking for cracks in the pavement floor. He looked under the tool cabinets and dragged away small shop machines to examine the ground, but found nothing unusual. Then he wandered over to the garbage bins and pulled them aside. There, in the pavement floor, was a crack he had never paid attention to. With pickaxe and a shovel, he began chipping away, until a slab of foundation lifted. While peering into the hole, he reached down and pulled up a wooden box, dusting the surface with his hands.

Back at his kitchen table, he banged a hammer at the old rusty lock, and it finally broke free. Curiously rummaging through old miners' tools, he began to pull out a pickaxe, a gold pan, a sluice box, a flume, and a trammel. Then he came upon a map of old Canada, dated 1923. There was a large X marked over northern Manitoba, with a faded, hand-scribbled message, "Titanium." It was an area where his company was searching for metal deposits, but titanium was not one of them. This could make his company very rich, he thought.

He had laid out the contents on the table when he noticed a false floor at the bottom of the box. With crowbar in hand, he lifted around the edges, until the wood planks gave way, and he gasped! Old Canadian $100 bills were neatly batched in rows, tied with twine. He sat down and began counting them. There was $20,000 in all! A smile crossed his face.

The World Awakens

Ushaya did indeed make the trip, flying 3,000 miles over the borders of Mexico, the US, and Canada. When she arrived home, the first thing she did was unravel clover from its cloth, hoping it had survived the journey. The petals shone a soft violet hue. She retrieved soil and a dozen clay pots from her shed, and planted clover and sprinkled water over them. Then she placed the pots around her house, with two of them by her bedside tables.

The next day, she called up Jerome and said, "I know what the kids can do at the assembly. Brad is a wizard in computer programming, a side hobby of his. Devon is experienced with video, and Meg is a great amateur photographer. After all, who is going to man the cameras? I don't see Irena or Carlos standing behind cameras, do you?"

"A good idea," replied Jerome, nodding. Then he asked, "How is your hand? Are you all right?" She raised her hand, showing only a thin white scar.

A week later, the kids joined her in a Zoom call. "What? Cameras and computer equipment?" they cried out.

Ushaya replied, reassuringly, "Your talents will be useful at the assembly," as she gazed at the beautiful crystal.

Devon remarked, "We call it Sparky. When the kids are away, we let it float, and sometimes, it beams out laser lights in geometric patterns around us. We know it's special, but we still don't know what it is."

"You gave us a gift," said Meg.

"No, you found it," said Ushaya.

Meg shook her head and said, "Actually, Devon found it."

Devon argued, "We *all* found it."

Brad brought forth his map, and they gazed in awe at the large X. He told the story of old man Harvey, and how he had found a wooden box under his garage floor. "If we find titanium up there, man, I will be rich. Thanks for the great gift, Mom," he said, smiling.

"No, you found it," she said, shaking her head.

He argued, "It all started when you lifted my truck in the driveway. Definitely, life works in mysterious ways."

"That it does," she replied, staring out.

"Brad, what are you going to do with the money?" asked Meg.

He replied, "I don't know. Once these bills are cleared through legal collectors, I'll hold onto them, for they can only go up in value."

"What about Stan? How is he doing?" asked Devon.

Ushaya chuckled and said, "He is head over heels in genius thought. Matter of fact, the suits for the queen and prince are ready for pickup." They chatted for an hour before signing off.

Days later, Ushaya flew to Stan's place, and was greeted by Lucy at the front door. Speaking in perfect English, in robotic syntax, Lucy bowed and said, "It is nice to see you. Please enter." Ushaya entered the mansion, totally flummoxed.

Stan raised his voice. "I told you it was in the works. Come, join me in the sewing room," he said, and sprinted up the grand staircase, motioning her to follow.

Lucy was flying down the hallway when she asked, "Are you also a robot?"

"I don't think so," replied Ushaya, as they whizzed up the narrow, winding staircase to the second floor. Doors opened to the familiar hum of sewing machines, and they followed Stan to the last aisle on the right side of the room. He pulled out two swatches from a cabinet, and suddenly stopped and said, "Excuse me, I have to write this down," and began tapping obsessively on his iPad.

While waiting, her eyes fell upon a strange sight in a nearby alcove. Inside a glass booth stood a medieval English knight, in full armour, under a soft light, covered in chainmail, wearing a crested helmet, holding a shield in its left hand and a lance in its right gauntlet. The inscription below read: "Circa 1462, Saxony." She gazed at the magnificent armour, imagining the man who had once long ago fought in battle for his king, wearing this very suit. "Wow! Don't these things belong in a museum?" she asked.

Stan looked up, distracted, from his iPad, and said, "There are many collectors around the world who specialize in medieval relics, and there's quite a story on how I acquired this one, but that's for another time."

They soon arrived at the sewing machines, which were busily whirring away, and sat down at the table, before his laptop. Stan began tapping images in the air, explaining, "These two swatches, when combined, will make better suits than what Carlos wore." Suddenly, he became distracted again with another idea, and began furiously typing notes into his laptop.

Lucy brought out suits and vests for the queen and prince, and, looking at Stan, said, "You shouldn't ignore your guest."

He slammed the laptop shut. "Of course, my apologies," he said. A voice commanded from the computer, "Beginning countdown sequence. Programs not ejected properly, I repeat, programs not ejected . . ."

Meanwhile, Ushaya flew in FastMo down the winding stairwell, and Lucy easily matched her. She went into SuperMo, flying through the hallway, and Lucy matched her. She realized the drone had tracking ability, and said, "Sorry, Lucy, but this is where I leave you," and disappeared in HypeMo. Foop! Gone.

Antennae rose from her head, and Lucy looked around, perplexed, clicking and clacking, pacing the hallway. Where did she go? By then, Stan had caught up with Lucy, and he chuckled, while holding the suits for the queen and prince.

For days on end, Ushaya drew maps on parchment paper, for Carlos and Brad, and Meg and Devon, showing the locations where their gifts were found. She hand-scribbled the GPS coordinates, at the top and bottom, of each parchment paper. She was no artist, and her drawings may have looked like kids' treasure maps, with a large X and scribbled names of landmarks, highways, and mountain ranges, but she didn't care. They'll get the general idea, and most importantly, the secret coveted coordinates, which she decided not to reveal, until their assembly meeting. After all, if they knew of the exact locations in advance, it could start a race, with one country having an advantage over another, before she had completed her journey around the world. This way, it would be a level playing field. She pondered the events of the last nine months, convinced she was in some kind of zone, whenever she found a gift, perhaps led by the source of the Blue-ray light. But then she wondered if more gifts were coming, as she rolled the maps into scrolls, tying them with red ribbons and placing them in the treasure chest, under lock and key.

A week later, Jerome glanced at Ushaya and Carlos across his screen, while shuffling papers on his desk. He asked, "Are these reports true?" They nodded, and Jerome fired the reports across the world, waiting for the coming storm.

Ronald blasted Prince Muzaffar of Saudi Arabia, "Of course I can trust her. If I say it's important to meet this woman, then it's damn well important, you know that. Read the reports again. It is very serious," and he hung up.

Dumbfounded, Muzaffar called up Jerome and Carlos.

Jerome called the queen and prince.

The queen and prince called up Ronald and Carlos.

Jerome called up Irena in Germany, and Yadgiri in India.

Ronald called up Yaegar in Russia, and Zhangwei in China.

Jerome called up Hashimoto in Japan, and Mimbauwe in Rwanda.

Mimbauwe called up Ronald and Muzaffar.

President Carlos called up the queen and prince, to confirm airline tickets and hotel arrangements for mid-February, compliments of Mexico. He asked, "Are you sure, you are ready for her arrival?"

Prince Herb wheeled around in his wheelchair, and staring across the screen, replied, "We are not only ready, but are coming in disguise." Queen Julia nodded in agreement.

That night, Ushaya climbed into bed and turned off the light. Violet luminescent leaves of clover floated upon green stems in pots by her bedside tables, and she soon fell asleep.

Jerome called up Carlos, the following day, and said, "My apologies for not getting back to you sooner. How was your visit with Ushaya?"

Carlos repeated the words he'd said to Ronald, "Maravilloso, my friend."

Chapter Eight

Her Majesty Queen Julia II
and His Royal Highness Prince Herbert

The Queen and Prince

Julia was wandering down corridors of a cathedral, not far from Windshire Castle, when she asked, "Are you sure this is the right location?" She wore baggy beige pants, an oversized grey coat, and brown boots and gloves. A black fur hat was tied with black ribbons to her chin, and a grey scarf was wrapped around her face, to complete her disguise.

"This is the place," said Herb, wheeling around in his wheelchair. He wore a brown wool cap, an oversized brown coat and black boots, with a pair of sunglasses, and a grey scarf, obscuring his face, to complete his disguise.

Ushaya was floating through the cathedral alcoves, studying her coordinates, when she heard, "Psst, over here." Startled, she turned and peered at two peasants beckoning her, and, approaching them, she whispered, "I don't recognize either of you."

Julia quipped, "It is a good thing we recognize you."

Ushaya glanced down the corridors and asked, "Is the bay window open, as agreed?" She wore a silvery suit with a cream-coloured suede hat and beige poncho. Wisps of silvery-black hair streamed down on either side of her face.

Herb looked at her and replied, "Yes, the window is open, as agreed."

She pulled off her goggles, and brought out leather straps from her pack, and began wrapping them around his legs and torso, moving swiftly.

"What are you doing?" he protested loudly.

Tightening the straps, she replied. "We are not walking twenty minutes to Windshire Castle, as planned. It is too risky, for tourists will soon arrive." She strapped a wide piece of cloth around Julia's waist, attaching it to her belt. Then she gripped the wheelchair handles, and, glancing to her right, she said, "My Lady, please take my arm."

Speechless, Julia wrapped her arm in hers, and soon, they swooped along the corridor and out, up, up into the grey, wintry British air, with Herb hanging on for dear life.

Ushaya said, "Please forgive my manners, for I have not properly introduced myself. My name is Ushaya Landau, and I am most pleased to meet you." Doves burst from a nearby rooftop into the sky.

Julia clutched her handbag, as she gazed at horses in the distant, snowy pasture. Then she glanced down and wryly said, "I feel like Mary Poppins."

Herb spread out his arms, his scarf beginning to unravel from his face, as he cried out, "Wonderful! Absolutely glorious!"

They blissfully glided over steeples and rooftops, and sidewalks and dead-grassed boulevards, and, minutes later, flew right through the open bay window, landing in a large private salon. The room was filled with pictures and stately furniture, and a chandelier hung from the ceiling.

They removed their coats and scarves and sat down on sofas, around a fancy coffee table, inlaid with flecks of ivory. Still dressed in baggy pants, Julia served up English tea, along with a delectable array of chocolates and tortes, upon fine English silver trays.

Conversations bubbled in high spirits, and an hour had gone by when Herb picked up papers from the table, and began, "We have read your reports and wholly support your mission."

Julia took a sip of tea and said, "We look forward to meeting your kids, and Stanislav, too, whom you write so fondly of."

"Do you have a name for this mission?" asked Herb, as he bit into a chocolate nugget.

Ushaya shook her head and replied, "Not yet, but if you have any ideas, please share them with the assembly." They continued chatting about all sorts of topics, and it wasn't long before the subject of Brexit came up. Ushaya took a sip of tea and asked, "What are your thoughts around this?"

Herb answered, choosing his words carefully, "We are on the fence. Of course, we would like our countries to be united, but there are logistical problems around trade deals and such. And should this go through, we are concerned for the pound sterling devaluing, and a host of other fallouts that might occur."

Julia reached for a tart and said, "I wish our politicians would stop bickering and get on with it. The back and forth infighting is just dreadful, and, frankly, most worrisome."

Herb placed his teacup down and turned to Ushaya and said, "The British Commonwealth enjoys good relations with many countries in the Middle East, so why Saudi Arabia?"

Ushaya picked up a biscuit from a gold-rimmed plate and sat back in her blue velvet chair, trimmed with silver edgings, and replied, "The Middle East is a hotbed of issues, no matter where you go. So, I simply decided on the biggest country." She changed the subject, suggesting, "Would you like to fly? I've brought your suits."

Herb lowered his voice and said, "If we could have the pleasure some other time, that would make this old man happy."

Julia agreed. "Let us savour this moment."

Ushaya took another sip of tea and asked, "If you had one wish in the whole world, what would that be?"

Anticipating this moment, Julia rose from her seat and went to the ornate buffet across the room, and pulled out a carefully prepared speech, and gave it to her prince.

Herb cleared his throat and began, "Regarding Brexit, it is our firm belief that, no matter the outcome, we are moving toward a more beneficial and stronger alliance with all European nations." He paused for a moment, and then continued with the next item, "We wish success with your mission, Ushaya, that leaders will make it to your assembly meeting. We also wish continued prosperity for our four children and seven grandchildren. We wish the oceans be cleaned up of garbage and plastics and toxic chemicals. And to find a cure for cancer is another great wish of ours. Our final wish is that my dear cousin, whom I shall not name, would stop talking, blabbering on about this and that. It drives us both crazy."

"Surely, the last wish was not on the list," said Julia, frowning.

"It is now," he said, placing the paper on the coffee table.

Julia turned to Ushaya and said, "I know this is more than one wish."

She smiled wryly, "That's OK. Everybody keeps doing it."

Something about Ushaya charmed the queen—her soft yet commanding voice, her smile, her affability, her down-to-earth and yet gracious manners, that she felt they would become friends, and said, "Please, do not refer to me as 'My Lady.' Just call me Julia."

Herb piped in, "And call me Herb."

Ushaya looked around the salon and asked, "Would you like me to demonstrate strength?"

"There is no need. You have covered it very nicely in your reports," Julia replied.

Herb looked around the salon and said, "Besides, we might discover dust balls." They chuckled.

Julia carried on, "Have you been in contact with the Blue-ray light, since your first encounter?"

Ushaya became visibly agitated, and cried out, "Not once has it revealed itself. It is my greatest anguish, and I must find the Source!" She pounded her fist on the coffee table. It split in two pieces, crashing upon the carpet, with teacups, plates, cutlery, and food flying in every direction. In shock, apologizing profusely, she began picking up shards of china, strewn across the floor. She gazed at the broken table, and sputtered, "I'll pay for this, your majesty."

"It's an heirloom that cannot be replaced," said Herb, matter-of-factly, while glancing at broken chards of china on his lap, and cake splattered on his clothes.

Julia shot a glance at her prince, who occasionally was known to make indiscreet remarks in front of new company, and said, "This is not an heirloom, but a replica, and frankly holds very little value. Do you not remember when we purchased it at the auction ten years ago?"

Without a skip, Herb replied, "Ah, yes, I remember now. It was shortly before you gave the Throne Speech in the House of Lords." They apologized, profusely, for their error, expressing their deepest assurances to not fret over such trifles, and that every item was completely replaceable.

Ushaya watched Julia pick up the smashed teapot and asked, "Do you have a broom?"

"We have many things in this room, but a broom we do not," she replied.

"How may I help you, then?" she asked.

"Do not worry, we will have this cleaned up in no time," said Herb.

In the surreal atmosphere of the salon, having fallen down a rabbit hole, they sat around the broken table and continued in light conversation, ignoring the mess around them. Julia piped up, "Would anyone like more tea? I can make it in a jiffy."

Ushaya glanced at her invisible watch and replied, "That's very kind of you, but it's almost noon, and I must bid you farewell. I have enjoyed our time immensely, but do not wish to overstay my welcome."

Wheeling his chair around, Herb followed her to the bay window, with his queen by his side. "What are your plans for your stay?" he asked.

Ushaya put on her gloves and replied, "I plan to visit the famous Birkshire Moors, 300 miles north of here, and should get there in a few minutes." He glanced at the mess on the floor and at the tea stains on the wall.

Ushaya looked about solemnly and asked, "Should I put this incident in my report?"

"Please do," said Julia, with a twinkle in her eye.

Floating farther from the window, she bowed and said, "It's been a glorious day I shall never forget," and with goggles on, she slowly disappeared like an apparition, into the grey horizon.

Herb felt his queen's hand in his and said, "Forgive my blunder, my darling. What is an heirloom, in exchange for the opportunity to fly," and together, they continued staring out the window.

The Ring and the Monster

Ushaya had just reached the Birkshire Moors when it began to snow heavily, and so she veered southwest under more agreeable skies. A lone building appeared in stark contrast to the vast, empty farmlands and snow-covered fields. She circled around what appeared to be an abandoned foundry or forge of some kind, judging by its ancient stonework and tall chimneys. Curiosity got the better of her, for she had to find out why it was empty and boarded up with "No Trespassing" signs. Not a soul was in sight. There were no parked cars, and snow had not been plowed from walkways. How old was this place and who owned it?

She peered through dirty windows, wondering how to get inside. Then she rose to the rooftops and peered into a tall tower, thinking this might be a good entry point. She slowly descended down the shaft. Musty air and strange odours hit her nostrils that she could not identify, and she coughed. A colony of bats burst out, startling her.

She descended farther into darkness toward a glimmer of light, and fear gripped her, and she asked herself, *What if I can't get out? Is this a foolish mistake? What am I doing in a chimney?* Then it came to her: the Zone. She could never identify the moment until after she had found a gift. This time, she paid attention for clues that could lead her closer to the Source, and with renewed courage, she continued down the shaft, toward the light.

Daylight streamed through windows when she landed on a huge wind turbine that had not been in operation for decades. With senses piqued, she jumped through the network of pulleys, passing along a plank walkway, flanked by ropes. She silently floated over the great space, and stopped, amazed at the scene before her.

The compound was huge. Three large steel vats stood propped on steel legs in the centre of the room. Vaulted ceilings, made of wooden beams, spanned high above. To the left of the vats were rows of workstations and benches, with tools lined up on the walls. To the right of the vats stood ten-foot cabinets, continuing row after row, toward the windows. She pulled off her hood, and listened. All was quiet, not a rat or a mouse stirred. Abandoned webs hung over machinery, and the floors were covered in dust. She pulled out her phone and saved the coordinates. She floated to the workstations to her left, and picked up a small scythe through the cobwebs, studying it for a moment before placing it back down, next to a wrought-iron poker. Then she floated to the three metal vats, forty feet wide and twenty feet deep, and peered in. They were empty.

She began floating among the rows of ten-foot shelving, running her hand along drawers and knobs. Curiosity got the better of her, and poking here and there, she pulled out one drawer on the left, wiping off the dust. It held scraps of metal, and she closed the drawer. On her right, she opened another drawer. It was filled with loose screws and bolts and metal plates. She turned down another row and pulled out a drawer to her right. There, she found a dusty leather-bound logbook, and opened the pages. It appeared to be a recordkeeping of sorts, with tick marks alongside scribbled, faded names. *Perhaps workers' schedules*, she thought. The entry date was 1593. She closed the logbook and slid the drawer shut. Farther down the row, to her left, a drawer jutted out slightly from the cabinets, and she tried opening it, but it was stuck. With one final yank, something flung to the ground, twirling like a penny, emitting a high, soft ringtone, before coming to a full stop.

She removed her left glove and picked it up, and, blowing off the dust, held it between her fingers. It appeared to be a ring as black as onyx, and she wondered what it was made of, perhaps stone or metal, but she wasn't sure. She placed it on her left ring finger, and, to her amazement, it began to shine brightly, yet cool to the touch. *How magnificent*! she whispered. Then she removed the ring to examine the inside surface, looking for an inscription, but the shine faded to black, and she could no longer see. She placed it back on her finger, and again, it began to shine brightly. She was dumbfounded.

Suddenly, a large door slammed, and she heard the sound of chains being dragged across the floor, followed by horrible screeching howls and heavy breathing, echoing through the rafters. She was not alone, and, quietly, she closed the drawer and put on her glove, wondering if it was some kind of creature. She cautiously peered above the cabinets and got the fright of her life!

A massive black blob of oily sludge-like substance, forty feet tall and twenty feet wide, was lumbering along the rows, projecting tentacles, in and out, like a snail, and yet morphing its mass, like an octopus. To her horror, the thing slowly stood up, transfixed, staring right at her, yet with no eyes.

She ducked down behind the cabinets in shock, mouthing silently, "Monster." The sound of heavy breathing came closer, and what was that stench? She covered her nose and mouth, barely able to breathe through noxious fumes of sewage and chemicals, mixed with dead, rotting things. More concerning, the thing was heading her way.

She floated past two aisles and down the next row, toward the windows. As she peered around the corner, covering her nose, she caught sight of the Monster's tail disappearing around a corner, leaving a trail of goo. It was gaining on her. Through watery eyes and the smell of stench, her heart began to pound in her chest. Screeches reverberated through the air. She didn't know what was worse, the stench or the screeching, and began to tremble.

Locked in battle, zigzagging up and down the maze of rows, both picking up speed, she came upon a terrible surprise. The Monster was on the other side of her cabinets! It was cunning, and now she was trapped in the last row between the windows to her left and the turbine blades in front. She looked for a way out, her eyes darting back and forth, her heart pounding. The Monster closed in ten feet around the corner. She looked up at the rafters.

Five feet . . . time stood still.

Four . . . she held her breath.

Three . . . terrified.

Two . . . BANG!! Shattered glass sprayed into a thousand pieces in every direction, as she flew in HypeMo to a dead stop a mile away. Breathless, she pulled up her goggles and examined her body. There were minor surface cuts to her suit and gloves. In great pain, she gazed at the swelling in her right arm and realized it was broken. Her forearm limped helplessly from her elbow at a twenty-degree angle. Pulling out clover from her pack, she gently plastered a few leaves over the wound, and then wrapped her arm in gauze bandages. Howls echoed across the open fields. With broken wing, weak and exhausted, she slowly glided back to her hotel, grateful for calm grey skies.

She collapsed on the couch, with screeching howls, still ringing in her ears, and looked at her arm. She knew this pain, only too well, from when she had broken her left forearm, years ago, which took months to heal. Slowly, she sat up and unravelled the gauze bandages. Leaves of clover stuck to the sweaty, swollen skin, covered in bruises. *I must get to the hospital at once! But that would jeopardize my mission*, she thought. With intense focus, she grabbed her right forearm and stretched, twisted and pressed, all at the same time, screaming in agony . . . click! Tears ran down her cheeks in instant relief, as she gazed at the arm, already much straighter, and she slapped on more precious clover and bound her arm tight.

Hours later, she sat in one of the dens, peering at the ring with a magnifying glass, under a reading lamp. It bore inscriptions that she could not understand. Painstakingly, she drew the symbols onto a piece of paper. Where they Greek or Arabic, or Sumatran? She wondered. Her research on the symbols showed no tangible results. She placed the ring back on her finger, and it began to glow. Feeling hungry, she called up in-service delivery. A young man apologized that it may take an hour, as they were extremely busy. Minutes later, there was a knock on the door. Surprised that her food had arrived so soon, she gave the waiter a generous tip, and sat down to bangers, mash and green peas. With the pain subsiding, she continued researching online for symbols of the ring, but came up empty-handed.

As she lay soaking in a hot tub, filled with essential oils, with her wounded arm on the ledge, she pondered the horrors of the foundry. Occasionally, she would glance at the ring, glowing softly on her finger. After her bath, she floated to the boudoir, ignoring her itchy back, and put on her nightgown, and slipped under the duvet covers. The bedside clock showed 9:00 p.m. All night long, a black blob was chasing her down streets, in one nightmare after another. Thrashing about in her blanket, she awoke in a sweat, and sat up in bed. It was past midnight.

Count Theobald, the Archivist

After her morning Eggs Benedict, courtesy of in-service delivery, she began browsing online, searching for ancient English foundries. She keyed in the coordinates, and voila! There it was, the stone fortress, staring back at her. Shuddering, she scrolled down to read its history. Blake Moore Foundry began operating in 1593, the same year in the logbook, she thought, and she continued reading.

King Robert (1548-1628) commissioned Aristocrat Blake Moore, son of Earl of Durham County, in 1590, to build a foundry to bolster war efforts against the Scots and the Irish. Blake Moore, who was experienced in metallurgy, rounded up the very best men in the kingdom and set them to task. It took three years to complete, and by 1593, the foundry was supplying the finest swords, battle-axes, hand cannons and all manner of weaponry. It was the only foundry of its day that served both as foundry and forge, producing non-weapons, such as clocks and blacksmithing tools for the local regions.

King Robert married Lady Sarah from the House of Two Door, who bore him two daughters, Mary and Jane, and a son named Edgar the Young. During his reign, he promoted religious tolerance between Roman Catholics and puritan Anglicans, and while France descended into political and religious turmoil, England did not. Arts and culture expanded under his rule, but levying taxes upon the rich drew great disfavour from the aristocracy and subjects of the Royal Court. His crowning achievement came at the Battle of Boises in 1603 against the Spaniards and the Danish, both vying for the northern isles, and together with the Irish and the Scots, they quashed the invading ships at sea. Ushaya sipped her coffee and continued reading.

In gratitude, the king gave his eldest daughter, Lady Jane, in marriage, to Prince Patrick, son of the king of Scotland, Thomas VI, thereby, securing a fruitful alliance. Trade routes rapidly expanded across the channel, between England and Scotland, prospering both nations. Hailed by many esteemed historians, as one of the greatest kings in English history, he was a wise and just ruler, much loved by his people, during his forty-year reign, whose only apparent fault was speaking with a lisp.

Upon his deathbed, in one final great move, King Robert signed the *United Kingdom's Act* in 1628, thereby effectively joining Scotland and Ireland with England. He passed away peacefully at the age of eighty, from complications of gout, with his long time Queen consort and his children by his side. His son ascended the throne as King Edgar I, at the age of fifty-three. Ushaya took another sip of coffee and continued reading.

The foundry passed through many hands over the centuries, and during the *Reform Act of 1837*, the year that England had abolished slavery and updated child labour laws, a fire broke out. Count Albert of Southeast Essex County rebuilt the foundry and sold it to entrepreneur, Baron Barnard in 1856, thereby, transferring powers to the house of Stanwert. Tragedies fell upon his family—illness and stillborn children, murder, bankruptcy, typhoid fever, and intrigues with the members of the Royal Court.

The most prosperous times came in the late 1800s, when the foundry was forging iron castings and blacksmithing tools until 1899, when mysteriously, it stopped operating. Rumours circulated about an eccentric old countess, who spent her last years shuttered in her castle. No one knew for sure who owned the foundry until 1981, when reports surfaced of a Count Theobald Dunsmure, embroiled in legal battles with the courts, and to this day, it stands abandoned.

Blurry-eyed, Ushaya looked away from her screen. As fascinated as she was with its history, not much was written about the actual foundry and its layout. She must examine original blueprints, and after several calls, she reached the National Archives of London.

The clerk advised, "First, you must fill the online form, and at the end, click 'Special.' Then choose 'Examine Period Documents.' It will take up to six weeks to process your order."

"Really?" asked Ushaya.

"I'm afraid so, with special period documents, yes," said the clerk.

"Thank you for your advice," said Ushaya, and she hung up, "Like bloody hell!" Her arm was healing nicely, and all suited up, she flew to London. Modern architecture graced the lobby, as she made her way to the front desk. Ms. Claire Booth, a middle-aged clerk, greeted her, "Welcome to the National Archives of London. How may I help you?"

Ushaya came to the point and asked, "What floor and area of the building holds special period documents, such as blueprints of the Blake Moore Foundry, which was built in 1593?" A tall, lean grey-haired man stood behind the clerk, and looked up from his cabinets. Their eyes locked uncomfortably.

Claire replied, "Special documents are held in the west wing on the third floor," and pushed a form into her hands, "Fill this in, and we can get started." While pretending to fill in the form, Ushaya disappeared. Surprised, Claire turned to Theo, the archivist, and said, "The lady I just served, she disappeared before my eyes. Where did she go?"

He shut the cabinet door and said, "Excuse me, I'll be right back," and swiftly walked across the hallways, passing cafes and reading lounges, until he reached three elevators, one of them resting on the third floor. Impatiently, he pressed the button, over and over.

By a stroke of luck, Ushaya had entered through the locked-down "Special Documents" door, on the heels of a male employee, who had forgotten something, and quickly left, leaving her all alone. It was a gigantic room, filled with coloured modern steel containers, tightly packed, row after row. While darting in and out of the aisles, with sunglasses on and a hood over her head, careful to avoid security cameras, she decided to play a game with the ring, asking, "Down this aisle?" It merely shone. "OK, how about this one?" It shone lukewarm. As she weaved through the rows, the ring began to glow hotter, until she hovered before a container, with a file name, "GAD1500-RMD1900." It required codes and swipe cards to open. She banged her fist on the container, muttering, "Of course, these are modern times. How stupid of me!" Now she was trapped, for she could not open the container.

A door slammed, followed by heavy breathing and quick footsteps. With heart pounding, she ran down the row, and when she turned the corner, she froze. The archivist stopped dead in front of her. "Who the hell are you, and how did you get in here?" he barked.

She didn't know what to say, at first. "My name is Stella Partridge, and I cannot divulge my reason for being here," she said, stepping back.

He said, mockingly. "So, you managed to infiltrate our high-security system. Show your identification papers."

"I don't have any," she said.

"Take off your sunglasses and show yourself!" he demanded.

"I cannot do that either," she said. With eyes locked, they circled each other, the silence palpable between them.

He looked up and down at her grey suit and beige poncho. She wore sunglasses and silver sneakers, and a hood covering her face. Impressed with her astonishing feat of bypassing all security, he asked, "You are looking for blueprints for Blake Moore Foundry, is that it?"

She strolled down the aisle, realizing that he had more than a mere interest in the foundry. The ring glowed softly on her finger, and she dropped her hand to her side, out of view. The power of persuasion filled her very being, as she stood in front of the container. She removed her sunglasses and pulled down her hood, exposing her face. With eyelashes fluttering, she replied, "Yes, but I cannot open it."

As if in a spell, he swiped his card and punched in the codes. The container opened, and he pulled out one drawer that contained ancient manuscripts. "What exactly are you looking for?" he asked.

She replied, "I am looking for all blueprints that were made between 1593 and 1899, before the foundry was abandoned."

"Normally, documents are viewed in a private room," he said.

She fluttered her eyelashes and said, "I prefer to view them here, if you please."

He sifted through the documents and laid out the only three blueprints in its history.

"May I hold them?" she asked.

He nodded.

The first was an old drawing, dated 1598. Three large vats were visibly marked, but the rest of the foundry was unrecognizable. She placed the document down on the tray and moved to the next print, completed in 1746, the year the wind turbines were built. She placed it down on the tray and moved to the final blueprint, made in 1856, during the last expansion years. She clearly recognized the row where she had found the ring, and asked, "Have there been rumours of a magic ring in its history?"

His eyes widened and he said, "Why, yes, a legend circulated in the early 1600s, of a ring forged by fire and rare metals, during a revival to transmute lead into gold, called the Ring of Power, but no such ring was ever found. Why do you ask? This is not common knowledge."

Fluttering her eyelashes, she sweetly asked, "Do you have a document of this legend?"

He sifted through the drawers and pulled out a fragment, written in old English, and laid it on the tray.

Sensing both were searching for the same thing, she asked, "Why are you interested in the foundry?"

He announced, "I am Count Theobald Dunsmure, the last descendent of the House of Stanwert. My heritage has been plagued by legal issues since 1899, and therefore, I have not yet claimed my rightful heir to the property."

She asked, "Have there been rumours of a monster in its history?"

Theobald recoiled, sputtering, "What do you know of such things? It has never been written, only passed down orally, about mysterious disappearances, and that the foundry was haunted. Who are you?" He reached for his radio to call in security.

Ushaya said, "We are destined to meet again," and with those words, she disappeared.

He glanced at the tray, and the fragment was gone! He shut the drawers and swiped his card, and ran to the exit, hollering, "Code Black. I repeat, Code Black. Suspect is a senior female in a grey suit and beige poncho, in possession of stolen archival property." Impatiently, he pressed the elevator button, and then ran down corridors, passing shops and lounges, until he arrived at the front desk. "Quick, search for a name, Stella Partridge," he barked at Claire.

She dutifully searched through her database, and responded, "There is no such name."

Theo pounded his fists against the cabinets, realizing his error, as sirens wailed in the distance. How would he explain that his swipe card had opened the archives, allowing a strange woman to enter without a signature? How would he explain that the suspect was not entered into their system? An investigation would soon open, exposing every breach of law, stacking up against him. He would surely lose his job, and perhaps end up in jail. No, no, he had to call off the police somehow, he thought, and, turning to Claire, he said, "Create a profile for Stella Partridge. I don't care what you do, just put her in the system."

For the next hour, Theo sat across from two policemen in a private room, explaining his elaborate fake story, while pointing to some other document in his hand. "As you can see, officers," he concluded, "I found the document among blueprints in the same drawer. It wasn't stolen, after all. Frankly, I am most embarrassed to say, it is a false alarm, and I do apologize for taking up your time." In the end, the officers accepted his statement and left.

But more trouble came when his superiors ordered a viewing of security camera tapes. Theo sat with three investigators in a high-security room, studying the recordings. He held his breath, as his superiors watched him and Stella circle each other in their first encounter. But they moved on, more interested at what happened at the container site.

"There, stop the tape," said one investigator, and they all peered into the screen.

"It's like she disappeared," said another investigator. They played the tape over and over. There appeared to be a glitch, but they could not find any tampering with the analogue signals. Theo showed them the fake document, and with no evidence of wrongdoing, his investigation ended.

Ushaya watched him step out from the meeting room, able to keep his job, and then whisked away in HypeMo.

He picked up his briefcase and coat at the front desk, and hurried out of the building, suspicious that Stella knew something about the ring.

Claire called out, "Is everything all right, Theo?"

The Ring wields its power

The plane soared across the Atlantic Ocean, as she gazed silently out the window. At long last, she arrived back home in her little Crestfield town. Clover plants were thriving and growing taller, much to her relief. She transplanted cuttings into more pots, and sprinkled them with water. That afternoon, she texted Julia and Herb: "I have arrived home safe and sound, and will be in touch. P.S. I have found a gift for you." They waited patiently for her report.

As days went by, extraordinary things began to happen. When she greeted people in the streets, they would entirely agree with her, no matter what she said. She negotiated new terms for a mortgage that had been refused six months ago, and had now gotten it. While standing in long supermarket lineups, a new stall would always open, and she would be the first in line. She began to realize the power of the ring.

One day, while resting her elbow over her neighbour's fence, she said to Emily, "We should have coffee some time."

"I would love that," replied Emily, although she was a tea drinker. Precious Mimi sat wagging her tail by her feet.

Ushaya took the ring off her finger, and the old crab was soon yelling about dead branches in her backyard, and the little doggy was yapping and snarling. She slipped the ring back on her finger.

Emily gazed up and said, "Isn't this a lovely winter's day?"

Ushaya looked up at the bright blue sky, and replied, "No it's not. It's about to rain." Clouds thundered and lightning struck. Emily and her doggy hurriedly ran inside their house.

Feeling ashamed for having played childish games with a ring worthy of much more power, Ushaya slowly trudged through the snow, back to her house, deep in contemplation.

US President Ronald Thump had entrusted Ushaya to keep the Gemball safe in her hands until the assembly meeting. One day, while sitting before the Gemball, she asked, "Where do you come from?" The entire surface turned into some kind of alien landscape, like inside a cave or the inside of a large whale.

She then asked, "What is the purpose of the ring?" Army legions rose up and were about to go into battle. She did not know what that meant.

"What is the monster from the foundry?" she asked. An apocalyptic scene emerged. Under dark skies, rivers of toxic chemicals and garbage were dumping into seas and oceans, much like molten rock, moving down an erupting volcano. Dead whales and dolphins washed up on shores. Smokestacks plumed fire and brimstone into the air, while human corpses stacked up high across a burnt-out landscape. She shuddered, wondering what that meant.

She asked, "What is the Ancient Relic, that I found in Mexico?" A scene emerged with dozens of frightened people entering a white light emanating from the stone statue, and then they disappeared into the relic. She did not know what that meant either.

"What about the twelve spheres in Canada?" she asked. A jumble of images appeared that seemed to make no sense: first, a charioteer upon a fluffy cloud, followed by hands, rolling a sphere across the floor. Then the scene changed to armies of ghoul-like creatures, exploding into fragments. She did not like what she saw, thinking of Echo Canyon, where she and her kids' encountered those black ghosts.

"What are the frogfish?" she asked. A scene opened to frogfish sun tanning along sandy shores of the Gagnon stream. The scene seemed silly to her, and she muttered, "Are you playing games with me?" She shut the ball off and walked away.

Late that evening, hushed voices spoke through the phone. Professor Alan Bromwell whispered, "I'm in." He was a historian and a close colleague of Theo, the archivist. He had a keen interest in Theo's heritage, and for years, they had been gathering information on the Blake Moore Foundry.

Theo replied, "We go as planned." They were about to break into the foundry.

The Monster wields its power

Days later, Ushaya sat before her computer, looking at Julia and Herb in her screen, who were gazing back at the ring glowing upon her finger. "It is my gift for you," Ushaya solemnly said. They listened, in horror, to her stories of the monster and the archivist, and yet were intrigued by the ring. Two hours had passed, and they ended their call.

A week later, Ushaya was gazing again across the screen at Herb and Julia, who appeared grim. Herb spoke first, "We've been following news of a disturbing event, published in the weekly *North of London* paper, shortly after you left. It's about a gruesome quadruple murder in the very Blake Moore Foundry that you spoke of in your report. We will send the file now."

Ushaya opened the file and began reading about archivist Theobald Dunsmure and Professor Alan Bromwell, along with two police officers, found at the Blake Moore Foundry site, identified only by their dental remains. As the story went, Ms. Claire Booth, who was personal assistant to Dunsmore, had become suspicious of his strange behaviour in the days following up to the event. She decided to follow Dunsmore and Bromwell, as they took a long country drive, keeping a safe distance behind, until they arrived at the foundry. After parking her car on the other side of the compound, she peered around the corner, and witnessed them breaking through chains on the door, using special cutting tools, while two police officers stood by. When the four of them entered the foundry, suddenly, she heard screams. Alarmed, she cautiously walked over to the entrance and peered inside. Four puddles of muck and sludge lay on the floor in a bloody mess, and she ran away, alerting the police, reporting a strange stench coming from the foundry.

Ushaya stopped reading and looked up, and said, "This is dreadful news. Theo was the only clue to the mystery of the ring and the monster. I promised him we would meet again, and now this." She lowered her head. "I wonder if there is a connection with the black ghosts in Echo Canyon."

Julia replied, "Perhaps. And what is the link between Theo and Alan?"

Ushaya cried out, "Why does the monster want the ring, and now that the ring is no longer in the foundry . . ."

"It may go looking for it," Herb completed the sentence.

Ushaya whispered, "What if I am the one in danger?"

Julia pondered a moment and replied, "My senses tell me that the monster cannot venture out. Otherwise, it would have done so already. Perhaps the ring protects you, after all."

Ushaya had learned how to harness the ring's power of persuasion, and announced, "One day, this ring will be yours. By virtue of authority, I grant you immediate powers to secure the abandoned property and take over title from its only heir, now deceased, bless his mortal soul." She leaned back in her chair, adding, "Use whatever means you deem necessary, and choose your members wisely."

Julia and Herb could barely keep up with their royal duties and functions, so swamped they were, with phone calls and emails for weeks thereafter. With great swiftness and miraculous divine intervention, the abandoned Blake Moore property was secured under a new secret title, by royal decree. With equal swiftness, Julia and Herb secured a team of six detectives and forensic experts to begin their investigations with the local police.

One day, Jerome was gazing across the screen at all three—Ushaya, Julia, and Herb. "Are these reports true?" he asked. They nodded, and he emailed the reports to all the assembly leaders across the world, and sat back in his chair, deep in thought.

Days before departing for Germany, Ushaya picked up Irena's suit from Stan's place. He babbled on about a new invention that she could not understand, and had to rely on Lucy for interpretation, "Oh, really? A centrifuge fused with plasma and ionized particles?"

That evening, Ushaya drew Britain's landscape on a piece of parchment, marking a big X over Blake Moore, with coordinates above and below. She sat back sipping wine and smoking a cigarette. Then she securely tied the scroll with a red ribbon, and brought out the blue treasure chest and placed it among the other gifts. The ring shone on her finger, as she thought of her upcoming visit with the chancellor of Germany—grateful for an all-expense-paid trip, with the finest in-service accommodations, including unlimited spa and massage treatments.

Chapter Nine

German Chancellor Irena Klassen

Touchdown Berlin

The plane was an hour late, waylaid by heavy fog. Patiently shuffling through the lineup, a male attendant advised Ushaya that her baggage had been pulled for inspection, and to please come this way.

Ushaya asked, "*Stimmt irgendetwas nicht*?" (Is there something wrong?)

He ordered her to unlock the suitcases, and she obliged. Rummaging through her belongings, staring at ropes, suits, goggles, masks, and a pickaxe, he asked, "*Was ist das*?" In broken German, she explained that her hiking group was planning to scale the Zugspitze Peak in the Bavarian region. While staring at the ring on her finger, and seeing how fit she was for her age, he stamped her passport and said, "Sie konnen gehen." (You are free to go.)

She couldn't wait to get out of there. In a private outdoor alcove, she strapped on her backpack and clipped the suitcases to her belt. It was eight degrees Fahrenheit, and the fog was beginning to lift. With goggles on and coordinates set, she flew in SuperMo to the grand Hochenstein Hotel, not far from the Bundesmarck Palast, where she was to meet the chancellor.

Her grand suite was decorated with modern and traditional art, and one wall was painted in gold, and there were massive floor-to-ceiling windows. Flames flickered from a fireplace, surrounded by a large, carved wooden mantelpiece. The kitchen came equipped with the latest gadgets. A welcome tray filled with chocolates and a fine bottle of wine sat on a marbled island.

She floated along hallways, hung with chandeliers, and entered a den, where she drew back velvet curtains to view the city lights. She continued down the hall to the boudoir. Luxurious bedding draped over a queen-size bed, and two venetian-style doors opened to a balcony with wrought-iron railings. She was pleasantly surprised to see a floral-coloured, old-fashioned claw-foot tub, with golden faucets, next to a Jacuzzi hot tub and sauna room. Returning to the great space, she chuckled, "All that I need—no more, no less."

The following day at noon, she flew through a Bundesmarck window and, pulling down her hood, she nervously extended her hand, and said, "It is a great pleasure to meet you."

Irena shook her hand, replying, "My pleasure more, and please make yourself comfortable," and gestured her toward a couch. Irena oozed genuine warmth. She was a down-to-earth yet classy lady, Ushaya thought, observing her in a smart business suit and shiny loafers, and with a fine set of pearls draped around her neck.

Irena returned from the kitchen with a platter of sandwiches and piping hot sausages, and remarked, "You may be right. Flying through a window could be the best way to visit the leaders in secret."

Ushaya watched her leave for the kitchen and called out, "I'm glad you agree."

Irena called back, "I'd like to offer you a beer on this special occasion." With lagers in hand, she returned and sat down beside her.

They conversed for hours about the weather, about Ushaya's kids, about their favourite vacation spots, and their interest in art and music. Ushaya learned that Irena's husband, Finn, was a molecular biologist and professor at Humboldt University in Berlin. She also learned that they had no children. While stabbing at a sausage, and not used to fine beer, she said, "I have forgotten my German, and as they say, if you don't use it, you lose it."

Dabbing her mouth, Irena pressed a button on her laptop, asking, "You don't mind a bit of background music?"

"Not at all," she replied.

"I am keen to learn more about Fast, Super, and HypeMo. You were in contact with professors. What did they say?" Irena asked. She held a PhD in physics and genetic engineering. They debated equations and formulas for a while. Then Irena asked, "How can you surpass the sound barrier and still be alive?"

Ushaya shrugged and replied, "The only way is to wear a titanium exoskeleton. No, seriously, this is why I need to be studied, to find out what's going on. It's all a mystery."

Irena asked, "How can you defy gravity?" A classic song by Leonard Cohen came through the speakers, "Dance me to the end of love." Slightly tipsy, they got up and began swaying to the music. "I believe he was born in Canada of Jewish descent," whispered Irena. Suddenly she felt Ushaya's arm around her waist, and together, they floated across the room. Astounded, peering down at the floor, while twirling through outstretched hands, she noticed the ring glow softly on her finger.

Arm in arm, they floated out the window. Irena gasped, hanging on tightly, staring at the grounds below, the cold air penetrating her clothes, as they rose above the Bundesmarck rooftops, and up into the grey skies. Ushaya asked, "If you had one wish what would that be?"

With outstretched hands and a twirl, Irena faced her and said, "I do not wish for a No-deal Brexit." Gliding and swaying in the breeze, she added, "I do wish for a stronger European Union, but all sides must make concessions at the negotiating tables. I also wish for rapid advancement in DNA and genetic engineering," and pausing, she said, "It's quiet up here."

As they descended, gliding over rooftops, Ushaya smiled and said, "I shall not be looking for a gift, for I have already found one."

"What is that?" wondered Irena.

"It is myself," she replied, "Your country should be headquarters to test the powers and study this body of mine. There will be blood tests, head scans, DNA extractions and eye tests, and God knows what else. Each country would have their satellite base, but one country must be the central hub."

Irena was surprised and said, "It is a fantastic gift, but one that holds great responsibility and needs approval from the leaders."

"I am hoping they will accept—that is, if you accept first?" inquired Ushaya.

The slipped back through the window, continually swaying to the music, and twirled around with hands clasped behind their backs. Ushaya whispered, "I'd like to dodge a flying bullet one day."

Swinging one last time, facing each other, Irena looked quizzically into her face, "Dodge a bullet, ja?"

"Absolut," she replied, and together they danced to "the end of love".

CHAPTER NINE

Ushaya goes to Jail

With three days left to her visit, there was time to see Dresden, her birthplace. How so much had grown, she thought. An hour later, Ushaya was sauntering along the main downtown boulevard, when suddenly, car tires screeched and people screamed. Four masked men ran out of a bank into a grey sedan, and were whisked away. With great speed, Ushaya caught up with it. She noted its license plate, and flew alongside the vehicle and caught a glimpse of the robbers with their masks down. One man pointed a gun at her, and she disappeared back to the scene of the crime.

The robber hollered, "Who the hell was she?"

The driver looked out his rear-view mirror, and said, "I don't know. We better let the boss know." They ditched the vehicle in a river and drove away in a getaway car.

Moments later, police cars had surrounded the crime scene. The Polizei were questioning witnesses among the crowds in the street. Commandant Hermann Mueller, of Special Task Forces, pointed to a woman in a poncho, and hollered, "*Du da druben! Was ist Ihr Geschaft hier*?" (You there! What is your business here?)

Ushaya proudly walked across the street, and replied, "I have the license plate number, and I saw the robbers' faces."

The commandant eyed her suspiciously, and said, "*Ich habe gesehen, wie du das Auto gejagt hast. Vielleicht bist du bei ihnen und sie haben dich verlassen, ja*?" (I saw you chasing the car. Maybe, you are one of them and they left you, ya?)

"Nein, ich war nicht bei ihnen," said Ushaya, who couldn't believe the accusation against her.

The commandant immediately turned to his officers, and ordered, "*Verhafte diese Frau*!" (Arrest this woman!)

Not knowing why she was targeted, she desperately pleaded in broken German, blurting, "Ich bin innocent! Ich haben the license plate gesehen! Ich haben information fur Sie! Ich bin in Dresden geboren!" His men thought she was a loony-tune and, following orders, they handcuffed her and forced her into the vehicle.

At the station, her backpack, poncho, and iPhone were confiscated, followed by fingerprinting and mug shots. Then she was strip-searched, had all her human rights taken away, with fingers intrusively probing into every orifice of her body. Oh, the indignity of it all! She muttered to herself.

Meanwhile, across the city, in her office, Detektiv Erika Schultz, from Special Internal Affairs, was glossing over the case file on Commandant Mueller. A secret investigation had been underway for many months, linking him with a string of crimes that never got solved under his watch. While Erika was pondering the latest jewel heist, the phone rang.

It was Inspektor Gerd Auerbach. He said, "*Mueller hat eine altere Frau in Gewahrsam. Ich mochte, dass Sie auf der Station nachforschen, warum er so interessiert ist. Es konnte ein anderer Fallkerl sein.*" (Mueller has a senior female in custody. I want you at the station to investigate why he is so interested. It could be another fall guy.)

"*Eine altere Dame? Sie ist wahrscheinlich eine normale Burgerin*," said Erika, surprised. (A senior female? She's probably an ordinary citizen.)

Gerd sighed and replied, "*Das ware meine Vermutung. Kommen Sie besser so schnell wie moglich hierher*." (That would be my guess. Better get here as soon as possible.)

"*Sofort Sir*," she said. (Right away, sir.) She packed her briefcase and made her way to the underground parking lot. It would take an hour to reach the station, depending on traffic, she thought, looking at her watch.

While trapped in some jail cell, crouched in a corner, pondering her nightmare situation, Ushaya could easily escape this pop can, but decided to help with the investigation. The door opened and a German guard snapped, "*Komm mit mir*!"

The guard led her to a dingy interrogation room with two chairs and a desk. A single light bulb dangled from the ceiling. In the room sat the very same commandant she had met in the streets, who motioned for her to sit down, and the door clanged shut. She knew now she was in trouble.

In perfect English, he began interrogating her, over and over, "State your name. Where are you staying? Why are you in Dresden? Why do you wear a grey suit, if not to escape detection as you rob a bank? Why did they leave you behind?"

Ushaya kept changing her story, realizing she was dealing with a crooked cop. "I don't remember," she said.

He wheeled her chair around and glared into her face, and said with menace in his voice, "Then we shall start again. What is your name?"

Erika greeted Inspektor Gerd at the station. He closed the door of his office and pulled down the shades, and spoke: "*Ushaya Landau, weiblich, 65 Jahre alt, kanadische Staatsburgerin, geboren in Dresden.*" (Female, aged sixty-five, Canadian citizen, born in Dresden.) He pulled up files on his screen.

Erika glanced at the notes. "Apprehended on suspicious links with a jewel heist that took place at the Langstraat Bank at 10:00 a.m., March 17, 2019, detained in Block Nine, cell room No. 15." She asked, "*Was hast du sonst noch an ihr*?" (What else do you have on her?)

He brought up more files and replied, "*Sie ist Touristin und ubernachtet im Hotel Hochenstein.*" (She is a visiting tourist and is staying at the Hochenstein Hotel.)

She quickly moved to the door, for time was of the essence, and turned to Gerd, and said, "*Eine Freude, Sie wiederzusehen. Eines Tages werden Sie gut entschadigt. Wir sind nah dran, aber wir brauchen mehr Beweise.*" (A pleasure to see you again. One day, you will be well compensated. We are close, but we need more proof.)

He waved his hand dismissively, and said, "*Alles, um diesen Bastard zu Fall zu bringen.*" (Anything to bring this bastard down.)

Erika swiped her card and entered Block Nine. While wandering along the corridors, she found Ushaya's cell and peered in. It was empty. She headed straight for the stairwell and ran down two flights to the interrogation rooms, while calling for backup.

Meanwhile, Ushaya had not been cooperating with the commandant. Suddenly, he punched her in the face, sending her reeling across the floor. She pissed herself. The liquid ran down her suit and blood trickled from her mouth. He picked up the chair and ordered her to sit. Slowly, she got up and sat back down. Unclipping his baton from his belt, he began to swing at her, and missed. He swung again and missed. *I will not be hit again*, she thought, and scrambled out of the chair, realizing a different kind of monster before her. They circled one another, and he lunged forward, and she jumped back two somersaults, landing in a corner.

Mueller smacked his baton in his hand, and said, sneering, "Kung-Fu chop-chop? Let's see what you can do with these boys," and motioned four guards into the room. One carried chains. Another held a baseball bat, and another, a cleaver, and the fourth held electric cables. The ring glowed white hot on her finger as they circled her.

Chains lashed out, and she caught them with bare hands. While bringing the guard forcibly toward her, she shoved him into the guard with the cleaver, and both fell to the floor, and the cleaver slid across the room. Mueller lunged forward. She jabbed hard into his side, and he fell to his knees. Electric cables squeezed around her neck, while at the same time, chains wrapped around her left arm. Her head smacked hard into the guard behind, WHAM! He loosened his grip. She grabbed both their chains, and whirled around, WHOOP, WHOOP, and suddenly let go. They hurtled in the air and hit the wall and fell, slumped on top of each other. One howled in pain with a dislocated shoulder, his arm dangling limply, the other writhed in agony with a broken knee. She high-kicked Mueller in the chest, POW! He keeled over. A guard lunged toward her, swinging his bat. WHACK! The bat flew from his hand, and, twisting his arm, she gave it a sharp blow. The arm snapped in two. CRACK! "Ah!" he cried out. She tossed his body across the room, landing it on top of the others. THUD! With crazed eyes, the remaining guard ran toward her, hurling his cleaver. She caught it mid-air. Suddenly, he staggered back, shocked to see the cleaver embedded in his stomach. With one quick push, she sent him flying on top of the others, and they moaned in agony. Mueller crawled across the floor to his drawer and pulled out a gun.

Erika ran down the hall and stopped in front of the door, and peered through the small window. It was a scene she did not expect to see. A pile of guards lay in a heap of jumbled legs and arms, in one corner. A baseball bat and chains were strewn across the floor. She quickly entered and exclaimed, "*Was ist denn hier los*?" (What is going on here?)

With gun in hand, Mueller pointed to Ushaya, and said, "She attacked us!" Ushaya sat crouched in the centre of the room.

Erika turned to the guards and hollered, "Aus! All of you!" To Mueller, she commanded, "Put that gun down." One by one, the guards filed out, limping and moaning. She glanced at the guard with the cleaver in his stomach, dripping blood across the floor, and sarcastically said, "Be sure to seek medical help," and shut the door. By then, four heavily armed backup guards had arrived and were waiting outside.

She slammed her briefcase on the table, and raised her voice at Mueller. "From now on, we take over this investigation. Hand over the files, you're finished." Ushaya moved to the back of the room.

Slumped in his chair, Mueller slid the report across the table, and said with a snarl, "You will hear from my superiors."

Erika leaned over the table, staring him in the eye, and spoke. "Chains and a baseball bat? That's excessive force, in direct contravention of the laws of this country."

"It's a high-profile case, and I was simply using scare tactics, until she," he said, pointing at Ushaya, "attacked us, and we barely defended ourselves. In case you haven't noticed, we are the ones injured here." He got up, brushing past Erika, and said, snarling, "*Wir haben Schmutz auf Sie. Erinnerst du dich an diese Nacht? Sie haben das Ende noch nicht gehort. Ich kenne Leute in hohen Positionen.*" (We have dirt on you. Remember that night? You haven't heard the end of this. I know people in high places.)

Erika flinched. "*Ist das eine Bedrohung*?" she calmly asked. (Is that a threat?) He silently glared at her on his way out, and left the room.

She motioned Ushaya to sit down and spoke in perfect English: "I am Detektiv Erika Schultz, and before we begin, is there anything you need?"

"I need to pee," she replied. A guard guided her to the lavatory, and then returned her to the interrogation room.

"You have a right to a phone call," said Erika, who handed her a phone and got up to leave.

Ushaya asked, "Where am I?"

She answered, "You are detained in the Obere Klappen Polizei Hauptquartier," and left the room.

In her jumbled brain, trying to remember, Ushaya hurriedly punched in the untraceable number. The phone rang three times, and Irena answered, "Hello, is that you, Ushaya?"

With a trembling voice, she whispered, "Yes, it's me."

"Are you all right?" asked Irena, most concerned.

"No, I am in jail at the Obere Klappen. I was arrested this morning, on trumped-up charges connected with a bank heist."

"How dreadful! Look, I can pull some strings and get you out," said Irena.

Ushaya replied, "I want to help with their case. I have some information. Look up Commandant Hermann Mueller. He's a bad cop, and I was interrogated by him."

"Are you hurt?"

"A little bit."

Irena gasped, "You must get out immediately!"

"No, wait," she said, "A special operative, by the name of Erika Schultz, is working secretly to bring him down. She is my angel, who allowed me a phone call. Look, give me twelve hours. If you haven't heard from me, then send in the brigade." The door swung open, and in walked Erika, and Ushaya hung up.

Erika offered her a sandwich and juice, but she wasn't hungry. Then she pulled out papers from her briefcase and laid them next to the commandant's report, and said, "I know you have been through a terrible ordeal, but I have to ask some questions."

Ushaya glanced up at Erika, who appeared to be in her mid-forties, slim of build and five-foot six tall. She wore an expensive-looking white blouse, a beige business jacket and a pair of wide pants. Her polished, sturdy shoes were black. She had short blonde hair, and her dark-brown almond eyes emanated warmth and kindness. There was no wedding ring on her finger, and she wore a gold bracelet on her left wrist.

While massaging her swollen face and wiping dried blood from her mouth, Ushaya asked, "Is this a bad cop-good cop scenario?"

"I assure you it is not," said Erika, clasping her hands on the table. "My first question is, how can you afford to stay at the Hochenstein Hotel at 10,000 Euros a night?"

Ushaya answered with a lie. "I inherited some money from my late uncle. It may sound eccentric, but after a hard day climbing mountains, it is nice to come back to some luxury, wouldn't you say?"

Erika sat back, intrigued, and asked, "How did you manage to subdue four guards?"

Ushaya replied, "I learned Chinese martial arts in my youth, and that training stays with you. And I swear, I was attacked first," she said.

Erika asked, "You described the suspects. Tell me how that happened."

She replied, "I stepped out from an alley and saw them get into a grey car, and that's when they pulled down their masks."

Erika scanned Mueller's papers, and then looked up and said, "None of what you say is in his report. In fact, he claims you got kicked out of the car and started chasing it."

"It's a lie, Erika. Just think," argued Ushaya, "If the police arrived after the bank heist, how could he have seen me chase a car? They would have been long gone."

"Mueller was in the area at the time on another call, and I have confirmed this with the district," said Erika, noticing the ring glowing on her finger. "Nice ring you have," she said.

"Thank you." Ushaya looked down at the table.

Erika began to reveal more. "We have been investigating Mueller for some time. He has been implicated in a number of robberies throughout Europe."

"But why me?"

Enchanted by the ring's glow, Erika replied, "We suspect you were meant to be a fall guy, a tactic he uses to further his agenda. The robbers had likely alerted him, and that's why you were targeted in the crowd."

"What exactly was stolen?"

"Fifty million Euros' worth of jewels," she replied. "This bank has some of the highest concentrations of valuable jewels from around the world." She pushed a deposition form in front of her and said, "You are a victim here, and have every right to file a grievance, and I urge you to do so. It will strengthen our case."

Ushaya pondered for a moment, for she was on a secret mission herself. She replied, "Let me think about it. Right now, I just want to get back home." That night in her jail cell, she ate her sandwich and drank her juice.

Meanwhile, Irena made a call to an old trusted friend, General Leopold Reiner, of elite German secret service. She whispered into the phone, "*Wir haben hier eine Situation.*" (We have a situation here.) She told the story of Ushaya's incarceration, and concluded, "*Warte zwolf Stunden. Ihr Team muss sich moglicherweise nicht engagieren.*" (Wait twelve hours. Your team may not need to engage.) She paused and said, "*Tatsachlich lade ich Sie zu unserer geheimen Organisation ein. Ushaya hat Superkrafte; Ich werde es spater erklaren.*"

(Matter of fact, I am inviting you to our secret organization. Ushaya has superpowers; I will explain later.)

They were once lovers in their youth, and from time to time, had crossed paths in civic duties. It was a friendship based on trust and understanding, but for the first time, Leopold wondered what she meant. "*OK*," he said. "*Zwolf Stunden geben mir Zeit, ein Team zusammenzustellen*." (Twelve hours will give me time to assemble a team.)

That night, Irena joined her husband in bed, and with arms wrapped around her, Finn whispered, "*Ist alles in Ordnung, meine liebe*?" (Is everything all right, my dear?)

She gazed into his face and said, "*Nein, nicht alles*." (No, not everything.)

"*Was bedruckt dich*?" (What's bothering you?)

Snuggling closer, she whispered, "*Kann ich noch nicht sagen. Es ist nur Politik, weisst du*?" (I cannot say yet. It's just politics, you know?) The phone rang again from Internal Affairs, and she got out of bed to answer the call.

The next morning, Ushaya's cell door opened wide. Erika motioned to Ushaya and said, "You are free to go and can collect your belongings."

Ushaya walked out of her jail cell to her first taste of freedom, with guards standing on either side. As they walked briskly down the corridors, Erika offered, "I would like to personally escort you to the airport tomorrow, to ensure you safely board your plane. Again, I urge you to sign the grievance report."

"I will think about it," she said.

Mystified, wondering if there was more to her than she had realized, Erika said, "We will need to contact you with further questions, do you understand?"

"*Absolut*," she replied.

Back at the hotel, Ushaya was plastered in clover, while a wonderful masseur was soothing her aching body, soothing her mind, and soothing her soul.

General Leopold Reiner

A stealth fighter jet stood waiting in a field the following day to take Ushaya home, courtesy of Irena. Dressed in uniform, General Leopold Reiner greeted her. Upon his chest were pinned the highest medals of honour. He had broad shoulders and blue eyes, and stood six feet tall. His blonde hair was neatly cropped under his cap, and lines on his face told stories of many battles to protect and serve his country. For a man in his fifties, he appeared strong and healthy, as he brought her suitcases on board.

An approaching vehicle shut off its engine, and Erika stepped out. Ushaya extended her hand and said, "Thank you for coming alone, and for everything you have done."

Erika glanced at Leopold, and back at Ushaya, wondering if she was on some high-level mission. "Why have you brought me here?" she asked.

"It was you who insisted on escorting me to the airport," replied Ushaya, as she climbed into her seat. She turned to Erika and said, "We will meet again." The engines roared, and the door slid shut. Erika stepped back, watching the jet take off and disappear into the horizon.

They were soaring 2,000 miles an hour, across the Atlantic Ocean, at a 20,000-foot altitude. Leopold glanced at Ushaya, who was not wearing goggles or a respirator mask, and said, "I've met with Irena and have read the reports. It all seems too fantastic to believe."

"I can understand that, sir," she said, gazing out the window.

He pulled out a helmet from a latch box between them, insisting, "You should, at least, wear this." Obediently, she placed it over her head and adjusted the mouth guard.

He began, "So it all started with a strange blue light, is that right?"

Ushaya tried to humour him with a rhyme, "Indeed, it was a scary sight that night."

He picked up her cue, and asked, "And you couldn't put up a fight?"

"I was in fright and my face turned white."

"Try as you might, the light was too bright?" he asked, with a twinkle in his eye. They chuckled.

For hours, they swapped stories, back and forth, and while charting a path along the sixty-sixth parallel, passing under Greenland, seeing nothing but ocean below, Ushaya asked, "How heavy is this jet?"

"About 20,000 kilograms," he said.

"Can you translate that to pounds?"

"About 45,000 pounds, why?" he asked.

Gazing out the window, she replied, "I'd like to fly this baby."

He chortled, "Have you flown a plane before?"

"No, I haven't," she said, turning to him, "But I once flew a caboose, the same weight as this plane."

He scanned his hand across the sophisticated equipment, and said, "A caboose is one thing, but you don't know a thing about this aircraft."

"I mean, out there," she said, pointing a finger. After a long pause, she realized, he was in a state of crisis, and said reassuringly, "If you can bring this jet into slow speed, I will jump out. After I am steady, you shut off the engines. If something goes wrong and I can't do this, just turn on the engines, and I will jump back in."

Torn between logic and facts, theory and plausibility, supposition and certainty, ignorance and knowledge, and fear and trust, Leopold turned to her, and said, "It's cold out there."

The ring shone brightly, as she put on her gloves. He flicked switches on the control panel, and checked the weather report. It showed sunny skies ahead. With his right hand on the throttle, he descended to a lower altitude, and set his craft into slow speed. Then he turned to her and said, "I will allow this, but on the first sign of trouble . . ." his voice trailed.

With ear buds on, she jumped out of the aircraft and disappeared below. Her hands pressed up against the underbelly, avoiding the hot jet streams on either side. Once steady, she commanded, "I am ready, Leopold. Shut off the engines."

Sweat poured down his face as he relived every precious memory of his life, memories of making love with Irena, so long ago, on cold winter nights, memories of competing at family barbecues, as to who could cook the best sausages, and memories of his fishing buddy, who caught "the big one." He relived memories of gunfire battles and explosions on foreign soil, while delivering emergency food and supplies to local civilians in need. Images filled his mind of a long, illustrious career, going down in flames, with the remains of a once great fighter jet now strewn across the ocean floor, only to be discovered twenty years later. Then he remembered Irena's words, "Ushaya is more powerful than you think—trust her instincts." He punched the sequence codes to a full dead stop, turned on the backup internal systems, and held his breath.

They dropped rapidly. Suddenly, the jet lifted, and he heard her call out, "Eight-hundred kilometers an hour." He glanced at the flickering lights on his instrument panel, when he heard, "Sixteen hundred." As he gazed down, enchanted, at the ocean whizzing by below, he softly whispered, "We are really flying."

The radar beeped out a warning signal, breaking his dream-like spell, and he straightened in his seat. Flicking several switches, he said, "Oncoming plane, Ushaya, bearing east, head on, you better get in."

By then, icicles had formed around her helmet, and her hands were stuck to the belly of the jet. *Indeed, it was cold out the*re, she thought. Through muffled voice, she sputtered, "Gladly!" The jet came to a standstill, and she jumped into the cockpit. He immediately fired up the engines and veered northwest across the sky.

Leopold placed a thermos of hot coffee into her frozen hands. He shook his head and said, "You really do have the power. Irena was right about you."

Ushaya replied, through chattering teeth, "You have shown great bravery and trust."

"You can take your helmet off, if you wish," he said.

She took off the helmet and placed it in the latch box. Tousling her dark flowing hair, she said, "Nothing will go wrong. You're safe with me."

He sternly raised his voice, "As second officer under my command, I am the one to say *you* are safe with *me*."

"Nice craft you have," she said, smiling.

Indeed, it was the finest in the fleet, capable of twice the distance of most jets before needing to refuel. He soared upside down. He flew sideways with his right wing tip in the air. He plummeted, creating figure eights in the sky, and then soared back up. He flicked several switches at the same time. The cockpit filled up with shooting lasers and colourful lights, like a disco ball on a dance floor.

In awe, Ushaya cried out, "Is this part of the program?"

"No, one day, I just discovered it," he replied, and they howled in laughter.

They continued a steady course across the ocean, chatting all the way. Their first stop was in Ottawa, to refuel. Then they pushed on westward across the provinces, and finally landed in an empty field, near her home. With suitcases on the ground, they stood silently facing each other.

"Will you join Irena's team? She would be extremely pleased if you do," said Ushaya.

Leopold pulled off his cap, and ran his hand through his blond hair, and said with a twinkle in his eye, "If I can teach you how to fly this jet."

"Splendid! Welcome to the assembly," she piped up, shaking his hand.

"I am certain, Erika will come on board," he added.

She replied, "We accept nothing but the finest, ja?"

Suspicion

One day, weeks later, the doorbell rang. Ushaya went to answer it, while floating two feet above the floor. Erika stood at the front steps with a bouquet of flowers in her hand.

Ushaya gushed, "Oh, these are lovely! Please come in and make yourself comfortable," and she motioned Erika to the couch while she placed the bouquet in a large vase on the dining table.

Erika watched her disappear and reappear with two beers and a tray of small sandwiches, which she set on the coffee table. They chatted for two hours, then Erika placed down her beer mug, and said, "I have been instructed to keep this brief. I want you to know, we have infiltrated the criminal hub, known as *Blaue Juwelendiebstahl von Dresden* (Blue jewel theft of Dresden), and have arrested over twenty men and women—one of them that commandant of yours."

Ushaya slowly set her beer down and announced, "Take my arm."

In awe, Erika floated out the front door, past the gargoyles, to the bottom of the driveway. She got into her car and started the engine, and then rolled down the window.

Ushaya asked, "Are there any questions about the case you wish to ask me?"

"There are many questions, but not about the case. I look forward to meeting again," said Erika, rolling up her window.

Ushaya waved as she drove away, and called out, "Welcome to the assembly!"

The following day, Ushaya visited the local garden shop, where the clerk filled an order for two angel statues, to be delivered to her home address. Then a text came in from Stan: "Mimbauwe suit ready for pickup."

Meanwhile, the remaining leaders, who Ushaya had yet to visit, became suspicious of what was happening, and held a secret meeting.

Yadgiri, from India, spoke first, "Are they infected with some kind of virus or mental illness?"

"I thought this nonsense would end with the queen and prince, but it did not," said Saudi Prince Muzaffar.

Yaegar, from Russia, gazed across the screen and said, "Germany wants to be headquarters. Can you imagine?"

"They claim to fly at great speeds," said Mimbauwe of Rwanda.

Zhang Wei, from China, suggested, "It might be some kind of drug."

"However, we must admire her courage in solving a crime," reminded Hashimoto of Japan.

Voices raised, and one boomed louder, "That, too, could be a hallucination!" There was silence.

Yaegar advised, "Things may not appear as they seem. We need to investigate further."

Yadgiri gazed at Mimbauwe, and said, "You are next." Mimbauwe stared back, wide-eyed.

As he lay in bed that night, memories swirled in his mind—memories that shaped the man he had become. Mimbauwe was born into a poor village, rife with superstitious voodoo practices. He had seen the horrors in his youth, of women raped and albino arms cut off. During economic downturns, he had witnessed gunfight battles, and crops and houses razed to the ground, and he had survived through the worst genocide, committed by the Hutus against the Tutsi people. When he became president of Rwanda, he vowed to be a better leader than his predecessors. Then he pulled the covers over his head and fell into a restless sleep.

The following night, music was playing from speakers, and candles were glowing throughout Ushaya's house. She had finished marking a big X over Berlin, on parchment paper, and another X over Dresden. GPS coordinates were hand-scribbled, above and below. She sat back in her chair at the kitchen table, and took a sip of wine and a drag from her cigarette. Then she tied the scroll with a red ribbon and hid it in the treasure chest. Suitcases were packed and ready to go, and she wondered what adventures awaited in Africa.

That evening, while standing naked in front of the bathroom mirror, she gazed at her left hand. It was healing nicely, bearing only a thin white scar. Her right arm had stretched out straight, no longer needing clover. But when she peered into the mirror at her itchy back, she went into complete and utter shock.

Six-inch scales were rising from either side of her spine, and when she flexed her muscles, the wings stood on end! She reeled backward, slamming into the bathroom door, and flew naked down the hall to the living room window. As she stared out at the full moon, shrouded in wisps of cloud, she wondered what was happening to her. She returned to the bedroom and slipped into her nightgown. As she lay in the dark, soft violet leaves glowed from clover pots by her bedside, while the ring glowed softly on her finger. Was she in denial? Definitely, but tomorrow was another big day.

Chapter Ten

Rwandan President Mimbauwe the IV

The Challenge

Mimbauwe insisted, "Too dangerous to fly through a window. The compound is heavily fortified."

"SuperMo," reminded Jerome, adding, "You heard what happened in Germany. You're not backing out, are you?"

Mimbauwe turned quiet and said, "With all due respect, sir, might you be infected with a virus of the mind?"

Ignoring his fear, Jerome proposed a challenge: "If you don't want her to fly through the window, I bet she could walk right through the main doors and find you. Remember the Archives of London?"

He chortled, "Impossible! It's one thing at the archives, but quite another thing here."

Jerome pressed on, "She will need instructions on how to find you, and the rendezvous spot, that's all."

Mimbauwe leaned back in his chair, folding his hands, and replied, "I will take you up on your challenge. We shall see what she can do."

"Good!"

"All right then!"

"Wait. I have to clear this with Ushaya," said Jerome, and they signed off.

"What??" Ushaya frowned.

Jerome apologized, "I got carried away."

With hands clasped, she slowly looked up and said, "Tell him I need directions across the entire complex, entering from the far west, not from the centre."

"Are you sure you are up to this task?" he asked.

"It's just one building, not miles across the sky," she replied.

Meanwhile, Mimbauwe had opened a large book of blueprints, wondering if he had already become infected.

Ushaya landed at the Kigali International Airport, during its usual rainy season, but weather forecasts showed sunny skies, with median temperatures of seventy-five degrees Fahrenheit. It was a large, modern airport, filled with many travellers. A sea of coloured faces passed her by, and she felt like the minority. While following signs in Kinyarwanda, French, Swahili, and English, she found everyone to be helpful, including the many roaming guards.

The following morning, she hid in tall palm trees, gazing through binoculars, studying a building. The House of Parliament was eight stories high, with grey and white-checked balconies, and above the roofline, was a concrete block with four white murals. Another set of buildings stood in front of the parliament building, with green rooftops and white facades, in a series of unequal heights, creating a pleasing architecture, marked by four large red mural designs. On either side of the main doors stood two large national flags. There were twenty points of entry around the main building, and it was heavily guarded, as the president had said.

She read the instructions again, "Enter from the west, passing two guards, and at the end of the corridor, bypass two more guards in front of double-set doors. This leads you through the Dignitary's Lounge and Welcome Hall security area, and there will be many people milling around. Pass through the legislature wings and executive offices. Turn left at the third corridor, pass the library, and at the end, bypass two more guards. An elevator leads to the top floor. Turn right and follow the hall past the kitchen and housekeeping quarters, and at the second left corridor, take the private elevator up one floor, then left, right, left, right . . ."

She phoned up Jerome and said, "I'm ready to enter."

Jerome phoned up Mimbauwe and said, "She's on her way."

Soon, she got lost, wandering left or right. Quick! Guards were coming. Hiding in an alcove, until they passed to her left, she then stepped out to her right.

Five minutes later, there was a knock on the door. Mimbauwe answered it.

Ushaya bowed and said, "It is an honour to meet you, your Excellency."

Stunned, he shook her hand and replied, "It is with great pleasure and my honour also. Please, just call me Mimbauwe, and do come in. May I take your pack?" He motioned her to a chaise lounge, covered in a zebra print, placing the pack by her side. Then he sat across from her on a chaise lounge with a lion print.

She observed a tall, slim man, dressed in a navy suit, wearing a white shirt and red tie, aged mid-sixties, with lines etched on his face of battles lost and won. His hair was short with salt-and-pepper curly locks, and he wore thick, black-rimmed glasses. Serious and intelligent, he was often scorned by critics for his impatience and suppressed emotions, and for the deaths of political opponents, which Mimbauwe had flatly denied any involvements with. He was known to sleep only a few hours a night, and exercised during the day. He clearly doted on his family, and was known to read academic texts and foreign newspapers.

A tray of fruit lay on the table. He poured Urwagwa beer into their glasses, and spoke in a high, gravelly voice, tinged with an accent that she could not discern, "I trust your flights went well and without incident, and that you are settled in your hotel suite."

She replied, "I am most pleased with the service, it is excellent, thank you."

"If there is anything else you need, you have only to ask," he said.

She took a sip of beer and remarked, "Hmm, this is delicious." Her eyes gazed about the room, resting on a mask upon a wall.

Soon, they were standing before a wall of masks, with beers in hand. Mimbauwe began to speak, "They are from many countries. This Bwoom mask, of the Kuba people, comes from the Congo, and this Dogon mask comes from Mali. This one is a Maasai mask from Kenya, and this one is a Baule mask, from ancient cultures of Ghana. Here, we have a Zulu mask, which was gifted to me by the Zimbabwe government, on one of our state visits." On and on, he explained their origins. Fascinated, she stared at a wooden mask, from Botswana, with tufts of hair and bulging eyes.

"Do you collect masks?" he asked.

She smiled and said, "No, but I do collect dust balls. You should see my place."

He chuckled, motioning her. "Come, let's sit down. I have read the reports and understand that an assembly meeting will take place later this year."

She nodded and said, "That is the plan, after my visit with Yaegar in Russia. God willing that it happens."

Conversations flowed back and forth about politics and economic developments. They talked about his improved health-care system, and his efforts to eradicate diseases afflicting his people. They discussed his aggressive tactics to save wildebeests from poachers in neighbouring Tanzania. He had introduced safe drinking water and improved infrastructures throughout his country. He eliminated child labour with a series of laws. They talked about freedom of speech, and women's rights, and deals with guerrilla warlords, and about foreign trade, and then they stopped talking. There was silence.

"I understand you have a family?" Ushaya inquired, forking a piece of mango into her mouth.

He reached for a slice of avocado and replied, "Yes, I am happily married to my wife Sylvie, and we have one son and one daughter. My son, Simba, sits on the Rwandan Development Board, as board member, responsible for investment and entrepreneurship for young African business leaders. My beautiful daughter, Anitha, continues to champion a variety of social causes, from women's empowerment to education and poverty eradication."

Ushaya took a sip of beer and placed it on the table. Pausing for a moment, she said, "I have brought your suit. Shall we fly together?"

He didn't believe that he would agree to this, but moments later, he found himself stepping back into the room, patting his suit and vest, posing. "It feels comfortable enough. How does it look?" he asked. She gazed at his sturdy pair of shoes, and nodded approvingly.

He didn't believe, as he watched her secure ropes between them. Soon, a pack was on his back and a water bottle by his side. Nor did he believe, as he put on his visor and gloves, and flew up, up into the sky, gliding a hundred miles an hour, northbound, into the Land of a Thousand Hills, swooping through deep valleys, while holding onto ropes, gazing in awe at the sheer natural beauty all around him.

She pointed to a herd of buffalo, thunderously running across the savannah grasslands. He pointed to a gorilla, entering a national park. She pointed to a passing grey shoebill, awkwardly flapping its wings in the air. They heard the roar from a pride of lions sitting in the grasses below. Ushaya landed and peered closely at one lion, yawning wide, staring back at them. Mimbauwe spoke nervously, "We need not look into the lion's mouth to understand its roar."

She pushed off into the sky, and swinging his ropes, parallel to her side, she asked, "How do you feel?"

Mimbauwe spread out his arms, exclaiming, "I have no words to express, except, perhaps, free."

"I shall not ask for your wish, for I already know," she said.

"What is your wish?" he asked.

The question took her by surprise, for she had not thought about it before. She answered, "I wish for the end of world hunger," and she continued, "I ask for world peace, but is it possible, given our many differences? I do wish for less disparity between the wealthy and the poor, and my last wish is to discover the source of these powers."

He said wryly, "Those are a lot of wishes. I only asked for one."

"Indeed," she said, smiling.

Mimbauwe glided effortlessly across the sky, wishing this would never end, but alas, he heard Ushaya call out, "Let us return." They soared across southern skies at one hundred miles an hour, chatting pleasantly all the way back to his palace. He began to believe, pointing east to the distant Serengeti plains, and west to the Nubago wetlands. The sky turned grey above, as they passed over Lake Muhazi and the Kigali Genocide Memorial. When the parliament buildings came into view, they slowed down and hid in nearby tall bushes. While observing numerous guards and tourists milling about, he whispered, "How are we going to reach the window?"

"HypeMo," she replied.

"How fast is HypeMo?" he asked. In one blink of an eye, he stood in his private chambers, dizzy and in shock, clutching his chest and catching his breath. Ushaya studied him with intent, for this was the first time she had flown a human in HypeMo. A broad smile crossed his face.

The following morning, Mimbauwe called her up. "I trust you had a good night's sleep?"

"Yes, and you?" she asked.

He replied, "Very well, thank you. I am completely amazed, and will contact Prince Muzaffar and insist he meet with you."

"I'm very glad to hear that. Welcome to the assembly," she said.

He suggested, "There should an interim online meeting, before you complete your journey."

She nodded and said, "That's a good idea. Let Jerome know that."

"What are your plans for the day?" he asked. She replied, "Lake Victoria is supposed to be beautiful. It's about 300 hundred miles east of here; I should get there in a few minutes."

He believed her, and said, "Have a safe and wonderful journey. I cannot express how happy I am for yesterday, and I regret my initial doubts, and look forward to meeting you again."

"It's good to doubt," she said, adding, "Yesterday was magical for me, too."

"Consider your trip to Saudi Arabia all expenses paid."

"Thank you, that is most kind."

Lady of the Lake

Lake Victoria used to claim the lives of thousands of boaters each year, due to treacherous weather conditions from moisture build-up and warm currents and frequent thunderstorms. With better warning systems in place and access to more life jackets, the death toll had plummeted, but hundreds still perished each year. Famous for its islands and sheer natural beauty, it is home to many small villages, dotting along the shores, whose inhabitants derive their livelihood from the lake's bounty.

While gliding over zebras and gazelles grazing in fields and baboons sitting in treetops, Ushaya noticed men on the ground with rifles aimed at a lone ailing rhino standing in the open plain.

She would have none of that! Swooping down, she confiscated the weapons from their hands. The men looked at each other, confused, wondering what had happened to their guns. She glanced back at the rhino, pleased that the poachers had been stopped in their tracks. "At least it gets to live another day." About to throw the rifles into a nearby stream, she realized, they were not rifles at all, and cried out in shame, "Oh no!" Immediately, she flew back and lay the guns down, and disappeared, watching from a distance. Stunned, the men picked up their dart guns and took aim. The great rhino slumped to the ground, and they attended to its wound, which had become infected from a recent hyena attack.

When she reached Lake Victoria, the winds began to pick up. Storm clouds gathered and waters swelled and frothed in undulating swirls. Thunder clapped and lightning struck, and the rains came. She lay her pack under a canopy of trees, deciding to wait out the weather, then noticed a fishing vessel struggling in thirty-foot swells a mile into the lake. Waves crashed all around them, and then suddenly, the vessel nose-dived and capsized!

Immediately in HypeMo through pounding rain, she reached the sunken boat. Eight bobbing heads struggled to keep afloat. She took one deep breath and swooped into the cold waters.

The men went into complete shock at what they saw. Their boat rose up, majestically turning on its side, gushing out water, and was soon set afloat upon the waves. Arms wrapped around two men, transporting them to the vessel. She plunged into the swirling waters and brought two more men on board.

In awe and fright, they yelled in Swahili, "*Pale*!" (Over there!)

She jumped back in and brought two more on board. The boat rocked violently, as the men slid across the floor. One pointed, "*Pale*!" She dove into the waters and brought one man on board. Frantically looking about for the last man, one of them called out, "*Huko*!" (There!)

Totally submerged underwater, the last man thought he was going to die, when suddenly he felt himself lift up, up, up. While gawking at a woman in a grey suit with wet dark hair streaming down her face, he heard all his men cheer! Under angry skies, the vessel floated above the waves and was soon transported safely to shore. Drenched in the torrential downpour, they gazed at the female apparition gazing back at them, before they saw her swiftly disappear across the lake.

Sulimon Seeds

She soared eastward over Tanzania, over Kenya to Mombasa Island, grateful for the hot, arid air that dried her clothes. Then she came upon a perfect stretch of sandy beach, along the Indian Ocean, and, circling a rock, she landed. Boulder outcrops dotted the land behind her. Not a soul was in sight and she sighed and said, "Finally, some peace and quiet." While wiggling her bare toes in the sand and soaking in the sun's rays, she watched birds play dare games, running to and fro, with gentle waves lapping the shore. An hour went by, and she brought out a sandwich and papaya juice.

Suddenly a man approached from her right, walking along the sands, not fifty feet away, and she stood up from her rock, sensing the Zone. It was the same state she had felt when entering the chimney at Blake Moore Foundry, just before finding the ring of power, and so she paid attention.

He stopped ten feet in front of her and said, "Madame Butterfly, my name is Sulimon. What is yours?"

She folded her arms and asked, "Why do you call me that?"

"You circled the rock like a butterfly," he replied, in a smooth, deep voice.

Time stood still. While barefoot and with her hair in a complete mess, she gazed up at the six-foot demi-god before her. His skin was a golden brown, and his beard was black, and layers of gold hoops hung around his neck. He wore a white turban inlaid with precious gems, and a green and beige patterned vest with a red sash around his waist. Baggy orange pants of silken cloth swirled around his legs, down to green sparkly slippers upon his feet. She began to wonder if he was a genie from a magic lamp, and, unfolding her arms, she said, "My name is Ushaya Landau. What is your business here?"

A dazzling white smile broke across his face, and he replied, "I am a merchant from far and wide, and I bring gifts." He opened his vest, displaying pockets on either side, exposing his golden bare chest.

Distracted at first by the smooth skin, she broke her stare and began examining the many trinkets in his vest, asking, "Do you have a gift worthy for a great leader? He is most noble and wise."

Replying in a deep, velvety voice, he said, "All these are worthy gifts. Go ahead, you can touch." He nodded approvingly.

She hesitantly reached out and touched a fishhook with colourful feathers, asking, "How can a fishhook be a great gift?"

Sulimon answered, "It is the law of attraction, capable of rallying forces to his side and putting his commands into policy."

Moving on, she touched a small sword. "What is the meaning of this?"

"Absolute power, great protection, capable of smiting one's enemies."

She touched a bronze coin. "And this?"

"Great economic prosperity for his country."

The ring shone brightly on her finger. It was hard to choose, she thought, as she passed a small skull dangling from a chain, and another pocket holding a set of keys. Then she eyed a pouch, and asked, "What's this? May I hold it?"

He placed the pouch in her hands and said, "These are seeds, but no ordinary seeds. They grow into trees and shrubs and flowers, but they also manifest thoughts. Your leader must be very careful what he wishes for, when he plants a seed."

She opened the strings and poured different seed shapes and sizes into her hand, and asked, "How many are there?"

"A hundred, but thousands of possibilities."

She placed them back in the pouch and said, "I will take these. What shall I pay you?"

"One hundred franc."

Rummaging in her pack and finding some coins, she dropped them into his open hand, and said, "It doesn't seem like much for a valuable gift."

"A simple transaction will suffice."

While jiggling the pouch between her fingers, she began to have second thoughts—a bag of seeds? How would that compare with clover or the Gemball, or the spheres or the ring? She looked up, and he was gone. Where had he gone? Floating frantically about, she called out, "Come back! Who are you and what is the Blue-ray light! Do not abandon me like this, I demand to know!" But he was nowhere to be found.

Out of Control

Three days had passed since her arrival in Canada, and feeling more settled and caught up on errands, she began to prepare for her friend Mandy's visit. She also made a call to her gardener, Wally, to arrange a backhoe to excavate the back of the property, for a gazebo and a fire pit. She continued witnessing the twelve spheres switch positions in the recreation room, wondering what they were all about.

While sitting one day before the Gemball, jiggling seeds, she asked, "What powers do these hold?" Colourful striations swirled across the surface, and a desert appeared, transforming into tall trees and beautiful flowers. Then images changed to African soldiers squatting with rifles behind an impenetrable wall of thick bushes, their best defence from encroaching enemies. She did not know what that meant. Colourful swirls gave way to an image of Mimbauwe signing an important document to join African nations, before it faded back to opaque.

Ushaya poured the seeds into an oven pan on the kitchen table, and with a sharp knife, she separated them into groups by shape and size, counting 106 seeds in all, giving them names such as "long and slender" and "flat and round." She returned from the greenhouse with a bag of soil and six small pots, and began to plant the first seed. While patting down the soil, her mind began to wander, thinking how it would be nice to have a cat, but with her busy schedule, it could not be possible. Suddenly, a bright green two-inch sprout shot through the soil, and she heard "meow." Looking down to her right, a fluffy grey and white three-month old Maine Coon kitten sat on the floor, gazing up at her with soft green, slanted eyes and tall, pointy ears. She picked up the kitten and placed her on the table, asking, "Where do you come from?"

Absentmindedly pressing a seed into the second pot, she thought, "Good thing it's not a dog, that would be a disaster." A green sprout shot through the soil, and she heard a soft "yap." To her left was a three-month old German shepherd pup, looking up with floppy ears, sweet brown eyes, big paws, and wagging tail, with a pink spot on his nose and a clip in his ear. She placed him next to the kitten, asking, "Where do you come from, little fella?"

Then she remembered the words of Sulimon: "Your leader must be careful what he wishes for when he plants a seed."

The following morning, she flew into town with her newfound pets snuggled close to her chest, their little heads peering out of her vest jacket to enjoy the view. There were pots and soil to purchase, and pet food and kitty litter, spatulas, toys and beds. Everywhere she went, clerks cooed, petting their soft faces. "What are their names?" they asked.

Ushaya pointed, "He is Ralph and she is Chloe."

In a sweet voice, one clerk replied, "Nice to meet you, Ralph and Chloe."

With shopping bags strapped to her belt, she flew back home, with little heads bobbing blissfully across the sky. They followed her everywhere, into the laundry room, into the garden and onto the front porch. They sat on her shoulders, while she worked on the computer. Little "accidents" occurred and she would guide Ralph to the newsprint on the kitchen floor. She showed Chloe how to dig in the litter box, using her front paws. She watched them devour their food and lap their water, and she phoned the local pet clinic to make their first appointment.

The next morning, the two plants grew four feet high with lush leaves, and she had to transplant them into bigger pots, wondering what to do if they kept growing. By the end of day three, they were seven feet tall and she jokingly wondered if this was Jack and the Beanstalk, only these were seeds, not beans.

She planted the remaining four seeds, blanking all thoughts from her mind, but when she came to the last seed, she had a thought and smiled.

The following day, two plants grew ten feet tall, reaching her ceiling, and four plants grew four feet high, one growing Canadian fifty-dollar bills, furled up like new leaves, and she exclaimed, "A money tree!" But then she moaned, "I should have thought of $100 bills." Plants exploded all over the place, and every day, she flew into town to buy bigger pots and more soil. Soon, seeds were dropping on the floor, sprouting right there! It was getting out of control. She could barely move around the house, and cried out, "What am I going to do?" And, worse, her friend would be arriving that day.

There was only one thing to do, and that was to plant them outdoors, but where? Out she flew with a shovel and two plants, fourteen feet high, gliding to a nearby alpine meadow. After planting them, she flew back and got two more. This went on all day, and by late afternoon, she gazed at the instant little forest she had created.

As she stepped out in her dirty overalls, with the last two plants, Mandy suddenly showed up at the back door. "How can you carry them, aren't they heavy? Do you need help?" she asked.

Ushaya stammered, "No, no, good to see you, why don't you come in and look after Ralph and Chloe, while I deliver these plants to my neighbour. I will be right back."

Mandy affectionately picked up Ralph and Chloe, as she stared at the debris and soil strewn across the living room floor.

Two hours had passed over a glass of wine and a plate of cheese and crackers, while Mandy talked about her life. She and her husband had two cruises planned for that year, and a fourth grandchild was on its way. Her pottery business had finally taken off, and sales were brisk. "Enough about me. How about you, Ushaya? You look great, by the way." She stopped talking.

"Well, you know, I am just living the retired life and thoroughly enjoying it," she replied, showing pictures of the kids on her laptop, careful to leave out details. She so badly wanted to reveal her secrets, but this was not the time.

Mandy gazed at Ralph and Chloe sleeping in her lap, and whispered, "They are so adorable." The time had come for her to leave, and as she drove away, they blew kisses and waved, promising, one day, that Mediterranean cruise together.

A full moon was rising when Ushaya visited the enchanted Sulimon Forest. Trees swayed in the gentle breeze, and flower bushes had sprung up, thick and lush. A lark sang his lonely evening song. Birds nested in trees and squirrels peeked out from tree trunks. A young speckled deer sprang over a rock, disappearing into the underbrush. Bullfrogs croaked in marsh reeds, and the air was filled with crickets chirping their song.

She wondered, *How is this possible? Only six seeds and yet all this forest*? If the seed was a tree, then a variety of trees sprouted. If the seed was a bush, then different bushes sprouted. When she turned down a pathway, a money tree came into view, unfurling Canadian fifty-dollar bills. A gust of wind shook the money to the ground, and, chuckling, she collected them all and sat in the grass, counting $5,000!

Meanwhile, a concerned Mimbauwe called up Jerome, asking, "It's been weeks since I have heard from her. Is she all right?"

"Give her more time," Jerome assured him.

Ushaya practiced her powers to stay in shape. One day, she soared west across the Pacific Ocean at 3,000 miles an hour, landing in the Hawaiian Islands. It was a great milestone, the first time she had travelled non-stop over water.

Another day, she witnessed two mountaineers scaling a rock face, 500 feet tall. Something went horribly wrong, and they began to slip and tumble, and she swooped in, and carried them to safety, upon a nearby ledge. Then she bowed to the man and woman and flew away in FastMo, leaving them both stunned.

One warm evening in Vancouver, two rival street gangs were about to shred each other in an underground parking lot. Ten men and women got out of cars, slamming their doors shut, armed with semi-automatic rifles and pistols, but the deal went horribly wrong. In the first round of bullets, their weapons suddenly disappeared from their hands. Confused and suspicious, the gang members lunged, punched, kicked, strangled and slammed their bodies to the ground. All bloodied in the end, shouting at each other, they got back in their cars and sped away. The confiscated weapons lay mysteriously on a constable's desk at a nearby precinct. An officer got up from his desk, and said, "Sergeant, have a look at these."

While browsing his newspaper, one morning, Mimbauwe caught a headline story. Legends grew about a Lady of the Lake who had saved eight fishermen from treacherous waters. Local inhabitants began making talismans shaped from straw, wood, and alabaster, and sold them to fishermen to protect them at sea. Tribal artists began making masks of the Lady of the Lake and, soon, news spread across African countries. Mimbauwe looked up from his newspaper.

The next day, he sat at his computer, and said to Ushaya across the screen, "So, it was you."

"I couldn't let them perish now, could I?" she responded.

Mimbauwe smiled and said, "On the contrary. I am awarding you the highest medal of achievement, the Order of Honour, for your exemplary service."

She humbly bowed and said, "I am most happy to serve."

"The Sulimon Forest video you sent me is extraordinary," he said, shaking his head.

She jiggled seed packages in front of the screen. "Only six seeds were planted to create the forest. There are a hundred more seeds left, and they are my gift for you." Then she brought forth a bush into view. Already unfurling money leaves, she added, "Take the money."

He insisted, "No, they are Canadian dollars—you keep them, and as for the remaining seeds, please bring them to the assembly meeting."

Chloe appeared on screen, meowing. Then Ralph jumped into her lap, yapping.

Mimbauwe broke into a smile and offered, "We will pay for all food and veterinary expenses for your new family."

Days later, Jerome looked up from his reports, gazing at Ushaya and Mimbauwe on screen, and said, "A virtual meeting should take place after your visit with Prince Muzaffar to discuss logistics for the assembly meeting. We need cameras and computer equipment, and tables and chairs."

"Food and drinks and cutlery," added Mimbauwe.

Jerome nodded and said, "I will discuss with Irena, but I'm afraid most provisions will fall on her to provide."

"That's a lot on her plate. What about car rentals and hotel arrangements?" asked Ushaya.

Jerome thought for a moment, and replied, "Perhaps Yaegar could oversee those details. He knows Germany well."

Mimbauwe offered, "I shall bring African masks for an added touch to the occasion." They ended their call.

Ronald adverts a Disaster

One day, Ushaya sat before the Gemball in her living room, while Ronald tuned in through her screen. Suddenly, he predicted a disaster in China. A mud landslide was about to engulf whole villages in the Guangdong region, and he warned Zhangwei. In good faith, Zhangwei ordered troops to the area to evacuate the locals and secure its borders. Days later, a huge mudslide came tumbling down. Although possessions were lost, 70,000 lives were saved in the disaster. The people of China hailed their great leader for his great vision, and Zhangwei called Ronald to thank him.

Hashimoto of Japan also called Ronald. "I commend you on your prediction."

Ushaya called up Julia and Herb, wondering if they had heard any more about Blake Moore Foundry.

Herb began, "Our team continues to investigate the connection between the two officers and archivist Dunsmure and Professor Bromwell."

Julia spoke next, "Our detectives heard howling screeches coming from the foundry. It is our firm conclusion that we must kill the monster."

"At least, we know it hasn't left the place. I will have to go back in again, only this time, with Special Forces," said Ushaya.

Herb assured her, "You will have the finest in the world at your side."

Ushaya said, "This must occur after our assembly meeting. In the meantime, the foundry must be battened down."

"Our teams have already secured the premises," said Julia.

"Nice work," replied Ushaya.

Meanwhile, Carlos called Ronald to congratulate him on his prediction. "The Gemball is extraordinary."

Ronald beamed, "Any more thoughts around the ancient relic?"

He sat back and said, "I think it's more than an idol of an ancient king."

"Like what?" he asked.

Carlos answered, "I had a dream one night. While uttering a secret word, I pressed on one paw of the jaguar reliefs, and nothing happened. Then I touched the back of the relic, and a bright light opened to a new world, or should I say, dimension. I cannot explain."

Ronald insisted, "You should share this with the assembly meeting—it might be an important clue. Do you remember the secret word?"

Carlos nodded and said, "I do."

Jerome called up president Yaegar of Russia, insisting, "We need your expertise on board. We cannot do this without you. You complete the circuit. I assure you, you will not be disappointed."

Yaegar sat with folded hands on his desk, gazing across his computer screen, surprised that he had now agreed to be in charge of car rentals and hotel accommodations for the assembly meeting in Germany.

One day, Ushaya received a text from Stan: "Suits are ready for Prince Muzaffar." The following morning, she arrived at Stan's mansion and was greeted by Lucy the robot, who said, "Welcome, please come in."

Ushaya looked around perplexed, and asked, "Where is Stan?"

Lucy replied, "I am in charge here, for my master is nowhere to be found. He is confused and needs guidance. I prepare the meals and do his laundry. I make his bed and scrub the floors, and dust the place, and pay the bills. He's been terribly negligent in his duties."

A week later, Ushaya was sipping her morning coffee, while rocking back and forth on the front porch swing. Ralph and Chloe were resting in her lap, as she began reading the newspaper. A tense standoff took place among Turkey, the US, Russia, and the Kurdish army, in northern Syria. Russia cut a deal with Turkey, swooping in with their troops, while US troops vacated the territory. There was another article about a major forest fire raging across Southwest Australia. Sighing, Ushaya moved onto the Life section of the newspaper.

Days later, Ushaya dropped off Ralph and Chloe at Wally's place, along with their toys and food. Suitcases were packed and ready to go. Mimbauwe's scroll was tied with a red ribbon, and together with the seeds, she tucked them among the other gifts, and locked the blue treasure chest and hid the key. That evening, her little dragon wings had now dried off from the shower, and not wanting to think about them, still clearly in denial, she turned off her bedside lamp and fell into a restless sleep.

Meanwhile, Mimbauwe no longer cared what bug or voodoo spell he was under, and called up Muzaffar, and looking across the screen, he blurted, "You must meet with Ushaya. It is true what they say. I know, because I flew with her."

Muzaffar sat back in his chair, wondering what new troubles had come to his kingdom.

Chapter Eleven

Saudi Crown Prince Muzaffar ibn Abdullah Al Wahalab

A Man of many disguises

Ushaya studied her reflection in the mirror of a private lavatory at the King Khalef Airport. Dressed in royal Arab garb, compliments of Stan, a glittery soft blue chiffon scarf covered her black hair, fastened with a brooch at the neckline. A silver ribbon circled her head with a ruby clinging to her forehead. Layers of soft blue and white silks swirled around her body, fanning out at her feet. A purple sash was draped over her right shoulder and tucked into a braided belt.

With sunglasses on, she whisked in HypeMo through the airport to a waiting chauffeur. After showing him her passport and destination hotel, she stepped into the stretched limousine, while he placed her luggage in the trunk. Beige leather seats and gold door handles adorned the interior. A small chandelier hung from the velour ceiling. Insulated in the silent atmosphere, she watched the bustling Riyadh city go by through tinted windows. A cool breeze brushed pleasantly across her face, as temperatures soared outside to ninety-five degrees.

The chauffeur wore the customary beige suit and tie. Swaths of braided red and brown cloths wrapped around his head, hiding most of his face. Occasionally, he would glance at his passenger through the front screen console, while he drove south through neighbourhoods filled with white and yellow alabaster houses as far as the eyes could see.

She had practiced a few words in Arabic, and, pressing the intercom, she said, "*Anah yawm jamil.*" (It's a nice day.) Silence. *Not much for small talk*, she thought.

"*Ah, naeam, niema*," he replied. (Ah, yes, yes.)

Must have been her accent that threw him off, she thought. She began to wonder why they were driving across flat desert terrain when the chauffeur suddenly stopped the car and opened her door, and ordered, "Get out!"

Shocked, she stepped out, and he sped away, leaving her stranded with all her luggage in the middle of nowhere. She couldn't believe a chauffeur would abandon her like this. Was she in the Zone already?

The limo stopped a mile away at a small mosque, and the driver threw off his headscarves. It was Prince Muzaffar himself, watching intently through high-powered binoculars, determined to expose her for the fraud she was. After all, there had to be some trick, and maybe he might find some clue. Considering himself a realist, he wondered why leaders would fall for a flying woman story, and now, Mimbauwe was infected. Ridiculous! This was the test, he thought. What would she do so far from the hotel? He peered into his binoculars.

Suddenly, security forces closed in on Ushaya from the south that he had not anticipated. He had cleared all security from the area, and began to worry, for foreigners were not allowed, and turning on his engine, he was ready to intercept. Indignant, Ushaya reset her GPS and clipped the luggage to her belt, and before his very eyes, she disappeared into thin air, poof! He peered again in disbelief. Screeching tires came to a halt, and four men scrambled out of their cars, scratching their heads. Where did their target go?

Muzaffar realized his plan had backfired. It was not well thought out. He did not anticipate guards. He didn't think how Ushaya would react, as he placed an innocent Western woman in jeopardy, thereby, tarnishing his image worldwide. He didn't trust his allies, the ones who could have helped him the most. And, worse, they had agreed to meet the following day, in disguise, at a local café. There would be a lot of explaining to do. Slowly, he returned home, deciding, "No, it cannot wait until tomorrow. I must call her today."

Al Shafiz Hotel was a palace, filled with exquisite furnishings. Ushaya walked along glittering mosaic-chipped floors, passing velour chairs flanked by tall palm trees and square columns. She stood a while, in front of a golden wall, hung with tapestries, before weaving her way to the front desk. While gazing at the glass ceiling, seventy feet above, she marvelled at the sun's rays refracting rainbows across the entire lobby.

She stepped into the penthouse suite with her luggage, and began looking around. To the far right, a waterfall trickled from a bronze background wall, rippling into a blue marble base, filled with white pebbles and goldfish, swimming in the water. To the far left was a large archway into the kitchen, inlaid with tiny mosaic patterns across its walls. The floor was alabaster white. Little curtains covered the windows, and a small vase with gardenias lay on the countertop. Rich patterns of ethnic cloths covered the steel-surfaced cupboards, and a framed photo of King Khalef hung on a wall. On a long wooden table sat a basket of fruit. The kitchen appeared quaint and more subdued in décor than the rest of the suite.

She floated to the great space and pressed a button. Wall-to-wall shades withdrew to panoramic views from the fiftieth floor. High-rise buildings, in the latest architectural designs, clustered everywhere, unlike she had ever seen before. She emailed Jerome, as was customary to do, "I am settled in a lovely penthouse suite."

Jerome emailed Muzaffar, "I've heard word, and all is well."

An hour later, the phone rang on her secret hotline, and she answered, "Hello?"

"Ushaya, this is Prince Muzaffar. I know it is not protocol to speak before we meet, but there is a misunderstanding I must clear up with you. First, how do you like your suite?"

"It's wonderful, the scenery is spectacular. Mimbauwe is too generous," she replied.

"I trust your flights went well?" he inquired.

"My flights were pleasant, but I have to tell you something. I had a horrible experience with a chauffeur who picked me up at the airport and . . ."

"May I interrupt, please? I was that chauffeur," he said. There was silence.

"But why?" she asked.

Muzaffar replied, "I was certain the leaders were all going mad, lost in some fantasy gone haywire, so I did not believe, until I saw you disappear. You can be assured, when the guards were closing in, I was ready to intercept. I wish to make up for your pain and suffering. Will you forgive my transgressions?"

She paused for a moment and said, "It is good to doubt, and I believe this happened for a reason. So, we have already met."

He asked, "Is it possible to not mention this incident in your report, and keep this matter between us?"

"Of course, I understand."

"I want to say how beautiful you looked today."

She blushed, "Thank you, your Highness."

"Just call me Muzaffar."

She suggested, "Shall we meet this afternoon to become better acquainted, and I can teach you the ropes? We will be more prepared for tomorrow 's meeting at the café."

Enchanted, under the same spell as the others, Muzaffar gave instructions through an eastern window and waited for her arrival.

Desert sandstorm

The following day, dressed in a full-length blue burka with a mesh across her eyes, Ushaya sat at the outdoor café, glancing over at Muzaffar. He wore the common white thaub and loose pants. Swaths of woven cloth wrapped around his head to hide his face and beard, and a pair of leather sandals completed his disguise. Their vests hid under their robes, and ropes lay discreetly between them under the table. The place filled up with single men, reading their newspapers, and families chatting incessantly.

It was noon and stiflingly hot. Fanning herself, Ushaya glanced over the menu, not understanding any of it. "You look totally unrecognizable," she whispered.

"So do you," he replied, adding, "I am amused to be incognito. No one recognizes me, which is refreshing." A waiter arrived, and he ordered kabsa and coffee, for two.

The waiter returned with plates of rice and spicy-cut lamb, trickling with tahini sauce, and placed them on the table. As they dug into their meals, he asked her, "Why have you chosen me? I wonder how other Mideast countries will react, down the road, especially Iran."

She sipped her delicious coffee and replied, "I chose you, because you have the biggest country. As for the others, we shall cross that bridge after our assembly meeting. Right now, we have the powers on our side."

A loudspeaker blurted out the mid-day Prayer Call, and everyone in the café unfolded their carpets and curled into balls, with heads facing Mecca. Muzaffar gave her a carpet, and they both knelt together. Among their concealed ropes, he whispered, "Foreigners need not kneel."

She whispered back, "I'm with you, and besides, do I look like a foreigner?"

He glanced at her burka and said, "Point well taken."

Something about the whole experience struck a deep chord in her. Transported to some place in time, she let the sound of the voice lull her rhythmically, in guided prayer. Then she began muttering to herself, "Why five times a day? Why not once a day, or once a month?" She remained prostrated, respecting their religion and laws of the land.

At the end of prayers, the café began emptying out, and he paid for their meals.

She whispered, "Now is a good time. *Daeuna natir maea.*" (Let us fly together.)

Before he could object, up, up he soared, 200 miles an hour, clutching his ropes. What a sight they must have looked to anyone from the ground, two blue and white ghosts, blazing across the sky.

She lifted her veil, careful not to expose too much skin under the relentless, unforgiving sun. He pointed to a camel caravan, trudging around a dried-up river bend. She pointed to shifting sand dunes in the distance. He let go of the ropes and spread out his arms, and cried out, "*Allah akbaru*!" (God is great!)

They landed on a high, rugged plateau and sat with legs dangling over the edge. Ushaya pulled out two peaches and water bottles from her pack and said, "You landed very well. I'm impressed." While chatting away in small talk, they soon engaged in politics and Mideast conflicts.

Muzaffar bit into his fruit and began, "Although our countries are united under a common religion, there are many different interpretations of the Qur'an. I would like to think we all get along, in spite of, our different agendas." He took another bite of his fruit, adding, "I used to think the axis of evil was Iran and Turkey and ISIL, but I wonder now."

“Why do you say that?” she asked.

“Politics are complicated,” he replied.

“Indeed,” she said.

Muzaffar continued, “The world is moving from oil to solar, wind, and other products, but we still need oil for many things. Nonetheless, we are working with industry players toward renewable energy.”

She agreed, “Our very vests and shoes are made with oil products. Everything around us is touched by oil. No, it’s here to stay, for sure. And with all the power and wealth you possess, you can make this transition happen and prosper.”

“Do not forget oil reserves around the world that we compete with, but Iran is my biggest issue.” He took a swig from his water bottle, adding, “And I want to quash rebel groups.”

She shook her head and said, “Yes, ISIS is terrible.”

“ISIS is another matter,” he said. “I am talking about the Houthi rebels in Yemen that attempt to undermine our policies and destabilize the regions. But I am tired of this war.” He stopped and pointed to a falcon, majestically gliding its wings across the sky.

She turned to him and said, “I understand you have a Vision 2030.” Soon the topic of women’s rights came up.

He waved his hand and replied, “You are right to say that 50 percent oppressed means a country operating at 50 percent capacity. I believe in that. That is why I have been pushing for reforms to improve education for women, and to change laws around guardianship. Women can now drive cars. But our muftis and clerics wish things to remain the same, so it requires a delicate balance.”

She got bolder and said, “Are you aware of the migrant issue?”

“What issue?” he asked.

“Thousands of migrants from India, Pakistan, Bangladesh, and Indonesia come here to work in your country and end up in bonded slavery, their visas taken away. They live in deplorable conditions and get beaten and don’t get paid, and . . .”

“Those are exaggerated reports, perpetuated by Western media,” he said, warning her. “You are concerning yourself over internal affairs that you should not meddle in.”

Undeterred, she said, "You are expanding tourism to Western countries, which is great, but the migrants who come here, they suffer."

He finished his last bite of fruit and tossed the core into the air, and said, "I will look into the issue."

Ushaya took a sip of water, and while gazing out at the desert, whispered, "Thank you. If reports are exaggerated and it turns out to be a hundred, then it's still a hundred too many. You have given me a wonderful gift. It more than compensates for yesterday."

He replied, "I am pleased my debt is paid with such swiftness." He looked to her and asked, "Tell me, what more have you on the source of the Blue-ray light?"

She answered, "I fear we are pawns in a game with a more powerful enemy out there. We must unite and prepare."

"What kind of enemy?" he asked alarmed.

"The monster," she replied.

"Yes, but in spite of the monster, do you not think your gifts are benevolent?" he asked.

She leaned in closer and said, "Maybe so, maybe not."

"How do we prepare?" he wondered.

She admitted, "I do not know yet." The ring glowed white hot on her finger, and, turning to him, she asked, "If you had one wish in the whole world, what would that be?"

Dust clouds rose in the distance. A sandstorm was heading their way, and he calmly replied, "We must move quickly."

Whipping sand and debris soon engulfed them, and with visors and gloves on, she hollered, "Hang on!" They soared 300 miles an hour, with the storm chasing at their heels, as he held onto ropes for dear life.

Muzaffar's headscarf disappeared into the wind, and Ushaya, grateful for the eye shield and burka, barely made her way back safely through his palace window.

Al-Zall Market

At noon the following day, Ushaya was circling the heart of Riyadh when she swooped down into a marketplace. She had always wanted to visit a famous bazaar, and here was her chance. Courtesy of Stan, she dressed in a long beige robe that covered her arms, with a navy-blue scarf wrapped around her head, exposing her face. The place was packed with locals and foreigners, jostling in front of stalls. There was so much to see. As she peeked through a crowd at one booth, there lay an exotic array of gemstones, gold bracelets, watches and bronze hanging bells. The next booth was filled with ornamental oil lamps, and one caught her eye. She asked, "*Kam yukalif hadha*?" (How much does that cost?)

The man replied, "Seventy-five Riyal." She was now the proud owner of an oil lamp! A great souvenir to take home, she thought, and placed it in her pack.

Children were chasing through the crowds, while parents were hollering in a cacophony of languages that she didn't understand. But she didn't care, for she was having so much fun. At one booth, carpets lay across tabletops. Another booth had curved swords in decorative yellow sheaths, and, moving on, she joined shoulder to shoulder with customers, standing in front of ceramic pottery in blue and yellow designs. Amid loudspeakers and tinkling coins and ringing bells, she wondered which way to go, and turning to her left, she entered an open market, passing stands of neatly arranged eggplants, potatoes, and dates.

She continued moving through the crowds, passing caged chickens, flapping their wings, and a booth of dried lamb meat, strung up on ropes, when a bauble caught her eye at the next stall.

Suddenly, a man bumped into her, and they stumbled toward the ground. He wrapped his arms around her waist, breaking her fall. By then, a throng of people had surrounded them. The ring glowed on her finger, and the last thing she wanted was attention, and she quickly disappeared into the dense crowd. She tried making her way back to the bauble, but could not find it, and the irony didn't escape her. She had travelled thousands of miles, and here she was, completely lost within twenty feet!

A familiar aroma wafted through the air, and she followed the scent to a nearby alley, where an old woman, clad in a black abaya, sat before a cardboard menu. She pointed at the menu to order kabsa, and the woman prepared the meal, and Ushaya paid her. While savouring every last bite, gazing at the crowds, she noticed a door next to the kiosk, and the same old woman encouraged her to enter.

Ushaya entered the shop and stood at the front counter, asking out loud, "Hello? Anybody here?" There was silence, and she looked around the shop. Arabic clocks were ticking on a wall to one side. She floated past tables filled with jewellery and gemstones, and while she was passing puppets, neatly propped upon shelves, an old man suddenly appeared through the beaded curtain. He caught her levitating for a split second before she quickly descended.

In broken English, he asked, "Sorry you wait, you look for something?" He was dressed in baggy pants and a white cotton shirt. He had a short-cropped white beard, and his blue eyes sparkled from a deeply lined face.

She curtsied, drawing her headscarf closer, and replied, "I seek a gift for a great leader."

He did not understand, and out came her iPhone and Google voice translator, and he was surprised to hear her voice translate into Arabic.

She soon realized her request must have sounded ridiculous. Wide-eyed, he whisked to the front door and locked the shop from inside. "Please, I have something," he said, and then disappeared through the beaded curtain.

Twenty minutes passed, and there was still no sign of him. She peered nervously over the counter. *What if he is calling the police to take me to some jail hellhole? Then, I will be outta here in HypeMo*, she said to herself. Expecting any second for men to burst through the door, she wondered, o*r this is a PTSD moment*?

The air was still, save for ticking clocks. She floated to a tray of fine cloths, and then placed them back down, and when she moved to the puppets, the old man burst through the beaded curtain, carrying a long bundle, noticing her float again.

Dang, she thought to herself, and quickly landed.

He said nothing as he unravelled the cloth bindings from a carpet and spread it across the counter. It was eight feet long and four feet wide, a tapestry with silk delicate fringes along the edges. A golden thread shimmered across ancient battle scenes and beautiful turreted palaces, across flowers and trees and valleys and riversides, amid swirling geometric designs.

She asked, "What is your name?"

He replied, "Akbar. What your name?"

"Ushaya."

"Where you come from?"

"Canada."

She handed him the phone, and he asked into the voice translator, "Do you have husband? Children?" And they passed the phone back and forth in conversation.

"I have two children and two grandchildren. My husband, Eddie, passed away six years ago."

"I am sorry to hear." He paused. "Farida and I are happily married for fifty years. We have seven children and thirteen grandchildren."

Ushaya smiled and said, "You are a lucky man. I gather you are Persian?" He nodded politely, and they turned their attention to the carpet. They continued passing the phone back and forth, translating their dialogue. "What is the story of this carpet? How old is it?" she asked.

"Its history is mostly lost," he began, "Legend says it was gifted by Cyrus, the great Persian king, to an ancient Arab Bedouin tribe to calm down the two regions, after several raids back and forth."

She asked, "How did you come across it?"

"In my youth, while travelling through the Ad Dahna Desert, I once met merchants who sold nothing but carpets, and I fell in love with this one, and they themselves knew little of its history. I paid a hefty price for it."

"What is special about it?" she asked.

Akbar answered, "Something strange began to happen. The carpet kept disappearing to different places in our home, and we became afraid, for we had not moved it. So I wrapped it up and stowed it in the back of my shop, and it has not been unwrapped until now."

"That's some story," she said, suspiciously. While grazing her hands over the soft surface, she asked, "What is this golden thread?"

He replied, "It gave us dreams, both amazing and frightful, to even stare at it. Yet, I believe it is a gift, worthy of a great leader."

"It is truly beautiful. I will purchase it. How much do I owe you?" she asked.

"You owe me nothing, just take it," he said.

She insisted, "I always pay," and pouring out the contents from her pouch, she shoved the money across the table. He was surprised. Then she asked, "Does it have a name?"

He replied, “It is simply called the Carpet with the Golden Thread.”

“Not bad, but may I call it Akbar?” she asked.

He shrugged and said, “If you wish, but the leader should decide.”

They said their goodbyes, and Ushaya stepped out into the bustling crowds. The old woman smiled at her, and she smiled back. Akbar bowed and closed the door. With coordinates set and the carpet strapped to her backpack, she flew in HypeMo over the marketplace, toward her hotel, wondering if this was a scam, and the carpet was only ten years old.

Ishtan the Carpet

She unravelled its cloth bindings and laid the carpet over the table in the living room, and stood back to admire its beauty. Then she floated to the kitchen to make a pot of coffee. While humming a tune, she picked up a piece of fruit from a basket and was about to take her first bite when something caught her eye. The carpet lay on the kitchen floor entry. She stopped humming, feeling rather spooked. Flapping it in the air, she lay it back down in the great space and dragged a table on top, and floated back to the kitchen to pour a cup of coffee. About to take her first sip, she saw the carpet was back again.

Suddenly, it stood up eight feet tall with fringes shimmering. She let the cup go from her hand, and it smashed into pieces on the floor, spilling coffee everywhere. Trembling, watching it move toward her, she yelled, “Don’t come any closer!” It stopped and turned horizontal, floating around the kitchen table.

Slowly edging along the counters, she squeaked, “Who . . . what are you?” It came closer, pressing against her knees, and she shrieked and fell on top. They floated out of the kitchen into the great space, passing the waterfall and down hallways, and back to the great space, and then stopped in mid-air. She stepped off and reeled around. “What magic is this? Do you come from the source of the Blue-ray light?” she asked.

Standing vertical, it nodded. She could have sworn it meant “yes.”

“Do you come to harm us?” she asked.

It shook back and forth, and she took it to mean “no.”

She sighed, motioning it to the couch, and said, “Let us sit down.” Side by side, they sat down, and she was amused at how the carpet sat like a human, draped over the couch. "Well this is awkward. A "yes" is a nod and a "no" is a shake back and forth, is that right?" she asked, and it nodded.

"How about a maybe?" It rippled once.

"How about absolutely no?" It sprang from the couch and flattened its body to the floor.

"How about absolutely yes?" It sprang up vertical and shimmered in the air.

She paced the floor, pressing on, "How about if I am in danger, like a warning sign?" It wrapped around her body, as if protecting her, and then let go, standing back.

"Who are you and where do you come from?" she asked. It spread its fringes wide, revealing the golden thread, and twirled around the room and stopped, slightly swaying in front of her.

"That's a nice story, but I have no idea what you're talking about," she said, turning to the kitchen. The carpet followed her. She found paper towels and began to mop up the coffee spill. The carpet brought out a dustpan from the cupboard, and with its fringes, shovelled up the broken shards. While crouched together on the floor, she whispered, "Are you male or female? I will rephrase: Are you male?" It nodded.

Floating to the living room, no longer afraid, she cheekily smirked and said, "You are not the only one around here who can fly." He nudged at her feet. Obeying him, she sat on the carpet, cross-legged, and, together, they flew out the sliding doors over the city landscape. "May I call you Akbar?" she asked. He rippled once.

"You realize, I will gift you to Prince Muzaffar." He twirled and twirled. Giggling with glee, she hung onto his fringes, zigzagging among skyscrapers, passing man-made ponds and white mosques. They flew and flew, and eventually landed back on her balcony, standing side-by-side to admire the view.

One time, she stormed out the kitchen, and said, "You have not told me where you come from. Can you write with a pen in English?" He nodded.

"Why didn't you tell me?" She pulled out a pen and paper pad from a nearby desk, and pointed to the blank page on the coffee table.

The carpet paused a while, and then began to write: "I am a shape-shifter and telepath from another universe. My name is Ishtan, and I come from Lazantis, a planet trillions of years old, with many life forms, alien to your own. Our terrain is as varied and beautiful as yours. We have similar atmosphere and revolve around a larger sun, and have day and night, as you do."

His fringes moved swiftly across the page, as he continued, "Many species live on planets beyond our solar system. We have had our share of wars among nations, but over time, we learned to live in harmony and prosper through trade. My descendants come from powerful overlords. We are the Titans, the guardians who protect the records of knowledge and memory of all life forms on Lazantis."

She gasped, "So, your name is Ishtan."

He nodded.

"How do you know English so well?"

Ishtan wrote, "I write and speak all tongues," and flipping the page, he continued, "Our sun is dying. We have ten million years left, before we must vacate our planet, so we began the search for a new home. But a great evil invaded our solar system from a faraway galaxy, the dark underlords, called the Gogolan. They attacked many planets before reaching ours, eradicating all memory, all records, destroying cities, setting worlds ablaze, and turning inhabitants into mindless slaves. Many species escaped to asteroid outposts and space stations."

"How dreadful!" she cried out.

He turned a page and continued, "We formed a federation called the Zogar, and the Titans sent out secret missions to infiltrate the underworld. It was dangerous work and no easy task, but in the end, we achieved our goal and stole their secrets. Armed with this new knowledge, we waited for them. But, the Gogolan came in far greater numbers than anticipated. They set our world on fire, and we lost millions of lives. Our planet descended into chaos between good and evil."

Ushaya returned from the kitchen with a bottle of wine.

He continued writing, "We are shape-shifters, capable of turning into objects, like a chair or a pebble on a beach. We took on the Gogolan forms and used their weapons against them, and in the end, quashed the enemy, winning the war. A thousand years passed, and a Kisga'a Shield was erected. It holds a powerful beam that surrounds Lazantis to this day, and we shared this knowledge with our celestial beings to protect them from invasion. Millions of planetoids are safeguarded against the Gogolan, who were using asteroids as breeding grounds. Still, outbreaks occur in the Bartuk quadrant and continue to be a threat to this day."

She sipped her wine and lit up a cigarette, motioning Ishtan on.

"After the war, we resumed our search for a new home, and our ship encountered a rare phenomenon, the 'Cosmic Fold,' a moving ripple between parallel universes. We had heard of species crossing over and returning with wondrous stories of the cosmos beyond. So we entered the Fold, landing just outside your solar system. It was not long before we discovered your beautiful planet, which you call Earth, and for hundreds of years, we have been observing it. The ancient relic, a powerful Titan, was the first to enter your planet."

Ishtan got up, pacing the floor, clasping his fringes behind him, and then returned back to the couch, and wrote, "But so have the Gogolan. Five hundred years ago, a young disgruntled Tanzoik, on his way to becoming a great Titan, betrayed us all. His name was Phyteus Quaal. He joined the enemy with promises of supreme domain over galaxies, but he soon learned it was a ruse. The Gogolan only wanted the exact coordinates of the Fold through which we entered, for they knew that a fraction off would send them into another universe, in error. Gripped by the Gogolan's power and under extreme duress, Phyteus confessed the codes of the Kisga'a Shield. They tried to extract knowledge of his other powers, but he managed to escape and return to Lazantis, in hopes of clemency. Our Tribunal of Justice was not so forgiving and banished him to where the banished ones go. However, he escaped centuries later, and was never found."

Ushaya took another sip of wine.

Ishtan continued, "Four hundred years ago, cracks compromised the Kisga'a Shield, and a young Gogolan penetrated the Fold, landing on Earth. We overrode the codes, and immediately summoned a Master Titan, the Ring of Power, and together with Sparky, they imprisoned the monster in a cloak and shield. As long as the ring remained cloaked, the monster could not follow the ring's trace signature."

Ushaya gasped. "So the monster at Blake Moore is a Gogolan!"

"Yes, by wearing the ring, you set it free, searching to destroy the Titan, but she is much more powerful."

"The ring is a female?"

"We have male and female species, as you do."

She stubbed her cigarette in a saucer plate and poured another glass of wine.

Ishtan turned another page, and continued, "The monster is a wounded Gogolan, who has lost most of his powers. Fully grown, they are massive black beings, the size of buildings, with bright, narrow yellow eyes and sharp, pointed teeth. Their bony fingers emit lightning bolts of terror that do nothing but destroy. Their shrieks make all creatures tremble."

She gasped again. "They attacked us in Echo Canyon! But they were small creatures, and we barely got out alive. She zapped the air, pfft, pfft! Nothing happened.

Ishtan wrote, "Those were the gogolytes, the young ones. There was another breach in the Kisga'a Shield, and hundreds of them entered your atmosphere. Your DNA held traces of the Titans' energy fields, so they locked onto you and your kids. You were immediately given the power to 'zap,' as you call it." He continued writing. "Know that we were there with you, during your escape, for the speed you were going, the gogolytes could have easily overtaken you. Sparky destroyed every gogolyte and overrode the codes and fortified the Shield, and then hid in Meg and Devon's backyard, ready to be discovered by them."

"Sparky is also female?" she asked. He nodded. She began pacing, puffing on another cigarette, and asked, "Why didn't you destroy the monster centuries ago?"

He wrote, "A wounded Gogolan would rather evaporate than be captured, but this one wanted to live. We sent word to the Zogar federation, and they sent a medical cargo ship to retrieve the monster, in order to study it. The first ship got lost in the Fold, and the second ship did not make it through, for the Gogolan destroyed it. A third ship is on its way, armed with the latest technology, and should arrive on Earth in less than a year."

Ushaya continued pacing, and asked, "Why is the ring allowing the monster to roam freely in the foundry?"

He wrote, "Your people want proof of its existence—but rest assured, it cannot escape. Only those who dare enter the foundry are in danger."

She stopped pacing and said, "It is true. I am the only one who witnessed it, and there is doubt among our leaders that it even exists. We are bringing in a team to destroy it."

Ishtan shook his carpet body, as if chuckling, and wrote, "You will not be able to kill it with your weapons."

"Not even a bomb?" she asked.

He answered, "It will only anger it, but try as you might. Be sure to wear the ring when you enter."

"I plan on it," she said, pausing, "Why did the detectives and forensic experts not get attacked?"

"He was studying them."

"What is the monster's name?" she wondered.

"Bokal," wrote Ishtan.

Floating back and forth, drinking straight from the bottle, puffing on her cigarette, she cried out, "This is dreadful news. Good and evil aliens on earth? You have got to be kidding me!" She became irate, flinging her hands in the air. "You may be under a dying sun, but you go searching in some other galaxy and . . ."

"Universe," corrected Ishtan.

"And spy on us for hundreds of years, and now an enemy is waiting outside the door? Tell me this isn't so."

Slowly, he wrote, "Should the Gogolan make another attempt to enter earth, we have one big advantage over them."

She plopped down on the couch, exasperated, "What is that?" she asked.

He continued writing, "They are not familiar with a briefcase or a flower or a piece of rock on your planet. We are objects that have no meaning to them. The twelve spheres you found in Jerome's stream, Ronald's Gemball, the healing clover and the ancient relic, the ring and Sulimon Seeds, are all helpful to your own world, as you will soon discover. But, they also serve as our disguises. I found this carpet, which once belonged in the royal looms of the palace of Cyrus, the great Persian king."

"So you are an entity that resides in this carpet, a Titan," she said.

He wrote, "We are all Titans who have come with powerful creatures from our world. Shortly before the attack in Echo Canyon, a breach in our Shield revealed a strange anomaly, alarming us to begin the grand mission. We summoned the Blue-ray light that scanned the world over, and eventually the light settled over the mountains you call home. There were many contenders, and your energy emitted a frequency that resonated with our cause. We had hoped to place powerful gifts in the hands of your leaders; thus, you have been chosen to bring about the gathering."

"Why me, an ordinary citizen living my own life?"

"The Blue-ray light makes no mistake."

"What is the Blue-ray light?"

"A most supreme being."

"Are you taking over our minds?"

"It is never our intent. You have free will. We only guide to bring about the gathering. What you and your leaders do with the powers is your choice."

She became saddened, and replied, "You come with a dark tale of a dying sun, a mass migration, and an invasion. I wish I hadn't known all of this and could just live out my simple life."

He wrote, "Ushaya, you have come far, but if you wish, you may return to mortal state. This would mean searching for another contender to fill your place."

She straightened up, staring at him, "Hell, no. I like flying. But my kids have been dragged into this—how could you?" she asked.

"Those were your choices, and they hold great powers and are protected. Would you have it any other way?" he asked.

She raised her voice. "Why did you wait until now, when you could have come forward while my kids were terrorized by the gogolytes in Echo Canyon?"

"Because I was stuck here in Saudi Arabia!" he wrote, feverishly.

Realizing Ishtan had a sense of humour, she smirked and asked, "Is Stanislav one of us?"

He answered, "Yes, he was our first encounter before you. He holds power of Genius, who came knocking on his door, selling swatches of cloth. Lord of Innovation and Technology, a great Titan he is."

"How can a bunch of seeds and a Gemball help our leaders?" she asked, incredulous.

"One day, they will learn how to unlock the powers. Their combined strengths are greater than yours, for you alone cannot execute the plan," he replied.

Floating back and forth, and intoxicated, she slurred, "This is tremendous pressure on us. We have no clue about the powers and what this is all about. You already know, so show us the gifts, and we can start right away."

Ishtan wrote, "The gifts have little meaning in context of pure information. Their discoveries must form part of your experience. A dictionary is a book with many words, but until one searches for a word, it has no importance." He continued, "The time has come to gather our forces. We come in peace and wish to be accepted by your peoples, for we, too, are looking for a home. Your species holds great promise for advancement, and this is why we bring gifts. Have you noticed your powers increasing, Ushaya? You have shown remarkable bravery, and we commend you."

"What do Titans really look like?" she asked.

"You have learned a great deal today—it is enough."

"Where is your spaceship hiding?" He was silent.

"What are the frogfish?" He remained silent.

"The butterflies in Mexico, are they Titans?" He put the pen down and rested his fringes.

Inebriated and overwhelmed, she slammed the bottle on the table, and punched a fist through a wall. "I need to take a walk," she said, and flew out the balcony window.

Ishtan sat back in a sofa, reading a newspaper. A while later, she returned, staggering about the room. He looked up and said, "You must control your emotions, Ushaya."

While clumsily sitting at her desk, attempting to write her report, she barked, "Don't go trolling me about my emotions." Then she realized she had actually heard Ishtan speak. He snuck up behind, leaning over her shoulders. She minimized the file, staring at the blank screen, and said, "If you do not show me, then I will not show you." Sulking, he flopped to the floor.

She muttered, "I'm talking to a friggin' carpet. What has become of me?"

Ishtan the telepath

Ushaya could not wait another day to speak with Muzaffar, and so arranged a Zoom meeting that evening. He looked across the screen, asking, "Is everything all right?"

"Yes and no," she replied. Then she began her tale of the Al-Zall Market, how she had met old man Akbar and his carpet, called Ishtan, which flies and communicates. She went on about strange beings from another universe, called the Titans, who come bearing powers to uplift humanity. In a jumble of incoherent words, she continued, "An evil force, called the Gogolan, under a dying sun, contained a Shield, and gifts are hidden on our planet, and I asked Ishtan many questions, but he refused to answer." She emailed the notes to Muzaffar, and said, "Look, I did not write this, Ishtan did."

He read through the neatly written notes, and then slowly folded his hands on his desk. "You expect me to believe this?" he asked, incredulous.

"I will demonstrate," she said, and she sat cross-legged upon the carpet, gently swaying in front of the screen.

His eyes narrowed, and he replied, "But everything that touches you, goes with you."

She stepped off the carpet, and proudly announced, "Meet Ishtan, the carpet with the golden thread, my gift to you." Ishtan bowed before Muzaffar.

Feeling silly, Muzaffar bowed back. With hands clasped under his chin, he silently gazed at the carpet. Ishtan flinched, moving side to side. Muzaffar raised his brows and stared back intently. Ishtan shook his head. Muzaffar leaned forward, with one hand on his hip and the other in the air, as if expressing a thought. Ishtan twirled and flung out his fringes, and then sat back down. Completely annoyed, with folded arms, Ushaya looked away, and then stared back at them. They were still engaged in silent communication.

Muzaffar spoke out loud. "We speak telepathically. It is truly amazing, Ushaya. I believe you are right to say there is an entity that resides in this carpet. He tells me that you wore a beige robe and a navy-blue headscarf when you entered Akbar's shop. Is this true?"

She looked at Ishtan, blurting, "Why didn't you tell me you could communicate telepathically? It could have saved you from all that writing."

Ishtan's voice BOOMED in her head in a communiqué called Silo, "I told you I was a telepath, and you never asked, but the good prince did."

Muzaffar turned to Ishtan, and without moving his lips, he asked in Silo, "What language do you speak on your planet?"

"Temseth," replied Ishtan.

A heated three-way Silo convo flowed, with hands and fringes gesturing wildly, as they fired glances back and forth, discussing the upcoming assembly meeting. Setting up a task, without moving his lips, Muzaffar nodded to Ushaya. "Pick up that bronze falcon statue behind you, and bring it to the table." In Silo, he commanded Ishtan, "Fetch me the urn on the pedestal, by the alcove." Obeying, they went about their tasks and lay them on the table.

Ushaya raised her brows at Muzaffar, and said in Silo, "All nations will want to work with you, in exchange for a carpet ride, don't you think?" Suddenly, they burst out laughing at the absurdity of it all. Ishtan shook his "shoulders" uncontrollably.

Muzaffar wiped his tears and spoke out loud, "You are leaving tomorrow, is that right?"

She nodded. "Yes, boarding the 10:00 morning flight. Shall I bring the gift to you now?"

None of the leaders wanted to be the first to accept a gift prematurely. He replied, "No, keep Ishtan safe in your possession until the assembly meeting."

She was concerned, wondering, "It's a long journey home, filled with airport conveyor belts, if you know what I mean. I worry what will happen to him."

Muzaffar sat back in his chair, quietly thinking a while, before he spoke. "There is a change of plans and you will receive details shortly," he replied.

She apologized for the hole in the wall. "I got overwhelmed and . . ."

He waved his hand and said, "Do not worry, it will be taken care of," and, leaning forward, he added, "Thank you for a beautiful experience, Ushaya." Turning to Ishtan, he said, "I look forward to our next meeting, and may you both have a good evening." They ended their call.

Muzaffar paced the floor, pondering Ishtan's words: "I am here to protect you from enemies and will counsel you in your day-to-day matters, as you desire."

While digging into her meal of fatir and muhammara and rice, Ushaya offered food to Ishtan. He refused, crossing his fringes, leaning to one side.

She asked in Silo, "Then what do you eat?"

He answered, "I absorb the sun's rays by day, and the moonbeams by night. I feed on oxygen and gases, and on lightning bolts, dust storms, and raindrops in the sky. From microbes in the earth's soil to invisible frequencies that fill your atmosphere, I feed on it all." She quietly munched away, pondering his answer.

Late that evening, a text arrived from Muzaffar, with instructions to meet Captain Faisal and Lieutenant Hassan, at ten o'clock the following morning, 300 miles north of the hotel. Her return flight was cancelled, and a private jet would be waiting to take her home. With coordinates set in her phone, she turned to Ishtan, who was sitting in his favourite sofa, and asked, "Have you been on a jet plane before?"

He shook his head.

The Zone

It was springtime, and Ushaya was delighted to see tender leaves sprouting throughout her gardens, grateful for Wally, who had taken care of her plots, while she was away. Her contractor had finally finished the upper level of her property, after months of waiting. Passing through the arched cedar arbour, she admired the new garden beds, promising bluebells and roses, daisies, foxgloves, primrose, lilies and violets. Birds fluttered and splashed in a stone pedestal to her left. She walked along the red brick path, passing the angel statues, and entered the glass greenhouse, to check on Sulimon plants and Clover pots, that needed transplanting.

Ralph and Chloe were completely enamoured with Ishtan, chasing him around the house. When they got too frisky, nipping and swatting at his fringes, he would simply hide. Sometimes, they would catch a ride upon Ishtan, with Ralph yapping away and Chloe curled into a ball, purring loudly.

Days went by, and Ushaya began to settle into normal life, enjoying everyday pleasures. One afternoon, her neighbour, Emily Barker, invited her for tea. Mimi sat calmly in her lap, while conversations flowed back and forth, and, soon, they were bitching about the economy and rising gas prices. At one point, Emily broke down, sobbing in her hands. She missed her late husband, who had passed away ten years earlier with cancer. Ushaya rubbed her shoulders, trying to console her. At the end of their visit, they stood at the doorway, hugging each other, promising to keep more in touch. Ushaya realized, on her way out, that she was not wearing the ring, which was safely hidden in its velvet case.

Ralph turned out to be very chill, a nice balance to her frenetic lifestyle. Except for flights in the air, he would lie most days over the edge of the couch, with his big furry ears, satisfied, to watch the world go by. Chloe, on the other hand, was a chatty kitten, following her everywhere, getting into all kinds of mischief. One day, while snipping stems of clover in the greenhouse, Ushaya caught her digging in Sulimon pots, and chased her out.

A week later, a text came in from Stan: "Suits for PM Yadgiri of India are ready for pickup." With Ralph and Chloe tucked in her front vest jacket, she flew across the skies and landed at his doorstep. When Lucy opened the door, Chloe immediately hissed. Lucy freaked out and hissed back at her, while Ralph yapped uncontrollably.

Stan arrived in time, commanding, "Lucy, let them pass," while motioning Ushaya to come in.

She slowly edged past Lucy, asking, "What's this all about?"

He carried her pack to the couches and replied, "Lucy can draw from memory of a cat or a dog, but she has never met one in real life."

"Never?" she asked, laying Chloe and Ralph down by her feet.

He whispered, "Look, she is processing now." Lucy sat motionless on the couch, with antennae scanning the new intruders.

Her enchanted visit ended with a beautiful sari, carefully rolled into her pack, along with a new laptop for Ishtan. Ropes were strapped around Ralph and Chloe, and, soaring home under puffy white clouds, she looked upon their tiny vests and goggles, and smiled.

One day, Ushaya sat before her laptop, ready to channel Ishtan's voice. Her first question was, "I often went into a state, just before discovering a gift, and I called this the Zone. So what is the Zone actually?"

He replied in Silo, "You are correct. It is a state of alignment to a higher purpose, where you sense something is happening, and to pay attention, for you are about to have an encounter."

She typed his words into her laptop, and then asked, "What about Stan? Was he in the Zone?"

He replied, "Twice. The first time, when he met Genius at his door, selling swatches, and the second time, when the two of you flew together and encountered Lord of Innovation and Technology. Without him, we could not have travelled this far."

She asked, continually typing, “Was Brad in the Zone when he found the map?”

Ishtan moved to the family photos on her credenza, and said, “Yes, another great Titan. The map guides us through the stars. After all, what use is a spaceship without a map? Now, Brad steers whatever course he desires. It started with the big X over northern Manitoba. Imagine the power of the map.”

Ushaya became distracted with thoughts. The house insurance needed updating, and she should bring out her dinner from the freezer. She took a deep breath and went back to her dictation, asking, “What about Sparky? Were Meg and Devon in the Zone?”

Ishtan picked up her thoughts and pulled out the frozen dinner and set it on the kitchen counter, replying, “Yes, their commitment paid off, for Sparky is a Master Titan. Her laser beams unite us all in a powerful grid to keep the Kisga’a Shield in place. She is the electromagnetic frequency that makes it all possible. She is our personal Wi-Fi, so to speak. Sparky can also destroy enemies in a flash.”

Ushaya continued transcribing, asking, “What about the gogolytes in Echo Canyon? Were we in the Zone?”

He replied, “Sparky destroyed them all and that is how you managed to escape. Yes, you were all in the Zone.”

“What about the frogfish?” she asked.

Ishtan sniffed the fresh-cut tulips on her dining table, and began, “You came across a TV program, while browsing brochures in your hotel, and you chose the Canadian Shield, remember?” She nodded. He continued, “They are master creatures that led you to the Titans. It is the only place on earth with that many Titans. Yes, you were in the Zone.”

She asked, “What do the spheres do?”

“Ah, the mystery of the Twelve Titans,” he replied, “It will be up to your own Prime Minister Jerome, when the time is right.”

“What about president Ronald of USA?” she asked, madly typing away.

Ishtan placed the frozen dinner into the oven, setting the timer, and said, “In the US, you chose the Everglades. The alligators are catalysts and master creatures, which led you to the Gemball, a great Titan with a special mission. He is the all-seeing visionary and expert info gatherer. He can reveal events in the present and into the future, and because we are telepaths, this is how we know so much."

Ushaya paused for a moment, and asked, "OK, what about the ancient relic? Was I in the Zone?"

He began chopping lettuce for a salad, calling out from the kitchen, "You chose Mexico, and we sent butterflies, another catalyst. They are many creatures that led you to the jungles. It is there you discovered the ancient relic, and a great Titan he is. He is your planet's record-keeper of all history that has come before, in every country, of every civilization that rose and fell. The relic is like a large mansion with many rooms. Whoever dares enter the statue, does so at their risk, for one could be transported into time, anywhere, and be stuck, if one does not know how to return. The relic is our last refuge, where we can hide, if necessary. Remember, I told you that the ancient relic was the first to enter your planet."

Ishtan mixed the salad ingredients and placed the bowl on the dining table, and continued, "Another great Titan had yet to be discovered. Due to your impatience, a razor-sharp plant forced you to return to earth. By the way, she enjoys the name Clover. On our planet, she is called Xrpreschew."

"Better stick with Clover," suggested Ushaya.

While gazing out the patio doors, he said, "In Britain, you encountered a snowstorm. By sheer good luck, you changed direction and discovered the foundry, where a Master Titan was waiting. A shelf jutted in the aisle, attracting you to the ring. When you wore her upon your finger, a wounded Gogolan appeared, the only one that entered your planet, controlled by the ring and Sparky's beams. The ring unites our forces under her command; we take orders from her. She has cloaking powers, which is different from shape shifting, and she cloaks our spaceship on your planet. She has many other powers, but this will suffice, for now."

"Will you finally reveal the location of the spaceship?" she asked.

Ishtan chuckled and said, "Whoever can find the Titan spaceship, we promise to fly that brave soul in a solar excursion."

"What is the ring's name on your planet?" she asked.

"Vrodomuschgaz," he replied.

"Better stick with the Ring," she said, rapidly typing.

While pacing back and forth, he continued, "In Germany you were truly tested. An unexpected robbery occurred, and we had every confidence that you would prove your valour, and in the end, your leaders agreed. Why even now, Irena is rallying your allies to join headquarters."

He paced some more and said, "In Rwanda, you chose Lake Victoria as your destination, but it was far from where Sulimon had been waiting for you. He created the perfect storm, and you rescued the fishermen. Knowing that you would have to dry off, he had hoped that you would fly eastward. Sulimon is a great Titan over many master creatures. You chose the bag of seeds, a worthy gift, and he was most pleased."

Ushaya stopped transcribing, and said, "Why did he not meet me in Lake Victoria? You seem to control my every move."

Ishtan sat down next to her, and replied, "There is always free choice, as I have said. All we do is guide you to the gifts, not force you. It is our Universal Directive."

She sat back in her chair and folded her arms, and asked, "What would he have done if I had decided to dry off at the hotel, instead?"

Ishtan answered, "Sulimon would have waited patiently for the next opportunity. After all, you could have decided to visit the far eastern coast, but didn't. Instead, you ended up saving eight men stranded in a lake."

Her eyes slit, and she said, "Yes, but that was because Sulimon created the perfect storm."

"You decided on Lake Victoria," he said. There was a long silence.

Realizing she was now the one writing the report, instead of Ishtan, the irony didn't escape her. She went back to her laptop, and asked, "What about Al-Zall Market?"

He replied, "I shape-shifted several times—first, as the man who bumped into you, and then, the aroma and the old woman who prepared your food." He assured her, "Akbar is a real man who lives in your world. My carpet rested in his shop for many decades, and I longed for the day to be released from its bindings and be set free. I am the contact between our world and yours, given my talent for many languages."

"Are you a Master Titan?"

"I am on my way to becoming one."

"Who are the Master Titans again?"

He replied, "Sparky and the ring, and a third one you have yet to discover."

Overwhelmed by it all, she stopped transcribing and cried out, "So, while the powers were shape-shifting for centuries, what were the frogfish and the alligators doing? Just bumming around? What is the Gemball's name on your planet?"

Ishtan sat down at the table. He logged into his new laptop, and calmly replied, "Your journey is not over, and there is one more thing. Jake, the manager you met at Valhalla Outfitters, where you bought your first suits, is a Titan, a shape shifter and communicator par excellence. He was the catalyst that brought you and Stan together." A buzzing sound startled her; dinner was ready.

Days later, Ushaya sent her report to all the assembly leaders. Her son, Brad, was surprised to learn that his map was a Titan, and pulling it from its hiding place, he spread it across the kitchen table. He had never asked questions, like Mom did with Ishtan, and clearing his throat, he began, "Where is the rarest mineral deposit in Canada?"

The map sent a bolt of light to northern Alberta. It seemed to be communicating with him, he thought. He began asking trick questions. "Where is Goose Bay?" A flash flew across the surface and landed in Newfoundland. It was true, he thought.

"Where is Baker Lake?" A streak of light landed in Nunavut, northern Canada. It was also true. The map knew he was being tested.

Then Brad asked, "Where is the spaceship located?" The air crackled and sizzled, and a fiery orange-white ball blazed a trail all the way across the map, and off the edge. Panicking, he waved it in the air and laid it back down. The glow had disappeared, leaving the paper intact, with no damage. The answer appeared to be off the map, he thought. Excitedly, he called up Prime Minister Jerome and told his story, advising him that the Titan spaceship was not located in Canada. Jerome nodded solemnly.

The night before her departure for India, Ushaya sipped her wine and smoked her cigarettes. Flames flickered from the oil lamp, and music played out from speakers, as she sat in her living room. With GPS coordinates inscribed, above and below, and a big X over Al-Zall Market, the scroll was ready for her to tie it with a red ribbon and place it in the treasure chest. Turning to Ishtan, she said, "Time to wrap you up."

He clearly said no, insisting he could take care of Ralph and Chloe while she was away.

She decided, "All right, but when Wally comes around to do some gardening, you must stay quiet." Satisfied, Ishtan leaned back in his sofa, returning to his newspaper.

That same evening, while standing naked in front of the bathroom mirror, she examined her little dragon wings, running down her spine. She spoke to no one about this, not even Ishtan. She turned off the bedroom lamp, wondering what adventures awaited in India. The monsoon season had not yet arrived in Maharashtra. The ring glowed softly on her finger, and with Chloe and Ralph snuggled under the covers and Ishtan by her bedside, she fell into a deep sleep.

Chapter Twelve

Indian Prime Minister Yadgiri Mohendra

Rendezvous with Elephants

Yadgiri often rode elephants, in his youth, at the Naveshwar Reserve, where his entire family had worked, just outside their village in the state of Karnataka. His father was a warden and his mother was the head cook. His older brother and sister performed various tasks, from schlepping dried grass and dung to riding tractors throughout the compound. A political uprising forced his family to Maharashtra, and since then, they had settled into the Singli District.

During his term as chief minister, he had purchased a swath of land next to a wildlife sanctuary, and founded the Bageshwar Elephant Reserve, establishing a progressive new approach to elephant rides. With a dedicated team of teachers, zoologists, medical staff, and groundskeepers, elephants grew to love their handlers, and a special bond often formed between them. Rods with hooks or any harsh form of treatment were forbidden; instead, programs were designed to teach through kindness and repetition. One program, called Rescue Elders, took in abandoned older elephants from dire conditions, to heal them and integrate them with the herds. And since then, they'd tripled their staff and built new compounds, to keep up with the influx.

Not all elephants were suited for rides; instead, some elephants had developed different skills. Some played a game called Kickball. In a field, four staff players would kick four large red balls to four elephants that had to kick them back. They became quite experienced, kicking balls using their trunks and legs, and staff had to be on their toes!

Others played the tabla, a set of Indian drums. At first, sounds were dissonant, as the elephants tapped their trunks across the surfaces while pounding their feet. But over time, mantra-like rhythms and beats floated in the air. Three musicians joined in, playing a sitar, a khartal and a shruti box, and staff often circled, swaying and clapping to the music. The songs were compiled into a CD, called "Meditations of a Wandering Elephant," with the proceeds from their sale funnelled back into their programs. The CD soon became a big hit.

Others learned Hindi and English. Specialists in animal linguistics were employed to teach them words, such as "apple" and "tree," and phrases, such as "Go for walk" and "Come and play."

It began with four elephants, standing behind desks in the large "schoolhouse." One specialist stood in front of the class, tapping a pointer to a white board, scribbling down words, while an assistant stood by the elephants. Four fruits lay on a large table before them—an apple, a banana, an apricot, and a mango.

The specialist motioned Pranit to come forward and take the apricot. Pranit lumbered over to the table, studying the fruit. With his trunk, he picked up the apricot and put it into his mouth and sauntered to his desk.

"Very good," said the specialist. She turned to Arjun, a young elephant, and said, "Come eat apple." Arjun lumbered over and ate the apple, and sauntered back.

"Come eat banana," she motioned to Meera, who picked up the banana.

"Come eat strawberries," she said to Dhwani, who was shuffling her feet, swishing her tail back and forth, bewildered, for there was only a mango. The specialist smiled, and brought out a bowl of strawberries from under the table, and laid it on top. Happily, Dhwani scooped up the fruit and sauntered back.

Special treats, like sweet rice cakes, tree bark, and watermelon, were placed on their desks for homework well done. One day, Pranit found his neighbour's food more appealing, and swiped it into his mouth. Meera complained loudly. The assistant removed the bark from Pranit's desk and gave it to Meera, plus two extra treats, and none to the first, who complained bitterly. Elephants learned about consequences that day.

Lessons graduated in complexity, to emotions, such as love, fear, and anger. One day, staff learned what elephants feared the most. Borrowed from local wildlife sanctuaries, cages of a tiger, a hyena, and a king cobra snake were unloaded from flatbed trucks and arranged side by side. The elephants backed away, having encountered them in the wild before. But when a nearby backhoe dug a hole in the ground, the elephants reacted with the most fright. Immediately, the instructor wrote down on cue cards, '*Chhed ka dar*', in Hindi, and '*Afraid of hole*', in English.

While elephants jostled and played in the fields, a specialist would show large cue cards with the words, '*Play a Game*', in English, and '*Ek kḥel khelo*', in Hindi. Everyone at the reserve was encouraged to use these cue cards. At first, the elephants were confused with two different phrases, but eventually caught on, becoming the first in the world to understand two languages.

Specialists learned a great deal from their pachyderm friends. One day, while walking along a dirt road, with her young male companion, Falguni spoke in Hindi, "*Aap dukhee hain aur apanee maan ko yaad karate hain.*" (You sad and miss your mother.)

Omkaar curled his trunk around her, and let go.

"She sick, but medicine good. You see her soon," said Falguni.

The elephant picked up the pace at the good news, then suddenly raised his tusks to the grey sky, and ran for cover under the canopy. Falguni glanced up and shrugged, "No rain today . . . tomorrow." A cool breeze rustled through the trees, and raindrops sprinkled on her face. Hurriedly, she followed Omkaar to the base just in time, before the torrential downpour hit the compound. The reserve's success story not only gained attention across India, but also Sri Lanka, Indonesia, Malaysia, and Africa.

Fast-forward twenty years: Yadgiri was standing by two elephants shifting back and forth in the grasslands of the wild sanctuary, waiting for Ushaya's arrival. Peering through binoculars, he waved at the spectre in the sky that was swiftly descending toward him.

Ushaya landed before him and brought down her visor and removed her gloves and savannah hat, and, extending her hand, said, "I am most pleased to meet you, your Excellency."

Enchanted, Yadgiri unwrapped the scarf from his face, and shaking her hand, replied, "Very nice to meet you, at last. But please, just call me Yadgiri."

Ushaya looked at the sky and said, "Nice day for some fresh air. At least we have no rain."

"How were your flights? Are you settled in?" he asked, while observing her, dressed in tight-fitting beige pants and a fashionable green khaki jacket. She wore a belt around her waist, sturdy shoes upon her feet, and a backpack, slung across her shoulders. Her hair was wrapped in a bun, with wisps of silvery-black hair falling on either side of her face.

She replied, "Flights went smoothly, and my accommodations are beautiful. Muzaffar is too generous." She observed a man in his sixties, with a cropped white beard, soft, deep eyes, and a broad smile. He wore loose-fitting brown khaki pants, a white, long-sleeved shirt, and a brown vest. Yadgiri was known to be complicated, both humble and arrogant, trusting of few people, and an ascetic with strong Hindu beliefs. He was popular and unpopular, both nationally and internationally.

While petting his elephant, his voice almost lyrical, he said, "These two sisters go everywhere together. Meet Gita and Rajneesh."

"I never rode one before," said Ushaya, as she glided her hands along the massive legs, looking up at Gita, who was adorned with bells and braided cloths, and a red-and-blue blanket draped over her back. A large basket was tethered to leather straps around her body.

"It will be most pleasant," he assured her, as he climbed up onto Rajneesh. Settled into his basket, he rolled up the ladder, and encouraged her to do the same.

A trunk curiously reached inside her pack, and Ushaya giggled. Ancient eyes met hers, and Gita slowly lowered her front legs. Ushaya levitated cross-legged and gently settled into her basket. The two elephants flapped their ears and shuffled their feet.

Yadgiri looked at her and said, "In all my years, I have never seen a human fly. And, I have never seen Gita kneel before someone she had not met before." Lightly tapping Rajneesh, he smiled and said, "Elephants never cease to amaze me. Welcome to India, Ushaya."

She smiled back, as he guided them across the plains. The air buzzed with insects, and monkeys screeched from nearby jungles. A large python slithered away from Gita's feet. A swarm of bees buzzed around Rajneesh, and she quickly slapped her tail to shoo the menace away.

As they trudged on, Yadgiri began, "The elephant has been revered in our culture for thousands of years, and they must be treated with the greatest respect. Hindus worship Lord Ganesha, the Supreme Deity, who embodies the form of an elephant. We are banning current rides across the country under new legislation, called the *Elephant Protection Act.* Many new reserves are forming, following this new model of wellbeing. Also, rides are limited to two people only, the guide and one tourist." He continued, "We are rolling out campaigns to transition workers from this industry to other forms of employment, even encouraging them to be part of the new reserves."

"That's good news, and I commend you," said Ushaya, staring down from her high perch upon Gita, feeling she was guiding a moving mountain.

He asked, "Are you aware that elephants can paint on canvas?"

She replied, "I hear their artwork can fetch quite the price, and I would love one for my collection."

They chatted about their families and their hobbies, about their successes and failures, when soon, their conversations turned to politics. Knowing how little she knew of India, he asked, "From your Western perspective, what issues come to mind?"

Ushaya thought for a moment and began, "Well, there is the conflict with Pakistan over your move to annex Kashmir and Jammu, by revoking Article 370, sparking fears of ethnic cleansing, especially, among the Muslim population. Hundreds on both sides of the conflict have been killed in clashes."

Yadgiri sipped papaya juice from his canteen and said, "It is part of a broader national agenda, where we seek to open the region to all faiths. Religion is complicated, Ushaya."

"Indeed," she said.

"What else comes to mind?" he asked.

Ushaya thought for a moment and replied, "Well, there is the *Citizenship Amendment Act*, allowing citizenship to illegal immigrants living in the country, but barring Muslim descent. There is a rumour that you are turning India into a Hindu state."

Gazelles stood in the distance, flicking their ears, staring back at him with their doe-like eyes. He said, "I am most certainly not turning India into a Hindu state. What I am doing is fulfilling my campaign promise, a policy very popular among my supporters."

"Are you kicking Muslims out?" she asked.

"That is not possible," he retorted.

"How many are in your country?"

"About 200 million."

"Then what recourse do you have?" she asked.

Yadgiri took another swig from his canteen and spoke. "I have many Muslim friends, Ushaya. That is not the point. The law grants citizenship to minorities—such as Sikhs, Buddhists, Jain, Zoroastrians, and Christians—who face religious persecution."

Ushaya looked across at Yadgiri, sitting in his basket, and said, "On the one hand, you absorb Muslim-majority Kashmir into India, on the other, you exclude undocumented Muslims from automatic citizenship. Two different things, I assume."

He replied, "Politics and religion are complicated matters."

"Indeed," she said.

Their elephants continued trudging across the savannah fields. They lumbered past wild peacocks, pecking the ground. Ushaya gulped from her canteen and wiped her mouth. She closed the cap, and said, "I'd like to fly you. Are you ready?"

The two of them scrambled out of their baskets and landed on the ground, next to their elephants. With ropes strapped through his vest, and with visor, gloves and ear buds on, Yadgiri peered at her and said, "I have been practicing the 'Forward, Back, and Stabilize moves, that you wrote about in your reports.'" Suddenly, he levitated forty feet in the air. A rush of adrenalin pumped through his veins. His face flushed, and he held his breath, gazing in awe. They were about to soar when his elephants lifted their trunks in the air, prancing up and down, with ears flapping wildly. "Do you think they can come along?" he asked.

"Impossible, I refuse to frighten them," she replied.

He said, trying to convince her, "You did say that what touches you goes with you."

"Yes, but elephants?" she asked, incredulous.

He whispered, "If they become frightened, then immediately bring them down. Besides, they might wander away."

Ushaya couldn't believe his reckless suggestion, but had an idea, and said, "Get out your landing gear." Three, two, one, forward, back, and stabilize. It was a perfect landing! Working swiftly with ropes and hooks from her pack, she created two double-knotted large nooses and slipped them around the elephants' heads, and clipped the large hooks to her belt. She returned Yadgiri to his basket, unclipped his hook, and sat back in her own basket. Shocked, he objected to being separated.

She smiled and said, "What touches me goes with me, right?"

Up, up, they soared into the warm winds, the elephants in awe, with euphoric smiles, and large ears pinned against their bodies, and trunks straight out into the rush of air. While cruising at 100 miles an hour, at 4,000 feet altitude, Yadgiri hung onto his basket and hat. Ushaya held the reins, guiding them over plains, turning into hills and lush forests, and sugarcane fields, stretching across the panoramic view. He pointed to cormorants in the sky, and she pointed to crocodiles on the banks of Krishna River. He pointed to the Western Ghats mountain ranges, and, with a glint in his eye, cried out, "Who says elephants can't fly!" Gita released a big plop of dung, and Ushaya watched it fall to earth.

He pointed to a herd of elephants, pacing back and forth, in distress. "What is happening down there?"

"I don't know, let's check it out," she said, and slowly landed in the nearby grass. They scrambled out of their baskets and approached, careful not to be trampled by an agitated herd, thrashing their trunks, wailing, and stomping, kicking up dust. Closer and closer, they crept, until they reached a deep hole and saw a baby calf, sloshing in the mud, too weak to stand up. "Oh no!" she cried out.

"We had much rain last week. I will alert the authorities," he said. While peering down at the helpless baby, he asked, "Can you save him?"

She circled the pit and said, "The hole is very narrow. It requires delicate precision. One wrong move, and we are buried alive." She removed her jacket and iPhone, and handed the items to Yadgiri. Circling one more time, she slid down the sides, with muck falling upon her as she descended. It was a tight squeeze, and the baby stirred in the darkness. Yadgiri held his breath for what seemed like eternity. By then, Gita and Rajneesh had joined the group, pacing back and forth. Suddenly, Ushaya rose out of the pit, caked in mud, with the baby on her back, and gently laid him on the ground. Gradually, he got up on his wobbly feet, as the herd surrounded him.

They followed the elephants, on foot, to a nearby stream. While the elephants frolicked in the water, the matriarch suddenly sprayed Ushaya completely. She was free of mud but now soaked to the bone! Yadgiri laughed hysterically. One by one, they crossed the stream, raising their trunks, bellowing out their trumpet calls. The sounds rippled down their spine, as they watched them disappear into the forest.

Up, up, faster they flew, with Gita and Rajneesh in total glee, cruising 200 miles an hour, at 3,000 feet altitude. Ushaya called out, "If you had one wish, what would that be?"

Yadgiri looked down below and said, "Stimulate the economy to create more jobs." He gazed at the distant mountains and said, "Improve infrastructures and create a universal health care." He crossed over Krishna River and avocado plantations and said, "Advance foreign interests to become the global power we should be."

"Most noble goals," she said, checking her GPS.

He glanced at the landscape and said, "Look around you, it appears all things are possible." She turned to him and silently nodded. Adjusting his ear buds, he asked, "An evil force is held in check by a shield and a ring. According to Ishtan, a wounded monster is about to beam out into space. So, what is happening here?"

The elephants slowed to a dead stop in mid-air and she said, "We must take Ishtan's word seriously. If this is an illusion, then I will humbly disappear and no one will find me. But look around us. Is it just a dream?" He gazed down at wild peacocks perched in tamarind trees, proudly displaying their plumage. The elephants pushed on, as she continued, "I believe aliens are truly here, bearing gifts. And the Gogolan?" She quoted words from the Bible, Psalms 23:4, "Yea, though I walk through the valley of the shadow of death, I will fear no evil, for thou art with me; your rod and staff comfort me." She blurted, "Yadgiri, you must join us to find the source of these powers."

"Do I have any choice?" he asked.

"You always have choice," she replied.

"Then I accept the invitation," he said.

She smiled and said, “Welcome to the assembly, an alternate world awaits us.” The grounds whizzed by, as Gita and Rajneesh spread their feet and ears, ready for landing.

He could find no words, except, “What plans do you have for your stay?”

She replied, “I’d like to visit the Malakshwar Shiva Temple and the famous Shrine of the Sufi Mystic, Faluddin Shakti. Not far from there is the Muslim mosque, Haji Baba Masjid, and if there is time, I would like to see the Palace of Sultan Aga Khan.

“Yadgiri?”

“Yes?”

“I have no clue where this journey is taking us.”

He recited the wise words of Rumi, “As you start to walk on the way, the way appears.”

“Perhaps I should do more walking,” she quipped, and they both chuckled.

While hugging Rajneesh and Gita one last time, at the Bageshwar gates, Ushaya turned to Yadgiri and said, “It was magical, and I shall never forget.”

He offered, “Do come in for a change of clothing.”

She replied, “Thank you, but as you know, we are here in secret. The hotel is not far; I will be there in a few minutes.” She put on her visor and asked, “May I call you tonight?”

“Please, anytime,” he said, watching her fade into the distant sky. With GPS in hand, he opened radio frequency to the wild sanctuary officers. “The hole is a hundred miles from here, I’m sending coordinates now,” he said. There was a pause, and he barked, “Yes, yes, we travelled 200 miles, round trip, in two hours. Just get down there.” He dared not explain how, observing Gita and Rajneesh rubbing their bodies against tree trunks, on their way back to base camp.

Dagger meets Water

Hot water ran down her body, soothing her soul. While contemplating the events of the morning, she stepped through the glass shower doors and dried herself off, put on her housecoat and slippers, and wrapped a towel around her head.

She wandered through the hotel suite, room after room, each filled with luxurious furnishings and rugs on wooden, mosaic-patterned floors. She passed through a courtyard with cascading waterfalls, flowing into a basin on her left, and ornamental trees to her right. She opened thick wooden doors and floated into a library of wall-to-wall books, neatly stacked on three sides. Linen curtains graciously spilled onto the floor, as she stepped out through glass doors to a large balcony, and stood, gazing at the magnificent view from her fifteenth-floor penthouse suite. She returned to the great space, observing the splendour all around, and sat down, wondering. *It seems each leader wants to outdo the other.* Not that she was really complaining. While eating her meal of bhakris and masala dosa, she planned out her itinerary for the day.

By mid afternoon, dressed in a fresh safari outfit, she headed north 300 miles to her first destination, the Shrine of Sufi Mystic Faluddin Shakti. Halfway into her journey, her GPS started giving conflicting readouts. Frustrated, she landed in the town of Bedvanti, to figure out the confusion. The promenade was filled with hundreds of people. Turning into an alley, looking for a private spot, she met a young Indian boy, about twelve years old, selling trinkets at a kiosk, wiping sweat from his face. She offered him a bottle of lassi, and he drank the whole thing down, as she studied his wares, wondering why he wasn't in school.

The boy offered a trinket in return, and pulling out a dagger from underneath the tablecloth, he secured it to the strings on her backpack. Surprised at his sudden gesture, she turned to thank him, but where did he go? The kiosk stood empty. A young Indian mother with three children turned the corner and stood in front of the same kiosk. Ushaya couldn't leave without buying a bauble.

While scuttling down stone steps of the promenade and along the stony wall, stretching hundreds of feet, she found a bare patch among debris of man-made waste, and sat down in the sand. Beyond the sand and rock lay a stretch of lowland forest. She turned the twelve-inch dagger in her left hand, admiring its beauty, and felt it had the weight and look of iron. A gold-speckled curved hilt was encrusted with small jewels, and underneath was a round copper sphere, engraved with strange symbols. While running her fingers down the blade, she remembered the confused GPS, and absented-mindedly struck the dagger in the sand.

Deafening sounds filled the air, and the earth rumbled, breaking up all around her. The wall and sandy barge disappeared like a domino effect, sucking trees and bushes into a deep chasm. Violent waves heaved, spraying in the air, frothing in furious frenzy, filling the wide gap with water, overflowing the banks of the promenade. Everyone scattered, crying out in Hindi, "*Bhookamp*!" (Earthquake!)

She grabbed the dagger and backpack, and ran with the crowds along the promenade, in total mayhem and confusion. People were crashing into kiosks and vegetable carts, trampling over fallen bodies. Children were crying, separated from their families, amid screams of terror, ringing in her ears. All of a sudden, it became strangely quiet. Pushing and shoving through the crowd, she came upon a sight that she did not believe.

Hundreds of people were splashing in blue waters, laughing, grateful for some relief from the hot sun. Some hung onto floating tree branches, propelling them with their feet, and some did the backstroke, while others plugged their noses, sinking their heads underneath. Several called forth, in Punjabi, to the hundreds standing on the edge, "*Adara ā'ō, iha śānadāra hai! Savaraga tōṁ ika barakata*!" (Come in, it's wonderful! A blessing from heaven!) One by one, people jumped into the river, then whole families jumped in, while crowds mingled about, amazed and confused.

Ushaya did not make it to the Shakti palace or Shiva mosque or Sultan's tomb, so shook up was she. Instead, she disappeared in SuperMo, reappearing a hundred miles south, cruising over plains and hills, and began wondering if it was a coincidence. The thought gnawed at her, and she had to be sure. Swooping to the ground, she retrieved the dagger from her pack, and remained crouched, observing her surroundings. A small village was nestled in the hills to her left. Forest groves meandered along the right, and a valley stretched for miles before her. Holding it in her left hand, and with all her might, she thrust that dagger into the ground.

The earth rumbled and the ground split with a terrible sound, sucking in fields, boulders, and trees. Thunderous waves sprayed furiously in the air, frothing, churning, and crashing. Countless birds shot in the sky, and gazelles frantically galloped to safer ground. She escaped along the banks, deflecting tree after tree, which toppled upon her, and rose high above the mighty roar, coughing and spluttering. The waters calmed into gentle ripples, across a winding river, a mile long. All became peaceful.

She knelt over the riverbank and splashed water upon her face, and then collapsed, spread-eagled, in the grass, realizing Ishtan was right. She was getting stronger. Jerome's voice boomed in her head, "I have discovered what the twelve spheres can do," followed by Meg and Devon: "Sparky is our lucky charm." And the queen and prince: "It may go looking for you . . . We have secured the premises." Visions danced in her head, of frogfish and alligators, the ancient relic and clover, the Gemball and Ishtan, and the Ring of Power. Visions of the Blue-ray light swirled like a Sufi dance, round and round, round and round, round and round and round, as she fell into a deep slumber.

By late afternoon, flies buzzed around her head, and, groaning, she swatted them away and sat up, staring at the newly terra-formed river, which sparkled like diamonds under a sunny sky. While she floated along the winding river, recording the scene with her phone, cars began to approach from the distant village. It was time to head back to the hotel, she thought, hoping the GPS was now working.

That evening, Ushaya had arranged a Zoom meeting with Yadgiri, and told him the whole story. Then she showed him the dagger, and said, "Look at this."

He gazed into the screen and gushed, "It is beautiful. I am not familiar with the design." Then he said, "I heard about the earthquakes. So, it was you."

She solemnly nodded and replied, "My gift for you." There was silence.

He waved his hand and said, "Keep it safe while in your possession. I look forward to receiving it at the assembly meeting."

"Yadgiri?"

"Yes?"

"I worry about passing through airport customs. Surely, I will be pulled from the lineup."

With folded hands, leaning back, he said, "There will be a change of plans. Details will arrive shortly." And they ended their transmission.

Yadgiri placed an urgent call to his trusted friend and confidante, the minister of waterways, who was a master of ancient languages, to come at once to his secured hotel regency. He sent another urgent message to the IAF squadron, knowing exactly the man to call.

Swami Gupta Maharaj

With two more days left to her visit, Ushaya planned on staying low. The following morning, she bumped into an acquaintance in the main lobby. Phoebe was a plump woman in her mid-forties, and quite attractive, with long, wavy brown hair and side-sweeping bangs. They had first met upon her arrival at the hotel, while standing in front of a painting, and soon had struck up a bond over tea in one of the hotel cafes. Smartly dressed in an elegant suit and shawl and high-heeled shoes, Phoebe had the manners of an aristocrat, yet appeared warm and caring and down-to-earth, when she spoke. She was a diplomat for the Indian Foreign Service, on a mission with officials in Maharashtra to discuss territorial relations of the region. "Where are you heading?" asked Phoebe.

Ushaya appeared downcast, and said, "Oh, for a walk. I had the shock of my life yesterday, was caught up in the earthquake, did you hear about it?"

"Yes, it's all over the news. How dreadful!" replied Phoebe, "Come, join me at my suite and tell me all about it."

While sitting in her suite, Ushaya told her story, careful to leave out details. "Then, I saw hundreds of people swimming in the river . . ."

Trying to ease her shock and deep brooding, Phoebe went onto her laptop, looking for activities to do, and came upon a site, Palm and Card Reader by Swami Gupta. "Let's have our fortunes told. He is famous around here," she said.

"Na, I'm not interested," replied Ushaya.

"Oh come on, it'll get your mind off things. I'll take you shopping after," Phoebe said, knowing how much Ushaya enjoyed shopping. An hour later, they met in the lobby, holding small bouquets of marigolds and lotus flowers. "These are offerings to the swami, and he also accepts money," she said.

They zigzagged through busy streets, passing hundreds of people, among the honking horns and colourful rickshaws carrying passengers along crowded roadways, when they soon came to a red and yellow door. A disciple of Swami Gupta greeted them.

She whispered to Ushaya, "There is no lineup, just our luck." The disciple motioned Phoebe in first, while Ushaya waited outside. A lineup was beginning to form.

Not long after, Phoebe stepped out in a happy daze, exclaiming, "He is amazing! You're going to love him."

The disciple motioned Ushaya in. She bowed and offered the swami her flowers, which he graciously accepted, placing them in a vase, among the dozen others, before motioning her to sit down.

Sitting cross-legged on the carpet, she observed an Indian man in his forties with long hair and beard, clothed in a beige robe, and wearing beads around his neck. His deep almond eyes held the wisdom of many years of spiritual training, upon a face so kind and serene.

He asked in perfect English, "May I see your palms?"

She lay out her palms on the low-lying table between them.

As he turned her hands gently back and forth, he said, "You are left-handed?"

"Yes, mostly left-handed, but I write with my right hand."

He pointed to vertical lines under her ring fingers, and said, "You have many gifts to show the world." She nodded, quietly surprised.

"Have you broken a bone recently?"

"Yes. How do you know that?" she asked.

"This scar on your left hand, you have escaped death many times," he said. She nodded, for it was also true.

From her left thumb, a horizontal line crossed the entire palm, and he warned, "Beware, there is an evil force that seeks to undermine your plans, but a great force will also support and guide you." He pointed to parallel fate lines, rising vertically in her right palm.

The ring glowed on her finger, and she asked, "What kind of evil? Are they aliens?" Their eyes locked.

He peered down at two crossbars, cutting the life lines in both palms, and replied, "The evil I speak of comes from many sides. You must guard yourself, even from colleagues."

Then the swami brought out a deck of cards, a combination of Tarot and Indian mythology. He advised her to shuffle thoroughly and spread them face down, in a mishmash jumble on the table. While gliding his hand across the cards, he turned over the World card, and said, "You have travelled far and wide, seeking the world over, like a lost child dazed in the light of wondrous adventures, but you have yet to find what you are looking for." He motioned her to pick a card, and she pulled a Chariot with Four Horses. He said, "The answers you seek will come swiftly."

He pulled an Eastern image of a religious ascetic, floating cross-legged, above a square pit, and warned, "Beware, the crystal pool. It is dangerous. Do not enter." She did not know what that meant. She pulled the Strength card, and he looked up and said, "A great battle is coming that requires all your strength."

By then, Ushaya was sure an encounter with the Gogolan was imminent, and she asked, "Will we succeed?"

He turned over an Eastern image, the Page of Staves. It showed a magnificent being on a white horse, riding a crest of violent waves, reaching down with one hand into the waters, to lift up a drowning man. "It depends on how united your colleagues will be against the evil that confronts them. Judging by this card, there is hope," he replied.

It was the shortest, yet most profound reading of her life. She pulled out her pouch and emptied its contents, and gently shoved the money across the table. A piece of folded paper slipped under the doorway. He handed it to her and said, "It is addressed to you."

Ushaya opened the paper and read, "Emergency came up, and had to leave. All is OK. Take a taxi back to the hotel, and I'll reimburse you, will explain later. Phoebe."

She bowed to the swami, thanking him for his counsel, and he bowed in return.

While passing the hotel front desk, a sweet voice called out, "Mrs. Landau? An envelope for you." Thanking the clerk, she opened the letter on her way to the elevators, and read, "Please forgive me. I have been immediately called to New Delhi to meet with the high commissioner of the UN, and I cannot miss this meeting. Pray that I catch this flight! P.S. We have our contact info, let's stay in touch, dear heart. Until we meet again. Phoebe." Ushaya folded the paper and pressed the penthouse button.

Jagpal and Nadin

That same evening, Yadgiri called up Ushaya, and said, "You will meet with Captain Jagpal Dhar, Special Forces, and he will fly you home. He is an expert in metals, and perhaps, could identify the source of the dagger."

"Splendid," she said.

"And I have chosen my close advisor, minister of waterways, Nadin Joshi, who has agreed to join our allegiance. Show him the dagger also. He is an expert in ancient Indian languages, and perhaps could decipher the symbols. They are very much looking forward to meeting you."

The following morning, a jet plane stood waiting 500 miles east of her hotel in an open field. The captain was gazing through his binoculars.

"Anything yet?" asked the minister, looking about.

"Nothing . . . Wait," said the captain, pointing to the western sky.

An apparition descended toward them, dressed in a blue sari and silver scarf, draped around her head, carrying two large metal suitcases. Landing, Ushaya pulled down her visor and introduced herself in Hindi, "*Mera naam usha laandau, hai aur mujhe aapase milakar bahut khushee ho rahee hai.*" (My name is Ushaya Landau and I am most pleased to meet you.)

Enchanted, the minister shook her hand and said, "It is our pleasure also. My name is Nadin Joshi. Yadgiri has told me much about this mission, in our short time together, and I am most intrigued." She observed a bald-headed man in his fifties, with round, speckled glasses, who was slightly overweight, dressed impeccably in a beige suit, white shirt, red tie, and brown shiny shoes.

The captain held out his hand and said, "Please call me Jagpal." He was dashingly handsome in his captain's uniform, appearing to be in his forties, with jet-black hair, styled like a movie star, flashing a smile, showing pearly white teeth. While placing her luggage inside the cabin, he turned to her and said, "I must say, you look very beautiful in your sari."

She blushed and said, "The truth is, Stanislav had an occasion for this sari, but it never happened."

"Of course, you were too busy with mud holes and earthquakes," beamed Nadin.

"Perhaps this *is* the right time," said Jagpal, as he pulled out a camera from one of the compartments, asking, "May I take some pictures? It would be a fine send-off for Yadgiri." The shutter clicked away, and on a timer, all three stood in the frame. Click! Click! Click! While stowing the camera back into the compartment, Jagpal ventured, "I have a cousin who Stanislav may be interested to meet. Darshit is an aspiring artist and master weaver who is struggling to enter the garment industry."

"This is not the time for business talk!" said Nadin. His face flushed as he pulled out a handkerchief from his right pocket, dabbing the sweat from his forehead.

Turning to Jagpal, she replied, "I'll put in a good word, when the time is right."

He bowed and said, "I am most grateful."

Nadin advised, "We leave you in peace. Please make yourself comfortable. When the plane has reached altitude and switched into autopilot, we will come and join you."

She adjusted her scarf, and demurely propped herself on the rounded couch for a snooze. The engines roared, and, soon, they were airborne.

Eventually, the jet plane secured in autopilot, and the men crept back in, peering at her. "Did you have a nice rest?" asked Jagpal.

"Yes, thank you," she replied, straightening her sari.

They brought forth tea, crackers, cheese, hummus, and olives, and placed the trays on the table. Nadin handed her a package and said, "Please accept this gift from Yadgiri."

She unwrapped the paper, and stared at a painting, signed by Rajneesh. Two elephants were brush-stroked across the upper half of the canvas, with their trunks stretched out, one slightly ahead of the other. Blob figures with round heads sat in squares boxes upon their backs. A bright yellow circle rested in the upper right-hand corner. Near the bottom of the painting was a river, meandering through a grove of trees. She cried in glee, "Oh, that rascal! Yadgiri didn't tell me that his elephant could paint. It's gorgeous!" She placed the picture on the table. Together, they stared at the title: "Fly Light—Trees Small."

Jagpal pointed to one blob and said, "That must be Yadgiri, you can see his beard."

"Look at the spikes coming out from your back, Ushaya," said Nadin.

"They are like the rays of the sun," Jagpal said.

She was quietly horrified. How could Rajneesh know about the wings on her back? "Yes, the rays of the sun," her voice drifted.

Conversations flowed back and forth, about their jobs and families and friends, about the highs and lows of their lives. They listened to her adventures, about the time when she smacked up her car, and about the time when the kids dropped to earth, escaping a military plane. While dabbing her mouth, she got down to business, and said, "I will bring out the dagger," and disappeared before their very eyes. The men sipped their tea, wondering where she had gone in such a small space, when, she suddenly reappeared. Unfolding a cloth, she laid the dagger in Nadin's hands.

A bead of sweat fell down his cheek. Dazzled by the jewels in its curved hilt, he turned the blade, studying the intricate glyphs around the sphere.

"Do the symbols make any sense?" she asked.

Nadin replied, "It appears to be from two different centuries and cultures. The blade is similar to the Katars, during fourteenth-century Tamil, of the Vijayanagara Empire. The sphere resembles those of the ornamental Kila stakes of the Vedic traditions, but the glyphs are not any language I know of." He continued studying it and said, "Yet, some characters resemble Zoroastrian and Bodo. We will need to examine it further."

"What do you think it's made of?" she asked.

Nadin handed the dagger to Jagpal, who began studying it. He said, "It has the weight of iron, and its colour suggests a hint of cobalt. The blade's composition appears to be made of nickel, which strongly suggests extraterrestrial origin, in other words, a meteorite. With a fluorescent X-ray spectrometer, we can take a better look." He began to wonder, "What would happen if I should strike the dagger into the floor, right here?"

She smiled wryly, and replied, "I wouldn't advise it sir, unless, you want to be at the bottom of a rescue mission."

"This is no time for frivolity. Give me the dagger," retorted Nadin.

"I am merely curious," said Jagpal, studying the blade some more before handing it over.

Nadin leaned in and said, "I cautioned Yadgiri on its use. A great many things must be considered, before terra shaping. It's an environmental concern for the entire country."

Ushaya apologized. "I was reckless, I didn't mean to . . ."

"You were merely being curious," interrupted Jagpal. He got up and saluted, "Time to check the instruments."

Nadin placed down his teacup and said, "You did not take precautions when you flew Yadgiri and the elephants over the sanctuary. In this day and age of surveillance cameras, you have to be most careful." She had to agree, nodding her head. He dipped a cracker in hummus and continued, "You travel across the world, using your own name. If you want your mission to be in secret, you must create an alias. You cannot use your name."

She defiantly crossed her arms. "But I'm a nobody, unlike the leaders," she said. "Whatever I do, I will keep my own name. I had already changed my name once, while stuck in the Archives of London."

Jagpal's voice announced through the intercom, "Touchdown to refuel at Hobot Airport at the Mongolian border."

They pushed on through the far regions of Russia and touched down again, by the Sea of Okhotsk. Over the Bering Sea and Alaska, they continued their flight to BC, all the while in lively debates, discussing the dagger's power. Day became night, and night became day. They laughed and played board games, and ate, and slept.

The jet landed at 08:00 hours in a secluded valley, and, disembarking, they stretched their legs, breathing in the fresh Canadian air, as the sun rose over the hill, bathing its morning glow across a field of alpine blooms. To the east lay the mouth of the Selkirk River, flanked by mountain ranges on either side, cascading into the distance.

Nadin gazed around and gushed, "It's breathtaking." Jagpal's camera clicked wildly away.

Ushaya took their arms and began floating in the air, "Shall we do a fly-about? Hang on tight," she said. Before they could object, they were soaring along the river, zigzagging through mountain ranges, at fifty miles an hour. In a state of shock, Nadin clutched her arm tightly, with no ropes to hang onto, the cool breeze blowing through his clothes, and his red tie flapping in the wind.

Jagpal was in his glory and cried out, "Yaahoo!" He pointed to waterfalls, rushing down the gorge. Nadin pointed to a mother bear and two cubs, walking along the pebbled beach. They flew over a mountain range, and suddenly had to hide in trees, for Ushaya had forgotten about the little town below. Cars drove along the highway, as people busily walked along downtown sidewalks, heading for work. A small aircraft flew overhead. While they sat in the trees, Nadin wiped his brow and straightened his tie, looking down at his ruffled suit.

"How do you feel?" she asked.

"Extraordinary," was all he could say.

She turned to Jagpal and asked, "How do we get out of here? I suggest, we back up over the mountain and move along that corridor, around the bend."

He surveyed the land, and said, "No, I say we move along the railway tracks and over that hill."

"Why do you say that?" she asked.

"Look up behind you," he replied. A logging truck was slowly driving along the dirt road, directly above them. They hatched their escape plan, and off they flew, undetected over the hill. Jagpal took pictures of his legs, dangling in the air. He took pictures of Ushaya and Nadin, waving into the camera, with thumbs up, and in glorious exaltation, the three soared across the majestic skies.

When they arrived back at their jet plane and were seated in the cockpit, Nadin suddenly found his voice, giddily babbling on. "It was incredible," he said. "I cannot believe it, I . . . *we* actually flew, do you realize that, Jagpal? Ha, ha, and the rush of speed, and the wind and the mountains, I could almost touch the clouds. We were going places, far and wide."

"Yes, we travelled twenty miles," Ushaya smiled wryly.

The engines grew louder, and Jagpal said, "This valley is as beautiful as you. I look forward to meeting again."

Ushaya saluted and called out, "Welcome to the assembly," and watched them blaze a trail across western skies.

Show and tell

So happy to be home at last, Ushaya hugged her furry friends and chased them up the front steps. Ishtan the carpet stood at the doorway, gazing at her sari, and said, "I see you had quite the adventure."

That evening, Ushaya and Ronald were in a Zoom call. Ushaya tapped the Gemball, and Ronald gazed long and hard across his screen. The following day, he called up president Zhangwei of China, and proposed, "Look, we'll drop the steel tariffs and the WaWa sanctions, that is, if your gift is worthy of trade. What do you say?"

Though grateful for his astounding prediction of the earthquake disaster, Zhangwei asked, "Oh? What makes you so confident?"

Ronald replied, "Something shiny is in them hills, it wasn't too clear, but I know something is coming your way."

"We shall see," he said prudently.

Days went by, and Ushaya got a text from Stan: "Suits ready for pickup."

The following morning, she arrived at his mansion, and Lucy invited her in. "Where is Stan?" she asked.

Lucy replied, "He is nowhere to be found, but left instructions. Check your email for details." She handed her Zhangwei's suit and gear, plus a parka, along with an evening gown and blue slippers. She uploaded a new voice tracker program into her iPhone, compliments of Stan.

Then one day, Western leaders logged on in the middle of the night, and Eastern leaders logged on during the day, to join the online meeting.

Jerome began, "I am pleased we are gathered here today. The purpose of this meeting is to share what we understand about the gifts so far. I now introduce the great inventor, who has made our journeys possible. Welcome Stanislav Kominsky!" Everyone applauded.

Stanislav bowed to the screen and said, "I am honoured to be here on this special occasion." He had just brought out his latest brainchild, a steel contraption with centrifugal force that would revolutionize every household, when suddenly Lucy came into view, clicking and clacking. Immediately, he shoved her from the screen.

"What was that?" Jerome inquired.

Ushaya quietly rolled her eyes.

Lucy appeared again, and Stan tried to swat her away, but in the end, she stood by his side. Resigned, he told the truth, "She is my AI project, a part of my contract with CSIS."

The group gawked at the robotic creature, flailing its scrawny arms, a robot that spoke in perfect English, "My master is being reminded to be honest and truthful, qualities he has taught me. I have overwritten his mind and taken control of household duties."

Feeling embarrassed, Stan chuckled and said, "Give her control of the house, and now she wants my mind."

Jerome was annoyed and said, "This is classified information, Stan." He turned to Ushaya and asked, "Do you know anything about this?"

Flustered, not knowing what to say, she lowered her head and replied, "I have met her many times." The group fell silent.

Stan came to her rescue, piping up, "Meet Lucy, who can protect and serve! Jerome, if trouble should come our way, as Muzaffar and Ushaya say, then I would recommend Lucy join as a new member. We may find her useful; she could be an excellent decoy, among other talents."

Leaders scrambled on board, pledging billions of dollars toward mining and renewable energy projects. Some were willing to share technology secrets in exchange for working with Lucy. Pleased with new offers pouring in, Jerome cleared his throat and said, "It's nice to meet you, Lucy."

Clicking and clacking, Lucy bowed and said, "Likewise." Everyone applauded.

Jerome announced, "We must move on. Without further ado, I now introduce Meg and Devon." All eyes were on the kids.

Sparky, the crystal gem rested on Meg's outstretched right palm, its dazzling rays emitting rainbow colours. Devon tapped Sparky two feet into the air, and everyone gasped. Rounding the crystal back in her hand, Meg said, "We have discovered something. One time, I was looking for my lost keys. I looked everywhere, but could not find them. Then, Sparky beamed a light to the buffet at our back entrance, and behind, on the floor, were my keys."

Devon spoke next, "One day, we were planting tomato seeds in our garden, and for some reason, she decided to beam around them. In five days, they grew three feet tall, with little green tomatoes. This shouldn't happen for another three months." Everyone applauded.

"Let us know of any new developments," said Jerome, and he turned to Brad to take the floor.

Brad showed the map to the screen, and said, "Northern Alberta has great potential for mining, but we also discovered unknown trace elements, yet to be identified, very strange. Jerome has agreed to meet the CEO of my company, Tony Calderon, and by comparing core samples with the spheres, we hope to find some answers."

Yaegar of Russia asked, "What is the name of your company?"

Brad replied, "GeoFindX, Inc."

Ushaya brought forth the twelve spheres and spread them across the table, and two spheres switched positions before their very eyes. Jerome smiled and said, "I believe we have formed a useful alliance." He reluctantly admitted, "According to Brad, the Titan spaceship is not in Canada." Soft murmurs sounded among the members.

Zhangwei asked, "Have you observed three or more spheres switch at the same time?"

Jerome shook his head, for he couldn't recall such an incident.

Ushaya quipped, "Hell, no, and I hope not. It's enough keeping track of two balls," and they chuckled. She then put the Gemball upon a white velvet cloth, and, tapping it once, it began to glow. They all gasped.

Ronald gazed across the screen at the Gemball, and suddenly cried out, "A disaster is coming our way, just south of Houston." The group leaned into their screens, astonished to see fire explosions and black smoke.

"What is happening?" asked Mimbauwe, president of Rwanda.

Ronald replied, "An oil spill in the Gulf of Mexico, killing thousands of fish and marine life, and a dozen workers dead."

Carlos, president of Mexico, broke in, "Which pipeline? Give us a name, the location."

Ronald continued concentrating on the Gemball across the screen, and said, "It's called . . . called Manchausen Group. I've never heard of them."

Muzaffar of Saudi Arabia offered his best experts to assist with any cleanup, "We know a thing or two about pipeline explosions."

"Thank you, thank you very much," said Ronald.

Carlos's voice boomed, "We need to shut this pipeline down, now! How soon will it happen?"

The Gemball grew pale, and Ronald replied, "I suspect a week or two."

"That's not much time," said Prince Herbert.

Ronald blasted, "How the hell do I shut down a pipeline?"

PM Hashimoto of Japan glanced at Irena and said, "Our countries are big investors in Manchausen Group. Leave it with me. I know the CEO quite well." Irena silently nodded.

Jerome turned to Ronald and said, "Keep us informed, as new details emerge." He then motioned Ushaya to continue.

She slid a clover pot into view and turned off the lights. It began to glow. Silently gazing at luminescent violet leaves suspended on bright green stems, she whispered, "These precious leaves healed my hand in Mexico. They healed my broken arm in Britain, and they healed my swollen face in Germany." The members were so awestruck with the clover plant, that she waited a while before turning the lights back on. From the treasure chest, she brought out the ancient relic, and carefully unwrapped the cloth. They stared at the half-man-half-beast statue.

"It's magnificent," said Devon.

"Truly exquisite," said Stan.

Carlos ripped his shirt open to reveal his tattoo, and everyone peered at the replica inked into his skin.

Jerome cleared his throat, and announced, "I now introduce the queen and prince."

Julia spoke first, "We are content with Ushaya wearing the ring. Meanwhile, our team is monitoring the Blake Moore Foundry. Samples taken from the sludge found at the murder scene show DNA traces of every element known to man, which quite baffles them. We will update you on further news."

Herb spoke next, "The monster has not left the building. As noted in our reports, we seek an elite task force of six of the finest recruits from around the world, and together with Ushaya, they will enter the foundry to kill the monster."

"As I understand, this takes place after the assembly meeting," said Mimbauwe.

Herb replied, "Yes, and their training should take place at German headquarters." He looked over at Irena across his screen.

Irena's voice rose above the clamour. "We are beyond impressed with Ushaya's courage and strength, as she continues to seek the source of her powers." Murmurs sounded. While gazing at the faces of Zhangwei, Hashimoto, and Yaegar, who had yet to come on board, she continued, "We were once skeptical, like you, but we ask that you reserve judgment until you meet with her." She brought up a document, and announced, "I have formed a Document of Intent for all members to sign, agreeing that Germany be headquarters to study Ushaya and the gifts of power. Take your time to reflect upon this important document. You have all the way up through our first assembly meeting to decide." All murmured in response, and Jerome motioned Ushaya to continue.

From a wooden box, she brought out Sulimon Seeds, neatly packaged in plastic pouches. She jiggled them between her fingers before laying them on the table. She then slid a young money tree into view, and everyone gawked. Plucking one fifty-dollar bill, she unfurled it for them to see, and said, "We must be careful not to pick the fruit too soon."

Jerome raised his brows and said, "Waiting for the ink to dry?" They all chuckled.

Stan said, "Those will be unmarked bills. How can they go into circulation?"

"We'll bring in a new series," replied Jerome.

Mimbauwe warned, "We must not be too quick to plant these seeds. They will have grave consequences if we choose the wrong path."

Zhangwei agreed, "The growing dollars will impact the monetary system and create economic catastrophe, worldwide."

Suddenly, Ralph and Chloe appeared, sniffing the screen, and they all cooed and aahed. Jerome motioned to Prince Muzaffar, for it was now his turn.

Muzaffar spoke: "I have flown with Ushaya and know what she speaks of. I now introduce, Ishtan the carpet with the golden thread."

Ushaya spread Ishtan's carpet wide; it rippled like the waves of a babbling brook. With fringes shimmering, Ishtan peered into the screen, and everyone recoiled. Words BOOMED in Silo, "The kids are on the right path about Sparky. The power is in her transmission ability. She IS the Kisga'a Shield. On our planet, her name is Quazaik."

Queen Julia was surprised and said, "Did I just hear that Sparky is Quazaik?"

"I heard she is the Kisga'a Shield," said Hashimoto.

Yaegar piped, "I heard the same message, loud and clear."

Meg trembled at the sight of Quazaik, resting in her hand.

Everyone was talking over each other, and Muzaffar raised his voice. "Our biggest concern right now is Bokal held in captivity, until a cargo ship arrives. I agree with Julia and Herb, we must destroy any threat to our existence." More soft murmurs followed.

Ushaya moved on with their conference call, and brought forth the dagger from its cloth, for all to see. The group hushed in awe at the sight of its beauty. Yadgiri shook his head and said, "We dare not demonstrate its power."

Zhangwei had sat quietly, before he said, "Ushaya, I would be honoured to meet with you." Hashimoto and Yaegar also agreed to meet with her. Applause erupted.

Jerome announced, "Ladies and gentlemen, let us conclude our meeting, and reflect on what we have learned so far. We will meet again, as soon as possible." And one by one, they signed off.

A catastrophe was averted thanks to Hashimoto. He spoke with the CEO of Manchausen Group about a leak, and threatened him, "We will pull our stocks, unless you investigate." Allied planes from around the world flew over the Gulf of Mexico. Indeed, a faulty crack from a pipeline joint was sputtering oil, leaking into the ground. Panicked workers shouted out commands. Days later, the pipeline was back in operation, humming like a fine-tuned machine, pumping out endless barrels of oil.

Ronald and Carlos emailed everyone, "Thank you for your support, and a special thank you to Hashimoto!"

The night before departure to meet with president Zhangwei, Ushaya took a drag from her cigarette, while listening to her favourite melodies. Candles glowed throughout her house. She had finished marking a big X over Bedvanti, where she had first met the dagger, and GPS coordinates were inscribed above and below, on parchment paper. It was no secret where the earthquakes happened; nonetheless, she tied a red ribbon around Yadgiri's scroll and placed it in the treasure chest. Then she carefully laid the dagger on top.

Under a moonless, starry sky, Ushaya and Ishtan rocked, back and forth, on the front porch swing, with Chloe and Ralph by their sides. Ishtan spoke in Silo, "I shall take care of the Twelve Titans and Sulimon Forest, while you are away. Are you bringing the Gemball with you?"

Ushaya shook her head and said, "No, it must stay behind."

"What about the relic?"

"It stays behind."

"And the dagger?"

"It must stay."

"And the clover?"

She took a sip of wine and replied, "The clover comes with me."

"You go with no other?"

"The ring will be my other companion."

Ralph sauntered down the front steps and stopped to sniff the air. The odd light shone from houses below, as he gazed over their sleepy town. Chloe sat regal by a gargoyle, her tail curled around its claw, her head held high, with tall ears listening, her green eyes staring into bushes at seemingly nothing.

Ushaya pointed up and whispered, "Look, the Big Dipper."

Ishtan pointed to somewhere in space, and said, "See that nebula? It is where we entered the Fold. A pulsar neutron star went super nova, so we circumvented the Orion Arm through the Milky Way, and, passing through many asteroid belts, we stumbled upon your solar system. That's when we discovered your pretty blue planet." Suddenly, a meteor streaked across the black sky, burning out as quickly as it came.

Chapter Thirteen

Chinese President Zhangwei Qi-Wan

The Longyou Caves

Ushaya would meet Zhangwei at the Longyou Caves, south of Hangzhou, near China's eastern border. Hangzhou is known for its wealth and culture. It is the home of many writers, artists, and poets, along with silk industries and fertile rice-growing fields. With a population of ten million, it is truly a beautiful city.

Also present at their rendezvous, would be three high-ranking agents from the MSS, new members who have agreed to join the allegiance:

Agent Beilin, a woman in her mid-forties, with long flowing black hair, wearing silver-lined glasses, was from Internal Security and Anti-Reconnaissance Division. Her side passion was the art of bonsai, even entering into competitions.

Agent Xiang, a chubby man in his fifties with slicked-back hair, was head of the Science and Technology Investigative Division. He enjoyed kite flying in his spare time.

Then there was agent Minghua, a tall and slim man in his mid-forties, with black-cropped hair and a birthmark on his right cheek, who was from Secret Service, a captain of the PLA Air Force. His passion was calligraphy, but he hadn't picked up a pen in years.

Ushaya reviewed their profiles for the last time, and shut down her laptop to prepare for the long journey ahead. Five thousand miles stood between Crestfield and Hangzhou, and weather forecasts were looking fair.

She said her goodbyes to Chloe and Ralph, and reminded Ishtan that Wally would be tending the gardens. With suitcases strapped to her belt, she soared west across the Pacific Ocean at 5,000 miles an hour, taking the odd midair break to enjoy the view. She was impressed with Stan's new GPS voice tracker, calling out directions, "Turn left and bank south 500 miles . . .

"Avoid oncoming plane and rise 2,000 feet . . .

"Descend 1,000 feet, and maintain course, for 3,000 miles . . .

"Cloud turbulence ahead, rise 1,000 feet . . ."

Scared out of her wits, flying in complete darkness, through time zone after time zone, passing over Japan and the East China Sea, the voice-tracker continued guiding her through the cityscapes, "Turn right-north twenty miles . . .

"Steady west 100 miles . . .

"Hard left-south forty miles . . .

"Soft-right two miles over the bridge . . .

"Veer left and scale down that tall building . . .

"Population density ahead. Back up, change course and go right . . . left, over, under . . . "

Relieved to be standing before the Qiantao Hotel, an hour later, at midnight, she felt proud of herself. Two records were broken that day, the longest flight over water, and in the dark.

The grand hotel was magnificent, just like the brochure boasted. A long shawl covered her suit, while two porters, dressed in buttoned-up red uniforms, carried her luggage to the front desk. Throngs of people mingled in the foyer, mostly speaking Mandarin. A male clerk, dressed in a navy suit and cap, asked, "Madam, would you like a porter?"

Using her new voice translator, she replied, "That's all right, I can manage. Thank you." He provided her with several brochures and a list of amenities.

She swiped the key card and entered her penthouse suite. Hundreds of lights glittered through crystal rods, suspended from the ceiling in the grand space. Bronze, red, and black furnishings filled room-after-room. *They had to quit outdoing each other*, she thought, wandering past an indoor pool.

She emailed Jerome that she had arrived, safe and sound. While standing naked over the bedroom balcony, she shook the dust from her suit, and then took a shower. Her itchy dragon wings were growing, and trying not to think about them, she turned off the lamp in her bedroom, and fell asleep.

The following day, Zhangwei and his secret agents stood at the back of the Longyou Caves, sealed off from the public.

Agent Beilin pointed at a spectre in the sky, which was closing in rapidly. "Is that her?" she asked.

Agent Xiang peered through binoculars, trying to contain his excitement. "It appears to be human," he replied.

"Then it must be her," said president Zhangwei, shielding his eyes.

Ushaya landed before them and pulled down her hood and visor. She extended her hand to Zhangwei, and said, "I'm honoured to meet you, your Excellency."

"My greatest pleasure, and please, call me Zhangwei," he said, then turning to his agents, said, "Allow me to introduce Agents Xiang, Beilin, and Minghua." They all shook hands.

In full salute, his agents guarded the entrance, as Ushaya and Zhangwei entered the caves. He clearly stated, "I do not wish to discuss politics. Not about Hong Kong or trade embargoes, or sanctions or human rights, or jailed dissidents. Nor do I want to discuss the Uyghur re-education camps or the WaWa Telecom issue, or any other political matter."

Wandering through lit caves with fifty-foot ceilings, she nodded and replied, "We are on sacred ground—why talk politics?"

As he led her through the caverns, he said, "I have visited these caves many times, and they have never ceased to amaze me. Drained from a riverbed in 1992, many of these grottoes are unconnected and are considered to be over 2,000 years old. There is no historical record of their construction, which is surprising, given how our people have kept records for thousands of years. Furthermore, these caves have maintained their structural integrity." Pointing all around, he continued, "As you see, the walls are covered with chiselled parallel markings, symbols still not deciphered by our experts that, therefore, remain a great mystery."

She gazed at sandstone pillars covered with inscriptions, and said, "Seems like alien technology, doesn't it?"

Zhangwei had often pondered that very same thought. He stepped onto the next plateau, which led to another chamber. Together, they stood at a large floor-to-ceiling pillar.

She asked, "If you had but one wish, what would that be?"

Zhangwei paused a moment and replied, "To build a nation based on the fourteen principles of our foundation. Have you read any of my books?"

She replied, "I have read only one, *China Renaissance*. It is comprehensive and lays out your vision very well."

While circling a column, he began, "I wish to gather the best minds to concentrate efforts on world issues. The problem is, we are all splintered in too many roundtable discussions. We should focus on three targeted projects that the whole world engages in, and give ourselves a five-year timeline to achieve our goals."

He moved to another pillar, and she followed. He further explained, "For instance, the garbage patch and plastics in the ocean that can be turned into renewable products, and animal farming, are the most pressing issues of our time. We had learned from the Israelis, who have perfected vast eco-systems of fish and produce farming, instead of taking from the land and oceans, which will surely deplete them. This is how we manage to feed 1.4 billion people. But there is more work to do." He went on, "In five years' time, we will have gained tangible results, something to be proud of. Then we can decide on the next three pressing issues, and so forth."

While weaving through cave structures, he continued speaking, "This starts a global movement, from mining to production of goods into households, from marketing and merchandising to education and new sources of employment, which leads to further understanding about climate change, and so forth."

They stood side by side along the roped walkway of the main chamber. "I aim to uplift the standard of living for all our citizens," he said, "and my final wish is to improve our space program." They fell silent.

Ushaya realized that he could be quite talkative when something interested him. She also realized he was a leader with great vision, recalling what she had read about him—his humble beginnings, growing up in a poor village, where his own father was jailed when he was young, through the years of turmoil during the Mao Zedong revolution, before his rise to power through the ranks of the Chinese Communist Party. She quietly remarked, "Those are noble goals."

They ended their tour and slipped out the back entrance. Zhangwei had a surprise in store for his new recruits. Ushaya pulled out five visors from her pack, and announced, "Hang on tight. It's time for a fly-about." With Zhangwei and Beilin to her left, and Minghua and Xiang to her right, they wrapped arms and up, up, up, rose in the air. Their fears soon turned to awe, as they glided northbound to the nearby forest. Glorious vistas stretched in every direction, from city skylines in the west to rice paddies in the south, and the sea to the east. They turned back to the caves, gliding over the terrain at fifty miles an hour.

Xiang smiled and said, "When I was young, I used to fly kites, wishing I could fly, too. Now, here we are; my wish has come true. Remarkable!"

Zhangwei reminisced, "When I was young, I wanted to be a pilot."

Ushaya revealed, "When I was young, I wanted to be a language interpreter for the UN."

"When I was young, I wanted to open a restaurant; instead, I fell in love with the art of Japanese bonsai," said Beilin.

Zhangwei remarked, "You make the best hotpot in the country," and everyone agreed.

Minghua was once a calligrapher in his spare time, translating old scripts, but he had let his talent go dormant since his wife died seven years earlier. "Perhaps I should take it up again," he thought out loud.

As they descended rapidly over the landscape, they heard, "Get out your landing gear." Three, two, one, and landing perfectly, they broke out in jubilee! Ushaya pulled down her visor in great relief, and said, "Well done, it was dangerous work. We broke a record with five of us and no ropes."

Zhangwei turned to his agents and announced, "Welcome to our allegiance." Their meeting ended with Ushaya, arm in arm with Zhangwei, ready for takeoff. He looked, one last time, at his agents, and said, "See you later," and they flew away.

While blazing a trail across the sky toward HoChing Palace, halfway to Hangzhou, he hung on for dear life, exhilarated, flying at 200 miles an hour, with the rush of warm air whipping past his face. Zhangwei hardly noticed the time gone by, as they flew over a parade in one of the local towns. The bands were marching to the same tune, in national union—such power to watch, he thought. They slowed to a full stop, in mid-air, to enjoy the view. Migrant starlings swarmed ahead, shifting this way and that, breaking apart and joining again in hypnotic displays. Such a marvel to behold, and smiling at each other, they continued descending, zigzagging among skyscrapers before swooping through the eastern open window of his palace.

They spent the day together, ordering in meals of hotpot, rice and dumplings, and steamed vermicelli rolls. Ushaya demonstrated HypeMo, much to his delight. He showed her a room filled with ancient Chinese pottery and artifacts. They discussed Stan's vision for the working class in the garment industry.

That evening, they stepped out of a taxi, with the agents by their side, and entered the Zijin Grand Theatre to watch the famous Wan Lin production, the "Dancing Swan." Zhangwei was wearing spectacles, a long grey wig, and Manchu-style moustache, and was dressed in a fine Chinese suit and white shirt, disguised as an esteemed university professor. Ushaya was dressed in her lovely silk gown and blue slippers, with a flower in her coiffed hair, and was holding a small Chinese purse. They took their seats in the balcony. Enthralled, she watched dancers move across the stage, such exquisite style and grace, such colour, that she couldn't be more amazed. She turned to Zhangwei, to her right, and whispered, "It is like a play within a play, have you noticed?" Final curtains fell, ending the evening in rapturous applause.

Agent Minghua, on her left, asked, "What plans do you have for your stay?"

Ushaya replied, "I'd like to see the Terracotta Army in Xi'an. It's only about 800 miles from here." She paused and said, "But I do not know what I am looking for."

Agent Beilin, who sat left to Minghua, quoted words of Lao Tzu, "The wise man knows what he does not know."

Crowds spilled out of the theatre into the street, and they hid in an alcove. With arms linked, they all floated away, disappearing into the night sky.

CHAPTER THIRTEEN

Flight of the yellow crane and the golden orb

Canaries sang outside her bedroom window. Ushaya yawned and stretched and rolled over in bed. Soon after her morning shower, she ordered breakfast, while browsing through Terracotta Army brochures.

At almost noon, and ready to go, she glanced at the label inside the parka vest, "Made in Canada,"—courtesy of Stanislav, the inventor, and she smiled. With a backpack and visor on, she flew, northwest, to the city of Xi'an. Halfway through the journey, while passing over mountain ranges, her voice tracker advised, "Unidentified bird ahead." As she closed in, the voice tracker announced, "It is a crane."

She glided alongside the bird, fluttering her arms playfully to show the many ways she could fly. The crane responded, showing its own prowess. It dipped its head, up and down, and so she copied. The bird repeated, and she repeated, wondering if it was some kind of mating ritual. She hoped not! *Must be a male bird*, she thought. Then she realized it was a female bird, fluttering her eyelids, ever so coyly, as they both flew into the Zone. Mesmerized by her graceful movements, with a flutter in her tail and a downward dip of her middle wings, Ushaya frolicked over mountain peaks, chasing the bird through chasms and gorges, passing lakes and rivers of such breathtaking beauty!

When she turned a mountain corner, she suddenly lost the bird. Where had it gone? She frantically scaled, high and low, along the jagged mountainside. To her left, there it was, resting on a precipice, in a deep, narrow crevice that dropped 800 feet. She inched her way on the right and sat on a ledge, fifty feet across from the bird. Carefully, she zoomed in, taking pictures, while it was preening its feathers. Slowly, she brought out a sketchpad and pencils from her pack. It looked up at her, and she froze. Ruffling its feathers, it went back to preening.

She drew as best as she could, first drawing the head, beak, and eyes. Then she drew the red crest, and gradually worked her way down its yellow body, and golden-brown tail feathers, ending with thin legs and pink webbed feet. She named her new sketch, simply, The Yellow Crane.

Suddenly, it spread its wings and flew away. Sadly, she watched it disappear into the sky, and then packed her gear and floated out of the crevice, into the cool air. She turned around, one last time, and noticed something on the precipice, and gliding back, she picked up a large, yellow feather that was left behind. As she tucked it between her breasts, something shiny caught her eye, to the left.

She floated deeper into the gorge, where massive patches of shiny foil-like substance stretched over jagged, stony outcrops, emitting a golden glow in the darkness. As she glided her hands along the surface, feeling its rubbery and smooth texture under the touch of her fingers, she pried off a six-inch square, surprised at how easily it peeled from the jagged rock, and then she stood on the small precipice, examining it. It behaved like plastic as she stretched and stretched the material, until it became the size of her body. She lay the sheet on the precipice, and gathering the edges, squished it together, like putty, punching it down with her hands. She continued rolling it over and over into a ball, until it became no bigger than the tip of her thumb. Staring at its luminescent glow, she decided to call it the Golden Orb, and placed it in one of her parka pockets.

She pulled off a small toothpick sliver from the rock face, and using her fingers, she stretched it outward until the strange material was once again the size of her body! Then folding the material over and over, reducing it to a tiny sliver in her palm, she wondered, *what is this stuff?* Carefully, she wrapped the golden sliver in cloth and placed it in another pocket.

Ishtan's voice BOOMED in her head, "You have found the gift—well done, Ushaya. That Titan Orb that you hold can produce 20,000 spacesuits, and has many other uses that your people, one day, will discover. The yellow feather belongs to a Tanzoik, a young Titan." Then all went silent.

Stunned, she never reached the Terracotta Army; instead, she returned to her hotel. While busily researching online, she discovered there were thirty-five crane species in China. She took notes of their habitats, how common they were, or how rare, what regions you could find them, and interesting facts. But none of the images appeared to match the exact crane she had seen. She had an idea, and late that afternoon, she flew to a hardware shop she had discovered in Hangzhou City, to collect a few tools, thankful for her voice translator.

The following day, no longer able to contain her excitement, she arranged a Skype call with Zhangwei. He appeared on screen and said, "Hello, Ushaya, how are you today?"

"I am well, and you?" she replied.

"I want to say how thrilled I was yesterday, and can assure you, my agents were equally enthralled."

"As was I, and I am most pleased to have met them."

"What gives me the pleasure of your call?"

Ushaya told the story of the yellow crane and Ishtan's voice transmission. She brought up the ball, no bigger than the tip of her thumb, to the screen and announced, "Meet the Golden Orb." He gazed at its golden aura.

She continued, "Of course, this material is not an orb. It adheres flat across the mountain's rocky surface, but watch what it can do." With a kitchen rolling pin, she began spreading the orb across the surface of her desk, stretching and yanking and rolling, working her way outward from the centre. She wrapped it over the chair and across the floor, and continued rolling up the walls until the room was plastered in this mysterious substance. She demonstrated, using scissors and knives, cutting through the material, but it would not cut.

"So, I went into town yesterday, and bought a chainsaw and blowtorch," she said. The chainsaw buzzed up and down the material, but it did not cut. Then she fired the blowtorch flames across the material, but nothing happened.

Zhangwei was fascinated. "Perhaps it needs something more powerful, like a photon laser," he suggested.

"Perhaps," she replied, and began peeling the material from the walls, folding it over and over, punching it down into a ball, until it was no bigger than the tip of her thumb.

She brought out the tiny sliver and said, "Watch what this can do." She stretched the material until it wrapped her entire body, like a spacesuit. Zhangwei stared in wonder, as she unwrapped it from her body and punched it down until it became a tiny sliver between her fingers.

Then she brought out the yellow feather and said, "According to Ishtan, it belongs to a Tanzoik, a young Titan." She emailed the drawing of the crane and the photos she had taken, and said, "These are my gifts for you."

Zhangwei sat back in his chair, recalling memories from his childhood, "When I was eight years old, I once met a crane in the backyard of the compound where I grew up. Every day, it would visit me, the whole summer long, and I would feed it corn and earthworms dug from the gardens. We became friends and would chase each other and play by a nearby pond. But one day, while following it into a forest, I lost the bird, and remembered crying to my parents."

"Is that so?" she softly murmured. They wondered what the Golden Orb was made of, and agreed that the only way was to get the material into a research lab. She added, "Remember, there is a lot more where this comes from . . . by the way, you should give it a name."

He pondered a moment, and replied, "I shall call this material Kunfu, and the yellow crane, YangXi."

"As you please."

"I insist on a private jet for your flight home."

"No, let me fly alone, as planned. Weather is looking fair, and I promise to safeguard your gifts to my utmost ability."

Zhangwei nodded his approval.

Precious Memories

The following afternoon, Ralph and Chloe jumped into her welcoming arms, and together, they frolicked up the driveway to Ishtan, waiting at the front door. Ushaya brought out the golden orb and sliver from her pockets. Ishtan nodded and offered her a cup of tea, in anticipation of her arrival.

In the hazy days of summer, she had time to relax in her gardens, reading a mystery novel. Some days, she would fly with Ishtan into the clouds, to enjoy some peace and quiet. Other days, she would visit Sulimon Forest. She no longer bothered to consult with the Gemball, and only occasionally, brought out the dagger and the ancient relic from the chest, to admire their beauty. The ring was hidden in its velvet case, for her thoughts were far removed from Blake Moore Foundry.

One day, while sun tanning in her lawn chair, waiting for her brother and sister and their spouses to arrive, Ushaya heard the RV vehicle turn off its engine in her driveway, and went down to greet them. They were only staying a short while on their way to the US.

Sister Amelia and her husband Paul were the first to step out of their RV. Amelia gazed up at the gargoyles, and chuckled at Ushaya, "Whoa, do these beasts help you sleep at night?"

Brother Kevin stepped out of the RV and bent down, petting a six-month old German shepherd dog, wagging his tail, and said, "This must be Ralph. He is one handsome dog."

Kevin's wife, Maria, was the last person to step out of the RV. She picked up Chloe into her arms. The fluffy grey-and-white Maine Coon cat purred away. "She's beautiful!" she exclaimed.

As they wandered through the house, Amelia asked, "What are all these plants?"

Ushaya replied, "This is clover and this is clover, and this one is clover, part of the Xrpreschew genus . . . and this one is a philodendron . . . and this one is Sulimon's Breath, an African plant."

Amelia's husband, Paul, asked, "Are you starting a clover patch?"

All day long, they laughed at Paul's jokes, swapping stories, while food and drinks flowed out from the kitchen. An exotic carpet lay under the coffee table, and marvelling at its beauty, Maria asked, "Where did you get this?"

Ushaya gazed down at Ishtan the carpet, and replied with a lie, "In New Zealand, when I visited the kids."

That evening, while sitting around the fire pit toasting marshmallows, as the music played through outdoor speakers, they began reminiscing about childhood memories. Brother Kevin said, "Remember when we went fishing and our four-horsepower rowboat capsized? What, we had to be in our teens." His wife Maria was gently petting Ralph and Chloe, snoozing in her lap.

Ushaya took a sip of wine and said, "Yeah, Horseshoe Bay. We had so much crazy fun. But Kevin, we didn't capsize, remember? The boat got caught in a thick lily patch, and all we did was bail out buckets of water."

Amelia was stoking the fire, watching embers disperse in the air. She shook her head and said, "That's not how I remember it. You guys were picking out snakes from the lily marsh, and I fell overboard screaming." A heated conversation erupted, each trying to remember exactly what had happened, when Paul cracked a joke, and everyone laughed. Soon, they headed for bed, for it was midnight. Maria carefully laid the sleeping Ralph and Chloe onto their cushions by the couch.

The following day, Ushaya and her family drove into town in their RV, to check out Valhalla Outfitters. Amelia and Paul were avid kayakers, and Ushaya introduced them to manager Jake, knowing secretly that he was a

Titan. They all shook hands and followed Jake, who pointed to a motorized kayak that was on sale, explaining, "This kayak holds storage units and a place for your phones. It comes equipped with GPS and warning systems and paddles, but also a motor to guide you safely through turbulent waters to shore. And underneath is a set of motorized wheels to help portage across land." And he concluded, "They're on sale, 30 percent off."

After studying the brochure, Amelia and Paul nodded and said, "We'll buy two kayaks."

"Right this way," said Jake, winking at Ushaya on the way to the till.

Brother Kevin had become a marathon runner to get in shape. He bought running shoes with zero-drop and carbon fibre plates, allowing for buoyant steps and greater speed. His wife Maria bought some nifty sunglasses. Jake helped load the kayaks on top of their RV, and by late afternoon, after farewell hugs and kisses, Ushaya watched her family drive away to their next destination.

Days later, Jerome was shuffling reports on his desk, gazing at Ushaya and Zhangwei across his screen. "Are these true?" he asked. They nodded, and he fired the reports across the world to the other leaders. He then opened a new file on his laptop, titled, 'Twelve Spheres and the Gifts of Power."

Meanwhile, Stan called up Ushaya and said, "Hashimoto's gear is ready for pickup." She arrived the following day at his mansion, and left with the gear, and a kimono, for herself.

Then one day, tragedy struck. Ushaya's dear friend Mandy suddenly passed away from a heart defect. Ushaya flew to Revelstoke to attend the funeral, and met her surviving husband, and family and friends, in a "celebration of life" ceremony.

When she arrived back home, she lit candles throughout the house and sat on the couch, with tears in her eyes, deeply missing her friend. Ralph nestled his snout into her lap, and Chloe curled up beside her. Ishtan the carpet brought her a glass of wine and cigarettes. She reminisced about the times when they took foolish risks as children. They'd walk along train tracks and jump off to watch a train whiz by, blowing its whistle. One time, they raided the toffee dumpster, down the lane from where they lived, and were chased away by the owner of the factory. They'd sneak into a nearby junkyard, pretending to drive in burnt-out discarded cars, as they sat behind the wheel among shards of glass.

She remembered Mandy's wedding day, and was present at the birth of her first child. Mandy was in the hospital when Ushaya had her foot surgery. Ah, so many memories to cherish.

Late that night, Ushaya tied Zhangwei's scroll with a red ribbon and placed it in the treasure chest. Carefully tucking the golden orb and sliver inside red velvet pouches with strings drawn snug, she then laid them among the other gifts. She wrapped the yellow YangXi feather in cloth, and laid it on top, before locking the chest.

That same night, while brushing her teeth, Ushaya called out to Ishtan, who soon arrived at the bathroom, with the door wide open. She did not want to talk yet about her dragon wings; instead, she began, "Did you know that the Chinese invented paper, the mechanical clock, tea, rice fields, gunpowder, and the compass? They also invented silk, umbrellas, sunglasses, kites, and parachutes, and flares and rockets, and porcelain, acupuncture, playing cards, and the fishing reel. And did you know that both China and Japan invented the toothbrush?" She swished her mouth one last time, and spat in the sink, and looked up at Ishtan, and said, "Lucky you, you don't need to brush your teeth."

A week later, more tragedy struck. Zhangwei and his wife, Sung Yee, stood under umbrellas in the pouring rain, attending a state funeral for Kenshin Huang, a close friend and party member, high in the ranks of the Politboro. As they gathered with a group of dignitaries, a full gun salute shot in the sky, and a funeral procession followed, to lay Kenshin's body to rest.

For days after, Zhangwei wrote letters of condolences to Kenshin's family. He sat before a box of photographs, and began bringing out memories of when they had first met as children. They both used to chase the crane in his backyard, and sifting through photographs, he found one photo of the crane, and it was almost identical to the crane Ushaya had encountered. He sat back, mystified. He reminisced about the times when he and Kenshin had been forced into hard labour during their teens, as part of a campaign by Mao Zedong, for educated youth to experience a peasant way of life. They had plowed fields and schlepped cow dung, and ground millet by donkey. Then he began to weep, in memories of the bird he once lost.

His wife appeared next to him, glancing in the screen, “What is it, my dear?” she asked.

Startled, he looked up at her and said, “It’s nothing, Sung Yee, just some childhood memory.”

While caressing his arms, with her face close to his, she asked, “When was the last time we had a holiday together, just the two of us?”

Wiping his tears, he gazed up into her sweet face.

Chapter Fourteen

Japanese Prime Minister Hashimoto Ochoa

Tea ceremony

One early morning, with luggage strapped to her belt, Ushaya checked the weather forecast. It showed partly cloudy with a few showers. That didn't matter, she thought. She would just fly above the clouds. Then she blazed a trail, westward, over the Pacific Ocean, at 5,000 miles an hour, passing through time zone after time zone, frightened in the dark, listening to her voice tracker. Finally, she arrived at midnight, an hour later, at the Takahama Garden Resort in Wakasa Bay.

She had never bowed so much in her entire life. First, she bowed to a couple walking in the streets, and then she bowed to bellhops and chauffeurs, standing in the circular driveway. She bowed to a lamppost and bowed to a stray cat on the sidewalk. She bowed to porters and to the front-desk clerks, before retiring to her penthouse suite on the third floor.

She chuckled at the Japanese self-cleaning toilet, while sitting on the throne, enjoying the jet streams and warm air, drying her bottom. She then removed the bathroom slippers from her feet, and donned another pair of slippers, and stepped out in her housecoat, floating down the hall. From high wooden beams to floral printed wallpaper, her entire suite was graced in simple Japanese designs, which she found most refreshing. She floated into the boudoir, where bamboo dividers, and rice paper shades and lanterns adorned the room, and, slipping between the sheets of her comfy bed, she slept the night away in dreamless sleep.

The morning sun filtered through the room, as she drew up the shades and pushed two windows open to breathe in the salty air. Little sailboats floated in the bay, as birds circled above. She dressed in a skirt and blouse, and wrapped a scarf around her head. With a pair of walking shoes and sunglasses on, she explored the grounds, passing beachside lounges, and came to the edge of the waters, lapping the seashore. She stood, gazing a long while, at the serenity all around her, before heading back to the resort. In the foyer, a female musician was playing a koto, a thirteen-stringed Japanese zither. She bowed to the musician and continued past the black couches and tall bamboo plants. She bowed one more time at the front desk clerks and porters, and pushed the elevator button to her floor.

By mid-afternoon, she was dressed in a kimono and sash, with a wooden pick through her coiffed hair. With her backpack on, she flew across the sky, and landed on the steps of the Oshu-Seki Imperial Tea House.

Hashimoto bowed deeply, and she bowed in return. He bowed and she bowed again. He was dressed in a hakama and long skirt over his kimono, with white socks on his feet, as he gestured her into the teahouse. She removed her silver sneakers, and entered. They washed their hands and rinsed their mouths, and soon were resting their knees upon takami mats, in front of a low-lying table.

In quiet contemplation, Hashimoto opened the ceremony by lighting the incense burner and pouring matcha tea into their cups. The ceremony was normally done in silence, yet he began to speak, "The Japanese are descendants of the hunter-gatherer Jomon tribe, 6,000 years ago. Out of the Yangtze Delta, China, in 200 BC, an alchemist and explorer by the name of Xu Fu, who we refer to as Jofuku, travelled to our islands, and introduced art and pottery and rice paddy fields to the Yayoi people of the time."

Fascinated with the history of Japan, she gazed at the ikebana flowers resting on the table, and said, "I understand your JAXA space agency collaborated with the University of Nairobi of Kenya, to launch your first outer-space satellite from the Japanese Experiment Module at the ISS."

Hashimoto brought forth meals of sweet wagashi on Oribe plates, and replied, "Yes, and I might add that three symbols of the Yayoi people still prevail today. They are the bronze mirror, the bronze sword, and the royal seal stone, with texts in the Kanji language, still not entirely deciphered.

There are numerous temples commemorating Xu Fu's achievements throughout Japan."

She asked, "May I hold your cup?" He nodded, motioning her.

She flung both teacups in the air, and on their descent, she caught them, matching velocity so deftly that they landed in her hands, without spilling a single drop. Then she placed them back on the table.

Staring in wonderment, he softly said, "Let us no longer talk about history, and certainly not WWII atrocities, or the Shogun warriors who ruled for 600 years, nor about politics, for that matter."

"Of course, we are in a sacred ceremony," she replied, adding, "Let's talk, instead, about cherry blossoms, that your country is so famous for." It turned into politics. Japan had increased forestation, but a longhorn beetle plagued cherry blossom trees, mired in policy and political errors.

She changed the subject and said, "Let's talk about fishing." It led to politics about dwindling harvests, due to overfishing, and sanctions against whaling.

"Let's talk about high-tech industries," she said. Due to political errors and lack of foresight, several industries were in decline, such as automotive, nonferrous metals, shipbuilding, textiles, and electronic equipment.

Ushaya set her teacup down and said, "Let's talk about your family."

He said, "My wife, Miyuki, and I have been happily married for thirty-three years, and we have one daughter, Kioko, who is in politics and . . ." he stopped talking and gazed at her. Then he got up and retrieved a GO board game from a shelf and set it on the table.

"Is this part of a traditional tea ceremony?" she asked.

He replied, "No, but there is nothing traditional about this ceremony."

"I don't how to play," she said.

"I will teach you," he said. He had once been a GO champion in his youth.

While examining black stones in a bowl, Ushaya picked one and laid it on the board. He made his move with a white stone. She dipped chopsticks into her meal, and made her next move with a black stone. They continued filling up the board, each expanding their territories, while invading the other, collecting liberties. Then she was in "atari," caught and captured, one stone after another, and his prisoner pile soon heaped up. Although, she had lost the match, he was impressed with the game.

She took a sip of tea and said, “It is time to fly.” They cleared up dishes and stored ritual items into cupboards.

Hashimoto loved his flip-top visors, which were outfitted with windshield wipers and made especially for him, courtesy of Stan. Dressed in his suit and vest, and Ushaya still in her kimono, they blazed a trail across grey skies, hinting of rain.

He catapulted into a series of acrobatic manoeuvres, navigating through city traffic lights, this way and that. The butterflies in his stomach moved to his throat, and, no longer able to find his voice or his body, suddenly, he flattened against a building wall. Ushaya scouted out corridors, left and right, and, like two Ninjas, they scaled up the tall building and flung high, landing on a rooftop.

As they leaned over a ledge, admiring the city views, she asked, “Do you agree the monster should be killed?”

He replied, “I do, we cannot wait for a spaceship to arrive,” and turning to her, said, “Have you noticed how Brad receives answers from his map, and Meg and Devon from Quazaik, and Ronald from the Gemball? Since Sulimon seeds grant a wish, perhaps it is the same with the twelve spheres.”

“I had never thought of that. You may be right,” she said, and, gazing at him, added, “I am nearing the end of my journey and I am tired. What advice do you have to help me succeed?”

Hashimoto quoted a passage from Lao Tzu:

“The Sage has no intention
So he cannot fail
Since he grasps nothing
Nothing is lost.

The Sage understands
People fail on the verge of success
So with that in mind
He is as diligent at the end as at the beginning.”

He looked at her, while leaning over the ledge, and said, “You must be proud that your kids are joining the assembly. The map and the Quazaik gem—their gifts are extraordinary.”

She smiled and said, "That I am."

"What are your plans for your stay?" he asked.

She replied, "I'd like to visit the Shungun-ji Temple, not far from here, and the Katsura Imperial Japanese Garden, and a monastery or two, if there is time." Checking her invisible watch, she added, "I shall visit the Sagano Bamboo Forest in Kyoto, before it closes at midnight."

Dark clouds gathered and raindrops sprinkled. Hashimoto flipped down his windshield wipers, swishing raindrops back and forth, and off they flew, heading for his palace. In ecstasy, he heard her call out, "If you had one wish in the whole world, what would that be?"

He answered, "Send the Fukushima nuclear waste from their meltdown fusion reactors onto rockets into space, past Pluto. It should be safe by then. It is ironic that our sun is nothing but a ball of nuclear explosions, feeding all life on earth."

"You have no more wishes?" she asked.

He glanced at her and said, "You only asked for one wish."

They blazed a trail through a maze of buildings and flew into the palace window, landing in his private quarters. With visors and hoods down, they silently bowed, and bowed again.

Yokuru! Yokuru!

Twinkling lights lit pathways through the Sagano Bamboo Forest when Ushaya came upon a crossroad and stopped. She was still dressed in her kimono, and had her silver sneakers on, and a backpack slung over her shoulders, when she met an old woman, dressed in a traditional Japanese kimono, gazing out from a nearby bridge. Sensing the Zone, she said, "Hello, my name is Ushaya. I am wondering which way to go."

The old woman smiled and said, "My name is Akemi. Either road leads somewhere."

Ushaya thanked her and began walking down one path, then turned and asked, "Is there a monastery worth visiting?"

Akemi replied, "A faraway Zen Buddhist monastery, called the Kinkaju Temple, is most worthy of a visit, but it is not open to the public. Perhaps, you should visit the nearby Nipon Temple." She wandered away, her silhouette disappearing into the forest.

A crescent moon was rising in the evening sky. Ushaya set a course for 200 miles east to the Kinkaju Temple, unsure of what to expect upon her arrival. She landed, crouched, on a wooden-arched bridge over a pond, connecting gardens to the temple grounds. Pagodas, lanterns, and decorative cloths hung throughout the pavilions. As she floated across the bridge, more and more monks began to surround her. Astonished to see her fly, they asked, "Who are you and why are you here?" Head Abbot Wu-pen came forward from the crowd of thirty monks, and bowed.

Thankful that they spoke in English, she bowed and said, "My name is Ushaya Landau, and I seek a gift for your leader." She eyed a nearby large boulder, and, picking up the rock, placed it in another spot on the grounds. Wiping her hands, she said, "There, much better aesthetics, don't you think?"

The monks whispered amongst each other, and Wu-pen nodded in approval. He summoned monk Genjo from the crowd, and they all followed him through a maze of corridors until they reached the inner temple. Genjo opened an old manuscript upon an altar, and said, "We come from the ancient Yayoi people. China's first emperor, Qin Shi Huangdi, sent Xu Fu, with his followers, to look for the elixir of life. The Qin Emperor wanted to become an immortal and live forever." He turned a page and continued, "They landed in Shingu and did not return to Qin. The farming techniques and knowledge, that Jofuku brought, improved the quality of life for our people. We are keepers of the Yayoi tradition."

Abbot Wu-pen brought forth a stone slab from its elaborate housing, and laid it on a wooden table. It was twelve inches tall and twelve inches wide. As they gathered around, he said, "The ancients discovered the Yokuru Tablet under the sacred Kiji Mountain. These glyphs have been only partially deciphered, and they remain a mystery to this day. We know the tablet is made of iron, uranium, aluminum, and titanium, but traces of unknown elements baffle our expert scholars, who wonder what gives it its deep-red colour." Ushaya marvelled at the golden glyphs, shining out from the deep-red tablet.

Monk Kiyoshi said, "Tonight we perform a sacred ceremony, 'Glory to Yokuru.' It happens every hundred years and you are welcome to join us."

Monk Nobu added, "It is written that if a winged messenger visits on this day, it is an auspicious sign."

The air bustled in subdued excitement, as they prepared for the ceremony. Large Taiko drums pounded in slow rhythmic beats. Monks swung incense burners back and forth, by their sides, as they paused at a bowl of water lilies on a pedestal to sprinkle water to bless the land and sky. They bowed to the bronze sword and mirror and the royal seal stone along their path. Wu-pen unwrapped the Yokuru Tablet and gave the cloth to monk Kiyoshi. With torches lit and drums beating, they began their procession across the bridge to the gardens, while Ushaya floated alongside them.

Suddenly, clouds formed and thunder clapped, and lightning struck the bridge, setting it on fire! Horrified, with mayhem everywhere, they ran in every direction, ducking under strewn pieces, flinging across the grounds, while fires raged across the wooden planks, which crumbled into the pond. Then the rains came.

The monks scrambled to their feet, and stood, transfixed, under the pouring rain, watching a red metallic bridge assemble across the pond, creaking and groaning with such frightful sounds. A piece of metal from the bridge fell to the ground, and Genjo picked it up and hid it in his robe. Thunderclouds dispersed from the sky, opening to twinkling stars and the crescent moon above. A mist rose from the bridge, and it was a sight to behold. Kiyoshi cried out, "Yokuru! Yokuru!"

While hiding in nearby bushes, Ushaya heard, "Psst." Startled, she turned around.

"Come this way," whispered Abbot Wu-pen, leading her back to the temple. From his robe, he brought forth the Yokuru Tablet and put it into her hands. "Take it," he said.

She refused at first. "It belongs to the temple."

He bowed and said, "The door has opened, and you must go through it."

Genjo was hiding behind a column, and was not pleased at what he had overheard, not pleased at all. Traditions going back thousands of years must remain the same, and now their most sacred object was being removed from the temple. He had studied his whole life, and for what? He peered inside his robe at the Yokuru fragment that fell from the bridge, and quietly slunk away.

Ushaya was flying across the night sky, her clothes still soaked from the rains, her hair streaming down her face, when she heard Ishtan's voice, "Good work. You have found the rare element to build a starship."

The following day, she called up Hashimoto and recounted her story of the Kinkaju Monastery. She then brought out the Yokuru Tablet, and softly said, "According to Ishtan, the bridge is made of spaceship material, just like this tablet. This is my gift for you, or should I say, a gift from the temple." There was silence.

Hashimoto gazed intently at the tablet, and said, "It is beautiful. I am not familiar with the glyphs. Do you think the Titan spaceship is in Japan?"

She lit a blowtorch and, blazing a stream of fire across its surface, the Yokuru Tablet remained intact and cool to the touch. "Perhaps," she replied.

"The bridge must be sealed off from outsiders."

"Agreed."

"You must take a private jet home."

She refused. "I can tuck Yokuru in my suitcase without the hassles of a long flight."

Ushaya's yellow eyes turned slanted, and her face morphed into some kind of dragon. Wondering if he was imagining things, Hashimoto quietly said, "Ushaya, thank you for our time together, it has been most extraordinary." And they ended their transmission. He sat back wondering a long time, when there was a familiar tap on the door. "Come in, my dear," he called out.

Miyuki entered with hot tea and biscuits, saying, "You have been buried in this room a while, and I thought you might like a break."

Hashimoto had forgotten to minimize the image on his desktop. Miyuki leaned in and asked, "Who is she?"

He answered with a white lie, "Stella Partridge has become high commissioner for the Japanese Embassy in Canada. I am scheduling a visit with Jerome to meet her." Miyuki happily went on about a family visit, coming soon. "Ah, yes," he said, placing his teacup down.

Days later, he summoned high officials, with the hard task of explaining the truth of their mission. General Satoshi Ito, from the Tenth Brigade, and astrophysicist Professor Yoki Fuji, both swore allegiance to the un-named secret organization. Soldiers were sent to seal off the perimeters of the monastery. Monks began revealing bits of their encounter with a lady in a kimono, and soon, each side was dropping clues of the covert operation, and both sides were equally amazed. Legends grew around the Yokuru Tablet, and reports leaked that the bridge would be removed for spaceship material and replaced by a wooden replica.

A week later, Jerome was gazing at Hashimoto and Ushaya across his screen, when he asked, "Is this true?" They both nodded, and he fired the reports across the globe. Then he added another entry in his laptop: "Spacesuits and now starships."

Summer barbecue

The day before the family arrived at Brad's place for a summer barbecue, Ushaya and Brad made a visit to old man Harvey, timing it just right, when Nurse Caroline would be away on errands. Harvey sat in his wheelchair, with the oxygen tank hissing rhythmically.

Brad held his bony hand and raised his voice, "I promised to introduce you to my mom, Ushaya."

Harvey shook her hand and said, "No need to holler, my friend. I have good ears."

He watched Ushaya tie leather straps around his legs and torso, and secure his oxygen tank to his wheelchair. With ropes attached to Brad, up, up, they gently glided into the sky, over suburban rooftops and farmers' fields and rolling hills. Harvey pulled the tubes from his nostrils and breathed in fresh air, excitedly pointing to a fox, running across the terrain. Brad pointed to a flock of starlings, circling a barn. Soon, they headed home, and whooshed through the door, landing back in the living room. Ushaya gave him some clover, leaving him with instructions on how to apply the magic leaves.

"Who are you?" asked Harvey.

"I do not know yet," she replied.

The following afternoon, they all gathered in Brad's backyard. Ushaya's grandkids Chelsea and Tyler greeted Harvey in his wheelchair. Meg and Brad set out food platters on tables, and steaks and corn sizzled on the grill, while Devon strummed tunes on his guitar. Everyone was happy to see each other. Into the evening, the adults became more inebriated, talking about their secret mission in cryptic ways. Ushaya began floating to the gardens, and Harvey stood up, pushing his wheelchair across the grass.

Tyler cried out, "Hey, you guys, are you seeing this?" Nobody seemed to care or even notice.

Chelsea whispered to Tyler, "Something strange is going on."

"Keep your eyes peeled," he whispered back, as they continued stoking their sticks in the fire pit.

While Brad was holding his map, a fiery ball blazed across the surface, landing in Alberta. He turned to the kids and asked, "Would you like a lesson in paleontology?"

Meg blew Quazaik from her hand and said, "Or, how about a lesson in aerodynamics." Devon continued strumming his guitar.

Tyler and Chelsea ran to the house, wondering if their sodas had been spiked with some kind of drug. They raced down the hall to Chelsea's bedroom, and pulled back the curtains, to the barbecue, and stared out. It was almost midnight when Nurse Caroline wandered into the fray, and, with locked arms, they all floated, disappearing into the gardens. Chelsea and Tyler glanced at each other in complete shock.

The following day, Tyler noticed cryptic words exchanged at the breakfast table. "Is your map OK? I thought it was on fire," said Devon.

"Just a piece of flying ember, it's all right," said Brad, knowing the kids had seen too much.

"My quartz crystal shone in the flames, did you notice?" Meg asked.

Tyler blurted, "We saw you levitate to the gardens."

"Even Harvey and Caroline, we saw you guys fly," added Chelsea.

Devon feigned surprise and said, "You must be seeing things. No one can levitate."

By that afternoon, Ushaya announced that she had to leave that day, as there were many things to do back home.

"Why can't you stay longer? You're retired," said Chelsea.

Devon looked up from Brad's map and replied, "Your grandma is going on a world cruise."

The family gathered in the living room, where Ushaya presented a gift to Chelsea: a gold locket on a delicate chain. Chelsea opened the clasp to a beam of radiant blue light, an ornamental keepsake that Stan had created. Everyone gasped.

Ushaya said, "This light has changed my life; it is a part of me. Whenever you need my help, all you have to do is call my name, and I will come for you."

Chelsea gave her a long hug and said, "Thanks, Grandma."

With a twinkle in her eye, while rummaging through her duffel bag, Ushaya said, “Now, let me see, what could a fourteen-year-old want?” Tyler stood by with a sheepish grin. Out came a motorized flying hoverboard. They watched him fly out the door, into the fields, with knees bent, as he glided over the pond, zipping here, there, and everywhere, before landing back on the front steps. “Where did you get this?” he asked, totally amazed.

Ushaya replied, “Stanislav the inventor, it’s a prototype. The patent is not out yet, so you must keep this a secret.” She winked at Meg and Devon. With luggage loaded into a waiting taxi, they waved at Ushaya and watched her drive away.

Days later, Ushaya picked up suits and gear from Stan’s place, for president Yaegar of Russia. By that evening, candles glowed throughout the house. She took a drag from her cigarette. With a red ribbon tied around Hashimoto’s scroll, and the Yokuru Tablet wrapped in cloth, she tucked them in the treasure chest.

While studying her naked body in the bathroom mirror, she saw two-foot dragon wings with webbed spikes, had grown out from either side of her spine. Her skin was turning scaly, and her jaw was protruding forward. Once again, her eyes turned yellow and narrowed into slits, staring out from the mirror. Mortified, she slammed back into the bathroom door, crying out, “What am I becoming?”

She fled naked to the living room, wondering if she was the one floating or if the new wings were guiding her. She turned off lamps and blew out candles, and returned to the bedroom, and slipped under the covers, with her wings folded tight. Ralph and Chloe were sound asleep by her side. The yellow in her eyes began to fade. Although she felt strong and healthy, and sound of mind, she still had not spoken to anyone about her dragon wings, not even Ishtan, who lay dormant by her bedside. Was she still in denial? Definitely, she thought. But tomorrow was a big day, the final leg of her journey—Russia.

Chapter Fifteen

Russian President Yaegar Volkov

Touchdown Vladivostok

She soared over the Bering Sea, taking frequent breaks, while listening to her voice tracker, through time zone after time zone, and finally landed in Vladivostok. The hotel looked like a spaceship, standing on steel legs. A hologram concierge greeted her, "Welcome to Hotel Galactic, please come this way." She followed the hologram through dimly lit hallways, passing space beams and futuristic architecture. Track lighting ran along the walls, and robotic gizmos buzzed in the air. The ceiling twinkled with the stars of the Milky Way. Her suite was no less amazing. All rooms were designed à la space modules, in cool bright lines against white and grey backgrounds, with sculptures suspended from ceilings.

Her wings had dried off from the shower, and, grateful that they no longer itched, she dressed in her housecoat and moved to the kitchen, to place an order on the large console. Out plopped a butterscotch ice cream cup with a spoon, and she floated to a round-shaped room with white walls, and slumped into a red couch to watch late-night Russian TV. Bleeps and commands sounded off: "Program is now over."

The slumber room came equipped with a glass-encased capsule, with luxurious bedding and crisp linen lining the walls. Climbing in, she set the wake-up time and pressed a button on the inside console, to a female voice, ringing out, "Initializing sequence, Beta four, deep space sleep." An arched dome slid over her pod, setting off oxygen mist. Lights turned off and the ceiling opened to a scene of stars, and she drifted into deep space sleep.

The following morning, she met president Yaegar at a nearby restaurant, as had been decided. He sported a man's wig, a brown moustache, and black-rimmed glasses, and was dressed in a long-sleeved, checkered shirt and brown blazer, looking like a scholar, to complete his disguise.

She wore shades and a kerchief tied under her chin; her lips were painted a dusty rose. She came dressed in beige velour, tight-fitting pants, dark brown, fashionable shoes, and a cream-coloured blouse, with a shawl draped around her shoulders. The ring glowed softly on her finger, and she wore a fancy bracelet on her right wrist. She looked like a movie star.

A waiter was about to pour water in their glasses when she whispered to Yaegar. With raised brows, he asked the waiter to fill only a quarter of the glasses, and no ice cubes. Soon, small bowls of warm, sweet kasha, and plates with boiled quail eggs and fresh fruit appeared in front of them.

While digging into her fruit, she asked, "It's August here, yet cool for summertime. Can't you do better than this?"

Yaegar spooned into his kasha and replied, "We have been busy on the western front with a stimulus package for annexed Cermia, to integrate the people into the Russian way of life. After this, I will get right onto your request."

She cut into a boiled egg and said, "There are many sanctions against your country. What impact is that having?"

"Are you a reporter?" he asked.

"What we speak of will not go into my report," she replied.

"Politics are messy, Ushaya."

"Indeed."

He said, "I am pleased with the growth of our GDP. We have reduced poverty by half in our country, and of course, we continue with our efforts."

She said, "And I also commend you on your efforts to end the Syrian war. I assume this strategy has helped Russia secure a greater presence in the Middle East."

"That it has," he replied, "But more work needs to be done for the Syrian people. Our Russian special forces continue to provide arms, training and protection against rebel militants. We have China, Iraq, Saudi Arabia and Belarus, and several other countries in support of our war efforts. However, our actions draw disfavour among our western allies."

She nodded and said, “I understand, you are the world’s largest exporter of natural gas and a big producer of petroleum.”

He spooned in a mouthful of blueberries and said, “Since the breakup of the Soviet Union, the state has taken over the oil and gas industries, and we have encouraged enterprise by reducing taxes on profits, benefitting our country.”

She took a sip of water and said, “Great accomplishments. And I understand that Russia will be launching Soyuz MS-13 spacecraft on its first mission to the ISS in 2020, is that right?”

“We are looking forward with great anticipation,” he replied.

Ushaya continued, “You have some of the world’s best cyber intelligence. I heard that some prestigious hacker units had fallen out of favour with the US, due to interference in Ronald’s election campaign, resulting in loss of diplomatic posts in the US, and the inability for Ronald to lift sanctions.”

Yaegar waved his hand and said, “Russian hackers did not interfere in their elections; this is just hearsay, to destabilize the relationship between our two countries.”

She changed the subject and asked, “Why come down so hard on peaceful protestors? Your people no longer have the freedom to express their views. What are you afraid of?”

He dabbed his mouth with a napkin and replied, “Large-scale demonstrations, opposing the very fabric of our constitution, are not acceptable. There is a real and present danger of mass unrest, turning into chaos and anarchy.”

“You fear a loss of power, which is understandable,” she said.

He forked into his quail egg and said, “What would your government do, if millions protested in the street under Jerome’s leadership? I am sure, he would bring in the army to restore order.”

She finished the last of her delicious kasha and said, “Well, if you listen to the people during times of peaceful demonstrations, you have a better chance of a win-win situation. But if you let the storm waters overflow the bridge, you can be sure there will always be a rebellion on your hands.” The ring glowed softly on her finger when she asked, “Do governments rule or do they serve?”

Yaegar replied, “Both, where appropriate.” He spooned the last mouthful of his kasha and sat back, dabbing his mouth, before he continued, “We are redefining what it means to be Russia, not the least, by observing what works and does not work in other political systems. Discarding values that do not uphold the national sentiment, while embracing emerging new markets toward capitalism and trade, is what we strive for."

"What constitution do you speak of, an emerging form of Communism?" she asked.

"An emerging something new," he replied, glancing at the ring glowing brightly on her finger.

Ushaya dabbed her mouth and concluded, "I thank you for our candid discussion. Let us no longer talk politics."

"I think you would make a good spy," he said.

She glanced at her invisible watch and said, "Too dangerous for me. So, shall we fly?" They clinked their empty glasses in a toast.

Soon, they were cruising at 300 miles an hour, dressed in their suits, hanging onto ropes, passing over cities and towns, gliding over the Trans-Siberian train clacking along the railway tracks. Up, up, into the sky, they continued their flight over plateaus, valleys, and winding rivers, toward the Sikhote-Alin Mountains.

A cool customer, Ushaya thought, but Yaegar was clearly enjoying the ride. He pointed to a Siberian tiger, running across the field. She pointed to a bear, fishing in the river. He pointed to a valley below, and asked, "Could we land here? I have been in these parts." Three, two, one, and they landed ecstatically, throwing off their hoods and visors. He twirled his hands in the air and gushed, "Do you ever tire of flying?"

She chuckled and said, "Never. The scene is always changing."

Yellow field flowers carpeted the valley floor, and a river wound its way on their right. He led her over rocks and dried moss, toward the forest, recounting his tales of adventure. "I once caught a big pike in this very river," he began. "And while riding horseback through the forest, I once encountered a lynx, and a big cat it is." Careful not to step on mushrooms peeking up through the forest floor, he dipped his head under lichen that clung to overhung branches, and whispered, "Do you have binoculars?"

She handed him binoculars.

He pointed and said, "There, a speckled guillemot bird, on the rock. It's far from the sea, where it normally inhabits," and he gave back the binoculars.

Ushaya peered in and said, "I didn't know you enjoyed bird watching." Suddenly, a wild boar broke out from the bushes, squealing, hoofing rapidly to their left. They stood back, looking at each other. Rustling in the leaves, a leopard appeared, staring at them.

"Huh!" she recoiled.

"Shhh," he whispered. The leopard sprang into the forest, stealthily hunting its prey.

When the danger had passed, they climbed onto a boulder. She pulled out two flasks filled with kompot, and asked, "If you had one wish, what would that be?"

He took a swig from his flask and replied, "To expedite clean-up of our water systems, filled with chemicals, due to Soviet-era dumping, and to reduce deforestation, due to aggressive logging, resulting in soil erosion. And I wish that all hospitals would have indoor plumbing and running water."

In disbelief, she asked, "No plumbing and running water?"

He sighed and said, "It's a national disgrace, and I aim to rein in our billionaire oligarchs, to chip in toward infrastructures around the country." He ended with a final wish, "We must find a new form of energy to get into space. Our Soyuz spacecraft has been operating for decades, but we cannot continue to burn fossil fuels alone. It is an inefficient way to travel, and at huge costs to the environment."

Ushaya looked down in contemplation and said, "Let me get this straight: indoor plumbing for everyone, and a new form of energy that gets us into space?"

They jumped off the rock, and Yaegar plucked a tiny purple flower from the woodland floor. Giving it to her, he said, "From one nature enthusiast to another."

"Thank you." She smiled and tucked the little flower into her lapel.

Elixir

The following morning, Ushaya soared in the cool air for 900 miles, reaching the Stanovoy valleys, where she lit down fifteen minutes later, in an alpine meadow. While relaxing among the wildflowers, she pondered his words: "It's a national disgrace, I aim to improve infrastructures around the country." Her phone rang. It was Jerome, and she answered, "Hello?"

He said, "You must follow protocol. You did not check in when you first arrived. I heard it through Yaegar."

"My apologies, I got distracted," she said. Suddenly, winds picked up, and staring at a massive tornado, funnelling down the valley, she said, "Jerome, I've got to go. A tornado is heading my way," and she hung up.

It was a rare sight in these parts. She could fly away, she thought, but this was her chance to test the golden sliver. She rapidly spread out the sliver, stretching it this way and that, until she was wrapped into a cocoon, waiting, wondering if she could survive a tornado. Howling winds grew louder, as the tornado sucked up all objects along its path, and suddenly, whoosh! She lifted, swirling among trees, rocks, and dust. Shaking up and down like a washing machine, she cried out, "Ahhhhhhh . . ." Not a soul heard her cries, and while spinning round and round, she had a revelation . . . and a moment of peace washed over her.

Then, spiralling downward, she hit the ground hard. THUD! Coughing and spluttering, she steadily rose to her feet, as the tornado raged down the valley, fading into the distance. She peeled off the sliver from her body, realizing it had protected her, for there was not a dent in the material. And rolling it between her fingers, until it became a tiny sliver, she placed it into her vest pocket. With a half-joke smile, she said to herself, *I'm no longer in Kansas, but where am I*?

She looked around, finding herself on a large block of granite, rising 600 feet from the earth's floor. There were no birds, no wind, no insects, no sound, nothing. Around the perimeters stood tall, dead trees, and mountains rose into jagged limestone peaks, covered in a light dusting of snow. As she staggered across the mesa, she came upon a fifty-foot round pool, filled with a liquid mercury kind of substance. The smell of ozone and strange chemicals wafted in the air, and she wondered what it was. Certainly, it did not look like ordinary water, she thought. Then she remembered the words of Swami Gupta: "Beware the crystal pool. It is dangerous. Do not enter."

She descended to the ground and broke off a twelve-foot dead branch, and landed back on the mesa. Slowly, she dipped the branch into the liquid, farther and farther, until six inches were left in her hand. When she pulled up, there was nothing left, just the stump! It had simply eaten the rest, like quicksand, with no ripples at all. The entry point turned blue, then back to silver.

She thought, *How odd—some kind of elixir of sorts*. She threw the stump into the pool and flew to the mesa floor, and broke off a thirty-foot dead branch, and tried again. Down, down into the liquid it went, until six inches remained in her hand. She pulled up, and the rest was gone! This time, she laid the stump on the granite surface, and had an idea.

While chipping away at the granite rock with her pickaxe, she lifted a slab, and slowly dipped it into the pool, and then slowly brought it back up. The liquid dripped off the stone slab, leaving a white ash film, but it did not destroy the rock. She laid the slab on the granite surface, next to the dead tree stump, wondering why this place had not been discovered before. All she knew was that she dared not touch it! Pondering upon the liquid substance, she decided to call it Elixir.

Ishtan's voice BOOMED in her head, "Good work, Ushaya. You have found the third Master Titan. The ring has cloaked the pool for centuries, but as you stand before him, he can now reveal himself safely. He is the fuel from our universe to yours, and the map holds the coordinates. The tornado was a powerful creature." All became silent.

Stunned, she immediately soared back to Vladivostok, searching for a hardware store in the downtown core. When she entered a shop, a middle-aged clerk with large breasts upon a large frame greeted her. "*Ya mogu vam chem-nibud' pomoch*?" asked the clerk. (May I help you?)

Through her voice translator, Ushaya inquired, "I am looking for a glass jar and a metal lid. It has to be a metal lid."

Amused at a customer in a grey suit, with a backpack, holding a strange device in her hand, thinking, she was one of those "weird ones," the clerk responded in English, "You wish a glass jar and metal lid?"

"Yes, and tongs and a long metal ladle," Ushaya said. "And a steel case and chain, please."

"We should have these things, let's see," the clerk replied. She led her down one aisle after another, and while placing items into a cart, asked, "Where do you come from?"

"BC, Canada," she replied.

"I have relatives in BC, descendants from Doukhobors. They are a little crazy, but good people," said the clerk, and, leaning closer, she whispered, "They are into all sorts of things, if you know what I mean."

"Is that so?" said Ushaya, glancing at her.

"Perhaps you might know them," said the clerk.

"Regrettably, I do not," she said. She paid for her purchases, and, thanking the clerk, left the shop.

The clerk shook her head, muttering. "*Vy vstrechayete vse vidy, dazhe v Kanade*." (You meet all kinds, even in Canada.)

Ushaya returned the following morning to the Stanovoy Mesa. While floating above the pool, with tongs grasping the glass jar, she carefully spooned in Elixir with the ladle. Then she landed on the granite surface and screwed the lid tight. This would be the litmus test, she thought. She held her breath and turned Elixir upside down, and . . . nothing happened. Relieved, she turned the jar upright.

With not a shake or a tremor, she soared across the skies, with the jar of Elixir and the tree stump and granite slab in the steel case, chained to her wrist, wondering where she had gotten the steely focus. But one thing was for sure. She was holding the most dangerous substance known to mankind. How were they going to unlock its secrets? Perhaps Yaegar would find the answer. Back at the hotel, placing Elixir upon a metal pan, as a precaution, she wondered, *How am I going to bring Elixir safely back to Canada? Hmm, he is a male, according to Ishtan.*

There were two calls to make, the first to Jerome. She recounted her story of the tornado and the Kunfu sliver that protected her. She went on about Ishtan's telepathic communiqué, and also, about a gift she had found for Yaegar, but did not reveal what it was. "You will have to wait until we send in our reports. I was just touching base to say I am OK," she said. They hung up, and the next call was to Yaegar.

He gazed across the screen and smiled, "How is your day so far?"

She shoved a jar in front of the screen, and replied, "I have found something. Meet Elixir." She recounted the tornado and the Kunfu suit and the Elixir pool. She recounted her telepathic encounter with Ishtan, and the hardware store. Then she showed the dead tree stump, explaining that only metals survive, and organic substances do not.

Yaegar said, “Try a piece of cloth, and see what that does.” She returned from the kitchen with a towel in her hand, and he snorted, “The whole towel can’t go in the jar.”

“It will dissolve, just watch,” she replied, and slowly dipped the towel into Elixir, until only a fragment was left in her hand. He observed the liquid turn from blue to silver, and was amazed. She dipped a plastic spatula into the Elixir jar, and then pulled up the remaining tip. The rest had dissolved.

“Try a metal object,” he suggested.

She returned with a stainless-steel fork and dipped it as far as she could go, and then pulled up. The fork, lined with a silver coating of Elixir, remained intact. She placed the fork next to the spatula and towel remnant on the pan. As long as they rested on a metal surface, they were safe. “What is this stuff?” she cried out, and, lowering her voice, “According to Ishtan, it is the fuel that will get you into space. There’s much more where this comes from. It’s my gift for you.” There was silence.

Then Yaegar said, “You will not travel back to Canada on your own. Stand by for more details,” and they hung up.

In deep contemplation, he calmly picked up the phone and dialled two loyal comrades to immediately join him in a high-security Kremlin meeting, instructing them to clear their schedules of all obligations for the next week. Neither of the comrades had met each other before.

Several hours passed, then Kapitan Nadiya Isankova walked in, Yaegar’s trusted confidante and an ace pilot with the Russian Aerospace Defence Forces. She was an attractive woman in her thirties with bright blue eyes, long eyelashes, and short brown, stylish hair, dressed in a smart-looking blazer and white blouse, and high-heeled shoes. Nadiya and Yaegar shook hands and sat down.

Viktor Smirnov, minister of energy and mines, entered the room. He was a tall stocky man in his mid-fifties, wearing spectacles, holding a briefcase in one hand, dressed in a dark-blue suit and matching tie, and shiny black shoes. All three shook hands and sat down.

Shuffling papers on his desk, Yaegar had the hard task of explaining the reason for their meeting. With folded hands, he began, “Let’s start from the beginning . . .” Several hours later, Nadiya and Viktor silently saluted each other in the hallway, with not a word between them, before they went their separate ways.

Ushaya continued writing her reports, ordering in meals, while observing Elixir. She had come to the end of the circuit, at last, and with suitcases packed, she went to bed for a good night's rest.

Game of Skolgi

The following morning, a small Il-86 jet plane waited in empty fields, 400 miles north of Vladivostok, to take her home. Dressed in her grey suit, with suitcases by her side, and a metal box chained to her right wrist, she descended to the ground and introduced herself to Nadiya and Viktor, "*Menya zovut Ushaya Landau. Ya ochen' rad poznakomit'sya s vami.*" (My name is Ushaya Landau. I am very pleased to meet you.)

Nadiya and Viktor shook her hand and took the suitcases on board, glancing at each other, before closing the hatch. Soon, the engines roared and they were airborne. Fully aware of the cargo she was carrying, Nadiya was instructed to fly straight as an arrow, with no fancy manoeuvring. When the plane had settled into autopilot, she joined Ushaya and Viktor, who were chatting in the lounge. Plates of borodinsky bread, cottage cheese, chopped apple, nuts, and raisins were set upon the table, along with pitchers of kvass.

Nadiya and Viktor spoke in English, and enjoying a hint of Russian accent, Ushaya cheekily piped up, "I hear that Russian is one of the hardest languages in the world to learn. Does that mean the Russian people are difficult?"

Viktor stared into his drink and replied, "Complicated, but not difficult."

Nadiya took a sip of kvass and said, "I might add English is also difficult."

"So, we both are difficult," said Viktor wryly. Their glasses clinked, breaking the icy mood, and lively conversations ensued, in which they learned much about each other. Nadiya had a twin sister, whom she adored. Viktor was born in Ukraine and grew up with seven brothers. They were fascinated with Ushaya's tales, watching her float about the lounge, with the ring shining on her finger.

Viktor asked, "Where is Elixir?"

Ushaya placed the steel case on the table and sat down. They stared at the case. Yaegar gave strict orders not to open it; after all, if something should go wrong . . .

Ishtan's voice BOOMED in their heads, in a telepathic communiqué, "The ring's cloaking powers are protecting you." There was no denying it. Each heard his deep, calm voice. Bewildered, they looked at each other and began communicating in Silo.

Viktor clearly heard Ushaya's thoughts and pulled out family photos, proudly showing them around. In Silo, Nadiya nodded to Ushaya, who obeyed her request and disappeared into the cockpit, and they were amazed. They all sat back down in the lounge, staring at the case, and were tempted to open it, but shook their heads, nervously chuckling. Engines droned across the sky when Nadiya returned to the cockpit to check the navigation instruments. After landing at a secret base in the Koryak Range to fuel up, they pushed on, over the Bering Sea.

To pass the time, Viktor brought out a board game, called Skolgi, a game of luck, wit, and strategy, using twenty trump cards and forty common cards. Sixty-four squares moved in a spiral on the board, ending at the centre. The point of the game was to be the first to reach the centre. One could only pull three trump cards in a game, so one chose them carefully. They usually contained beneficial instructions, but not always. The common cards indicated the amount of moves to make on the board.

Each square had instructions, like 'move two spaces forward' or "Move four spaces back," which could be helpful to the player or not. Every square gave three choices: obey the command, draw a trump card, or decline the move, in which case, the player would go back three spaces. This may be the best strategy, depending on where they were on the board.

Viktor and Ushaya set their pawns at the top square of the spiral and flipped a five-ruble coin. Whoever got the two-headed Eagle started first. Viktor got the eagle and pulled a "No. 7" from the common deck, and, counting seven squares, placed down his pawn. The instruction read, "Move one space forward."

Ushaya drew a "No. 1" common card and placed her pawn on the first square. The instruction read, "Move ten spaces forward." "I'm off to a good start," she smiled.

"The game has only begun," said Viktor.

They played this move and that move, and, an hour later, Viktor won. They played again, and he won again. They played a third time, and Nadiya won.

At last, their jet landed on the ridge, before Ushaya's front yard. The Ring of Power cloaked their aircraft to ensure safe passage of the deadly Elixir fuel. No wind or atmospheric disturbance was detected when they disembarked. Viktor and Nadiya were stretching their legs, soaking in the beauty all around, when Ralph and Chloe raced down the driveway, smothering them with sloppy kisses. Together, they walked up the driveway and met Ishtan the carpet, who was waiting at the door. Ushaya placed the steel case down by her side, and asked, "So, how were Ralph and Chloe?"

"A mighty handful, I would say," he replied.

She smiled and said, "Welcome to having pets."

In awe of a walking, talking carpet shimmering in the doorway, Nadiya and Viktor shook hands with Ishtan's fringes. In Silo, Ishtan replied, "My pleasure, also. Thank you for returning Ushaya and Elixir safely." He brought the luggage into the house, with Ralph and Chloe following.

Ushaya wrapped Nadiya and Viktor's arms into hers, and announced, "Time for a fly-about. Hang on tight." Up, up, airborne, they cruised a hundred miles an hour over mountaintops, descending through mists of cloud into the valley below, whizzing past forests, weaving along dried-up riverbeds and abandoned mining outposts and railway tracks, covered in overgrown grass.

With a broad smile, Nadiya cried out, "Isn't this glorious?"

Terrified, almost speechless, hanging on for dear life, with his tie flapping in the wind, Viktor replied, "Yes, quite wonderful."

They headed back to the ridge at the end of Ushaya's property, where Nadiya and Viktor entered their aircraft, under cloak. Ushaya stepped away, saluting, "Welcome to the assembly." She listened to their engines silently whir into the sky.

Neighbour Emily Barker peered through her curtains, observing Ushaya dressed in some suit, bowing to thin air, and wondered what was going on with her.

Give me that damn thing!

One October morning, on her way to the kitchen, Ushaya stopped before Chloe and Ralph, who were lounging on the couch. Eight months old, and adorable as they were, Ushaya announced, "All this flying is making you fat and lazy. From now on, we're getting our daily exercise." Ralph jumped off the couch, stretching his legs, and wagging his tail excitedly. But Chloe revolted. She had grown into a large, grey-white Maine Coon cat, with yellow diagonal eyes and tall, upright ears, emitting wisps of stray hairs. Ushaya gazed at her most beautiful cat, and put a harness on her, and dragged that Chloe out the door for their morning walk, along the ridge pathway. Romping freely among glorious autumn leaves, turning crimson and orange, and while sniffing this tree and that tree, Ralph raised his leg for a pee. Chloe walked trepid along the dirt path, clearly annoyed, shaking the mud from her paws.

The mist rose up the mountainside, and the air smelled so fresh. Sunday morning church bells rang in the valley below, calling out to the faithful in communion and prayer. Ushaya began to miss her mother and father, who had passed away many years before, and reminiscing upon precious memories, growing up with her siblings, she began to understand the love and sacrifices her parents had endured, during their lifetimes. Church bells continued ringing, calling out to her soul's longing for answers about the Blue-ray light.

The following day, Ushaya dropped Ralph and Chloe off at Wally's place, her gardener down the street, and instructed him that they must get their daily exercise, and then she left. Wally noticed strange things going on when he put out the garbage by the curb. Chloe sprung out from his second floor window, and over the neighbour's rooftop, like a flying squirrel, and soon appeared, purring, around his legs. He was surprised and yet relieved.

Ralph escaped from the house, sniffing through a pile of dead leaves in his front ditch. Digging in the soil with his front paws, he dragged out something the old gardener had long ago lost and forgotten about, and, strutting about the yard, with his head held high, the dog held the precious object in his mouth.

Wally said, "Good boy, now drop it." Chasing him up the street, he hollered, "Give it to me!" The whole neighbourhood witnessed the commotion. Emily glanced out her window. Helen Chu stared out her window from the upper ridge. A young couple stopped raking their leaves, and children stopped playing road hockey, as he ran by, hollering, "GIVE ME THAT DAMN THING! JUST DROP IT!" One wondered who was getting the most exercise.

Prowling about Emily's yard, Chloe caught a large rat in her claws, and then let it go. Stunned, the rat scampered into the bushes. Emily gathered her yappy Mimi in her arms and stared out the window, but saw nothing.

Final preparations

One mid-October day, Jerome ordered a conference call to finalize preparations for the assembly meeting. One by one, the leaders tuned into their screens, and soon, lively conversations went back and forth. They had agreed to meet at the end of October, during Halloween. Issues over security, computer setups, and the place of rendezvous were resolved. They would meet at the Liebschon Estate in Germany, one of Irena's properties that rarely hosted dignitaries, and all employees of the estate would be given a one-month holiday. They discussed coming incognito, and how to get away for four days without anyone knowing their whereabouts, under oath of secrecy and media blackout. Yaegar of Russia had secured hotel and limousine reservations, and Mimbauwe had decided on which African masks to bring to the occasion.

Irena agreed to provide most items, such as, food, flowers, cutlery, tables and chairs, and electronic equipment. Submissions poured in from around the world to gather the finest elite forces to destroy the monster. They agreed that Lucy would join as a member. They also agreed on a name for their secret organization—the Lazantis Project, code name TLP—and, one by one, they signed off.

A week later, Ushaya called Jerome, her voice barely audible, "I discovered something about the spheres after my visit with Hashimoto," she said, and quietly whispered Hashimoto's idea.

"Really? Anything I desire?" he asked.

"Yup," she said, nodding. And they hung up.

It was a chilly October morning when Ushaya arrived at Stan's place. A number of items lay on his coffee table. He opened lids from two narrow wooden boxes, each scooped with six round holes, lined with green felt, to hold the twelve spheres. Locks were bolted on the outside of each box, and he placed the two keys in her hand.

Next, he picked up a titanium cube for Elixir, and said, "This can only be opened by three sequenced moves. If done correctly, you will hear a click and the lid will slide off." He pointed inside the chamber, and said, "Place the jar in here. Then you must reverse the sequence to close the lid. Now you practice."

It was an impossible task, Ushaya thought, because there were no distinguishing marks across its smooth surface.

"Look closer," said Stan, guiding her.

She practiced over and over, opening and closing the cube to get the sequence right. Then she exclaimed, "I got it!"

He brought forth a brown sheath with magnetic flaps, asking, "Did you bring the dagger?" She pulled it from her pack, and they hushed in awe at its beauty. Carefully, he wrapped the sheath around it, explaining where the magnetic flaps attached.

Lucy picked up a steel tube by its handle, and laying it in Ushaya's hands, said, "This is for Ishtan the carpet." She continued, "On the keypad, are 100 characters from a mix of world languages. You are to punch in three sequences, each ten characters long." Lucy then gave her a piece of paper with the codes. Another impossible task, thought Ushaya, staring at glyphs and strange symbols on the keypad, and she glanced at her paper list.

"You have to memorize the codes before you leave," said Lucy.

Stan waved his hand and said, "Cut her some slack. Remember, she is mortal."

A week before their assembly meeting, disaster struck! Stan broke his leg in two places when he fell off a ladder, attempting to change a light bulb on the front deck. The ambulance came and dispatched him to the nearest hospital, and a complicated surgery followed. The surgeons were not sure how well his leg would heal. Recuperating back home a few days later, he feared he would not be able to join the assembly.

Immediately, Ushaya flew to Stan's place with a box of chocolates and some clover, and Lucy let her in. Stan was wheeling around in a wheelchair, in great pain, popping pills, with his right leg stretched out, held with pins. She set to work, plastering clover upon his leg, and said, "This ought to do it," instructing him to change clover bandages in twenty-four hours.

Feeling some relief, and wishing her well on her journey, Stan said, "Godspeed. I shall tune in by satellite."

She assured him, "Don't worry, you will be up in no time. I will see you both at the assembly," and she flew back home. Miraculously, his leg began to heal within days, to the surprised surgeons, as he hobbled about with his cane. The leaders cheered, ensuring a jet plane would be waiting for him.

Meanwhile, Meg and Devon pulled the drawstring cloth that held Quazaik, and placed the gem in a metal box. Brad rolled up his map and carefully placed it in a tube. Stan packed his suitcases, with the help of Lucy. Ushaya lowered the Elixir jar into the titanium chamber and locked the cube with a carrying chain. Examining the gifts one last time, to ensure they were neatly arranged, she covered them with a heavy cotton cloth, and locked the treasure chest and hid the key.

Then she went down her list, "Bills paid. Check.

"Clover pot. Check.

"Ropes, vests, suits, goggles, and gloves. Check.

"Laptop and agendas. Check.

"Dead branch, ladle, chainsaw, air gun, and blowtorch. Check."

That evening, Ushaya had just dried off after a shower, when she called out to Ishtan. He soon arrived, floating before the open bathroom door. With yellow eyes and protruding jaw, she pointed to her wings and said in a deep, throaty voice, "What are these?"

"You are becoming a young Tanzoik, learning how to shape-shift," Ishtan replied, and floated back down the hall.

Wrapped in her housecoat, she whisked down the hall and stopped him dead in his tracks, and with piercing eyes, commanded in a hoarse voice, "Time to wrap you up." Soon, Ishtan's bindings were secured and he was placed in a metal tube, locked in with combination codes. As she lay in bed that night, it was a long while before the yellow faded from her eyes.

Chapter Sixteen

The Assembling (Day One)

Incognito

End of October . . .

US Captain Trevor Kelly, a fresh recruit from Air Force One, landed his jet plane in Mexico. Aged thirty-five, slightly overweight with a stocky five-foot-eight frame, he wore his uniform and a cap over short-cropped blonde hair, with a silver stud in his right ear. An amiable sort of fellow he was, talkative, bright, and ambitious, and most important, a loyal companion to Ronald.

President Carlos boarded the plane with an unkempt wig and beard, wearing sunglasses and beaded necklaces. He wore a tie-dyed shirt and headband and baggy pants, and sandals upon his feet, looking like an old-time hippy.

Next pit stop was Andrews Air Force Base in Washington, to pick up Ronald. With his trench coat and gloves, shades, black shoes, and a crew-cut salt-and-pepper wig and a pencil-thin moustache, he looked like a high-class gangster. He turned to Trevor and said, "Good to see you," and turning to Carlos, he said, "You look ridiculous."

Carlos chortled. "So do you."

Ushaya and Stan were waiting with their suitcases on the ridge, at the edge of her property, when Captain Trevor landed the jet, cloaked under the ring's power. He stepped out and nervously shook their hands, and said, "I am honoured to meet you; at your service."

Emily stared out her window, wondering who these people were, with a pile of luggage, sitting at the end of Ushaya's driveway. Mimi yapped uncontrollably on the couch. She went over to pick up her doggy, and returned to the window, and by then, they were all gone. Where did the suitcases go?

Stan came as himself, no need for disguise, with his white goatee, blue-tinted shades, and long white hair neatly combed across his shoulders. A white silk scarf draped over a two-piece beige suit, trimmed with silver edgings, and he wore pointed lapels and silver cufflinks. Exuding elegance and flair, he walked up the ramp, holding onto a dragon's head cane, with Lucy by his side.

Ushaya walked up the ramp, smartly dressed in a maroon-coloured jacket and skirt, and shiny, low-heeled loafers, with her hair tucked under a grey-coiffed wig, wearing sunglasses and holding a briefcase.

They continued east, landing in Manitoba, to pick up Brad and his map. Old man Harvey became a wiser old man. Clover had cured the disease from his lungs, and he no longer needed the oxygen tank, and had begun walking again. Nurse Caroline had given up her nursing job and moved in with Harvey. They waved at Ushaya and Brad, who disappeared under the cloak. From the nearby field, dead brown grasses swayed under the loud roar of a plane, lifting in the sky.

Next stop was Ottawa International Airport, VIP wing, to pick up Jerome. While the plane refuelled, Jerome turned to Brad and said, "You didn't come in disguise."

Brad shrugged, replying, "Nah, not doing that shit."

"Oh, you rebel," said Ronald, slapping his back.

Carlos snickered at Jerome.

Jerome glared up and down at Carlos, and said, "You look ridiculous."

"So do you," snorted Carlos. Trevor and Ushaya stifled a cough.

Jerome shot a glance at Ronald, and said, "You look marvelous, my dear."

"What can I say?" replied Ronald, pulling off his gloves.

Jerome stumbled up the ramp in high-heeled shoes and nylon stockings, wearing a floral dress with ample bosom, and a blonde, wavy wig, and heavy make-up upon his shaven face. He entered the plane, and away they flew, across the ocean to Berlin.

Captain Jagpal was stationed in New Zealand when he got the call. Meg, prepared for cool weather, dressed in a pair of black slacks, runners, and a turtleneck sweater. She wore sunglasses and a long curly black wig, to complete her disguise. Devon dressed in casual pants, a shirt and jacket, and wore an eye-patch over his left eye, plus a cropped beard and a brown-coloured man wig.

"May I take some pictures?" asked Jagpal, and the camera clicked away. They continued over Australia, over Sumatra and the Bay of Bengal, and landed at the Delhi Airport, to refuel and pick up Yadgiri. Disguised as Sherlock Holmes in a tweed suit, with an Inverness cape and deerstalker hat, Yadgiri boarded the plane, holding a gentleman's pipe. Jagpal hardly recognized him in heavy makeup, with his beard now tinted brown.

"Nice to see you, Jagpal," said Yadgiri, and, turning to Meg and Devon, said, "What an honour to meet you, at last." He kissed Meg's outstretched hand and warmly embraced Devon. The kids chuckled at Yadgiri's disguise. Jagpal raised his camera, but Yadgiri refused. "No pictures please."

Their plane touched down at a private landing strip just outside Riyadh. In walked Prince Muzaffar, disguised as a Jewish rabbi, garbed in a black top hat, black business suit, and striped tie, with a full grey beard, hiding his own. With thick eyebrows and round spectacles, he held a book in his right hand. He insisted on group pictures, and while they gathered around, the camera clicked away. They soared across the Mediterranean Sea and over Eastern Europe, toward Berlin.

Meanwhile, Kapitan Nadiya Isankova was stationed in Japan, when she got the call. She bowed to Hashimoto and said, "I am honoured to meet you." They pushed on to Beijing to pick up Zhangwei, then across the tundra to Moscow, to refuel and pick up Yaegar. As they soared over Belarus and Poland, they sat back sipping sake, courtesy of Hashimoto's private stock.

Zhangwei wore a pointed bamboo coolie hat, a white peasant shirt, and a pair of black cotton pants. He wore sandals on his feet, and held a sickle in his left hand, looking like a farmer rice picker. A happy face Chinese mask completed his disguise. Hashimoto sat in his "ninja-yoroi" outfit, totally swathed in black, from his soft shoes up to his hood, carrying a katana sword across his back. Yaegar wore a bald cap and handlebar moustache, beige leggings, laced-up boots, a tight black-and-red singlet, and a bulging jockstrap under compression shorts, looking like a professional wrestler. The three leaders raised their glasses in a toast.

German General Leopold Reiner landed his plane on a private airstrip outside Kigali. Stepping out, he shook hands with Mimbauwe, and said, "Nice to meet you," trying not to stare. Mimbauwe was dressed in dreadlocks, a pair of shades with gold chains around his neck, and flashy rings on each finger. He wore tight black pants and a colourful vest, and polished brown shoes, and was disguised as an aging rap star. They soared northbound over Chad and Algeria, and all of Europe, before finally landing in the VIP wing at London City Airport.

Leopold saluted, trying not to laugh. Queen Julia walked up the ramp wearing an eighteenth-century frock over a long, buttoned dress, appearing as a middle-aged African housemaid for a rich cotton plantation owner. Her face was covered in black soot under a grey-coiffed African wig. A teacup, saucer, and creamer were glued to a tray in her left hand, completing her disguise.

Prince Herb wheeled up the ramp dressed as an old-time American cowboy, in a deerskin vest and canvas pants, and a red-checkered shirt. He wore a wide-brimmed hat and pointed leather boots, while swinging a lasso in his hand, ready to rope anything that got in his way. Leopold broke into hysterics, slapping his thighs, when suddenly, a noose tightened around his neck, and he was gasping for air. They flew east to Berlin.

That evening, they arrived, one by one, at the Kleinberg Hotel, greeted by Chancellor Irena and Detektiv Erika, both in disguises. The hotel sat among boutique shops on a wide, cobblestone street, lined with bare trees and black wrought-iron fences.

Erika wore a "spooky tree" costume with bare branches and tree stumps. A paper full moon hung above her head, and a black cat with an arched back was glued to one of the branches. A small light shone through the moon, down the costume, accenting its spooky atmosphere.

Irena wore "daytime, nighttime." Her right side was a business suit, half a jacket and matching pant leg, down to a loafer shoe, and she held a briefcase in her right hand. Her left side was half a pyjama top and pant leg, down to a slipper on her foot, and her left hand held a teddy bear. With make-up carefully applied to the right side, and none to the left, she wore a coiffed hairdo on the right and messed-up hair on the left, to complete her disguise.

They mingled with tourists in the lobby, silently nodding at each other on their way to the front desk, where clerks were chuckling at customers dressed for Halloween. "*Ich mag Ihr Kostüm*, Sir," smiled one pretty clerk, handing Yaegar his room key. (I like your costume, sir.)

"*Danke*," replied Yaegar.

They ordered food and removed their costumes to settle in for the night—except for Ushaya and her helpers. She sat behind the wheel of a mover's truck, with Brad now wearing a Joker's mask, and Irena by her side. With Meg and Devon in the backseats, she hit the open highway and soared in FastMo across the black skies. The truck was filled with laptops and video cameras and printers, and chairs and tables and trollies, and food, flowers, and tablecloths. It carried tools, hammers, mops, rags, sweepers, pails, garbage bags, and everything else the assembly could think of.

They arrived at the grand Liebschon Estate and went to work, like little elves. Meg swept the marble floors, while Ushaya dusted the large crystal chandelier. Irena lined up three-foot tables and chairs, in an arc, across the room, with a longer table for Julia and Herb. Then she placed a metal trolley by each station. Meg followed behind with tented nametags for each table, starting with Brad at the far left. Then she emptied food containers in the kitchen, adjacent to the grand space. Ushaya stored medical supplies in the utility room down the hall. Brad and Devon carefully arranged African masks on walls and pedestals across the room. Irena cut flowers into vases and arranged them on white tablecloths, along the buffet table, while Meg draped chiffon bow ties around the edges of the buffet table, for an elegant touch.

Devon set up Meg's stationary camera, facing the assembly, while Brad set up laptops and power bars on each table. Then they installed a computer screen to the floor, facing the members. By two large patio doors on the left side of the room, Brad shoved extra laptops under his table and began downloading programs from his network drive to his three screens, ensuring everything was ready to go. Exhausted, they flew back for a good night's sleep. All the while, the Kisga'a Shield quietly surrounded the hotel, as they slept.

First business of the day

The following morning, Ushaya and her elves arrived at the estate to set up the remaining items, this time bringing their overnight bags. Meg brought out small china plates filled with croissants, scones, jam, and clotted cream. She laid crackers, cheese, sausages, fruit, and yogurt, upon each table. She then brought out fine cutlery, water pitchers, glasses, and cloth napkins for each station.

Ushaya followed behind, placing the agenda proceedings upon each table, in a finely bound blue dossier, with the initials "TLP" embossed on the front covers. She shoved the locked treasure chest underneath her own station, next to Ishtan's tube, along with the small wooden crate with clover. Then she shoved a large suitcase, filled with ropes and gear, and asked, "Are we ready?"

Irena turned to the kids and asked, "I think so, what do you think?"

"I'm ready," said Devon, adjusting his video camera.

Sniffing flowers on the buffet table, Meg looked up at Brad, and said, "We're ready."

Ushaya flew back to the Kleinberg Hotel, greeting the remaining leaders at the back of the hotel. Dressed in their best attire, they discreetly boarded a large motorhome and headed out into the morning sky. While staring at the scenery whizzing below, they soon arrived, dazed and stunned, at Irena's estate, and began mingling about the grounds.

Meanwhile, across the field, a retired couple was gazing out their farmhouse window, to enjoy the morning view. "Susie, I swear I saw a motorhome fly and land on Irena's estate," said Stephan.

"Are you crazy? Your eyes are failing you," Susie said, and, staring closer, "I see a bunch of people hanging around."

He gazed out the window and whispered, "Let's investigate." He was an old army guy who had once lived in the US, and had parachuted many times in his youth into enemy territory on secret terrorist missions. They hurried along the dirt road, over the hill, and slunk into a ditch. While peering through binoculars, Stephan whispered, "Oh, shit, is that the American president?" Ronald was sharing a joke with Prince Muzaffar, while Mimbauwe was chatting with Zhangwei, as they entered the main doors. Stephan scanned Carlos and Jerome, who were gesturing wildly with their hands, and then he passed the binoculars to Susie.

She peered in and said, "What the hell, I see the queen and prince talking to some weird flying object. And look! There's Yaegar of Russia. He's with some dude in blue sunglasses."

"Let me see," said Stephan, and peering in, "Something definitely is going on." Hashimoto of Japan gazed in their direction, and they immediately ducked in the ditch, and all went silent for some time. "We'll come back tonight," whispered Stephan, and they scampered over the hill across the fields, heading home.

The leaders had freshened up in their quarters, while Devon began filming the grand entrance that was about to begin. Ushaya and Irena stood waiting at the door. The first one to enter was Jerome, dressed in a two-piece blue suit, a white shirt, and a violet tie.

"Hello," said Ushaya, smiling.

In walked Stan with his dragon cane, carrying a steel box. Irena ducked as Lucy fluttered about her head, and said, "So glad you could join us."

"Come along, Lucy," said Stan.

Ushaya shook Hashimoto's hand and said, "I liked your costume."

He bowed and said, "I liked Prince Herbert's."

Irena shook hands with Ronald. "Nice disguise," she said.

Ronald felt rather pleased, and said, "I liked it myself."

Ushaya shook hands with Zhangwei who entered next, and said, "What a great costume."

Zhangwei replied, "I liked Mimbauwe's."

Yadgiri shook hands with Irena, and said, "Yours was my favourite."

Ushaya greeted Carlos of Mexico, and said, "Loved your costume."

"I liked Yaegar's," replied Carlos.

Mimbauwe walked in, and shook Irena's hand. "I liked Queen Julia's," he said.

Julia wheeled her prince through the door. Ushaya turned to Herb and said, "Hashimoto liked your costume."

He looked up and said, "I liked Jerome's."

"Nice to see you," said Irena, shaking hands with Prince Muzaffar.

Dressed in his signature thobe and bisht, with his red-checkered keffiyeh and agal, wrapped around his head, he said, "I liked everyone's disguise, but if pressed to decide, I would say Erika's, and I told her so." He added, "It is a shame she cannot be here today. She is a fine young woman."

The last member to walk through the door was Yaegar of Russia, dressed in a slick, two-piece grey suit, white shirt, and blue tie. He shook Irena and Ushaya's hands.

"Well?" they asked.

He leaned in and said, "I liked Ronald's."

Meg guided them to their seats, while Brad busily showed them their laptop programs. Conversations and light chatter gradually quieted down, until one could hear a pin drop; the silence was palpable.

While shuffling papers on her table, gazing at world leaders across the room, stage fright set in for Ushaya. She glanced behind at Meg, who nodded encouragingly. She glanced to her right at Devon, who gave the thumbs up. To her left, Jerome motioned her to proceed.

"Ahem," she stood up and said, "My name is Ushaya Landau. Welcome to the Lazantis Project—TLP, for short." No one flinched an eye as she floated across the room, continuing, "Thank you for arriving incognito. That is a feat in itself. For the record, there are eighteen of us in this room, and I would like each of you to introduce yourself." One by one, the members stood up and said their name and sat back down, including the kids, including Lucy. It was a stiff and formal address.

Jerome stood up and announced, "Ladies and gentlemen, we gather here at this extraordinary event for Ushaya to present the gifts, and to discuss the manifesto and our plans going forward. The agenda before you outlines a very packed two-day program with much to cover. At this time, I would like to thank the members and Ushaya for making this all possible." He sat down, and the assembly applauded.

While buttering his croissant, Yaegar called out, "Ushaya, how would you get out of a steel-encased locked vault?"

"With difficulty," she said, still floating. "I should not be in that situation in the first place."

"At what speed can you now fly?" asked Zhangwei, scooping into his yogurt cup.

"Five thousand miles an hour. Not as fast as a rocket can," she replied. They chuckled.

"How fast can a rocket go?" asked Herb.

Ronald stood up and said, "Twenty-five thousand miles an hour. I've watched the NASA videos." He sat back down.

While cutting into his sausages, Mimbauwe piped up, "I have been meaning to ask, how slow is SlowMo?"

Ushaya sat down at her table, contemplating, and then spoke. "Have you ever watched water boil on a stove? It's that slow. About one inch every ten minutes."

Lucy sprung from Stan's table, landing in front of Ushaya, and clicking and clacking, she asked, "Where does love go when love dies?"

Ushaya replied, "Perhaps love never dies, but simply transforms into something greater than itself."

"And what about hate?" asked Lucy.

Stan stood up and said, "Hate is a destructive emotion that eventually consumes itself. That is the difference. Hate contracts and love expands." Lucy returned, wondering: why all the applause?

Jerome stood up and announced, "We have many questions, but we must continue with our program. The first business of the day is to cast our votes on the best disguise. The top prize is a Lamborghini, your choice of colour. The runner-up gets a legacy Accutron watch."

They pulled out pens and paper from their agendas and quietly pondered, while Meg went around with a silver tray, collecting their votes. Brad kept meticulous score, ticking checkmarks by each name; it was a close race. He stood up and said, "The winner is . . ." Drumroll . . . hands thumping loudly on tables . . . "The winner is Jerome!"

Jerome stood up amid applause, and, adjusting his tie, smiled at Brad and asked, "Who is runner-up?"

Looking at his score sheet, Brad cried out, "Yaegar!" More applause. Yaegar stood up, pleased to add another watch to his already large collection. Meg pinned a gold TLP insignia to the winners' lapels.

It was noon when Jerome announced, "The next item on the agenda is our group flight, but first take your time to finish breakfast." Murmurings sounded across the room.

Roger that

They returned to their quarters to gear up in suits, vests, and gloves. Some members stayed behind to clear up dishes from each station. A while later, the leaders returned to the assembly room, chuckling at the sight of each other. They had learned that some members would not fly. Julia and Herb would not fly, nor the kids, but Lucy would. Julia explained that the long flight had tired out her husband.

Herb nodded and said, "Another time; besides, the kids will have company."

Ushaya brought out ropes and hooks from her suitcase. Brad placed an audio device, nicknamed the "Com", upon her lapel and gave each member ear buds. Meg pushed back tables to one end of the room, while Devon's camera continued to roll.

While contemplating the order, from left to right, Ushaya commanded everyone to stand in a line, starting with Stan at the far left, and Lucy at the far right. Ropes were looped through their vests, starting from their left sides and back around their right sides. She inspected her troops one last time, and returned to the centre, where she looped the tail end ropes through her vest into triple knots, and then clipped the two large hooks to her belts. Tethered in ropes, the group faced Julia and Herb, and bowed.

"Ladies and gentlemen," Ushaya began. "Our historic flight will go down in history. We have witnesses in this room, Her Majesty the Queen and Prince Herbert, and Meg, Devon, and Brad." She continued, "Thirteen of us will fly. I shall refer to my left and right sides as my "wings". The first helmsmen and last wing tips will feel the flight more than anyone else. That is why I have chosen this order." She glanced to the far left of her. "Stan, are you sure you are ready for this?"

He replied, "Absolutely, I insist. My leg is healing. Besides, we're mostly flying, right?"

They were shuffling their feet, patting their suits, and adjusting their ear buds, when Carlos cried out, "With all this rope, it would be incredible that we could levitate at all."

"Thought transference, remember?" reminded Jerome.

Meg said, "Mom can lift whatever touches her at will."

"What is our combined weight?" asked Zhangwei.

Ushaya pulled out her phone from her vest pocket, mumbling, "175 x 12 = 2,100 pounds. Add in for good measure, 100 pounds for rope and Lucy's weight." She looked up and said, "Just over a ton, a piece of cake."

Hashimoto wondered, "What about bodily functions, like you know, if we have to go?"

Yaegar replied, "Those urges suspend in mid air. Besides, we are only flying fifty miles."

Ushaya said, "We won't be like birds, you know."

Ronald asked, "What about gravity?"

Yadgiri shot a glance at him. "You're asking this now?"

"So how are we going to fly?" asked Muzaffar.

Suddenly, they levitated ten feet and flew in tight formation across the grand space and down the hall, into a large parlour, and then returned to the assembly room. Ushaya descended, spreading her "wings," and called out, "Land, forward, back, and stabilize!" Some landed awkwardly, swerving back and forth, and one member stumbled. Lucy was the only one who landed perfectly. Over and over, they practiced their moves, rising and descending. Meg and Brad opened the large patio doors, and with the wings of a gliding bird, Ushaya led them into the open air and cried out once more, "Are we ready?" Thundering like a Riverdance across a stage, they landed in total unison, thump, thump, thump! The witnesses chuckled. Ushaya's invisible watch showed three o'clock, and she commanded, "Goggles on!" And with a final salute, they soared up and away.

Meanwhile, at the farmhouse over the hill, Stephan was peering through his binoculars at the V-shaped formation in the sky. He turned to his wife, and said, "Look, Susie, a flock of geese."

She peered out the window and said, "Get your eyes checked, those are people flying."

He retorted, "Get your own eyes checked," and, peering back, sputtered, "Holy shit." Witnesses silently watched the leaders disappear into the sky.

They soared over towns and hills and winding rivers, cruising a hundred miles an hour. Elation filled their very souls, as they ascended into thick clouds, amazed at the beauty all around them. They gasped at the vast expanse, as far as the eyes could see, and into the great silence, they flew and flew.

Ushaya pressed her Com, and said, "Roll call, everyone, making sure you're OK. Left helm Jerome, are you all right?"

While hanging onto one rope, he replied, "Doing great. Roger out."

"Right helm Yaegar, how are you doing?" she asked.

He spread out both arms and answered, "Very fine. *Eto Rodzher.*"

To her second left position, Ushaya asked, "Muzaffar, are you all right?"

He was silent at first, and then asked, "Have you and Ishtan flown this high before?"

"Many times," she replied.

"Well then," he broadly smiled, "*Hadha rujar.*" (That's a Roger.)

To her second right position, she asked, "Mimbauwe, how are you?"

Staring into the vast empty sky, he quietly murmured, "Roger out."

To her left third, Irena broke into song, "The skies are alive with music," and with voice trailing, added, "*Das ist ein Roger.*"

To her right third, Yadgiri beamed, "I wish my elephants were here!"

Left fourth, Carlos clutched his chest, "My heart has no words for . . ." his voice faded.

Right fourth, Hashimoto had an idea, blurting, "Stan, we must talk of a new device for laptops."

Left fifth, Ronald spread his arms in glee. "Let's move faster!" he cried out.

"We will in time," said Ushaya.

Right fifth, Zhangwei quietly said, "I feel most, most . . . Zen."

Her final left-wing tip was Stan, who was struggling to keep the line straight, with his legs fluttering in the wind, his body wobbling back and forth.

Right sixth, Lucy looked at him and said, "Master, you are holding your ropes too far ahead. Pull back, with elbows bent close to your body, and keep your legs together."

Stan obeyed, and as the left wing straightened out, he felt more in control. Glancing at Lucy, he said, "From now on, call me Stan, not master."

Steering the right wing, Lucy proudly announced, "Then Stan it is. Roger that."

In tight formation, they descended into thick clouds, hanging onto ropes for dear life, through turbulent atmosphere. When they came out the other side, Ushaya spread her two wings, gliding effortlessly across the skies. The cool autumn air brushed their euphoric faces as they continued their descent. All the while, at the Liebschon Estate, the witnesses were watching their flight through the overhead screen.

A cathedral came into view in the valley below. Ushaya asked, "Irena, what is that cathedral again?"

Her voice crackled through the airwaves, "*Munsch mar Bruhachen.*"

They were about to land at the steeple grounds when two custodians showed up, walking along the corridor, so they re-routed to the opposite side. As they peered over the stony wall, Zhangwei whispered, "The coast is clear."

Three, two, one . . . touchdown! Exhilarated in a cacophony of voices, feeling like they had landed on the moon, they stepped over ropes to greet each other with high fives, shaking hands, weaving in and out of the crowd. While chatting excitedly, moving in closer and closer, they soon found themselves tangled in a jumble of ropes, unable to move. En masse, their packed bodies shimmied three feet to the left, and then shimmied five feet to the right. They couldn't free themselves. "We're stuck!" cried out Ushaya.

Two antennae rose up from the crowd. Scanning their positions, Lucy commanded Hashimoto, "Swing your left rope over Zhangwei, and Zhangwei, step under Ronald's rope." They obeyed. She continued, "Hashimoto, duck under Carlos's ropes." He was now facing Yadgiri.

Lucy continued, "Irena, swing the left rope over Mimbauwe and squeeze past Yadgiri." Irena was now facing Muzaffar.

"Jerome and Ushaya, untangle your joined wrists, and now turn to your right. Then take both your ropes and duck under the first person you see." Jerome was now facing Irena, and Ushaya was next to Yaegar.

"Stan, swing your rope over Ronald, and Irena, change places with Jerome." Under, over, and around, she continued her commands, until their mess of ropes finally loosened up. The group cheered.

"Well done, Lucy!" beamed Jerome.

Relieved to have her wings back, with leaders tethered in the right order, Ushaya announced, "Let us return. Are we ready?" In unison, they put on their goggles and flew up and away. Good timing it was, for the custodians were about to turn the corner to investigate the commotion, only to be met with silence. They hurried down the corridor and around the bend, and looked at each other, perplexed.

Ushaya calmly said, “Picking up speed . . . 100 . . . 200 . . . We are now approaching 300 miles per hour.” Carlos clutched his chest, while Ronald was in ecstasy. The cold air whipped across their frozen faces, all the way back to the estate. As they floated through the mansion doors, the witnesses showered them in confetti, welcoming them back to earth. Amid jubilation, while removing their ropes and gear, Jerome announced, “Let us freshen up after a hard day’s work, and convene in two hours for the next part of our program—the gifts.”

Brad’s map

Two hours later, when everyone was seated in the assembly room, Jerome motioned Brad to rise.

He pulled the map from his tube and rolled it out on a table. Everyone could see through the large screen that it magically revealed German territory. Brad began, “There are lots of mineral deposits waiting to be discovered, Irena.”

She smiled and said, “That’s exciting news.”

He walked over and offered the map to her. “I’m sure, we all have the same question on our minds: Is the Titan spaceship in Germany?” He added, “The map only answers in the country where it is currently located.”

Jerome said, “We already know the spaceship is not in Canada.”

Irena thought the question was a good idea, and holding the map, she asked out loud, “Is the Titan spaceship located in Germany?” A bolt of fiery light sizzled and crackled across the surface, followed by a trail of smoke, disappearing over the edges. It was a negative, and she gave the map back to Brad.

They all wanted to try Brad’s map, in exchange for anything his heart desired—his own casino, a private jet, the best stock options. “You just name it, and you’ll have it,” said Ronald.

Brad was taken aback and said, “Uh, one step at a time.”

From the treasure chest, Ushaya presented Brad’s scroll, and said, “My son, you hold a powerful Titan in your hands. As a member of TLP, you have an important role in sharing what discoveries you find about the map, and we all look forward to learning more. Do you accept your new role and responsibilities that surely will arise?”

Brad said, “I do.” They all applauded.

Meg and Devon's Quazaik

Jerome motioned them to take the floor. Meg opened the metal box on her table and brought out a drawstring velvet cloth. Shaking out the contents, a sparkling crystal rested upon her right palm in a sea of radiant colours. Devon tapped Quazaik ten feet into the air. The group hushed in awe.

Meg began, "She not only beams out coordinates, but anything in her field gets an energy boost. Why, just a month ago, we were renovating the back of the house, trying to figure out where posts and walls should go. It was a struggle for us, because the math was not adding up. Quazaik beamed around the room, and equations entered our heads, and decisions were made like crazy, and the layouts aligned perfectly."

Devon said, "One day, while we took Quazaik out for a country drive, an oncoming truck swerved into our lane. We thought we were goners, then lasers beamed around us, and we drove right through the truck, like a ghost, avoiding a head-on collision."

He blew at the crystal, and, one by one, the leaders tapped Quazaik, as it floated by. Quazaik landed in Ushaya's outstretched palm. Rainbow sparkles radiated from its core, as she tapped it in the air. Lasers engulfed the room in one big geometric design, and then Quazaik returned to Meg's palm. The leaders excitedly offered trades in exchange to hold Quazaik, for even a day, promising villas in southern France, capital funds to expand a chain of spas, where Meg could be the CEO, and yachts and a private island for Devon, and the list went on.

Meg and Devon traded with Brad's map, right there and then, wondering if the Titan spaceship was hiding in New Zealand. Brad could not refuse. A bolt of lightning flashed across the surface of the map, followed by fireballs, right off the edges. It still showed German territory.

As he held Quazaik in his palm, Brad asked a burning question, "There are glitches in our network security protocols to make this mission airtight. What am I missing?" Suddenly, he was bathed in a geometric design, and he began keying new code and algorithms into his computer, "Excuse me," he said, "I need to get this down . . ." The group murmured in excitement.

From her treasure chest, Ushaya laid the scroll on the table. Facing Meg and Devon, she said, "A Master Titan is in your hands. I ask you now, do you honour this power, according to the mandates of our manifesto, and are you ready and willing to sacrifice, in your loyal duty to our cause, to offer Quazaik in mutual cooperation for exploration and discovery?"

They replied, "We do." The assembly broke into great applause.

Stan's Gift of Genius

Jerome stood up and announced, "Welcome, Stanislav Kominsky, and Lucy, who keeps him sane." Amid chuckles, Stan brought a box onto his table, and, unlocking it, pulled out a new invention. The assembly gasped, not sure what it was.

He began, "This, ladies and gentlemen, promises a new form of energy for every household. Do you know that energy can be generated from snowfall? With some modifications to the triboelectric nanogenerator, I have made it to be very thin and easy to operate. The cab generates its own electricity and . . ."

Lucy interrupted, clicking and clacking, "This is my invention. He is trying to take credit for it."

Stan gave her a sharp look and said, "Lucy, we've been through this before." Then he stood up and gave his speech about the virtues of Genius, and how grateful he was to be at the receiving end of its power. He swore allegiance to the Lazantis Project, offering assistance however he could. Lucy sat quiet, knowing all too well that look he gave her, which meant she was in trouble.

Ushaya presented his scroll and said, "It is a great honour to have you and Genius amongst us," and turning to the members, she said, "I remind you all, it started with Stan." Everyone applauded.

Jerome's Twelve Spheres

Ushaya laid out two narrow boxes on Jerome's table. Unlocking the latches, she removed the tops to reveal the twelve spheres. "They are yours to hold," she said.

In awe, Jerome held two spheres in his hands. Suddenly, four spheres switched positions before their very eyes. They all gasped.

While floating back and forth, Ushaya continued, "Whatever thought or command, it will be yours. Go ahead, Jerome, release one sphere and use your imagination."

The assembly hushed in silence, while Jerome fell deep in thought. Then he rolled an emerald-green sphere across the floor, commanding, "I want six Roman soldiers on six white horses."

Electric static crackled through the air, and a strange portal opened. Everyone jumped up to make room for six Roman soldiers on six white horses, who strutted through in full armour, carrying shields, battle axes, spears, javelins, and swords, with horses snorting and hoofs thundering across the floor, as they lined up behind Jerome's table, and stopped. A voice called forth, "I am Centurion Pilus Thebas, and we await your command."

Jerome ran his hand across a horse's mane, smelling its scent and feeling the warm breath from its nostrils upon his face. He called out to Pilus, "Stand by for your orders." By then, the group had gathered around him, and he whispered, "It seems so real."

"This is some kind of illusion," retorted Zhangwei.

"But what if it's not, and we have six Romans and six white horses on my estate?" said Irena, worried.

"An illusion, eh?" said Jerome. He began thinking of a nursery rhyme, and changing it up a bit, he rolled a cobalt sphere across the floor, commanding, "I want six pretty maidens with six white geese."

The portal opened, and in came six pretty maidens, chasing geese squawking all over the room, with feathers flying, as members veered away from nipping beaks amidst the cries of frustrated maidens, who were clearly not in control. A goose jumped on Brad's table, flapping its wings, nearly knocking his computer screens to the floor. He grabbed the bird, struggling to keep it still, before releasing it to the floor. The geese waddled under tables, overturning trolleys and chairs, fluttering and quacking through the crowd, and the leaders themselves tried their hands at catching them. Roman soldiers ogled the pretty maidens in the chaos, and dismounted their horses to come to the rescue. One soldier bent down on his knee, asking a maiden for her hand in marriage. Blushing, she accepted his proposal. Another soldier caught two geese under his shield, while another, with his bare hands, scooped up several by their feet, with their wings flapping wildly in protest. Eventually, the geese were rounded up into the maidens' hands, and the soldiers remounted their horses.

Jerome stared at Pilus and announced, "The Goose Rebellion is now under control. Well done. You shall return in victory with honours bestowed upon you, with chattels of land and titles worthy of your bravery."

Ushaya shot a glance at Jerome, perturbed. He whispered, "You told me to use my imagination." He then rolled a black sphere across the table, commanding, "Return at once to where you belong."

The mysterious portal opened, and to everyone's surprise, one by one, the horsemen and maidens disappeared with their geese into thin air. The assembly fell silent. Meg and Irena began sweeping the floor, while others picked up feathers, pleased to have a souvenir. All three spheres returned to their boxes, much to Jerome's surprise. They straightened the trollies, chairs, and tables strewn across the floor, before settling back in their seats. Zhangwei began clapping, followed by Stan and Irena, until the whole assembly erupted in applause.

Jerome turned to Ushaya and asked, "The frogfish in the stream, where is this place exactly?"

From her treasure chest, she brought out the scroll, and replied, "This will show you. I ask you now, do you accept this gift?"

Jerome unfurled the scroll and studied the map, gazing at coordinates, above and below. Then he rolled the scroll back up, and said, "I accept."

Ronald's Gemball

Ronald's face was bathed in an orange glow, as he held the Gemball for the first time.

"Go ahead, ask him a question," said Ushaya.

While peering intently, Ronald began, "Yadgiri, I see you are about to cancel the Golden Shakti Tower contract and some other real estate investments in your country."

Yadgiri blurted, "How did you know that? I was going to talk to you about this in private."

While images swirled, Ronald glanced at Muzaffar, and said, "You are about to cancel a contract in renewable energy sources between the US and your country, giving the contract to a neighbour, thereby excluding us in the loop, and I won't say which country." Prince Muzaffar sat back in quiet annoyance.

Ronald passed the ball to Carlos and said, "Here, amigo, have a look."

Carlos tapped the Gemball. "I feel uplifted . . . Dios mio," his voice faded, "Oh, that rascal nephew of mine, he is up to no good again." He turned to Ronald and said, "I see you are having trouble completing the wall."

Ronald held out his left hand and said, "The ball, please." The assembly murmured.

Ushaya warned, "You may become obsessed the more you gaze into it, so you must use prudence and reverence. Remember, I have not won the lottery yet."

Jerome suggested, "Let's trade sometime, just for a few days."

Ronald didn't skip a beat, and replied, "You've got yourself a deal." He became curious about the Titan spaceship, and offered Brad, "Let's trade right now, my Gemball for your map."

Brad could not refuse and gave him the map, replying, "I think it has to be done on your own soil, but here goes."

"We shall see," said Ronald, and, holding the map, he asked, "Is the Titan spaceship hiding in the USA?" A fiery ball blazed across the surface, and, sure enough, it only showed German territory.

All eyes turned to Brad. He gazed into the Gemball and spoke. "I see . . . I see a submarine moving along an ocean floor, which is releasing methane gases. Something is down there, but I can't see what." His voice faded. He tapped the Gemball twice and handed it to Ronald, who gave him back his map.

Ushaya presented the scroll to Ronald, and said, "I ask you now. Do you accept this gift?"

He stood up and gave his power speech: "I personally want to say how thrilled I am to be here with all you good folks. This exciting new chapter will make us great. It will make America great. When the City Chiefs won the Super Bowl in Iowa last year, I remember how proud I was for our nation. It's how I feel today, and that ain't no fake news."

Irena corrected, "It was in St. Louis, Missouri, not Iowa."

He sat back down and said, "I accept." Great applause erupted.

Jerome motioned Ushaya to continue with the next gift.

CHAPTER SIXTEEN

Clover and the ancient Relic

Ushaya placed a clover pot on Carlos's table. The kids turned out the lights and closed the patio curtains. In the darkness, iridescent violet leaves glowed on green floating stems. Everyone hushed, for there were no words to describe its beauty.

Carlos said, "I give clover to us all, no need for trade. Furthermore, if clover healed Ushaya, old man Harvey, and Stanislav, then it should work for our dear Prince Herb. So, I ask you, would you like to receive clover right now?"

"Why, yes, I suppose," said Herb, surprised.

Three snips of clover floated across the room, resting upon Prince Herb's head and down his spine. While he discreetly buttoned up his shirt and jacket, Ushaya said, "He must refresh with new leaves in twenty-four hours."

"Give him as much as he needs," said Carlos.

A powerful surge tingled through Herb's body, and he began to rise from his wheelchair. The kids turned on the lights, and, to everyone's amazement, he was still standing. Julia sprang from her chair to help her husband down to his seat. She turned to Carlos and said, "We look forward to future trades that will prosper both our nations." Great Applause.

From her treasure chest, Ushaya brought forth the ancient relic and placed it on Carlos's table. The group stared in silence at the magnificent half-man, half-beast statue.

"Go ahead, it's yours to hold," said Ushaya.

Ronald reminded him, "Remember that dream of yours."

Carlos nodded, as he held the relic. The beast stared into his eyes. While quietly whispering the secret word "Quetzalpoca" under his breath, he pressed against a paw of the jaguar relief spanning down the surface, but nothing happened. He felt around the back of the relic and pressed against the stone surface, and nothing happened. He continually whispered the word, and, moving his fingers a fraction of an inch, he pressed again. Suddenly, a chamber door opened, radiating a bright white light across the room. The assembly hushed in fright.

He asked Ushaya, "What do I do now?"

"Your guess is as good as mine," she replied.

Carlos slowly poked a finger through the door, and quickly pulled away; all seemed fine. He slid his hand through and continued, until half his body disappeared into the lighted doorway. Then he quickly pulled away. Everyone gasped in awe.

"How is that possible?" cried out Yaegar.

"Did you see anything?" asked Irena.

Carlos answered, "At first, I saw a brilliant white light. Then I was standing in jungles, hearing war cries from an ancient tribe descending upon me." Everyone fell silent. Curious about the Titan spaceship, he offered Brad the relic, in exchange, for his map, right there and then, and asked, "Is the Titan spaceship hiding in Mexico?" A splay of fireworks blazed across the surface of the map, followed by black smoke over the edges. It only showed German territory. With the chamber still open, streaming out light from the relic, he said to Brad, "Go ahead and enter." Everyone hushed.

Hesitant at first, Brad slowly slipped his elbow through the door, and then slipped his head and half his torso through the chamber. Suddenly, he pulled back and staggered across the room, awestruck and amazed, at what he'd seen. "First there was light," he said. "And then I heard the roar of a dinosaur, I believe a triceratops, if I am not mistaken." Carlos uttered the secret word and the chamber door closed, and the light was gone.

"Extraordinary!" everyone cried out.

Ushaya handed Carlos his scroll, asking, "Do you accept these gifts?"

He gazed at the clover pot and the ancient relic, and stood up and said, "I accept." The assembly broke out enthusiastically, wanting to trade with him. He waved his hand in the air and replied, "We shall see, when the time is right."

Dinner break (Two hours)

A lavish banquet feast was brought out from the kitchen. In walked Yadgiri, carrying plates filled with beef stroganoff and steamed vegetables, and dahl and rice bowls. Irena arranged cutlery, plates, and glasses on the table, while Zhangwei laid out plates filled with toasted bread sticks, cheeses and olives, and fresh-cut fruit. Queen Julia soon followed, with mashed potatoes and chicken cordon bleu. Lucy the robot brought out Mideast halawa bel-jubn, and German cakes and American pies. Meg brought out red and white wine, and sparkling water, beer, spritzers, and lemon tea. Then she lit the three tall pillar candles across the buffet table.

While strolling about with a plate of food in her hand, Ushaya noticed members carrying swords and revolvers, hidden in jackets and sleeves, and complained to Jerome, "Do you realize that several members are carrying weapons?"

He shrugged, unconcerned. "Probably ceremonial," he replied.

"What next, a grenade?" she whispered.

"You are overly paranoid," he said, shaking hands with Hashimoto.

She pondered out loud, "We had not discussed bringing weapons to the assembly. We can't even get on an airplane with a toothpick, let alone . . ."

Yaegar interrupted, apologizing to Ushaya before turning to Jerome. "I do not wish to intrude, but your spheres are rolling off the table. May I help?" Jerome glanced at his balls, which were rolling across the floor.

Ushaya excused herself. "I shall leave you two to your business." She turned around, wondering where Brad was, hoping he wasn't hiding, as usual. On the contrary, he was entertaining several leaders in lively debates. They soon settled back into their seats with food and drinks.

The Ring of Power

Jerome announced, "All rise to our Majesty Queen Julia II and Royal Highness Prince Herbert." Everyone stood up, and then sat back down. Ushaya presented a black velvet case to the queen, "Go ahead, wear the ring," she said.

Julia slipped it upon her right ring finger, and it began to glow. The assembly hushed.

Ushaya asked, "How do you feel?"

"I'm not sure," she replied. Then, slowly, she stood up and announced, "Ladies and gentlemen, we have many amenities, from hair salons to barber shops, to toys and souvenirs, to movie theatres and fitness gyms, and gaming rooms, to name just a few. You are sailing on the finest cruise ship these oceans have ever seen." The assembly agreed.

She continued, "It's a beautiful sunny morning, so take a stroll along the decks, and relax at one of the five swimming pools on board, and enjoy a free drink on the house." They all cheered.

Happily nodding at first, Ushaya began to see through her ruse, and sharply gave her the stink eye.

Ashamed at her abuse of power, and attempting to correct her errant ways, Julia announced, "Ladies and gentlemen, we are *not* on a cruise ship." They all agreed.

She added, "And it is not morning, it is daytime." They all agreed.

Flustered, she said, "I meant to say evening, not daytime!" They empathically agreed. She sat down and quickly passed the ring to her prince.

Herb placed the ring on his finger, and it began to glow. A power surged through his very being. Healing clover was working its magic as he stood up from his wheelchair and said, "I think we should all hold the ring."

"Do you think that is wise?" asked Julia.

Herb flung the ring on the table; it twirled like a penny before coming to a full stop. He said, "If we are to be one for all and all for one, then everyone here should know its power." In silence, one by one, they all held the black ring between their fingers, before passing it down the line.

Ushaya lowered her voice, asking, "What about the monster, the Gogolan. What news do you have?"

Julia replied, "It remains in the northeast sector of Blake Moore, where it likes to hide. The main entrance is central south, so that may be an advantage to you and your team, when you enter again."

Seated by then, Herb addressed the assembly, "As you know, a six-man team will meet with Ushaya in Germany for military training exercises."

Irena glanced around the room and said, "Thank you for your submissions, we are processing applications, and will let you know, in due course."

Ushaya presented the scroll to the queen and prince, and said, "I ask you both, do you accept this gift?"

Julia gazed at her husband, duke of Eldenbrow, her long-time lover and friend, father of her children, great confidante in the duties of the royal family, and member and advisor of the assembly.

Herb turned to his beloved wife, mother of his children and grandchildren, and long-time lover. And proud to serve the monarchy, he insisted, "Now wear the ring."

With a weighted responsibility she had never known, Queen Julia placed the ring back on her finger. It shone bright hot as she stood up and said, "We accept, one for all and all for one." The whole assembly erupted in standing applause.

Ushaya was in her glory, rambling on about this special moment in history, when suddenly, she stopped talking and stared at Ronald. "Will you please put that ball down? We need your attention here," she said, crossly.

Ronald continued gazing, then replied, "I see Yadgiri is about to remove one of our attachés from his diplomatic post, a Mr. Abdul Zahir, whom I personally endorsed."

Yadgiri had had enough of Ronald's indiscretions, and stomping over to the buffet table, he threw a piece of cake in his direction, but missed. It hit the ancient relic instead.

"How dare you!" Carlos stood up, indignant.

Ronald quietly turned to Jerome, and said, "Better put your balls away."

Suddenly, Muzaffar and Carlos pulled out short swords and clashed in a duel across the floor. With swords locked, Carlos hissed, "You never came through with the last shipment of gas."

Muzaffar snarled back, "You never came through with those construction projects in my country, as we agreed!" They released their hold and continued duelling across the room.

Brad quickly stuffed the map in his suitcase under the table. Yaegar began dancing on tables, bare chested, swinging his shirt, and then pounced toward Zhangwei, who simply moved aside, sending him crashing into a line of chairs. The whole assembly was on the move. Zhangwei tapped Ronald's shoulder and threatened, "If you place one more sanction against China, you will live to regret it," and he swung a punch. Ronald stopped him with his arm, snarling, "You son of a bastard," and jabbed him hard in the chest and stomped on his foot. "AGHH!" Zhangwei yelled out in pain.

Ushaya tried to calm everyone down, "Ladies and gentlemen, look at your . . ." —Wham! Annoyed, she wiped the pie cream from her face and flicked it across the room, forgetting her strength. It landed on Mimbauwe, and soon the two were in a shouting match. Devon continued filming through the crowd, while ducking objects whipping through the air, when he began to home in on Ushaya. She turned to him, her face morphing into some kind of creature, as she growled, "Get the fecking camera out of my face!" She shoved him into a group, sending them flying across the floor. While Devon was picking up broken camera pieces, Ronald shoved him hard, and, hurling around, Devon punched him in the gut. Ronald stumbled back and pulled out his gun, and shot aimlessly in the air.

BANG! Mayhem! A scene in chaos, throwing cake, food, chairs, laptops . . . punching each other . . . WHAM! POW! THUD! UGH! Muzaffar pierced Carlos's shoulder, and Carlos thrust his sword into his right thigh, and they both fell to their knees.

Yaegar dropkicked Stan and snapped his arm in two. Staggering to his feet, Stan kicked Yaegar in the groin. Shocked with pain and rage, Yaegar lifted Stan and hurled his body, spread-eagled, onto the buffet table. Everything came tumbling down. Hot food spilled across the floor, and tablecloths caught on fire from the lit candles. Meg slapped Brad across his face and he slapped her back, both hollering insults at each other. Swinging punches at each other, Jerome and Yaegar stumbled over Carlos and Muzaffar's bodies. Carlos and Muzaffar both cried out in pain. Ronald was chasing Meg through the debris when she picked up a broken board and slammed it on his head. Down he went, seeing stars. Bodies flew into pedestals and chairs, and tables went flying through the patio doors, smashing to pieces in a spray of broken glass. Devon's body was pinned to the floor, with Mimbauwe throttling his left side over and over, in the smoke-filled room, while African masks burned in the fires that raged up the curtains and across the walls.

Fire alarms were about to set off, but Quazaik cut the signal before the overhead sprinkler system could activate and alert the authorities. Instead, she beamed around the room. Lucy caught her signal and yanked two fire extinguishers from their housings, and began spraying down the place. Everyone coughed and gagged through the smoke and steam. Frantically looking about, Lucy found Brad fist fighting with Zhangwei, and urgently said, "Brad, tell your mom to go to the queen."

Brad managed to break away, and, sloshing across slippery floors, found his mom, and yelled, "Lucy says go to the queen."

Ushaya cried out, "What?" Yaegar and Hashimoto were about to charge at her. As soon as they closed in, she stepped aside, and, BAM! Their bodies slammed hard, tumbling to the ground.

"Go to the queen!" hollered Brad.

While searching through the crowd, ducking flying objects, she found Julia, who was shocked, sitting in her seat. Ushaya yelled, "Please do something!"

"What can I do?" Julia insisted. The ring shone bright hot on her finger.

Jerome wheeled Herb round and round, until they both crashed to the floor. Herb cried out, "The whistle! The whistle!"

Julia brought out a whistle from her purse and handed it to her.

Ushaya hollered, "Why on earth do you carry a whistle?"

Julia hollered back, "Why on earth do you carry a tourmaline rock?" Amid terrified screams, her hat flew off her coiffed hair, rolling down the aisle. Hashimoto stepped on it, embroiled in a fistfight with Mimbauwe, chop-chop kicks in the air, and he brought Mimbauwe to his knees. "AGHH!" he cried out.

"For God's sake, Ushaya, blow the whistle now!" commanded Julia.

Immediately, Ushaya flew to the shattered glass chandelier, barely dangling upon exposed cables, from the ceiling. She gazed down at garbage and food strewn across the floor, at the broken patio doors and burnt-out curtains, at holes punched in walls, covered in black soot, at tables and laptops and the TV console, smashed to pieces. She gazed through the haze of smoke at Irena's hands around Yadgiri's throat, strangling him until he was about to pass out, and, pursing her lips, she blew the whistle, "Wheeeeeeeeeeeeeeeee eeeeeeeeeeeeeeeeeeeeeeee, yip!"

Everyone stopped.

Moans and groans echoed across the room, as the wounded lay writhing on the floor. Others wandered in a daze of destruction, with torn clothes and faces covered in bruises and soot. Jerome was crawling on all fours, searching for his spheres. Meg pulled the treasure chest from underneath a pile of broken tables, and Devon found Ishtan's tube, lying in a corner of the room. Zhangwei staggered toward the Gemball, which was resting among the fallen pedestals. Yaegar wandered through mangled laptops and food sludge, and from the rubble, he picked up a sphere. While sifting through debris, Ronald retrieved the only surviving African mask, and blew away the dust.

Brad stumbled upon his charred suitcase, and, opening the latches, was relieved to see that his map was safe. While crouched on the floor, he searched around for a computer screen, and found one that was only partially damaged. Attaching it to his network drive, he fired it up. It worked. The video files were saved. *Great good luck!* he thought.

Jerome and Irena helped Herb back into his wheelchair, while Hashimoto found one sphere ball in a lump of beef stroganoff, splattered on the floor. Lying among the ruins, Julia patted down the soil in the broken clover pot and gave it to Carlos. He sputtered, "Yes, please, we need clover."

Ushaya solemnly descended, asking, "Is there a doctor in the house?" No one came forward.

"Is there a nurse in the house?" Silence.

Irena said, "I have medical training."

Meg offered, "I can help."

Yaegar nodded and said, "I also have medical training."

"As do I," said Hashimoto.

Ushaya returned from the utility room with medical supplies, and soon, the four "nurses" began administering clover over everyone's bruised and broken bodies. They applied neck braces and arm slings, and bandages around their heads, torsos and legs, while others began sweeping the floor, picking up debris.

Ushaya spoke to Irena. "Permission to bring in the backhoe, stationed on your property, so I can get rid of the garbage."

"I don't have the keys," Irena said, adjusting Yadgiri's neck brace.

"I don't need them," Ushaya replied.

"Well, don't damage the floors, they were newly tiled." Irena turned back to the wounded, clearly in shock, for the floors were already damaged in the fire.

The broken patio doors swung open, and everyone stepped aside, watching a backhoe enter the estate, rounding up garbage and debris into one corner. Suddenly, Ushaya lost control and the eastern wall came crumbling down, exposing the outside courtyard, and destroying parts of the kitchen. Irena quietly moaned.

On her final return from several dumps into field containers, Ushaya noticed a red dot on her suit and quickly bee-lined to its source. Noticing two people hiding in a bush, she commanded, "Who are you? State your names!"

Caught by surprise, shaking like a leaf, he lowered his infrared camera, and said, "My name is Stephan, and this is my wife Susie."

Ushaya's voice boomed, "Where do you come from?"

"Over the hill," quivered Susie.

Ushaya descended to the ground and whispered, "My name is Ushaya Landau. What you have witnessed tonight is top secret, do you understand?" The couple nodded in silence. She raised her voice. "Now go home. We will be in touch." As they hurried away, she called out, "Welcome to the Lazantis Project!" Faster over the hill they ran, with flashlights flickering wildly in the dark.

Yaegar was rinsing his mop in the utility room sink when he quietly said, "I feel most ashamed."

"I am just as guilty," replied Ushaya, wringing rag cloths under hot water in a separate sink. She asked, "Do you think it was the ring?"

Jerome entered, hearing her last words. While washing his face in the sink, he mumbled, "One for all and all for one."

Soon everyone vacated the assembly room and had retired to their private quarters, to recuperate.

No Sleep Tonight

That evening, healing clover was taking effect, like a strong morphine injection, and they all wandered back into the assembly room. Dressed in casual clothing and a headscarf, Julia entered, wheeling in her prince, followed by Zhangwei, who was covered in clover and limping with an injured foot.

Irena and Jerome were preparing whatever food they could find in the kitchen, while Meg and Yaegar found two rickety tables in storage, and set them up. Brad and Devon boarded up the exposed crumbling wall and the broken glass doors, using staple guns and large plastic tarps they had found in the utility room, for a cold chill was seeping through the estate. Hashimoto arranged leftover wilted flowers in Styrofoam cups, placing them on the buffet table, while Jerome managed to find some plastic forks and knives, and neatly arranged them at one end. With patches of clover over his bloodied left eye, Devon began filming, using his backup video camera, ready to roll, take two.

Stan walked in with his dragon's cane, wearing an arm sling. Carlos staggered in with clover upon his bandaged shoulder, followed by Yadgiri in his neck brace. Muzaffar walked in, holding his crutch, with Clover all over his body.

A tattered TLP agenda lay on the table, along with a pen and piece of paper. Quazaik hovered high in one corner, watching the scene below, while Lucy stood at the entrance.

Ushaya greeted Lucy at the door, and silently floated past the food platters to join the members huddled around a table. Suddenly, she slammed her pen down, breaking it in two, and went into a rant, "We ought to be ashamed of ourselves! Carlos and Muzaffar with stab wounds, and Mimbauwe with cracked ribs, and Yadgiri in a neck brace, and Stan with a broken arm. Ronald has a head wound, and Meg has gashes on her face, and Devon has a bloody eye, and Zhangwei has an injured foot. Herb survived the whole ordeal, thank goodness!" She stopped, out of breath, and, looking around, asked, "Who else is injured?"

The ring glowed softly on Julia's finger, and trying to lighten the mood, she said, "I lost my hat, and my heirloom brooch is destroyed." Everyone was deeply saddened by this great misfortune.

Yadgiri admitted, "I provoked it from the start with that piece of cake, was aiming for Ronald and missed. And I am very sorry for my behavior."

Ronald folded his arms, taking it all in stride, and replied, "It's easy to miss. We are only a few thousand miles apart." They all chuckled.

Carlos said, "You are forgiven. The relic has survived." Yadgiri was relieved.

Ronald said, "Actually, it's my fault. I should be more mindful before I speak."

"As should I," said Julia, "We now realize the power of the ring." Everyone agreed.

Meg interrupted, "Are you OK, Mom?"

Ushaya gazed down and replied, "I sustained no injuries, except for my pride." They quietly asked each other for forgiveness, and after a moment of silence, Jerome piped up, "Let us enjoy our last meal of the evening."

While circling around meagre leftovers on a makeshift table, Yaegar thought there was no need to fight over rations, and allowed Irena to take the last slice of bread. He was about to reach for the lone pickled onion on a plate when Stan snatched it up and plopped it in his mouth. Meanwhile, Mimbauwe began telling Ronald the story of the last surviving mask in his hand: "Queen Idia, mother of Esigie, ruled in the 1500s. With her magic powers and medicine knowledge, she helped her son rise up to be a great warrior on the battlefields."

"You don't say," said Ronald, munching on a carrot stick.

Ushaya took Devon's camera from his hands. "Go on, enjoy yourself," she said. Devon thanked her and joined Meg, who was chatting with Muzaffar, who had taken a shining to Quazaik, which was resting in his hands.

Ushaya continued filming, eavesdropping on Irena and Jerome. "I am assembling my team of doctors, physicists, and DNA experts," said Irena.

Jerome added, "I am assembling a team of geologists, environmentalists, and astrophysicists, as we speak."

Hashimoto joined in, "Botanists, mathematicians, and scientists, perhaps fifty members from each country."

Zhangwei joined the group and said, "More like a hundred, including military expertise."

Hashimoto turned to Stan to discuss that new device for computers, he had envisioned during their group flight. "You know how we are always hunched over our laptops, like old men, right?"

"What about it?" Stan asked.

Hashimoto replied, "Install slide bars to raise the screen a foot. When we are finished, we simply slide the screen back down before closing the laptop."

"That's tampering with patented property," interrupted Irena.

Ronald joined in, "We can do whatever we please. We'll build our own laptop empire and give the competition a run for their money."

Zhangwei quipped, "And which empire are you competing against?"

Stan interrupted, "Perhaps it is already being invented."

Jerome pulled Stan aside and whispered, "Have a talk with Hashimoto, will you? You do it best."

Ushaya gradually moved away, and began homing in on a fly on the wall that was rubbing its back legs together, seemingly unperturbed by the chaos around it.

The evening ended with several leaders clearing up food platters to the kitchen, and soon, two dishwashers were humming. Irena was the last to leave the assembly room, and gazing at the destruction around her, she turned out the lights, shaking her head, wondering how she was going to explain the mess to construction crews.

Devon sat in his private quarters with a cloverleaf over his left eye. While studying the video images, he frowned and said, “Ushaya, your filming was great, but the second half, you only caught a fly on a wall. I can’t use this material.”

“My apologies, I got carried away,” she replied.

“Wait, close in on it,” said Brad. Devon expanded the view and zoomed in.

“The details are incredible!” cried out Meg.

Ushaya yawned and said, “Today has been a disaster.”

“No, you did great work today,” said Devon.

Ushaya hugged the kids, and with a tinge of sadness in her voice, she whispered, “We all did.” Then she retired to her quarters.

As the wounded lay in their beds, Ronald staggered down the hall, plastered in clover and head bandages, and met up with Jerome and Irena. Meanwhile, Queen Julia tiptoed down the hall in her nightcap and gown, and was greeted by Yaegar and Hashimoto. Together, at the stroke of midnight, the West met East under northern skies that rained meteor showers over Germany. Nobody got enough sleep that night.

Chapter Seventeen

The Assembling (Day Two)

German headquarters (GHQ)

The following morning, they gathered in a parlour room. Jerome and Hashimoto brought in sofas and lounge chairs from other parts of the estate. Irena and Meg brought in nightstands and side tables. Brad set up his network drive, connecting the only remaining laptop to the TV monitor. The charred chest lay next to Ishtan's scorched tube, under a table. Finding clipboards in an office cabinet, Ushaya printed off eighteen agendas, and then stood by the parlour entrance to greet the members. Devon's camera continued to roll.

One by one, they arrived, Jerome with his twelve spheres, followed by Ronald and the Gemball. Carlos staggered in with his duct-taped clover pot and the ancient relic. Julia entered, wearing her finest new hat, with the ring glowing softly on her finger. She strolled arm in arm with her prince, who limped by her side, holding his cane. Quazaik and Lucy frolicked about in gleeful delight. In jovial spirits, all chatted away. Meg and Yaegar served hot coffee and tea into Styrofoam cups, along with honey and cream. Breakfast smells wafted from the kitchen, and everyone was mighty hungry. While studying their agendas, they soon turned quiet.

Irena opened first: "I have been informed that two new members will be joining my team."

Hashimoto asked, "Who?"

She replied "My neighbours, whom I have never met." She turned to Ushaya, and said, "Please explain."

Ushaya told the story of Stephan and Susie, and no one could believe that she would be so quick to choose outsiders. "Well," she argued, "They saw the whole thing and seem like a nice couple. I'm sure they will be helpful to our mission. Better to convert witnesses than have them spread unwanted rumours."

Irena loaded up blueprints on the laptop and said, "These buildings are suitable for our undertaking, and renovations are underway. From now on, they will be referred to as GHQ, short for German Headquarters, located near the ESA in Darmstadt." She scrolled to another image, and continued, "Ushaya will be studied at this location, the Rauschmark Gebaude. She has agreed to come to the GHQ every two months, for one week, and that way, we can plot her development. Of course, these buildings are not exclusive to our mission alone, for that would attract attention; therefore, national biochemistry, medical, and genetics research facilities will relocate here, giving us access to the best equipment they have."

"How are you going to relocate them without creating suspicion?" Stan wondered.

Irena replied, "High-ranking officials are being sworn in as we speak, who will oversee the transition. Underground facilities will be off limits, for our purposes only. We are formulating a plan on how to run daily operations, and we welcome your input." The members began contributing many ideas toward their mission.

An hour later, Irena glanced up from the agenda, and asked, "Ushaya, have you not added more to the manifesto?"

"No, I haven't," she said.

"Why not?"

"I've been too busy," she replied. The assembly took turns adding to the manifesto, and Ushaya was mighty pleased to have real experts do what they do best. They discussed the selection process for new members. It would be a great many people, sworn into oath, starting small and eventually expanding to 500 members. When they concluded their discussion, they sat back, drinking coffee and tea.

Herb thanked Carlos, who was sitting across the room, "What greater gift could I receive than clover."

Julia said, "The clover is extraordinary, and your generosity to bring it to the world is highly commendable. It will come back to you a hundredfold. And the dragon relic is a mystery to behold." Everyone agreed.

Herb corrected her, "Honey, it's not dragon, it's ancient relic." They all agreed again.

Ushaya wondered, "Why did you say dragon?"

Julia shrugged and said, "It was an honest mistake."

Ushaya cleared her throat, and pausing, she looked at Irena.

Irena glanced over the Documents of Intent, all signed by the members, and concluded, "TLP has now become official, and we will continue with our mission." Everyone applauded.

Soon, breakfast was served. Meg and Lucy brought forth scrambled eggs and clotted cream and strawberry jam, slathered on scones, along with cheeses, sausages, nuts, and fruits. Plastic cutlery and paper napkins and plates were laid out on the table, buffet style. When they had finished their meals and dishes had been taken away, they settled back in their seats.

Mimbauwe and Sulimon Seeds

Ushaya brought out a little pot with soil, and a box, containing Sulimon Seeds. Mimbauwe jiggled the pouches. Staring at them, he said, "So these grew into your forest."

She asked, "Would you like to plant one now . . . with a thought? But please, don't be like Jerome." They all chuckled.

While examining one packet, he noticed something, and said, "I think there is one seed that is different from the others."

"I suppose you're right," she said, and, sifting through the other pouches, said, "Matter of fact, it doesn't belong to any of these groups."

"Then I will plant this seed," said Mimbauwe. He opened the pouch, and everyone leaned over to see a large seed in his palm. It was dark purple, flat and pear-shaped. Gently, he pressed it into the soil, and cheekily announced, "This will grow into a large money tree by tonight."

They shook their heads and said, "No way!"

He shrugged and said, "We shall see." A bright green sprout shot through the soil, growing two leaves, and then two more leaves. They gasped.

Ushaya presented his scroll and said, "I ask you now. Do you accept this gift?"

He unfurled the scroll and quietly studied the coordinates. Then he rolled it back up, and said, "I accept."

Carlos asked, "This is your first plant—what are you going to call it?"

Zhangwei had an idea and said, "Why not call it Nesting Bird Tree?"

"How about Lazantis Blossoms?" suggested Hashimoto.

"Or Sulimon's Promise?" said Devon.

Mimbauwe thanked them and replied, "I shall call it Heaven's Gate." He got up and placed the pot in a corner, where it would be undisturbed by the meeting, and then returned to his seat. He was curious about the Titan spaceship, and traded one seed for the map, and Brad could not refuse. Mimbauwe asked, "Is the Titan spaceship located in Rwanda?" The answer was the same as always. It only showed German territory. He returned the map to Brad, and murmurs sounded across the room, while Brad gazed at a seed in his hand. Jerome motioned Ushaya to introduce the next gift.

Prince Muzaffar and Ishtan the carpet

She unravelled the carpet from its bindings and laid it across the table. Immediately, Ishtan sprang to life, his golden thread shimmering to an audience mesmerized by his beauty. He spoke in Silo, "I have a message from Zogar. They are extremely pleased we are gathered here, and there is much to learn from each other. Together, we shall make this planet a more heavenly place, with wondrous new inventions guiding you to the stars. You are awakening to the Age of Curiosity, to discover who you are, among your fellow creatures and so-called inert substances around you." They were shocked to hear him speak in their mother tongues.

Muzaffar whispered to Yaegar. Soon, a wingback chair was brought in from another room for Ishtan, who graciously accepted. He continued, "What you call inert is not as inert as you think. Gold and silver are living substances. Rocks and clouds are living substances, and so are mountains and caves. They appear to be inert, since you have not yet discovered how to measure their movements, nor understand their true nature. So tell me, is a thunderstorm or an atomic bomb inert?"

They asked him many questions . . .

"How old are you?"

"Three thousand years, which is young, for a Titan can live up to 20,000."

"Are you born a Titan or do you train to become one?"

"Both. I was born as one, so my training began early."

"Can a human survive on Lazantis?"

"Yes, the atmosphere is similar, but you require enzyme injections, in order to acclimatize."

"What do your species eat?"

"Titans feed on atmospheric energies, wherever we go. Most other species eat plants, nuts, berries, and rock ash, mined from the Uquak Mountains. Only a few species eat animal meat." He began floating across the room, greeting members. Transfixed by the golden thread, they touched his soft silk fringes, secretly wishing for a carpet ride.

Ushaya turned to Muzaffar and said, "The time has come to fly." With Meg and Brad's help, he sat upon the carpet, and as soon as he lay down his crutch, he began gliding around the room, to everyone's delight. He floated to the assembly room, with members following behind. Enthralled, he passed the crumbling wall and the smashed chandelier, hanging by a thread, and the next thing he knew, he flew out an open window into the sky.

Stephan was peering through his binoculars when he said, "Susie, check this out."

She got up from a pile of receipts on her desk, and peered in. "If my eyes are not mistaken, that's Prince Muzaffar, flying on some kind of carpet," she replied, and gave back the binoculars.

"Exactly," said Stephan, peering again. Then he lowered the binoculars, and they both stared out the window.

A dreamlike trance took over Muzaffar as he glided over farmers' fields, chalets, and hilltop churches. His red-checkered keffiyeh was flapping in the wind, with the cool breeze brushing past his face. Up, up, higher, gasping his last breath, he entered the clouds, and into the great silence they flew.

Ishtan spoke, "It is a great day for Titans. We finally meet in one place, after so many centuries."

Muzaffar didn't know what to say, except, "It is a great day to be flying on a carpet." With those famous last words, he hung onto his fringes, descending through turbulent clouds, where he met a black eagle, banking its majestic wings, as they flew in sync. They parted ways, and he continued descending over farmlands and countryside mansions. Soon, he found himself floating triumphantly through the window of the estate, to confetti raining down upon him from a cheering crowd.

Irena and Ronald helped him off the carpet, and, leaning on his crutch, he bowed to Ishtan and said, "I look forward to our fruitful alliance."

When they had settled back in their seats in the parlour room, Muzaffar became curious about the spaceship, and turned to Brad with an offer. Muzaffar held the map and asked, "Is the Titan spaceship in Saudi Arabia?" A fireball blazed across the surface and off the edges, showing only German territory, and the assembly murmured. He must take this up with Ishtan, he thought. Then Muzaffar gave the map back to Brad, and said, "I asked the map a question, and now, in trade, it is your turn for a request."

All eyes turned to the three kids as they sat upon the carpet, floating across the room, to everyone's delight. They glided down the hall, while members followed behind. Suddenly, Ishtan rolled them into a bundle, twirling and darting in and out of rooms, before whisking back down the hall to the parlour. The kids stepped off the carpet, dizzy and stunned. Breaking into chuckles, they exclaimed, "That was a hell of a ride!"

Everyone wanted to trade with Muzaffar. He waved his hand and said, "When the time is right."

Ushaya presented the tube, scroll, and secret passcodes, asking, "Do you accept this gift?"

He stood up again on his crutch, and replied, "I accept." The assembly broke into applause. Then Jerome motioned Ushaya to introduce the next gift.

Yadgiri's dagger

She gave the dagger into Yadgiri's hands, and, slowly, he pulled it from its sheath. Everyone hushed. As he turned the blade, he said, beaming, "Nadin and Jagpal are very excited to begin the research. They are gathering teams as we speak." He passed the dagger around so that all may feel its power. One by one, they held the dagger, running their fingers over the hilt and gemstones, over the copper sphere and down the blade. Even Lucy and Ishtan held the dagger.

Ronald opened first, and said to Yadgiri, “I’ll trade you for some of that water, and we’ll set up factories to make bottled water; it’ll be good for business.” Mimbauwe offered two seeds, desperate for some water. Muzaffar negotiated a deal, for his country also needed water. Meg and Devon offered Quazaik, in trade for the dagger, to replenish their garden pond.

Yadgiri was curious about the spaceship and exchanged the dagger for the map, right there and then. Brad could not refuse. Yadgiri asked out loud, “Is the Titan’s spaceship in India?” Bolts of light streaked across the surface, disappearing off the edges, showing only German territory.

All eyes turned to Brad, who was nervously wiping the blade with his shirt, to give it a shine, when suddenly, he lost control, and the dagger slipped from his hands and fell to the floor in a loud rattle.

Terrifying creaks groaned across the room, then, suddenly, a small fountain burst through the floorboards, gushing a spray of water. Horrified, they sprang from their seats, standing helplessly around the fountain. In awe and wonder, they moved in closer, with their Styrofoam cups, for they were thirsty. The fountain slowly disappeared, taking floorboards with it, into the abyss, as they silently stood around the gaping hole. Brad humbly lay the dagger in Yadgiri’s hands. While adjusting his neck brace, beaming, Yadgiri said, “Let us thank Brad for this little accident, for we have all drunk the water of life. How did it taste?”

“Pure,” said Devon.

“Sparkling,” said Herb.

“Fresh,” said Yaegar.

“Cool,” said Lucy the robot. All brows raised in her direction.

Ushaya presented the scroll and asked, “Do you accept this gift?”

Yadgiri returned the Dagger into its sheath. He stood up and replied, “I accept,” and great applause followed.

Suddenly, Meg pointed to Heaven’s Gate in the corner, which had now grown to five feet tall, sprouting buds that very much looked like money flowers. They crowded around the tree, and Jerome announced, “Let us take a short break to change into dry clothing.”

Zhangwei's golden orb

An hour later, with everyone settled in their seats, Ushaya pulled out a red velvet pouch and unwrapped the cloth to reveal the golden orb and sliver. Everyone hushed in awe. "Go ahead, it is yours to hold," she said to Zhangwei.

Zhangwei began squishing the orb, spreading it six inches every which way, and then passed it around, so that all may feel its power.

With a sparkle in her eye, Ushaya took her kitchen rolling pin, and began stretching the orb across the floor, across the tables and across the sofas. Everyone joined in, stretching, pulling it wider and wider, up three walls and over the TV monitor and curtains. The entire parlour room shimmered in a golden glow, covered up like a tent, except, for the one wall, where they all stood. Devon, Meg, and Jerome giddily walked up the strange material, and slid down the slope. Yaegar, Irena, and Lucy joined, sliding down the tent. Whoopee!

From her suitcase, Ushaya brought out a blowtorch and fired it up, whoosh! A hot, streaming flame blazed across the golden surface, but nothing happened. It remained intact. Then she demonstrated the chainsaw. The sound drove deep into their bones: whrrrr, whrrr . . . trying to cut through the fabric, but it would not budge.

"Extraordinary!" cried out Stan. Everyone joined in, peeling the cloth off the walls, folding it over and over, until it became a small ball, no bigger than the tip of one's thumb. Ushaya then gave back the golden orb to Zhangwei.

Ishtan spoke in Silo, "This little Kunfu orb can produce 20,000 spacesuits."

Zhangwei traded the sliver for Brad's map, and asked, "Is the Titan spaceship hiding in China?" A fiery ball blazed off the edges, and it only showed German territory. Then Zhangwei gave the map back to Brad.

All eyes turned to Brad, as he spread the tiny toothpick sliver between his fingers, working it farther outward, using the rolling pin, stretching it this way and that way. Soon, he stood in front of the assembly, enveloped in this strange stuff, looking like an astronaut, ready for takeoff. As he walked by each member, they touched the Kunfu material. He peeled off the strange stuff, squishing and rolling it between his fingers, and then returned the sliver to Zhangwei.

"Oh, I almost forgot," said Ushaya, as she pulled out the yellow feather from her bosom.

While holding the YangXi feather in his hand, Zhangwei began to quietly weep. Ushaya sat down, and the assembly grew silent. He blew his nose into a handkerchief, retrieved from his lapel, and dabbed his eyes, then said, "I once lost a crane, and now she is found."

Ishtan softly spoke in Silo, "She will show you the way. Choose wisely who you trade her with, for she is a Tanzoik, capable of superb navigation, using only her instincts. She is the map's lover."

Brad wryly smiled and said, "Romance among the stars?" Murmurs fell across the room, while Zhangwei gazed at his new-feathered friend.

"I knew there was something shiny in them hills," said Ronald, "Shall we make a trade for some of that Kunfu?" They all wanted to trade for a piece of that golden mountainside. Zhangwei stood up, limping, and replied, "When the time is right."

Ushaya presented the scroll and asked, "Do you accept these gifts?"

Zhangwei unravelled the scroll and glanced at the GPS coordinates. Then he rolled it up and said, "I accept." The assembly applauded.

Hashimoto's Yokuru

The members gathered around the Yokuru Tablet, which rested on a tripod. They examined the irregular edgings and the inscriptions, and were in awe of its beauty, of its deep red colour and golden glyphs.

Ushaya demonstrated the chainsaw across the tablet, but the slab remained intact. She aimed the blowtorch steadily for a minute, and then they all touched the surface, and it felt cool to the touch.

Hashimoto said, "The Kinkaju Temple is now heavily guarded. We have assigned a team to dismantle the red bridge and build a new one in its place. As you are aware, the entire monastery witnessed what happened that night, and so the monks have been sworn into oath of secrecy, and will act as liaison, between our mission and the outside world."

Brad handed Hashimoto the map, right there and then, and said, "I know you are curious, as are the rest of us. No need for a trade, so go ahead."

Ushaya and Hashimoto exchanged glances, confident the spaceship was hiding somewhere in Japan. Hashimoto bowed, and holding the map, asked,

"Is the Titan spaceship in Japan?" Bolts of light flashed across the surface and off the edges. It only showed German territory. Hashimoto was quietly surprised, and he returned the map to Brad.

Ishtan spoke in Silo, "Yokuru is lightweight and simple to produce in large quantities. Under intense heat, with the perfect mix of elements and alloys, we can build a starship. Once we manufacture the equipment and tools for the task, the product would be ready for the assembly lines."

Hashimoto asked, "What kind of elements?"

Ishtan replied, "Aluminum, titanium, osmium, iridium, rhenium, platinum, and uranium, combined with Yokuru and traces of iron, should get you well on your way."

Everyone wanted to trade with Hashimoto. He waved his hand and said, "When the time is right."

Ushaya gave him his scroll and asked, "Do you accept this gift?"

He bowed and replied, "I accept." Great applause followed.

Yaegar's Elixir

Jerome announced, "Ladies and gentlemen, we have come to the final leg of Ushaya's journey, with a great gift for Yaegar." He motioned her to proceed.

From her blue-faded wooden treasure chest, she brought forth the titanium cube. Several items lay side by side on her table, symbolizing the four elements of earth, water, fire, and air. Yaegar demonstrated with earth first. Gathered around the table, they watched him slowly dip the two-foot dead branch into the liquid, farther and farther, until only a stump was left in his hand. Elixir just ate the rest, like quicksand, and he placed the stump on the metal tray. Next, he poured a large pitcher of water into the cube, not spilling a single drop, and Elixir just ate it. He aimed the blowtorch flame directly into its centre, holding a steady gaze for a long time, and then stopped. Ushaya motioned him to hold the cube, and he held it in his hands; it felt cool to the touch. He then shot an air gun into the cube. Bang! A loud sound ricocheted across the room. Everyone recoiled, but nothing happened. The cube remained intact, and the liquid turned from blue to silver. In a final demonstration, he dipped a long metal ladle into Elixir, and then raised it. The ladle remained intact, dripping silver droplets, and he placed it on the metal tray. They all shook their heads in disbelief.

Brad offered Yaegar his map, and said, "There is no need for trade; after all, what could I do with Elixir?" Yaegar thanked him for his offer, and asked out loud, "Is the Titan spaceship in Russia?" Bolts of light and fiery balls blazed across the surface and off the edges. The map only showed German territory. They were all very curious by then, and Brad realized he was about to become a very busy man. Ushaya locked the cube, and placed the ladle and dead branch in the steel case.

Ronald was secretly jealous that Yaegar got a Master Titan, and began gazing into the Gemball. He looked up, smiling, and said, "I just asked where in the world is the spaceship hiding, but all I get is a hazy blob, against a black sky."

Yaegar was suspicious. After all, why was Ronald smiling? Did he discover its location and was keeping the secret to himself? He feigned a smile, and, thanking Ronald for his candid remarks, stood up and spoke: "I agree with Ushaya and Muzaffar that we may be pawns in a cosmic scheme. I do not doubt the extraordinary circumstances we find ourselves in, as we have witnessed." He turned to Ishtan and asked, "What elements need to mix with Elixir to create the fuel?"

Ishtan replied, "The fuel that you use is not possible for deep space travel. But a little bit of your liquid hydrogen and oxygen, together with Elixir, will be all that you need. This new fuel can run automobiles and many types of machinery." He paused and said, "By the way, Elixir has another important function. It is the portal, the gateway between your world and other worlds, including ours. When properly refined and contained, one can enter through the plasma pool. But you must use the map; otherwise, you could end up anywhere in the universe, with no way back."

Ushaya placed the scroll and cube into his hands, and said, "You hold a Master Titan. Do you accept this gift?"

Yaegar unfurled the scroll and studied the coordinates, above and below. Then he wrapped up the scroll, stood up, and said, "I accept." Everyone wanted to trade for a few drops of Elixir. Waving his hand, he replied, "When the time is right."

While milling about, during an hour's break, some were standing in front of Heaven's Gate, which was now seven feet tall, admiring its beauty. Others were chatting with Ishtan and Lucy, while Quazaik bounced around the room, occasionally resting on their shoulders.

The Summoning

The group dispersed, making their way to the kitchen and the great space. Zhangwei and Meg had returned to their quarters to freshen up. While lingering in the parlour room, Jerome privately pulled Ushaya aside, and said, "Muzaffar was concerned about breaking international laws, and the floods in India."

She had already gone through this with Minister Nadin, and replied, "Yes, I struck the dagger." Next thing she knew, she was ushered into a private den, down the hall, confronted by Yadgiri, Carlos, Yaegar, and the queen and prince. "What's this about?" she frowned.

Julia spoke first, "You broke many international laws. We are concerned about security breaches. You had brought Elixir, a deadly unknown substance, through international airspace from Russia to Canada, and then all across Europe, thereby, risking several nations at once, not to mention the oceans, full of life."

Yaegar agreed, "In retrospect, this was a very reckless move."

Carlos spoke next, "You brought indigenous plants from Mexico to Canada, and you dug up a relic from our soils, that did not go through due process and proper channels."

Jerome wondered out loud, "Where is Muzaffar? He was supposed to join us." They continued without him.

Herb pointed out, "You destroyed private property at Blake Moore and stole valuable documents from the National Archives, which resulted in a police investigation; not to mention, you left behind a monster."

Yadgiri shook his head and said, "The dagger created very big floods in India, and you planted African seeds on Canadian soil."

In disbelief, Ushaya wondered what Zone she was in. Then they heard a noise outside their room. Carlos opened the door, and they gathered around, watching Muzaffar whiz by on Ishtan's carpet, laughing down the hall.

"Now we know why he hadn't shown up," said Jerome.

"Yes, he appears distracted," mumbled Julia. She turned to Ushaya, admitting, "We are only joking about you breaking international laws. We are extremely pleased with the gifts." The group chuckled. Ushaya was clearly annoyed with her prank.

Herb raised his cane in the air, and said, "This merely shows how we need to set the highest security measures, under extreme radar. And there is much more work to do." They all had to agree.

Suddenly, Muzaffar and Ishtan burst through the door, apologizing for their tardiness, and sat down with the others. Straightening his robe, Muzaffar solemnly turned to Yaegar, and said, "Ishtan warns that Elixir should not be traded, lest it fall into the wrong hands."

Yaegar's face turned ashen. "Into whose hands could Elixir fall?" he asked.

Ishtan spoke in Silo, "Secret agents around the world will attempt to steal Elixir in covert operations. We have yet to determine who, in the realm of multiple possibilities."

They hashed out strategies to protect Elixir from getting into the wrong hands, from high-level transports to the GHQ, to fortifying the grounds in Russia. Yaegar glanced at his Accutron watch, and said, "This discussion should be added to the official report."

Nodding in agreement, they left the den to join the rest, who had congregated in the great space. It was time to wrap up their two-day rendezvous. Leftover food and equipment were packed into the truck, and suitcases were loaded into the motorhome. Furniture was rearranged throughout the rooms. Everyone agreed to chip in funds to renovate Irena's estate as soon as possible.

Irena wondered, "How will I explain the damages to my contractors?"

Julia advised, "Detektiv Erika should lead a team, following reports of vandalism and forced entry, where a fire broke out. Under high security and media confusion, all outsiders would be met with the same message, that a team is investigating the source, and in due time, reports would become public." Irena agreed to the plan.

"Look!" cried out Mimbauwe, pointing to Heaven's Gate. They surrounded the ten-foot tree, which was covered in lush, pear-shaped leaves and thick blossoms of money, dropping everywhere on the floor. Chuckling, gathering up the bills, they soon realized that the leaves were Euros. Of course, it had been planted on European soil.

"You can't take it back, it won't fit on the plane," said Ronald.

Mimbauwe decided to give Heaven's Gate to Irena. After all, his country grew different currency. Flabbergasted, she accepted the gift. He wasn't too concerned, knowing there were ninety-eight seeds left, and a host of possibilities. Stan measured Heaven's Gate with his measuring tape. It had grown to eleven feet while they talked!

"Poor thing, it must be suffocating," said Meg. Into the dark, over the hill they went, carrying flashlights and shovels, to plant Heaven's Gate among a grove of tall bushes.

Dishes were organized in cupboards, and floors were swept, one last time. Hashimoto tossed the remaining garbage into outside bins, and, scanning the dark for any suspicious activity, turned back inside. Hidden in nearby bushes were Stephan and Susie, glancing at each other.

They inspected each room to ensure nothing was left behind, and then boarded up the estate doors. While standing outside, mingling about, Ushaya noticed a red dot on her shoulder and quickly bee-lined to its source. Caught once more, Stephan brought down his infrared camera. Susie smiled nervously and said, "Nice to see you again."

Ushaya summoned them from their hiding place, announcing, "Meet Stephan and Susie!"

They sheepishly stepped out of the bushes, and Lucy the robot, was the first to greet them. In awe, they shook her scrawny hands. Then they shook Stan's hand, recognizing the dude in blue-tinted glasses. They curtsied, awkwardly, before the queen and prince, shocked to see Herb standing with a cane and no wheelchair. They shook hands with Muzaffar, dressed in full royal garb. They shook hands with Ronald, who introduced them to Zhangwei and Hashimoto. Yadgiri introduced them to Carlos. They shook hands with Mimbauwe and Yaegar, and soon met Brad, Meg, and Devon. Geometric lasers beamed around them when Jerome pulled them aside to explain their mission, "We have been given superpowers by an alien race of Titans from a planet called Lazantis, from another universe. There is a monster in captivity, but the Kisga'a Shield and ring hold it in place, and . . ." They could not believe what they were hearing.

In full glory, with golden thread shimmering in the dark, Ishtan BOOMED his voice in their heads, "Welcome to the Lazantis Project!" In complete disbelief, Stephan and Susie shook fringes with a floating, talking carpet. They twirled around and met Irena, who said, "We ask you now, will you join us? Take your time. You have the choice to join or not."

They gawked at the motley crew, bandaged from head to toe, staggering around on crutches, with clover patches upon their wounds, looking like the living dead. They nodded their heads, not quite sure what they were agreeing to.

"Splendid!" piped up Irena. "You'll be under my team. We shall, in due course, bring you up to speed, and ask you to sign the Document of Intent."

Stephan and Susie joined the group, and while chatting with each other, Julia whispered something to Irena, who then tapped a musical triangle, until they formed a circle around Ushaya.

Irena said, "Before we conclude our evening, it would not be complete without expressing our deepest appreciation for the powers bestowed upon us. As a token of our gratitude, and by no means equal, we now present you with a gift." Meg stepped forward and placed a flat package in her mom's hands, and receded back into the circle.

"Go ahead, open it," said Lucy.

Stephan and Susie glanced at each other.

Ushaya untied the bow and removed the paper wrapping to reveal a painted slab, gilded in bronze edgings. It was the coat of arms for TLP, with an olive branch weaving through its letters at the top. Below was an upright triangle, emblazed in gold, and along each side of the triangle were the words, "synthesis, conversion, and transformation." She began to realize that the triangle represented energy that could not be created or destroyed, only converted from one form to another. A zigzag lightning bolt ran along the left side of the triangle, representing the spark of Genius. Along the right side, a compass, protractor, and ruler joined together, depicting dimension and space. Below the triangle was a jumble of numbers, haphazardly etched into the slab, representing the foundation of creation. Ushaya looked up with tears welling up in her eyes, amid great applause.

That evening, Ushaya locked arms with Stephan and Susie to her left, and the queen and prince, to her right, and flew under the full moon, shining a path to Stephan and Susie's farmhouse.

Meanwhile, back at the estate, Muzaffar quietly commanded Ishtan to roll into his tube. He tried the combination codes, hidden in his thobe, but the tube would not lock. No matter, he thought, he would figure it out later.

Julia and Herb had returned to the estate, and joined everyone boarding their vehicles. Ushaya first flew Stan, Lucy, and the kids in the mover's truck, across the skies to the Brandenburg Airport. Trevor, Jagpal, Nadiya, and Leopold stood waiting on the tarmac runway. They discreetly took care of the mover's truck, while the members boarded their respective planes, waiting for the others to arrive.

An hour later, back at the estate, Ushaya flew the remaining leaders in their motorhome, with gifts by their side. They kept staring at the titanium cube chained to Yaegar's left wrist, for none wanted to travel with Elixir. To prove its safety, he flipped the cube upside down and turned it back upright. They recoiled in horror, but nothing happened. Yaegar shrugged his shoulders and quietly smiled.

Chapter Eighteen

Kill the Monster

The viral outbreak

January 2020 . . .

The Gemball predicted a viral outbreak in Nuwah, China. Suddenly, a pandemic raged across the world. Every country went into lockdown, and a second wave came, worse than the first. Then a fourth wave came, worse than the third. Italy fell into chaos. Armoured trucks lined empty streets, carrying the dead to mass graves. Although their nation was in lockdown and deep grief, the Italians sang out from their balconies in a show of solidarity. People lost their jobs; their livelihoods were wiped out. Economies collapsed and stock markets crashed. Stimulus packages were sent to millions who were unemployed, during a state of emergency. Citizens were forced to wear masks and practice social distancing.

Ronald caught the virus and self-isolated. Stan advised a genius idea to flatten the curve, but he wouldn't listen. New York City became the epicentre with the highest infection rates, and Florida authorities finally shut down their beaches, but it was too late—the virus spread across the US in greater numbers than anywhere else in the world. Ronald ordered troops to the US-Canada border.

Jerome retaliated, "Unnecessary!" He himself delivered a sombre message to Canadians from his podium, "My wife Kaitlyn has been infected and is self-isolating." On the eve of Brexit, British Prime Minister Karloff also caught the virus. Meanwhile a mad race began around the world to distribute vaccines. Ronald launched Operation Warp Speed, an incredible public health achievement. Under his new policy, vaccines were ready in nine months instead of the usual four years it takes to develop them.

Conspiracy theories abounded, and millions did not want to be vaccinated. Some feared that the new vaccine would compromise their health. Others were enraged at governments forcing a bio-chemical weapon into their bodies, against human rights to choose, especially since the vaccines were new and not tested for their long-term effects. Misinformation and new information kept plugging up the internet, and fear took over. Would there be a yearly booster shot? It became a "them and us" kind of thing, a modern-day witch-hunt. Anti-vaxers were forced to wear six-inch armbands like Jews in WWII, and had to endure the walk of shame, not being allowed in restaurants and public events, nor cross borders to other countries. Many lost their jobs or were put on leave without pay. Most annoying of all, the rules and restrictions kept changing on how to conduct one's daily affairs. Sometimes, citizens were allowed in public venues, and other times, they were not. Students sometimes went to school, and other times did not. People became weary of it all, and a growing dissent rose up across the world. Yet life somehow carried on.

Operation Underlord

Ushaya was bunkered for months at the GHQ, learning how to dodge a bullet and meet the elite forces, and to have her body tested at the Rauschmark Gebaude. She underwent a battery of tests: blood pressure, cell counts; nuclear magnetic resonance; X-rays; full physical; CAT scans; brain scans; ultrasounds; vitamin, mineral, and bacterial analyses. There were tests on cognitive and memory skills, then endurance, strength, and speed.

Dr. Caspar Hauser was surprised when she gave blood, for it was aqua blue. Examining her wings, he said, "Why didn't you speak of this before?"

"With whom should I have consulted?" she asked.

He replied, "You should have put it in the reports." He called in more colleagues, and now six doctors were examining her.

With yellow eyes turning slanted, she gazed over her shoulder, "Tell me, what am I to do?" she asked.

Dr. Hauser walked around facing her, and said, "We will do everything we can. May we take a small sample of your wings?"

Not long afterward, she began her training exercises to dodge a flying bullet. After many attempts, testing with a red powder named "ketchup," she was ready for the real thing. The trigger pulled back . . . Bang! In one quick reflex, she disappeared in HypeMo. The men staggered around the room. Where did she go? Sergeant Holmes, head of the team, looked up at the rafters, and said, "Congratulations, Ushaya, you dodged a speeding bullet. You may come down now."

One day, Irena sent out a secret missive to TLP: "A great many contenders were equal to the task, and a final decision has been made. Operation Underlord will proceed under a team called ACT, short for Alphior C. Tek, a mythological warrior, according to Lazantis legends, I am told." A six-man team would be Ushaya's backup to enter the foundry and kill the monster.

A month later, Ushaya was floating across the tarmac, greeting six elite commandos at a private airstrip, near the GHQ.

First, she met Indian commander-in-chief, Kumar Chandra, head of Land Regiment Special Forces. He was an expert in tactical grounds and reconnaissance, and was to lead the team. Guided down the line, shaking hands, one by one, Ushaya met African-American commando Wyatt Jackson from Delta Force, their top dog in amphibious operations, and also automatic assault weapons. There was Russian commando Yakov Petrov, specializing in intelligence gathering and surveillance. Next, came Arab female commando of the Royal Saudi Land Forces, Zainab Al-Khaled, an expert in ballistic missiles, chosen by Muzaffar. Chinese Chenglei Wang was an expert mapper and tactical officer. Canadian commando, Nakoteh Harrison of the Algonquin native tribe, shook her hand and said, "Congrats to you on dodging a bullet." He was their team's morale-builder, using words of wisdom and a calm voice, as only an Indigenous person could, but he was also an expert sniper.

She announced, "Goggles on and hang on tight." Over snowy fields and icy bridges and frozen rivers, they flew, linked arm in arm, passing towns, dotting the countryside, and soon, they returned to the tarmac, landing amid shouts of glee, tearing off their goggles. Ushaya smiled and said, "We broke another record. Seven of us flew without ropes."

In time, she got to know them, and they got to know her. One thing was for sure: she didn't know a thing about a Howitzer, a Colt 45 or an AK-47. There was work to do. Weeks went by, during which she learned about land weaponry, guns, artillery, mortars, grenade launchers, cannons, Kalashnikovs, DXL sniper guns, and hypersonic ammunition. They examined strategies, by rolling out maps of the foundry and studying computer simulations, while Ushaya taught them everything she knew about the Gogolan. They taught her the "rules of engagement."

She shook her head and said, "There are no rules of engagement here."

Nakoteh nodded and replied, "Good point."

Kumar said, "Tomorrow is our big day. Everyone dismissed. Get some rest. We deploy at 0800 hours."

Everyone was settled in their barracks joking with each other. Commando Zainab of Saudi-Arabia pressed the canteen button for an apple juice. She was not only intelligent, but also beautiful. Nakoteh struck up a conversation with her, hoping for a date, "Do you ever want to settle down and have two kids, and live in the countryside, like I do?"

Twisting the lid from her apple juice, she replied, "I'm a city person and I don't want kids."

Yakov piped up, secretly hoping for a date, "What do you do in your spare time? I like kite-surfing."

She took a sip and replied, "I like knitting." The men watched her wander down the hall to her quarters.

The following morning, a helicopter landed in front of Blake Moore Foundry, among swirling snowdrifts. They disembarked, with boots hitting the ground, dressed in exoskeleton suits and Kevlar vests, with ropes, goggles, helmets, and oxygen masks. They wore head beams and video cameras, and semi-automatics and sniper guns were strapped over their shoulders, while Zainab carried a bazooka, holding a formidable bomb.

They chatted a while with Captain Edmond Cole, head of the UK team on the grounds, when Kumar spoke into his Com device, "Man your stations. We're going in." The SWAT team crouched by armoured trucks, with semi-automatics aimed at the foundry. The ACT team floated through the open doors, and two officers closed the doors behind them.

They glided above rows of dusty cabinets, passing the three vats, with head beams cutting through the semi-darkness. Ushaya was allowed to wear the ring on this dangerous mission, which was now glowing on her finger. Kumar motioned to an opening in the northeast sector that Ushaya had not seen before. She nodded, and silently, they entered a labyrinth of confusing corridors, until they reached a large, empty, windowless chamber. They immediately spread flares across the floor and the chamber lit up. Suddenly, a door clanged shut, and chains dragged across the floor. Where was the sound coming from? The ring shone bright hot, cutting through the semi darkness. They looked wildly about, assuming their positions. A stench filled their nostrils.

Kumar whispered, "Stand back, easy does it."

A black, monstrous sludge appeared, looming over them, shrieking an awful sound. Trembling, with watery eyes and oxygen masks fogging up, they broke into a sweat, some wanting to puke. Ushaya immediately whisked them back to the entrance, and they took their positions. With eyes locked through their optics, aiming crosshairs on multiple targets on the beast, Kumar commanded, "FIRE!" A sea of rapid bullets blazed through the air, amid war cries and screeching howls. Smoky haze filled the chamber, as they continued blitzing hundreds of rounds per minute until they emptied their magazines. But their firepower only provoked more anger. Tentacles slithered across the floor, toward them, and Kumar commanded, "NOW!" The bomb discharged from the bazooka launcher . . . BOOM!! Everyone hurtled through the chamber from the explosion, and the monster blew up in a thousand pieces.

They staggered about in silence. It was all over. Oily patches of goo dripped from the domed ceiling and down the walls of the chamber. But to their horror, the black sticky globs slithered over their bodies and across the floor, joining together, and now the Gogolan was bigger than ever!

Immediately, they hightailed in SuperMo through narrow passages, with headlamps flickering wildly, slamming into walls, in total mayhem, as they continued firing down one corridor after another, with the monster hot on their trail. Freeze frame . . . Time stood still . . . CRASH! Out through a window, they escaped, with glass shattering into a thousand pieces. Kumar yelled to the ground patrol, "Retreat!" Terrified, with bone-chilling shrieks ringing in their ears, the SWAT team scrambled into their armoured trucks and sped away.

The ACT team collapsed on a snow-covered hill and threw off their oxygen masks, to catch their breath. Many were injured—a broken knee, one with a deep gash in his arm, and several with head wounds. Wyatt puked in the snow. They studied their suits to ensure no gooey residue had hitchhiked for a ride, and agreed that they may be contaminated and would need to be quarantined.

Chenglei of China sat back with a busted knee, in two places. "I guess, I am out of commission, sorry for this," he winced.

"Nonsense, you will be up in no time," said Ushaya, rolling out a thick layer of clover. She cut a hole in his suit and gently plastered leaves to his knee, and then bandaged it. She did the same with the rest of the team, plastering clover over their wounds. Then she plastered leaves and bandaged up her left hand. All their cameras were broken, and Zainab couldn't even find hers.

Commander Kumar threw down his helmet. "Shit, shit, shit!" he sputtered.

Ushaya rubbed her bruised knuckles, and said, "Don't be hard on them. This is just my second time, and only your first. Besides, the GHQ is recording our signal; they have the master tapes."

Yakov, commando of Russia, yelled, "Hey, I think my camera is working." They gathered around, watching the replay—more shuddering and puking in the snow.

Ushaya said, "We will nail this sucker—that is, if you want to do another mission." There was silence.

Kumar said, "You have shown great courage and strength. Count me in."

"And you have shown great strategy," she said, taking a swig of rum from her flask.

He looked around at his team, "Are you in or out?" he asked.

With fresh vomit still on his suit, Wyatt nodded and replied, "I'm in."

With head wounds, Zainab nodded and said, "Count me in."

Nakoteh spoke. "Next time, I will aim between its eyes." Chuckling in comic relief, they huddled together, amid screeching howls, echoing in the distance.

Frantic voices came through the airwaves. "Is everyone all right?" asked Jerome.

"Operation Underlord was not a success, but we are safe," replied Kumar.

Irena's voiced crackled. "Well done. Come home."

Herb asked, "How is the ring?"

Ushaya looked at her finger and replied, "Shining bright as the dickens."

Ronald asked, "What about the monster?"

"It's bigger than ever," said Kumar, "But we will fight again and take it out with nuclear warheads." Ishtan's voice BOOMED, "Our mother ship will arrive in six months. A nuclear head will only split it into many monsters. I insist, let us take it home."

Kumar deferred to the leaders. "It's your call," he said.

Members talked to each other, and soon were back on the airwaves. Julia said, "It is best the mother ship arrive. We will not resort to nuclear bombs and lose the foundry."

Kumar responded, "Roger that. We abide by your wise counsel. We're heading home." They packed their gear and slowly crept back to the foundry. Silently, they scrambled into their helicopter, and high-tailed out of there, watching the monster stare at them through the shattered window, screeching and howling.

A grand ceremony was held at the GHQ in honour of their bravery. In attendance were TLP leaders and sub-members, who proudly watched Ushaya and the ACT elite forces receive their Medals of Valour.

Eureka

All went well, at first, as they began assembling their teams and setting up labs and organizing strategies at the GHQ. Helicopters and planes flew overhead in every country. Carlos sent archaeologists to the clover patch, and they found the place where the ancient relic had once lain hidden.

Stan modified laptops with sidebars, to raise the screens, and together with Hashimoto and tech corporations, they signed a deal. Ronald joined Zhangwei with their corporations to do the same, and so the race was on. Who would be first? Ha!

Jerome invited Stan and Lucy to his residence, in anticipation of Quazaik's arrival, on loan, from Meg and Devon. Suddenly, Quazaik appeared in Jerome's hands, and they gazed at the sea of radiant shapes, mesmerized by the octagonal blue gem emitting effervescent rays.

Jerome asked, "How can I create affordable housing and improve the economic downturn for the middle class? Our Bay Street investors are worried about pipeline deals, and what about our health-care system, taking up 40 percent of our national budget?"

Stan asked, "I've been thinking of a new line of men's clothing. Should I go ahead with it?"

Lucy asked, "How do we fix the accelerator glitch in the nanogenerator?"

Not to be outdone by Lucy, Stan asked, "Can you tell us more about the Blue-ray light?"

Jerome asked, "How can I get Kaitlyn to bake my favourite pie, she keeps promising me?"

Quazaik beamed down one genius idea after another. Alas, Jerome had to return Quazaik, and it immediately disappeared from his hands. He then sent a team to the Gagnon Stream, in search of the frogfish.

One day, Muzaffar disguised himself as an ordinary Arab man, to find Akbar's shop in the Al-Zall Marketplace. The stunned Akbar simply bowed, when he was rewarded with enough riyal to live in great wealth. Then they whisked away on Ishtan's carpet, with garments flapping in the wind, up, up, into the sky, in total ecstasy!

Mimbauwe, president of Rwanda, traded two seeds with Yadgiri, for his dagger. When Mimbauwe struck the dagger across the Land of a Thousand Hills, he and three loyal commandos swam in the newly formed rivers, completely exhilarated and astonished. Then he returned the dagger to Yadgiri.

Meanwhile, crouched on their knees, Jagpal and Kumar planted seeds in the Thar Desert of Rajasthan.

"What were your thoughts?" asked Yadgiri.

Kumar wiped the soil from his hands, and replied, "No more hunger in India; enough food for everyone."

Jagpal brushed the soil over his seed, and said, "An end to the dowry system." Suddenly, sprouts shot up through the parched soil, growing four, eight, twelve leaves. Yadgiri gently tapped the dagger on the ground, and the earth sent precious water seeping through the soil. A week later, a new forest was dropping seeds. Insects buzzed and bustard birds flew overhead. Snakes slithered in nearby grasses, and field mice scurried through the underbrush.

Stan and Lucy were making their rounds to world leaders, who gratefully accepted their company, for a touch of Genius.

Zhangwei's team disembarked from helicopters, landing on the precipice. They peeled large layers of Kunfu from the jagged outcrops. When they returned to their lab facilities, they set to work, testing different elements to create the perfect spacesuit. With Stan and Lucy's help, his scientists began solving complicated formulas, unlocking the secrets, by combining Kunfu with thermoplastic polymers. Every day, they extracted samples from test tubes, and ran computer simulations, and wrote down their codes. Ishtan also arrived, on loan, courtesy of Muzaffar, and under his tutelage, they manufactured the machinery and tools to produce the first assembly line. Each day, workers waved at more trucks delivering technology and supplies onto factory docks.

One day, Brad arrived with his tube slung over his shoulder and a briefcase in his hand, glancing at the hubbub of activity. Zhangwei approached and said, "Welcome! I have been waiting for you." Brad shook Ishtan's fringes, and shook hands with Stan and Lucy. Zhangwei walked along with his entourage, showing them around the factory, mighty pleased at the new developments. At one point, he broke off from the group, inviting Brad into a small room. He laid the feather YangXi on the map, and the surface began to glow, as the map wrapped around it, and they both were amazed. Zhangwei asked, "Is the spaceship hiding in China?" It was a negative. He turned to Brad, and said, "Now, about that casino of yours . . ."

Hashimoto set to work unlocking the secrets of the Yokuru Bridge, in a vast underground facility, near JAXA Space Agency. With Ishtan, Stan, and Lucy's help, a hundred scientists smelted Yokuru into chemical pits, experimenting with elements, by trial and fire, until they finally created a product, ready for assembling. Jerome lent them a purple sphere, as a goodwill gesture, and from there, Japanese scientists manifested starship blueprints and the necessary equipment, to bring about their grand plan. While standing in the Yokuru facility, Hashimoto watched his teams build the interiors and the fuel chambers, and electronic components, with the most high-tech navigation systems they had ever known. They proudly named their new starship NODA.

Yaegar's army had secured the perimeters around the Elixir pool. The ring cloaked the surrounding area, while Quazaik beamed out protective rays. Now, all three Master Titans were engaged. His army scooped up large amounts of Elixir into steel vats, strung from helicopters. Loud chopper blades whirred across the sky, to the underground Zephron control centre, which was nearing completion.

Ronald sent the Gemball as a goodwill gesture, to secure friendly ties. But in truth, he was vying to be the first to get his hands on Elixir. Not to be outdone by him, Jerome, also vying for the coveted Elixir fuel, sent an orange sphere.

Russian scientists saw visions of a plasma ring, while gazing into the Gemball, and immediately, they began creating blueprints to match. Yaegar made powerful commands with the sphere, and the necessary equipment appeared! All three of them—Stan, Lucy and Ishtan—soon arrived, and they helped accelerate their progress, teaching them how to transform the Elixir energy into space fuel. They also worked, day and night, to build an upright titanium ring housing a liquid plasma substance. Complicated formulas and lights flickered around the ring, and they cried out, "Slava Zefronu!" (Hail to the Zephron!)

Yaegar and a team of scientists were standing behind a glass partition when Ishtan said, "This is the porthole to many dimensions, including our universe. Be sure to bring the map when you enter." World leaders were stunned, yet again.

Meanwhile, Devon bought a yacht and set sail to his private resort in the Fiji Islands. Meg opened up a string of spas, signing contracts with the biggest hotels on New Zealand's western coast. Brad bought a casino in Winnipeg, with ideas for expansion.

Twelve gnomes

Irena received a white sphere from Jerome, on loan, as a goodwill gesture. Her estate had been under Erika's command, with news reporters sniffing around, looking for a good story. One day, rogue detectives approached Stephan and Susie, asking questions. They replied, "We didn't hear a thing and saw nothing. It was quiet over the hill."

Renovations must begin at once, thought Irena. Remembering the time when Jerome had conjured up six Roman soldiers and six white horses, she decided to use her own imagination, and rolling the white sphere across her private dining table, she commanded, "I want a dozen gnomes to renovate the Liebschon Estate, overnight."

The following day, while she and Erika took a country drive, Irena requested Stephan and Susie to meet them at the estate. When they arrived, they walked through the brand new front doors, and gasped. Gnomes were whizzing about the grand space, in good spirits, singing, "Heave-ho, to work we go, work we go . . ."

They gazed in awe at shiny marbled floors and freshly painted walls, newly repaired. Brand new curtains drew back, on either side of the glass doors, and they looked up at the elegant chandelier hanging from the ceiling above. Kitchen counters and cabinets were rebuilt, and the hole in the parlour room was covered in wood flooring.

Four-foot gnomes with white beards were dressed in long-sleeved brown shirts and tattered pants, and elfin felt hats. They had just nailed the last of the baseboards, and with toolbelts around their waists, they gathered around the new arrivals.

One gnome, named Buggles, approached warily, asking, "You ain't trolls, are ye?"

Snarlyputtin, a halfling gnome, smaller than regular gnomes, jostled through the crowd, holding a shovel, "Don't reckon Orks, neither," he said.

"Nay, they are humankind," said Muldorf, stroking his beard.

Drendil looked suspiciously around, and asked, "You don't have cats, do ya? Them vermin like nothing better than to shred us apart."

Irena replied, "There are no cats here."

With a pick-axe over his shoulder, Runkelstin said, "You no waifish skinny pole. We like them built thicker. Aye, you be a pretty lass."

Irena blushed, "Well . . ."

Susie interrupted, "Where do you come from?"

"From the land of Feywald," said Dinkelroot proudly.

Suddenly, they all held their noses, staring at a gnome in grubby clothes and a ruffled hat. Bluenose blew his nose into a handkerchief, and tucked it in his trousers. Grunting at the offending gnome, he snarled, "You should have taken your monthly bath, sir Stinker."

Lowalk snapped his fingers, announcing, "Time to celebrate!" Immediately, the gnomes set up a banquet feast, singing, "Heave-ho, to work we go, work we go." The humans stood in awe, as gnomes whizzed about, setting up a long table covered in a white tablecloth. Soon, dishes and spoons were neatly arranged across the table, in front of wooden chairs. Three pillar candles lit up, along the table, and goblets were filled with mead and thistle milk. Out from the kitchen, came steaming plates of slow-cooked vegetables and mashed potatoes, along with dandelion and mushroom soups, sprinkled with a dust of acorn, and no meat dishes could be seen anywhere.

They sat down to a feast, chatting merrily, passing food down the table, and drinking their mead, while pipers played their flutes and piccolos. Stephan glanced at Bluenose, appreciatively, and said, "The food is delicious."

Muldorf raised his goblet to a toast, announcing, "Here ye, gather a feasting with humans, who are not so bad after all. It is an honour to be in thy presence." They thumped their fists loudly on the table, nodding their heads. Silly as gnomes could be, they continued drinking more mead, getting drunker and louder, as their comic antics made everyone laugh. Buggles poked at Dinkelroot, snorting, "Don't play with your food."

Stinker fell off his chair in gut-splitting laughter, grabbing the tablecloth on his way down. The pillar candles fell, lighting the cloth on fire! Immediately, Stephan returned with a fire extinguisher and hosed across the table. In the raucous, coughing from smoke and steam, Irena rose from her seat, tapping a triangle to get everyone's attention. The room fell quiet. She whispered to Erika, "Make this count."

Erika rolled the white sphere across the banquet table, announcing, "Thank you for your hospitality. Our bellies are fed, and our spirits renewed, but you must return, at once, to where you belong. And for your good deeds, take Heaven's Gate tree with you, in gratitude for your excellent work."

A portal opened, and in walked the twelve gnomes, carrying Heaven's Gate, stretched over their shoulders. Tables and chairs, cutlery and food platters were piled up high, and, soon, they disappeared into thin air. Zip! The portal closed. All was silent.

Stunned, Irena and her team ran over the hill to where Heaven's Gate was planted. While standing around a large empty hole, Susie said, "Nothing happened here, right?"

Irena shook her head, whispering, "Nothing at all."

"Good. Can I call off reporters and shut down the investigation?" asked Erika.

"Gladly," replied Irena, picking up the only two Heaven's Gate seeds left behind by the gnomes. Days later, she gave one seed to president Mimbauwe of Rwanda, special delivery, and he happily accepted it.

Meanwhile, the spheres returned to Jerome from their journeys, far and wide. Rubbing his cue stick, he stood back and aimed, striking the white ball into the triangle on his pool table. One sphere sank into a pocket, the rest swerved away. He forgot the command he had assigned the ball.

Where is Queen Julia?

Herb was strolling down a corridor of Windshire castle, feeling much better, thanks to clover. With Julia by his side, they entered a salon to greet his cousin, Greek prince, Paolis, who was pacing the floor. "Ah, here you are, old chap," said Herb, embracing him, "How long has it been?" Paolis was shocked, yet pleased, to see Herb no longer in a wheel chair. He graciously shook Julia's hand, and they sat down for a cup of tea. Herb explained his miraculous recovery, due to a medical breakthrough with a rare plant, discovered in Mexico. Once the excitement had settled down, upon hearing the good news, Paolis began yacking, as usual, about the latest gossip and inconsequential matters. They listened and listened, unable to get a word in edgewise, as he continued blabbering on about this and that.

Coming to his rescue, Julia slipped the ring to Herb. Paolis became unusually quiet, while Herb chatted away to his heart's content about this and that. It was time for Paolis to leave, and they escorted him to the door. As he drove away, Julia smiled and said, "That went well, don't you think?"

"Bloody well, I would say," replied Herb.

One day, while experimenting with the ring's cloaking powers, Julia became flummoxed. "Look, Herb, watch this," she said, placing the ring on her middle finger. The whole castle cloaked and disappeared. Maids, cooks, palace footmen, and employees were confused as they stared out at flat, empty space. Julia placed the ring back on her ring finger to restore order.

Herb had an idea, and placed the ring on his forefinger. It cloaked him.

"Where are you?" she asked.

He chuckled and replied, "Over here." She turned to see him standing by a bookshelf. He gave her the ring. "Now you try," he said. She placed the ring on her forefinger, and went invisible. Amused, he looked about and asked,

"Where are you?" There was silence. "OK, you can show up now." More silence. "Stop this game. I remind you, we are attending a ceremony this afternoon." More silence. He opened the salon door, and, peering down each corridor, cried out, "Julia, where are you? Enough of this nonsense!" A butler in an adjacent room raised his brows.

An hour before the ceremony, Herb found Julia in her dressing room. With a mix of anger and relief, he sputtered, "I was worried about you!"

A hat sat upon her coiffed hair, and a brooch was pinned to her jacket. With silk gloves on, and carrying her handbag, she walked out the door. "I didn't mean to alarm you, just wanted to see how long I could cloak," she replied, with slight annoyance in her tone. "And I saw many things going on around here at Windshire."

One autumn day, months later, the Zogar mother ship arrived, hovering above the Blake Moore Foundry, before hundreds of TLP members. A spectacular scene unfolded before their eyes, as the Zogar uncloaked for all to see. Above the foundry hovered a gigantic ship, in a series of strange, convoluted circles, joined together, around a tube-like core.

They watched the wounded Bokal thrash about in a glass-like cube, in muted sounds, being transported through a halo opening that closed behind him. Then the mother ship whirred into the sky and disappeared.

Everyone rejoiced to see the monster go. "So long . . . Sayonara . . . Good riddance . . . Adios."

Not long after, their lives started turning sideways. No longer threatened by a monster on the planet, the leaders became locked in power conflicts and personal battles of their own. Intrigue, espionage, murder, and mayhem soon followed. The Gemball had visions of dark times ahead. Their environments turned surreal, equal to their moods, and they began changing into characters from the depths of their psyche; indeed, they turned into strange mortal beings.

Chapter Nineteen

Descent into Chaos

Over our dead bodies

An abandoned ashram stood deep in the jungle, with domed rooftops, now reduced to rubble, once home to a famous yogi. While holding a mirror among the temple ruins, Yadgiri took a razor to his beard, keeping it cropped and neat, ignoring his grey, straggly hair, which had now grown over his shoulders. He patched holes with mud, across the temple walls, and hung curtains and Ganesha bells. Then he strung up brightly coloured strings of lights that never die out. It was a courtesy gift from Stan, giving him eternal light. He could choose which strings to attach, as he desired.

One alcove served as his sleeping quarters. Photos of family and friends, and the latest painting by Rajneesh, his elephant, sat on a dresser. He passed underneath clothes, hung on ropes between two pillars, and gazed at his upright dagger, entrenched in a nearby altar. In another alcove, a Puja brass plate sat on a stone slab, filled with rice grains, incense and marigold flowers. Outside the ashram sprang a small fountain, a place to wash his clothes and drink from its bounty.

Dressed in loose pants and a cotton shirt, and with a turban around his head and sandals upon his feet, Yadgiri fetched his rifle, for another day of hunting. That day, he bagged wild goat, and by that afternoon, he had turned it into minced keema, grilling seekh kebabs on skewers. One day, a sacred cow was grazing in the open field. About to take aim, he slowly put down his rifle.

He returned to the ashram, sat on a carpet, in front of a makeshift table, to check his laptop and smartphone, for incoming messages. Stan had advanced remote LAN interfaced programs into a separate matrix, using satellite technology, so that their laptops would never run out of power. Special forces camped around the ashram, camouflaged, protecting him.

One day, his three most trusted advisors came for a visit. While studying the GHQ reports, minister Nadin said, "Zhangwei has purchased swaths of Indian land to build large-scale factories, using our resources. He wants the dagger now, but intends to withhold Kunfu until the project is complete."

Captain Jagpal curled his lip and said, "An advantage to increase his power on the back of the dagger, for he will need water to run them."

Commander Kumar said, "Cheating us out of our own head start on the production of Kunfu, until much later."

Yadgiri snarled, "Over our dead bodies."

The thanks I get

President Carlos of Mexico kicked at the broken-hinged door of his burnt-out '65 white Ventura, with four flat tires, a red interior, and a partially caved-in roof. Stranded in wasteland, he stepped out of his car, grimacing under the hot evening sun, wearing a blue-green feathered Aztec headdress. An open, beaded vest revealed his tattoo across his chest, and he wore a tunic over a loincloth to cover his body. Adorned on both wrists were bracelets made with semi-precious stones, and upon his feet, he wore ancient sandals, wrapped up to his ankles. With dirty fingernails, he reached into his mouth and pulled out a loose tooth, spitting out blood.

Then he climbed back into his car, and, while chewing leaves of clover, he switched on the string of lights, to check his laptop and smartphone. He glanced over at the ancient relic, which was sitting on the battered seat next to him.

The leaders were not interested in trading for the relic, not even the queen and prince, he thought. They weren't interested in history, only their precious powers, and he had given his away. Angrily, he banged out a message, "Regarding the clover, you're welcome. If that's the thanks I get, then I shall refuse all future trades. Over and out."

One did trade with him: Yadgiri. The two Titans obeyed their commands and immediately switched position. Carlos now had the dagger, and Yadgiri had the ancient relic. While gazing at the exquisite dagger, Carlos struck the ground. A fountain sprang forth, and he drank thirstily from his cup, while splashing his face.

Meanwhile, Yadgiri and his men dove into the relic, transported back in time through a foggy atmosphere. As they hid behind a temple column, they watched disciples, bent over the Bhagavad Gita manuscripts, transcribing a dialogue between Prince Arjuna and Krishna, an avatar of Lord Vishnu. Nadin whispered, "It is true then. This happened."

A one-legged blind beggar hobbled across the mezzanine, speaking words they could not understand. Yadgiri searched his pockets, and brought out a coin and placed it in his hand. The beggar rubbed it between his fingers, bit into it, and smiled, for the coin was rare and could fetch a good price. He made a sign on Yadgiri's forehead, blessing him, and then hobbled away.

Someone was coming down the steps to their left. "We should go," whispered Jagpal. Kumar uttered the secret word, "Quetzalpoca", and at once, they floated through the misty fog into the white light, slipping through the relic, landing back at the ashram. They cheered, for they had lived to tell their tales!

Intrigued by their adventures, the leaders changed their tune and wanted to trade, but Carlos refused, waiting out for the highest bidder. Angrily, they turned against him, and left him to his own vices. With pistol in hand, Carlos shot a bighorn sheep, and by nightfall, was roasting its carcass over a fire pit. While sitting on a tree stump, his phone rang.

It was Yadgiri. "Look, we need more time, there is much more to explore," he said, adding, "You hang onto the dagger. Go create some rivers."

Carlos snarled back, "I insist upon its return. The relic is mine."

"What? I can't hear you," said Yadgiri, cutting him off.

Days went by, as Carlos struck the dagger into the parched soil, and each time, the earth split open, gushing forth waters into rivers and streams. Although satisfied with his new creations, he was disturbed by Yadgiri's betrayal, muttering to himself, "The thanks I get," and began planning nefarious activities in a revenge counter move.

Double Jeopardy

Prince Muzaffar lived in the Basra-Nafud desert, close to the border of Iran. Carpets and cushions lay scattered around his tent, and a string of eternal lights lit the walls in pleasing colours. At one corner lay his prayer rug, at another, stood a table and chair, holding his laptop and papers, next to a makeshift kitchen.

He pulled back the flaps from his tent and stepped out, gazing at sandstone formations huddled majestically under a cloudless blue sky. Except for his red-and-white checkered keffiyeh, he was completely dressed in black, and his beard had grown thick and bushy, and he had become strong and powerful. While mounted upon Ishtan, with sword and longbow by his side, he bagged Arabian Tahr for his meat, and by early evening, was braising it over an open fire. He turned to Ishtan, who was relaxing on the ground, and said, "Hmm, transmute these lands into oases."

Ishtan nodded and said, "First, you must get the dagger."

Muzaffar trudged back to the tent, hoping for word from Yadgiri. While scrolling through his feed, he had learned that Yadgiri would not trade, and immediately called him up, "What is this?" he asked.

"You cannot have the dagger," said Yadgiri. "I have a deal going on with Carlos, your precious water has to wait." Then Yadgiri hung up on him.

Muzaffar consulted with Ishtan, and then called up Carlos. While staring at his Aztec headdress, he proposed, "Yadgiri refuses to give back your relic, right? So let us trade Ishtan for the dagger. I could use water."

Carlos thought about it, and said, "It would be a great honour to be in Ishtan's presence and receive his counsel. But I want my relic back, and propose a counter-offer. I'll trade the dagger for Ishtan, if you can return the relic to me."

It was a stalemate situation, thought Muzaffar. He turned to Ishtan for more advice. Then he came back on the phone and said, "There may be a way to convince Yadgiri."

"How?" asked Carlos.

He replied, "Should the relic disappear, he would be defenceless, without power, enough to spook him, would you say? He would long for his dagger back, but without the relic in exchange, he would have nothing." Muzaffar continued, "Then what if the relic should reappear one day? What choice would he have, but turn to you? This may or may not work. In the meantime, you will have Ishtan, until the transaction is complete."

Carlos grinned and said, "You will not be disappointed with the dagger. Clover flourishes along the banks of my streams, and I was about to trade with Mimbauwe for Sulimon Seeds."

Muzaffar muffled the phone, to consult with Ishtan: "Can I trust him to not trade you?"

Ishtan whispered, "It would not be to his advantage, for I will come back to you."

Muzaffar returned to his phone and said, "I accept the offer." The deal was made, and two Titans switched position.

Carlos was now riding upon Ishtan, frolicking under the setting sun, when he asked, "You are a shape-shifter. Can you change into a horse?" Ishtan descended to the ground, and, continuing his flight, transformed into an Andalusian horse. Carlos was now galloping bareback, across the plains, in total ecstasy.

In his isolation, he found companionship, and understood why Muzaffar enjoyed him so much. Days idled by as they chatted about everything and anything, and Carlos learned much about Ishtan's planet. He asked questions about gas and oil trades, but Ishtan was loyal to Muzaffar, not revealing state oil secrets. Yet, the more Carlos hung around Ishtan, the more he grew to love him.

Meanwhile, Muzaffar struck the dagger, watching desert sands erupt in gushing waters, forming an oasis. An eternal fountain sprang outside his tent, and he was most pleased. One day, his special forces arrived. Commando Zainab, his most decorated officer from ACT, entered first. Beguiled by her beauty, Muzaffar bowed and said, "Welcome to my humble abode."

Captain Faisal and Lieutenant Hassan soon arrived, and Muzaffar shook their hands and said, "It's been a while since we last met."

Faisal asked, "How is Ushaya, by the way?"

Zainab added, "I have not seen or heard from her, since Bokal the monster was taken by the Zogar ship."

Muzaffar answered, "Nor have I, and I assume she is resting, after that ordeal." They soon joined together and walked around the oasis.

The dagger did this?" asked Zainab, amazed.

Muzaffar nodded and replied, "Now, you must lead your team on a dangerous mission—but this time, no need for a bazooka." All afternoon, back in his tent, they planned out their strategy.

Zainab and her two operatives quietly moved through the jungles, bypassing guards, and infiltrated the ashram while Yadgiri was asleep. They stole the ancient relic from the altar, and stealthily slipped away in the darkness.

The following morning, Yadgiri went into a panic, looking everywhere, wondering if this had been Carlos's doing. Or did his troops steal it? Paranoid, even of Jagpal and Kumar, he told no one of its disappearance. Without power, and defenceless, he knew this could spell disaster. He must do some sleuthing. He longed for his dagger back, but how?

Muzaffar rewarded his team with riches and honours, for their outstanding success, and concluded, "Stand by for your final mission. We strike in a few days." They saluted and filed out of the tent.

Alone, at his table, Muzaffar gazed at the half-man-half-beast statue. He wanted seeds, while he still held the relic. So, he called up Mimbauwe. "Are you interested?" he asked. "If so, we must keep this matter between us."

Intrigued, Mimbauwe replied, "I will give you two seeds." Two Titans switched position. Mimbauwe and his three loyal commandos entered the relic to realms of unreal beauty, transported in time to ancient tribes of Africa. They dipped in and out through its portal, enjoying the relic immensely. History had gotten it all wrong, they had discovered.

Meanwhile, Muzaffar planted two seeds and two thoughts, and watched sprouts grow so rapidly that by end of day, lush palms and olive trees swayed along the banks of his oasis. Reports of crude oil discoveries came in, which could make his country richer. He heard back from his private investors throughout the Gulf countries, ready to sign a deal for a new and bolder stock exchange, opening up markets previously closed.

Upon his word, Mimbauwe did, indeed, return the relic to Muzaffar. He said, "We discovered that early man did not originate in Africa. Man emerged from a landmass between what is now India and Sumatra, before it sank, during Earth's catastrophic changes." Then he wondered: "I am curious. Why haven't you entered the relic yourself?"

Wanting Ishtan back as soon as possible, Muzaffar shrugged and replied, "I just prefer seeds at this time."

"How are they growing?" asked Mimbauwe.

Saying nothing about the dagger, that was still in his possession, he said, "Date, olive, and fig trees grow among the palms, shading us from the sun, and I thank you." They both hung up.

Muzaffar immediately sent Zainab's team on their final mission, to return the relic to Yadgiri. Spooked and mystified, Yadgiri wondered why it had returned, and became suspicious. Such a precarious power, he thought. At least the dagger never left his side, and he opened a channel with Carlos: "I will have my dagger back, please." The two Titans switched position. The relic returned to Carlos, and Yadgiri got his dagger back.

Muzaffar now had the water and seeds he desired, and only traded Ishtan, once, for a double dip of gifts. Pleased with his strategy, he called up Carlos. While gazing at his feather headdress, he said, "I trust the powers are back with their rightful owners."

Carlos grinned and said, "I might add, Ishtan is back in your hands. He is most wise, and I very much enjoyed his company."

"We should trade again," said Muzaffar.

Carlos paused and said, "You were right. It was enough to shake up Yadgiri. Good work."

Muzaffar gazed at Carlos, remembering their duel at the assembly, and said, "Words are better than swords, would you say?"

Double-crossed

Weeks later, Mimbauwe called up Yadgiri. "I see the jungles are keeping you safe," he said.

Yadgiri nodded and said, "Our gods work in mysterious ways. Tell me, why do I have the pleasure of your call?"

He replied, "Muzaffar refuses Ishtan for my seeds, but I know he is interested in your dagger. Why don't you trade? Once he has water, he will come to me. If you agree to this, I shall tell you a secret."

"You badly want to fly with Ishtan?" asked Yadgiri.

"Absolutely," shrugged Mimbauwe, adding, "Don't you?"

Yadgiri thought, and said, "Upon my word of honour, you have a deal. Now, what is that secret?"

Mimbauwe leaned in and replied, "A few weeks ago, I *did* trade two seeds with Muzaffar, who had the relic. We entered wondrous realms into Africa's history, and beyond. Then I sent the relic back to Muzaffar, who has since given it back to Carlos, I believe."

Yadgiri turned ashen and whispered, "Muzaffar possessed the relic?"

"Yes, but for some reason he did not enter the relic, just wanted my seeds," he said. They soon ended their transmission.

Realizing he had been double-crossed, Yadgiri called up Carlos, hollering, "I will not trade the dagger for Ishtan. How did Muzaffar get hold of the relic? Who do you suppose Mimbauwe traded seeds with, huh?" He hung up on Carlos. In truth, Yadgiri very much wanted to ride on Ishtan's carpet, and began hatching his own devilish plot.

Livid with anger, Carlos called up Muzaffar, hollering, "Your job was to bring back the Relic and not do side deals. What if Mimbauwe had other plans? And now, Yadgiri knows."

Muzaffar replied, "I had no reason to mistrust Mimbauwe, but I was mistaken. However, I enjoy the trees that are growing around my oasis. As for Yadgiri, I no longer need his dagger. You should be thanking me." They both hung up.

Carlos planned to cancel all gas deals with Muzaffar, and create his own rich deposits on Mexican soil. He called up Jerome, and asked, "How are you thriving?"

Jerome answered, "With my spheres, I have everything I need. Actually, now that we speak, I propose a trade: one sphere for the ancient relic."

Carlos's face lit up, and he replied, "It is the reason for my call, but on one condition: only trade with me."

Jerome badly wanted the relic, so the deal was made. Two Titans switched position. Jerome now had the relic, and Carlos had one sphere.

World domination

Rains fell on tin can roofs of an abandoned shack in a forest along the Ontario-Quebec border. Trudging in boots across the muddy ground and carrying a kerosene lamp, Jerome reached his stockpile of half-baked commands, and tightened the blue tarp, to keep them dry. Scratching his head under a French toque, wearing lumberjack clothes, and rubbing his salt-and-pepper scruffy beard, he trudged back to his musty, one-room shack. Blankets and pillows lay neatly on his cot, and eternal lights were strung across the walls. Pictures of his loving wife and kids sat on a dresser. A group photo from Irena's estate sat on a shelf, along with a photo of Stan and Lucy.

The rain continued its downpour as he gazed out the window. While holding one sphere, he commanded a broom and proceeded to sweep the place, removing cobwebs and chasing mice out the door. Then he held another sphere. Indoor plumbing ran hot and cold water, and a sink, shower, and toilet appeared. "The heck with outhouses," he muttered. With another command, a fire crackled nicely in the potbelly stove, heating his cozy sugar shack.

By day, with shotgun, he caught a deer, and by night, mosquitos buzzed around his head as he watched the venison cook over the pit. Grateful for eternal fire, he wondered what more he could manifest, with almighty power at his fingertips.

Eleven spheres lay scattered on the ground when the phone rang. It was Queen Julia. "We have not heard from you—have you been checking your messages?" she asked.

He stood up from his log, and replied, "Why, yes, Your Majesty. I have heard disturbing reports of sabotage among our allies."

Prince Herb joined the call, asking, "What do you suppose they are up to?"

"I am not sure yet, so I propose a bold option," replied Jerome. "Allow me to wear the ring in exchange for two spheres, for just a few weeks. Something happened between Carlos and Muzaffar, that has become a bone of contention between them. Furthermore, Yadgiri and Muzaffar had a falling out too, over what, I do not know yet. I may be able to find out more, while wearing the ring—of course, without them knowing this little detail. With queries coming from me, instead of you, they will feel less threatened to reveal information. In the meantime, enjoy manifesting to your heart's desire. Shall I send a purple and orange sphere, would that please you?"

Julia had longed for a sphere, and now there would be two in her possession. She said, "You hold a Master Titan. Choose your commands wisely."

"One more thing," added Herb. "Only trade with us while you possess the ring."

Jerome nodded and said, “Also choose wisely. The spheres are not to be trifled with, as I have discovered.” Julia and Herb understood, and they all hung up. The Titans immediately switched position.

While gazing at the ring, Jerome called up Ronald, and said, “I want to know some things.”

Ronald replied, “Sure, bro, but first, I have important business to attend to. Give me a week. After that, we trade, but only trade with me.”

Desperate for the Gemball, Jerome replied, “Of course.” They hung up, and a smile crept upon his face. What great power was soon to be destined into his hands! With the ring and Gemball, he would be an unstoppable force to uncover Carlos and Yadgiri’s plots against Muzaffar—a feather in his toque, he thought. He sat back on the log, relishing the day when he would become the Almighty One.

The spheres were rolling around the pit. As he picked one up, he suddenly tripped, and accidentally dropped it in the fire. It sizzled and crackled. Panicking, he commanded another sphere to bring it back from the flames. It leaped out and landed in his hand, like a hot potato, and he dropped it. He gazed at his burns, and ran into the shack, and slapped clover on his wound. While bandaging his hand, he quietly whispered, “World domination.”

Bag those alligators

Ronald moved into a rundown hotel on the east side of NYC. The room was sparsely furnished, covered in faded wallpaper. A dirty single mattress lay on a spring-coiled frame, with bed sheets strewn across the floor. At one corner stood a rusty sink, toilet, and broken mirror, and from the ceiling dangled a lightbulb. Due to laziness, he had not yet strung up the eternal lights, which lay shining on the floor. As he stared into the mirror, rubbing his face stubble and cleaning the wax out of his ears, he realized he hadn’t dressed in weeks. In his undershirt and boxer shorts, he walked to the closet and brought out a pink tie and trench coat.

While spying through the curtains, he saw his aide, Stuart McCallum, coming up the street, and was hoping for good news. According to the Gemball, the two alligators in the Florida Everglades had distinctive white streaks along their backs, unlike any other in the swamplands. They would tell him the location of the Titan spaceship, if only he could catch them—a challenge Ronald could not refuse.

Every day, Stuart walked up the spiral staircase to the third floor, delivering burgers and fries, and cola drinks. He walked down the graffiti-ridden hallway, where dubious characters loitered about. He knocked on the same door, and heard four locks unlatch before it creaked open, and Ronald motioned him in with a quick nod.

"Well, have you found them?" he asked, munching on his burger.

Stuart replied, "Good news, we saw the very gators you speak of. They got away, but we are closing in."

Ronald stuffed his face with fries, hollering, "I want them caught and bagged. Remember, no harm must come to them. You have not forgotten how much I'm paying you—a handsome price—should you come up with the goods. If not, expect someone to go home in a body bag."

Just the gangster he always thought he was, Stuart asked, "Why so interested in a couple of gators? You've got your Gemball. With all due respect, sir, you should be running a country. You're shirking duties to our citizens. Appointments are filling your calendar. What are you going to do?"

Ronald gulped down his drink and belched, then asked, "Have you heard from Jerome? He should have sent me a sphere by now."

Stuart picked up a monocular and gazed out the dirty windows. He then placed it back on the table, and said, "Not yet, sir. Is there anything else you need?"

Ronald slumped into an old worn-out couch, yanking at his dishevelled tie. He removed his shoes, airing out his smelly socks, wiggling his toes, and replied, "That will be all. Dismissed."

Stuart heard the four latches click behind him, as he walked down the grungy hallway, passing a woman, lurking in a corridor, beckoning him for a dollar.

Ronald was planning nefarious moves, once he got hold of a sphere. So was Stuart, as he sped through city traffic, nearly hitting pedestrians. A man fell into garbage cans, lined up on a street, and straightening up, he hollered, "Hey, watch where you're going, buddy!"

Frogfish meet Jerome

While wearing the ring and gazing into the Gemball, Jerome had uncovered Yadgiri and Carlos's plots. With burning desire to hold court with Ishtan, he called up Muzaffar, in exchange for his secret. "I tell you to watch your back; they are plotting against you," he warned.

Muzaffar replied, "I appreciate the warning. We go as planned, my Ishtan for one sphere." And the deal was made. Soon, Muzaffar was holding a gold-speckled black sphere in his hand. His first command was for a blue Bugatti car that needed no gas to operate. It would be his wheels while Ishtan was away, he thought. With a new command, a freezer stood outside his tent, stockpiled with food. As he strolled through palm trees, he watched pavilions and walkways spring up along the banks of his oasis. He went back into his tent. Indoor plumbing—a sink, toilet, and shower—appeared.

Meanwhile, Jerome was riding, in ecstasy, upon Ishtan, as they flew over rivers and lakes. He pointed to the Gagnon Stream and asked to land upon the very rock on which Ushaya once sat. He gazed at springtime branches, hanging over a shallow stream, as a gentle wind caressed the leaves of trees, swaying in the breeze. "It is peaceful here. My team has not found the frogfish, no matter what season," said Jerome.

Ishtan stood at the water's edge, and said, "Now is the time."

Jerome retrieved a blue-speckled, green sphere from his pack. The ring shone bright on his finger, when he commanded, "Frogfish, come forth in fellowship." Suddenly, the stream bubbled. Frothy waves crashed along the banks, and hundreds of creatures appeared, with tails thrashing in the water, staring at him.

Ishtan glanced at Jerome and said, "You now have an audience. By the power of my translation abilities, what do you say?"

Frog heads and scaly fish bodies stood erect. Jerome cleared his throat and said, "It's nice to meet you. We are grateful for the spheres." They thrashed their tails, stirring up cloudy water, and stood attentively, clinging to his every word. While pacing the shoreline, he asked, "Tell me about you. Where do you come from?"

A frogfish came forward, and spoke in a deep voice, "My adopted name is Achak, in honour of the Algonquians, a native tribe from your region. I am caretaker over primitive life forms that live in the sediments of this stream. We come from Lazantis, as you already know."

Another came forward and said, "I speak for the native Cree tribe. My name is Gway-chiw, and I am a trickster. I protect the stream from intrusions, and overturn canoes when men dare enter."

"Do all of you choose native names?" asked Jerome, flabbergasted. They thrashed their tails, in agreement. With subdued excitement, he asked, "Are there any more spheres, hiding in the good sediments of your soil?"

Euyron, a female of the Huron-Wendat tribe, came forward, and spoke in French. He understood her perfectly, and wondered, "If there are no more spheres, then why do you still inhabit this stream?"

"For when you return them," said Euyron.

"Why would I do that?" he asked.

"One day, you will no longer need them," she replied. Suddenly, they all leaped in the waters and disappeared into the sediment.

Jerome quietly sat back, eating his veggie sandwich and sipping beer from his thermos. Ishtan was leaning against the rock, gazing at the trees, when he said, "You have the Gemball and the relic, and the ring and myself, in your hands, plus most of the spheres. It is a lot of power you are accumulating, but it is the wrong way to go. I know your thoughts." Jerome stopped chewing.

"Let me give you some advice," continued Ishtan. "The world domination you seek requires all your spheres at the same time. You do not need to trade." Back at the shack, Ishtan taught him how to harness the spheres. The more he hung around Ishtan, the more he loved him. But the day arrived when they had to return their gifts. Muzaffar was relieved to have Ishtan back, and Jerome was relieved to have his sphere back.

Piracy on the high seas

Carlos held a green-speckled gold sphere, commanding new oil deposits for his country. A portal opened, and wisps of black smoke emerged, disappearing into the horizon. Day after day, reports of crude oil came in, and gas and oil companies began mobilizing equipment to drill all over Mexico. Tired of his burnt-out car, Carlos had the sphere transport him back to his grand National Palace. From there, he made a series of commands. First, put an end to bullfights in Mexico. Next, round up drug cartels into custody, and put an end to police corruption. Next, pare back extravagant misuse of funds by the higher echelons of government, including his family. Would he gain allies? Would he gain enemies?

Meanwhile, Jerome was gazing at the relic, wondering if it was true. According to his studies in ancient Canada, the earliest settlements began 12,000 years ago, in the vast region of Beringia, across the Mackenzie River, in the Northwest Territories.

He dressed into winter clothing and heavy boots, and, pausing for a moment, he entered the relic, and swirling into the light, he found himself on rugged snow plains, as far as the eyes could see. He sniffed the fresh, crisp air, and saw in the distance what appeared to be an early human settlement. While he locked coordinates into the GPS, a giant polar bear leaped out from a snowbank, charging straight for him. He uttered the secret word "Quetzalpoca" and landed back in his shack, stunned and exhilarated. As he peeled off his winter clothes, he keyed the coordinates into his historical map program, and, voilà! It matched the findings of the Beringia region.

He sat back in his sofa, sipping tea, staring at the relic, thinking and thinking, wondering about reincarnation. It was a belief he rarely expressed to others, and now was the time to make a bold move, he thought.

Transported through the white light, he landed on a Spanish galleon, sailing across the Caribbean Sea. Rotting fruit and musty air filled his nostrils, as the boat rocked gently back and forth. Dressed in clothes, out of time, he hid behind barrels of rum. A drunken sailor sat up, squinting at him, slurring, "Deckhand, I know yer kin. Me sore eyes tell me, what they do, strip ya'?

"What year are we in?" asked Jerome.

The drunk snorted and replied, "Gone too long, have ya? The waves have swallowed all time, aye."

Jerome pressed on, shaking his shoulders, "Listen, what year is it?"

"It be 1695, ye best get ready for another attack," replied the sailor, and he slumped back to the floor.

A pretty maiden was strolling by, her frock in tatters, her golden wavy hair streaming across her shoulders, as she carried water jugs toward the stern to serve the crew. Jerome recognized her at once. It was the face of his future wife, Kaitlyn! He stealthily moved across the deck, past the gunwales, and rounded a corner. A pirate, dressed in full regalia, possibly a captain, cocked his pistol and aimed. Jerome raised his arms in surrender.

"Alfonzo, I ain't recognize ya'," said the pirate, shaking Jerome's shoulders, "Yar in rough shape, ye know who I am."

"Of course," was all he could say.

"Good boy, ye don't forget Bart Roberts."

Jerome beamed and said, "The greatest pirate that ever sailed the seas."

Bart drew down his pistol and commanded, "Ye best get properly attired; there be battle at sunset."

Obsessed with the relic statue, Jerome entered the light emanating from its backside, over and over, stealing away nights for tender love with his sweet Kaitlyn, once called Isabel. The ship plunged through stormy seas, landing at one island after another, as pirates plundered for gold and treasures, with the body count piling up along the shores. Alas, the time had come to exchange back their powers, and Jerome was disappointed.

Carlos asked, "Did you like the relic?"

Jerome was speechless at first, and then said, "We must trade again, one day."

"Agreed," said Carlos.

With three more balls to collect, Jerome had returned the ring to Julia and Herb, and, removing his pirate hat, he proudly bowed and said, "Your Majesty and Your Highness, by the grace of the ring, I have uncloaked Carlos and Yadgiri's plots against Muzaffar." He stared across the screen, wondering what was happening to them.

Julia sat upon an elaborate throne, made of stone carvings. She wore an ancient jewelled crown upon her head, and was dressed in a purple, flowing gown, while holding a gnarly and twisted wooden sceptre in her left hand. The ring glowed brightly on her finger, and a crow sat upon her shoulder when she spoke. "I am pleased to hear the news. However, there is trouble in the land. Your spheres opened to a viewing screen. It has come to our attention that you were unfaithful, doing side deals, while in possession of the ring, is that so?"

Jerome feigned ignorance, and replied, "I was under the ring's spell, please forgive my transgressions."

Herb joined the call, hunchbacked, wearing a Catholic robe. Raising a lantern to the screen, he pulled down his hood, and warned, "You will have difficulty getting back your last sphere."

Jerome abruptly disconnected the queen and prince. Pacing his sugar shack, he sat down before the Gemball, asking, "Will my sphere return to me?" A scene opened to a calendar, flipping pages—three, five, seven, and stopped at nine months. It alarmed him greatly.

Stuart McCallum

Ronald held the last sphere, commanding, "I want them caught and bagged!" Soon, word came back that Stuart's men had ambushed the alligators, using a net. Their tails had thrashed about in a pool of mud.

Ronald called up Jerome, and, appearing frantic, blurted, "I must see the Gemball before we do our final trade. It is a matter of urgency; it's about my wife."

Desperate for his sphere back, Jerome allowed him to gaze through the screen, but could not see what Ronald was looking at. Suddenly, his transmission went dead.

Grinning, Ronald cried out, "Victory!" The alligators had revealed the location of the Titan spaceship. All day long, he skipped with joy, fixing up his digs, attaching the eternal lights across the room, while humming tunes. Burgers and fries had magically appeared, and indeed, one sphere was all he needed for his every command. Now that he had discovered the spaceship coordinates, he was no longer interested in the Gemball.

Jerome called again, demanding that Ronald take back the Gemball, and Ronald refused. "You keep it. I am rather liking the sphere," he said, and hung up. Jerome sat back in his sofa, stroking his beard.

Ronald did not pay Stuart for his fair share, as promised, for bagging the alligators. In retaliation, Stuart called up Jerome and said, "I will get your sphere back in exchange for the Gemball." Jerome had no choice but to agree to the deal.

For once in his life, Stuart was in a position of power, and that pleased him. The opportunity came while he was lurking in the grungy hallway, hiding a crowbar in his jacket. With the key to Ronald's room, he waited for him to visit the lady tramp, a few doors down. Stealthily, he passed by their door and, hearing groans and soft cooing, quickly entered his room. He dragged the bed aside, and pulled back the rug from underneath, and, with his crowbar, lifted several floorboards. Slowly, he brought out a silver-sprinkled blue sphere from the hole in the floor. Gazing a long while, he whispered, "What beauty," before tucking the sphere into his satchel. He restored the floorboards, and returned the furniture. Then he made his way down the winding staircase, passing junkies flaked out in corridors. Hearing cries of pleasure about to reach a climax, he left the hotel.

Ronald returned to his room, and, upon discovering the missing sphere, became enraged! With neither the sphere nor the Gemball, he had no power, and he began to ponder his next move.

Stuart returned to his Manhattan condo and embraced his wife, Olivia. He looked into her lovely brown eyes while running his hand through her short, curly brown locks, remembering why he had fallen in love with her.

Dressed in casual leggings and a long-sleeved sweater, she moved toward the kitchen, asking, "How was your day at the office?"

"Business as usual," he replied as he entered his private quarters with the sphere hidden in his satchel.

They had been happily married for twenty-five years, but Olivia had been unable to conceive a child. After consulting with several IVF experts, they were advised that, at her age of forty-five, prospects looked slim.

They ate their meals by candlelight, and by late evening, were making love like never before, rolling between the sheets. She squeezed his shoulders as he penetrated deeper into her moist chamber of mysteries and sweet delights, thrusting in and out, until waves of euphoria released from their heaving bodies, crashing against the shorelines of their dreams—and they sighed.

The following day, they exchanged kisses in the driveway, and Stuart watched Olivia drive off to visit her cousin in New Jersey for a few weeks. Then he returned to his condo. Now was his chance, he thought, and, while holding the sphere, he commanded, "I want full payment rendered for bagging the alligators, plus a new post, as a senator, in the US Congress." A mysterious portal opened, and then shut just as quickly. Lo and behold, a large deposit appeared in his bank account.

Senator Lloyd Albany, an acquaintance of his, called him up and said, "I have looked over your portfolio, and it certainly appears you have been underrated for the skills you have. A vacancy has come up, and we would like to appoint you for the position. Would you accept the post?"

Stuart stammered, "Why, why yes, I would be most honoured."

All afternoon, he tripped the light fantastic, dancing around the condo, while listening to music. He vacuumed the rugs and took out the garbage, and even cleaned out the fridge. Then he held the sphere, and made his final command, "We wish to conceive a child." The portal opened, and in glided a baby carriage, resting on the floor.

Weeks later, Olivia arrived back home, and sat down with the good news. "I am pregnant, the IVF worked," she said, smiling. When she awoke the following morning, a baby carriage stood by the bedroom curtains. Giggling, she turned to Stuart, who was lying next to her, and whispered, "Oh, you shouldn't have. It's a bit early, no?"

True to his word, Stuart had returned the sphere to Jerome, and their Titans switched position. Now, Jerome had all his spheres back, and, chuckling, he said to himself, "The chickens have come home to roost—the prediction was incorrect." Or so he thought.

One day while gazing into the Gemball, Stuart called up Carlos and said, "Do not ask how the Gemball has come into my possession. All I know is that Ronald refused to trade for your relic."

"So, you wish a trade," said Carlos.

"Not for the relic, but for the clover," replied Stuart. "You see, I am in stage two leukemia, an incurable disease that will shorten my life. I have not told my wife Olivia yet, and we are about to conceive a child. Do what you will with the Gemball, for I no longer need it. All I wish is clover."

Carlos took pity on him, for how could Ronald not supply him with clover? But he also wanted the Gemball and so replied, "Your wish is granted."

Jerome had all his spheres back. Carlos held both the relic and the Gemball. Stuart had clover, and a baby was on its way. Julia and Herb wore the ring. Muzaffar had Ishtan, and Yadgiri had his dagger back. All was well in their kingdoms. Only Ronald was unhappy, but not for long.

Low-hanging fruit

Mimbauwe lived in a thatched-roofed hut made of cow dung and twigs, upon the banks of a river he had created months before, in exchange for the dagger. Razor-sharp leaves hid him from view. Using a machete, he cut through coconuts to quench his thirst, and to eat the pulp. He removed husks from macadamia nuts, and ate them, too.

Photos of his wife, Sylvie, and their two children hung on a wall in his hut, and a Zulu mask was propped on an altar. White tribal markings were painted on his face, and a bone was pierced through his nostrils. While wearing a loincloth and feathers through his braided hair, he hunted African wild dog with his spear, turning the skewered carcass over fire, by night, watching flames sear through its flesh. He devoured the meat and spit out the bones, and then ate the boiled cassava leaves and sweet potatoes, cooked over a charcoal grill.

He planted a seed and then flung his black-rimmed glasses into the fire, for he had now gained perfect vision. Some days, his three loyal commandos, Ngabo, Gasimba, and Bisangwa, would strip naked with him, and jump into the river, which was teeming with tilapia. Other days, he would hunt that fish for his breakfast. Strings of light lit up inside the mosquito nets, as he checked his hoard of Sulimon Seeds, which were hidden behind a fake mud-patched wall, next to his bed.

He called up Brad and asked, "Remember the seed I gave you at the assembly meeting? Did you plant it?"

Brad gazed at his nose ring and feathers in his hair, and replied, "That seed produced thorny bushes, which overtook my gardens, so I had to dig them up."

"What was your thought?" he asked.

"That my girlfriend, Cheyenne, become my wife," said Brad.

Mimbauwe roared with laughter, and said, "Then, clearly, my friend, you need two seeds of mine, in exchange for the map."

Brad paused and said, "Do you remember LHF, you know, low-hanging fruit?"

"What about it?" he asked.

"Let's set up your account, my gift to you, for helping me out," said Brad.

Days later, Brad planted the two seeds from Mimbauwe. Honeysuckle shrubs and magnolia trees sprouted throughout his gardens, and he was most pleased. Old man Harvey and Caroline waved to him from across the street, and he waved back.

Meanwhile, in possession of the map, Mimbauwe and his three commandos asked many questions about natural resources, yet to be discovered under their soils. They also asked if the Titan spaceship was in Rwanda. It was a negative response, so Mimbauwe returned the map to Brad. However, LHF produced astonishing information. His commandos tried breaking the encryption codes, but failed.

Gasimba was scrolling through the newsfeed when he said, "Look at this. Jerome once held the ring and the relic."

Bisangwa spoke next, "Yeah, and Stuart McCallum stole a sphere from Ronald in exchange for the Gemball, from Jerome. Then this Stuart traded the Gemball with Carlos for the clover."

Reading further, Ngabo said, "Yadgiri refuses to trade with Muzaffar, something angered him." He looked at Mimbauwe and said, "Your deal is off with Yadgiri."

"Then I must find another way to meet Ishtan," said Mimbauwe. He called up Zhangwei, but the line was busy.

Praying mantis and the floating globe

President Zhangwei roamed the Longyou Caves, dressed in ancient Chinese merchant robes made of green and orange silk, with wide, embroidered sleeves, and a yellow sash around his waist. Clothes hung in a fancy Chinese wardrobe, and a mat lay on the floor, along with blankets and pillows. While twirling his pencil-thin moustache, he gazed at photos of his wife, Sung Yee, upon an altar.

Commando Chenglei, his most decorated officer from ACT, entered the cave with Agents Xiang, Beilin, and Minghua. Each week, they provided him with enough food, and removed refuse, in an efficient system. Zhangwei checked daily reports on the progress of the Kunfu spacesuit material, which had now gone into production. He kept abreast of his party's on-goings, making commands from a distance and signing electronic documents when needed.

Although he had his books, the golden orb, and his feathered friend, YangXi, by his side, he thought it was time to improve his digs. One day, he called up Jerome, with an offer, "I will give Kunfu for one sphere."

Jerome could not resist his generous offer; world domination could wait. The two Titans switched position.

Zhangwei gazed wondrously at the blue and white-marbled sphere, which reminded him of Earth itself. Soon, indoor plumbing, a bathroom, and a kitchen appeared. He was careful not to disturb the integrity of the caves. Next, a freezer appeared, filled with food.

Meanwhile, Jerome received a tiny sliver, and angrily called up Zhangwei, "This hardly constitutes a fair trade. I want my sphere back."

"You are ungrateful," said Zhangwei. "That sliver will get you well on your way, and I am not finished yet." He hung up.

Fuming, Jerome paced back and forth while holding the sliver. He had let go a precious sphere yet again.

A week later, Mimbauwe finally got through to Zhangwei. "Greetings," he said. "How are you holding out in the caves?"

Zhangwei replied, "It is suitable for my needs. Rest assured, I am running my country quite nicely from here."

"Glad to hear that," said Mimbauwe. "And I enjoy the Belt and Road Initiative, which benefits both our countries."

"As do I—is this the reason for your call?" he asked, impatiently.

Mimbauwe replied, "Not quite. You see, I once traded two seeds with Muzaffar for the relic."

Zhangwei was surprised, "You held the relic?"

"Yes, and it was glorious," said Mimbauwe. "We sailed the seven seas, discovering many things. But Muzaffar refuses more seeds for Ishtan, whom I also desire."

"You still have the relic?" asked Zhangwei.

Mimbauwe devoured the last of his meat, licked his fingers, and replied, "No, it has been returned to Carlos. Did you know that Carlos once traded Yadgiri for his dagger? Jerome also traded one sphere for the relic. Are you aware that Stuart McCallum stole a sphere from Ronald in return for the Gemball from Jerome? Then this Stuart gave the Gemball to Carlos, for clover."

Zhangwei gazed at him and said, "Excuse me for asking, but who did what?"

Mimbauwe spat out the bones, and, wiping his mouth, replied, "I just know Yadgiri has his dagger back, and Carlos has both the relic and the Gemball."

"How do you know such things?" asked Zhangwei.

Mimbauwe answered, "Go talk with Brad, if you can find him. He went underground. I once traded seeds for his map. I admit the Titan spaceship is not in Rwanda, so I returned the map, but not before Brad taught me about LHF. This is how I know so much."

"So what do you propose?" wondered Zhangwei.

Mimbauwe replied, "I say, give some of your Kunfu to Carlos for the ancient relic. You will like the relic, believe me. Even Jerome almost refused to give it up, but wanted all his spheres back, for some reason." Zhangwei glanced over at the sphere, resting on the table, and said nothing.

Mimbauwe continued, "Muzaffar also wants the relic. If you trade for Ishtan, you do not need to give more of your precious Kunfu in this transaction. Go ahead and enjoy Ishtan—I hear he is a great companion." He paused and said, "This is where I come in. Before you return Ishtan to Muzaffar, why not trade with me for two seeds. Surely you know how potent they are. After my time with Ishtan, I will return him to you, and you do not need to trade Kunfu with me, either. You will have the triple pleasure of holding the relic, Ishtan, and seeds, for only one trade of your Kunfu."

Zhangwei narrowed his eyes, and said, "You wish to meet Ishtan that badly?"

"Do you not also?" he asked blithely.

Zhangwei sighed, "And the Gemball?" he asked.

Mimbauwe twirled his nose bone, and replied, "I don't think Carlos will give up his prized possession. You cannot have both powers. He will only trade Kunfu once, so you must choose, and I say the relic."

Zhangwei could bypass him, altogether, and deal directly with Carlos, he thought. But then again, Mimbauwe had a good point, and leaning into the screen, he replied, "You have a deal." They ended their transmission.

Carlos sat in his National Palace, most pleased with a large sliver in his hand, sent from Zhangwei, knowing it would produce a thousand spacesuits. He sent the sliver to his science team at the AEM space agency, to begin production, at once. But as days went by, he found himself slipping in and out of two realities, between TLP world and his everyday life. Calls came in from government officials upset with his radical reforms. Family members called up angry about their clawed-back funds, yet he held strong to his policies. A cool wind blew through the open window, ruffling papers on his desk.

Meanwhile, Zhangwei and his team entered the relic statue, and through the white light, landed back in time. Agent Minghua looked about and said, "We are still at the Longyou Caves." But when they stepped out, it was an entirely different landscape.

Agent Beilin recognized a small bonsai, growing nearby, and she whispered, "This tree has been extinct for thousands of years." They scurried along sandstone walls, and when they turned a corner, they suddenly backed up. Giant alien creatures were roaming about, with eyes hanging at the end of antennae protruding from their heads, sounding off clicks to communicate: click-click-click, clack-clack-clack, click, click. Some flew, their wings moving rapidly, creating a buzzing sound, while others stood on their hind legs. They were ten feet tall, and looked like praying mantises.

Commando Chenglei motioned the team through tall bone-like formations, such strangeness to the eyes, when they stopped and retreated behind a boulder. More mantis creatures were mining the earth, scooping up soil with their barbed-thorn legs, their bodies covered in sand granules, as they slathered soil onto the cave walls, with some kind of sticky spit, from their mouths.

Suddenly, the clicks grew louder, as the creatures closed in. Zhangwei uttered the secret word, "Quetzalpoca", and they found themselves transported through the white light, landing back in their modern caves.

Agent Xiang was grazing his hand along the walls, still unable to decipher the inscriptions, when he spoke. "So, aliens created these caves long ago. What kind of creatures were they?"

Minghua wondered, "What in these walls was so precious to them?"

Beilin prepared a hotpot feast for the men, and as they dug in, Chenglei said, "I think they were looking for a rare mineral, and these caves are simply a by-product from their mining expedition."

Day after day, they entered the relic, always landing in a different time and place. Zhangwei observed Marco Polo loading spices from docks onto a ship, and whispered, "So my ancestry goes back to the Silk Road, long after Genghis Khan, around year 1300."

Chenglei nodded and said, "The time when Emperor Zhao Mengfu ruled the Song Dynasty."

Xiang blurted, "We're talking 700 years ago."

One time, they hid behind a curtain, observing the Guangxu Emperor, under house arrest, tinkering with watches and clocks, a hobby that had fascinated him since childhood. The mystery of his death in 1908 was finally laid to rest when Empress Dowager Cixi entered the room. Very ill herself, she snuck a lethal dose of arsenic into a gold chalice and gave it to Guangxu to drink. Writhing in abdominal pain, vomiting, and turning blue, his swollen skin erupting in lesions, he staggered to his bed, and died a horrible death. Cixi sat by the struggling emperor, closing his eyelids with smug satisfaction. She now could reverse his radical reforms and reinstate her policies, before her own looming demise. There was a noise behind her, and she turned toward the curtain. By then, Zhangwei and his team were gone, and had returned to the present time.

While wandering through the caves, deep in thought, Zhangwei announced, "There is one more power to demonstrate. Come gather around." His team silently passed the earthen sphere to each other, as he made a command. To their surprise, a portal opened and in floated a large, lit-up world globe, rotating slowly in the air, tracking the powers with coloured dots.

Excitedly circling the floating globe, Beilin pointed to the queen and prince, and said, "Their dot is purple."

Minghua pointed to Jerome in Canada, and said, "He has two dots, a yellow and red, representing his Spheres and a Kunfu sliver." He glided his finger to China, adding, "We have two dots, a yellow and red, representing one Sphere and our Kunfu." Nodding in agreement, they pulled out their tablets, jotting down notes, talking back and forth.

Xiang glanced at Mimbauwe's pink dot blinking over Rwanda, and asked, "What does that mean?"

"It means Mimbauwe is about to make a power move," replied Zhangwei.

Chenglei pointed to Carlos in Mexico, and said, "The Gemball is royal blue," and gliding his finger to China, added, "We have his relic, and it is violet."

"Then, the blue dot must belong to Ronald," said Beilin. They looked at the US, and there was no dot.

They continued plotting their course across the floating globe, discovering that each leader had a different colour. Muzaffar had a dark green dot, and Yaegar had an orange dot. Irena was grey, and Hashimoto was teal. Around the Globe they went, until they came upon Ushaya. Her dot was emerald green, but there was one gold dot, near her dot, not accounted for.

Xiang asked, "Should we report this to the GHQ?"

"Not yet," replied Zhangwei. "We must examine the data further." Four dots blinked across the Globe . . . Rwanda, Mexico, Saudi Arabia and China.

Triple Swap Deal

Zhangwei called up Muzaffar to trade the relic for his carpet. Muzaffar wondered how he'd gotten hold of the relic, but in the end, he agreed. "OK, my Ishtan for the relic." Two Titans immediately switched position.

Zhangwei and his team were riding upon Ishtan, when a yellow crane glided alongside them. With tears in his eyes, he brought out the feather from his robe, announcing, "Behold, YangXi the crane. She has come back to us."

Ming-wua gazed up at the majestic bird, and asked, "Have you heard from Ushaya?"

"No, I haven't," he replied. "I assume she is taking a much-deserved rest." The crane descended and brushed her wings against the feather in his hand, and the feather transformed into a golden egg. Zhangwei knew what that meant, remembering the time when the map had wrapped around YangXi at the Kunfu facility. He said, "I must let Brad know that the map and YangXi are about to have a baby."

They returned to their caves in ecstasy, gliding upon Ishtan, and when they arrived, Zhangwei swaddled the golden egg in silk cloths, and laid it on the table. Brad was delighted with the news, and helped set up an LHF account for Zhangwei. Hours later, while scrolling through newsfeeds, Zhangwei and his team were shocked by their findings. Chenglei turned to Ishtan and asked, "Is there a mole? Who is watching us?"

Ishtan replied, "The LHF is a secret network, in the guise of conspiracy theorists. Ronald often referred to such things, as 'fake news,' but this is an insider job that began with TLP. The map and Gemball will give you answers."

They asked about the praying mantises, describing what they saw when they entered the relic.

Ishtan was surprised, and said, "They must be Zytokians. We have heard of such creatures. It will need the map and the Zephron ring in Russia, to enter the dimension where they exist, if they still do exist."

Zhangwei paced the floor, and said, "Yaegar would never agree to the Zephron."

Chenglei suggested, "YangXi would be a great help to her lover, the map, and Yaegar might agree."

"No, I will not send her on such a dangerous mission. She has a young one to protect," said Zhangwei. Try as they might, they could not figure out a way to enter the Zephron.

Xiang proposed, "We have Kunfu and also a sphere. Perhaps that will interest Yaegar. After all, Jerome will not release another ball."

Ming-wua agreed. "A triple deal—Kunfu, the sphere returned to us, and we gain entry into the Zephron."

Ishtan commanded, "Return to your palace at once. Take everything with you, and fortify the entrance. Yaegar is interested in Kunfu and the sphere, but I fear he may invade the caves, wondering why you wish to enter the Zephron at this time. It will not be good, what he discovers." He glanced at the floating globe, adding, "More powers are needed to appease him, and you are right, you can forget about the Zephron. By the way, if you do not return the sphere to Jerome before he gets wind of your intentions, he might rally with . . ."

Zhangwei pounded his fist on the table, hollering, "I will continue my deal with Mimbauwe, and keep the sphere until I trade with Yaegar!"

Ishtan shrugged his shoulders, and replied, "As you wish." Suddenly, Ishtan disappeared to Mimbauwe, and two Sulimon Seeds were now in Zhangwei's hand. The two Titans had switched position.

Beilin and Chenglei dug holes among the trees, outside of the Longyou Caves, and carefully pressed their seeds into the soil.

"What were your thoughts?" asked Zhangwei.

Beilin glanced up and replied, "Eradicate genetic defects among our people."

Chenglei spoke next: "Fly on the Titan spaceship."

Zhangwei clasped his hands and said, "The map says it is not in China; you may have wasted a thought." Green sprouts shot through the soil, growing three feet high, bursting with leaves.

Meanwhile, Mimbauwe and his commandos flew across the skies upon Ishtan, under the morning sun. Returned to their hut, they sat crowding around a low table, where Mimbauwe brought out packets of seeds, and said, "For your loyal service, I grant each of you a seed. Choose your thought wisely, before you plant." Sifting through the seeds, Ngabo picked a long and slender one, holding it in his hand. Bisangwa chose a flat, round one, and Gasimba picked a tiny black seed.

Ishtan spoke. "The seeds are as powerful as the twelve spheres. Both Titans grant wishes. You must harness your thoughts, and you have more than twelve seeds."

That afternoon, they jumped naked into the river, splashing about with Ishtan, who quite enjoyed getting wet. And the more they flew across the sky, the more they loved him. But, alas, Ishtan was returned to Zhangwei that very day, as agreed.

Chenglei glided his hand along the cave walls, and asked, "Are these a by-product of the Zytokian mining expeditions?"

Ishtan replied, "Judging by these glyphs, they went through a great deal of trouble to be simply a by-product. I would need more time to study the glyphs. There is something rare in these caves."

Beilin boldly asked, "Does anyone know the whereabouts of the Titan spaceship?"

Xiang added, "We planted a seed to be on your spaceship." They all fell silent.

"Life works out in mysterious ways," replied Ishtan.

Zhangwei continued his side deal, sending the relic to Muzaffar. A day later, Muzaffar returned the relic to Zhangwei, in exchange for his Ishtan back.

Zhangwei asked, "How did you like the relic?"

Muzaffar replied, "We had quite the adventure, and even tried to enter the future, but the relic did not comply."

"A great idea we had not thought of before. Perhaps it is the Gemball's domain," said Zhangwei.

Muzaffar said, "I hear Carlos has it."

"It is true, how do you know?" asked Zhangwei.

He answered, "Ishtan told me. How do you know?"

Zhangwei said, "I learned it through LHF. Brad taught me." And they both hung up.

Zhangwei and his team entered the relic, one last time, and made a precious discovery. He called up Carlos and asked, "Are you pleased with Kunfu?"

Carlos replied, "Very much so. We are manufacturing the prototype, according to your specs. And how was the relic?"

Zhangwei replied, "Extraordinary. You hold a great power."

"I know," said Carlos, smiling.

Zhangwei paused and said, "You are mistaken about your bloodline going back 3,000 years to a tribe, I believe you call Xialha?"

"What do you mean?" he asked, alarmed.

Zhangwei began, "Ancient tribes once built temples around bottomless ponds, under forest canopies in the Brazilian Amazon. High upon a rock sat the very ancient relic itself. This is the birthplace of your ancestry. You are off by 10,000 years, Carlos." He scanned his notes and looked up, and said, "I will send you samples of glyphs from their temples, and perhaps, together, we can decipher their language."

Annoyed that Zhangwei had found his ancestry, before he did, while holding his very own relic, Carlos said, "It would be an honour to collaborate. Now, may I have my relic back?"

"Of course," replied Zhangwei, and they both hung up.

Zhangwei gazed at the golden egg, swathed in cloth. He gazed at the sphere, and at the floating globe, tracking their power moves. Pleased with only one trade of Kunfu for Sulimon Seeds, and a double dip of Ishtan and the relic, he quietly murmured, "World power."

Dual reality, dual lives

Tired of his sugar shack, Jerome left his pile of half-baked commands under the blue tarp, and returned to his private residence, at 24 Sussex Drive, in Ottawa. Clean-shaven and dressed in a two-piece suit, he was stoking embers in the fireplace, wondering how to get his sphere back from Zhangwei, when Kaitlyn entered the salon. She dropped her bags, and they embraced. She looked at him and said, "You're home early. How was your day at the office?" She peeled off her jacket and went to the kitchen, to check on the Crockpot meal.

Then it struck him! He was living a dual life. What? Only a day had gone by? He could have sworn it was weeks, maybe months, and barely remembered what happened at the office that day. Time was altered. Pondering the frogfish, he called out, "I'm working on that trilateral agreement with frog—I mean First Nations Assembly."

His children burst into the room. The eldest son Sebastian, now aged seventeen, showed his arm and said, "We got vaccinated today."

Thirteen-year old Annabelle slumped into the couch, filing her fingernails, wearing a pink-green hairdo, a mini-skirt, fishnet stockings, and little boots on her feet. "Now, we won't get the virus," she said, with a bored tone in her voice.

Jerome stared at her and asked, "Did you go to school looking like that? Isn't there a dress code?"

Little eight-year old Adrian interrupted: "Daddy, did you get vaccinated?"

He tried hard to remember, "Uh, of course I did."

Sebastian picked up a silver-sprinkled blue sphere from the coffee table, and asked, "What is this?"

Jerome had forgotten about it—a most foolish mistake, he thought. It was the sphere that Stuart stole from Ronald, to give back to him, in exchange for the Gemball. Staying cool as a cucumber, he replied, "A gift from an old friend, while he was travelling overseas."

Annabelle jumped from the couch, and the kids gathered around, as she held the sphere. "It's beautiful. Wish I could have one, like this," she said. Then she placed it back on the table. Jerome watched a ball fling through the open portal behind them, bounce along the carpet with a thud, and roll under the couch.

Adrian asked, "What's that sound?"

Jerome looked around and replied, "What sound?" When the kids left the room, he was on his hands and knees, coaxing the ball from under the couch. He returned to his private office and made a command to both spheres. Only one sphere rolled off his desk. The portal opened, and in glided a bouquet of flowers. He hid the real sphere in his locked vault, and covered the replica in black velvet cloth, and placed it in a bottom drawer. Annabelle's birthday was next week, and this would make a perfect gift, he thought.

Shenanigans continue

The leaders continued living in hideouts and palaces while conducting their daily affairs, attending meetings, and making speeches. Meanwhile, they hurled every vice known to mankind at each other, in the alternate world of TLP. Sometimes, Muzaffar listened to Ishtan, but oftentimes, he did not. One day, he slipped back into reality, and was besieged with officials and family members trying to reach him. He attended the birth of his grandson. He watched a ceremony, for the official opening of a new skyscraper, and then he joined the Gulf consortium to discuss the new stock exchange. As soon as the documents were signed, he escaped right back to TLP, racing his Bugatti car across the desert. Commando Zainab, along with Captain Faisal and Lieutenant Hassan, were in the back seats, while Ishtan sat in the front. Fifty miles away, they stepped out of the car.

Yadgiri had let bygones be bygones, agreeing to a trade with Muzaffar, for he wanted that ride on Ishtan, and Muzaffar wanted another chance with the dagger, and so their Titans switched positions.

Muzaffar handed the dagger to Hassan, who struck the ground with such force that waters sprang forth, thunderously crashing into a lake. Sulimon Seeds were strewn by the handfuls from their car, as they drove around, deciding to call the lake Al-Akbar Buhayra, in honour of the man who brought Ishtan to them. Muzaffar allowed Zainab to strike the dagger, and strike she did! Thunder rolled across the land and the rains fell. They drove to the bluffs, where Faisal struck the dagger. A tiny waterfall trickled down the rocks, and they roared with laughter. Muzaffar knew of Yadgiri's plot against him, and sent that dagger packing right back to him, without the carpet.

Yadgiri was enraged, "Where is Ishtan?"

Muzaffar continued his power play with Carlos. He said, "I know your plot, but you see, you cannot go to my neighbours, disrupting oil prices, trying to weaken me. It is contrary to TLP conventions, as laid out in the manifesto, under *Article 16.1(b)*, which specifically states, "Interference in the business of other countries is strictly forbidden, unless agreed upon by mutual consent." Muzaffar lightened up, and said, "We don't need your gas trades."

Carlos's mouth twitched as he spoke. "Don't need your gas either," he said. "We have our own sources, now."

Muzaffar said, "Except mine are bigger, we have a lot more sand than you do. However, this is not the reason for my call. I wish to trade Ishtan for the Gemball."

"I thought you wanted the relic," said Carlos.

He had already experienced the relic, unknown to Carlos, and so ruefully replied, "I do. However, at this time, I wish for the Gemball."

Carlos sat in his palace, dressed in a fine blue suit, his hair groomed back. While fidgeting with his cufflinks, he said, "Let me consider your offer and get back to you." And they both hung up.

Zainab glanced at Muzaffar and said, "He might not agree—you were not exactly gracious."

Muzaffar shrugged and replied, "I want him to know what we know. And what he doesn't know, he doesn't know. But I do know he wants Ishtan again."

One day, Yadgiri called up Carlos, lamenting, "I know, we have double-crossed each other before, but I hope we are over that now. What must I do to get Ishtan?"

While fidgeting with his cufflinks, Carlos replied, "There may be a way. I, too, wage a vendetta against Muzaffar. He then called up Muzaffar, agreeing to the deal. Suddenly, Carlos was bowing before Ishtan, and he cried out, "We do not have much time. Go at once to Yadgiri!" Carlos did not send the Gemball to Muzaffar. Instead, he called up Ronald, and said, "I have something that is yours. Do not ask me how it has come into my possession, but you owe me one."

Tired of his hotel room, Ronald had long since returned to the Oval Office. A wide grin crossed his face, and he said, "Carlos, I am forever in your debt. How can I repay you?"

Carlos answered, "Give clover to everyone on your team, and allow me to gaze into the Gemball whenever I want. Those are my only demands."

Ronald thought for a moment, and, being in a generous mood, he replied, "I will do you one, even better. Brad taught me LHF, and I had learned that

Hashimoto doesn't want your relic; however, he wants my gemball, for a few days. In exchange, Hashimoto will provide me with Yokuru spaceship material, along with design specifications, a most worthy trade. Perhaps you can have a little Yokuru for yourself, and no need for the relic in this transaction."

Carlos nodded in agreement, and they both hung up. While pausing a while, he then called up Brad to secure an LHF account.

Thrilled to have his gemball back, Ronald realized how much he had missed it. He asked a burning question. Visions appeared, showing a binding agreement between Congress and executive committees, giving him more presidential powers. A smile crept upon his face, and he whispered, "World power."

Muzaffar did not receive the Gemball, and where was Ishtan? He was without power and became enraged!

Meanwhile, Yadgiri and his men whisked through jungles, passing guards who were in awe of a flying carpet. Up, up, they glided into the bright blue sky. Minister Nadin pointed to the beautiful Lotus Temple. Commander Kumar pointed to the Yamuna flood plains, and Captain Jagpal pointed to a flock of flamingos, gliding alongside them. Higher and higher, they flew, thrilled to see the distant, snow-capped Himalayan peaks, gleaming under the sun.

They returned to the ashram and invited the guards to join them. Everyone was amazed with Ishtan. All afternoon they celebrated, feasting and playing music. They would sometimes tease Ishtan with food, but he always refused, and they would roar with laughter. The more they hung around him, the more they loved him.

Ishtan, too, was enjoying the lively crowd and the attention he was getting. He turned to Yadgiri and advised, "The dagger is as powerful as the spheres, for it feeds all life on earth. It is the thought that counts, when you command the dagger." Everyone turned silent.

Kumar leaned to Yadgiri and said, "We should return to your palace." Regrettably, they sent Ishtan back to Carlos that very day, as agreed.

Carlos immediately sent Ishtan back to Muzaffar, and said, "I have changed my mind, no deal." They both hung up.

Muzaffar was annoyed with Ishtan, asking, "Where have you been all day?"

Ishtan was faced with a moral dilemma. Carlos had traded in good faith, expecting nothing in return, so he replied, "I flew here, there, and everywhere." Muzaffar packed his belongings and planted two seeds. Then he returned to his Arabian palace, taking Ishtan with him, leaving the Bugatti car behind.

Zhangwei and his team cleared all evidence from the Longyou Caves. They set up explosives and trip wires at the entrance, in case Yaegar tried to enter. When they returned to his private quarters, at the HoChing Palace, they observed dots flashing across the floating globe. The blue dot was now in the US, and they wondered what kind of deal Ronald had made with Carlos. Zhangwei glanced at the sphere on his desk, and spoke: "World power begins."

Meanwhile, Yadgiri had returned to his palace and was pacing the floor, wearing a turban and Hindu clothing. He called up Zhangwei and said, "Your factories have now reached completion. It is time to trade—your Kunfu for my dagger." The two Titans switched position. Zhangwei struck the dagger, and water flowed throughout the pipes, feeding his massive factories. Then he returned the dagger to Yadgiri.

While gazing at a tiny sliver of Kunfu in his hand, Yadgiri sneered, "You loathsome, despicable creature." Bilateral agreements were breaking down, left, right, and centre.

One day, Jerome sent a cobalt sphere to Mimbauwe in hope for a Heaven's Gate seed, a most prized possession. Then he learned of a triple blockade, along the Rwandan borders. Cargo trucks and merchants were forbidden to enter, from all sides. There was a tense standoff, with each president accusing the other of espionage and political assassinations.

Mimbauwe was tired of Uganda abducting citizens to support rebels bent on overthrowing his government, and with wars in the Congo, and their meddling in his backyard. So, he sent hundreds of armed soldiers to patrol the borders, behind thick, impenetrable forests, that grew from Heaven's Gate seeds. Rumours circulated among the Rwandan people, that Mimbauwe was going to use voodoo magic, in a surprise attack. It was on everyone's lips.

Mimbauwe stood in the battlefield, holding the cobalt sphere, while dressed in tribal clothing, with war paint upon his face, and a bone pierced through his nostrils, and feathers in his hair. Commandos, Gasimba,

Bisangwa and Ngabo, stood by his side, wearing the same ritual clothing, with bones pierced through their nostrils, and feathers in their hair. African drums pounded in rhythmic unison, along the borders, when Mimbauwe made a powerful command.

Heaven's Gate opened, like Moses parting the Red Sea, and 1,000 African warriors entered through the portal, in full ancient armour, carrying spears, arrows, battle shields, and swords, galloping on horses snorting, and hoofs thundering across the borders. In confusion and fear, the armies fled under the galloping hoofs, and, one by one, they fell to the ground, with swords pointed down at them. There was a ceasefire.

Mimbauwe stood before the sea of warriors, and announced, "Well done. You have controlled the rebellion. Return at once to where you belong, with honours bestowed upon you and titles worthy of your bravery. Lands of gold and myrrh await you, and kingdoms, filled with animals and women and song."

One thousand warriors and their horses strutted through the portal, and disappeared. Zip! Gone. A peace deal was struck among the nations. Mimbauwe did all he could for his people, and not one bullet was fired from his army the entire time. What voodoo magic was this? The soldiers lay down their weapons, shocked at his new power, and Mimbauwe was hailed a hero in his country.

Jerome was pissed off to no end. The nerve of him, using his very own thought, back at the assembly meeting, but a thousand times more potent now. He gazed at Mimbauwe across the screen and said, "I commend you on your great deeds."

"Now, who will be king," said Mimbauwe, beaming.

"When shall I get Heaven's Gate seed?" asked Jerome.

Mimbauwe replied, "You have enough seeds with Sulimon's forest, don't be so greedy."

Jerome demanded, "Give me back the sphere."

Mimbauwe twirled his nose bone and said, "I'm not finished yet. These things take time, as you know."

"You horrible sack of evil," snarled Jerome, and he hung up. Now, two spheres were on the lam—one in the clutches of Mimbauwe, and the other still with Zhangwei.

Mimbauwe chuckled to himself, "Rule the world." But he was losing seeds, and wondered how many were left. His men had counted seventy-six seeds. They planted one more, and left the hut to return to Mimbauwe's palace.

With each passing season, more and more agreements broke down, man pitted against man, as they dishonoured their vows, hurling commands across the world.

One day, Captain Trevor Kelly joined Ronald at the Oval Office. Ronald was yelling at Zhangwei, "Why, you bastard, take this!" He slammed down the phone, gazing at a tiny Kunfu sliver in his hand. With the Gemball resting on his desk, he looked up at Trevor and said, frowning, "Over my dead body will he get the Gemball."

Quazaik

Tyler and Chelsea were gazing at Dragon's Pond through the kitchen window, wondering what was so special about it. With Mom and Dad away, Tyler headed out the door, and said, "C'mon, let's go." Baxter the dog ran along with them, and when they arrived at the giant rock, he began to bark.

Chelsea asked, "What is it, Baxter?" He pawed at the fake moss covering the base of the rock. They rolled back the moss and peered into a hole. Tyler brought out a metal box, containing numbers and alphabets on the front lock. Chelsea asked, "What was that secret code again?"

Months earlier, Tyler had wandered into the garage and heard his dad mutter strange numbers and letters, over and over. He had hidden behind utility shelves, where he quietly picked up a pencil from the floor, and, looking for something to write on, found a tattered piece of paper on a nearby shelf. His dad continued muttering the sequenced code, as Tyler wrote it down. Then he'd stuffed the note into his shirt pocket, and quietly slunk away.

Tyler brought out the piece of paper from his pocket, to show Chelsea. It read, "Q8U3A1Z8A1I9K2."

She looked at him and said, "If you remove the numbers, the word spells out QUAZAIK." They stared at each other, and Baxter barked. They ran to the house and placed the metal box on the dining table. Carefully, they turned the dial to unlock the box, until they heard a click. Tyler brought out a velvet cloth, and when he shook out the contents, a sparkling crystal rested upon his right palm, in a sea of radiant colours and shapes. Chelsea gasped.

All day long, they played with Quazaik, running across the property, with Baxter in tow, barking and yapping. They returned to the house, chasing the crystal up the stairs and down the hall, with Baxter, following right behind them.

"What is this thing?" asked Chelsea, giggling.

Tyler said, "I don't know, but Mom will be home soon. We should bring it back to its spot and try again tomorrow." Suddenly, a car door slammed in the driveway. "Quick, hide it!" he exclaimed.

She asked, frantic, "Where?"

"In the attic," he whispered.

"Hellooo?" Meg called out. Nervously, the kids came down the stairs to greet her. "There you are," she said, smiling, "Your dad will be here in a few minutes, and he wants to take you on his yacht. Start packing, just some light stuff."

The kids protested. "But we have exams next week."

Meg lay down the groceries on the kitchen counter, and said, frowning, "You haven't been with your dad in a while. Don't you want to see him? Besides, he will have you back in a few days."

Devon's truck arrived in the driveway. He wiped his feet, greeting Tyler and Chelsea at the front door, then announcing, "I know a great fishing spot you guys will love, and I'll take you to a concert in the Fiji Islands."

Meg began emptying items from the grocery bags, into cupboards, and said, "My new outdoor spa just opened, with a waterfall, rippling over rocks into a pool. It's quite lovely."

Devon smiled and said, "That's wonderful." As he strolled through the gardens, he began to notice automatic sprinkler systems, spraying mist everywhere. There was fresh water in Dragon's Pond, and he called out to the house, "Meg, who installed these?"

She peered out the back door and hollered, "A local contractor."

Soon, the kids boarded the yacht and sailed away, worried out of their wits about Quazaik.

Later that day, Meg pulled back the fake moss and looked into the hole. It was empty. Frantically, she upended flowerbeds, and then sent an urgent message to Devon: "Someone stole Quazaik, she is gone!"

Devon answered his phone, "What do you mean, she is gone? I trusted you to keep her safe."

She hissed, "Yeah, while you gallivant about the Fiji Islands. Come to think of it, I checked yesterday, and she was here. Perhaps, you have taken it."

He snapped back, "Oh, so I have Quazaik? Whatever for?" He paused for a moment, and said suspiciously, "I saw a text from Yadgiri—what was that about?"

Meg was annoyed, for he had no business snooping in her phone. All she wanted was a sprinkler system and fresh water for their Dragon's Pond, and a waterfall for her new spa. Fed up, she had taken matters into her own hands, and arranged a trade with Yadgiri, explaining that Devon disappeared into the Fiji Islands, God knows where. She assured Yadgiri that, upon Devon's return, they would make another trade.

Yadgiri loved Quazaik, and was pleased to be in the presence of a Master Titan. He felt her protective rays raining down upon him, with one genius idea after another. He even found his missing gold ring, behind the bathroom toilet. Alas, they had returned their gifts, as agreed.

Meg answered with another lie, "He was just checking on me, to see how I was doing."

Devon grew more suspicious and said, "There is something you're not telling me, Meg. Maybe YOU have Quazaik." She cut him off and the signal went dead. He tried to reach her, but to no avail. Angrily, he steered his yacht around and headed back to New Zealand.

The kids watched the waves trailing behind the engines. They couldn't talk about what they did. What had they done!

Meg called her mom, but there was no answer. With bags packed, she headed out the door to meet the queen and prince.

When Devon returned from their sailing expedition, he immediately checked behind the dragon's wing. Soil was disturbed, and the hole was empty. He slammed his fists against the rock, and squatted to the ground, in a seething mix of rage and disbelief. Tossing and turning in their beds that night, the kids could not sleep. Meanwhile, Quazaik lay hidden in the attic.

To reveal or not to reveal

Meg walked briskly through the once-opulent halls of Windshire Castle, now transformed into a dark and foreboding fortress. Queen Julia was by her side, holding a sceptre, wearing a deep-crimson gown and a crown of deer antlers, upon her head. They passed scary sculptures, under black chandeliers, when hunchbacked Herb joined them, wearing a Catholic robe, holding a lit lantern, guiding them down the dark and twisted hallways, with the ring upon his finger.

They were debating the stolen Quazaik when Herb said, "I say, we send a team to New Zealand."

Julia disagreed, "Too much exposure to our cause. I say we loan the ring to Ronald. The Gemball will tell us who stole Quazaik."

Herb pulled up his hood, and passed the ring to Julia. With his face obscured in the darkness of his hood, he said, "It might also reveal the location of the Titan spaceship."

"Indeed," replied Julia. A large crow flew through the open window of their fortress and rested on her right arm. The ring shone on her finger. Thunder rolled and lightning flashed across grey skies. Wielding her power, she released the crow out the window, and sent a message to Ronald, "We trade the ring for the Gemball." The two Titans switched position.

At once, the Gemball floated into a chamber room and rested on a nearby pedestal. As they gazed into the swirling images, Julia said, "It appears, your own children hold Quazaik, in some room."

Meg was shocked, "Oh my God, that's the attic," she cried out.

"You should let Devon know," said Herb.

She nodded and said, "I will."

They asked about the Titan spaceship. Images swirled, showing only a vague blob in black skies. They were disappointed, wondering why it would not reveal clearly.

It was Meg's turn to ask a question. "Where is Mom?" she asked. All three were shocked, observing a dragon, wandering about in lit caves.

"Let us keep this matter between us, for now," said Julia, pondering.

Ronald wasn't so stupid to reveal the location of the Titan spaceship, before he gave Gemball to the queen and prince. After all, it was not the Gemball that knew the answer, but the alligators, ha! He discovered that the Titan spaceship was orbiting around Earth, cloaked, in the same thermosphere as the ISS. But he also made another discovery. The Zogar mother ship was stationed high in the exosphere, which meant that Bokal the monster had not left orbit. Ronald had a moral dilemma, should he disclose this to TLP, thereby, exposing the Titan spaceship's whereabouts? The ring glowed softly on his finger, and this told him the answer, and he decided to wait.

Julia called up Ronald and said, "Keep the ring, a while. We like the Gemball."

"And choose your commands wisely," said Herb, holding a lantern to the screen.

Ronald replied, "As you wish."

Days later, the kids broke down in tears. Chelsea cried, "We didn't mean to take Quazaik!"

"Dad mumbled a bunch of code, and we kept seeing you guys go behind the rock, and we were curious," said Tyler.

"It's all right," Meg comforted them in a group hug. "She is now safe with us."

"Now sit down," said Devon. "What we are about to tell you is top secret." They all sat at the table.

Meg began the story of the Blue-ray light, and how Grandma Ushi had received superpowers. She told the story of Uncle Brad joining in a card trick, and about their flight to Echo Canyon, and the gogolytes they encountered, and how they nearly collided with a military plane in the sky. The kids were in disbelief. Tyler piped up, "Remember my Black Rider kite? Is that why she was able to spin so fast?"

Meg said, "Yes, but she is much more powerful now."

"Where is Grandma?" asked Chelsea.

Meg clasped her hands, and, letting out a sigh, replied, "We cannot say yet. We are looking for her."

"With all these powers, how can you not know where Grandma is?" Tyler asked, incredulous.

Devon poured himself a stiff one and sat down, and said, "Listen, kids, there's more to the story." He revealed their secret TLP mission, and how world leaders had been given superpowers by an alien race of Titans from a planet called Lazantis. He continued about the monster in captivity, taken by the Zogar mother ship, and about the Kisga'a Shield and the Ring of Power, and about Ishtan the Carpet. Then he sat back in his chair, with final words, "Our planet is about to witness the greatest event in human history." The kids could not believe what they were hearing.

Meg placed Quazaik into Chelsea's hands, and said, "Go ahead and ask any question you like."

Dazzled by its radiance, she looked up and asked, "Any question?" Devon nodded.

Chelsea began, "There's this guy at school. I wonder if Travis likes me." Quazaik beamed out geometric rays, and suddenly, her cell phone rang. She answered, "Hello? Hi, Travis, how's it going?" She moved to the kitchen. "Your birthday party next weekend? Sure, thanks for the invite. See you then."

Meg and Devon smiled, as they presented the crystal to Tyler.

Tyler asked, "How can I pass this calculus exam, coming up? It seems impossible." Quazaik beamed geometric rays around him, and he was in awe. He got up from the table and said, "Excuse me, got to go," and ran up the stairs, yelling, "Go find Grandma!"

Mastermind

Eternal lights lit up a boxcar of an abandoned train in the Vorkuta Gulag, a hundred miles north of the Arctic Circle. President Yaegar of Russia had laid rugs upon the steel floors and built a metal fire pit underneath a shaft, allowing in fresh air from above. Clothes hung on cords stretched across the walls. Pictures of his wife Sofia and two children lined a shelf, together with precious mementos. The Accutron watch he'd won at the assembly sat alongside a picture of a Russian saint, among eternal lights, flickering in the dank, cozy atmosphere of his new home. His most sentimental possession was the titanium Cube, that held Elixir, and, after gazing at it one more time, he locked it back up in the vault. Standing before a washbowl, filled with arctic water, he glanced in the mirror, ready to groom his handlebar moustache with a straight razor, realizing he was almost bald.

It was minus forty degrees outside, and winds howled across the tundra as he stepped out of the train, wearing a woolly, thick-padded coat and thermal vest, and heavy leggings and boots. He rubbed his gloves together, breathing out visibly in the air, as his face hid inside a fur hat. He trudged across the frozen landscape with a high-powered telescopic rifle to hunt seal for his meat, and by nightfall, was turning the carcass over the fire pit. With what little kindling he could find, he smoke-dried the meat and strung it along one end of the train. The guts and remains were burned in the fire pit, which attracted animals to the site.

While trudging through the snow, one day, he stopped dead in his tracks. A lone black wolf was sniffing the air. He seemed to have lost his pack. Yaegar threw him a piece of seal meat, and thus begun a friendship, with the wolf following him everywhere he went. Together, Yaegar speared arctic char and mackerel, in fishing holes. Some days, they would chase each other, in frolic and play. He built a lean-to shelter at base camp, and decided to call the wolf, Borzov. One time, they lay flat over a ridge, observing two polar bears roaming in the distance. Perhaps, a male and female, he thought, and they quietly slunk away.

Enough play in his favourite hinterland, he decided one day. It was time to get down to business. Yakov, his most decorated commando from ACT, and best pilot Nadiya, and minister Viktor, all stared across their screens.

With folded hands, Yaegar spoke. "The next shipment is tomorrow?"

Nadiya replied, "We arrive at base camp at 0900 hours."

He glanced at Viktor and said, "It is my understanding that we must extract a rare element, elsewhere, that we do not have for the Elixir fuel."

Viktor said, "There are only two locations in the world, one in the Pantanal marshlands of Brazil, and the other in the Florida Everglades—can you believe?"

"And what of the Zephron ring?" asked Yaegar.

Viktor replied, "According to Olaf Meier, who heads our team of engineers, as you know, once we have the trace element, and with minor adjustments, it will be ready and operational."

Yakov saluted and spoke: "Permission to move forward, on your command."

Yaegar sat back, twirling his handlebar moustache, and replied, "I say we go for the Everglades. Permission granted."

Troops descended near the location of the alligators, in the Florida swamplands. This worried Ronald, who slammed back in retaliation. With the ring glowing hot on his finger, he barked, "You have no right to mine precious metals on US soil, without my consent. Call off your troops immediately."

Yaegar calmly said, "You know where the Titan spaceship hides, don't you?"

Ronald blasted, "If I knew, I would not tell you, and certainly, you will not find it here. Now, off my planet!" He hung up.

The power of the ring managed to ward off Yaegar, who moved to greener pastures, but not before pondering his last words, "Off . . . my . . . planet," which got him thinking. As he crawled into his makeshift bed, and was about to dim the lights, a call came in from Irena, speaking in a controlled voice, "It is time to release the Elixir. You are breaking every law of TLP." He hung up on her.

Meanwhile, drums pounded slow beats: Bong . . . bong . . . bong, reverberating across the land of Japan.

Hashimoto was dressed in a rakusu robe and pointed rice hat, while sitting with Buddhist monks, bent over manuscripts at the Kinkaju Temple, deciphering a long-lost legend. Candles flickered throughout the room, and the Yokuru Tablet shone from a nearby altar. A photo of his wife, Miyuki, and daughter Kioko, sat upon a shelf next to a group photo from Irena's estate.

Monk Nobu was scanning sacred texts with his ruler when he spoke: "It is written that a steel bird will one day fly from the sacred Kiji Mountain to rule the sun and moon and stars, in the heavens above." He glanced at the others and said, "This must be NODA, our starship."

Monk Kiyoshi asked, "When will it be operational?"

Hashimoto replied, "All we need is Kunfu suits and the Elixir fuel."

Nobu continued scanning text and said, "It is written that a traitor, among us, will repent."

The monks glanced at Genjo, who pulled out the Yokuru fragment from his robe. He bowed and said, "This belongs to the Temple. Forgive me, I did not know the Yokuru Tablet would return."

Wu-pen handed him a scroll, and laid a piece of cloth over his shoulder, and said, "It has been decided. Keep the fragment for your own temple, where you will become abbot, guiding new priests in the ways of our tradition." The monks began chanting, and Genjo continued bowing, chanting along with them.

Days later, Hashimoto sat alone in his private quarters at the temple, examining incoming GHQ reports, when he called up Yaegar and said, "You must trade Elixir, for a generous amount of Yokuru and the formulas, to build your own starship, an equal proposition." Yaegar hung up on him, and continued ice fishing at his favourite hole.

Another call came in. It was Zhangwei, who said, "Kunfu suits are ready, and we have a sphere. You once held a sphere to build your Zephron control centre, but Jerome will not release another ball, so here is your chance. The time has come to enter the Zephron ring, in exchange, for my gifts. Why else are we given such powers?"

Suddenly, Yaegar received a generous amount of Kunfu, in one hand, and the sphere, in the other. He looked up at Zhangwei and said, "We shall discuss the preparations to enter the Zephron at our next meeting." They both hung up. But Yaegar had no intentions of complying with the agreement. Ever since Ishtan's warning at the assembly meeting, so long ago, he needed the "all-clear" from Muzaffar to trade, but had yet to hear from him.

With enough meat left for Borzov, plus a small eternal fire, for warmth, Yaegar said his goodbyes, embracing the wolf one last time. Then he commanded the sphere to return his mementos and the Cube, at once, to the Kremlin Palace. That evening, while playing a sonata on his piano, he stopped, and sent that sphere packing right back to Jerome, not Zhangwei.

Jerome was exceedingly pleased. "Yaegar, why do I have the honour of your generosity?"

Twirling his handlebar moustache, he replied, "Too much for a growing superpower, like China. Better with you, where it belongs."

Jerome solemnly said, "I owe you one." And they hung up.

Yaegar sat back pondering his strategy. Better to trade with Jerome and many spheres, than with Zhangwei and only one sphere. He called up Zhangwei, refusing his demands, "Neither Elixir nor Zephron shall I trade," he said.

"You fool!" fumed Zhangwei. "Jerome is accumulating massive power, and once he has all his spheres, he will dominate the world. I learned this through LHF, and, by the way, Mimbauwe has the last sphere." Yaegar was about to hang up. "No, wait! I have something else," said Zhangwei, showing him the floating globe.

Yaegar stared in wonder, clearly impressed, "What is your price?" he asked.

"It would make a good addition to your control centre, of course, on loan," said Zhangwei, continuing, "Our team must be among the first to enter the Zephron, that is my price. If you do not honour our agreement, I will not give you the Kunfu specs."

Yaegar folded his hands and replied, "I am glad we have come to a landmark deal," and they both hung up again.

Days later, a chopper landed on the Kremlin rooftops. Brad stepped out, greeting Yaegar under loud, whirring blades. Settled in his private quarters, Yaegar offered him kvass. "I trust your journey went well?" he asked.

Brad took a sip and replied, "I enjoyed the private jet escort, thank you."

Yaegar shrugged and said, "The least we can do for a member of TLP."

Conversations flowed back and forth, in small talk, when things gradually took a serious turn. Brad pulled out his map and spread it across the desk, and said, "You want to know, right?"

Yaegar laid both hands on the map and asked, "Is the Titan spaceship in Russia?" It was a negative. He glanced at Brad. "Can I ask another question?"

"Of course, as many as you like. This is why I am here," said Brad.

"Is the Titan spaceship in orbit around planet Earth?" asked Yaegar. A trail of fire blazed across the surface and stopped high in the thermosphere, over the region of the Mojave Desert in the USA. Both were surprised. He turned to Brad and said, "Let this be our secret. I'm pretty sure Ronald knows, so that makes three of us."

"How would Ronald know? I haven't visited him yet," asked Brad, and then remembered, "I did teach him LHF, but I have already searched and cannot find anything."

Yaegar replied, "He may have discovered it through the Gemball, but the queen and prince also held the Gemball, and could not find the answer. There is something else Ronald knows." Yaegar was open with Brad about the new developments, to gain his trust and keep him close; after all, he wanted the map to enter the Zephron.

Brad was faced with a moral dilemma. Should he divulge the secret of the Titan spaceship's whereabouts to the queen and prince? Should he let Jerome know? Or Irena? But he, too, desired to enter the Zephron. Deciding to play his cards right, he set up an LHF account for Yaegar. In compensation for his long journey, Yaegar offered him a casino by a seaside resort, plus rights to a geological dig in the Amur region, where dinosaur fossils lie, and, most importantly, he offered him first dibs to enter the Zephron.

Brad returned to Manitoba. One day, he called up Ronald, who was furious. “There are moles in TLP!” he exclaimed.

“Apparently so, according to LHF, but we don’t know who,” replied Brad. Then he proposed, “Shall I make a visit with my map? Let’s see if the Titan spaceship is in the US, in exchange, that I may gaze into the Gemball.”

Ronald replied warily, “I heard you visited Yaegar. How did that turn out?”

“The spaceship is not in Russia,” replied Brad.

Ronald sighed and said, “Thank you for your offer, and I shall take you up on it, but right now, I have more important business to attend to.” They both hung up. Ronald released the alligators from their nets. They had done their job and were free to go. Brad was now convinced that Ronald knew where the spaceship hid. Why else would he turn down his map?

Weeks later, the queen and prince gave back the Gemball to Ronald, in return for their ring. And so it came to pass—Mimbauwe still held the cobalt sphere. Zhangwei lost his sphere back to Jerome, and his floating globe was now stationed at the Zephron control centre in Russia.

Plotting at the GHQ

It was dark and gloomy in her self-contained bunker, save for a large lit-up monitor, tracking world leaders, swindling, lying, and cheating across the world. Dressed in her nightgown, housecoat, and slippers, looking haggard, Irena brushed away straggly hairs from her washed-out face, as she brought out another beer from the fridge. Gone were the days of pearls and suits and polished loafers. She sat down with her laptop, waiting for Erika, Leopold, and Inspektor Gerd to arrive. Gerd had joined TLP, promoted by Erika for the good work in solving the jewellery heist. The buzzer sounded. With her remote, she let them enter, and the steel doors clanged shut behind them. Erika gave her a hug and glanced over at the eternal lights, lying in a heap on the floor. “I’ll get these set up right away,” she said.

“Oh, OK,” said Irena, feeling slightly defeated.

“When was the last time you ate?” asked Gerd, staring into the fridge.

“Yesterday,” she said.

“Hmm,” he began pulling out food and a fine bottle of Italian wine.

Leopold sat in full uniform, with Irena on the couch. They reminisced about old times, about the misadventures they had together. He gazed at her and whispered, "When I look into your eyes, you are as beautiful today as the day I met you."

She coughed, replying, "I hardly think so, it's been . . ."

He interrupted, "No, in every way."

She got up from the couch and said, "Excuse me, while I freshen up."

Erika turned on the stereo, and soon, they were grooving to an eclectic mix of music. Leopold helped Erika set up the eternal lights across the room, which lit up quite nicely, and they were both pleased. The three made small talk. With arms wrapped around Gerd, Erika rested her head on his shoulders, as he stirred vegetables on the stove, and then they tenderly kissed.

Leopold gazed at a photo of Irena and her esteemed husband, Finn, professor emeritus in molecular biology, attending the opening ceremony of the world's largest industrial show in Hanover. Another photo of the Liebschon Estate sat on a shelf, all members beaming, including Ishtan the Carpet.

An hour later, Irena entered the room to admiring glances, as she strolled about, dressed in a silk teal gown, draped over her shoulders, wrapping around her body, showing her curves, flowing down to the floor, with a V-neck plunge and ruffled sleeves to her elbows. A pin held her coiffed hair in place. Ruby teardrop earrings hung from her ears, and a set of pearls hung around her neck. With a dab of lipstick on her lips, she fluttered her eyelids at the eternal lights, twinkling about the room, and cried out, "Fabulous!" Leopold couldn't stop gazing at her.

They sat down to a feast of ravioli and roasted potatoes, passing fruit and vegetable platters down the table. Leopold made a toast: "To TLP, we shall prevail. One for all and all for one." Wine glasses clinked.

Irena glanced at the lit candles on the table, and quipped, "Let's hope we don't need the fire extinguisher."

"Not on my watch," growled Leopold. They all laughed as they dug into their meals.

Feeling in good spirits, her soul and body replenished, Irena dabbed her mouth, and tapped the triangle. It was time to make their call.

Thunder and lightning streamed across the wall monitor. They hardly recognized Queen Julia, wearing the ring, as she sat upon a throne more powerful than ever. Prince Herb emerged from dark corners of their castle, with Magus the crow resting on his arm. He pulled down his hood and spoke.

"Ushaya has turned into a dragon and is hiding in her house, transformed into caves, by which power, we do not know."

Irena interrupted, "Stand by, Ronald is about to join."

The screen flickered, and he appeared with the Gemball. Everyone welcomed him aboard. He flashed his famous smile and said, "It's good to see you folks. Sorry I am late. Have I missed anything?"

"We were just discussing Ushaya," said Erika.

Leopold turned to Herb and asked, "How does she look?"

He replied, "We only spoke briefly on the phone, before she hung up. Her voice sounded rough, but she assured us that she is resting."

Julia spoke. "Mimbauwe has lost the cobalt sphere in a recent coup, and no one knows who stole it."

Ronald thought a while, and said, "The Gemball is not giving a clear answer either."

"I understand that the Gemball has revealed the location of the Cube," said Leopold.

Ronald nodded and replied, "That it has. So what do you propose?"

Irena replied, "Ushaya must steal the Cube, Yaegar's most prized possession, as ransom, until he releases the Elixir."

Erika spoke next: "With her HypeMo power, it would be best that she do it alone. That way, no collateral damage."

"We will track her moves and stay in contact with her," said Gerd.

Herb added, "I do not need to remind you, this is top secret. Our plan must stay with us. We shall call it Operation, Intercept, No-Kill—OINK, for short."

"Agreed, no casualties," said Ronald. "If Mimbauwe accomplished it with 1,000 African warriors, so can we." All afternoon, they hashed out their plan.

"A bold strategy that I uphold," concluded Julia.

Irena announced, "Permission to move forward." Her clan thumped their fists loudly on the table, and the candlesticks nearly fell over. Julia looked at them and thought: Here were high officials, now acting like gnomes, but she could hardly criticize, given her own appearance.

Herb spoke: "We are about to see how the crow flies." Magus flew from his arm through a western window, as thunder rumbled and lightning flashed.

Enter the dragon

Transformed into a magnificent dragon, with piercing yellow eyes and sharp rows of teeth, Ushaya strutted about the cave, swishing her tail back and forth from her emerald reptilian body and golden-ribbed, scaly undersides. Ten-foot green wings spread out rainbow glitter, shining in the flickering flames from the fireplace. Corkscrew-like horns trailed out from her head, and nodes ran down her spine. Two nostrils breathed out steam from the end of her protruding snout, and fire spewed out from her jaws, depending on her mood.

Pleased with her midnight raids, she placed the cobalt sphere on the piled-high treasure of jewels, in a corner of the cave, among sparkling gems and stolen paintings. She stepped out to view the winter landscape, waiting for Wally's arrival. Gargoyles stood majestically guarding their territory, and angel statues stood silently vigil in the backyard.

Wally was trudging up the snow path when he ran behind a row of evergreen trees, trembling in awe. She motioned him with her claw, to come inside. The outside of the house remained the same, but when he entered, it was a large, brightly lit cave that led to several dark caverns. A treasure trove was piled high in one corner, and the whole room resembled a mix of ancient lore artifacts and modern technology.

It took all day explaining her dragon form and her plan, to an astonished Wally. He pet Ralph and Chloe, glad to see them again, and, together, they walked through dark caverns and entered a chamber, lit up with more treasures. Wally gazed into her yellow eyes and said, "I will take care of Ralph and Chloe while you are away, but for how long?"

"I do not know," she replied in a deep, gruff voice. Steam puffed from her nostrils, followed by bursts of fire. They wandered back through the caverns to the main open space, where she swooped up her furry friends into her claws, hugging them one last time. Then she watched them leave with Wally, down the steps, passing the gargoyles, until they disappeared along the ridge. Smiling a dragon smile, with nefarious ideas of her own, she returned to the cave.

The monitor lit up, and a transmission came in from Irena. "My, you have changed," she said nervously, "You look splendid, my dear. I trust you are doing well."

The dragon snorted steam, and with a deep voice, replied, "Why are you calling?"

Irena began, "There are three urgent matters. Quazaik is back with Meg and Devon, but her shield is weak. Spies swarm about their property. I hear Chelsea and Tyler are frightened, but rest assured, the ring is cloaking Quazaik."

Snorting more steam, the dragon hissed, demanding, "What else?"

Irena said, "Someone stole the last sphere from Mimbauwe. It should be returned to Jerome. Do you know anything about this?"

The dragon glanced at the cobalt sphere resting on her pile of treasures. Puffing out steam in annoyance, she answered, "I know nothing. Why else do you bother me?" Ushaya had often become cranky and impatient, since her transformation.

Trembling, trying to stay calm, Irena said, "The Cube is Yaegar's most prized possession. In spite of all our efforts, he refuses to negotiate the Elixir. We are summoning you on a dangerous mission to retrieve the Cube, as ransom. You must hide it in your caves; we can think of no other safer place. The queen and prince have personally endorsed our plan, and they will cloak you with the ring." Irena paused and continued, "You will have the codes to the vault, but can you still do HypeMo?"

Ushaya rested her dragon body on the floor, with wings tucked to her side. Her yellow eyes turned slanted, and she replied, "What must I do to execute the plan?" All afternoon, they hashed out details of the mission.

Irena concluded, "Erika and Gerd will track your moves and be your backup. In the meantime, we will throw Yaegar off his trail. If he should penetrate our defences, we will be ready." She paused. "Ushaya, when you return to your caves, hide it well." They both signed off.

The stolen cube

Laptops sat on tables amongst a jumble of equipment. Irena was pacing the floor of the bunker at the GHQ. Ronald sat in his Oval Office, staring silently across his screen, and Julia and Herb did the same from their fortress. The OINK team was on pins and needles.

General Leopold broke the silence, tapping coordinates in the air. "Initializing sequence, Ushaya is on the move."

"She is already at the Kremlin—can HypeMo do that?" asked Erika.

Julia replied, "There is only one power that can do that. She must have the cobalt sphere."

Gerd said, "She has now entered the chamber."

Ushaya swiftly passed a hallway, and entered steel doors that opened to another set of steel doors, and another, and another, until she came upon a chamber with a vault. Two burly Russians, armed with automatic rifles, stood at the entrance. Immediately, she transformed into a mouse, and scurried along the chamber walls, squeaking away. The men glanced over. One of them pulled out a stale piece of cheese from his vest pocket, and threw it across the floor. The mouse sat, nibbling on the cheese, watching them. The men chortled. It was the highlight of their day, in an otherwise monotonous job.

Suddenly, alarm bells rang off. Ergh! Ergh! Ergh! Ergh!

Ushaya entered the vault, in splendid dragon form, and quickly disabled the cameras with a blast of fire. More fire blasted across the steel keypad, melting the surface, and with one claw, she reached into the burnt-out hole and grabbed the Cube. Her other claw held the cobalt sphere, obeying her final command. The guards entered the vault, aiming rifles, set for "kill," but it was too late. A little mouse scurried away.

When she returned to her cave, she placed the Cube on top of her treasure pile. Smiling a dragon's smile, she said to herself, "Now that's real power."

Yaegar was livid, sitting in his private quarters, twirling his handlebar moustache. He wore sunglasses and a two-piece, silk grey suit, black shirt, and no tie. A call came in from Irena. She spoke solemnly, "We demand Elixir for the Cube." He hung up on her. Betrayed by them all, he went into shock. Soon, more guards surrounded the Elixir pool and the Zephron ring.

Ralph and Chloe showed up one day, following Ushaya, digging deep into her caves, creating passages and dead-end corridors. With the sphere, she commanded a series of rooms, filled with trip-wire booby traps and mirrors, reflecting into infinity. Some caverns flickered with lights, while others were completely dark.

They arrived at a chamber door behind a wall of granite, where she uttered the secret code, "EDUC101." The granite door slid aside, and she crawled in, with Ralph and Chloe by her side. The Cube sat on a pedestal, encased in a glass box. A set of eternal lights softly lit up the chamber room. On their way out, she uttered the same secret word, to close the granite slab, and they made their way through corridors until they reached the main cave. Then she sealed the entrance door, disguising it as a smooth, sandstone wall, to blend in with the surroundings.

Meanwhile, Jerome wondered where his last sphere went. He called the queen and prince, but there was no answer. Fuming, he called up Mimbauwe. No answer. He called up Irena. No answer. Frustrated, he called up Yaegar, and said, "Comrade, how go things?"

"Not very well, and you?" replied Yaegar.

"Not very well, either," he said. "Someone stole my last sphere from Mimbauwe. Do you know anything about this? I made several calls, but no one is answering—why is that?"

Yaegar leaned into his screen and replied, "Your so-called allies are traitors. They stole the Cube, in ransom, for Elixir." He paused. "Here I am acting in good faith, waiting to hear from Muzaffar, and they went ahead and stole the Cube."

Jerome was shocked. "I know nothing of this, which makes me think they have something on the cobalt sphere."

Yaegar narrowed his eyes and said, "Indeed. Only a sphere could accomplish this feat. Perhaps you know something, and this is just a courtesy call."

"It's not like that, I . . ."

Yaegar hung up on him.

Jerome angrily called up Ushaya, but there was no answer, and he slammed down the phone. He stared at the remaining spheres in his vault, wondering what move to make next. The stakes were high; he must have that last sphere.

The new arrival

There was a knock on the door, and Ushaya opened and then slammed it shut. Brad knocked again. She answered in a deep, raspy voice, "What do you want?"

He looked up at this creature, barely recognizing his mom, and replied, "Remember me? I am Brad, your long-lost son."

Bursts of fire released from her jaw, and, scowling, she let him pass. He stepped in, gazing at jewels and sparkling gems and watches and Faberge eggs and ancient Sumerian scrolls, piled high in one corner of her dragon cave. Among the treasures lay a jumble of masterpieces by van Gogh, Renoir, Matisse, Picasso, and other valuable paintings. Reports had emerged about a string of heists from famous museums around the world, and now he realized where they went.

All day long, Ushaya and Brad chatted, wandering through the caverns, exploring her new digs. Then they returned to the great space, where she offered a cold brew of ale to Brad, as they sat around the hearth before a roaring fire, crackling in the fireplace. Ambient Celtic music wafted through the speakers, and Brad envisioned being surrounded by dragons, fairies, and goblins, as he took a sip of beer. "Where are Ralph and Chloe?" he asked.

Gazing into the fireplace, she answered, "At Wally's place. He has everything they need."

He wondered, "Now, that you are a dragon, what do you eat?"

She replied, "I am no longer a mortal. Only oxygen is needed to feed the fire in my belly that balances the steam flowing through my blood. However, I quite enjoy hoarding, one mortal vice," and she pointed a claw to the treasures.

He glanced across the cave and said, "You must return them; they do not belong to you."

She stomped over to the treasure trove and pulled out a sphere, and placed it in his hands.

He held it for a moment, gazing at its beauty, and then gave it back to her, and said. "So, you have the cobalt sphere."

Smiling a dragon smile, she replied, "Beautiful, isn't it?" and placed it back on the treasure pile. Then she turned to him and said, "I have just returned from an important mission, to retrieve the Cube, now hidden in my caves, as ransom for Elixir. The world waits for the fuel, but Yaegar is being stubborn. Leaders have gone astray, and the Kisga'a Shield is weak. I must find the Zogar ship, and plead with these Titans, these Lazantians, to stop this madness, and to find the source of the Blue-ray light. This is why you are here, to enter the Zephron, with your map."

Brad shook his head and said, "There is nothing I would like better, but it's too early yet, too risky."

She relaxed her belly to the floor, with wings and legs tucked by her side, and spoke: "We will bring the sphere to a scientist by the name of Olaf Meier, in exchange for his expertise. He knows the entire control centre. Cameras will be disabled, and Olaf will operate under an alias, tracked to an unknown identity. Once your map gives him the codes, he will start up the Zephron, and then we enter."

Brad sputtered, "And leave the Cube? That is the most irresponsible and reckless move you could ever make! You are abandoning your post. What will Olaf do with a sphere? And how are we going to pass security, and all those white coats?"

She gazed at him, and said, "A plan is in place. At the precise moment of our arrival, there will be no one in the control centre. We have a deal that he will be allowed one command with the sphere before he must send it back to Jerome, return address unknown. As for the Cube, it is safe here."

"How can you trust him?" he wondered.

Her eyes narrowed as she replied, "An outstanding genius he is, with a good heart. We have been in contact for some time. I trust Olaf completely."

Brad was thrown into a moral dilemma. Should he reveal this to his allies, especially Yaegar? Yet, here was his chance. A wondrous adventure could await him—or certain death, he wasn't sure.

Ushaya made one final call, tapping the keyboard with her claw. Meg showed up on the monitor, exasperated, crying out, "Where have you been? Oh my God, what has become of you? I mean—I—you look beautiful."

Devon peevishly asked, "Is that a treasure pile I see? Typical dragon you are."

She breathed out fire and snorted steam, and proudly showed off her ten-foot wings and claws, and nodules, protruding down her back. Suddenly, Brad appeared by her side.

"Oh God, it's been a while, how are you doing?" asked Meg.

"Pretty good, all things considered," he replied.

Chelsea showed up on screen, and said, "My, what big teeth you have, Grandma."

She hissed, which quite frightened Chelsea. She thumped across the floor, swishing her tail, as she explained her plan. "This is our last call before we enter the Zephron. Leaders have gone astray. I must find Zogar to stop this madness!"

Devon gave his blessings to go forth, confident she had the power. Meg shook her head in disbelief, and said, "Do what you must, Mom, but remember to use both heart and mind—that is if you have a heart?"

"It is the seat of my magic," replied Ushaya.

Tyler showed up on screen, pleading, "Please come back. You can fly Black Rider anytime."

She gazed, hypnotically, across the screen, and said, "I look forward to that."

Chelsea choked up with tears, crying, "I already miss you. Please come back."

Ushaya huffed out steam from her nostrils and said, "I promise to fly you over New York City at night, upon my return." Chelsea sniffled.

"We love you," said Brad, and they disconnected.

"Nooooooo!" cried out Meg, sobbing in Devon's arms.

"Let them go," whispered Devon. "We have Quazaik, and they have the map. The leaders will know what to do."

Olaf Meier

Engineers were studying data at the Zephron control centre, a massive underground facility near the Elixir pool. Yaegar, Nadiya, and Viktor had unexpectedly arrived that day, with twenty soldiers. The floating globe was suspended in the centre, surrounded by an arc of floating screens and console stations. Scientists were eagerly showing them their latest developments on the Zephron ring, such as, plasma ejectors, now stabilized, with the right mixture, for return entry, and other complicated matters, when an announcement sounded off on all three floors: "*Kod golub', eto trenirovka, povtoryayu, trenirovka*." (Code Dove, this is a drill, repeat, a drill.)

It was the familiar evacuation drill, conducted every month. Hundreds of employees filed along hallways toward the stairwells, chatting incessantly, climbing up three floors to outside destinations. Nadiya and Viktor rubbed their hands, in the chilly morning air. Yaegar gazed at the distant granite rock containing the raw Elixir pool.

The compound was completely deserted, except for Olaf, pacing the control centre, expecting their arrival any second. Suddenly, Ushaya appeared in splendid dragon form, with Brad by her side. He proudly introduced himself, speaking in a heavy Russian accent, "Velcom to Russia. I am Olaf Meier. Is great honour to meet you." He turned to Brad, "I heard much about you, and yos map is crucial to our mission. Let me show you round."

Brad observed a man in his fifties, small in stature, wearing a white lab coat, with a head full of white, unruly hair. There were dark circles under his deep brown eyes, showing warmth tinged with sadness. But when he smiled, the lines of his face smiled with him. He was eccentric, to be sure, thought Brad.

Ushaya walked around the arc, gazing at the floating globe, showing emerald green and black dots, blinking over Russia. "Our positions are being tracked," she said.

Olaf said, "Do not worry. You see real image. Everyone else sees simulation."

She huffed out steam and said, "You are certain the Zephron is operational."

He replied, "Ninety-five percent, but you know, is not been tested."

"That's a 5 percent risk," Brad pointed out.

They gazed at the Zephron ring, twenty-feet round, with liquid plasma swirling across its surface, surrounded by a ring of flickering lights and strange symbols.

Olaf said, "Yaegar arrived this morning with his entourage."

Her dragon eyes narrowed as she replied, "An unfortunate surprise. No matter, we shall proceed. Be careful, when you leave." She gave him the cobalt sphere and said, "Only one command, and then return it to Jerome."

He looked up at her and said, "We must be quick. May the Zephron guide you safely, there and back."

In garbled voice, Ushaya called out, "Set course for Zogtyk," not realizing her error.

Destination codes shone across the map, and Olaf activated the titanium ring. Grinding sounds clanked, as the great wheel turned, and stopped. The plasma pool swirled in rainbow colours. Brad nodded to his mom, and, together, they entered the Zephron.

Olaf stared awestruck, whispering, "Is finally done."

An urgent call came in from Muzaffar: "The Cube is at Ushaya's cave!"

Ishtan spoke next. “Ushaya and Brad have entered the Zephron. A genius among your crew holds the last sphere, and is doing a fine job scrambling signals. Who might that be?”

Alarms set off, “*U nas narusheniye. Kod devyat'. Povtorite kod devyat'. Eto ne drel'.*” (We have a breach. Code Nine. Repeat Code Nine. This is not a drill.) Employees stampeded down stairwells, cramming into elevators, while Yaegar rallied elite forces around the compound exits, knowing, exactly who that might be.

With a fully automatic AK-47 strapped to his back, Olaf picked up his briefcase and placed the sphere in his white-coat pocket. Then he put on a balaclava mask and walked out the control centre, passing hallways, with scanning rays disabled. He reached a secret passageway to the underground parking lot, counting down 120 seconds under his breath.

With engines revved, Olaf drove his getaway car through the garage doors to the outside world, and was stopped by soldiers, aiming automatics at him. Tires screeched and gunshots blazed as he sped away, in a spray of bullets, zinging back and forth. Suddenly, his tires blew out—Damn! He jumped out of the vehicle and ran toward a generator, killing two soldiers on the way. Crouched behind the wall, heavily breathing, he brought out the sphere and made a command, “Let them know of Zogar.” About to make another command, he heard footsteps approach, and he aimed his rifle. Nadiya turned the corner and shot him dead. The sphere fell from his hand and rolled across the concrete ground.

Yaegar picked it up and walked over to the man with a bullet in his chest. Kneeling before him, he pulled off his mask, and began wiping tears from his eyes. Men gathered around as he spoke. “What a shame, he fired first. We have lost a great comrade today.” Nadiya crouched next to him, her head hung low, in remorse. Yaegar turned to her and said, “It is not your fault. The responsibility rests upon my shoulders.” Sighing, he stood up in the cold, frozen landscape. As he held the sphere, he said out loud, “Bring back the Cube,” and with a final command, he returned the cobalt sphere to Jerome.

High Treason

Ten Russian soldiers burst into the dragon cave under Commando Yakov's team. While sniffing fresh-fallen snow in Wally's front yard, Ralph's ears perked. He bolted up the street and entered the cave, with Chloe following right behind. Growling and baring his teeth, he circled the surprised men, who were staring at the intruders. He then flung himself into the air and pounced on a soldier, knocking him down. Another soldier shot him dead. In one final yelp, his lifeless body lay on the floor. Chloe slunk away, yowling and hissing. The same soldier aimed his rifle, but Yakov placed his hand over Andrei's rifle, and said, "Let the cat go."

Chaos broke out. Soldiers plundered the treasures, stuffing their packs with gems and shiny baubles, fist fighting in one-to-one combat, forgetting their honour to protect and serve. Yakov ordered his men to drop their treasures. Eyeing him suspiciously, they one by one lay down the loot. Lights flickered from the fireplace, showing their shadowy presence as they gathered around Ralph's lifeless body. In shock, they began shouting and shoving each other.

"Silence!" commanded Yakov. He turned to Andrei and said, "You are guilty of treason and murder." None of his men dared refute him.

Andrei spat indignantly on the floor and said, "It attacked our men. Ushaya compromised the mission and dishonoured our name. In case you have forgotten, our concern is the Cube."

Yakov snarled, "You shouldn't have killed the dog. The wrath of your deed will come back to haunt us. Ralph was Ushaya's companion, it was no ordinary dog."

Meanwhile, Chloe ran to Wally's house, yowling in pain.

Wally stopped rummaging in his garage. "What is it, Chloe?" he asked.

She led him to the cave, and they hid behind bushes, watching soldiers drag the struggling Andrei, with shackles around his feet, trudging up the snow-covered path, toward the angel statues. Forced to dig through hard ground and snow with a shovel, he wrapped the dog in a blanket and buried him.

Yakov said, "How do you wish to be executed?"

Standing before the mound, Andrei replied, "So, now you are judge, jury, and executioner." He paused. "Bullet straight to my head."

Yakov paced back twenty feet and aimed his Glock 19 and shot fifteen rounds of 9mm ammunition, emptying the magazine into his fallen body.

Blood splattered everywhere, and he quietly murmured, "Wish granted, thanks for betraying us." Vultures circled above.

Footsteps approached in the snow. It was Gustaf. "We have found nothing, sir."

They moved toward the dragon cave, with Yakov yelling at his men, "Tear this place apart. The Cube must be somewhere!"

Wally shrank back in despair. When all was quiet, he crept up to the burial mound and pushed Andrei's remains aside. Then he dug up Ralph and carried him down the path, glancing at vultures in the sky. Turning to Chloe, he commanded, "Go and give them what they want."

The soldiers smashed through walls with pickaxes and drill guns, and then explosives. BOOM! "Look here," cried out one soldier. With flashlights, they wandered through corridors, left and right, often reaching dead ends. Backtracking, they continued along passageways until they came upon a room of mirrors. They smashed the mirrors, only to find more mirrors, reflecting into infinity, and they realized it was another dead end. The men broke up and went their separate ways.

While wandering through caverns, Yakov saw Chloe in front of him, her green eyes glowing in the dim light. What a magnificent cat she was, he thought, as he followed her through one corridor after another, until they reached a granite slab. Chloe meowed audible English letters and numbers. Yakov was surprised when the granite stone slid aside. As he entered the chamber, he quietly gasped, for there sat the Cube on a pedestal. He looked at Chloe and said, "I am truly sorry for your loss."

She meowed cat sounds, and said, "Thank you for sparing my life."

Men yelled in the distance: "All clear . . . nothing here." Yakov hid the Cube in his pack and left the chamber, yelling out, "Nothing here. We come back with better equipment." The granite slab closed, and he turned to Chloe, and whispered, "I thank you, also."

A hasty gathering

Ronald called for an emergency meeting. Members joined on multiple screens, as he proceeded with the greatest speech of his life. "I see that Ushaya and Brad are not among us." Voices murmured, and he continued, "We are losing powers. How many spheres have gone astray on half-baked thoughts, and how many Sulimon Seeds, wasted on the battlefield?" Jerome and Mimbauwe nodded in agreement.

Ronald glanced at Carlos. "Have we not learnt from the ancient relic?" He turned to Stan and Lucy. "Does Genius not count for anything?" He looked about. "Good news, Quazaik has been found." Meg and Devon remained silent.

He glanced at Yaegar and said, "The last two spheres have returned to Jerome, thanks to you." The assembly applauded. Yaegar did not appear too pleased.

Jerome nodded and said, "I am beginning to understand the true power of the spheres."

Irena spoke to Yaegar. "So, you got your Cube back, is that right?"

Yaegar replied, "It is true, but with great sadness, I announce a few casualties." Shocked to hear the news, the assembly rose from their seats, in silence, for the loss of Ralph the dog, and Olaf Meier, and the soldiers killed in combat. Moments later, they sat back down.

Yaegar motioned to his group of scientists, and said, "I now introduce Pater Turgenev, who is expert on the Zephron ring." The assembly rose again from their seats.

Pater commanded a formidable presence, towering above the others at six-foot five, with a massive body and square face, resembling Frankenstein. His black hair slicked back from a clean-shaven face, and his brown eyes were soft, when he said, in a thick Russian accent: "Vis great honour to be heah."

Yaegar announced, "I release Elixir for Kunfu suits and Yokuru starship specs, as first steps toward reconciliation." Everyone applauded.

Glancing up from the Gemball, Ronald spoke: "It is time to reveal what I know. The Titan spaceship orbits around earth's thermosphere, cloaked and following right behind the ISS. Furthermore, the Zogar mother ship is stationed high in the exosphere. It has not left our orbit." There was silence.

"Congratulations on your discoveries," said Irena.

"Then the monster has not left our atmosphere," said Carlos.

Ronald gazed into the Gemball, and said, "Ushaya and Brad are in some strange desert."

"They wos headed for the Zogar ship, but I believeth, they landed somevere else," said Pater.

"So where are they?" asked Meg.

Queen Julia sat upon a throne, dressed in a splendid coral sequenced gown, with a small crown upon her coiffed hair. The ring glowed on her finger when she commanded, "Release Ishtan; he must find Ushaya and Brad."

Muzaffar brushed Ishtan with a carpet brush, and straightened out his fringes. He faced him and said, "Go bring them home, may Allah be with you."

Herb was dressed in his finest blue suit, with snippets of clover in his lapel and Magus the crow upon his shoulder, when he made a final command, "Let the dagger go with Ishtan." Yadgiri obeyed, and the dagger disappeared from his hands.

Ishtan and the dagger arrived at the Zephron control centre. Pater and his scientists shook fringes with a floating carpet, while passing the dagger around. Yaegar was pleased to see them again, and said, "You have your orders. Before you go, is there a message for us?"

Ishtan replied, "Quazaik is unstable. This means only one thing: the Gogolan are near." While floating before the Zephron ring, he picked up the map's signal, and said, "Pater is correct, these coordinates are not for the Zogar. It is another place."

Russian scientists were manning their stations, waiting for the final countdown sequence, when Pater hollered, "Then go vair they are!" Grinding sounds clanked, as the great wheel turned, and stopped. In whisked Ishtan and the dagger into the swirling plasma pool.

Scientists gathered in front of the Zephron, gazing at blinking lights around the ring. Yaegar murmured, "*Bog skorosti.*" (God speed.)

Chapter Twenty

Lazantis Falling

Land of Zytok

Three moons were silhouetted against a green-orange sky, as Ushaya glided to the bottom of a stone-ridged mountain. They could barely breathe, and the air was dry. Brad hungrily pulled out cashews and a bottle of water from his pack. "We should have come more prepared," he said.

While surveying the parched landscape, Ushaya replied, "Something is not quite right." Stone outcroppings carpeted the land with black thorns, rising from sunbaked grounds, among desert mounds and bone-like formations. There were no trees, water, birds, or animals.

Brad spread out the map. Compass points and strange symbols lit up. "Where are we? How do you read this damn thing?" he muttered. Suddenly, Ishtan and the dagger appeared. Feeling relief, Brad said, "Am I glad to see you—but why are you here?"

"We were summoned to find you," said Ishtan, and studying the map, he blurted, "This is the land of Zytok."

Ushaya stomped the grounds, spewing fire, and said, "Well, that's just great. I asked for Zogar."

Ishtan glanced at her and said, "You said Zogtyk, and there is no such place, so the map improvised." He gazed in all directions, wondering, "Something tells me the Zytokians still exist."

She could barely breathe, as she flexed her wings, asking, "What kind of air is this?"

Ishtan replied, "Same as earth, but less nitric oxides, so save your steam and fire."

Brad held the dagger, coughing and gasping for air, and said, "Guess what guys?" and he struck the dagger into the ground. Pools of water bubbled to the surface, and they all jumped in.

Ushaya splashed her wings joyously, and spoke in a gravelly voice, "Water, water, everywhere. Nor any drop to drink."

Brad was treading water, when he said, "Alone, alone, all, all alone. Alone on a wide, wide sea, and never a saint took pity on my soul in agony."

"Rime of the Ancient Mariner, by Samuel Coleridge in 1798," said Ishtan, lying on his back, soaking in much-needed moisture, gazing at three moons in the sky. The dagger bobbed up and down in the water, clearly enjoying the view. Suddenly, creatures skittered among nearby rocks. Ishtan perked up, whispering, "Shh, we are not alone." Ushaya raised her head, snorting steam.

Sounds grew in intensity: "Click, click, click, clack, clack, clack, click, CLACK, CLACK, CLACK," and an army of gigantic praying mantises, beetle bugs, mosquitoes, and houseflies, descended over the ridge, ambushing them. Fights broke out. Ushaya spread her wings, blasting fire in all directions, decimating creatures. Brad struck the dagger to the ground, and a wave of water drowned more creatures. Mantises grew in force, spitting threads from their mouths into a net, surrounding them. The insects took away their map and dagger, and pinned Ushaya down with more spit lines, anchoring her snout, wings, and feet to the ground. She pulled at her restraints but they would not budge. Ten-foot mantises stood around the net, in silence.

Ishtan set up a two-way communiqué, and spoke: "We are Titans from Earth, a place you once visited, and my name is Ishtan, and we come in peace."

A gigantic mantis, leader of all insects, came forward holding the dagger, as he stared at the strange, shimmering carpet, and said, "We are Zytokians. My name is Azgar. Why have you come?"

Ishtan replied, "We bring gifts in exchange for our freedom."

Glancing at the dagger in his forelegs, Azgar hissed, "What is this?"

"The source of life, we call water," said Brad.

A female nymph with grey wings, stepped forward and spoke. "I am Shenden, wife of Azgar." Pointing to the dragon, she said, "Legend tells us a flying serpent will one day appear from the sky, with breath of fire to save us.

Is she the one?" Defeated, chained to the ground, Ushaya could only snort. Brad glided his hands across her scales, comforting her.

A six-foot housefly appeared, rubbing his wings together. "You there! What kind of bug are you?" he demanded to know.

Brad answered, "Me? Uh . . . I am human. My name is Brad. What is yours?"

"I am Hork," replied Housefly.

Beetle Bug came forward, with the map in its front legs. With clicking sounds, he asked, "What is this?"

Brad replied, "It guides us through the stars."

Mosquito Enzo buzzed through the crowd and landed at the net, before Brad, and said, "You look anemic and could use a blood transfusion."

Brad turned to Ishtan and whispered, "This is some mistake. Can we get out of here?"

"Not without the map and dagger," he whispered back.

Hundreds of mosquitoes landed on the net, whining high-pitched sounds, in a frenzy of buzzing wings. Azgar lifted his barbed arm in the air to silence the minions. He stared at the human, with eyes turning every which way from antennae protruding from his mantis head, and said, "We are in famine. Superbugs have eaten our water supply, and thus, our lands lay desolate and bare."

Brad didn't know what to say.

Ishtan said, "A grave situation, indeed. Perhaps we can help. Meet our dragon friend, Ushaya. Her fire kills germs, and the dagger can restore your lands with precious water."

"Not so easy," said Azgar. "Superbugs stole a crystal beacon, hoarding it deep in their underground caverns. It carries the Phogram Ray, the most powerful shield in the galaxy. They do not even know how to use it, thankfully."

"What are superbugs?" asked Brad.

"Starworms," replied Beetle Bug, "Cunning creatures that bury water globules in the sand by stealing moisture from the air. Whoever they touch becomes diseased, and many of us have perished. We have no antidote, except for fire. Then they would die on the spot."

"Our planet was once bountiful with forests, flowers, and fruits, but now we cannot even light up a single fire," said Shenden.

Azgar nodded and said, "A long time ago, the Goguls came to trade their firepower for our beacon secrets, but they did not uphold their bargain, and . . ."

Ishtan interrupted, "The who?"

Suddenly, hideous brown turd-like worms sprang from the sands, their bodies thirty feet long and ten feet round. They writhed back and forth, screeching from their round mouths, showing a circle of sharp teeth, with ugly eyes and tiny flippers on either side of their strange bodies, and hundreds of tiny feet.

Panic everywhere! Mantises struck from behind, spitting out nets, and houseflies buzzed, mesmerizing them with their elliptic orbits. Poisonous gunk blasted from the mouths of starworms, and houseflies fell to the ground. Mosquitoes landed on their backs, drilling their proboscises to suck out blood, but the starworms rolled over, killing them instantly. Beetles swarmed over their bodies and were instantly shaken off and trampled on. The air sizzled with loud clicking sounds and screeching bellows, in a fight for survival.

Beetle Bug ran off with the map, but a large starworm raised half its body in the air and snatched the dagger from the escaping Azgar, and immediately dove into the sand.

All became silent, save for agonized squeaks from the wounded. The insects scooped up their fallen comrades and flew over the mountain ridge to their city dens. Ushaya snorted, her eyes fading in the struggle against the restraints. Brad crouched by her side, stunned in disbelief. He cried out, "Here we are in a land of bugs, and we lose the dagger and map. How is this possible?"

The sun descended below the horizon, lighting up a million stars in the sky. They could barely sleep. All night long, starworms rose from the sands, banging into the net . . . banging and banging. Ushaya watched helplessly, as Brad shrank back in fear, but the creatures could not penetrate.

The morning sun rose in a cloudless, orange sky, and a large council of insects was gathered in the distance. Lost in another dimension, languishing in prison, with no way out, Ushaya glanced despondently at Ishtan. His heart was heavy, too, for he could not speak of Ralph and Olaf's fate at this precise hour. Dipping in the pool, he wrung his carpet over Ushaya's scales, to cool her down, and said, "These are intelligent beings, with a life of their own, just trying to defend their land. There is more to learn from them."

The insects approached the net. It appeared that Azgar had decided to befriend the Titans. He said, "So, the dragon breathes fire."

"Yes," said Brad, "and she has sharp claws and big teeth, and she can fly."

"I see that," said Azgar.

Brad asked, "Why do you call them starworms?"

"Because they look like worms and are from the stars," quipped Azgar.

Shenden said, "Don't mind my husband, he is having a bad day. We believe they are an alien species that entered our planet hundreds of years ago."

Ishtan inquired, "You once visited Earth—tell us about the Longyou Caves."

Beetle Bug rubbed his front legs together, to clean off the sand, and said, "Is that what you call the place?" Insects were buzzing in the air.

Azgar paced back and forth, and replied, "It is true. Our ancestors were mining for the rare diosilica, a conductor that when heated in the sands, gives us our spit. They stayed a while, but then abandoned it for richer deposits elsewhere. Before they left, they planted a crystal beacon in the walls, for future generations, but we never understood why, for there was not enough diosilica to mine. We continue to study ancient logs and leaves for more answers, and thus the beacon remains in your caves."

Shenden spoke. "Our ancestors discovered three beacons on our planet. We have one, the starworms stole one, and it appears you have the third."

Brad looked at Ishtan, and said, "The Longyou Caves are a heritage site, so no one dared excavate beyond the walls."

Ishtan paused, and then spoke to the insects, "Are you saying the beacon is what transported your ancestors to Earth?"

Beetle Bug replied, "It's a powerful force shield and transportation device, once you know how to operate it. The Phogram Ray can also destroy enemies."

Hork threw up regurgitated food. "There, feel much better," he said.

"Mind your manners, we are in the presence of special guests," snapped Shenden. Mosquitoes buzzed overhead.

Ishtan inquired further, "Tell us what happened with the Goguls."

Azgar began, "A nasty lot they were. Had to be ten of them, according to legend. They behaved well enough, so our ancestors gave away the beacon secrets to the Goguls. However, the Goguls quickly left without giving us the firepower in return. Our ancestors soon realized their mistake. In their haste, they did not even question their intent, perhaps, feeling intimidated by their size and menacing eyes. Thankfully, they only gave the specs, not the beacon."

Shenden added, "The Goguls have been banned from entering our planet, hundreds of years ago, and since then, we have improved the technologies of our two beacons. Even if they try, they cannot enter."

Mosquito Enzo said, "Unfortunately, some time ago, the starworms stole one of our beacons, in a surprise attack, and thus, only one remains with us."

Never before had Ishtan felt such thrill rippling through his carpet body. He said, "I would like to study its specs. It may be the missing piece to our Kisga'a Shield. A Titan, named Quazaik, operates it. The Goguls, which we call Gogolan, are interfering with the frequencies, compromising the integrity of the shield's power. We fear an invasion."

"So, the Goguls are troubling you. Perhaps we could help, if you help us first," said Azgar.

Shenden announced, "Set them free." Praying mantises chewed through the net until it gave way. Released from restraints, Ushaya roared out fire and spewed out steam, stomping about, flexing her wings.

"Come this way," said Beetle Bug.

An amazing sight beheld their eyes, as Ushaya hovered before a majestic city of untold beauty sprawled out before them. It was the last stronghold, protected by their beacon shield. Lush forests and alien flowers grew along winding riverbeds. Sand mounds and tall, bone-like formations rose in clusters, toward the distant citadel. Grey spiral columns and drawbridges were embedded into the mountainside, among ancient tree roots, twining through fortress walls.

Azgar and Shenden entered the gates upon a dragon, floating across the mosaic-chipped road. Insects lined either side, holding wooden staffs and shields of green, round leaves, bowing at the majestic creature winding its way toward the citadel. More insects jostled among the crowds to watch the spectacle—polka-dotted ladybugs, grasshoppers, crickets, and butterflies. Gigantic ants locked together to form a drawbridge in honour of their arrival, allowing entry to their humungous caverns, which were filled with twinkling fireflies.

Ushaya followed them, through one corridor after another, until they reached a banquet feast set before them. Tall, chiselled columns rose up all around them, inscribed with ancient glyphs and repetitive etch marks, just like the ones found in the Longyou Caves. Hundreds of water globules clung to the walls, like soap bubbles. Ishtan and Brad were in awe.

Amid the drone of chatter and clicking sounds, young female beetles, wearing seed necklaces, were fanning palm leaves, giggling at young male beetles, who were making their way through the crowd, dressed in green tuxedo suits and leafy bow ties, serving algae, roots, and leaves on a tray—delicacies many could not refuse.

"What is this weird stuff?" muttered Brad, browsing along a wide-hollowed log. Twigs and moss were displayed on green leaf plates, next to dried-up bugs and mealy worms. He wandered over to the flea soup, stewing in a black greasy paste, when Mosquito Enzo bumped into him, slurping through a reed straw. "Here, try one of my blood drinks," he offered.

"Thank you, perhaps later," replied Brad, pushing through the crowd, eying berries at the salad bar. Ants walked about with trays of dead aphids, while cockroaches scurried underfoot, salaciously eating up the garbage left behind. Ishtan politely refused any food offered him; instead, he let young insects crawl over his carpet body, fascinated with his fringes.

Brad ate a few mushrooms at the salad bar. *They taste not half bad*, he thought.

Honeybees busily filled their buttercups with nectar from the gods. Young flies and ladybugs frisked about, chasing each other, while centipedes crawled up sandstone columns, to get a better view. Ushaya enjoyed the attention, too, demonstrating her fire and steam to an amazed crowd of spectators.

Brad barely hung onto the bar counter, overwhelmed by magic mushrooms. He glanced humorously at Ishtan, floating next to him, and sputtered, "Holy Toledo, you are Batman and I am Robin."

"Indeed, birds and bats once lived here," replied Ishtan, as he floated to nearby columns to study its glyphs.

Gazing at revellers, rejoicing in merriment, Shenden turned to Azgar and said, "I am pregnant."

Azgar sent out a frenzied signal across the hall. Everyone quieted down. Strutting about, he announced, "Great news: our fiftieth child will be born."

Shouts of glee erupted among the clicks and hisses, until Azgar flung up his barbed arm to silence them.

Shenden cried out, "How many are born on this day?"

Four hundred insects came forward, skittering across the floor, flying through the air, and crawling up cavern walls. Brad downed a Bloody Mary, and slammed the shot glass on the counter, ordering another. Mosquito Enzo obliged. Insects were buzzing in sexual frenzy, chasing and stumbling over each other, through the caverns, overcome with the nectar from the gods when, suddenly, water globules burst, raining down on them, sending everyone retreating to their private dens. Huffing out one last steam, Ushaya curled up her dragon body and closed her yellow eyes. Ishtan wrapped his fringes around the fallen Brad, who was slumped in a corner, and under twinkling fireflies, they fell into a deep slumber.

Counter attack

A six-inch, rocket-like contraption rested upon a bedrock altar in a secret chamber, deep in their citadel.

"May I touch it?" asked Ishtan.

Shenden nodded.

His fringes touched the crystal beacon, sending colourful electric currents running through his carpet body, when suddenly he disconnected and said, "It is indeed, the missing link that Quazaik needs." Turning to Azgar, he said, "I know what happened. Long ago, a wounded Gogolan by the name of Bokal broke through our Kisga'a shield and landed on Earth. Armed with the stored knowledge from your crystal beacon, he scrambled the signals and sabotaged the beacon's integrity, using a transformer. Then he sent the specs to the Gogolan warship. Too weak to make it back himself, we caught him in mid-air and transported his body to the foundry, under the ring and Quazaik's power."

Mosquito Enzo said, "You are dealing with old technology."

Azgar sat contemplating on a thin green leaf, and said, "Our beacon must replace the one in your cave. It will strengthen your shield."

Shenden spoke to Ishtan, "But you must return both beacons to us."

Ishtan bowed and replied, "Once we have the specs for the Phogram ray, I promise their return. You have my word."

"Not enough. What's in it for us?" asked Beetle Bug.

Ishtan glanced at Ushaya. From her claw, she lay the tourmaline down on the ground before them, giving up her precious stone, as extra insurance to seal the deal. Gathered around the strange rock, believing it held magic powers, Azgar got off his bladed, green perch, and announced, "We will proceed as planned."

"I must inform you," said Ishtan, "Goguls introduced the starworms to your planet."

Hork shook his head, muttering, "I always thought they were up to no good."

Brad blurted, "Holy Toledo!"

"I assume this will help you," said Beetle Bug, returning the map to Brad. They all gathered around, plotting their strategy to retrieve the dagger and the beacon from the starworms' lair. Two coordinates lit up on the map, showing separate locations, not far apart.

The Zytokians led them to a sand dune, where Shenden turned to Ushaya, and advised, "Use your mighty claws, and your mighty fire and steam, to blast a path, until you reach a large cavern, about 1,000 feet below."

Hork rubbed his front legs together, and his wings turned iridescent when he spoke. "The few survivors who returned talk of a wondrous place, filled with globules. But beware, the cavern has eight tunnels, like the arms of an octopus."

Stomping and snorting, Ushaya asked, "How do you know of such creatures? They live in the sea?"

"Remember, our planet was once fertile," replied Shenden.

Enzo said, "You must choose which tunnels to enter."

"The map will guide us," said Brad.

Azgar stood before them, and announced, "Go forth, brave ones, and we await your return." They retreated behind nearby rock formations, and there was a moment of silence.

Perched between dragon wings, clutching the map close to his chest, Brad had flashbacks of Echo Canyon, and thought: *Here I am, faced with another monster, and must save the world. Holy Toledo*. The magic mushrooms were wearing off, and it was no longer a dream, but a reality.

Ishtan commanded, "Go!"

Furiously digging into sand, her snout breathing fire and steam, with wings snug by her sides, Ushaya continued drilling, deeper and deeper, until they reached the great cavern. On full alert, they scanned in every direction. Giant ledges spiralled around the cavern to the ground, and hundreds of globules floated in pools of water, scattered among stone walkways, while strange-looking glow bugs floated above. Ushaya quietly pointed at the eight tunnels. Slowly unravelling the map, Brad quietly pointed to a nest of starworms, in tunnels five and eight.

Ishtan replied in Silo, "The dagger and beacon are in six and seven. Azgar says, we go for the beacon, first."

Brad shook his head. "No, we go for the dagger first," and suddenly he stopped talking. Screeches echoed from the tunnels, and Ushaya swirled around. Starworms swarmed down spiral pathways, heaving their massive bodies over the ledges, to quash her. In one quick reflex, navigating through falling bodies, she blasted out fire, left, right, and centre, killing them instantly. But she was outnumbered, as hundreds more clamoured up spiral walkways, surrounding her.

The leader stepped out on a precipice, a gigantic slug of a thing, holding water globules in its front legs. For a moment, he admired her dragon form. Then from his hideous mouth, showing a circle of teeth, he bellowed out the war cry, "Destroy them!"

They flew into the air, knocking Ushaya to the ground. Brad ran off and hid behind a column. Dozens of flying, yellow scorpions showed up, shooting poisonous arrows from their stingers, and Ishtan sprang up in acrobatic leaps and bounds, swatting arrows right back, killing them with their own venom. An army of leeches slithered toward Brad, as he ran and stumbled to the ground. Overtaken by blood-sucking creatures, lying there rapidly fading, Ushaya swooped in and burnt them to a crisp. Starworms closed in, and she flung Brad's lifeless body onto her back, and charged toward tunnel six, while Ishtan circled about, deflecting poisonous arrows. Her mighty fire sent giant creatures, guarding the entrance, scattering and screeching in the flames. She whipped through the tunnel, slamming into walls, while hordes of scorpions and starworms followed in hot pursuit.

Brad woke up in the mayhem, clutching a nodule down Ushaya's spine. Painstakingly, he pulled out the map from his shirt, and shouted, "Two hundred feet to your right!"

Ushaya swooped into a small cave, lit up with glow bugs. There lay the dagger, upon a stone ledge. Brad slid off her dragon body, and staggering over to the dagger, he flung it across the cave. A groundswell of water rose, plugging up the entrance, and starworms raged and bellowed from the other side.

All was quiet. Brad sat back exhausted, with head hung in great relief, holding the returning dagger in his hand. Ishtan leaned against the cave wall, nursing his wounded fringes. Ushaya pulled out a stash of clover from her wings, and gave it to them. Then she gathered glow bugs into her claw, and said, "They seem harmless enough."

"They may be spies," warned Ishtan. A rumble sounded from above, and debris fell to the floor.

Brad looked at the map, blurting, "They're digging their way in. We have to go." He wrapped the dagger in cloth and tied it around his waist.

Ushaya paced the floor, wondering, "How far to tunnel seven?"

He replied, "Seven hundred feet."

"How many guard the cave?" she asked.

"One hundred and twenty," said Brad, examining the map.

Ishtan asked, "What is the most direct route with no starworms?"

"Over here," said Brad, "But how are we going to get through?" Rumbling sounds filled the cave, with more debris falling to the floor.

Ushaya huffed and puffed a steady blaze of fire until a hole was large enough to enter, cooling it with her steam. Continually clawing and laboriously smashing through granite and mud, Brad struck the dagger to seal off the entrance behind them. He was grateful that the map shone coordinates in the dark. Dozens of glow bugs hitched a ride, as they forged on.

Halfway through, Ishtan gazed at the map, and said, "They are changing course and are about to intercept, fifty feet ahead."

Ushaya stepped back, waiting. Brad slipped the map inside his shirt, and pulled out the dagger. Ishtan stood ready for battle. Rumbles echoed across the tunnel, when suddenly, walls gave way and starworms stormed in, roaring, spewing out poisonous gunk. Ushaya blasted out fire, in one evasive manoeuvre after another, as creatures continued retreating through the tunnel. Scorpions flung a spray of poison arrows toward Ishtan, but he sent those arrows right back at them. Awful squeaking sounds came from the dying, as Ushaya forged on into the tunnel. Pounding on all four legs, straddling like a drunken sailor, she blazed out streams of fire, pushing creatures farther back, until she stumbled upon a small cave. There was an eerie silence.

Brad checked the map, and said, "They moved the beacon to another cavern, and we are surrounded by a huge nest of them."

Ushaya glanced wildly about, "Where?" she asked.

Hundreds of slugs dropped from the ceiling, and then crawled up their bodies. "Ahh!" cried out Brad. Ishtan vigorously shook his carpet, flinging slugs everywhere. Ushaya spewed bursts of fire, and hollered to Brad, "Where is the beacon!"

He pointed weakly, sputtering, "Next cavern over."

When they entered, there sat the beacon, silently blinking in an alcove. They swooped toward the light, and Ishtan picked up the beacon, and, while he held it tight, they made off through another tunnel, led by glow bugs.

Ushaya bellowed out, "They must be allies incognito."

Brad struck a wall of water behind them, as they continued their ascent. But on their way up, creatures ambushed Ushaya, spewing poisonous gunk upon her right wing, amid scorpion arrows, striking her dragon body, over and over. She stumbled and faltered in a blaze of fire, with sand walls caving in around them, on their race to the surface. With one final push, she burst through the sands into the air, and collapsed at the feet of Azgar, unconscious.

There was mayhem everywhere. Insects buzzed in great numbers, attacking creatures, surfacing from the mounds. Brad crawled behind a rock, and Ishtan flung the beacon to Azgar. As he held both beacons, Azgar fused the Phogram rays together, empowering both crystals, and geometric beams lit up all around them, fortifying their positions.

Wide-eyed in fear, starworms quickly retreated into the sand, with thousands of insects following in hot pursuit to their dens. Protected by the beacon shield, shooting Phogram rays, the insects destroyed the ungodly creatures in the underworld. They released thousands of globules from their nests, floating out of desert sands, bursting in the air, restoring the atmosphere. What a sight to behold! Exhilarated, the Zytokians breathed in fresh oxygen for the first time, in a long time, as the rains fell upon the land.

CHAPTER TWENTY

A grand farewell

Back at the Zytok citadel, Shenden rubbed the tourmaline rock under Ushaya's snout, like smelling salts, hoping to revive her. Brad tenderly patted clover over her wounds, while Ishtan examined her heartbeat and took her temperature. Ushaya woke up groggily, "How did I get here?" she sputtered.

Shenden replied, "It was a large group effort."

Ushaya looked over at Brad. "Are you all right?" she asked.

"Thanks to clover, I am," he said.

Several days had passed in healing, when a great celebration was announced, to rejoice in their massive victory. Thousands of insects, young and old, joined dancing and feasting in the great hall. The dagger created cascading waterfalls that flowed into troughs throughout the citadel. Young beetles, dressed in fine tuxedoes, were holding trays of dried-up baby scorpions, the latest delicacy, in the crowds, reminding everyone not to eat their stingers. Glow bugs and fireflies circled one another, seeing each other for the first time. Ishtan was conversing with Beetle Bug, while high official mantises were passing the dagger around. A heavily pregnant Shenden waddled through the crowds, with Azgar by her side, greeting butterflies and ladybugs. Cockroaches, centipedes, and grasshoppers hitched a ride upon Ushaya as she flew about the caverns.

Brad finished the last of his mushrooms, and, gulping down his last blood drink, he turned to Enzo, advising, "A fine cocktail this is, but it could use a touch of spirits."

"Like what?" Enzo asked.

Brad gazed out the citadel, pointing to young agave leaves sprouting below. Then he wrote out a recipe for tequila, and, handing it to him, said, "It will work like a charm." Enzo seemed pleased. Under three half-moons rising, they continued partying into the wee hours of the morning.

The following morning, the sun rose in a green sky, dappled with pink, puffy clouds. Deep in their citadel, Azgar removed a crystal beacon from the altar, and, presenting it to Ishtan, said, "It is time to repay you. We expect its return, along with the one from your planet, as promised."

Ishtan bowed and replied, "As I said, you have my word."

Beetle Bug wondered, "What powers does the tourmaline rock hold?"

Hork the fly interrupted, spewing out last night's dinner, and said, "Come back anytime. You are welcome here."

Enzo said, "I must see Earth one day. I am most curious about your mosquitoes."

Stumbling across the floor, hung over from mushrooms, Brad replied, "They are a lot like you, but way smaller."

Azgar said, "We shall not hold you any longer, for you have a dangerous journey ahead."

Shenden, wife of Azgar, bade them a swift farewell: "By the powers vested in you, return to your world."

Ushaya bowed to her new insect family, and said, "It's been a great honour to meet you all." Guided by the map, she flapped her mighty wings across the land to the Zephron gateway, where she paused before the entrance. Brad held the map and dagger, and Ishtan held the crystal beacon. Tired of being a dragon, her body weak, with no fire left, Ushaya longed for her human form, but wondered how she could morph without breaking down every cell of DNA in her body.

"You always had the power to return to human form; after all, you are a young Tanzoik," said Ishtan. Suddenly, he picked up a signal from the beacon, and said, "Zogar has powered up their weapons, and the Gogolan have penetrated our shield."

"Am I really a Tanzoik?" Ushaya asked.

Brad cried out, "This is not the time to discuss this. We must go now!"

Ushaya entered the Zephron as a dragon, and sucked into a slipstream of high-velocity pressure, her body broke down mass, matter, and volume, in a kaleidoscope of atomic structures, through a matrix of light and colour. The Zephron barely hung onto their signals, as she landed, in human form, on the other side, unconscious.

The Gogolan invasion

Debris lay scattered around the Zephron control centre. Medics whisked Ushaya on a gurney through the underground bunker to the operating theatre. They hooked her up with tubes, an oxygen mask, and a pair of electric paddles, which they attached to her naked body. Charging, clear, zap! No response. "Again," said Dr. Volga. Charging, clear, zap!

A medic hollered, "Blood pressure falling. She is losing vitals." He inserted a syringe into her arm. Her disfigured face was still transforming, and her back was bleeding. They cauterized the lines on either side of the spine, where wings once grew, and bandaged them with healing clover. They applied compresses to her swollen hands and feet, and clover ointment over her blisters. The heart monitor picked up a pulse, and they rejoiced!

The medics wheeled Ushaya into the Splunka Chamber to analyze blood and cell counts, and heart and kidney functions, and the contents of her digestion tract. They studied brain activity and her skeletal frame, and performed myriad other tests. The medics wheeled her back to her private room, hooked her up with intravenous drips and a heart monitor, which beeped a slow pulse, and did everything they could to stabilize her.

Brad sat by, holding her hand, worried out of his wits. "Will Mom survive?" he asked.

Dr. Volga looked up from her chart. With empathetic eyes, she replied, "There is brain activity, which means she is alive. But her pupils are unresponsive. I am afraid she has fallen into a coma."

"For how long?" he asked.

"Until further tests, we cannot say," she replied.

The dagger and Ishtan entered the Zephron control centre, where alarms were setting off a steady beep. Yaegar greeted them and said, "The situation is very grave. We have sealed the Zephron ring and have cloaked the Elixir pool. All personnel have been ordered below, for their safety."

Gazing at screens, Pater said, "It began in Canada. Just look at this."

A dark mass blotted the sun in a Gogolan trail of destruction across the world. Panic everywhere! People in the streets were screaming, "Ahhh!" Buildings destroyed . . . BAM! Fireballs! Country after country was besieged in untold horrors. People and animals were torn apart, limb-by-limb, and mountainsides were set ablaze in flames. Land over sea, and sea over land, the monsters quickly spread across the Atlantic Ocean, killing marine life, flattening cities across Europe, Africa, and the Middle East. Thousands more swooped into the Fukushima contaminated wastes, stored in tanks, feeding upon it like food, before blazing a western trail over Russia and China.

A frantic message came on screen from Meg and Devon: "How is Mom?" Their voices were drowned out by Jerome, who spoke next, "They're coming in by the millions, we must stop them." Hashimoto joined onscreen and calmly said, "The NODA starship is ready." More frantic messages came in from Carlos and Ronald, "Mayday! Mayday!" Queen Julia joined the call, commanding the dagger to return at once to Yadgiri. Yadgiri was mighty relieved to have his Titan back.

Herb joined onscreen, and asked, "Does the floating globe track their whereabouts?"

Zhangwei shook his head. "Only Titans, unfortunately," he replied.

"But the map does," said Brad, joining them, and they gathered around.

Ishtan brought forth the crystal beacon, and said, "Behold the missing key from the land of Zytok. It will fortify the Kisga'a Shield and shut down the porthole." He turned to Meg and Devon, and said, "Prepare Quazaik, on my command." He turned to Julia and Herb, and gazing across the screen, he said, "Wait on my signal before you cloak. First, a visit to the Longyou Caves," and with those words, he disappeared.

The grounds shook, and columns crumbled, while thousands of Gogolan were heading his way. Ishtan knew he must act quickly, and, as he felt along cavern passageways, his beacon suddenly beeped. He disengaged the rigged wires from the entrance of the cave, and set the explosives, before the wall. BOOM! Amid rubble and dust sat the very ancient beacon, quietly flashing. Carefully, he lifted the crystal from its housing and replaced it with the newer model, and then cried out to Meg and Devon, "Now!" They released Quazaik, which activated the shield. Chelsea and Tyler ran out to the front porch, gazing in awe at a spectacular blinding ray of light, zipping the faulty porthole tight.

Ishtan commanded only one word to Julia and Herb: "Cloak!"

The Gogolan warship was heading for the ISS. It was twice the size of Zogar, and was shaped like a stingray on steroids. Its massive shape was flat, grey, and round, composed of pectoral fins, joined at the head control centre, ending in a long, narrow appendage, trailing behind, armed for defence. Bright yellow eyes served as windows, peering out from dorsal sides, above the mouth's entry, for docking and disembarking. Gill slits emitted space fuel from its underbelly, mixed with the ancient beacon ray. Surrounding the ship's core were hundreds of long, bone-like stingers, spanning in every direction, ready for attack.

Under cloak and shield, the Zogar ship intercepted the surprised enemy by shooting Phogram rays in terrifying displays of rapid-firing lasers, amid gaseous dust clouds. Many Gogolan were killed on board, and parts of their ship were destroyed, with debris flinging into space. Mission accomplished.

Ishtan was relieved, as he looked about the caves one last time before returning to an anxious Muzaffar, waiting in his Arabian palace.

"*Allahu akbar*! You are back, a job well done," Muzaffar blustered, embracing the carpet, with tears in his eyes. While tenderly dabbing clover on his wounded fringes, he asked, "How is Ushaya?"

"In a coma, but stabilized," replied Ishtan.

Muzaffar wondered why the Zogar had not destroyed the Gogolan ship completely.

Ishtan said, "Quazaik is still building power. Besides, she needs all of us Titans to finish them off." They stared at the overhead screen, watching the horror continue.

Ravaging the lands across Canada, unleashing darkness, setting buildings ablaze, the monsters swept through army installations, in explosions of fire. They toppled the Statue of Liberty, crashing into the New York harbour. They toppled the Cristo Rey in Mexico, and Christ the Redeemer, in Brazil. Another front opened in the Far East, toppling the Motherland Calls statue, in Volgograd, and the Grand Buddha Temple in Guangzhou . . . both destroyed. They swept through the Varanasi pilgrimage site upon the Ganges River, home of Lord Shiva in India . . . destroyed. Thousands blazed across the Middle East, incinerating skyscrapers, mosques, and temples . . . destroyed. African dust bowls swirled upward from the deserts, lifting wildlife a mile high, which then fell back to earth, their carcasses hanging from trees, the grounds soaked in blood. Crops and fields were decimated. Fires raged along the autobahn in Germany, as monsters flipped cars in the air, smashing against guardrails . . . destroyed. Holland dikes . . . destroyed. Castles in England and Scotland . . . destroyed! Everywhere, people fled in fear and despair.

Torrential rains fell upon the earth, and frogs fell from the sky. Millions of birds swarmed in confusion, slamming into people and buildings, all over the world, falling dead to the ground. Locusts grew in great numbers across the lands, destroying crops. Wild animals entered villages, attacking people, running in every direction. Pestilence spread a hideous disease, and firstborns died in childbirth, and man pitted against man, committing horrible deeds, against each other, in a battle to survive . . . the ten plagues from the Bible foretold. Was this Armageddon?

While scavenging across the lands, the Gogolan plucked people from city sidewalks, from office buildings, from flattened homes, and from charred farmlands. Cruise ships overturned in the oceans, spilling people into the churning waters, boiled alive, among dead whales and aquatic sea life, bubbling to the surface. Corralled by the millions, across scorched fields, they were pierced with barbed wires, strung and nailed to posts, tortured by gogolytes, amidst anguished cries from the helpless, roasting alive under an evil fire.

From his palace headquarters, Yadgiri struck the dagger with such force that a wall of water a mile high rose up, drowning black masses, heading for Tibet and Nepal, flooding the mountain valleys below. Icecaps were melting under the monsters' fire, raising ocean levels.

Prince Herb wore the ring, when he made a powerful command to Yadgiri. Under cloak, Yadgiri hurled the dagger into the air, shouting, "Freeze!" The dagger struck the arctic grounds, instantly turning water back into icebergs and glacial fields, while Phogram rays smote countless enemies in the north. Another scourge headed for Delhi. Jagpal grabbed the dagger and ran out of the palace. "I have an idea," he yelled out.

Commander Kumar cried out, "No! What are you doing?"

Jagpal jumped into his Jeep and sped across the ruined landscape, his wheels riding over broken rubble, passing corpses, until he reached a clearing and jumped out. Staring at the black mass looming large ahead, he whispered, "Take this, you bastards," and he flung the dagger high into the air. Thunderous sprays erupted into the sky, sucking Gogolan into a whirlpool of water back deep into the ground, amid exploding fireballs. Suddenly, he was hit. One eyeball hung out from his socket across his scorched face. His left arm was blown off, and guts were spilling from his body. In agony, he slowly crawled to the whirlpool and flung himself in.

Yadgiri made frantic calls: "Jagpal, where are you? Come in, Jagpal!" The dagger returned, and for the first time, he felt its great sadness, and began to weep. Kumar removed his cap to his chest, in sorrow. Shouts of glee rose from the living, "Long live Yadgiri!"

It was 4:00 a.m., and the cellphone rang. Groggily lifting his head, Ronald tapped the Gemball, "What now?"

"They're heading your way," said Yaegar. Ronald saw a vision in the Gemball that might save the world, using the twelve spheres across the globe. He continued staring into the Gemball, when Stuart bolted through the door, blurting, "Let's go!"

The floors shook, and walls were crumbling as they whisked down several hallways to the escape elevators. One elevator wasn't working; they tried the other. Suddenly, a monster turned the corner and spewed out a firebomb, heading straight for Ronald, who was holding the Gemball. Stuart forcibly shoved him into the elevator, and took the hit! The doors closed, and his burnt-out corpse lay smouldering on the floor.

Elevator doors opened to Ronald's wife, Karina, and pregnant Olivia, standing among a host of politicians and dignitaries, surrounding him. Ronald was frantic, "Wait! Stuart!" They waited a full minute, but the door did not open. Thunderous rumbles echoed above, amid screeching howls.

"We must go," said Karina. As they swiftly jostled down the bunker hall, Olivia cried out, sobbing, "Where is Stuart, where is he?"

Fifty scientists and archaeologists were hiding in Carlos's bunker, while walls were collapsing all around them. They turned the wheel, opening the titanium vault, and there rested the ancient relic upon a pedestal. Carlos hugged his wife, Rosalina, and his son, Geraldo, one last time. Rounding up dozens of experts, he announced, "We stay behind to help the federation. The rest of you must enter the relic. It is your last refuge. The secret word will bring you back." They were hesitant at first. The Mexican palace rocked above, with Phogram rays blasting Gogolan in a pile of flying debris. "NOW!" he commanded. They whisked into the relic. When all had entered, his remaining team closed the titanium wheel from inside, and ran down a secret passage, carrying the relic to another bunker.

Countries joined in the fray, plugging up the airwaves in frantic communiqués. Queen Julia released the full TLP reports to all world leaders across the globe. Some believed in the reports, and others did not. The leader of New Zealand believed, but the leader of Australia did not. Brazil's leader believed, but Argentina's did not. The leader of Egypt believed, but Sudan's leader did not. Poland's leader believed, but the leader of France did not. Turkey's leader believed, but the leader of Iran did not. Muzaffar had the hard task of explaining to President Izad Hashemi the authenticity of the reports. For days on end, he tried to make him understand, but Hashemi did not believe his fantastic tale; instead, his country launched its first atomic bomb. A thousand more Gogolan rose up from the rubble.

Muzaffar furrowed his brows and said, "*Now* will you listen?"

All the world leaders came forward, asking how they could help. Prince Herb commanded them to shut down their arsenal of weapons, and cut off oil supplies and the electric power grids in their countries. They obeyed, and their countries went into darkness. This effectively cut off the power supplies from the Gogolan, which could no longer feed on empty energy. Instead, they went straight for the remaining countries of TLP, shining bright across planet Earth.

Back at the Russian control centre, Brad pointed to the map, and Yaegar called up Mimbauwe. "They're heading your way," he said.

Mimbauwe appeared on screen and said, "We have a visitor. Behold Sulimon." A majestic Titan appeared, and he was everything Ushaya had described: a six-foot demi-god with golden brown skin, wearing a white turban embedded with precious gems. His beard was black, and layers of gold hoops hung around his neck. He wore a green vest with a red sash around his waist, and baggy, orange pants swirled around his legs, down to green, sparkly slippers upon his feet. Their jaws dropped. He spoke in a deep, velvety voice: "Let no man underestimate the seeds. We must join in thought, and only then can we overcome this scourge."

Mimbauwe announced, "Observe!" Hundreds of aircraft dropped seeds from the sky, across Rwanda. Thousands of soldiers aimed high-powered rifles at the descending Gogolan, landing on their soils. Bloodcurdling screams, marked by a crescendo of gunfire, crackled through the air, in deafening sounds; suddenly, the soldiers were engulfed in thick forests of tall umbrella trees. Fantastic large canopies sprang up across the land, shielding the Rwandan people from the monsters' prying eyes. Quazaik arrived, beaming out geometric lasers, shooting Phograms rays. The enemy could not advance, for two Titans were protecting them.

The Gogolan immediately whisked to neighbouring countries, plundering habitats and cities in their path, but soon were stopped by more umbrella canopies, obscuring the lands underneath, while Quazaik followed, shooting more Phogram rays. Word quickly spread across Africa that Mimbauwe had executed another voodoo spell.

Meanwhile, back at the Russian compounds, the beeps from monitors and the hissing of tubes and ventilators were the only sounds in her room, as Ushaya lay in bed, rocking gently back and forth, to keep her circulation going. Intravenous lines fed life-giving nutrients into her veins, while doctors tended, day and night, replacing clover bandages when needed. Nurses washed away dragon scales and pus from her drenched body, and lab technicians swabbed samples every step of the way. Then they loosely wrapped her in a light sheet. Dr. Volga mapped her progress, analyzing incoming reports, streaming across multiple monitors.

In a surprise move, Stanislav the inventor, summoned Jake from Valhalla Outfitters, to watch over Ushaya. He flew in like a hurricane, under the darkened sun, bypassing security, and appeared at the control centre. Russian scientists bowed to another great Titan. Glancing at a gold dot blinking on the floating globe, Jake spoke, "Still operational, I see."

Pater blurted, "So, you are the missing dot, unaccounted for, that Zhangwei spoke of."

In awe, Yaegar shook hands with Jake, and said, "Right this way."

Brad rose from his chair and said, "What a great honour to finally meet you."

Jake shook his hand and replied, "The honour is mine." By then, doctors and nurses were crowding around in Ushaya's room, gawking at the new arrival. Wearing stylish clothes, Jake appeared as a young good-looking man, with blue eyes and long lashes, and a blonde haircut, swooped to one side of his face. He glided his hands over Ushaya's body and, looking up at the crowd, said, "Please excuse us. We need to be alone." Everyone filed out of the room.

Jake pulled up a chair and sat down beside her. While holding her hand, he whispered into her ear, attempting contact, "Remember your first suits at Valhalla? You looked fabulous, my dear. You have travelled a long way since, donning all manners of disguise, in search of the Blue-ray light. But know that your dragon form is testimony of the young Tanzoik you have become." Jake proved to be a communicator par excellence, giving words of encouragement, as he rambled on, "I'm a bit of a doctor myself—not the fighting kind—really, more like a confidante. When I was a young Tanzoik . . ."

The final solution

Joined together in a virtual meeting at the Zephron control centre, TLP members gazed across their screens. Meg spoke first, who held Quazaik in her hand. "So, we lead the Gogolan to one place."

"And bring down their warship in one blow," added Devon.

Irena, Chancellor of Germany, nodded solemnly and said, "Elixir pool will be the target."

Pater the scientist, said, "Is brilliant idea."

Yaegar asked, "But how?"

Ronald looked up from his Gemball, and said, "The twelve spheres."

Suddenly, each leader held a sphere in their hands. Jerome of Canada spoke next, "If our thoughts count, then let us rein them in."

A flurry of ideas followed:

"The dagger creates a whirlpool," suggested Yadgiri of India.

"Sulimon cuts a forest path," said Mimbauwe.

Ronald piped up, "The Gemball will be one step ahead."

"Kunfu suits are fully assembled," said Zhangwei.

Hashimoto of Japan said, "NODA starship is ready for battle."

Prince Muzaffar stared at his white sphere, wondering, "How do we ward them off? They will pick up our scent, like bloodhounds."

"Stan's Genius," replied Ishtan.

"Ah, yes, a great Titan you are. What have you to say?" asked Prince Herb.

While fumbling with a new contraption, Stan said, "I am not a Titan . . . Genius is, and . . ."

Lucy the robot cut him off. "Ladies and gentlemen, this is a Nano Disrupticon. It will scramble their signals and create an illusion, throwing off their plans."

By then, Kapitan Nadiya and minister Viktor had arrived at the Russian control centre. They spoke with Yaegar: "Everyone is secured below, sir."

"Good work," said Yaegar, adding, "Why don't you join Station Three? They could use a few hands on deck." They saluted and walked away. He returned to the meeting, hunched over the map. Glancing over at Brad, he said, "You have a great Titan."

Pater was tapping keys across his console when he said, "No human has entered the Zephron and returned from the land of Zytok, as you did."

"That I did," said Brad, feeling a moment of pride, but then he frowned, "Mom is human, too, isn't she?"

The queen and prince were sitting on thrones, side by side, dressed in full royal regalia. Magus the crow was resting on Herb's shoulder, while the ring glowed brightly on Julia's finger. Rallying forces with international pride, Julia said, "We must remain steadfast with our collective thoughts. Yet no battle has been fought, without the agile minds of the brave, who dare to think differently, if it so helps the collective mind."

Herb spoke next: "Therefore, we say, use your autonomy, if you must, to command your sphere, as you see fit, for what matters in the end is the sweet taste of victory!" Applause erupted in gleeful shouts.

NODA Starship

Zhangwei of China was holding his sphere, when he uttered a powerful command. Sixty warriors from around the world beamed to the NODA tarmac in Japan, all geared up in Kunfu suits, under a mission dubbed NODA-TLP1.

Captain Haru Kai-shek paced the ground, scanning faces of men and women, standing in salute. Unlike most Japanese soldiers, he wore long black-and-white hair, neatly combed over his shoulders, and a Katana sword, tucked in his belt. Aged forty-six, he was slim and short in stature, about five-foot five, and with an angular face, pointed ears, and sparkly eyes, he bore the striking features of an elf, and yet spoke in a deep, commanding voice: "The defining moment has arrived, the moment we have been waiting for all our lives. The sacrifices you make are to the highest cause. So, gather yourselves and all your courage, and, together, we will crush the enemy, until they are destroyed, or we die trying. To live or die! What will it be?" Great cheers erupted, to the beat of distant Japanese drums. He concluded, "A word from Prime Minister Hashimoto Ochoa." They bowed to the overhead screen.

Hashimoto spoke: "A most dangerous journey lies ahead. The Kunfu suits will protect you; after all, they are made from Titan material. No doubt, we are in capable hands, but the mission cannot proceed without Ishtan." He held up his sphere and made a powerful command to Ishtan, "Join now in battle."

Muzaffar proudly brushed his carpet body with a bristle brush, and straightened out his fringes. He pinned a TLP insignia on his "lapel." With final words, he said, "You leave me once again. May Allah guide you and return our troops home safely."

NODA was the finest starship the world had ever seen. Equipped for deep space travel, it was shaped like an elongated oval, in different shades of grey, gently narrowing to a conic nose. Two metallic arms jutted from either side, spinning wheels in colourful lights, transmitting signals to the power grid in the hull. They affectionately called the wheels "Spinners."

The teams busily boarded through the cargo bay, wheeling in equipment across metallic floors, passing shipping containers and the escape hatch, toward engineering modules, amid shouts and barking voices: Go, go, go! Housed at the far end of the lower deck were habitation and observation rooms, leading to the kitchen and mess hall, and, beyond that were private sleeping quarters. Hours later, they emerged from their quarters, returning to engineering pods shaped like beehives, surrounding the power grid, in preparation for battle. Attached to their hip holsters were Phogram phasers, with two settings: one to stun, the other, to vapourize.

The upper deck contained the main bridge, with viewing screens spanning a large control centre. Officers were busily manning their stations when elevator doors whisked open. In walked Captain Kai-shek, in a Kunfu suit, and wearing a sash across his torso, emblazoned with international symbols. The officers saluted. "At ease," he said, as he sat in his captain's chair.

Lieutenant Jiao Chang, of Taiwanese descent, came fresh out of the academy before rising through the ranks, to join TLP. She was young, smart, and attractive—small in stature, with short black hair and straight bangs. Tattoo designs emanated from her eyes, and her lips were luscious and full. Tapping keys on her console, she turned to Kai-shek, and said, "Shield deflectors holding."

First Officer Angelo Kruger, born of German-Italian descent, was a tall, burly man, sporting a thick moustache and a head full of curly brown hair. In his spare time, he enjoyed sculpting and making beer. While manning his station, he flicked switches on his console, and said, "Phogram rays, ready to engage, sir."

Second Officer Isaro Kayumba began her career at the Rwanda Space Agency before joining TLP. Mature in age, with wisps of grey running through her coiffed hair, she was known for her knowledge of ancient voodoo spells, as a side hobby. While examining data and sensor arrays across multiple screens, she said, "Cloaking device enabled."

Engineer One Jules Bergeron was a blonde French-Canadian in his mid-fifties. He had spent six months on the ISS, analyzing spacecraft designs, before he joined TLP. He was a good friend of Stanislav, too. Stationed on lower deck, peering out at the great, whirring wheels, his crew opened 'Com' with the bridge. Bergeron said, "Propulsion systems are now online, and Spinners are operational. Igniting Elixir plasma fuel through the manifold chambers. It's now travelling along running boards to the power grid. Mon Dieu, what a sight this is, Captain."

"On screen," said Kai-shek. His crew watched in awe. He swivelled his chair, and, facing Ishtan, said, "What have you?"

Ishtan was tapping fringes in lightning speed across his console. As Engineer Two, responsible for the ship's diagnostics, he looked up and replied, "All systems go."

Chief medical officer, Dr. Ricardo Aguilar-Gonzalez, was a man in his late forties, born of Mexican descent. With short, black hair, combed behind his ears, he was slightly overweight and short in stature, yet youthful in appearance, with a round baby face. As he stood by Ishtan, he became flustered and said, "Dios mio, do not move those fringes so quickly, you might create an accident. You're not even wearing a Kunfu suit. What happens if you get injured?"

Ishtan blithely remarked, "I'm sure my fringes will be in good hands."

Navigator Ethan Kaaka, born of Australian-Maori descent, was a cadet, who rose through the ranks to join TLP. Early family life was not easy for him. At eight years old, he watched helplessly as his younger five-year-old brother Lucas slip from a rocky shore and drown in a river. The event sent his family into turmoil. Father up and left, seeking comfort in liquor and women, and gambling their fortunes away. Mother became clinically depressed, popping pills, locked in memories of tragedy and loss. His parents ignored the young Ethan, who grew up angry, joining rebel gangs in his teens, with a cavalier attitude and a mischievous smile, always looking for adventure in the wrong places.

The day Ethan turned twenty-seven was the day that changed his life. He became an air force pilot, and, now aged forty-seven, twenty years later, here he was, steering a starship into battle. He had long red hair, which combed across his shoulders, and he had a Maori moko tattoo inked on his right cheek. Ignoring protocol, in typical Aussie fashion, he wore his Kunfu suit open to his waist, exposing another tattoo on his chest. His eyes scanned across maps and instrument panels, making one final sweep, when he spoke. "Setting course for upper stratosphere, coordinates, bearing 100 degrees north and 90 degrees east."

"Release diatomic thrusters," commanded Kai-shek.

"Aye, aye, sir," said helmsman Bob Dawson, an American born in Dallas, Texas. He began his career in the marines, rising to commander of USS guided-missile destroyer Artemis, Class II, before joining TLP. At age sixty-four, he wore a Stetson hat, a remnant of his youth, growing up on a horse ranch, and his face was covered in lines and scars. But under that rugged façade was a sentimental man of sorts, with a soft spot for causes, both great and small. Flicking switches and raising control levers, he steered that NODA through Japan's gigantic bunker, and out into orbit. Within seconds, they reached destination, holding position in the exosphere. Three warships cloaked in triangle formation: the great Zogar, the Gogolan, and the NODA.

"Incoming transmission, sir," said Ishtan.

"Open frequency, on screen," said Kai-shek. They gazed in awe at the sheer size of the ship, with convoluted circles spiralling around a massive, tube-like core.

Ten aliens appeared on screen, and one came forward, and spoke: "I am Bahar, commander of Zogar. There are 300 officers on board this vessel. We commend you earthlings. What you have achieved is beyond extraordinary, and I assure you, we stand by, united, ready to act on your final commands."

The entire crew stared out in disbelief at what could only be described as Light Beings. Flaming golden wings spread from their ephemeral, shimmering bodies, emitting swirls and wisps of blue-grey aura, spiralling down to a sprinkling of bright lights. Antler-like protrusions rose from their oblong-shaped heads, into blue and red gaseous auras. Their lips were thin and straight, and two charcoal eyes gazed out with such beauty, that the crew could not describe. It was a sight to behold.

Kai-shek rose from his chair and said, “I am Haru Kai-shek, captain of NODA, and our vessel holds sixty officers. Please accept our apologies, for we do not speak Temseth.”

Ishtan gazed up at Bahar and replied, “No need for apology. We understand very well.”

Trapped

Gogolan were circling the half-destroyed Windshire Castle, where Prince Herb stood in a dark salon, wearing the ring. Queen Julia was by his side, with Magus resting upon her shoulder. Both held a sphere. The entire UK went under cloak, and the air filled with electromagnetic disturbance, amid shrieks and rumbling, dark clouds from above. Hushed in silence, citizens looked up at the sky.

Another front headed for New Zealand, and Julia commanded, “Prepare Quazaik. You are now cloaked.”

“We are ready,” replied Meg and Devon, nervously holding Quazaik in their trembling hands. Their kids Chelsea and Tyler joined together in thought.

A third front circled above the Zephron control centre. Brad pointed to the map and said, “Yaegar, they’re right above us.” Nadiya and Viktor and the entire Russian team stood at their stations. Pater glanced up at the floating globe showing leaders in position. Tension filled the air.

Yaegar said, “They’re after Master Titans. Why are they not attacking?”

Kai-shek commanded from the NODA main bridge, “Put Ronald on screen. I want to know their plans.”

US President Ronald was sitting in his Oval Office, when he looked up from the Gemball and said, “They will form a star-like formation around the world. I’m sending locations now.”

"Downloading, as you speak," said Ishtan, stationed on the NODA.

Each leader held their sphere, when Jerome spoke from his Ottawa residence. "Easy does it. Keep thoughts steady," he commanded.

"Phogram rays on target, sir," said Angelo from the NODA.

Bahar appeared on screen from the Zogar ship, and said, "Ready to execute Phase One."

"NOW!" commanded Kai-shek.

Quazaik beamed a gigantic geometric grid around the earth.

"Initializing Nano Disrupticon," said Stan, as he stood in his mansion, with Lucy by his side.

Their plan worked, at first. Monsters were swarming in confusion through a vortex of energy fields to illusory destination points. But something faltered along the way—a thought, a glitch in their programs, they weren't sure, for suddenly, ten Gogolan surrounded Prince Herb, eying the ring on his finger, and the sphere in his left hand.

Trapped, Herb stood before the enemy for the very first time. Winds howled through the castle. Magus beat his wings, and landed on a window ledge, which distracted the monsters. In that split-second, Herb flung the ring to Queen Julia, with a final command, "One for all and all for one!"

She immediately cloaked, but Herb and the surrounding area remained exposed. Gogolan descended upon him, as he held his sphere in a fiery clash of Phogram rays, under Quazaik's Shield, and, soon, the room filled with smoke and fire. The monsters were decimated, except for one, which was wounded, lurking in smoky shadows. Coughing through the flames, Herb climbed over fallen roof timbers, and called out, "Julia, where are you?"

"Over here," she whispered.

Terrifying screeches filled the air, and "AAHH!" He sputtered a final command, but it was too late. Snatched into enemy jaws, his burnt-out corpse lay on the ground, as a Phogram ray struck the Gogolan, vapourizing it completely.

Coughing, stumbling through the flames, in her scorched gown, her face covered in soot, Julia fell to her knees before the charred remains of her beloved husband, and began to weep. Fires grew all around, amid falling debris. Suddenly, his golden sphere gleamed through the rubble, and she placed both spheres into her pockets. The ring shone bright hot on her finger, as Magus cawed out thrice. With a heavy heart, Julia lifted Herb's charred body and flew out the window, cloaked with the familiar by her side. A distance away, they turned around and watched the castle crumble under fiery flames, until there was no more.

Trapped again

The Zephron control centre shook, amongst flying debris. Pater turned ashen, staring at dozens of black dots blinking on the floating globe.

"What does that mean?" asked Viktor.

He answered, "It means we have a breach. The internal matrix is rigged with some kind of virus, affecting our programs." Scientists frantically rerouted the primary systems to the backup mainframe.

"Then we are trapped," said Brad.

Yaegar commanded, "Get Kai-shek on screen. The Zephron ring must never fall into their hands."

Eerie clanging echoed around them, amid shrieking howls. Bang! Crash! Dozens of Gogolan stormed the facility, blasting doorways in the air, with almighty fire, clashing with Phogram rays, under the Kisga'a Shield. Everyone ran for cover, some burnt to a crisp. Ahh!!!

The titanium wall was melting away, under Gogolan fire, exposing the Zephron ring. Nadiya let out a loud whistle, using her two fingers, "Wheeeeeeeeeee, yip!!!" They stopped and stared in her direction. A Phogram ray struck them down, to finish the job, but not before a ball of fire spewed from their mouths. Her burnt corpse lay smouldering on the floor. All fell silent.

Coughing and spluttering through the smoke, they came out from hiding, picking up scraps of metal and wire, among the rubble. Brad stood in shock, clutching his map, assessing the situation. The Zephron ring had survived the insurgency, and two stations remained operational, but the floating globe was decimated, gone. Ushaya was unharmed, safe under Jake and Dr. Volga's team. Yaegar knelt before Nadiya's corpse and wept—another loss he could barely endure. Then he became enraged, and hollered, "Everyone on screen!"

Kai-shek appeared and said, "It is with great sadness I hear of your loss."

"How could this happen?" asked Julia, choking back tears.

Stan blurted, "I detected no glitch in the Disrupticon."

Meg wondered, "Quazaik followed every step of the way—so what was missing?"

Jerome asked, "Have our thoughts faltered in some way?"

Ishtan looked up from his sensor array, and, turning to Kai-shek, said, "We have done no wrong. The Gogolan have gathered a mutant task force, capable of withstanding extreme temperatures, as witnessed at the titanium wall. They disrupted the Shield's defence, and if so, there must be more of them."

Bahar came on screen and said, "Recalibrating their signals and overriding frequencies, as we speak."

"Adjusting incoming data to the mainframe power supply," said engineer Jules.

"Phogram rays now fully charged," said first officer Angelo.

Second officer Isaro Kayumba said, "Cloaking device enabled."

Lieutenant Jiao Chang turned to Kai-shek, and said, "Shield deflectors holding."

Ronald gazed up from the Gemball and said, "They are about to change formation."

"Course correction," said navigator Ethan.

Julia was hiding in the ruins of a burnt-out chalet, with Magus on her shoulder, when she commanded, "Release the Disrupticon." Quazaik rebooted.

"Engage," said Kai-shek.

"Aye sir," said helmsman Bob.

Sulimon forests lit up illusory pathways across the skies, enticing monsters whizzing through entwined branches in hot pursuit of the NODA, when an awful sound split the air. Imaginary gigantic boulders rose up, as if on steroids, flexing muscle, blowing out bits of rock from internal thermal combustions of fire . . . thundering, stomping, lumbering toward them. Besieged on two fronts, the Gogolan blasted, fire for fire, upon its new foe, while simultaneously fighting the NODA.

Suddenly, a massive fireball struck one Spinner, knocking out circuits, sending their ship, spinning lopsided, through forest pathways. Emergency alarms set off. Everyone on the NODA flew into the air, slamming into barrels and walls, and sliding across floors. Tubes broke from their housings, hissing wildly across the engineering bay. Elixir fuel was spilling out from the grid's containment field, leaking across the floor, while monitors blinked intermittently. As soon as they had steadied their craft in a trail of plasma clouds, they were suddenly invaded!

Out of nowhere, Gogolan appeared, with menacing yellow eyes and sharp-pointed teeth, screeching and spewing fire. Soldiers stealthily moved among the shipping containers, with phasers set on high, killing a dozen in surprise attacks, before manoeuvring in position, around the power grid.

A strongman team dashed madly about, yanking water guns attached to hoses from the walls, and began blasting high-powered jet streams into the Gogolan, who did not care much for water. After all, water subdues fires, but then again, fire evaporates water. Their guns were no matches for their firepower, pushing back against the jet streams, eating up the water. All hands on deck fired their phasers, locked in final battle to death, soon realizing they were outnumbered.

Teetering back and forth on the main bridge, commanders reeled in chaos across the floor, colliding into consoles and chairs, amid fire and smoke, and sprinkler systems, raining down on them, while firing phasers, striking monsters here, there and everywhere. The Zogar overrode the invading code sequence and was about to power up, when suddenly, the unexpected happened. A strange apparition swept through the NODA and vapourized the Gogolan!

Silence fell on the ship, save for sparks frizzling from transformer blowouts and broken steel clanging, echoing across the hull. Emergency lights flickered intermittently. Coughing and hacking, Dr. Ricardo and his team lined up the injured on stretchers, along smoky hallways, as there was no more room in the medic bay.

Kai-shek scrambled into his burnt-out captain's chair, with a broken foot and injuries to his face, annoyed with Bahar, sputtering, "So what happened this time?"

Bahar came on screen and said, "We do not know. Neither side can claim victory for this. We are investigating the source."

Dr. Ricardo came on screen, blurting, "Captain, we have twenty wounded, and unfortunately, ten casualties, all from the lower deck. In all honesty, sir, it's a miracle we didn't have more. The Kunfu suits did a fine job protecting our vital organs, unlike Ishtan, who did not listen."

Ishtan suffered burns across his carpet, and quipped back, "I am sure my wounded fringes will be in good hands." He turned to the captain, and said, "A variant strain mutated from the original virus, but the Zogar took care of that. Your ship is now repairing itself."

"Damage reports," commanded Kai-shek.

Jules came on screen, with head wounds, hobbling on one injured leg, as he said, "Pods two, three, and six sustained heavy damage. Power to the thrusters is down 30 percent, and thermal optic transmissions are intermittent, throughout the ship, at best. But wait! The grid is repairing itself."

"Explain," said Kai-shek.

"Fuel injectors are passing Elixir through backup manifold chambers to the Spinners, which are now stabilizing. Computer modules are rerouting programs through pods one, four, and seven, to the mainframe. It should work now, mon Dieu."

"All systems back online," said Ishtan. The entire bridge was bathed in Light Beings, shimmering across the screen.

Lt. Jiao Chang, with a broken right arm and burns across her jaw, slid back in her chair. Blood trickled from her cracked lips. As she lit up programs across her console, she glanced at Kai-shek and said, "Shields are up, sir."

Officer Isaro was transmitting data across multiple screens, ignoring the burns to her hands, when she turned to Kai-shek and said, "Cloaking device operational."

"Thrusters now enabled," said Bob, with a broken leg, a gash across his face, and his Stetson hat nowhere to be found.

With singed hair and a dislocated shoulder, Angelo said, "Phogram rays are powered up, at your command, sir."

Navigator Ethan sustained several injuries—burns across his chest, loss of sight in his left eye, and bone exposing through burnt-off flesh from his nose. "Targets moving west, sir," he advised.

Jerome, who was stationed in his private quarters in Ottawa, stared at Light Beings across his screen. While holding his sphere, he said, "Keep thoughts steady, everyone."

Kai-shek raised his voice in command: "All roads lead to Rome. Engage."

"Yes sir," said Bob, steering NODA through Sulimon forests, with millions of Gogolan in hot pursuit.

Meg and Devon and their two kids stood by Dragon's Pond, holding Quazaik amid howling winds and ear-splitting static, crackling in the skies. Phogram rays shot out terrifying flashes, while Quazaik beamed out geometric grids across the earth, clashing with forces, trying to break them apart. The Gogolan were unable to penetrate the NODA Shield, as long as Meg and Devon and their kids stood united in thought. Little Baxter peered out from behind the boulder, barking incessantly at the sky.

Brad and Yaegar were staring at the map, while stationed at the control centre. The whole of eastern Russia blotted in one black stain.

"Uncloak the Elixir pool," commanded Julia. Yaegar solemnly obeyed. She turned to Yadgiri, and commanded, "Strike the dagger." And with the full power of the Titans, they waged all-out war.

A gigantic whirlpool appeared in the sky, sucking Gogolan into a vortex of swirling liquid, to their demise, screeching, clashing with NODA rays, in terrifying displays of firepower, until all were consumed in the poisonous Elixir fuel.

Citizens around the world trembled in awe and fear, gazing at the skies. Zogar struck the final blow, beaming Phogram rays into the cloaked Gogolan warship, smashing it to smithereens in a cloud of gases, sending debris into space.

Thus all ended in the Stanovoy Mountains of Russia. The NODA landed in a field, and the crew disembarked, dropping to their knees upon a scorched earth, simmering in flames. The Gogolan were destroyed. THE BATTLE WAS WON!

The Great Reconstruction

Everywhere was mass destruction, and 500 million were dead.

Stench and black smoke plumed in the air. Sounds of moaning echoed around the planet, as people wept in deep mourning, burying their dead. Sirens wailed in every city, town, and village. Citizens around the world set to work cleaning up the devastation, looking for missing loved ones among the rubble and ruins. They posted messages on billboards and websites. Some reunited, but many never returned. Wailing walls were erected, etched with names of the innocents who perished, and mourning continued day and night for ninety days.

All over the planet, the Titans helped rebuild their cities and towns, while Dagger busily replenished the oceans, rivers and lakes, providing much needed fresh water. Then one day, seas and oceans cooled under the sun's rays, breaking through dark clouds. Coastal fishermen spotted a pod of whales on the ocean's surface, spouting water in the air, and cried out, "Look!" Antarctic seals and penguins gathered in large numbers, barking and squawking uncontrollably, for there was a lot to talk about. Arctic polar bears emerged from icy waters, shaking their fur. Animals everywhere, staggered in shock, many of them wounded. Deer stood in burnt-out forests, flicking their ears, foraging for the occasional twig or leaf. Foxes scampered among burning embers, in search of earthworms. Elephants bellowed out trumpet calls, and lions roared, across the scorched plains of Africa. Insects and birds sought shelter among rocks and crevices, wherever they could find refuge. Small rivers and streams dried up around the world. Luckily, the frogfish had survived the war, hiding in sedimentary soils of the Gagnon Stream in Canada.

Sulimon Seeds sprinkled across the skies, carried by winds, to forests and farmland fields. Industry and food production resumed, to feed the hungry populations, and like a phoenix, rising from smouldering ashes, the earth began its great reconstruction.

One day, fifty people emerged from the ancient relic statue and stood about the Mexican burnt-out palace. Carlos broke down in tears, embracing his wife Rosalina and son Geraldo. He wandered through the crowds, shaking hands with fellow members of his team, so glad they had returned, and yet he noticed their stunned faces, and asked, "Pray, tell me, what did you see?"

They recounted fantastic tales from beyond, as they split up into groups through different portals of time. Kingdoms had sprawled out before them as they wandered among the ancient peoples of the past, caught up in mayhem and intrigue, and the worshipping of deities. They told tales of empires lost with little trace of their existence—Atlantis, Lemuria, Mythris—and inventions were lost to wars, famine, and earth's cataclysmic changes. Many of his team members returned with an artifact in their hands, such as, dinosaur bones, amulets, and codex manuscripts. They told stories of a lost empire in the Brazilian jungles where they had discovered the very ancient relic statue, upon a stone altar. One archaeologist stepped forward, presenting a piece of chipped knee, off the relic, and said, "This is proof that we were there."

Carlos frowned, studying the ancient relic in his hands, and said, "How is that possible? It is intact."

His son Geraldo said, "Perhaps another generation repaired the damage."

Someone added, "We must search for hairline fissures that may have been missed."

"But that is also not possible. You only got there months ago," said Carlos.

Rosalina squeezed his arm, and replied, "My dear husband, I realized something while lost in the maze of time. Do you know that timelines alter multiple realities? They are not fixed on a singular path, as we suppose. Yes, the past influences us today, and we are the result of past actions. But cannot the present influence the past, like the seeds we are now planting for the future, as we speak? The truth is, all past, present, and future have open fields upon which we plant."

Carlos was dumbfounded. She left as housewife and mother and came back a philosopher. As he whisked through the bunker, he wryly said, "What you have done would have been a death sentence in the past, but we are in another reality, called modern times. Send in your reports. The world will be interested to hear of your exploits . . . uh, adventures." He stopped and turned to them, and said, "But a great many things happened while you were away." He told the story of the Gogolan invasion. They were shocked to hear that five hundred million people had perished, and that much had been destroyed. Carlos concluded, "But in the end, we conquered them, with the help of Light Beings."

Geraldo asked, "What about clover?"

He answered, "Clover is doing a fine job, healing the wounded, even animals. Come, I shall show you what is happening. There is much to tell." They stepped outside the palace to a half-destroyed Mexico City, which was rapidly rebuilding before their eyes.

Jerome placed a wreath on the steps of the Ralph the Dog monument, erected on the northeast grounds of Parliament Hill in Ottawa, in honour of his great sacrifice. Twelve spheres circled above, in elliptical orbit. Jerome stood by Stan, Lucy, and Commando Nakoteh, among a hundred dignitaries, watching a twenty-gun salute fire into the air. All heads hung low in solemn expression.

Ronald sat at his new oval desk, in the West Wing of a partially rebuilt White House. He clung to the hope that Stuart was still alive, somewhere, as he tapped into his screen. It lit up and Ronald said, "14-0-7 Control . . . Request open frequency on line six."

"No incoming message, sir, he's a no-show," replied the dispatcher.

"All right," he said. "Patch me to the GHQ." He sighed in resignation to the truth of Stuart's demise.

Ushaya had been transported to the GHQ months before. Sub-atomic particles were no longer destroying her organs, and all bodily systems appeared to be functioning and in stable condition, yet she remained in a coma. Physicians and scientists were gathered around a conference table, discussing her condition with Meg, Devon, and Brad, who sat listening with intent. The map lay on the table, and Quazaik floated about the room. Irena was in deep conversation with Leopold, while Erika and Gerd were conversing with Jake. As they chatted, Ronald came on screen.

Irena said, "Our thoughts are with you at this difficult hour. When is the celebration of life to honour Stuart?"

Ronald answered, "In two days." He paused and asked, "How is Ushaya?"

Dr. Caspar Hauser replied, "She remains in stable condition. Her hair is growing again, although now mostly silver. We will have a full report by end of week."

Stuart McCallum had died heroically, in battle, defending his president. Dressed in black, holding an umbrella under the pouring rain, Ronald blew his nose into a handkerchief. Heads of state and a host of dignitaries stood by with US Captain Trevor Kelly and commando Wyatt Jackson, of the ACT team. Alongside them stood Olivia holding an infant in her arms.

Stuart's symbolic casket was lowered into a burial chamber, inside an elaborate tomb containing his favourite items. Drums beat to the sounds of a full orchestra, and organs playing medieval fantasy music in lilting, rhythmic tunes. It was Stuart's favourite kind of music. When the eulogy ended and crowds began to disperse, Ronald trudged over to Olivia. As he gazed at the infant son in her arms, he said, "Logan is a fine choice for a name. His father's legacy will live on." Then he held her hand, and softly said, "If there is anything you need, you only have to ask." Olivia nodded a half-smile, with eyes filled with tears.

He trudged back with his entourage to the waiting limousines, and, soon, the convoy rolled down the streets. Huge crowds lined either side, holding paper mâché globes. Some carried signs that read, "We love you, Gemball." Others carried signs that read, "We love you, too, Ronald." Ronald gazed out the tinted window of his limousine, deep in thought, with the Gemball by his side.

A procession of limousines drove slowly through Moscow streets, lined with Russian crowds on either side, until they reached the Kremlin necropolis. Yaegar and commando Yakov placed several large wreaths on the steps of cenotaphs, where Nadiya and Olaf's remains laid to rest, along with soldiers killed in battle. A twenty-gun salute fired in the sky, in honour of the brave heroes, who'd sacrificed their lives to the Motherland.

Another procession continued, late that afternoon, through the streets of Saint Petersburg, ending at the Vrata Iskupleniya (Redemption Gates). Yaegar and commando Yakov placed a wreath on the steps of the cenotaph, erected in memory of Ralph the Dog. Then they joined Pater, Viktor, and high officials, all with heads hung low, in solemn contemplation.

Yadgiri held the dagger, wrapped in ceremonial cloth, in both hands as he stood by Commander Kumar and Minister Nadin, along with dozens of officials, under pleasant October skies. They buried a golden coffin, covered in red roses and lotus flowers, in memory of Captain Jagpal Dhar, who was enshrined in a mausoleum. A full gun salute was fired in the sky, in honour of their hero, who'd sacrificed himself to India, preventing total invasion. The photos he took became immortalized, and hung in Mumbai's Vidya Pratishthan Museum, in the state of Maharashtra, open for public viewing.

Captain Kai-shek and the NODA crew joined Hashimoto in the city of Kyoto, Japan, standing before a large Yokuru monument, etched in ancient scripture. Alongside them stood monks Wu-pen and Genjo, as they watched a full gun salute fire in the evening sky, to celebrate the arrival of Light Beings. Fireworks followed all over Japan, to crowds enraptured by the dizzying array of lights. Thousands of Japanese citizens took to the streets, chanting, "NODA . . . NODA . . . NODA." Thousands more released floating paper lanterns into rivers and streams, in hauntingly beautiful displays of magical delight.

A bronze statue named "*Umunsi wo gutangaza Afurika*," (Africa Proclamation Day) was erected in the heart of Kigali, Rwanda. It stood forty feet tall, depicting a collage of African faces of the young and old, male and female, representing the different ethnic groups of Africa. Present at the statue were Mimbauwe and Sulimon the Titan, and commandos Ngabo, Gasimba, and Bisangwa, along with a host of dignitaries. Across the lands of Africa, in every country, in every household, every man, woman, and child had received a seed to unify, in thought, set for April 5, 2023, on their calendar.

Ngabo wore a wooden Botswana mask, and, scowling at Mimbauwe, he said, "Unified in thought, or total chaos."

Wearing a Baule mask, Gasimba blurted out, "Do you think this is wise?"

"With all due respect, sir, this is political suicide," said Bisangwa, who was wearing a Bwoom mask.

Mimbauwe replied, "I have fulfilled my promise to Africa. Now the people will decide." Africans danced and drummed across every country, from coast to coast, from the northern Sahara Desert to South Africa's windswept plains. They danced through city streets, towns, and farmland fields. They danced across jungles and savannahs and seaside villages.

Mimbauwe put on a Dogon mask and said, "I am well aware of the risks. Either we unite or chaos prevails. And if chaos prevails, then heaven help us."

Sulimon opened his vest, offering, "Would you like another gift?"

Mimbauwe reminisced the time when Ushaya once stood before Sulimon so long ago, wondering which gift to choose. He hummed and hawed, and said, "How about that fishhook with colourful feathers?"

"Wise choice," replied Sulimon.

A dome-shaped mausoleum stood in the heart of Riyadh, Saudi Arabia. The qabr al'abria' (Tomb of the Innocents), was made of white alabaster and graced with two large grey and black doors, and beautiful stained-glass windows and tall minarets. A lit-up corridor and passageway led to a golden crypt that was filled with human and animal ashes and surrounded by elaborately designed walls. Daylight shone through vaulted ceilings, refracting colourful mosaics across the marble floors.

Commando Zainab, Cpt. Faisal, and Lt. Hassan stood before the mausoleum, with throngs of dignitaries dressed in fine traditional Arab garb. Ishtan's shimmering carpet stood floating by Prince Muzaffar's side. The daylong ceremony ended with a twenty-gun salute to commemorate the blood of the innocents spilled in the Gogolan War. Muzaffar decreed a day of fasting and prayer, and the peoples of the world obeyed.

Guards patrolled the titanium wall surrounding the Longyou Caves, where the crystal beacon lay deeply buried. Geared up in Kunfu suits, Zhangwei and his entourage, along with dignitaries, stood before a tall, bone-like archway, erected in honour of the Zytokians. Commando Chenglei and Agents Beilin, Xiang, and Minghua, stood by the golden egg, which was not yet hatched, and rested on an altar, wrapped in red silk. Mother YangXi circled above, keeping a close watch.

Hundreds of thousands of citizens circled around the titanium wall, watching from a distance. They erected food stalls and kiosks, selling trinkets and wares—everything from binoculars and cameras to coolie hats and sunglasses, children's toys, baby food, blankets, and toiletries. Pavilions sprang up in parkland settings, housing public toilets and showers, and emergency first-aid stations. Tens of thousands of families pitched tents and brought campers and set up lawn chairs in designated campgrounds, all waiting for the show to begin. Celebrations continued for three days and nights, with wondrous firework displays bursting in the skies, with no trail of smoke, to an amazed crowd, sitting in lawn chairs, with sunglasses on, catching performances with their cameras and smartphones.

Light Beings

HRH Prince Herbert died in battle, defending his queen and the ring . . . defending his country . . . defending the world. A horse-drawn carriage carried his casket, covered in draped cloths and medals of honour, through the streets of Wexshire County. Magus the crow circled above the long, sombre procession, which was lined with citizens on either side. A cavalry of horsemen strutted down cobbled streets, followed by regimental marching bands.

Scottish bagpipes came a-piping, amid Irish flutes a-playing, to the beats of snare drums, as musicians played out wistful melodies from their accordions.

Albert Wallis, dean of Wexshire, and Archbishop Roland Carmichael of Cranbury conducted the funeral services. Queen Julia accepted the folded cloth placed in her hand. Herbert's remains were buried in the royal vault of St. Elworth's Chapel. A twenty-one-gun salute shot in the sky. Julia decreed nine days of mourning, and many businesses shuttered across the UK.

One day, Julia stood alone on a bridge overlooking Tranquil Pond, feeling grateful that her family and friends had survived the war. Tears streamed down her face, in memories of her dear husband, which filled her with both joy and sadness at the long life they had together. Whispering words rustled through leaves of a nearby oak tree, giving her the strength to carry on.

She called forth to the Titans and their creatures: "Release your bonds from your hosts. You are free to live among us. Welcome to Earth." She removed the ring from her finger and flung it into the pond, sending circular ripples across the still waters.

Planes flew overhead and fireworks were set off all over the world. Titans transformed into Light Beings before the leaders, radiating different colours, shapes, and sizes. Out of Tranquil Pond arose the ring as a Light Being to an astonished Julia, who was bathed in its glow and beauty.

Irena was sitting by Ushaya, who was still in a coma at the GHQ, when she noticed a finger move, ever so slightly. Suddenly, a Light Being appeared with a body shimmering and radiating beautiful auras of light. "Guten Tag," said the Titan, in a soft female voice, "My name is Phylina. I come from Zogar with a gift. Ushaya wished that your country be headquarters for genetic advancements, and this wish is now granted."

Close to tears, Irena asked, "Will she not survive?"

"She will live. She needs more time," replied Phylina.

Irena sighed with relief and said, "That is the greatest gift of all."

Meanwhile, Stan was rebuilding his winding staircase at his mansion, which had been damaged in the war. With hammer, nails, and a tape measure in his toolbelt, he picked up the circular saw and cut another two-by-four. Lucy the robot handed him the cordless drill. As he nailed the slab of maple wood into the staircase, he wondered where Genius was. Perhaps, it was in him, he thought.

There was a knock on the door, and, dusting his overalls, he went to answer it. There stood Jake, as a Light Being, Lord of Innovation and Technology, reaching his ephemeral hand into his, with a new swatch of fabric. Stan and Lucy gazed in awe at his beauty.

Mischa, the Elixir Light Being, showed up one day, floating about the Zephron control centre, with two heads and two sets of flaming wings, amid swirling gases, surrounding his twin light bodies. Four charcoal eyes gazed down at Yaegar and Pater, who stood in awe. All day long, their team of scientists gathered around the twin male Titans, to advance their technology on the Zephron ring, while learning much about Lazantis.

The two alligators from the Florida swamplands rose up, turning into strange, alien creatures, fluttering like butterflies, across Mexican skies.

Frogfish were not ready to show their true light bodies. Rather, they were enjoying their new forms, sunbathing on rocky shores along the Gagnon Stream. They had sunglasses on as they relaxed their webbed feet in the water, and rested their flippers behind their heads. One of them spoke in French, "*Notre travail est fait.*" (Our job is done.)

"Oui," said another, and they continued sunbathing.

Three hundred Light Beings from the Zogar ship were free to roam amongst the people, as they went about their daily lives. One day, a young Israeli couple was walking along the Jordan River Promenade when, suddenly, they looked up, delighted to be in the presence of a Light Being. In Seoul, South Korea, CEOs were conducting a roundtable meeting in a high-rise office building when two Titans entered the room. So they offered them a seat at the table. Lab technicians, working at the CERN nuclear institute in Zwitzerland, gave a nod to Lazantians, as they came and went. While pulling bread from the oven, a startled Afghani housewife turned around, and, facing a Light Being, she smiled. In Zimbabwe, farmers were plowing their fields, waving their hats in welcome. In South Australia, miners emerged from rock quarries, bowing in reverence before Light Beings.

July 9, 2022, was proclaimed World Encounter Day (WED), the day the Gogolan were annihilated, the day the world encountered Lazantians. The peoples of the Earth rejoiced, "Long live Titans! Long live Lazantis!"

One day, Ishtan arrived at the Zephron control centre, disguised as the carpet. Brad arrived with his map and, together, they entered the Zephron, to return the two crystal beacons, as promised. The great wheel turned, while Yaegar, Pater, and the whole science team watched them slip through the plasma ring.

Brad rode upon Ishtan's carpet, weaving through underbrush and oversized, lush fern leaves of a forest that had grown all around them. They were amazed at how much the land of Zytok had been restored. Alien-like flowers sprouted everywhere. Creatures flew in the air under pink-orange skies filled with puffy white clouds. They continued their journey, heading to the citadel, where a crowd of insects was awaiting their arrival. Azgar and Shenden were the first to greet them.

Shenden said, "We are pleased you have kept your promise. You are always welcome here." Azgar was now holding all three beacons.

Brad presented a vial containing a few frightened mosquitoes to Mosquito Enzo. "Take good care of them," he said.

"They are so tiny," said Enzo, holding the vial in his forelegs, studying the new arrivals.

They were invited to a feast of dead aphids, mites, and roaches, along with tree bark across the banquet log. Brad and Ishtan began to hear something—what was that sound? It was the sound of music that had long died out, and was now revived, across the great hall. Ladybugs buzzed their wings, in tandem, with cicadas drumming their abdomen, among the chorus of crickets, playing their reeds and singing their songs. Brad tapped his foot to the rhythm, while Ishtan danced and swirled among hundreds of insects, skittering across the floor. In the merriment, Beetle Bug, who was standing next to Brad, offered him some mushrooms, but Brad politely declined. Instead, they struck a conversation about the map, as Brad spread it across a granite slab. Beetle Bug was intrigued to learn of an ancient fallen tree, a treasure trove of leaves and worms they have not yet discovered in a faraway forest.

Hork the fly joined them, asking, "How is Ushaya the dragon? I found out she is your mother, although you don't look anything alike."

Brad replied, "Mom has turned back into a human, like me, and she is in a coma, fighting for her life."

"That's too bad," said Hork, "She should have stayed a dragon, a much better creature than a human."

Brad looked at him and said, "Thanks for cheering me up." He wandered over to a lookout ledge, and gazed over the landscape.

Mosquito Enzo joined him and said, "That tequila recipe you gave us makes a great drink, but unfortunately, it has been seized by good-for-nothing ants. They are no longer building their hills. Since then, worker bees have encroached upon the lands, stealing our tequila, injecting the nectar into illegal flowers. We had to send in the army of wasps to raid their compounds, to restore order in our empire."

"Is that so?" said Brad, feeling slightly guilty.

Azgar guided Brad and Ishtan through the catacombs of dead mantis officials, until they arrived at an underground chamber. Retrieving the tourmaline rock from a hole in the sandstone wall, he gave it to Brad and said, "It is of no consequence to us. You may have it."

From the great hall, Ishtan and Brad bade the insect family goodbye, in a grand finale of buzzing wings and cicadas drumming. Shenden spoke to Brad, "May your mother survive, and she is welcome to come anytime, as dragon or human, it does not matter."

Brad spoke with tears in his eyes, "Thank you for cheering me up."

Soon the great wheel turned and Brad and Ishtan entered the Zephron ring, landing back on Earth, to an awaiting team of Russian scientists. Yaegar and Pater welcomed them home.

The tourmaline rock had returned to Ushaya at the GHQ, resting in her folded hands. Irena sat by her bedside, when she looked up at Brad and said, "It's nice to see you again." They both gazed down at Ushaya in deep slumber.

Phyteus Quaal

Phasers were aimed at a group of gogolytes, huddled in the Baumann's Cave, and a German SWAT team ordered them to come out with their hands in the air. Filing out, one by one, they cried, "Please, we are defectors, we mean no harm. If anything, we can help." There was no screeching, no fireballs, only yellow eyes cast downward.

A German general hollered, "*Verhafte sie*!" (Arrest them!) With phasers locked on "stun," the gogolytes fell to the ground. Hundreds more were discovered around the world, in abandoned caves and mineshafts. Flushed out from their hiding places, they were apprehended and detained in one big facility at the GHQ.

Ishtan was summoned to assess the situation, and floating as a carpet in front of the overcrowded cells, he was greeted by Irena, Erika, and Leopold, when he began examining the new inmates. "Let them go," he said. "They are harmless. Just poets, artists, and intellectuals."

Erika chortled, "I didn't know gogolytes could be poets."

Leopold handed Ishtan a green cartouche with black symbols confiscated from one of the inmates. "Can you interpret this?" he asked.

Ishtan began reciting:

"*Great fires kiss the sun that give us life by day*
The moon's cooling mists temper our hearts by night
We give thanks to another tomorrow to show us the way
Out of sorrows we carry in our flight."

Irena commanded the guards, "You heard what Ishtan said. Release them."

Hundreds of black, ghostly apparitions filed out of jail through the courtyards, toward freedom, passing Leopold, who snarled, "We'll be watching you."

A lone gogolyte wandered through the streets of Amsterdam, ostracized by everyone he came in contact with. People eyed him suspiciously, not wanting anything to do with him. Here he was, a migrant on an alien planet with no identity, scavenging through garbage bins for what scraps he could find, with no place to call home and no job . . . just drifting aimlessly through the Netherlands. Despondent, he sat down on a city bench questioning his future, when a ten-year-old Dutch girl sat down beside him and said, "I'll be your friend. I'm not afraid of you."

Flashing his yellow, toothy grin, he gazed down at her with soft yellow eyes, and spoke. "Really? What is your name?"

Dressed in a school uniform, wearing a backpack, with her hair braided in pigtails, she looked up at him and said, "Makayla. What's yours?"

"Phyteus Quaal," he replied.

All afternoon, he showed her games from his planet, like eating fireballs and performing the disappearing act. Makayla giggled in delight, showing him games from her planet, like hopscotch, and then badminton—swinging her racket against the birdie over the net in a nearby badminton court.

Suddenly, her mother showed up and shrieked, "Get away from that monster!"

While her mother dragged her away, Makayla cried out, "Mommy, he is not a monster, he's my friend!"

Sad and dejected, Phyteus sat back down on the bench, ready to accept his fate, for he knew the moment his name was uttered, they would be coming for him.

"ALL RISE!" said commander Bahar on the Zogar spaceship. A group of Light Beings floated around a horizontal bright-white disc, containing records of their case. Convoluted vault-like structures rose up amid rising and descending columns, hissing steam in the alien atmosphere. Fifty Light Beings lined the grand corridor of Tribunal Hall, observing the shackled gogolyte float in a force-field cage, hauled up before the Elders.

Bahar opened the proceedings, "You managed to escape from planetoid Calatraz, the highest-security prison in the quadrant, and now, claim yourself a stowaway on the Gogolan warship, undetected by Quazaik and all of us Titans. How is this possible? What have you to say?"

Phyteus said, "Honourable Elders and Members of the Council, for hundreds of years, in deep remorse for my actions, I had spent much time contemplating. Years in captivity have made me realize what truly matters as a Tanzoik: to uphold the oath of honour and integrity, free of vice and greed, and, above all, defender of creatures both great and small." Ignoring pangs of gogolyte hunger, he continued, "Over time, my powers grew, and one day, I met an inmate advanced in age who came from the rare Placidus tribe, who was wrongfully incarcerated in the first place. He was most wise and held many secrets, and he knew how to break out of prison through connections with the Gogolan."

Defence council female Elder Xoda scanned the disc, and said, "This would be Warnock, correct?"

Phyteus nodded and continued, "The Gogolan invaded the compounds, rallying prisoners to their cause, and little did I know I would be heading for planet Earth on one of their biggest war ships. I used my powers to transform into a gogolyte and joined their mission, waiting for the chance to redeem myself at the right time. Whatever happened to Warnock, I do not know, for I never saw him again."

"He does not speak like a gogolyte," murmured a Light Being.

"Indeed, more like a Tanzoik," said another.

The battle of offence and defence continued.

Offence council male Elder Konak said, "Let us not forget the accused is responsible for millions of deaths on Lazantis."

Defence Xoda slammed back, "He vapourized the Gogolan on the NODA. Does not saving human lives count in his defence?"

Konak countered, "He escaped from prison, another crime against the state. We cannot be sure of his true intent."

Xoda said, "Our reports have proven, without a shadow of doubt, that he lured millions of Gogolan through Sulimon forests into the dagger's funnel of death."

Bahar said, "If you are truly Phyteus, then show yourself."

Light Beings gave way, floating back, gawking at the gogolyte in the golden cage, as he transformed into a Tanzoik Light Being. Wisps of dark smoke and gaseous clouds swirled around his ephemeral body, and his eyes flashed out neon lights in every direction, and they recognized the face of Phyteus Quaal. Realizing that he was more powerful than they had anticipated, the Elders broke away to deliberate over his sentence, in confidence. It was a while before they returned to the disc.

When the counsel reassembled, Bahar spoke, "We have decided that you, Phyteus Quaal, stand before us accused of war crimes, which will not be struck from your record. However, you may be exonerated of these crimes equal to the good works you have demonstrated, but only under one condition. You must gather all intelligence on the gogolytes who remain on earth, for we are not entirely sure of their intent. If you accomplish this to our satisfaction, you may earn your freedom. Go now, you have your mission, but know that we are watching you."

The crowd murmured as the force field lowered from his cage. His shackles released from his body, and, stepping out, Phyteus bowed and said, "It is the highest honour to be serving Lazantis again, and I will not disappoint you."

Months later, Phyteus and Makayla were playing hide-and-seek in a nearby forest. Phyteus hid behind a tree and said, "I am not really a gogolyte, but I cannot show you my true self yet, for I am on a secret mission."

Hiding behind another tree, Makayla asked, "What do you mean?" He floated to her and whispered in her ear. She hushed in awe. "Really?"

Chapter Twenty-One

Final Frontier

Two spaceships were stationed in the Mojave Desert ready to onboard leaders for their solar excursion. Ronald proudly cut the ribbon in a ribbon-cutting ceremony, before a cheering crowd of hundreds of thousands standing in awe, across the landscape under a clear blue sky. Guards were posted outside each entrance, ticking off names of Lazantians and leaders boarding their respective craft.

Zogar invitees

Ronald walked up the ramp with Captain Trevor Kelly, and Commando Wyatt Jackson from ACT, gazing at neon lights blinking across the Gemball's ephemeral body. Queen Julia walked up the ramp with Magus on her shoulder and Master Titan by her side, radiating concentric rings in the air. She held a photo of Herb in her hand, knowing he wouldn't want to miss this for anything in the world.

Ushaya lay deep in slumber, dressed in a lilac satin gown and silver slippers, with beaded jewels around her coiffed silver-and-black hair, holding the tourmaline rock in her folded hands. Irena and Dr. Hauser wheeled her bed up the ramp with the help of Leopold, Erika, and Gerd, followed by Stephan and Susie, gazing at Phylina the Titan, enraptured by her splendour and beauty.

Brad walked up, mesmerized, by the Map Light Being. Two charcoal eyes burned out from his glorious ephemeral form. Meg and Devon and their two kids, Tyler and Chelsea, walked up the ramp, in awe of Quazaik Light Being, as sparkling rays beamed from her crystalline angular body. Lucy and

Stan followed next. Antennae rose from Lucy's head, taking in every detail of swirling mist clouds, surrounding Jake's light body.

Carlos walked up the ramp with Ancient Relic and Clover Light Beings, their effervescent bodies glowing with such beauty he could not describe. Yadgiri walked up the ramp, carrying a photo of Jagpal, with Kumar and Nadin by his side, with Dagger Light Being shimmering in swirls of cosmic dust.

A guard could not recognize one Light Being and asked, "You with Mimbauwe?" The Light Being turned into a demi-god, wearing a turban and golden rings around his neck, with green slippers on his feet.

Mimbauwe answered, "I'd like you to meet Sulimon."

The guard looked up in awe, and ticked off their names on his clipboard and let them pass. Commandos Ngabo, Gasimba, and Bisangwa, soon followed behind, boarding the Zogar ship.

NODA Invitees

Captain Kai-shek stood at the landing dock, greeting members dressed in normal attire over Kunfu suits. The first to arrive were Muzaffar and old man Akbar the merchant, praised for bringing Ishtan to the world. Commando Zainab and Cpt. Faisal and Lt. Hassan followed behind, gazing at Ishtan Light Being, enraptured by his exquisite beauty.

Hashimoto and monks Genjo, Wu-pen, and Nobu greeted Kai-shek, as they came on board, completely in awe of Yokuru Light Being, with wisps of smoky hues swirling around his light body. Zhangwei walked up carrying the golden egg in a reed basket. Commando Chenglei, along with agents Xiang, Beilin, and Minghua, stood by his side. They shook hands with Kai-shek and boarded the NODA, while Kunfu Light Being whisked up the ramp, as a golden orb, with YangXi the yellow crane, by his side.

Mischa, the Elixir Light Being, glanced down at dense human forms with a mix of curiosity and respect. Yaegar and Pater looked up at his two heads and four charcoal eyes, while commando Yakov Petrov and minister Viktor Smirnov brushed their hands across his twin light bodies, as he floated by.

Jerome and commando Nakoteh Harrison followed, grinning from ear to ear, as twelve little Titans glided up the ramp, with flaming wings emitting sprinkles of light from their ever-changing forms.

Great visionaries and entrepreneurs were invited, too. Ephron Musk and Bezo Jeffrey, Sir Richard Bransard and Sir Darwin Attenbrow, walked up the ramp, in total euphoria. Following behind them were Bilbo Gates, Rupee Durmoch and Rowan Buff, shaking hands with Captain Kai-shek, as they boarded the NODA.

The last to arrive were Phyteus Quaal, holding Makayla's hand as they strolled up the ramp. Dressed in a little Kunfu suit, she gazed up at her new Tanzoik friend. Her parents stood watching from the crowd, with tears rolling down their cheeks, sending out prayers.

Ushaya's sister Amelia and husband Paul, and brother Kevin and wife Maria, were bathed in the glow from the ships. Alongside them stood old man Harvey and Caroline, holding hands. Swami Gupta and Phoebe looked up and smiled. Ronald's wife Karina stood by Olivia, holding her six-month old, Logan, next to Brad's girlfriend, Cheyenne, all gazing at the ships.

Hashimoto's wife Miyuki and their daughter Kioko were chatting with Sung Yee, wife of Zhangwei, while Jerome's wife Kaitlyn and their three kids were chatting with Irena's husband Finn. Behind them were Carlos's wife, Rosalina, and son Geraldo, along with a host of archaeologists, all chatting away.

Dressed in fine Arab garb, Muzaffar's wife Zahra bint Mansur and their four children wandered through the crowd, meeting up with Mimbauwe's wife, Sylvie and their two children, Simba and Anitha.

Farida, Akbar's wife, and their seven children and thirteen grandchildren, began clapping rhythmically. Clap, clap, clap . . . clap, clap, clap . . . clapity, clapity . . . clap, clap, clap . . . clap, clap, clap. Monks beat Japanese drums. Yaegar's wife Sofia and their two children took endless videos from their smartphones, while Julia and Herb's four children and seven grandchildren waved arms in the air, as one does in a rock concert.

The peoples of the earth watched in great anticipation. Chinese villagers gathered around laptops, and African bushmen gathered around their laptops. Millions gathered in the Mexican El Zocalo Square, watching a large televised screen. The same happened in London, Paris, Berlin, and Tehran, and all over the world. Hundreds of news reporters wandered through the crowds, filming and flashing cameras, for this was their big day. They were about to send world leaders into space!

The clapping and drums stopped. Ramps lifted and hatches shut tight. Convoluted circles lit up, spiralling around Zogar's massive tube-like core, while Spinners spun from the NODA.

Voices joined around the world: "Ten, nine, eight, seven . . ." A flash of Blue-ray light streaked across the sky.

"Six, five, four, three . . ." Steam hissed from their hulls.

"Two, one . . . Now!"

Two spaceships whirred silently into orbit, as crowds cheered in exaltation, shielding their eyes from the sun.

Beyond the sun

Ronald sputtered, "Hey, look at this, just look at this." The Titan spaceship was orbiting in the same thermosphere as the ISS, both flashing signals in welcome. The Zogar and NODA ships passed the dark side of the moon, hurtling into space toward Mars, leaving their pretty blue planet far behind.

Massive quantum processors, attached to mainframe computers, were stationed along the Zogar's tube, amid tall columns rising up and down, containing green liquid plasma fuel. Light Beings greeted newcomers, who arrived on moving floors, rising and descending like elevators without walls or doors. More moving floors carried passengers to various walkways throughout the ship, lit up in beams of light.

Peering into blackness from an observation deck on the Zogar, Tyler piped up, "Look, Mars."

Devon blurted, "It is indeed a red planet." Everyone on board became excited, glued to observation screens.

Ronald joined Chelsea, who was in awe. "See those tracks down there? That's when Rover *Perseverance* landed in 2020," he said proudly.

Meg stood by Quazaik, who was sparking out rays from her angular form, and asked, "Do you miss Lazantis?"

Quazaik gazed at her through charcoal eyes, and replied, "Our planet will still exist for thousands of years. Perhaps you would like to visit one day."

Dr. Hauser and Irena were stationed in a private pod, watching over Ushaya, when Jake dropped in and said, "Go ahead and enjoy the ship, I will stay with her. Don't forget your locator. It will guide you back." They picked up their metallic devices and, thanking Jake, went on their merry way.

Brad was jumping floor to floor, rising up and down along the Zogar tube, filled with people and Light Beings, when he called out, "Hey, has anybody seen my map?"

"I think he went that way," said Lucy, whizzing by."

"Thanks," he replied, and turned direction.

Yadgiri was staring into the blackness from an observation deck. Standing next to a Light Being, he asked, "Hello, what is your name?"

"Dagger, don't you recognize me?" he replied.

Queen Julia crossed adjacent floors to greet Irena and Dr. Hauser, when Magus cawed twice and flew ahead of them. Irena whispered, "Step off here, your majesty. We have something to show you." They followed the crow down corridors, until they reached a dimly lit cavern lined with vertical sleep pods, row after row. As they wandered among the rows, some pods held Light Beings who were deep in repose, while others were empty. Dr. Hauser whispered, "This is where they go to recharge."

Rumours soon spread about Bokal the Monster, held in captivity at the back of the tube, out of sight and blocked off from the rest of the Zogar ship.

Meanwhile, on the NODA starship, Nakoteh and Yaegar were peering into the void from an observation deck, when Nakoteh said, "In the beginning, God created the heavens and the earth, and the earth was without form. Darkness fell upon the face of the deep, and the Spirit moved across the waters. And God said, 'Let there be light.'"

"You know the Bible," said Yaegar.

"Not really," he replied.

Officers were manning their stations on the NODA main bridge. Alongside them was Ishtan, scanning sensor arrays across his console, with Jerome by his side. While gazing into the cosmos through the viewing screen, Jerome spoke wryly, "You once told me I needed all spheres for world domination. You were right."

Kai-shek sat back in his captain's chair, and smiling, said, "Mission accomplished."

Muzaffar was wandering through NODA corridors when he met Phyteus for the first time, with Makayla by his side. He asked, "So, how do you like the gogolyte form?"

Phyteus replied, "As much contempt as I have for them, there is a part of me that enjoys it."

"In what way?" he asked.

He quipped, "Spewing fireballs from my mouth and zapping from my bony fingers gives me a new sense of power I had not experienced before."

Muzaffar smiled and said, "I see you have Ishtan's sense of humour." He turned to Makayla and said, "And you, little princess, welcome aboard."

She looked up at his bushy beard and Arab garb and replied, "You dress funny."

He chuckled and said, "Don't we all."

Visionaries and entrepreneurs were standing around the power grid on the NODA, discussing commercial space flight tourism with engineer Jules. "If we could acquire this new technology," said Sir Richard Bransard. He was a business magnate extraordinaire and founder of *Vestal Voyager*, an American company specializing in hardware components and computer mainframes to operate space vehicles.

"With permission from TLP, of course," added Sir Darwin Attenbrow, a celebrated broadcaster from the UK, who brought to the world the wonders of nature, through his many TV documentaries.

"Imagine what new discoveries await us," said Ephron Musk, a charismatic visionary, who founded *PlanetaryX*, a company that built and launched rockets into space.

"Different flights for a different price," said Bezo Jeffrey, founder of *Horizons Galactic*, a company that was building space pods around the planet. Jeffrey envisioned a future where millions of people would live and work in space for the benefit of Earth.

Bilbo Gates was a worldwide philanthropist and founder of *NanoBotix*, a leading organization in nanobot technology to help cure human diseases. He nodded and said, "TLP would get a cut of the proceeds."

"Many people would become wealthy," said Rupee Durmoch, a business magnate and media tycoon. Among his many holdings in film and satellite television, he owned *Foxhound Telecom*, a multi-national TV channel, based in New York City.

Rowan Buff nodded and said, "My wealth would go to those in need." He was one of America's most successful investors, who amassed huge fortunes while defying prevailing investment trends, and he was also a philanthropist—giving much of his fortune away to social and worthy causes.

Jules shrugged and replied, "Sounds like a plan. I'm sure TLP will listen to your proposals."

They continued their sojourn, travelling through space, until they reached Jupiter. Everyone gasped at the sheer size of the planet. It was massive! Thirteen hundred earths could fit into Jupiter. The Great Red Spot came into view in the southern hemisphere amid gaseous storms swirling stripe clouds around its core. Blue electric auroras circled above the northern hemisphere. While navigating through its seventy-nine moons, they paused before Ganymede and Europa, two beautiful moons, each with distinctive worlds, before continuing their sojourn into space.

The NODA followed Zogar, orbiting icy rings around the mighty Saturn's golden-white globe, another massive planet that could hold 700 earths. A pink aurora circled the southern hemisphere, and they gasped at such beauty! Navigating among its many moons, they paused before the green Titan, an icy rock where bodies of liquid had been found, according to the Cassini-Huygens space probe.

They ventured farther into space, until they reached Uranus, a gigantic icy-blue planet with rings, rotating on its side in opposite direction than most other planets, spinning with twenty-seven moons orbiting in its gravitational field. They gasped at such strange beauty!

Into the blackness, they reached Neptune, orbiting a massive electric-blue gas planet, and everyone fell silent. Blazing a trail beyond Neptune through the doughnut-shaped Kuiper Belt into the band of celestial bodies, navigating through thousands of asteroids and icy objects, and shooting comets, they exclaimed, "WOW!"

Pluto came into view, an icy dwarf planet the size of earth's moon. The largest of its five moons, Charon, was so big they orbited each other, like a double planet. They exited the Kuiper Belt, venturing farther into space across the Milky Way in HypeMo, and only slowed down to observe sights of the cosmos—and what wondrous sights they were.

Four light years from earth, the closest star, Proxima Centauri, a pretty red dwarf star, much smaller than the sun, came into view in the Alpha Centauri system. Stationed on the NODA starship, Ishtan announced, "Aliens exist in these quadrants, similar to your own kind. Perhaps conditions are favourable for terrestrial life forms like yourself."

Eight light years from earth, in the constellation Canis Major, the Dog Star Sirius—a binary star twice the size of the sun and the brightest star seen in the Earth's night sky—came into view, and they were amazed!

Seven thousand light years from earth, Susie peered through an alien telescope from the Zogar observation deck, and whispered to Stephan, "What a beautiful cluster of moons among gaseous clouds."

He peered into the telescope, and said, "No, my dear, those are Pillars of Creation in the Eagle Nebula; get your eyes checked."

Steering clear of deadly gas cloud formations and exploding stars and burnt-out globes, their starships sped through interstellar space, whizzing through dust particles and asteroid belts until they reached the edge of the Milky Way galaxy, and stopped.

"Look, Andromeda!" they cried out. Two million light years from earth, Andromeda is a massive, lopsided blue cluster of trillions of suns, spiralling to a bright white core. Stationed for a day to take in the sights, they pushed on farther into space toward their final destination, saving the best for last.

Twenty million light years from earth, they stopped to observe a flat-shaped disk, like the rim of a sombrero, which shone with such brilliance across the vast expanse that the eyes could not see, and they cried out, "WOW!" It was located in the Virgo cluster of billions of suns that contained both the Milky Way and Andromeda galaxies. Stationed for two days, they soaked in the sights before returning home.

Speeding through the universe, they arrived back in their solar system, circling their almighty sun, exploding in gaseous nuclear fusions, and they thought how so small their sun was and how puny Earth was. Yet, filled with millions of life forms, it was the only home they knew, and they returned from the cosmos with a newfound sense of gratitude and awe. Their sun loomed large as they navigated around Mercury, exclaiming, "Ah!" It was a tiny grey orb, slightly larger than Earth's moon, mottled with electric-blue patches, like a pretty marble. Circling goddess planet Venus, they exclaimed, "Oh!" It was the size of Earth with a surface hot enough to melt lead—a hostile environment, where nothing could survive in its thick, acidic atmosphere. A week had gone by when they landed back on Earth.

Three . . . two . . . one, hatches opened, hissing steam. Light Beings carried Ushaya, deep in slumber upon her bed, down the ramp, and one by one, the astronauts walked out in silence, stunned, to a cheering crowd.

Out of coma

One eye opened to a tiny fruit fly resting on the bed rail. The other eye opened to smiling faces she recognized at once.

"Welcome back," said Irena.

Pulling tubes from her nostrils and needles from her wrists, Ushaya slowly sat up, wondering, "*What happened? Where am I?*"

"You are at the GHQ and have been in a coma for over a year," said Dr. Hauser.

Staring down at her body, she saw she no longer had yellow eyes or a protruding jaw, or magnificent wings or huge claws. She was human again.

Jake placed a glass of water next to the tourmaline rock on her bedside table, and said, "You need to drink this, special order from Yadgiri and the dagger."

She looked at Jake, confused, and said, "What are you doing here, and what do you know of the dagger?" She shakily reached out for the tourmaline rock, "And how did this get here?"

"Rest awhile, you've been through a long journey," said Leopold.

Erika handed her a dossier and said, "We leave you with this full report."

Irena placed her hand on her arm and said, "Let us know if you need anything. We'll be back soon to check on you." And they filed out of the room.

Days went by, and while reading the report, Ushaya learned of the Gogolan invasion, and was deeply saddened by the five hundred million who had perished. She learned of Jagpal and Prince Herbert, who did not survive, sacrificing their lives to help save the world. Skimming through pages, her eyes rested on the story of Phyteus Quaal, and she was amazed. Skimming more pages, she was astounded by the Light Beings and the NODA starship.

One day, Brad and Ishtan visited her, and filled her in with adventures from the land of Zytok.

She sat up in bed, musing, "Ah, it is coming back to me now. Azgar and Shenden, and whatever happened to Mosquito Enzo?"

"He is caretaker of a few mosquitos we brought from Earth," replied Brad.

She chuckled and said, "That will take his mind off bloodthirsty intentions."

Brad asked, "Do you remember the starworms?"

She shuddered and replied, "Only too well." And, holding the tourmaline rock, she said, "So you managed to get the rock back from the Zytokians."

"Azgar said the rock was of no use to them," he replied.

She turned sad and said, "I wish I had remained a dragon to help in the war."

"You have brought back the beacon, and we won the battle," said Ishtan.

"And the dagger? What happened to him?" she asked.

Ishtan replied, "He is busy delivering door-to-door water."

Brad said, "You flew around the galaxy with us. Do you remember?"

She shook her head and said, "The last memory I have is of leaving Zytok." She gazed at Ishtan, whispering, "Can you show me your true light body?"

He transformed into a magnificent being, shimmering from head to toe, with deep blue eyes and a blue halo above his head. Colourful wisps swirled among twinkling lights, up and down his golden frame. A streak of light shone diagonally across his ephemeral form, just like the carpet had. Wow! *He must be a good-looking dude by alien standards*, she thought.

Ishtan spoke through thin lips: "While fighting the Gogolan on our planet, I was nearly split in two, and this light is the scar I bear to this day."

She was surprised and said, "You never told us it was a battle scar. I am sad to hear of your suffering. Still, it is a thing of beauty."

"That it is," he replied.

Brad unfurled the map for them to see. A Light Being rose up with flaming wings and sprinkling lights, ablaze in red-hot fiery wisps, spiralling down his ephemeral form. His eyes were charcoal and his lips were thin. "Wow!" Ushaya cried out.

Meanwhile, Yaegar of Russia called up Mimbauwe of Rwanda, for a favour. He asked, "What seed can I present to Ushaya, when I have to break the bad news?" Mimbauwe sent him his most powerful seed, and Yaegar thanked him.

Days later, Ushaya sat up in bed, discussing the report with Yaegar and commando Yakov. She learned what happened to Olaf and Nadiya, and quietly spoke. "I only met Olaf for a short time. He was a brilliant scientist."

"And a good friend of mine," said Yaegar, adding, "He may go down in history as the first to operate the Zephron, but I am deeply saddened by his loss."

"He left a body of work behind that helped defeat the Gogolan," said Yakov.

Ushaya felt sad and said, "What happened to Olaf is my fault."

"Do not blame yourself. It is the fault of many, blinded by war," said Yakov.

She sat back and sighed, reminiscing on the time she flew with Nadiya and Viktor on a jet plane to bring back the Cube to Canada. With a slight smile, she said, "Nadiya beat us in a game of Skolgi."

Yaegar whispered, "And she beat the Gogolan in their own game, saving the Zephron ring."

Ushaya paused and said, "So Nadiya killed off Olaf, am I to understand that, sir?" Yaegar hung his head.

"And what happened to the Cube?" she asked.

Yaegar replied, "It is on display in a heavily guarded shrine in Saint Petersburg, a popular tourist spot. The monies we collect are funnelled into programs to help senior citizens in Russia to live out a good life."

Then she learned what happened to Ralph. "Nooooooooooooooooooo!" Her sobs echoed throughout the hospital, and doctors and nurses walked down corridors with heads bent in silence.

Yaegar presented her with a potent seed. In near hysterics, she cried out, "What are you saying? No one can bring back Ralph!"

Yakov tried to calm her down and said, "However you choose, we only know it is very potent." Sniffling, she looked down at the round, prickly white seed in her hand.

Months of rehabilitation followed: learning how to walk and regain her strength. Her memory was coming back to her, and she began to eat and drink, which set off chemical reactions from the brain to her toes, initializing all bodily functions. She puked in the toilet, and nurses helped her back to the bed. Endless tests were performed, and only shadow marks remained down her spine, where wings once were.

Daily conference calls came in from members of TLP. Jerome appeared on screen, one day, and said, "The frogfish refuse to turn into Light Beings; they rather enjoy their new forms."

"It's their right, I guess," replied Ushaya.

Julia came on screen, one day, and said, "Yes, I am managing without Herb. It isn't easy though."

Ushaya hung her head and replied, "The whole world misses him. You are not alone."

Julia thought pensively and said, "I had a dream last night. He was flying his own starship through space." The crow cawed upon her shoulder.

"Perhaps, he did," said Ushaya.

Yadgiri called up one day and asked, "Do you like it? It's Jagpal's favourite photo of you and Nadin flying through the mountains, with thumbs up."

Gazing at the framed photo hanging on the wall, with tears in her eyes, Ushaya replied, "I remember the moment well . . . thank you."

Carlos of Mexico called up one day. "You know, clover is 'lover' with a 'C' in front," he remarked.

"I never thought of that, and your point?" she asked.

"No point," he replied.

"I hear the clover has gone into mass production."

"Yes, and creating chaos with health insurances around the world."

"Continue the good work," Ushaya said, smiling.

Zhangwei called up, asking, "So how does it fit?"

While admiring her form in the mirror, wearing a Kunfu suit, she patted her silver hair with wisps of black, and replied, "It's a big improvement from the golden sliver."

One day, Muzaffar came on screen, beaming. "Guess who dropped in." Ishtan appeared as a carpet, lounging in his favourite chair, reading a newspaper.

"I see you are still catching up on the latest. Anything new?" asked Ushaya.

Ishtan folded the paper and placed it on the table, and replied, "A massive meteor, on collision course with earth, has been diverted into space."

Weeks went by when Ronald arrived at the GHQ, presenting the Gemball, as Light Being. Enchanted by neon lights blinking across his ephemeral body, Ushaya whispered to Ronald, "What is his alien name?"

"I can never pronounce it," he whispered back.

The Gemball replied through thin lips, "Ibnagoschdakotallulah."

"See, I told you so, completely unpronounceable," said Ronald.

The Gemball smiled, "Call me Dakota, for short."

A month had gone by when Ushaya called up Mimbauwe and said, "Thank you for the seed, but I have no idea what to do with it."

He warned her, "Your wish is your command; however, be careful what you choose. What manifests may be beyond comprehension."

Hashimoto called her up, asking if she ever wanted to turn back into a dragon. Ushaya admitted, "I haven't tried, not even interested."

Becoming stronger each day, she continued reading incoming reports. Yadgiri sent her a painting signed by elephant, Rajneesh. It was a scene of Rajneesh and Gita floating in space, among twinkling stars and a crescent moon, and she smiled.

The golden egg hatched, ruffling its fuzzy little brown feathers, cheeping, with mother YangXi standing by. Zhangwei announced to the world, "We have a baby boy." As proud father, the Map Light Being offered Brad the honour of naming his new hatchling.

Brad thought a while and said, "How about Compass?" And they were pleased.

Hundreds of Light Beings gathered in the great hall of the Zogar ship. Commander Bahar elevated Ishtan to Master Titan in a grand ceremony that was televised around the world, in honour of his great achievements. He not only proved himself as a great engineer, but also mastered universal languages, as a smooth operator between parties, while demonstrating grace under fire, with the strength and bravery of a true warrior. Prince Muzaffar was mighty proud.

Olivia happily settled into motherhood with her young, lively toddler Logan. Nakoteh and Zainab became lovers, moving to a chalet in the Swiss Alps. Ronald set up water bottle factories in India, signing agreements with Yadgiri. Stan and Hashimoto beat out the competition, inventing sidebars to raise laptop screens.

The Yokuru Tablet remained in the Kinkaju Temple. Two monks were leisurely walking across the bridge when Wu-pen broke the silence and said, "Legend has now come to pass."

Genjo nodded and replied, "Recorded over 1,000 years ago."

Brad knelt on one knee in front of magnolia bushes in his backyard and presented a ring to Cheyenne. She cupped her mouth, happily accepting the proposal, and they embraced.

"Of course I will hear his proposal," said Stan, speaking with Yadgiri about Jagpal's cousin Darshit, who wanted to get into the garment industry.

Jake became friends with an older, wiser, male Light Being he had met on the Zogar. Flying around earth, united in blended bodies, they landed on Easter Island, near Chile, admiring statues carved in human figures with oversized heads. Zubaak said, "They are similar to a race of beings on our planet."

"Yes, the Tahuki," replied Jake.

The gogolyte defectors had integrated into society. One day, a group gathered in a park-like setting, where they exchanged information about their new world, while playing gogolyte music. People passing by would stop and listen to strange, haunting lilts from their long metal rods striking the ground, drawing up sounds from the depths of the earth. Phyteus was roaming about, disguised as a gogolyte, when an attractive female caught his eye. He said, "Hello, my name is Quaal, Phyteus Quaal. What is yours?"

Demurely fluttering her yellow eyelashes and flashing a perfect row of sharp-pointed teeth, she replied, "Nirivanja is my name."

Meanwhile, Russian oligarchs signed agreements with president Yaegar, to fund plumbing and running water in all hospitals across the country. They agreed to sell their super yachts to foreign investors, funnelling the money back into their economy to build up infrastructures and create new jobs and increase GDP output, making Russia stronger, in exchange, for a trip through the Zephron ring.

Back at the farmhouse across Irena's estate, Susie peered one evening through a long-range telescope from a bay window. Shaking her head, she said, "No, Stephan, that is Orion's Belt. Get your . . ."

"Don't even say it," he interrupted.

Dragonfly

The day arrived when Ushaya was released from the GHQ, and her first mission was to visit New Zealand for a family reunion. Old man Harvey and nurse Caroline were invited to the celebration. The air filled with excitement as Caroline set up long tables and chairs. Meg finished decorating their backyard, placing flowers on the table, while Devon was strumming his guitar. Baxter the dog was barking and wagging his tail at Quazaik, who had transformed back into a sparkling gem, floating above Dragon's Pond. Harvey was barbecuing fish and vegetables on the grill, and Brad and Cheyenne brought out plates of food. Brad's map was not present at this occasion, for he was busy with his own family.

Chelsea and Tyler ran toward Ushaya, who was the first to arrive, followed by Ushaya's sister Amelia and husband Paul, and brother Kevin and wife Maria. In warm embraces and tears of joy, they gathered around the table and sat down to a feast, when suddenly, the last to arrive was Ishtan the Carpet.

As they dug into their meals, passing food trays down the table, Chelsea giggled at Ishtan and asked, "Can you change into a donkey?"

He changed into a donkey. "Hee-haw," he said, kicking up his hind legs. They all chuckled.

Tyler asked, "Can you change into that alien you saw in the Alpha Centauri system?"

Ishtan changed into a humanoid figure, a beautiful goddess-like creature. Her skin was tanned, her face long, with wide-oval eyes and thin brows, a small nose and wide lips and small ears. She wore a golden-bronze headdress, which draped down both sides of her face, to a long neck upon a slender body with large breasts. An elaborate choker circled her neck, attached with loops to an exquisite low-cut, tight-fitting gown made of red velour and swirling golden designs—down to a set of whirling wheels in place of feet. They were shocked! A shawl in the same colour as her dress draped around her elbows, and she held a black triangular device in her slender hands. They all ate their meals in silence.

Days went by in dream-like states, everyone enjoying their reunion, as they wandered about with drinks in hand, joining in activities, like lawn bowling. Of course, Amelia's husband Paul would crack a joke, here and there. "Knock, knock," he said.

"Who's there?"

"White."

"White who?"

"White don't we play another game of lawn bowling?" They all groaned.

Gathered around the outdoor bar, Paul, Kevin, and Harvey were discussing the latest sports news, while Amelia, Maria, and Caroline were mingling in the gardens, discussing recipes. Brad and Cheyenne were walking along the ravines of the property, while Ushaya and Ishtan sat in lawn chairs, admiring the view. Sipping her wine, Ushaya asked Ishtan, "How can I fly the grandkids in HypeMo?"

"Ask Jerome for a sphere," replied Ishtan.

That night she flew Chelsea and Tyler over New York City, a promise she meant to keep. Tyler gasped at the city lights. Chelsea pointed to a statue of a Light Being. No longer in dragon form, Ushaya smiled and said, "It's good to be back to my old self again."

"And what old self is that, Grandma?" asked Chelsea.

The weeklong festivities came to an end. In final hugs and tears of joy, Meg and Devon waved them all goodbye. Jerome's sphere transported them back to their homes, and Ushaya returned to the mountains, where another celebration was about to occur.

A month later, she united with Stan in marriage, which took place in the grand space of his mansion. Large screens were erected, televising the event around the world, and Light Beings also joined in, listening to music play, as Ushaya descended the winding staircase, with a blue sparkly veil that covered her silver-and-black coiffed hair. She wore a blue satin gown that trailed behind her, with long white gloves to her elbows, and silver sling-backed shoes upon her feet. In her hands, she held a small bouquet of peonies, while Lucy, who was to give the bride away, accompanied her.

Stan wore silk tan-coloured pants that creased elegantly around his ankles, and chestnut-brown, pointy shoes. His thin moustache and goatee were trimmed and his long white hair combed across his shoulders. A silk red scarf draped over his white satin shirt and velvety-tan jacket, with coattails trimmed with silver edgings, pointed lapels and ruby cufflinks. Their eyes locked before they joined together in front of the altar.

Jake was chosen to preside over the ceremony. Appearing in earthly form, he began his speech: "Together in holy matrimony, to have and hold through thick and thin, for better or worse, through sickness and health, for richer or poorer, to love and cherish till death do you part, according to the

Creator's ordinance, I now pronounce you husband and wife. You may now exchange powers."

Lucy brought forth two sapphire rings upon a golden cushion. Stan placed a ring upon Ushaya's finger, and Ushaya placed a ring upon his finger, and they kissed. Applause erupted across the screens amid confetti raining down on them. A month of merriment followed—making love and drinking iced tea and wine. While wandering through his gardens, she excitedly discussed their honeymoon trip through the cosmos on the Zogar!

Then one day, Ushaya returned to her dragon cave alone. It was half-destroyed, covered in soot, with blown-out shattered windows and caved-in corridors. Treasures lay under a heap of rubble and dust. The gargoyles had fallen to the wayside in pieces on the front lawn, and the backyard was flattened, void of trees. Her gardens and greenhouse had been incinerated, yet the two angel statues had survived, slightly leaning to one side.

An old man limped up the driveway and she invited him to the front porch. He lay down his crutch and sat on the stone steps, grunting in pain. Removing his cowboy hat, he said, "My name is Duke. I live down the street. So you are the Ushaya everyone talks about." He had the deepest blue eyes and a face covered in lines. She offered him something to drink, and he replied, "Nah, I'm good. Actually, I'm here to bring sad news."

Wearing a simple dress and loafers, she sat down next to him, and bracing herself, she asked, "What is it?"

"Wally didn't make it. He had a heart attack while taking care of Ralph. Everyone around here knew that he dug up Ralph's body from the mound, when the Russians came invading your cave. Ralph was making a slow recovery, but then the Gogolan swept through this place, and now we don't know what happened to either of them; their bodies were never found."

"How dreadful," she whispered.

"Emily Barker, she died too. Her charred remains were found in the back of her property, the house totally destroyed. Her Mimi dog ended up on my doorstep, lost and scared. Then Chloe showed up skinny and hungry, so I took them in and did what I could, taking care of them and all. They should be coming around soon." He stood up and put on his hat, and said, "Sorry to break the news, ma'am. Best get on my way." Ushaya thanked Duke for dropping by and gave him some clover, and watched him limp down the driveway.

When she entered the cave, a surprise was waiting for her. A brand new computer console sat on a new dining table, with a large screen lit up in multiple squares. Several of TLP members had joined in, and, gazing across the screens, she asked, "Where are the Titans?"

Nakoteh replied, "They packed their bags and left Earth for good, searching for another planet."

Ushaya chuckled and said, "I don't blame them." Among the rubble, she glanced up at a chandelier. She had always wanted one, but now her head bent down in sadness.

Muzaffar asked, "You don't like the chandelier?"

"It's beautiful, it's just . . ." her voice trailed off.

"You miss Ralph and Wally," said Carlos.

Tears welled up in her eyes. "There are many things I do not know," she replied.

Zhangwei quoted the words of Lao Tzu, "*The wise man knows what he does not know.*"

"And the wise man knows what he *does* know," said Mimbauwe, and turning to Ushaya, "Why don't you plant that seed? Go on, we will wait. The GemBall will follow where you go."

Queen Julia was standing in a salon of a newly built castle, in honour of Prince Herbert. Photos of Herb and world leaders hung from all four walls of the salon. The ring of power shone bright on her finger, and Magus the crow sat upon her right shoulder. She retrieved a wooden box from the buffet drawer and pulled out a whistle—the same whistle from the assembly meeting, so long ago—and placed it on the mantelpiece above a small fire flickering from the fireplace. Then she stood back, and with a final command, said, "Carry on."

Ronald was sitting in the Oval Office, with his gemball, when he called up Jerome, and said, "The Grand Plan is about to hatch."

From his Ottawa residence, Jerome struck a cue stick across his pool table, and pocketing the white sphere, he replied, "Good to know."

Wandering through her backyard, Ushaya knelt before the mound, where Ralph's body once laid buried. Memories drifted through her mind of Ralph frolicking through autumn leaves, and the times he yapped while riding on Ishtan, and when Lucy met Ralph and Chloe for the first time at Stan's place. She chuckled at reports of Wally chasing him up the street with something precious in his mouth. Then she felt remorse for leaving Wally, Ralph and Chloe to fend for themselves, before entering the Zephron ring. How selfish of her! She now realized what should have been done. Alas, that is what regrets do, she thought. They bring some of life's greatest lessons. One cannot turn back the hands of time, the *ifs* and *could haves* and *should haves* . . . it is what happened and is still happening today, and life moves on in mysterious ways.

Suddenly, Chloe and Mimi showed up! In shouts of glee, Ushaya hugged them close to her bosom. They frisked about, and when they had settled down by her side, she gazed at the prickly white seed in her hand. She reminisced about the time she stood over skyscrapers in Kyoto, admiring the view, when Hashimoto quoted a passage from Lao Tzu, "*Be as diligent at the end as at the beginning*," and with great intent, and perhaps, mixed with a dose of trepidation, she planted that seed into Ralph's empty grave.

Suddenly, a green sprout shot through the soil, and there was a small yap. A little German shepherd doggy rose from the mound, with a pink dot on his nose and a clip in his ear.

"It must be him!" she cried out, chasing after Ralph back to the caves, with Chloe and Mimi following behind. With tears of joy, she exclaimed, "Who says only cats have nine lives!" Ralph ran down a corridor of her caves, and giggling, she ran after him.

Irena spoke across the screen: "It's physically impossible."

Yadgiri quipped, "Yeah, like the gnomes on your estate."

"It must be a descendant of Ralph," said Zhangwei.

Yaegar shrugged his shoulders and said, "Let her believe, if it makes her happy."

Stan slightly smiled and said, "You don't know my Ushaya."

Days later, she was swinging back and forth on the front porch, with the tourmaline rock in her hand, while listening to music she'd heard many times before. Suddenly, she entered the Zone, and the rock fell, landing on the porch. Transformed into a dragonfly with magnificent translucent turquoise wings, buzzing and clicking, Ushaya flew toward the Blue-ray light, streaking across the evening sky.

Little Ralph yapped around the gargoyle ruins, with Mimi and Chloe chasing after him, swatting their paws, and then they stopped and sat attentively, looking over the valley. Angel statues stood silently sentient in the backyard. Dragon's misty breath descended along the winding river through mountains cascading into distant valleys, and together, they watched the sun set on the horizon, promising a new dawn for mankind.

Lightning Source UK Ltd.
Milton Keynes UK
UKHW010953060223
416537UK00007B/1506